THE
PLAGUE
TALES

THE
PLAGUE
TALES

ANN BENSON

Delacorte **Press**

For Robert,
in honor of twenty years.

Published by
Delacorte Press
Bantam Doubleday Dell Publishing Group, Inc.
1540 Broadway
New York, New York 10036

Library of Congress Cataloging in Publication Data

Benson, Ann.
    The plague tales : a novel / by Ann Benson.
        p.   cm.
    ISBN 0-385-31651-8
    1. Civilization, Medieval—14th century—Fiction.   2. Plague—Fiction.
I. Title.
PS3552.E547659P58   1997
813′.54—dc21   96-47246
                                                                            CIP

Manufactured in the United States of America
Published simultaneously in Canada

June 1997

10 9 8 7 6 5 4 3 2 1

BVG

Acknowledgments

I wish to acknowledge the fine work of both Jennifer Robinson and Peter Miller in helping bring this book to print. Jackie Cantor's remarkably gentle and astute editing improved it immensely, as did the comments of Arnold Silver, Linda Cohen, Robert Benson, Robert Glassman, and Ariel Glassman. I am grateful to them all for their efforts on my behalf.

Prologue

Clutching a musty book to his chest, Robert Sarin lowered himself carefully into a rickety wooden rocking chair and shifted his stiff joints until his position was tolerably comfortable. Once settled, he placed the book in his lap and folded his hands over its cracked leather binding. He rocked slowly, his mind consumed with worry about how he would make it through the next day, and then the one after that, without stumbling over some terrible problem that he did not have the wherewithal to anticipate. He stared blankly at the ancient woman in the nearby bed, whose own unmoving gaze was focused upward on the straw ceiling as if she were searching for signs of some small verminous creature, one foolish enough to reveal itself in her pristine home.

Out, damned rat! she used to say when an unsuspecting rodent would stray into her protectorate, and the son keeping vigil by her side, though old himself, could still recall the sound of vengeance in her laughter as she planned the intruder's demise. When he was a child, the force of her will would sometimes scare him so badly that he would scramble under the bed in which she now lay, then peek out timidly and stare up at the straw.

Out, indeed, the damned rats would go, he remembered, always departing with suitable haste, for his mother was not a woman to be trifled with in her prime. Even in the infirmity of her tenth decade, as her skin thinned to translucence and her eyes grew dull, the keenness of her mind had not deserted her. On the edge of death she still clung to life with all the fierce tenacity of one summoned too soon to the precipice, one who would shatter the bell before allowing it to toll in her memory. She was not ready to jump into the void yet; he thought, with some sadness, that she would never be ready. She had told him often, her voice brittle and bitter, that she had not finished her work on earth. And despite his awe of her, he was always certain that she loved him well. She had taught him everything he knew, and *he* was not ready to let her go.

He could see the veins through her parchment skin and wondered how the walls of her heart, themselves by now as delicate as paper, could keep those veins blue with blood. Her face, in youth so clear and firm, was a mass of folds and wrinkles, all spotted with the strange dark growths of age, unwanted splotches of taupe flesh that appeared one day

1

and established themselves, then rudely invited their cousins to camp alongside them. Her chest rose slowly, almost imperceptibly, and then fell again. With each repetition the interval between the peak and the valley of her breath lengthened a bit, and soon, Sarin knew, the gap would lengthen to the point that the rhythm could no longer be maintained.

Was that all? he wondered. *Just a disruption in the rhythm?* Surely, he thought, it must take more than that to bring almost a century of constancy to an end. He pulled a feather bookmark from between the pages of the book and reached out, placing it in front of her mouth and nose. Every few moments the feather's delicate tendrils would stir just slightly from her weak breath. But after a few more protracted and halting breaths the stirrings finally ceased, and the feather remained motionless in his hand. He held it there for what seemed to him like a very long time before he was fully convinced that his mother had passed. Then he lowered his head and cried quietly, his tears falling like soft rain on the book's mold-chalky cover.

He raised his sad eyes and looked over her still body to the window on the other side of the bed. Several pairs of eyes looked in, their shapes oddly distorted by waves in the uneven glass. He looked from one to the next until he had connected with every pair. There he saw the unmistakable look of fear, the pain of uncertainty. His mother had been their champion, their protector, and with her passing it should have fallen on him to take up the cause. But the violence of his own birth had robbed him of some of the mental skills he would otherwise have inherited from his mother, and before she slipped into her final descent, she had arranged they would instead champion him.

She had told him that the book contained everything he needed to know to make a proper job of what lay before him. He looked down at the musty old volume and started to open it, then realized with some panic that he had pulled out the feather marking the page where she had said he should begin. The hot, shameful fear of failing her flooded through him. How could he have lost the page? She had been so careful to mark it for him.

He began at the very beginning, and turned the pages carefully, muttering to himself, scrutinizing the ancient writings for familiar words. On the early pages the once-black ink had faded over the centuries to a dull brown not much darker than the stained page to which it had originally been applied, and it was a difficult task to make out the letters. The hand was spidery and foreign-looking, and written in a language he could not read; though his mother had tried several times to teach him, he never could manage to grasp it. Feeling very stupid, he moved impatiently through the pages until he came to the place where the writing was in the language he could read; the ink was much darker, though lighter yet than the most recent entries. He did not stop to read until he came to the place where the fresh ink was coal-black and the edges of the letters still crisp, and the writings were in the familiar hand of the woman who lay dead on the small bed. There, he read slowly and carefully to be sure he understood everything clearly, for he wanted very much to do it all just right when the time came.

She had told him there would come another task for him to do, one that would require more of him, and that everything he needed to know could be found in the book. The task would come to him, she'd said, because it had not come to her, although she could not say just when it would happen. He hoped with all his heart that he would find the courage and strength to carry out his part in the same way she would have, had it come in her time. He glanced up at the eyes in the window, and nodded very slightly. In unison the watchers repeated his gesture, acknowledging their complicity.

It was something, he thought. He prayed it would be enough.

Zero

April 2005

J ust as Janie Crowe was closing in on contentment, something went *clunk* in the machinery of the world and everything ground to a painful halt.

"Don't you think it's ironic," said the woman in the airplane seat next to her, her voice nasally distorted by the small speaker in her protective mask, "that it was something so simple? I mean, think of all the cataclysmic possibilities. It could have been a nuclear accident. A comet landing on the earth. Some terrorist group with a truckload of chemical weapons. But no. Nothing dramatic like that. It was just stupid bacteria."

"Go figure," Janie replied dryly, hoping her disinterest would be made clear by the tone of her voice. When would this pain-in-the-ass woman run out of sad stories about all the disagreeable things that had happened to her since the Outbreaks, and stop her pissing and moaning? Janie decided that if she was subjected to a continuation after the "lunch" break, she would interject a few of her own favorite Outbreak anecdotes. The woman's tales of inconvenience were sure to seem trivial in comparison.

The plane bumped its way across the Atlantic, heading for London. Janie thought to herself, *No more cancer, but we still have turbulence.* A steward walked slowly down the aisle, unaccountably surefooted as the aircraft lurched up and down, and handed out to each of the plane's passengers, a small squared box of a nutritional supplement designed to suppress hunger. Another steward followed close behind him, passing out what the airlines called "sterile intake devices," a medically correct euphemism for what were once called plastic straws. At forty-five Janie was too young to remember the time when straws were made of rolled waxed paper; all the straws in her lifetime had been plastic. She was sure there had been a time when straws were, naturally enough, made of straw, hence their name. She shook her head silently and sighed, thinking about how things always seemed to change, and that the changes were seldom pleasant.

She glanced over at her suddenly silent seatmate, who was slipping one end of the straw through a rubber hole in the base of her sterile mask. As Janie watched, she shoved the straw upward until it was within reach of her lips. Then she shoved the other end into a small rubber gasket at the top of the box, which closed snugly around the straw and formed an airtight seal. The woman began sucking gleefully, emitting a series of rather suggestive noises, which Janie could hear through her headgear. The woman looked up, saw Janie giggling over the noise, and quickly shut off her own sound transmitter. She gave Janie an embarrassed little smile and then looked away again, preoccupied with her now-silent intake ritual.

Good, Janie thought, *that'll keep you quiet for a while. You don't know how lucky you are, lady. If you'd started in on me again, I might have to tell you my own troubles. Like how I used to be a surgeon, a good one, and how I used to have a wonderful family, but they're all gone now, and how I was forced by an unsympathetic bureaucracy to be retrained for something else, and I'm middle aged and alone and I'm back in school again.*

She turned off the listening device on her headgear and attacked her own liquid meal. The silence gave her the feeling of being underwater—she could hear some sounds, but they were muffled by the tightness of the air seal. The dead sterile air inside the headgear did not conduct sound well. She closed her eyes and imagined that she was in some quiet forest of tall conifers, and that the only audible interruptions were occasional birdcalls and insects buzzing, which she conjured from memories of childhood excursions into such places. The peace was wonderfully soothing.

Not so fortunate were the stewards, who were forced to listen to the rubbing of one stiff plastic surface against another as the passengers shifted for comfort in their ungainly sterile suits, heavy, restrictive garments intended to keep any microscopic American beasties corralled so they couldn't invade the sole surviving piece of what had once been the United Kingdom. It was a sound only slightly less grating than fingernails scraped down a blackboard. To the unfortunate people charged with overseeing the comfort and sterility of the passengers, this and every other transoceanic flight sounded like some weird crystalline crinklefest.

The plane's passengers stood in line outside the customs area at Heathrow Airport. Janie looked up at the mezzanine for the hundredth time since the passengers from her flight had gotten into this line and made a detailed visual examination of the green-suited Biocop who had been standing there, barely moving, holding his chemical rifle in the same ready position for the last two hours. It was pointed directly at the waiting line of incoming passengers and it never wavered. As she watched, the cop straightened himself up and raised his hand to the side of his head to adjust the volume in his earphones. After a few moments of intense listening he looked toward a nearby mezzanine door and within a second or two another Biocop came out, then moved quietly along the mezzanine catwalk and stood next to the first cop. After a brief interchange the first Biocop started walking away, and the new one trained his weapon in the same direction.

Janie nudged the woman next to her, the same one who'd verbally terrorized her on the flight. The woman was so bored with the wait that she had resorted to memorizing the headlines scrolling onto the huge television screen ahead of them. She turned in Janie's direction.

"Look," Janie said, pointing to the mezzanine. "The Changing of the Guards."

After three hours in line Janie finally reached a customs agent, a stony-faced middle-aged man who smelled of garlic and behaved as if he was in need of a strong antacid.

What a pissy job, Janie thought to herself, and considered momentarily that slightly less luck in the medical reassignment lottery might have forced her into something like customs work. She was suddenly more appreciative of her situation—at least she would be using some of her original surgical skills in her new work when she completed her forensics certification. The business she would attend to on this trip to London was the last piece needed before she could start the final application process, and when her certification application was accepted, it would mark the beginning of a new life, one cleansed of all reminders of her old life. One by one the cracked pieces of the person Janie Crowe once was were being replaced by the sound pieces of the person Janie Crowe would soon be. There were days when she thought this was a good thing, and days when the loss of each piece, however cracked it might be, seemed like a little bit of death. She was too tired to think about what kind of day this one was turning out to be.

Her group was waved forward to a long table where her luggage and boxes were lined up for inspection. An agent asked her, "What is the purpose of your visit?"

"I'm here to do some scientific research. An archaeological dig."

"What is the purpose of this research?"

"I'm completing certification for forensic archaeology."

"And how long will you be staying on our fair island?" he asked with a smile. Janie read it as a challenge to give the wrong answer.

But she was prepared for this question, as she had been coached by a U.S. Department of Foreign Travel official, one she had bribed handsomely to help smooth out the wrinkled process of obtaining a postOutbreak overseas travel permit. She answered in the least damaging manner.

"About three weeks, if all goes well." She could see the smile fade from the agent's face. He had just lost an opportunity to make a bodyprint of an unsuspecting visitor. He was clearly disappointed.

"Well," he said, "that's nice. But if your visit extends beyond four weeks you'll have to report to the Ministry of Identity to be bodyprinted. We have to issue you a card, you understand, and we must print you in order to do that."

He handed her a small booklet and advised her to read it. "These are the regulations for international visitors," he said. "You will be held responsible for all of the material, so please read it carefully."

As the agent examined the contents of her suitcases, Janie wondered to herself if there would be a pop quiz on visitor regulations. She chuckled quietly, but her gaiety faded as she realized that her toothpaste, deodorant, and moisture cream were all being confiscated. Her hair spray, shampoo, and conditioner were also gathered into the yellow plastic biosafe bag for quarantine. She was given the option of paying for shortterm storage and reclaiming the items on leaving the country, or allowing the items to be destroyed in a biosafe manner. Considering the cost of storage, she opted for destruction.

"I think I might want to buy some stock in a British toiletries maker," she said to the examiner.

He smiled politely, but she could see the clear delight in his face as he disposed of her expensive personal-care items. As he continued his examination of her toiletries pack he took out a small bottle of acetaminophen and set it aside, completely apart from the other confiscated items.

"What's the problem with the acetaminophen?" Janie asked.

"Available only with a prescription here," he said. "Aspirin and ibuprofen too."

She looked at him in wide-eyed disbelief, her mouth open.

"I don't make the policy, miss. I just enforce it. You might ask the chap at the next station."

After her personal luggage was finally cleared, the agent opened the box containing Janie's digging equipment. He poked around for a few minutes while Janie held her breath and watched. Then he looked up at Janie with a disgusted expression as if to say, *I didn't need this today*, and spoke into a hand-held walkie-talkie.

"Bring out the scanner, please."

As she let out the held breath, Janie muttered a soft flurry of unsavory invective, none of which was intended to convey her appreciation of this agent's concern for the safety of his countrymen. Her empty stomach, long since finished with the liquid meal she'd received on the plane, gurgled out its objection to the additional delay.

A tall portable laser scanning machine was wheeled from a nearby door by a green-suited cop and positioned at the foot of the table. The agent pushed a few buttons and the rollers started moving, carrying the scanner forward so that it passed directly over the table and the items laid out there.

Janie watched and whispered to herself, *Please don't let the buzzer go off . . . please don't find anything. . . .* And blessedly, nothing showed up. No uncataloged bacteria, no parasites, no fungi or viruses. Janie thought she was home free, but the examiner decided to prolong her agony by asking some questions about the unusual assortment of tools.

He pointed, and she answered. *Surveying equipment. Micrometer. Biosafe storage bags. Protective eyewear. Biosafe gloves. Soil plugger.*

He stopped there and picked up the meter-long metal tube in his gloved hands and turned it over while he examined it. It was a huge version of the garden tool used to plant bulbs for tulips and daffodils, and it seemed to pique his interest. He commented, "My mum has one like this. A bit smaller, though."

She thought to herself, *Your mum may have a Mickey Rooney. But I have a Kareem Abdul Jabbar. Different league altogether.*

But she smiled pleasantly and said aloud, "How lovely. It's nice to know people have the same interests all over the world."

This seemed to please him; he smiled back and said, "Well, that's all, I think. You can take your things through that door over there." He pointed to his left. "You can join the queue for your medical clearance."

As Janie closed the boxes he waved and said, "I hope you have a lovely visit." Janie waved back at him and turned to go.

As she headed toward the next line with other members of her group she muttered under her breath, "I'd settle for uneventful," knowing that it was not likely to be the case.

Soon she was waiting again, but this time the line seemed to move more quickly. Janie looked at her watch as she shuffled forward in a state of semiconsciousness. *Over twenty-four hours . . .* she thought. *All I want to do is get horizontal.* She peered forward around the people in line, her eyes barely open, and watched wearily as traveler after traveler presented his papers to the examiner, then held out his right wrist. The gloved examiner passed the wrist quickly under a bright blue light to disinfect it, then placed the entire hand into an opening in the front of a small computer; it reminded Janie of an old-fashioned automatic teller machine. She thought nostalgically about the one that used to be in the lobby of her dorm at med school. She'd had many wonderful conversations around that machine. *ATM-side chats.*

After every examination of an international traveler this Heathrow Compudoc machine would automatically debit the user's home country account for the cost of the procedure. Their American accounts would show the debit within a day of their arrival in England, and Janie was grateful that the mercurial credit exchange rate was favorable at the moment. She noticed as she waited that there were several machines but only one examiner. The line was very long; all the travelers who'd been passed through the large number of customs desks in operation were now funneled into this one line. It reminded her of the Sumner Tunnel in Boston. Or a blood clot, with platelets piling up all around an obstruction.

"They seem to be shorthanded today," she commented to the woman behind her, who yawned and nodded her agreement.

Finally it was Janie's turn. The examiner said, "Passport or card, please."

And as she was still uncarded, she handed him her passport. He flipped through the pages and said, "And what is the purpose of your visit, Ms. Crowe?"

Janie's shoulders slumped in fatigue; she thought, *Haven't we been here before?* But rather than irritate this man with protestations about repetition, Janie simply gave him the information again.

He entered some of the information from her passport into a computer, and a screen with her health and travel history appeared almost instantly. "And how long will you be with us?"

Between her hunger, exhaustion, and growing impatience, Janie was about to explode, but forced herself to remain calm. *Just play the game, Crowe,* she reminded herself. *You're almost at the goal line.* She managed to maintain self-control, and once again politely gave the examiner the information he wanted.

"Thank you, miss," the man said. "May I please have your wrist?"

She unbuttoned her shirtsleeve and held out her right wrist. The disinfecting light was surprisingly cool; for some reason Janie had expected it to feel warm. It was almost a pleasant sensation, at least until he took her arm and placed it in the machine's opening. Then she felt the surgeon's natural fear of hand injury, and had to breathe very deeply to avoid panicking and pulling away. A flexible metallic clamp closed in on her wrist, adjusting itself automatically to fit her specific size and shape. Once she was secured, the examiner pressed a few buttons.

"All set, now," he said, and Janie tensed up as she felt the vibration of the current passing through her flesh. It was over in a second, and the man said, "Should be just a moment for the readout."

She began to relax again. The machine still had her wrist, but it was no longer being subjected to the tests and readings of a few moments ago.

A piece of paper emerged silently from a slot at the base of the machine's front panel. The examiner tore it off and scanned it quickly. He smiled and said, "Healthy as a horse. All your proper immunizations, no infectious diseases." Then he grinned wickedly and said, "And you're not pregnant."

She glared back at him as the clamp on her wrist automatically loosened. *Asshole*, she thought. *You know perfectly goddamned well I've been sterilized. It's right there on that screen.*

"Next," he said, and the woman behind her moved forward for her turn.

As she rebuttoned her shirtsleeve, Janie watched the man do his little shtick with the woman, and as he pronounced her immunized, noninfectious, and unpregnant, Janie saw the "MD" after his name on his ID badge. *Please God*, she prayed silently, *don't ever let it come to this. I'll die before I let them do that to me.* As he was finishing up with the woman, Janie remembered to ask him about aspirin as the previous examiner had suggested.

He laughed sarcastically and said, "Well, the pharmaceutical manufacturers have to make their money somewhere, now, don't they? They can't make it on antibiotics anymore, so they convinced the powers that those over-the-counter painkillers aren't as safe as they were once touted to be. Got a whole new bunch of regulations put in place. And of course, they're all more expensive now, since the manufacturers have to recoup the cost of dealing with the regulators. That's bureaucracy for you. You'll have to get a prescription if you need aspirin."

He stamped the woman's entry papers and handed them back. "You're all set here," he said. "Follow the yellow stripe to exit."

Her group of passengers moved away from the Compudoc area and each of them spent a few moments reorganizing his or her separate belongings. Suddenly loud angry voices came from the area they'd just cleared, and everyone looked back to see a young man struggling with the machine, trying to get his wrist free. The examiner advised the people in line to move away from that Compudoc and led them to one of the empty ones Janie had noticed earlier. When the area was safely cleared, the examiner spoke into a walkie-talkie and stepped back himself. Soon four walls slid up through the floor of the examination area, enclosing the Compudoc and its protesting captive, who would remain there until Biocops came to take him away for "more detailed examination." The doctor ignored the young man's pleas, said, "Next!" and a nervous-looking woman stepped forward to the adjacent machine.

Janie looked at the woman next to her and grinned with great satisfaction. "Maybe he was pregnant," she said, and went outside to look for the person who would be awaiting her arrival.

One

A lejandro Canches wiped the beads of sweat off his brow with a muddy arm, leaving a dark smear of dirt across his forehead. The iron shovel standing upright in the pile of dirt beside him was a superb tool, one a poorer man could not have afforded, but it was much too heavy for use on such a sultry night in Aragon. He rested one arm on the shovel's handle and then leaned over it, resting for a moment, wishing with all his heart that the work before him could have waited for cooler weather. *But alas*, he thought, *it cannot.*

As his apprentice looked down from the edge of the hole, nervously vigilant against unwanted discoverers, the physician Canches took up the shovel and began once again to thrust it rhythmically through the soil. The hole deepened, and the pile grew higher, until finally, the tip of the shovel struck something solid, sending a jarring reverberation up through his aching shoulders into his bent spine. He quickly tossed the shovel aside and called to the boy to jump into the pit with him. Using only their hands, they shoved the dirt away frantically, hoping that they'd finally reached the wooden box, the ultimate goal in their clandestine effort.

Suddenly the apprentice gave a loud yelp and clutched one hand with the other. Alejandro stopped clawing and took the boy's hand in his own; he could feel a large splinter in the palm, but he could not see it through the steamy darkness.

He hissed at him to keep his voice down. "If we are discovered at this task, neither of us will have any need of hands! Forget your pain for now, and get back to work! I'll tend to it when we're back in the surgery."

Alejandro could not see the look of fury on the injured boy's face. Steeling himself against the throbbing agony of the wound, the boy returned to the work, reluctantly pawing at the clods of dirt, and fuming with resentment at his master's insistence that he continue without regard to his considerable discomfort.

"Here!" said the physician with great urgency. He was separated from his prize by only a few inches of dirt. "Help me clear this away!"

Together they exposed a small section of the box's surface, where the top met one side. Alejandro probed with his fingers along the edge until he located a crack; smiling triumphantly into the darkness, he picked up the shovel and forced it into the narrow space, hoping that the nails would slip free; to his great disappointment, the wood had not yet rotted enough to loosen its grip on the iron spikes. Soon, he knew, they would be rusted and it would be an easy task. Unfortunately, he did not have the luxury of waiting for nature to do his work.

Together they gave a mighty push downward on the handle of the shovel, and the top came loose with a loud crack. They grabbed the box top and heaved upward with all their strength while balancing tenuously on the exposed edge of the box, heaving and straining as they did. Alejandro's shoulders and arms were nearly useless with fatigue, but he would not stop now, with success so near and time passing too swiftly.

With one final mighty effort they yanked the top free and set it up on the firm ground beside the opened grave. Perched on the sides of the box, with dirt sliding down around his feet, Alejandro leaned over as far as he could and grabbed the body under the shoulders, inching it upward while the boy slipped a long strip of coarsely woven cloth underneath its back and then out on the other side. They did the same under the knees, then climbed back to the edge of the hole. Alejandro grabbed the ends of one cloth and the boy grabbed the other; they pulled upward, grunting and swearing, until the body finally rose. Once it cleared the top of the pit, they slid it sideways and laid it down on undisturbed ground.

Panting from exertion, Alejandro lay back for a moment to catch his breath. When he could speak again, he patted the dirty corpse with something not unlike affection and said, "So, Señor Alderón, my departed friend, we meet again. I have looked forward to this meeting." He leaned forward so his face was near the corpse's head and whispered, "And before I put you back in the earth, I swear to you on the bones of my own ancestors that I will know what killed you."

He had known this man and had treated him, with a lack of success that he regretted bitterly, for his final torturous malady. Carlos Alderón had been a blacksmith in Alejandro's hometown of Cervere in the Spanish province of Aragon, a good man who had forged the very shovel with which his coffin was reopened; he had in all likelihood also forged the hammer and nails with which it had been sealed shut.

Alejandro recalled the once huge man, who before his illness had been strong and healthy, a blessing that the physician believed to be God's reward for a decent life of honest labor. Though they'd had only rare contact with each other prior to Carlos' illness, Alejandro had admired from afar the way Carlos had lovingly guided his hardworking peasant family to a position of comfort and prosperity in Cervere, enabling them to rise far above their humble beginnings. There had been a good marriage for the daughter, and plenty of work at the forge for the

sons; the wife had grown respectably plump and had taken on the cho-
leric temperament appropriate to her elevated social position.

So when the devoted patriarch first began to cough up bits of
blood, he was not overly concerned for himself. After all, he had once
told Alejandro, God had been good to him, and he had no reason to
think his good fortune would not hold. But his coughing had not diminished after the usual fortnight of affliction, and the spittle grew more
bloody each day. His wife treated him with herbal potions and eucalyptus
teas with only temporary success. Reluctantly, Carlos went to see the
local barber, who after a brief examination of the spittle wisely told
Carlos that his problem was beyond his limited experience.

Still panting beside the shrunken corpse, Alejandro remembered
the day when the big man had appeared at his door, cap in hand, seeking
treatment for his frightening symptoms. Carlos had been visibly nervous,
not knowing the proper behavior for such a situation. It was forbidden
for Jewish physicians to give medical treatment to any Christian, and
though the Jews were not treated especially well in the town of Cervere,
they were tolerated without undue malice. Alejandro's wealthy and successful family was well regarded within the Jewish community, which had
resulted in advantageous marriages for his younger sisters (although he
himself had managed to slip out of the matchmaker's grasp), and he was
hesitant to jeopardize their position by engaging in a forbidden association.

So Alejandro was understandably wary of this new patient's presence when he showed up at the door. He had never treated or even
touched a Christian, except in medical school in Montpellier, and even
then he had never touched a *decent* Christian, only convicts and whores,
who had no choice but to stand still. It would mean terrible trouble for
his family if the local clergy got wind of it. Notwithstanding all of this,
and highly competent physician though he was, he was far too compas-
sionate and youthfully ignorant of the consequences of his behavior; he
lacked the hard wisdom that would have made him turn Carlos Alderón
away. He foolishly welcomed him, and resolved to give the big man his
best effort.

He tried every known treatment for lung maladies, including bleeding, purging, enemas, and exposing the patient to moist vapors, but
nothing worked. He had rolled a parchment and placed one end of the
tube on the man's chest as he had been taught to do, then listened at the
other end. What he heard was terribly puzzling to him, for one of Alderón's lungs sounded clear, while the air wheezed and whined in and
out of the other one. Alejandro began to suspect that one of the lungs

held something that the other did not, but could not confirm his suspicion except by looking into the man's chest. *If only I could see inside him,* he had thought at the time, in terrible frustration. He watched helplessly as Carlos' body grew frail and his spirit weakened. The former giant finally died looking like a shrunken leather sack full of bent and broken twigs.

As he and his apprentice now lifted the body onto their cart, it still seemed heavy, and Alejandro wondered if they would have succeeded had the man died of some injury that had not withered his flesh. They tossed fresh hay over the body and arranged the shovel and a few other tools around the pile. Then they pulled their rough hoods up so their faces were partially hidden, hoping to look like farmers passing through town to an early market.

They were both hot and dirty and miserably afraid of being caught, and the dangerous journey back to the surgery would take nearly an hour on the rutted roads. Nevertheless, the boy whined bitterly about the sliver in his hand, which was still throbbing viciously; his plaints and lamentations had the unwelcome effect of further agitating the already skittish mule. Alejandro retrieved a bottle of strong red wine from under the seat and instructed the boy to drink deeply, knowing that the wine's dulling effect would wear off by the time they were required to move the body again. He got no resistance from the boy, who guzzled the wine down as if it were aqua vitae, and the last he would ever taste. Thereafter they traveled more quietly, depending on the diminishing moonlight to illuminate the path. The nervous mule balked at navigating the dark terrain without benefit of a lantern, and the physician thought many times during the journey that he himself could have pulled the cart faster.

Just before dawn they finally guided the cart into the stable attached to Alejandro's home and locked the sturdy doors behind them. Leaving their gruesome cargo hidden safely in the stable, they traversed the dark passageway into the house by the light of a lantern. Every step brought an aching reminder of the night's exertion, but the physician remembered that he had promised to look at the boy's wound as soon as they were safely in the surgery, and would not allow his aches stop him.

He held the boy's hand under the light of the lantern and examined it carefully. "I regret that I could not tend to you sooner," he apologized, his regret deepening when he saw the severity of the wound. The boy squirmed, agitated by the pain in his hand, which even his drunkenness could not completely obliterate. Alejandro tried to hold the hand steady as he prepared to remove the splinter, but every time he touched it, the boy tried to jerk it away.

"Be still, boy—I cannot get a firm purchase on this God-cursed splinter!"

Shocked by Alejandro's blasphemous order, the boy complied, but the damage was done. The splinter snapped off at the opening to the exit wound, leaving a substantial piece still inside.

Alejandro washed the dirt and blood from the boy's hand and poured wine over the wound to cleanse it further. He had long known that wounds cleaned with water and treated with wine were more likely to heal without festering, although he had no explanation for the curative powers of the regimen. To numb the pain Alejandro dabbed oil of clove on the wound, which caused the boy to wince and draw a sharp inward breath.

"The sting will subside quickly," he told him. "Now, stay still while I wrap that hand. And drink more wine now. It will help you to sleep." The physician prayed silently that the boy would not lose that hand, or even his life, from the festering that would certainly follow.

As the sunlight's first rays edged over the horizon, Alejandro lay down on his bed, his energies entirely depleted. Vivid dreams of Carlos Alderón shattered his fragile sleep; the nauseating specter in a tattered black shroud chased him relentlessly through the dark treacherous woods. Alejandro was always one step out of the blacksmith's reach as he plunged forward into the unknown forest, lurching clumsily over endless obstacles, his leaden limbs struggling as if mired in a weed-choked swamp. He wanted only to drag himself out of that swamp and lie down a to a long rest.

Jarred by the terrifying dream, the physician's exhausted body twitched spasmodically, powerless to rouse itself and escape the unsettling pursuit. On and on he fled, Alderón's ghost racing behind him, with no safe haven ahead. True rest was still far, far away.

The midday sunlight was pouring through cracks in the shutters covering his narrow windows when the exhausted physician finally opened his eyes again. He rose stiffly from his bed, and was instantly reminded of the previous night's labors with every attempt at movement. His shoulders had never felt such agonizing pain. *Fool*, he thought, *how could you possibly work that hard without suffering later?* He went to his chemical cabinet and found a salve of menthol and camphor, which he rubbed onto his shoulders.

The water he splashed over his face refreshed him only slightly; it had been drawn from the well the day before and was unpleasantly tepid. In his current condition of disarray, he thought it unwise to leave his home, even to go to the well, for he was still in his previous day's mud-caked clothing. He quickly stripped off his wrecked garments, and wiped himself clean with a cloth dipped in the remains of his water. Ordinarily a fastidious man, Alejandro was sincere in his desire to set an example of cleanliness, which he hoped would inspire his patients to maintain a similar state, at great benefit to their health. In his current filthy condition he could hope to be inspirational only to certain barnyard animals.

He tucked his long black hair into a hat, and donned a simple shirt and plain trousers, then grabbed two wooden buckets. When he opened the door, the heat's intensity assaulted him, reminding him of how truly awful his day's work was going to be.

The sun was at its highest point in the sky, and its rays poured mercilessly down onto the town square, baking deeper cracks into the already parched earth. Shielding his eyes from the glare, he made his way around a corner to the common well.

He found to his dismay that it was surrounded by Christian women collecting fresh water for their basins and new gossip for their wagging tongues. A small roof shaded the well, providing some relief from the debilitating heat for those gathered under it. Alejandro stood back in the sunlight and waited his turn, making a feeble but unsuccessful attempt to hide his impatience. When they noticed his fidgeting, the women stepped aside reluctantly, wishing to prolong their own shaded stays at the well before returning to the demands of their families.

He hung one of the buckets on the hook and lowered it into the well. How cool the sound of the splash was as the bucket hit the water far below; how stinging the pain in his shoulders as he cranked the bucket, now heavy with water, back up again. *I should wake the boy*, he thought. *Such duties as this are his, not mine!* Then he remembered the apprentice's wounded hand, and decided to let him sleep until his assistance was required for the more demanding dissection. Cursing the bad luck that had led to the splinter, Alejandro stumbled achingly back to his house, teetering under the weight of the water-filled buckets. When he returned to the well again it was with only one bucket. He repeated the task until the large basin in his surgery was completely filled.

He was relieved to be finished, for he dreaded the prying eyes of the Christian women. Each time he returned to the well, a young girl in a rough dress tried to catch his eye, and each time he quickly looked away from her, not wishing to encourage her curiosity. She had been staring at him seductively, showing unmistakable interest in him. He did not acknowledge her attention or return her coy smiles, hoping she would end her silent but obvious advances if he ignored her.

Alejandro had no way of knowing that, dressed as he was in European-looking attire, he might be considered attractive by members of the opposite sex. Among his own people physical beauty was not necessarily considered to be an asset, and he paid little attention to his own. But he was tall, and well muscled despite his wiry slimness, with well-formed, angular features and smooth olive skin. He had a kind face, but his expression was usually serious and pensive. Rarely did he smile or laugh with abandon, for he was usually too busy pondering some weighty medical mystery. When he did smile, his amber eyes would seem to sparkle with dazzling brilliance, for only when he was truly happy would he give up his somber countenance, and the contrast was always startling, even to those who knew him well. And of those intimates, there were not many, for he was shy and kept to himself except when pursuing his profession. He was the sort of mysterious and enigmatic man who might appeal to a young girl lacking the sophistication to appreciate his finer qualities, but his innocence and lack of experience were such that he failed to understand his own allure. He didn't notice when the girl at the well began to whisper secretively to one of her companions. She had recognized him, despite his unusual attire, and was curious.

Back safely in his surgery, he began to prepare himself for the unsavory task before him, the dissection of Carlos Alderón's body, which would either confirm his suspicions that the origin of Carlos' disease was not the presumed imbalance between his lungs and his heart but something more clearly defined and observable, or give rise to a host of new questions. He was both repulsed by the foulness he knew he faced and excited by the prospect of discovery. It was not often that he had such an opportunity to learn. He had seen only four dissections during his entire time in medical school; after succumbing to intense pressure from secular quarters, the Christian pope had reluctantly given permission for each medical school to perform one dissection per year, abrogating the Church's official ban on such procedures. On those dreadful yearly occasions, the entire student body would gather in an open area to view the procedure as a barber-surgeon opened the cadaver, then took the body apart bit by bit over a period of three days. Putrefied organs were offered to the students for closer observation and detailed study, while the professor remained a safe distance away and described things he could not see firsthand. Quoting Galen, whose written words were to medicine as the holy Torah was to the Jews, professors would pass along what Alejandro had later discovered was frequently erroneous information, for what was taught had been written many centuries before. *We have learned so much since then*, he would always think as he witnessed the procedures. *Surely we can do better than this!* He wanted the truth about the human body, and he wanted to see it more closely for himself, to draw his own conclusions based on his own observations. This, he knew, was the only way he would get what he wanted. He would have to steal his knowledge when no one was looking.

Alejandro gathered his tools together, wishing he had an even better knife than the fine one he owned. He also cursed his lack of time, for he would have liked to examine as much of the cadaver as possible. He awakened his apprentice, and together they ate a light meal of bread and cheese before the work should take away all desire for food.

He checked the boy's wound again, and as expected, it had begun to fester. But the boy could function well enough to be of some value; he would have little choice if they were to make the progress needed. Alejandro applied another drop of clove oil to the wound, and they prepared to dissect the body.

They tied cloth masks filled with aromatic herbs over their mouths and noses, which would delay the inevitable time when they'd be forced to abandon their work because the smell overpowered them. They carefully removed the hay and set it aside for the return trip to the graveyard, then lifted the body with the rough cloth strips and carried it back to the surgery. As the windows were already shuttered against prying eyes, they were forced to light torches to provide serviceable light, which quickly increased the already overwhelming heat. After placing the remains of Carlos Alderón on the table, they carefully removed the layered shroud and set it aside for later rewrapping.

Already shriveled and wasted at burial, the body was now skeleton-like. What remained of the flesh was the color of a fish's belly. The gnarled fingers and curled toes were tightly clenched as if holding precious jewels, the bones nearly visible through the thin skin. It was gruesome, and Alejandro could not completely escape the grip of nausea. Stinging bile rose up in his throat and he had to turn his head to breathe before his stomach could find peace again. Yet despite the heat, the stench, and his own visceral fear, the young physician could barely contain his excitement. He was astonished by the depth of his own morbid fascination with this dead thing, which no longer bore even a slight resemblance to humanity, and disturbed by his own ungodly eagerness to desecrate it.

He made a long incision down the center of the corpse's chest. At the top and bottom of this incision he made two more cuts, then pulled aside the flaps of skin and muscle to reveal the rib cage. Grateful that his work was not hampered by the blood that would have flowed from such cuts had the patient been alive *(but, oh, he thought, what he would give for that experience if it could be painless!)*, he cracked open the breastbone with a chisel, taking care not to spoil what lay beneath it, then pulled the breastbone completely apart at the center. A new blast of foul odor rushed out. Ignoring his returning nausea, he peered into the body cavity and looked closely at the lungs. Their size was noticeably different. *I knew it!* he thought, his excitement building. He palpated the large lung; his fingers slid around on the slimy surface. But he could feel that it was hard and firm, and he wondered how air could be absorbed through such an apparently immovable mass. In contrast, the smaller one was soft and pliable and, despite the grayish color, resembled a dried apricot in shape and texture.

He cut open the larger lung, and was reminded of slicing meat; when he cut into the smaller one, he found the texture to be quite different. Instead of being firm and unyielding, it was still somewhat pliable. This made absolutely no sense to him; he had always assumed that as both sides of the chest rose in unison, so both lungs should be the same. So despite the abomination that lay before him, Alejandro smiled behind his mask, and his eyes sparkled with excitement. It was one of those rare times when he was truly happy, because he knew he had discovered what caused the death of Carlos Alderón.

The inside surface of the smaller lung was dark and almost sooty in appearance, in keeping with the popular medical theory that poisoned air could be responsible for creating certain imbalances. He wondered what dark poison had invaded Carlos Alderón's lung, causing it to muster its own defense by throwing up a large shield. He did not understand why this hard armor should lead to the body's death.

Puzzled, he pressed the lungs aside to reveal the dark brown heart, still firm to the touch, covered with patches of a white greasy matter that pulled away easily, not unlike the suet farmers added to their chickens' feed to fatten them. This heart was very much like those he had seen in the open chests of living animals. Señor Alderón had lived a peaceful life, and Alejandro therefore assumed that his heart would not be diseased, because he would logically have displayed some indication of foul temperament while alive. Despite their huge differences, and the difficult secrecy of the treatments, Carlos had never said an unkind word to him. Alejandro deplored his lack of experience with human hearts, but thought anyway that this one looked rather large, which was consistent with its owner's pleasant demeanor.

He wiped his befouled hands on a cloth and then rinsed them in water. After drying them carefully Alejandro sat down at a nearby table and took out his writing materials—a fine quill and a small bottle of blackish ink, and a leather-bound journal of parchment pages, his "book of wisdom," as he had taken to calling it. It was a gift he had carried with him to medical school in Montpellier, a last blessing from his father before he had sent his only son into the hands of Christians for an education he did not really want his son to have. Alejandro had always sworn to himself that he would make his family proud of him despite their objections to letting him enter the Christian world; he was determined to show them that his endeavors were worthy. The book now contained many careful sketches and pages of precise notes, to which he referred constantly in his work. He turned to a fresh page and carefully inscribed the words and images that would allow him to recall his observations of the inside of Carlos' chest at a later time, when that knowledge might be beneficial in the treatment of another patient.

His deep concentration was interrupted by the boy's insistent tapping on his shoulder, reminding him of their need to be brief. He finished his writings and set the book aside, then went about the grisly work of replacing each lung in its original position while the boy repositioned the limbs so the remnants of the cut shroud could be gathered around them again.

He went to the window and peered out through a crack to determine the hour. "The sun will set in a short while," he said to the boy. "We will be able to rebury the corpse tonight." He was immensely relieved that his self-imposed ordeal would soon end. "Soon we will be able to open these shutters and let this evil smell escape into the darkness," he added. The boy said nothing, but nodded his agreement.

They changed back into the traveling clothes they'd worn on the previous night, even though the garments were indescribably filthy. The clothing they had worn during their examination of the corpse reeked of death and decay, smells that could not be removed by even the strongest soap. They bundled it up in the corner of the stable for later burning, for it would draw curious attention to do so on such a hot night.

They brought the rewrapped corpse back through the passageway into the stable, and placed it in the rear of the cart. When they had carefully arranged the hay over it as before, Alejandro opened the stable door and brought the mule around to the front of the cart to be hitched up, only to discover by its refusal to cooperate that the mule's tempestuous temperament had not improved in the day that had passed. *Surely this beast does not have an overly large heart,* thought the doctor in disgust, *for its disposition is small and mean.* With some stroking and soft words the mule was finally gentled. Alejandro quickly tightened the leather cinches around its belly while he had the opportunity.

After their hours of work the boy's hand was once again throbbing, and he began to snivel and complain, moaning that his pain was intolerable.

Though he was impatient to be off again, Alejandro sent him back into the surgery for a bottle of wine. While he waited for the boy to rejoin him, he led the mule out of the stable onto the path leading to the road.

The cooler evening air was ambrosia to his seared lungs. He felt as if his throat and chest were on fire from the cloying stench of the surgery and the hot air he had been forced to breathe over the long course of the day. He gulped in great loud lungfuls of the sweet night air. Hearing only his own rasping breath, he failed to hear a movement nearby.

"Jew."

Alejandro froze, the young woman's voice having shocked him to stillness. *How had he not known someone was there?*

Again she said, "Jew!" louder and more forcefully. Without looking he knew this voice belonged to the girl who had eyed him so immodestly at the well. *Surely,* he thought, *she would not risk being found with me, especially in the dark!* Without speaking he looked at her, and their eyes locked.

"Do men of your kind usually respond so ungraciously when addressed by a lady?"

Alejandro kept his voice low, his tone deliberately unfriendly. He did not want this girl to mistake his intentions. "Lady," he said, allowing her a title of respect he felt was surely undeserved, "men of my 'kind' do not allow themselves to be in the company of a young woman when it is ill advised by the inequality of their stations in life." He hoped she would think he was implying that she held a loftier position by virtue of her Christianity; he did not want to explain his true meaning.

She laughed, tossing her long dark hair in a manner meant to excite him, and said, "I do not consider it a sin to enjoy the company of a good-looking man, even if he is unaccountably attired as a beggar. When I saw you this morning at the well, I thought you meant to please all the ladies. I do confess that your appearance pleased *me*. But now it is another tale! Tell me, are your patients not paying you, or do you travel this evening to a masquerade?"

Alejandro invented a quick tale that he thought might appease her curiosity. "I am traveling to a remote place to gather certain medicinal herbs that bloom only at night. The terrain is difficult and I will surely ruin my regular garments."

Smiling seductively, she stepped close enough to place her hand on his rough cloak as if to examine the quality of the fabric. "And this garment is surely beyond ruination," she said. He cringed, stiffening visibly, and she laughed mockingly at his discomfort. She continued to handle his cloak, slowly drawing her fingers down the front edge until her hands were near his waist, all the while keeping her eyes locked on his, searching for a signal to proceed with her exploration. He remained expressionless, still frozen with fear; he swore at himself again for having been careless.

If the apprentice came back, he knew she would be shamed into running away. *Surely*, he thought, *she will not allow a witness to see her here with me.* He fidgeted, and pulled away from her. *Where is that God-cursed boy?*

She frowned a little, realizing that he was resisting her advances. She deliberately reached for his waist, and pulled him back again.

"Señorina," he said nervously, "surely this can do no good for either of us. Are we not both forbidden by our Gods to be together in this way?"

She laughed and answered, "I am forbidden by my God even to be with a man of my *own* faith, unless he is chosen by my father, and I am properly married to him. I would be disgraced before the entire town if I were to approach a Christian man this way. But I know that *you* will not tell a living soul if I am unchaste with you. My father would demand your death, and the governor would surely accommodate him."

"Señorina . . ."

Laughing again, she added, "Besides, I am told that Jews are different in their manhood from Christians, and while I will not admit to knowing much about how a Christian man is, I do admit to curiosity. . . ."

As she continued her seduction, he felt his manhood rising against his will. *What disloyalty is this?* he demanded silently of his stirring loins. *You would rise for this strumpet?*

He said again, "Señorina, I beg you . . . do not do this . . ." but she did not remove her hand. As she laughed and slipped her hand into the space between his breeches and his belly, he grabbed her wrist and pushed it away. In his fear he held it too tightly, unintentionally causing her sharp pain. She cried aloud and gripped her injured wrist in shock.

The skittish mule paced nervously back and forth to the limit of his restraints. Trapped as he was by the girl, Alejandro had paid the difficult animal little heed, though he could see that the beast was agitated. On hearing her cry the mule reared up, determined to rid himself of the confining leather straps. The cart to which he was harnessed tipped sideways at an odd angle, and Alejandro watched in horror as the hay tumbled out at their feet, followed by the loosely wrapped body of Carlos Alderón, which landed at the girl's feet, its shroud dislodged from the face. The shriveled blacksmith lay staring up at the young girl as if in disbelief at her brazenness.

Her screams could be heard throughout the entire village and voices of alarm rose rapidly up in response. The apprentice, having sufficiently doused his pain, ran out of the stable just in time to see the girl running toward the square, her skirts flying out behind her, and to hear her shrieks of terror.

Alejandro knew instinctively that he could not escape. The girl would run to the constable and the priest would be called out to attend to the desanctified remains.

The apprentice looked pleadingly at him, not knowing what to do. No one had seen him with Alejandro during the course of their adventure; the physician waved him off urgently, and he ran away in great relief, narrowly escaping the ordeal of a trial and possible execution.

Alejandro dropped down to his knees, tired beyond all experience. He knew his life was forever altered, and he prayed to God for the strength to see him through the terrible days and nights to come. As he heard the approaching commotion, he covered his face with his hands, and wept bitter tears.

Two

J anie and her assistant sat at a small round table in her London
hotel room, a small efficiency with a kitchenette and sitting area.
Intended to accommodate the service for a minimal tea, the table
wasn't quite up to holding an entire scientific research project. It overflowed with piles of disorganized paperwork, which would ultimately be
gathered together in a coherent fashion and rewritten to create a doctoral
thesis, one that Janie sincerely hoped would make it past the critical—
but she had to admit, fair—eye of her thesis advisor back in Massachusetts.

"If John Sandhaus could see this mess, he'd have a conniption fit,"
Janie said.

"Sorry," her assistant said with a hurt look.

"No, no, I don't mean to imply it's your fault," Janie quickly added.
"I knew there would be this much paper. It's just that right now it
doesn't have that 'career-saving' look I'd hoped it would. It looks like one
of my early medical-school projects. Completely disorganized." She
worked her way through one of the piles of papers, looking for a specific
piece that she expected would have been folded into quarters because of
its large size. As she plowed through the various letters of permission,
geographical surveys, computer prints, and other odd scrawlings on
pressed cellulose, she could see that just about everything she'd expected
to find done by the time she arrived had in fact been done.

She found the piece she was looking for and unfolded it over the
rest of what lay there. It was a detailed geographical map of a portion of
London, a good chunk of which had been involved in the Great Fire of
1666. As part of the final thesis Janie would compare the chemical content of the soil in the burned sections against that of the unburned
sections, and the final dig sites were laid out carefully on the map before
her. Most of the sites were marked with red X's, indicating that permission to dig had been acquired and that the necessary paperwork was
already completed. A few were marked with the green X's that meant
permission had been given verbally, but the papers still had to be chased
down.

"Wow, you've been busy, I see," she said. "Really, Caroline, this is
nice work."

Caroline Porter beamed, pleased to receive Janie's acknowledgment of what had been a marvel of organization on her part. "I know when you look at this mess"—she gestured at the table—"it doesn't look like much. I was hoping to get it all into a binder before I picked you up at the airport, but it just didn't happen." She laughed a little. "I was counting on your plane being late."

Janie smiled. "Not usually a bad bet these days. But the flight went off without a hitch. Thank God, because the woman sitting beside me was a real yakker. I finally just shut off my earphones. I wish the etiquette for that stuff were more developed."

"Maybe you should e-mail Miss Manners."

Janie laughed. "Dear Miss Manners: How can one, with proper sensitivity and empathy, courteously silence one's rude and irritating airplane seatmate?"

"Gentle Reader," Caroline said, "One may whack such boors politely over the head with the buckle of one's seat belt."

"But then all the other passengers will be pissed off at me because the seat-belt alarm will sound."

Caroline smirked. "If we only ran the world, no one would face such dilemmas . . . but back to the dilemma at hand." She pointed to two spots on the map. "These two owners are away. One should be back tomorrow and the other is due in over the weekend. I have messages waiting for both of them." Then she sighed. "But this one"—she pointed to a small undeveloped area south of the Thames—"this one's going to be tough. His name is Robert Sarin. He's a very old man and he's the 'caretaker,' whatever that means, of this area." She drew her finger around it on the map. "This could be the fly in the ointment. I spoke to the man at some length yesterday before I picked you up at Heathrow. He's just not budging. And he doesn't seem to have a really good reason why he won't give permission. Tell you the truth, I don't think he's got all his bolts tightened. Seems a little slow to me."

"Do you think it will help if I give him a call myself?"

Caroline pondered for a moment before answering. "It certainly can't hurt. But I don't know why he'd give you permission if he won't give it to me. He doesn't know either of us. Maybe we should tell him about all the other people who've said yes."

"Good idea. Maybe he'd feel more comfortable if he knew what good company he'd be in by letting us dig." She shuffled through the papers until she found the list of property owners. "Lady this, Lord that, the tenth earl of whatchamacallit . . . a pretty impressive group, wouldn't you say?"

"Impressive," Caroline said. "But I don't know if it's gonna help you much. I think this guy Sarin will be a tough nut to crack."

Janie's eyebrows furrowed. "I'm getting a headache," she said. "Shit."

"I have some ibuprofen," Caroline offered, smiling.

Janie's eyebrows rose up in a look of surprise. "How'd you get *that* in?" she asked.

"The toe of one shoe. I brought four pairs but he only looked through two of them."

"Congratulations, I think. But don't get caught with it."

"I'm not planning to. I'll get you a couple." She went next door to her own room and returned in less than a minute. She handed three tablets to Janie and poured her a glass of water.

Janie swallowed them quickly, then leaned back in her chair as if in anticipation of some wonderful high that would soon take hold of her. "Ah, *drugs*," she said with a sigh. "Somehow I think the drugs we used to have were a lot more fun than this."

Caroline smirked. "Back in the 'good old days'?"

Janie said nothing, but responded instead with a brief and very strained smile. In her mind's eye she saw her neat home in the foothills of the Berkshire Mountains, her husband and daughter smiling from a porch swing as they rocked back and forth. She heard the buzz of June bugs and felt the sultry heat of a New England summer. Lawn mowers and children squealing with delight as they ran through sprinklers. Laundry, snow tires, the morning bathroom ritual of three people who were accustomed to living together. Then it faded, and she was alone again.

"Janie, I'm sorry. . . . I didn't mean . . ."

Janie tried to dismiss Caroline's concern with a wave of her hand. "It's all right, Caroline," she said. "Life goes on. And you shouldn't have to tiptoe around me. I don't expect you to run everything you're going to say to me through some sort of 'appropriateness' filter. We've got enough to think about as it is." She looked up again and smiled. "And thanks for the ibuprofen," she said. "I appreciate your parting with a little bit of your supply." Then she looked away again.

"No problem."

There was a small but uncomfortable silence between them for a few moments. Janie finally broke it by saying, "Okay, now that I've dealt with one headache, let's get on to the next one."

"Right," Caroline said. "The unbudgeable Mr. Sarin."

Janie sighed deeply. "He could really screw this whole project up. I need that soil sample." She spaced two fingers half an inch apart from each other and displayed them in front of Caroline's face. "I'm *this close* to getting certified. And I'm really getting tired of being unemployed."

"Maybe you could call John Sandhaus and see if he'll let you change the dig sites."

As she neatened the piles of papers, Janie said, "Attila the Advisor? Fat chance. He didn't even want me to come to London in the first place. 'Why can't you find something to do *here?*' he asked me. He'd love a chance to drag me back again and make me dig up something in the United States."

"They don't make this stuff easy for you, do they?" Caroline said.

"No, they don't," she said with a sigh. "But don't get me going on that. I haven't got enough time to wallow in it today." Then her expression intensified. "Tell you what," she said. "We'll get started on the first bunch of digs this afternoon. No time like the present." She pointed out several *X*'s in one neighborhood of London. "That way we can get them to the lab for analysis and I'll feel like I've actually accomplished something."

She poked through another pile of paper and then said, "I assume you've got the authorization papers for the lab somewhere in here. . . ."

Caroline moved one or two things and extracted a sheaf of pages, stapled together in one corner. "You were looking in the wrong pile," she said, smiling.

"Great," she said, taking the papers from Caroline and stuffing them in her briefcase. "While we're out, we'll swing by and take a look at this field. We should probably go ahead and place the marker, just in case, if we can do it without this Mrs. Sarin seeing us. Is the geography such that we can sneak in there?"

"There are a couple of big trees and it's surrounded by a sort of thicket. I wouldn't exactly call it woods, but the place is pretty private. I think the dig site will land pretty far from the cottage."

"Then I think we should risk it. And while we're there, maybe I'll get some ideas for how to change this guy's mind."

Janie slammed her pencil down on the tabletop in frustration, nearly breaking it, bruising her fingers in the process. It was an unusual display of temper for a woman customarily so self-possessed, but one that she felt was entirely justified. When the elderly caretaker of the property had, without offering an explanation, politely but firmly refused her own plea for permission to dig, she'd resorted to nearly *begging* him, and then she'd called everyone she could think of who might have the authority to overrule him. Her ear ached from a day of unproductive telephoning. She couldn't find a soul in any of England's thousand or so ministries willing to countermand Sarin's stubbornly immovable position.

What annoyed her most was the old caretaker's continued unwillingness to give her a reason for his refusal. Having seen that particular piece of ground during the previous day's fieldwork, she couldn't say that there was anything terribly precious about it. It was just an ordinary field, very slightly sloped, with a lot of weeds, unruly shrubs, and a few notable rocks. There was an old thatch-roofed stone cottage at the far end of the field in which Janie thought the caretaker probably lived. The one remarkable feature was a pair of old oaks, almost leafless, that grew from opposite sides of the dirt drive and met above it, twisting together in an ancient embrace. It was a sad and tired-looking place, not quaint and charming as she'd expected it to be. "I can't imagine what kind of care he thinks he's taking," she'd commented to Caroline at the time. "The place isn't exactly Kensington Gardens."

Janie walked to the refrigerator in her small hotel suite and selected a ripe nectarine. With a small sharp knife she sliced carefully through the smooth amber skin; the ripe flesh pulled gently away from the pit with little effort. *Such a simple pleasure,* she thought, *one of those things you take for granted until all these changes make them hard to get.* It was wonderfully juicy—she had to suck and bite at the same time to keep the juices from dripping onto her clothes. She ate it slowly, savoring the sweet juices, remembering a time when she would have eaten two or three such nectarines in a day without giving a minute's thought to where they came from. She licked her fingers, wiped her hands on her jeans and picked up the phone, then dialed the English eight-digit number, which left her American index finger dangling in hopeless anticipation of the ninth.

The phone rang twice in rapid succession; she could just barely heard it ringing through the wall separating her efficiency from Caroline's. Then she heard the familiar voice saying, "Hello?"

"Look sharp, darlin', this is your boss calling, and I'm in, to borrow a local phrase, a ripping bad mood."

"Oh, fabulous. Just what I need today, the boss in a bad mood. What is it now?"

"Same thing as yesterday," Janie said. "*Bureaucratus nervosa.* No known treatment. Invariably fatal."

"Explain to him about involuntary vasectomies, Madam Surgeon."

Janie chuckled. "I don't know if they're doing them in England yet. And I'm not a surgeon anymore, in case you forgot, which is why I'm doing this *stupid stupid* project in the first place. I should have listened to John and dug up something local. I think we're just going to have to pay our Mr. Sarin a visit."

The old caretaker closed the fragile book carefully when he heard the sound of the approaching car. He pulled the lace curtain aside and looked out through the uneven glass of the window in his ancient cottage. Shading his eyes against the late afternoon light, he tried to view the field beyond the old oaks through the eyes of his arriving visitors. *What were they seeing?* he wondered, feeling suddenly nervous. *Could they possibly know?*

His dog stood next to him, his head tilted curiously, wondering what his master was looking at. "They're here, old chum," he said, and patted the dog's head. "They're finally here."

He watched the two women intently as they got out of their rented car. They were both well dressed; he thought anyway that there was a look of prosperity about them. The taller one was clearly older than the small one. Her dark hair was chin length, casually cut, and tinged with a bit of gray at the temple. She had a pleasant face, but wore an expression of quiet worry; he saw the telltale tiny lines between her eyebrows and wondered what this handsome and obviously blessed woman had to worry about. She had long slender fingers, he noticed, and her hands moved gracefully as she unfolded a map. The other one was younger, petite and red haired, and her face was a mass of freckles. *One leads, the other follows*, he thought.

As he watched them move closer together, the differences between them seemed more pronounced. They studied the map for a moment, pointing here and there and exchanging a few comments he could not hear. Then they walked the length of the pathway, both wobbling a little in their dressy shoes as they proceeded over the worn stones of the path to the cottage door. He smiled, liking the looks of them, and admitted to himself that he was eager for some company. He had made only a few friends throughout the years. Now the closest of them had gone quite simple with age, leaving the caretaker with little opportunity to satisfy his need for occasional society.

He had gone to the grocer's for a tin of biscuits, a rare treat in his normally mean household, and had set out the best of his linen and service. He'd had to refold the napkins to hide a few spots; he hoped they wouldn't notice when they used them. It had occurred to him as he laid out the accoutrements of proper hospitality that these might be his last callers, and though his upbringing had been odd and isolated, it was nevertheless quite proper. He was sad that he could not give them what they had come to get, but was determined to give them the most graciously rendered disappointment he could arrange. He only wished that he knew better how to care for his home now that his mother was gone. He hadn't properly cleaned it, and it was beginning to look a bit of a mess.

The anticipated knock finally came. He left the window and shuffled to the wood plank door. He opened it to two very feminine smiles of anticipation.

"Mr. Sarin? Robert Sarin?" the tall one asked.

"Indeed." He smiled and nodded.

"I'm Janie Crowe and this is my assistant, Caroline Porter."

"Come in, please," he said, gesturing inward. The tall one had to stoop to enter; the small one stepped nimbly over the threshold without bending. He motioned them to sit, but as they headed for the chairs, he noticed that there were things scattered all over them. He shuffled over to the chairs, saying, "Oh, sorry, let me get those," and quickly scooped up what he could, a pair of socks and a sweater, the dog's leash, which he hadn't hung on the wall as his mother always did, a soiled plate with a fork resting in its center. Once everyone was comfortably settled, pleasantries were exchanged and they partook of the modest refreshment.

"Mr. Sarin," Janie began when they'd all set their teacups back into the saucers, "I'm grateful that you agreed to give me the opportunity to pursue this matter further. As I explained on the phone, I'm conducting an archaeological survey of this section of London." She nodded in Caroline's direction. "Miss Porter is assisting me in that endeavor. We need to collect a meter-deep plug about ten centimeters in diameter, which will be divided into layers and analyzed for purposes of scientific research."

Scientific research, she thought to herself. It was the most effective catchphrase in her persuasive repertoire. Janie knew from past experience that very few people could resist the feeling of importance gained by participating in "scientific research." To her disappointment it didn't have the desired convincing effect on Sarin.

He set his teacup back in its saucer and cleared his throat. "I'm sorry," he said. "I really am. But as I've already told you, I'm afraid that it will be quite impossible."

Janie furrowed her brow involuntarily. "Mr. Sarin, if I cannot acquire this last sample, all my previous results will be invalidated. This is very important to me. I'm sure you know that travel between the United

States and Britain is quite difficult these days. Might I ask why you cannot accommodate me? It seems a rather rigid position, considering the simplicity of my request."

There was an uncomfortable moment of silence; he struggled with himself over what he could reasonably offer as an explanation. He knew he wasn't good at thinking; his mother had told him so. He would give them the reasons, the ones he'd memorized in his childhood, the same ones he'd had no occasion to use until now when he was well into his dotage. They could never be expected to understand. He himself sometimes did not understand, though his whole life had been spent in the study of this place and its history. There were days when he devoted many hours to wondering about the care that had been put into this rocky field over the centuries. A branch would fall, and it would be dragged away in the night. Somehow the acorns were always picked up, though he himself never saw to it. People other than himself, people he rarely saw and hardly knew, were devoted to it as well.

"Mrs. Crowe," he began carefully, for he wanted badly to do a good job of explaining, "no one has ever disturbed the soil here. It is a condition of the will by which the property was deeded to the city of London that the ground never be broken. This cottage and the immediately surrounding gardens were built prior to the deeding, and are exempt from the restrictions, but since then nothing of the sort has been done."

Janie ran through her options mentally. She was quite unaccustomed to obstacles such as this. Sarin's refusal seemed to carry the weight of some unnamed higher authority, and she was stumped.

"Have you ever been told a reason for this restriction? It seems rather extreme."

He was diplomatic in his response, more diplomatic than one might expect from a man with his limited faculties. "I couldn't say what the reason is." *Wouldn't say*, he thought to himself, although he knew the reason like he knew the king's first name. "I'm afraid I won't be of much help to you in that area."

The silence that followed was weighted with finality. There was nowhere to go from here. It was the mandate of someone long dead and the caretaker could not countermand it even if he were of a mind to do so, which Janie doubted he was. She placed her teacup on the table, and stood up slowly, straightening her skirt as she did so. Caroline followed her lead and rose, her eyes darting anxiously back and forth between Janie and the caretaker, waiting to see who would make the next move. The old man remained seated for just a moment after they stood, staring off to the side and making small silent movements with his lips, little rehearsals of phrasing. Caroline looked at Janie, who showed her own confusion with a shrug.

"Well," Janie said, hoping it would get his attention, "I appreciate your time and the lovely refreshments. Perhaps we shall meet again sometime."

Her words worked in the intended manner. Sarin rose up slowly and responded with great care. "I'm quite sure we shall. And I'm really very sorry I couldn't be of more help."

"Thank you," Janie said, and they left.

Outside in the car Janie sat fuming behind the wheel for a moment and stared out at the field. She *needed* this sample to validate all the others, and if she didn't get it, she'd have to start the thesis process all over again.

"We'll steal it," she said, and turned the key.

Janie and Caroline stood at the edge of the field waiting for their eyes to adjust to the darkness, both dressed in black with sooted faces to match. Yet despite the cleverness of their attire, Janie felt very small and humble as she and Caroline proceeded toward the center of the field, placing each foot carefully, testing the darkness for unseen obstacles. Janie carried the long metal soil plugger, and Caroline the canvas bag in which they would stow the soil sample. The field was bumpy, and despite her careful steps, Janie stumbled; she lost her balance momentarily, and as she struggled to regain it, the soil plugger clanged against a rock. Unimpeded by trees or buildings, the sound echoed out over the field like a clarion announcing their arrival.

Mouthing silent curses, Caroline quickly reached out and grabbed the tube to still its vibration. They stood in silence, their hearts beating wildly, and squinted through the darkness, searching for signs that they might have been discovered. There was nothing to see but the silhouettes of the two massive oaks and the clumps of trees around the perimeter, some hiding the small cottage from easy view.

Yet Janie imagined the presence of unseen watchers. She could feel them, like stalking animals, encircling their position on the field. But there were no golden pairs of eyes, no breath sounds, and no low growls; the only sounds were occasional city noises, so she touched Caroline's arm and they proceeded, their senses on full alert, toward the place where they expected to find the beeper.

Thank God we surveyed before we approached Sarin, Janie thought, *and thank God it hasn't rained since we positioned the beeper.* Its thin sound came out of the darkness, faint but clear, so they turned in the direction of its apparent origin and headed toward it.

At ground zero they quickly assembled the plugger, and began twisting it down into the rocky earth. It was hard physical work, and soon both women were sweating despite the night's relative coolness. When the plugger was finally submerged to the proper depth, they stopped to rest for a few minutes.

Across the field in the old stone house the caretaker woke from a rather extended afternoon nap. He took a quick look at his watch, and cursed himself for having slept right through the best part of the evening. He hadn't realized, when he sat down in his rocking chair, how much the encounter with the two women earlier in the day had taken out of him. For several hours he'd slept like the dead.

He went to the basin and splashed his face with some cool water, then dried it briskly on a rough towel. His dog was still lying quietly by the door, waiting patiently for his "afternoon" walk.

Sarin offered his patient companion a bowl of fresh water, and the dog lapped it up, looking afterward at his master with something akin to a smile. The leash was lying on the floor where Sarin had dropped it earlier to make room for his visitors to sit down, and the dog pointed to it with his nose, his tail wagging furiously.

"All right, my friend, I understand," Sarin said. He wondered why he never had any difficulty communicating with his canine companion, when human beings were such a challenge. "I'll just get a sweater and we'll be off." He tucked a pipe and some matches into his pocket, and the pair went out for an evening walk.

The dog sniffed about for a bit, looking for just the right spot to leave his mark. He lifted his leg and christened a low shrub, then moved on eagerly. The caretaker struggled along behind him, slowed by the stiffness of his aged joints. The perimeter of the field was about half an hour's walk, providing they came upon no unexpected distractions re-quiring attention, like teenagers smoking their smelly dope or other such nonsense.

Their progress was undisturbed until the dog suddenly stopped and turned his head toward something out on the open area. He raised up his ears, cocking his head slightly, and hushed his panting. Somewhere high overhead a hawk shrieked out its predatory intent, and the confused dog looked up, first into the sky, then at his master, who reached down and patted him reassuringly on the head. They continued circling the field, experiencing no more interruptions until ten minutes later, when the dog raised his ears and whined again.

"What's this?" asked the caretaker, pulling the leash up short. "Is something out there, chum?" The dog strained against the restriction and tried to pull the old man toward the center of the field. The caretaker followed his lead, and was soon puffing to keep up.

Caroline stood up and stretched, ready to begin the removal process after their short rest, when her attention was grabbed by something bright in the distance on the other side of the field. She squinted, and her focus sharpened. A *flashlight!* She tapped Janie's shoulder and whispered, "Over there! Look! A light!"

"*Shit!*" Janie muttered under her breath. "He must have heard us when I banged the plugger! If he sees either of our faces, we're screwed." She looked around in the darkness and saw a group of trees that might provide some cover, if they could reach them soon enough. She grabbed Caroline by the arm and began leading her in that direction.

"The plugger!" Caroline whispered urgently. "What if he sees it?"

"Then he sees it. There's nothing we can do about that now. The handle's about as far down as it can go, so he might not. Let's just hope he's too simple to figure out what it is, if he does."

They scurried to the trees and looked back toward the place where they'd left the buried plugger. After ducking behind a large tree trunk, Janie let out the breath she'd been holding, unaware, since fleeing from the dig site on the field. They stood and watched as Sarin and his dog walked around the area in a random path, searching for something in a very disorganized manner. And though Janie knew that stealing a tubeful of dirt was scarcely illegal, Sarin's pointed refusal to allow it made the act of digging up this small bit of earth seem terribly immoral to her, an outright and blatant affront to the old man's dignity. She felt more ashamed than afraid, as if she were violating some ancient and obscure code of honor.

And as the minutes passed, and Sarin continued his aimless meanderings in the dark, Janie began to feel inexplicably cold, as if icy fingers were walking one over the other up her spine. Goose bumps rose up on her appendages, though they were all clothed. There was only a light wind, yet all around them the leaves began to rustle. Her senses issued strange warnings to her body, a feeling that they were not alone on the edge of the field.

She looked around quickly to see if her goose bumps spoke the truth. There was no one to be seen, just dark pillars of wood topped by unruly masses of swaying leaves, but Janie could not slow her heartbeat or stifle its insistent pounding in her ears. She could not stanch the cold sweat now dripping down between her breasts.

Finally the light stopped its meandering path, and was still. They heard the caretaker's dog panting as it strained against the leash, and then the old man called out, his voice defiant, "I know you're out there. I *know* it." Then his tone softened, and he said more quietly, "I wish you would just leave me alone." He turned, his shoulders slumped in silhouette, and headed back toward the cottage, the dog at his side, and was soon gone from view.

Janie stepped out from behind her tree and Caroline followed close behind her. They stole back out onto the field as quickly and quietly as they could, and pulled up the plugger with its treasured earthen contents. When it was safely stowed in a canvas bag they headed out, and as she turned the key in the door lock of the car, Janie was overwhelmed with relief that the task was behind them. But a nagging undertone of something else disrupted her peace of mind, a terrible, shameful feeling that she had done something she simply shouldn't have done.

Sarin sat trembling on his shabby divan, the faithful dog at his feet. He'd added another sweater, but could not seem to get warm. Tonight he would allow the dog to sleep on top of the bedcover, a rare treat for his companion. He spoke aloud to the dog, having no one else with whom he could share his fears.

"They've come at last, old friend," he said, "but there's nothing in the book about what I should do! It just says there shouldn't be any digging. . . . Oh dear, oh my . . ." he moaned. "Mother always said they would come, I just hoped it wouldn't be so soon. . . . I'm not ready yet. . . ."

Old fool, he thought to himself, *you've had a lifetime to prepare and still you're not ready?* He thought about his mother, who had prepared for their coming before him, and was glad she had passed over so she wouldn't see his cowardice when the critical time finally arrived. "Americans," he said to the dog. "I know so little about Americans! Now they've taken their bit of dirt and gone away again, and I don't remember what I'm supposed to do now!" Tears of frustration filled his eyes, the wet rage of a very simple man who faced a very complex task, one which he was expected, by demanding ancestors, to complete successfully. *How disappointed they would be to see me now*, he thought.

"They'll be back again, I'm sure of it," he said to the dog. "I just don't know when." He reached over and sank his fingers into the warm ruff of fur around the retriever's neck, and gripped it like a child afraid of losing his way. "We'll just have to try to be ready for them when they come again."

Two days later, Janie awoke from a fitful sleep to the shrill double ring of the telephone. She threw off the bedclothes and stumbled barefoot over the cold floor to the phone. She exchanged greetings with the lab technician on the other end of the line. Hearing the undisguised enthusiasm in his voice, she listened carefully through her early-morning haze to be sure she understood him, for he was talking very fast. She could imagine wild gesticulations at the other end of the line, rapid hand movements intended to convey his excitement. She grunted out a few sleepy but appropriate questions, heard his animated response, then politely ended the conversation. She pulled on a pair of socks and padded noiselessly to the bathroom to splash some cold water on her face, then warmed a cup of yesterday's leftover coffee in the microwave and brought it with her to the phone.

She dialed Caroline's suite. "Rise and shine, sleeping beauty," she said to her assistant. "We've got some unexpected work to do. There was something other than just dirt in that last tube."

Three

Alejandro awoke confused and disoriented in a dark and musty-smelling space. As his head slowly cleared, he cast his gaze randomly around the void, but found nothing on which he could easily focus. The only light came through a thin vertical crack in what he took to be a wall an indeterminate distance away. He groped toward it on hands and knees, and was dismayed at how quickly he reached it. A small, ill-fitting door allowed the teasing sliver of light to come through. Roughly square, the door was just large enough to accommodate him on hands and knees. He could not remember if he had crawled through of his own free will; if not, he thought he must have been shoved through with a good deal of force.

He stood up, taking care not to rise too abruptly lest he strike his head, for he was still unable to see a ceiling. At his full height he pressed himself against the wall that contained the small door, and began working his way to his right side, keeping his body flat. Slowly he groped his way around in one direction, and finding no corner, he made the assumption that the room was circular. His suspicion was confirmed when he suddenly found himself back at the trapdoor again.

He dropped to his knees and began to feel the floor. The surface was rough stone, large flat pieces fitted together with narrow gaps between them. He could feel no vegetation growing in the cracks and there was no discernible wetness, which only made him more aware of his great thirst and his immediate inability to satisfy it. His stomach growled, crying out to be filled, and though both sensations were bothersome, he was more concerned with determining the gravity of his situation than with satisfying the immediate needs of his body. He suppressed the distracting feelings of hunger and thirst and concentrated on discovering more about the place in which he was being held captive.

He lay down on the floor, stretching himself out to his full length with arms extended beyond his head, and found that he could just touch two surfaces. He repeated the same action several more times in different directions, and got the same result. From this he was able to determine the rough size of his enclosure. Then he stood on the very tips of his toes, reached up over his head, and jumped as high as he could. His fingers touched only air.

It is some kind of pit or tower, he thought, but concluded from the low level of the entering light that he could not be underground. And while the enclosure's apparent dryness did nothing for his thirst, he knew he would fare better without the dampness that fostered disease in many of the prisoners he'd examined as a student. He would not develop the pleurisy of wet confinement. He was certain that his eyes would soon adjust to the lack of light, but at present he could see very little—if he held his arm at full length away from his body, he could barely see his own hand. He twisted it back and forth in front of himself, feeling the small rush of air created by the movement, but seeing almost nothing. So Alejandro sat down with his back to the wall, eyes wide open, and waited for his vision to improve. Gradually it did, as he'd expected, but there was nothing to see.

He watched the thread of light at the door carefully, trying to notice any changes, dreading nightfall when he would be in total darkness. The angle of the light entering through the crack did not change, so Alejandro assumed it was not direct sunlight, but diffused light coming through a hall or passageway outside the trapdoor. But as the hours passed it did begin to grow dim, and he resigned himself to many long hours without full use of his senses. It was stunningly quiet in his pit. *If this were a prison*, he thought, *I would surely hear the cries of other inmates.*

By nightfall he could no longer ignore his senses. His parched throat screamed for water, his empty stomach groaned out its misery almost constantly. Sleep eluded him as his mind raced with worries of all the grim possibilities he faced. He recalled with visceral clarity the fate of a man who had been convicted before him of robbing a grave. The magistrate, after consultation with the local clergy, had come up with a logical and fit punishment for the crime: the criminal was buried alive, left to ponder his misdeed as he died in the very setting in which it had been committed. And that criminal had been a Christian. Alejandro could not even imagine what they would do to him, a Jew, for the same offense.

How can I convince them that my act was not a criminal one, that I only sought knowledge that their pope in his ignorance forbids me to acquire in a more reasonable manner? I have not robbed a grave, but borrowed its occupant for a while. I would have returned him no worse than when he went in originally. Still, he reproached himself for hours on end, not for his deed, but for the stupidity of having been caught. He searched his memory for something he could have done to avoid detection, but found nothing; his capture had been a matter of simple bad luck. His sense of injustice grew stronger as the night passed, and by the time the early threads of light came in through the door cracks, he was filled with grand schemes for saving himself.

His resolute determination was dashed when the small door was jerked open shortly after dawn, allowing an explosion of bright light to pierce his eyes, forcing him to shield himself from the painful illumination, which by then he craved almost as much as physical sustenance. A bowl of water and one small loaf of hard bread were quickly placed inside, and the door slammed shut again. It all happened so fast that Alejandro was caught completely unprepared. He had a thousand questions to ask of his keeper, but in a flash, the opportunity was gone.

"Have mercy! Please tell me where I am! For the love of God, allow me a candle. . . ." He desperately wanted a drink, but he knew that he had to plead his case before his keeper got too far away. He shouted his pleas over and over again until it became evident to him that there was no one there to hear him. He sank down on his knees, humbled by his inability to gain the attention of his captor, and downed the pitiful meal, licking the bowl with his dry tongue to gather every precious drop of the water.

Another whole day and night, he thought, assuming the worst. The thought of another silent, dark, and solitary day filled him with desolation. If he should lose control of himself during this ordeal, he knew that it would not be his body that betrayed him first, for his mind would become so desperate for a vision or a sound that it would begin to invent its own. If it came to that, he was sure he would prefer death to madness. The ultimate indignity was that he lacked even the means to end his own life.

In the center of a huge salon two men stood facing each other across an ornate oak table. Despite the imposing proportions of the room it was remarkably quiet, an effect of the numerous soft rugs and tapestries with which it was decorated.

The bishop politely gestured to his guest to take a seat. The elderly Jew bowed slightly in acknowledgment of his host's invitation, then carefully rearranged his robes and lowered himself into the chair. His posture was stooped, partly from years of bending over account ledgers and record books, and partly, the bishop suspected, from something far more burdensome. Avram's movements were unsteady, and his voice nearly trembled. The image he presented was not what the bishop had assumed of him from their years of correspondence.

Bishop John of Aragon had been Monsignor John, newly dispatched to his post by His Holiness Pope John XXII, when Avram Canches was just joining his family's lending business as his father had ordered him to do. He remembered the bitterness he'd felt on the day when it had been determined that he would not be allowed to pursue what would have been his choice of professions. "Let your brothers work with their hands," his stern father had said as he led Avram to the ledgers. "Your hands will hold a quill." He knew it was the reason he had succumbed to his own son Alejandro's pleas to pursue the study of medicine, despite his own grave doubts about the wisdom of it. He understood now his father's despotic behavior, and wished that he had found the strength to be so stern with his own son.

He and Bishop John had exchanged hundreds of letters since that day, all of them regarding the monetary concerns of the Christian Church. In an arrangement that had been hugely beneficial to both men, Avram had guaranteed that the worldly prelate would always have the cash to finance the elaborate rituals that his priests conducted, and had done so with consistent integrity, never voicing his personal opinion that God is not concerned with a man's clothing or the surroundings in which he worshiped. He was glad to collect his interest, and kept his cynical judgments to himself, and after years of association, Avram had come to feel a sort of wary esteem for the prelate.

The bishop held a similar favorable opinion of Avram, but was surprised to see before him a man who did not seem capable of conducting his business in the firm manner that had always been Avram Canches' trademark. They remained silent for a long while, eyeing each other, each redrawing the speculative mental image developed from years of wondering what the other might look like.

The bishop eventually spoke first. "You are not as I imagined, my friend. I had thought you would tower over me. You are a forceful businessman, and I would have sworn you were a giant."

The small, frail man replied, "Eminence, forgive me if I disappoint you. I can only hope that my mental powers have not shrunk with the years, as has my body."

"I suspect they remain gargantuan," the cleric said, laughing. "Now you must allow me to offer you some refreshment. Your journey was not short, and we are no longer young."

The bishop signaled to an acolyte, who returned a few minutes later bearing an ornate silver tray filled with breads, cheeses, and fruits.

Bishop John blessed the food in Latin as Avram spoke a few words in Hebrew; their eyes met over the candle flame as they simultaneously finished their brief devotions. The bishop then poured two goblets of

wine from a silver decanter. He held one up to the candlelight, savoring
the rich color of the wine through the glass. Handing it to his guest, he
said, "So, Avram, here we are, face-to-face at last after so many letters. I
am curious to know your reason for such a long journey."

Avram, visibly nervous, did not speak, but fidgeted with the knife,
clumsily cutting a chunk of cheese off one of the rounds on the tray
before him. Perceiving Avram's discomfort, the bishop sensed an opportunity to gain an advantage, however small, that might be used to good
purpose in the future over his creditor, so he pressed him further, feigning sincere concern for the man's well-being. "Please, Avram," he said,
"surely you know I am far more than your host at this simple meal. If you
have need to speak of difficult matters, do so without fear. You are in the
house of God, and you will find acceptance here."

Ignoring the pain in his old bones, Avram struggled to assume an
air of dignity and strength, and managed to squirm up a little taller in the
ornate chair. He thought to himself that it had probably cost the annual
tithes of fifty peasants to purchase this masterpiece. He observed as he
shifted his position that there were twelve such costly chairs carefully
arranged around the table. *They might have been a worthwhile expenditure
if one could only find some comfort in their seats,* the old Jew thought.

He cleared his throat. "Your Eminence," he began cautiously, "I am
sure that your 'advisors' have sent word that there has been trouble in our
town of Cervere."

The bishop eyed Avram suspiciously. *How does he know of my spies?*
he wondered. "Ah, yes, my advisors . . ." he said deliberately. "I recall
hearing that there was a problem of some disruption recently . . . a
grave robbery, was it not?" He knew full well that a Jew had been arrested
for robbing the grave of a recently deceased Christian tradesman. The
bereaved family was properly outraged and demanded immediate justice.
The bishop had not yet been told the details, however; he needed more
intelligence about the incident that Avram had laid before him. By coming so soon the Jew had taken away some of the bishop's usual advantage,
and John resolved to express his displeasure to the abbot in Cervere. He
felt ill prepared to continue, but did not wish to betray a weak link in his
famous network, a network he hadn't thought the old Jew would even
know about. *What more does he know, this wily old fox?* the bishop
wondered.

"Your Grace," Avram continued, "I regret to advise you that to my
eternal shame, the robber is my son."

The warmth drained from the bishop's face immediately. Neglecting impolitely to excuse himself, he rose up from his chair. Why hadn't

his spies been more specific about this? *I should excommunicate the incompetent fool who let this advantage slip from my fingers!* he thought angrily. *The old Jew was smart indeed to come forward with this admission, for he has deftly undercut me!*

He walked away from the table and stood staring out the window for a moment, his arms crossed, as if protecting himself from some great evil.

Avram could see that the bishop was angry, but what he could not understand was the reason. *Perhaps I have shown myself too soon,* he thought. He began to fear that his mission to save Alejandro would fail. Steadying himself against the edge of the table, he creaked to his feet and moved shakily around the table's edge nearer to his fuming host.

"My son is a physician, who took the great risk of treating this Christian at the man's own insistence, even though he knew it is forbidden. The poor man was dying horribly of a wasting disease, and my son made a noble effort to ease the suffering of his final days. He tried all known cures, expending his time on the patient's behalf. All he took in payment was a shovel. A shovel, Your Grace! He was compelled to examine the man's body in order to learn the cause of the malady. He does not believe that he has committed a crime."

He paused, hoping for a sympathetic response from his adversary, getting only an icy stare. Gathering his composure, Avram continued, "Surely he is not guilty of grave robbery. Had he not been stopped, he would have returned the body to its proper burial place, and was indeed on his way to do so when he was caught. Nothing was taken; the body was intact."

"Nevertheless," John said sternly, his eyes never leaving Avram's, "even Moses teaches that it is a sin to covet that which belongs to another man. Wise men of all religions have deemed that a man's body is among his most cherished possessions. How could a crime be greater than stealing the home in which a man's soul resides during his earthly walk? Why should he be excused from his evil deed, simply for saying he did not himself consider it to be evil? To determine the nature of evil is the privilege of God alone, certainly not that of a lowly Jew."

"I admit, Eminence, that Alejandro's deed was rash and ill considered. We Jews also believe that the body is a sacred gift from God. But he has always thirsted for knowledge. He will stop at nothing to gain it. If anyone is deserving of punishment, it is I for having allowed him to believe that he could live without the humility that is proper for our people. I am old and near the end of my life. I beg you, consider the crime to be mine. Confer his punishment on me instead."

The bishop looked at the old man, the unmet friend of many years, now suddenly transformed into an unwanted enemy. He saw a fragile, tired, and defeated soul, damned to eternal fire for his beliefs. He believed himself to have been a protector and sponsor of the Jews in his bishopric; this betrayal of his benign patronage was an outrage beyond all forgiveness. As his eyes burned into Avram's he hissed, *"How dare you allow your son to betray our trust?* I have always permitted the Jews of Aragon to live peacefully, in *convivencia.* His Holiness has entrusted me with the responsibility to carry out his policy of tolerance of the Jews in my dominion. How could you have allowed your son to make me look like such a failure? If *I* cannot control the Jews in Aragon, your people may find themselves confronted with a less sympathetic keeper!"

Avram remained silent. *So,* he thought, *he fears losing his power.* This was the open wound he needed in order to proceed. Avram knew that he could make the bishop look very good indeed. *But I must not waver,* he thought, *or he will not agree!* He changed his demeanor immediately from pleading to reasoning. He stood straighter, and spoke in a firm voice.

"Your Grace, I am well aware of the favor we Jews have enjoyed under your protection, and we are grateful for our prosperity in your realm. We, too, have made an effort to live in peace with all Christians, in the fervent hope that men of all faiths might experience the richness of tolerant cooperation."

The bishop looked directly at Avram, wondering why his attempt to intimidate him had failed. "Go on," he said suspiciously. "I am not sure I understand you yet."

Avram pulled a thick scroll from one sleeve of his robe. "Eminence, I have brought with me the record of the bishopric's accounts with the House of Canches. It would be my pleasure to review the accounts with you at this time. Perhaps we can be seated again, and resume our meal. We both have much to ponder, and I, for one, will think more clearly on a full stomach."

After a few seconds of wary consideration John gestured to the seat across from his. Avram gratefully sat down again, as did his host. They ate in silence, each one's mind racing with imaginative schemes for manipulating the other. How much could be gained? How little need be given up? The two men, armed with the wisdom of long lives and rich experiences, prepared to joust as warriors seldom did, their only weapons being their wits. The bishop was suddenly confronted with the glorious possibility of sending to Avignon sums far in excess of what he had told the pope to expect. He would be viewed as an excellent manager, a careful trustee, valuable to His Holiness for his shrewd stewardship of the tithes of Aragon. Avram wondered how much he could demand of the bishop in return for the cancellation of the Church's vast debt to his family. He would gladly give up this asset in exchange for Alejandro's life and a chance for him to begin anew in some other place. But the bargain could not simply be limited to Alejandro's release from prison. Avram would press for his safe passage out of Spain with a trustworthy Christian escort, one who would protect him on the long journey.

The bishop called the acolyte to clear the table of the meal and asked for more candles. After they were placed in the candelabra and lit, he sent the young acolyte away, and the two old men sat together, ready to conclude their unsavory business.

Avram began to recite, almost from memory, the speech he had prepared, should it be God's will that he needed it. "I have long appreciated Your Grace's patronage of my family. I am, of course, shamed by the terrible dishonor my son has done to you in failing to respect the repose of your Christian dead. While I am aware that I cannot possibly repay your generosity for allowing us to serve you these years, I would like to give you a small demonstration of my appreciation and esteem."

The elderly Jew then pulled open the scroll in front of the bishop to allow him to view the accounts. John studied the entries intently, carefully reviewing the long columns that listed the year of each loan and the amount owed. Some had been settled long ago, but a sobering debt remained unpaid. Even setting aside the interest, and assuming no new debts were to be added to the old, the Church would require several years of healthy tithes just to pay off the principal. Cursing himself, the bishop regretted that he had let the Church's debt to this shrewd man get so out of hand.

Avram once again rolled up the scroll and, keeping it just out of the flame's reach, held it over the candle, making the meaning of his previous statement clear to the watching bishop. "Perhaps it is time for me to reconsider these debts," he said. "I am sure we could work out an acceptable arrangement."

The bishop understood. "My friend, you are too kind. I could not possibly accept your generous offer without a gift of my own to you. Perhaps I can be of service to your family in its time of need."

Avram Canches made his proposal, his voice now stronger and more insistent. "My son must be released from his captivity, with guaranteed safe passage to Avignon. He will require an escort, and since I have no influence with your people, I will depend on you to arrange for a suitable guide. It must be someone you know to be completely trustworthy. I will, of course, reward him handsomely for this service."

The bishop could not believe his good fortune, and had to make an effort to hide his excitement. These requests were inconsequential, and easily arranged. "And there will be no further demands after this service is rendered?"

Avram raised himself up to his full height, mustering all the dignity and strength he could find in his weary soul. He looked the bishop straight in the eye and declared boldly, "Your Grace, this service has more value to me than anything else in your power. My son has merely stumbled on a stone in his path. The remission of your impossible debt is a small price to pay for his life."

Smiling almost scornfully, Bishop John of Aragon said to Avram Canches, "Then we are agreed to this bargain, Jew. Burn the scroll."

They both watched in silence as Avram held the parchment to the flame, filling the room with the nauseating odor of burning flesh, completely in keeping with the ignoble business being transacted therein. When the scroll was completely consumed, Bishop John turned to Avram and said, "I will contact a soldier named Hernandez on your behalf. He has served me well on many occasions. He is a tolerant and patient man, and he will be glad for your employment. But I warn you, when he learns he is to be escorting a renegade Jew, his price may be a drain on your riches."

Avram knew that he would ransom his own soul for Alejandro's freedom. He doubted that even the greediest soldier of fortune could demand what he was capable of paying for his son's safe passage. "Then, please, Your Grace, in deference to our long history, make a good bargain for me."

"I will do my best," the bishop said. "A messenger will be sent to you at first light. Details of the arrangements will be given to you at that time."

Avram bowed slightly as a gesture of his thanks. He bade the bishop good-bye, thinking it sad that they would never have contact again, for the squalid nature of their final exchange had ended their friendship forever. He had, before today, cherished their correspondence. It was a game well played between worthy adversaries, and he would miss it sorely.

The bishop walked with Avram to the door of the great room, as if to bid him farewell. To Avram's surprise and disgust he proffered the ultimate insult to the venerable Jew: he held out his ringed hand, waiting for Avram to bow in a supplicant kiss.

Avram looked at Bishop John in a glower of defiance. He stared down at the proffered hand, wishing he could show his disgust by spitting on it. But even though it would feel like a gift from God to be able to show his scorn, he knew it would do Alejandro no good. He swallowed his revulsion and stooped down, then made the required gesture of supplication. He rose up again, glared for a moment at the bishop, and then walked out.

The bishop called his acolyte with the pull of a bell cord. The young man entered the room, silently as always, and approached the senior cleric in reverence.

"Brother, send the cook out to look for that scoundrel Hernandez. No doubt he will know which tavern the rogue frequents."

"What shall the cook tell him, Eminence?" the young priest asked.

Bishop John scratched his chin for a moment, lost in an effort to come up with a plausible story. "Hmm," he said, "with Hernandez one must be careful to make the proper appeal and, of course, provide the proper enticement." He pondered for another moment, then said, "He is to be told that his services are required for an important journey on behalf of the Church. Tell the cook to hint that the purse will be an unusually fat one. And that I will expect him within the hour." He waved his hand in dismissal. As the young priest bowed his way backward out of the salon, the bishop said, "Send in my scribe at once."

The bishop waited for his scribe on his balcony, where he spent a few moments gazing up into the night sky and wondering, as always, at the majesty and mystery of the heavens. *What force,* he wondered, *could summon the strength to propel the sun in its daily journey around Earth?* He had heard that there were lands far to the north where at one time of year, the sun never left the sky, and at another time it barely made its presence known. He marveled that the ball of fire could hop so whimsically around the heavens. *Surely,* he thought, *it bounces off God's very fingertips.*

All too soon he was interrupted by the arrival of his scribe, who, after kissing the bishop's ring, arranged himself and his writing materials at the long table. The bishop dictated.

"The bearer of this scroll and his traveling companion are hereby granted safe passage by His Eminence, John, Bishop of Aragon."

The scribe handed him the scroll, to which he applied his personal seal. "Now for the next letter," he said, and began to dictate.

To the Most Reverend Father Joseph of the Order of St. Francis,

Brother, I greet you in the name of Christ our Savior. By the grace of God and to His greater Glory, I have negotiated terms of an agreement with the Jew Avram Canches to relieve the Holy Church of its financial obligation to the House of Canches. In appreciation for his kind indulgence, I have agreed to release his son Alejandro, now in your keeping and charged with the heinous sin of grave robbery, into the hands of Señor Eduardo Hernandez, who will present himself to you with my seal. Señor Hernandez will escort the vile young Jew outside our dominion, never again to intrude upon the peace of our region.

Notify the remaining family of Avram Canches that they are also banished from Aragon, and henceforth forfeit their claim to any interest in businesses located within our bishopric. The family will be required to quit their residence by sunset two days after your receipt of this letter, and any goods or property not disposed of prior to that time shall become the property of the Church, to increase her treasuries for the great work of God our Almighty Father.

Before releasing the young Jew, you will brand him so that all who see him shall know he is a Jew. He shall never malign Christian society again.

May God be with you in these important tasks. You do the work of Christ and His Virgin Mother Mary, and God will reward you well.

John, Bishop of Aragon

He applied the seal again. The scribe wrote one last letter of introduction, and was dismissed with a blessing. A soft knock was heard not three minutes after his departure, and the acolyte announced Señor Eduardo Hernandez.

Again, the light faded, and again Alejandro spent a night of thin sleep. As the first glimmer came through the cracked door frame, he readied himself for the arrival of his miserable meal. Though his body ached with hunger and thirst, it was not the prospect of nourishment that inspired him. Crouching just next to the door, eyes ever on the crack of light, ears searching for the smallest sound, he waited patiently for the return of his keeper. Every few minutes he would stretch one leg, then the other, and shake his arms about to keep himself alert and prepared.

He knew that he would have to shield his eyes from the stab of light that would momentarily blind him when the door was finally opened.

The faintest hint of footsteps sounded, sharpening his senses immediately. As they grew louder, Alejandro's heart beat nearly out of his chest in anticipation, its heavy pounding almost drowning out the cherished sound. The footsteps stopped, and he heard the bowl being set down outside the door. Cloth rustled, and the latch turned.

As the door opened, Alejandro brought one hand to his eyes, turning his head away, and blindly groped at the arm that came through the door. He felt the flesh of his captor, its warmth both thrilling and energizing. Then came the inevitable struggle, and he opened his eyes just as the arm pulled back. In the brilliant light, just before the door slammed shut again, he saw that the hand had dropped not a bowl or a crust, but a scroll.

Ignoring it for the moment, he cried out, "A word, I beg you, just one small word! Please, I beg of you, tell me what is happening to me!"

There was silence, but he heard no footsteps, so he knew his tormenter was still present. He almost missed the hushed words. "Be silent, or I cannot help you at all."

Quickly, Alejandro regained himself and, after wiping his face and nose on his filthy sleeve, responded, "God bless you, sir. I am desperate for knowledge of my situation!"

The tone of the voice darkened. "I prefer the blessing of my own God, Jew, as well you should. Listen carefully, for there is little time."

"Your forgiveness, please," Alejandro beseeched. "I will do as you say, only please tell me—"

"Silence!" the speaker hissed. "As you no doubt realize, I have brought a letter. From your father."

Alejandro groped around anxiously, finally finding the scroll. He tore off the ribbon hastily, but he could barely see the scribblings on the page. He said desperately to his jailer, "There is so little light; I shall not be able to read it."

The priest on the other side of the door paused for a moment. The father had not paid him well enough to provide light as well.

"Perhaps your God will send you some," the keeper said, and, laughing cruelly, he slunk away, knowing he would have to return later, when the prisoner was more calm, to give him his daily rations.

Alejandro sat with his back against the wall, the scroll clutched against his chest, and waited in pained frustration for his vision to adjust again. When he could finally see the thin line of light that came in through the crack in the door, he moved the parchment through its illumination a bit at a time, and the familiar scrawl began to reveal itself. His father had written in a language only a Jew could read, knowing the priest could not decipher it and that another Jew would not betray him with an accurate translation.

My Son,

Do not despair, for soon you will be liberated. I have arranged for your safe conduct to Avignon, where the pope's edict protects Jews from persecution. It is your best hope for survival. The priests will turn you over to a mercenary who will bear a package from me. Its contents will supply your needs for the journey. Guard your health and pray daily for the strength you will need in the coming days. May God protect you until we meet again.

Your loving father

Alejandro sat shivering with his back to the wall for the longest time after reading the letter. He tried to calm himself, knowing that his thirst would only be worsened by excessive excitement. As usual, his father was right. He would need to conserve his strength.

He was still sitting there a short while later when the door was opened again and his food and water set down, and he was left alone in the dark as before to cherish the taste of every crumb of bread and lick the bowl with his parched tongue to take up every last drop of water. He did not bother to make an attempt at escape, nor beg for words, but settled back to wait for his deliverance. He drifted off to sleep.

Alejandro awoke to a flash of what seemed like blinding light to his deprived eyes. He knew it was only the light let in by the opening of the trapdoor, but it seemed as if the sun itself were bearing down on his eyes with its fullest rays. He heard a voice calling to him, and he crawled quickly to the door, shielding his eyes until they were better acclimated.

The voice bade him crawl out through the small passage, and he did so gratefully, thinking that his time of rescue had come, eager to breathe some air that had not been fouled with the stench of his own excrement.

"Stand up, Jew" was the command. He did so, shakily, not yet having his full vision. Suddenly, he was slammed against the wall of the passageway, held in place at the shoulders by two monks. Another pushed his face to one side, exposing the surface of the cheek. It took only a split second for Alejandro to realize that the object rushing toward his face was meant to harm him, but it was enough for him to propel his body upward and loosen the grip of his confiners. Instead of its intended target the hot red brand landed in the middle of his chest, burning a hole right through the fabric of his shirt. He bellowed out a savage scream of pain.

"The face!" one of the captors said angrily. "We must do it again!"

But Alejandro, hearing their plan, began to writhe and thrash about so wildly that they could barely hold him. He clawed out like an animal and scratched one of his tormenters savagely on the arm, and the man promptly let go of him. He scrambled back into his cell, crawling like a newborn might wish to, back into the safety of the womb, a place where his captors would not follow.

The injured monk quickly assessed his wound, and while it was bleeding profusely, he knew it was not dangerous. He got to his feet and picked up the branding iron, thinking to try again, but saw to his disappointment that the red glow had faded. He dropped the evil instrument in disgust and slammed the door to the pit closed. "The chest will have to suffice," he said.

Alejandro fell limp as he heard their footsteps echoing down the corridor. He lay there for a seeming eternity, knowing he had been branded, feeling the searing pain of the burn and the raging anger of his humiliation. He was feverish, his entire body covered with clammy sweat in the dank stone room. He felt chilled one moment, and the next as if he were consumed in flames. He thought surely that this was the Christian hell, and he had been sent there as God's cruel jest. As if they could erase the mark his God had already set upon him, these evil men had felt it necessary to mark him again. He had foiled them this time and kept his face intact, but when they came back, as he was sure they would, they would not find a weak, compliant Jew. He would take them on, subdue them, and make his escape.

His food was brought again, and he ate like a wounded animal, seething in his desire to avenge this act of unbridled hatred. For two more days he did nothing but rest and eat, building his strength for the time when they would come for him. The yellow ooze that covered the circular wound began to harden into a crusty scab. Alejandro knew he was healing, and thanked God for the continuation of his life. He vowed to heaven that he would not waste it.

On the third day the door was suddenly opened at a time when he would not ordinarily be receiving food or water, and this time it was left open. The angry young prisoner waited patiently for his eyes to adjust to the light, gathering his determination as he sat in his cell. He peered cautiously upward and saw the silhouette of a crouching man in the passageway outside his cell, and decided to wait before making his move, hoping his new adversary would make some revealing move, show a weakness, or give himself away in some other manner. And when that imperfection showed itself, he would take full advantage of it; he would charge through the open door, and lash out at his captor in the full fury of a young man fighting for his survival.

The silhouette of the captor's head appeared in the open door. "Jew? Show yourself," a voice said.

He snickered from inside the pit, and thought to himself that he must sound deranged to the man on the other side of the open door. "Come in and find me, you stinking coward."

He heard deep laughter coming from outside the door. "You show an astonishing amount of bravery for a captive heathen," it said.

"Come in, then, and I will gladly show you just how brave a Jew can be."

"You think too much of my abilities, young man," said the voice. "I cannot see you in the dark. How then can I discern your bravery? One must have bright *daylight* to see the bravery of a Jew. Come now, have compassion on me, for I am a limited man. Show yourself."

Something unraveled inside Alejandro, some thread of sanity that he had managed to maintain in spite of his obstacles. The thread finally let go, and he roared in outrage.

"Then look at this, you Christian swine!"

He threw himself through the opening, rolled aside, and rose up quickly, crouching in an animalistic attack stance, ready to pounce on his captor.

The lone man waiting there laughed at the sorry sight of a ragged and filthy Jew snarling at him like a frightened beast. He slipped aside easily as the pathetic figure leapt at him in total disregard for his obvious advantages. "You will have to try again," he said, "although I warn you: I am a robust man, and you are no match for me."

But Alejandro paid him no attention whatsoever, and blindly charged again. Hernandez grabbed one of his arms, and swung him back around, then grabbed his other arm and squeezed them together behind the young man's back. Alejandro winced in agony as the burned skin on his chest was forced to spread to accommodate the extreme backward movement of his arms and shoulders. He was still at once, tears streaming down his face, quickly beaten, ashamed of his failure to do harm to his captor.

"Eduardo Hernandez at your service, my fine young peacock! And permit me to observe that you do little to dispel the belief that Jews are nothing but animals. Look at you, a pitiful sight, scratching and clawing like a woman!" He blithely spun Alejandro around, and faced him squarely.

"By the grace of God—yours or mine, who can tell?—I am here to escort you out of this hole to safety. I advise you to show me the respect owed to a gentleman of my obvious valor and chivalry."

Alejandro sank down to his knees, all his energy spent. Hernandez had to support him with his arms to keep him from crashing to the floor and, in doing so, realized how truly filthy Alejandro was. He turned his head away and quickly offered an opinion on Alejandro's condition. "You smell worse than a French nobleman, a state that will require improvement if I am to escort you all the way to Avignon." He laughed and said, "Perhaps I shall baptize you. It could do you no harm. Come with me, my fine young gentleman, and let us see to your new life. At least you can begin it in a state of cleanliness. Then we shall be able to see what other attentions you require."

Out into the blinding daylight they went, Alejandro stumbling along sightlessly, supported with surprising gentleness by the huge Spaniard who had come to rescue him. Hernandez literally threw his captive across the saddle of a waiting horse, then mounted another himself and took the reins of the one carrying Alejandro. They set out at a slow pace, Hernandez watching closely to see that his cargo did not slip off the horse.

A short distance away was a stream in a wooded area, shaded by trees and hidden from view. Hernandez lifted Alejandro off the horse and set him down gently. He immediately began pulling the rags off his body, but when he pulled the shirt up over the younger man's head, Alejandro cried out, and pulled his arms tightly in against his body.

"Come now, my friend. Modesty is a fine quality in a maiden, but it is wasted in a man!" He tried again to remove the shirt, but Alejandro spoke at last, saying he would remove it himself. He carefully worked off each sleeve, minimizing the pull on his wounded chest, then motioned to Hernandez to lift the remains of his once sturdy but now tattered garment over his head.

Hernandez gasped at the angry red circle just below Alejandro's neck. "Madre de Dios, young man, what was your crime?"

"I committed no crime" was the quick and angry response. "I am punished for seeking greater knowledge in an effort to improve the lot of all men who suffer needlessly from disease."

Hernandez recognized the zealot's fire in his voice. *Aha*, he thought, *so it was this one!* He had heard the local uproar over a tradesman's disinterment, reportedly perpetrated by one Cervere's Jews. And although Hernandez thought it best to leave God's business to God, he could not help but shiver at the thought of the decaying body under the physician's knife. He peered curiously at the wiry and exotic-looking man who had had the courage to do what he himself would never attempt. *Perhaps there is more here than meets the eye*, he thought with amusement.

He carefully guided Alejandro to the water's edge and bade him enter the cool stream. *He was lucky to survive that branding!* Hernandez thought. He had seen such a burn once before; it had festered to green and yellow, quickly consuming the bodily resources of the victim, who died delirious and screaming for water. He watched Alejandro dip himself in the water, and curiously peeked at his manhood to see the effect of the ritual that was done to all Jewish boys in infancy. Shuddering at the thought, he raised his eyes and noted how carefully the young man cleaned the circular wound on his chest. It caused him obvious pain, for he sucked in his breath and screwed up his face when the water touched the wound.

As he stood dripping in the stream, Alejandro turned toward Hernandez and asked if their supplies included any wine. Hernandez nodded and walked over to the tethered horses, removing a flask from one of the saddlebags. He was surprised to see Alejandro lean his body back and pour the entire contents of the flask over his chest, grimacing as he did so, letting it saturate the crusty circle.

"See here, young man! I am well paid for this duty, but not well enough to sanction your careless waste of good wine!"

The Jew had regained his wits, and said firmly, "I am a physician, and have observed that those wounds treated with ablution in both water and wine heal more quickly and perfectly than those left untreated. If you expect me to die of this injury and thereby lighten your journey, you must rethink your expectation. You will get no such compliance from me. It will do me far more good to wear this wine than to drink it."

Alejandro strode out of the water, with more strength now, refreshed by the removal of many days' filth from his body. His tattered rags were not worth burning; it would be a waste of good fuel to bother with them, so he left them in the pile where they had fallen on the bank of the stream.

"I presume that this package contains fresh attire?"

"Indeed, although I obtained it on my own, and know not whether its style will suit you."

Out came breeches, shirt, stockings, boots, vest, and hat. Alejandro had almost always dressed in the traditional robes of his people, and very rarely wore clothing in the European style. His last venture into stylish clothing at the Cervere well had ended disastrously, leading him to the miserable situation in which he now found himself. He hoped that similar clothing would not have the same disturbing effect on other people.

"Why, Jew, you look almost normal now. One might even call you handsome were it not for your curious hair."

Alejandro walked to the water's edge and peered down into the mirroring surface of the calm stream. He was surprised to see that Hernandez did not exaggerate. Except for his sidelocks he looked every bit the modern young European. He was shocked at his own impiety, and quickly stepped away, for it was unthinkable for him to *try* to look like a Christian.

"I would advise you to cut your hair, for it will only raise the interest of those we meet on our journey. It will be speculated that a Jew in Christian's clothing is running or hiding from something. This will not make our journey any easier."

Alejandro was horrified at the thought. "I cannot, for it will signify to other Jews that I dishonor our covenant with God."

"You will serve your God far better alive than dead, young man. I am paid to deliver you safely to Avignon, and I think you will arrive more safely without those telltale locks. Think again."

Not wishing to discuss his appearance any further, Alejandro asked for food, and Hernandez brought out a loaf of fresh bread and a hunk of cheese. Alejandro ate ravenously, prompting Hernandez to observe, "You eat as if it would be your last meal, Jew. Have you not known hunger before?"

Looking at his escort with undisguised wariness, Alejandro said, "My family has been fortunate."

Hernandez grunted. "Aye, I am aware of that." He handed Alejandro a small bundle wrapped in soft leather. "Your father bade me give you this," he said. "You are to open it before we begin our journey."

Stepping away for privacy, Alejandro untied the string that secured the package, gently unfolding each layer of the leather wrapping. There were several objects inside, and he examined each one in turn. The first was a purse of gold coins, more than he had seen at one time in his life. He fingered the disks and let them slip through his hands back into the purse, to enjoy the secure feeling of their weight, but took care not to let Hernandez hear their jingling. He would lack nothing on his journey to Avignon. His father had also sent a prayer shawl, a wickedly sharp knife, and the bishop's letter of safe passage to Avignon. There were some other personal items of clothing and hygiene, such as a comb and a small vial of oil of clove for toothaches and sore wounds. But most important, his father had sent his book, knowing that it was the most precious of his son's possessions. Alejandro held it reverently in his hands for a few moments before setting it down.

The last item in the package was another letter, sealed with wax for secrecy. Alejandro broke the seal and carefully unfolded the scroll.

My Dear Son,

Things have gone very badly for us. I have arranged your release, hoping that in the future you would contact us here with your whereabouts, but we have been betrayed by the bishop.

When I left him, it had been arranged that you would be safely conducted to Avignon by an escort (with whom you are now traveling if you are reading this letter). I burned the parchment that recorded the bishops's debt before his very eyes, thereby keeping my part of the bargain we made.

The swine has since ordered that our family must leave Cervere within two days, never to return. We have hastily sold our goods, and Uncle Joachim has bought the remaining debtor accounts from us.

My own spy bribed the bishop's messenger and reported the contents of his letter. Guard your face, that it is not scarred by the branding iron. Your mother is at her wits' end over your disfigurement. I have assured her that you will know how to heal yourself, and that disfigurement seems a small matter when compared to death. I hope you are not in pain, or suffering from a festering wound. Take ample care to wash it as you have so many times told me to do.

We will also travel to Avignon. If we arrive safely, we will leave word of our situation with the family of the local rabbi, who will also accept a letter from you to us.

Beloved son, you must understand that you are a hunted man. The family of Carlos Alderón has sworn vengeance upon you for your ungentle uprooting of their patriarch, and rumors are spreading that a renegade Jew is heading for Avignon, so you must conceal yourself. God will not punish you for staying alive. Do what you must to reach Avignon in safety, for there, God willing, we shall be reunited.

Your loving father

He felt a touch on his shoulder. It was surprisingly kind and gentle. "We should depart soon," he heard Hernandez say.

Alejandro rolled the scroll carefully, knowing he would come to treasure it. After placing the sheathed knife in the top of his boots and the letters in his vest, he retied the package and stowed it in his saddlebag. He mounted the horse, surprising Hernandez with his agility.

"Señor Hernandez," he said, "I beg you to indulge me for one more task. I am instructed by my father in his letter to deliver a message to the bishop before we depart."

Hernandez grunted his displeasure, but did not argue with his young employer. He turned his horse in the direction of the bishop's palatial monastery, and they proceeded at a fast trot.

Alejandro astonished himself with how quickly he took to riding a horse. It was not his customary practice, for most of his traveling had been done by mule-drawn cart. They rode quickly over the bumpy, dusty roads, and before he knew it, they were at the very monastery where his father had struck the fateful bargain with the bishop.

He leapt off the horse, again surprising himself when he landed on his feet, and gave the reins of his horse to Hernandez, then slipped away toward the door of the monastery. Before entering, he took out his knife and cut off his forelocks, letting them fall where he stood. He watched as the locks of curly black hair drifted to the ground, the last vestige of his attachment to this place and the beloved people of his family and community. As the curls hit the dirt at his feet he became a new man with a new life, and a past he could no longer admit to.

He left them where they landed and walked boldly to the monastery's massive doors. Alejandro greeted the monk who opened them in Spanish, saying that he had a message for the bishop from one of his creditors and that it must be delivered personally. But the monk said the bishop was in prayer and could not be disturbed.

More likely in bed with a sweet young companion, Alejandro thought to himself, thinking of the stories he'd been told. Taking the letters out of his vest, he showed the monk his safe passage, with the bishop's own easily recognized seal, and then the letter written in Hebrew, saying that he alone knew the translation.

Seeing that the bishop's own hand had granted this man the right to pass, the monk admitted him. He wondered at the contents of the long missal written in the heathen hand delivered by such an unlikely messenger, then decided that it was better left to the bishop to ponder it. He led the young man to the door of the salon, and knocked softly.

"Enter," said the bishop.

The monk waved him through the great door into the richly appointed room. Alejandro was momentarily awestruck by the grandeur of the furnishings, and looked around in wonder.

The bishop eyed him with suspicion as he studied the room. "Well, young traveler, God be with you. May I be of service?"

"Sir, I have a message of some importance, written here on this scroll."

"Bring it here, then, and let me see it in the light."

As Alejandro approached the man, he reached into his vest and retrieved the scrolled letter. He handed it to the bishop, who spent a moment untying the ribbon before he unrolled it.

He looked up at Alejandro with a puzzled look and said, "What joke is this, a message in the heathen script of the Jews?"

"It is a letter of appreciation from your great admirer Avram Canches. He wishes to thank you for your kindness and fair treatment."

A look of grave fear spread over the man's face, which pleased Alejandro. The bishop shrank back, knowing he was about to come to harm. Alejandro wasted no time, but pulled the knife out of his boot and plunged it deeply into the chest of the recoiling cleric.

As he regarded the limp form on the floor before him and watched the blood spread over the front of the rich robe, Alejandro wondered how he, a physician and healer, could so calmly end the life of another human being. He had sworn above all to do no harm, and here in this luxurious room he had done the ultimate harm without flinching, and with a complete lack of mercy. He saw himself in a mirror. *Who is that imposter?* he said silently to his own alien reflection. Taking the scroll from the bishop's hand, he tucked it into one pocket of his shirt, then wiped the betrayer's blood from his knife and replaced it in his boot. As quietly as he had entered, he slipped out again, closing the door behind him. With no indication that anything was amiss, he passed through the abbey halls and rejoined Hernandez outside, where they turned their horses to the east and headed toward the road to Avignon.

Four

J anie and Caroline stood at a table in the main laboratory of the Microbiology Department of the British Institute of Science, surrounded by glass and brushed chrome and white plastic laminate. The lab was housed in an old building with old characteristics: high ceilings, tall windows, resident echoes, *maybe even a ghost,* Janie thought. Awestruck and overwhelmed, they stood in the center of a room that had both the dignified authority of age and the intimidating power of technology. "I've never seen anyplace like this," Janie said. "My God, what I wouldn't give to play in here for a month."

The technician who'd summoned them there to look at what he'd found in the last tube of dirt laughed aloud. "Just make sure there's no one from Biopol looking over your shoulders. And if you're really going to play, they make you put playclothes on." He pointed to a nearby rack of biosafe equipment, all of it the same nasty bright green Janie had seen on the Biocops in the airport.

"Not my color," she said with a grim smile.

"Not anybody's," he said, smiling back flirtatiously. "I don't know who picked it, but they should be tried for conspiracy to commit visual mayhem."

"Conspiracy to give headaches, at least," Caroline commented.

The technician was charming in a very urbane and thoroughly British way. "Quite," he said. "Now, I believe this little tidbit might be of interest to you." He handed Janie a small piece of fabric, roughly circular, the approximate size of the tube in which he'd found it. "From the shape of it I'd say you sliced right through it when you twisted that tube into the dirt."

"I'd say it got pushed a bit before the fibers gave," Janie said. "See these little serrations? It had to have turned a bit in the soil for that to have happened. There must be a bigger piece down there still."

As she held the scrap in her hand, all of Janie's previous shame over absconding with the "illegal" dirt gave way to the excitement of finding something significant in it. "It's in remarkably good condition," she said. She measured from the top of the tube to the marker showing where the item had been situated in the tube. "At this depth it could have been deposited more than five hundred years ago, but there's very little deterioration. Probably because the soil around here is so peaty. It keeps the air out. I bet we won't look this good when someone digs us up." She handed the small circle of fabric back to the lab technician. "We'll have some fun with this when we get back to the States."

"Would you like to take a quick look at it right now?" he asked.

A list of silent questions popped into her mind. *Who put it there? When? Where had it been before landing in its final resting place?* She considered all those unknowns and realized that the thrill of deciphering them was what made her forced switch from surgery to forensics seem less horrifying than the other possibilities. Still, Janie hesitated. "Maybe we ought to wait," she said. "Now that we've got all the soil samples we can get right to work on them. I don't want to get sidetracked by something that's not really part of the project, although I have to admit it *is* a nice little find. I might be able to work it into the thesis somehow, but right now I'm more concerned with completing the work that's already included in it." She looked directly at the technician. "We're ready to start the chemistry runs today, if you've got the time." She wanted, without pressuring him, to imply that it wouldn't break her heart to get a fast start on the lab work.

But the technician didn't seem to understand her. He said, "I've got a couple of loose ends to tie up here first before I can sink my teeth into your work. Monday would be better for me. Then I can give you a few days of my undivided attention and you can go home. But I've got enough time for a quick look at this right now if you want."

"Oh, come on, Janie," Caroline said, her interest obvious. "Let's just take a peek. What can it hurt?"

What could it hurt? she wondered. *Probably nothing. Still . . .*

She glanced over at the small circle of fabric and wondered why the sight of it suddenly raised her hackles just enough to sound some poorly defined internal alarm. She didn't understand what made her want to leave it alone, but clearly something was holding her back. She couldn't name it as anything other than a sense that it was in her best interest to leave that specific item alone on this particular day. But Caroline, in contrast to her more cautious employer, wanted to satisfy her curiosity immediately.

"It'll only take a few minutes," she said. "We've done all this digging, some of it under very *interesting* circumstances, I might add, and so far all we have to show for it is some dirt under our fingernails and a piece of fabric. We'll be spending all day Monday on that dirt. How about we loosen up and have a little fun with the fabric today?"

Janie was surprised by the undertone of frustration she heard in Caroline's comment. She sometimes forgot that Caroline was here because it was an opportunity to learn that she could not have afforded otherwise, an opportunity to travel that might never come her way again. She'd come over beforehand, at Janie's expense, to set things up, and had been diligent in completing her end of the bargain. Janie found herself feeling suddenly inspired again by Caroline's interest, so she gave in against her better judgment.

"I guess we deserve some fun," she said, "but let's be careful. We don't really have the right equipment, and this is *history* we've got here."

The technician led them to a computer setup near the center of the lab, and arranged three chairs so they would all have a good view of the screen. He powered up the system and secured the fabric with the suction provided by a light-duty vacuum. The fabric was quite a bit larger than the microscope's plate, so it required some readjustment. Janie watched and winced each time he rearranged it, wondering what microscopic goodies were being dislodged with each movement. Finally it was settled and they brought up the first magnification.

"The fibers are really in fine condition," she said. "That leads me to think it might be wool." But as they moved through the fibers frame by frame, she saw the telltale long striations that indicated the likelihood of vegetable origin and reassessed her opinion. "Maybe linen," she said, "although I don't think it would be this well preserved. Looks like if there was ever any dye in it, it has leached out over time. But there's very little variation in the overall color, so my guess would be that it was originally white."

The strange artifact called to her, beckoning her to come closer. She complied and leaned in toward the screen for a closer look. The more she examined it, the more her curiosity grew, almost against her will. "Can you bring it up a little more?" she said.

The technician responded by pulling down a menu with the computer's mouse. He clicked on the command for magnification and selected a percentage. Almost immediately the screen was redrawn, and the fibers reappeared at twice the previous magnification.

They examined that section, and again Janie asked for further enlargement. The tech obliged her, repeating the command at her request until each fiber filled the screen entirely. They scrolled up and down and back and forth, shifting the image on the screen, stopping occasionally to examine points of interest. *All things considered,* Janie thought, *there isn't as much to see here as one might hope,* but just as she was beginning to lose interest a startlingly clear single cell scrolled into the screen's field.

"Stop there," she said quickly, pointing at the image.

Both Caroline and the technician, whose name tag said "Frank," drew in a breath when they saw the cell on the screen.

"Let's take a closer look at that," Janie said, and Frank complied by once again raising the magnification, then centering the cell on the screen. The image was slightly fuzzy, so Frank activated the automatic focus.

But the level of clarity didn't satisfy him. With obvious excitement in his voice, he said, "If you have a few minutes I can get it even sharper for you. There are a couple of filters I can run it through."

"Go ahead," Janie said, too eagerly for her own liking.

He played with the mouse a little, then entered some numerical values into a field. Another wave of electronic correction scrolled through the image from top to bottom, leaving a perfectly clear bacterium in its wake.

It was a squat, bloated little torpedo, with spidery flagella streaming out from all sides. As she looked at its dead stillness, Janie could imagine the waving of those flagella on the live bacterium as it moved through the nourishing liquid in which it had once lived. From the lack of visible bloodstains on the fabric, she guessed that it might have been deposited in sweat, or tears, or perhaps saliva. She could test it in John Sandhaus' university lab for traces of those body fluids.

"Hubba, hubba," Frank said, grinning over the find. "What a lovely little specimen this is. Looks like some type of enterobacteria, although it's not anything I recognize immediately."

Caroline gave out a low whistle of amazement. "Very pretty, very pretty indeed."

Janie kept her thoughts to herself. *So simple and perfect, and so incredibly well preserved,* she thought. Uninvited, another thought slipped in. *Dangerous,* it said. She knew that she would pursue the story of this microbe further when they got back home, and thought it might even give them some additional information relating to her thesis. But it sent chills down her spine, and she didn't know why. Neither Caroline or Frank seemed to be experiencing anything like her reaction to it.

"Can we put some sort of marker on this spot?" she asked, wanting suddenly to be finished with it. "I'd like to be able to come back to this without having to review the entire piece again."

"I can put a chemical dye marker on it," Frank said. "We can section out a small piece and save it as a search file. You can reopen the file later and direct the program to search out a match on the piece, and you can take the same file back home with you and direct your own system to do the same. Most biomed programs are set up to find specific dyes. I can use a common one to be on the safe side. We can print out this view of it now if you'd like, and I can save the entire file for you to take back to the States on a separate disk."

Rationalizing to herself the exposure of their delicate find to potentially damaging moisture, Janie said, "It's probably been wet more than a few times in its history, so I don't suppose a little bit of dye will kill it. It's already good and dead anyway."

He nodded. "I'll mark it right now, then we should leave it undisturbed for a while to minimize the spread of the dye. If you want me to, I can pack it up for you so it can be sent out tomorrow."

"That would be great," Janie said, relieved to have the burden of export documentation lifted from her. "You're certainly a lot more familiar with your own bioexport procedures than we are. Could I ask you to make two prints of the screen? I'd like to send one to my thesis advisor in America. I'd like to get his opinion about it. He'll run the images through a few programs and there'll be lots of data waiting for us when we get back."

"No problem."

He turned on the 3600 DPI laser printer, then pulled down the file menu at the top of the screen. He clicked on the command to save the file. "Pick a name," he said to Janie.

After giving it a moment's thought she said, "Gertrude. We'll name it after my grandmother. She's the original source of my funding."

"Good as a name can get," he said as he typed in the letters. "Gertrude it is." He made two prints of the image and gave them both to Janie, with assurances that he would take good care of the original.

Janie and Caroline departed, and Frank was left alone with the mystery creature. He gathered together an assortment of staining tools and materials, including a tiny syringe with a flow inhibitor. Working under the same magnification, he eased out one tiny drop of dye, which flowed onto the fibers of the fabric, deluging the single cell. He used the mouse to draw a box around the dyed image on the computer screen, and directed the computer to save the enclosed area as a separate file. Then he left the scope and turned his attention to a list of waiting lab tasks as the dye was absorbed.

He came back a short while later to remove the sample from the microscope plate. But out of curiosity he decided to have one more look before putting everything away. He sat down in the chair and looked at the screen.

Gertrude had moved.

He looked again; it wasn't possible. The bacterium was dead and couldn't *possibly* move. He thought perhaps his memory of its original position was faulty. Without exiting the program, he pulled down the print menu from the top of the screen and directed the system to print the previously saved file. He watched anxiously as the page emerged slowly from the printer, then tore it away when it was finally complete and compared the printed page to the screen.

Gertrude had definitely moved. *She must have been just playing dead. . . .* He saved the screen image as a new file, this time naming it "Frank" after himself. *Must have been in spore state. . . .* He sectioned off the immediate area of the cell and cleared everything else off the screen, then saved this smaller file as Frank2, and exited the program.

He was brimming with excitement. This sort of thing didn't happen every day, and he couldn't wait to share what he'd discovered about the microbe. Digging quickly through a pile of loose paper scraps scattered over his desk, each one with some important tidbit not to be forgotten, he found Janie's hotel number and dialed it quickly. There was no answer at her extension after the clerk put the call through.

"Damn," he said. Deeply disappointed, he hung up and went back to the computer, wondering if she'd gone somewhere other than her hotel.

After a few moments of typing and clicking, the image of the bacterium was successfully transferred via modem into another system nearby, in which resided a program called Microorganism Identification Catalog, nicknamed MIC. Of all the people who worked at the Institute, Frank was the most intimately knowledgable about the nuances of this particular program, and he had it up and running in seconds. It contained files for thousands of known microbes in graphic image format, and was able to compare its own resident images to an imported image for the purpose of visual first-round identification.

He brought up the Frank2 file, then directed the program to search for a match. After a few minutes the system issued a pleasant beep, announcing its decision.

PRELIMINARY CATEGORIZATION: ENTEROBACTERIA

Right again, Frank! he thought to himself triumphantly, his excitement still building. He directed the program to deepen its search.

READING FILES FOR SUBCATEGORIES
Cedeacea
Citrobacter

E. coli
Edwardsiella
Erwinia
Hafnia
Klebsiella
Kluyvera
Morganella
Providencia
Proteus
Salmonella
Serratia
Shigella
Yersinia

Bloody hell, he thought. A *nasty little group!* Capable of inflicting a choice variety of intestinal maladies, most of which could either kill the host organism or make it pray for a quick death. The program continued its sorting procedures, filtering out the possibilities as each characteristic was identified and compared to the known samples. Finally, after a few moments, the computer issued a short electronic fanfare, as if to congratulate itself before announcing MIC's decision.

"Cute," he said aloud, though there was no one about to hear his opinion. "Very cute. So what do we have here?"

Yersinia pestis
98% probability of accuracy
Identification complete.

Not your common everyday enterobacterium, he thought to himself, *or I'd be more familiar with it. Yersinia pestis.* He remembered vaguely studying the *Yersinia* at one time or another, but it was apparently not active in Britain or he knew he'd have been getting memos about it. Frank left the console and walked to the far bookshelf. Selecting a volume, he ran his finger impatiently down the columns of the index, finally locating the desired entry. He turned quickly to the indicated page, and read the relevant material.

As he neared the bottom of the page, he let out a low whistle. "My God . . ." he said quietly.

He took the volume back to the computer and made a visual comparison between the book's diagrams and the organism on the computer screen. As he watched, the microbe shuddered, its sides heaving with the immense effort of moving after such a long sleep. Frank jumped back involuntarily and clutched the book to his chest as if protecting himself.

He set down the heavy volume. Keeping his eyes glued to the screen as if the microbe might jump right off and attack him personally in all its magnified ferocity, he reached around behind himself and groped until his hand came into contact with a chair. He drew it close to the computer and sat down carefully. He watched in fascination as the microbe continued to struggle, intrigued by its sinuous dance, wondering what it was trying to accomplish. This type of organism, among the most simple beings on earth, was limited to two major activities: it could either take in nourishment or reproduce by division. And it was definitely not eating.

She's trying to replicate! "You liked that little dye bath, didn't you, sweetheart?" he said. Obviously refreshed, Gertrude had shaken off several hundred years of stiff dormancy and was trying to resume her normal life cycle. He stared at the screen and watched in frustrated fascination as the creature's sides heaved without result, a tiny Houdini wrapped in chains, one moment away from the fatal gulp. . . . He almost wanted to cheer her on.

His concentration was interrupted by the ding of the autoclave timer and the sudden cessation of the low background noise that always accompanied its operation, not a noise Frank ever minded or even really noticed until it stopped and he realized how truly annoying it had been. Muttering curses under his breath, he looked at his watch, and realized that he had gotten lost in the American woman's tiny creature, much to the detriment of the day's schedule. He realized with some concern that he was living up to his reputation for lateness, a fault he vehemently denied he possessed at every annual performance review. There was still a list of materials to be gathered for an upcoming project, still mail to be posted, and he had not yet reached the discoverer of the distracting microbe on the screen before him. Quickly he dialed the number; once again, there was no answer. This time he left a message that Janie should contact him at the lab as soon as possible.

He looked at Gertrude again. She was still heaving and twitching. "Come on, girl, you can do it . . ." he whispered to the image on the screen. "Come on. . . ." But she finally settled back into her original position and stopped moving, exhausted by her efforts. She made no more attempts at reproduction for several very long minutes, and finally Frank reluctantly tore himself away. He crossed the lab to the door marked BIOLOGICAL COLD STORAGE, where he leafed through the printed directory of the contents, looking for a particular sample he needed to get thawing. He flipped through page after page of Latin bacterial names,

67

each one dated and coded for the location of its holding tube in the storage rack, his index finger running quickly down the alphabetical list. He stopped at *Palmerella coli,* a strain of enterobacteria developed to have cell parts that mingled rather freely with those of other cells. It was graciously generous with its genetic components and could be coaxed into exchanging plasmids with only the slightest provocation. A virile, potent, and vigorous bacterium with a dash of proper British hospitality. He made note of the storage location and closed the directory.

As he looked through the glass partition into the freezer area, he thought to himself, *A thousand agents of death, just on the other side of that glass, microbes beyond all imagination. One or two cracked vials in the wrong hands . . .* he didn't even like to think about it. Microbes were lying in wait, licking their lips, primed to assume their rightful positions in the food chain. *One little slip . . .*

He set those doomsday thoughts aside and sat down at the operation console for the robotic retrieval arm. *Just like a video game,* he thought naughtily, and easily found the sample he sought amid the small forest of tubes and canisters. He picked it up carefully and guided it to the pass-through for exterior surface decontamination. Looking back at the empty space, he let his imagination run wild and tried to envision what would happen if anyone discovered an empty slot with no marker. Hordes of Biocops in their strange green spacesuits with yellow biosafe sacks hanging from the waist would descend upon this place within minutes of the discovery. Every exit would be sealed, and no one would come in or go out until the Biological Police were absolutely certain that there was no possibility of further contamination. It would be fascinating to watch, he thought. Then reality set in again, with all of its burdensome honor. He gave in to it and placed a marker identifying himself as the person who'd removed the tube. There were, he knew, perfectly good reasons for all these precautions, and Frank understood them only too well.

He left the cold storage area and placed the tube in an upright holding rack in the work area adjacent to the microscope where Gertrude lay in repose. He looked again at Gertrude, and saw that she was still motionless.

He wanted to poke and prod her, to see how she would react, to encourage her to be everything she could be. But work was piling up all around him, regular duties requiring his full attention. *Don't let yourself get distracted,* he warned himself; *get these other things out of the way first.* Obligation came first, but he could feel himself being tugged by fascination. Ultimately, obligation won out. "Don't worry, darling," he said to Gertrude as he powered down the computer, "I'll be back for you later."

He left the fabric circle on the microscope and punched in the locking numbers for the security door as he went out. Halfway down the hall he realized that he'd forgotten the mail, so he ran back and placed his palm flat against the entry verification screen and waited for the click of the lock. A few seconds later the flat screen sterilized itself by sending a flash of high-voltage electricity through the metal-coated surface, announcing its intention to do so with a shrill beep. Frank was one of only a few people with unlimited access to this lab, although with some concerted effort the security guard could override the system. He considered the whole system a great big pain in the ass, and wanted something simpler. He'd been told by the lab's director that anything simpler would be too easy to break, and would therefore not suffice. So on occasion, when it suited him to do so, Frank simply left the door unlocked. And seeing that he would be gone only a few minutes, he decided on his way back out again that this could be one of those occasions.

Out on the sidewalk as he waited for a break in the traffic, Frank felt the warm sunshine on his skin, a welcome change from the cold gray concrete walls and stark fluorescent lighting of the lab. He stood still in the bustle of the noonday sidewalk and soaked up the sun's rays, which seldom blazed with such intensity in England. When he turned his gaze back to the street his field of vision was dotted with blue sunspots. He failed to see the standard black London taxi come flying around the corner at breakneck speed. As it sailed through the air rather rapidly, his last thought before colliding with the metal lamppost was *Bloody hell,* Yersinia pestis. *Fucking bubonic plague.*

As they faced each other across the breakfast table, Janie read aloud to Caroline the newspaper article about Frank's death. When she finished, she set the paper down and they were both quiet for a moment.

She shook her head. "No wonder he wasn't there when I returned his call. It sounded like he was really excited about something. Now we'll never know what it was."

"We were just with him yesterday," Caroline said. "What a tragedy, he was so young. . . ."

But Janie, though not untouched by the loss, had more pragmatic concerns. *It doesn't seem so terribly unusual anymore, people dying suddenly,* she thought to herself. "We'll have to get the fabric and the rest of the soil samples out of the lab and send them back to the States. We won't be able to finish up here. Let's head over to the lab right now and start making the arrangements. I don't want to lose too much time."

"It would be a whole lot easier if we could make the initial screenings here," Caroline said, thinking of the mountains of customs paperwork she would now be forced to fill out. "Maybe we still can. Let's talk to the lab director and find out if we can continue with someone else."

Janie's voice conveyed her increasing level of irritation. "I knew something like this was going to happen. I don't *want* to wait for someone to take Frank's place. I have a life back home that I'd like to resume one of these days. I haven't worked in two years, Caroline, and I'm getting incredibly rusty. I have to be out of here in a little over three weeks; you have even less time than that. I *do not* want to be bodyprinted!"

Caroline, usually so calm, tried to reason with her. "Unfortunately, you don't get to make that decision," she pointed out. "If they want to print you, they'll find a reason, whether you like it or not. I can understand your reasons for wanting to keep your body out of the system, but you have to realize that it's going to happen sooner or later. They'll get everyone. You're not going to escape. Neither am I. So you might as well just accept it."

Janie flushed with embarrassment. Caroline's typically rational response was entirely justified. She admired her assistant's willingness to be so forthright with the person holding the purse strings. She apologized immediately. "You're right. I didn't mean to make such a fuss. It's just that I have this dire dread of it. . . . I'm not precisely sure why."

Caroline smiled. "Contrition is very becoming on you. You should try it more often."

"I think I will," Janie said resolutely. "Now we should probably decide how to proceed from here. We have a few new circumstances thrown into the mix. I agree with you, it would be easier to get the analyses done here than to ship back all that dirt. We'll keep that as our primary goal. Hopefully we can persuade someone at the Institute to help us."

"Let's just go there. You know how difficult it is to get things done over the phone in this country."

"I think that's a good plan. We can go right after we finish here. No sense in waiting around for help to come to us. And on the way there don't let me forget to mail this print." She held up a sealed, addressed manila envelope.

"Is it going to John Sandhaus?" Caroline asked.

"Uh-huh. He'll give it a good workover. By the time we get back, we'll know Gertrude's shoe size."

"If the envelope doesn't get lost on his desk."

"There's always the possibility that it will. Everyone wants the poor guy to take a look at something. I'm just glad he keeps looking at my stuff."

"Lucky you."

"I know. He's a pain in the ass sometimes, but he's good at what he does."

They were about to cross a side street not far from the Institute when Caroline remembered that there was a postal machine at the end of it. She pointed down the narrow street and said, "If we go down this way, we can mail the print at that box on the corner and then just go in the main entrance to the Institute instead of the side."

"Why not?" Janie said. "A little variety is nice every now and then. And considering how this trip is going, some change will do us good."

They turned right at the next corner, mailed the print, and then turned left again. They found themselves facing the ornate and forbidding facade of the Institute's main entrance.

Janie stopped for a minute to study the large map of the facility posted in the main reception area. She ran her finger over the etched surface until she found the office she was seeking.

"Go ahead without me, will you?" Janie said to Caroline. "I've got a couple of things to settle with the billing office for the tests they're going to run for me. It should only take a few minutes. I have to straighten out a couple of issues relating to credit exchanges. I'll meet you in the lab as soon as I'm done."

They parted, Janie heading in one direction, Caroline in the other, toward the lab. When she arrived after a long walk down the Institute's labyrinthine hallways, she found the door unlocked and the huge room strangely silent. She stepped inside tentatively, feeling as if she shouldn't be there, and called out to see if anyone else was present. No one responded.

It was a huge and complex facility, with more equipment than she'd ever seen in any other lab. There were dozens of microscope stations. With a little searching she found the one where they'd taken their first look at the strange circle of fabric. It was still there on the platen, apparently undisturbed. She looked around further, and wandered off to one end of the large room. There she found an entire wall of refrigerated storage units, and wondered which one of them contained their samples.

She was just gripping the handle of one of the units when a security guard, disturbed by her sudden and unexplained appearance on his video display, came into the lab. He asked what her business was and how she'd gotten in.

"The door was unlocked," she explained. "I have some samples here for analysis. I need to make some arrangements for them."

"Oh, dear!" he said, then blanched upon realizing that the door to the lab had probably been open all night. "I'm afraid that the facility is closed today due to the death of one of the technicians," he said. "No work will be done until Monday. Only the administrators are in today."

She glanced back at the microscope and wondered what effect prolonged exposure to the air would have on the piece of fabric. "Look, can I at least put away one of my samples? I think Frank may have been working on it just before he had his accident. He would have stored it properly if he'd had the opportunity."

The security guard followed her to the microscope. After surveying the scene he shook his head. "I'm afraid it's quite impossible. I'm sorry, miss, but I can't let you touch anything until I get the proper authorization. You'll have to speak with the director," he said, and gave her the necessary directions to find the administrative offices.

He motioned her out the door and she reluctantly complied, but not without giving him a frosty stare as she headed through it.

Bruce Ransom looked anxiously at the clock and watched with dismay as the second hand jerked inexorably forward. Each tick represented a diminishment in the short period of time he had to complete the research outline he was working on. This morning he had considered calling Ted Cummings and postponing their meeting, but he knew Ted was anxious to get this project under way, in spite of the inconvenience caused by Frank's untimely demise. Bruce was beginning to get antsy over the work, too, mostly due to his sincere desire to have it out of the way so he could move on to the good stuff. It was boring work, a confirming replication of something he'd already done without the necessary documentation. But funding for the larger, more interesting work to follow was contingent on Bruce's submission of that documentation, so he'd agreed to do it.

He remembered how he'd felt the day he discovered that the "bodyprint" of any bacterium could be used to reproduce a three-dimensional holographic image; by running that "printed" hologram through another program for 3-D animation, he'd been able to make the little fellow dance a jig before his eyes. It was a remarkable little bit of trickery. If he'd been able to add a schnoz and a hat, he could have morphed the creature into the bacterial version of Jimmy Durante. He could record the movements he'd animated and study every little detail by stopping the action at any point in the routine.

No one had been overly impressed until Bruce explained that what he'd done was significantly different from other types of 3-D computer animation: his version was based on real, living beings, and he could replicate them down to the individual cells. He knew, because he'd helped to develop the technique, that an individual bodyprint could be parsed into the separate body systems, the circulatory system, the skeleton, the neurological map, etcetera, and that those systems could be analyzed separately. *What if,* Bruce had said to the board, *we could use this information to enable people who can't move their limbs to control their own bodies through customized computer robotics?*

And though Institute Director Ted Cummings had been jokingly described by one colleague as a "stunningly adequate" scientist, he recognized brilliance when it hauled off and slapped him across the face. Having housed no star-quality experiments for quite some time, the Institute sent its scientific machinery whirring into action, with Ted, a shrewd maker of political deals, at the helm, flawlessly manipulating the venerable establishment's rudder on a course of grant-winning presentations. Remarkably, he himself was doing the lion's share of the early lab work. This was a real detour from Ted's usual routine. Bruce suspected that this was Ted's way of including himself in what would surely be award-winning work without having to participate in the meatier, more demanding phase. The clamor of accolades was a powerful enticement, even for a talented administrator who rarely needed to pull on latex gloves to justify his paycheck. *Perhaps his contract is up for renewal,* Bruce thought cynically. Such personal involvement in experimental work was more than slightly out of character for a man whose last eleven years had been spent directing the activities of a very talented group of researchers, any one of whom could leave him in the dust in a lab setting.

One of Ted's more ingratiating personal qualities was a penchant for punctuality. So when Bruce's intercom buzzer suddenly sounded he was tempted to pick the thing up and fling it across the room.

God, how did I find myself fighting these deadlines all the time? No surprise, really. The Institute had recruited him right out of his residency. Bruce, who had already accepted a lucrative fellowship, gave it up to work in its state-of-the-art facilities. He'd never had a chance at private practice; he'd been sweet-talked right into a job in genetic research, a career path that he would readily admit had many benefits. The work was intriguing, he'd had lots of opportunity for travel and professional growth, and he had never been called out in the middle of the night to deliver the baby of a deadline.

Still, it had changed his life dramatically to follow this routine. He moved from Boston to California almost overnight, and eventually here to England, putting an abrupt end to his previous plan to settle into a nice safe practice.

Despite his previous inclination to launch the intercom on a quick trip to Jupiter, he pressed the button. "Yes, Clara, what can I do for you?" he asked, trying to sound ruffled but accommodating.

His secretary responded nervously, "Pardon me, Dr. Ransom, I'm sorry to disturb you, but Dr. Cummings just called from the lab. He's anxious for you to join him."

Oh, fuck, he thought as he pressed the button down. "It's all right, I'll be out shortly. Do me a favor, though, and call him back for me. Tell him I'll be on my way in just a minute."

He finished the section he had been dictating and printed it quickly. It wasn't as organized as he'd hoped it would be, but it would have to do. Feeling a bit rumpled, he went to his lavatory and checked his appearance. Satisfied that he wouldn't frighten anyone, he rushed out through the anteroom, file folder in hand, his lab coat flying out behind him, and promptly stubbed his toe on the leg of a chair.

"Son of a bitch!" he muttered to himself. This was not going to be an easy day.

Five

T hey rode at a fast pace for the rest of the day, trying to put as much distance as possible between themselves and Alejandro's town of Cervere, always keeping alert for sources of water. Alejandro adapted quickly to the rhythm of riding, and felt quite comfortable in the saddle. To anyone watching him he would not have seemed like the novice rider he was.

Noticing his charge's unexpected skill, Hernandez remarked, "You are born to the saddle, Jew. I think you waste the best in yourself in being a *medicus*. It seems to me a worthless pursuit, anyway, full of deceit and trickery. I come from the barber's surgery feeling worse than when I went in, without fail."

"Then you must abandon the barber and instead consult a physician when you have a complaint, for a well-trained one has knowledge no barber can dare to claim."

"One such as yourself?" Hernandez asked.

Alejandro *hmphed* cynically. "You may be assured that I am well trained, but I curse my own ignorance daily."

"Well, then, it is settled. You must take up the sword if your present work fails to satisfy you. You will find more satisfaction in it, I am sure."

Alejandro did not like the tenor of their conversation as it seemed to be developing. He put a little more distance between himself and Hernandez, moving a few feet farther away to make further discussion difficult. *Such nonsense,* he thought to himself. *How can any calling be nobler than mine? Why, look what I have sacrificed for it! And why does this rogue bother me with such drivel, when I have far more weighty things to consider?*

But Hernandez would not be put off. In the few hours they'd spent together, Alejandro had discovered him to be an extremely jocular fellow, a lover of discourse. As if he'd read the young physician's mind, the Spaniard guided his horse closer and said, "You will find no nobler work than soldiering, young man. You look to be one who could easily master the skills."

"And of course, you will be happy to teach me, I fear. . . ."

"And why not? What better time than a journey that may well prove treacherous?"

We do not have the time to luxuriate in the learning of skills, Alejandro thought to himself. *By now the murder of the bishop has been discovered, and I am even more a hunted man than before.* He wondered if Hernandez suspected him. He had said nothing, and did not act like a man who was escorting a fugitive he knew to be the murderer of a bishop. While they traveled quickly, Hernandez had not guided them into a state of flight; they traveled openly, without hiding, and Hernandez was friendly to all who passed.

"I think not," Alejandro finally said to Hernandez's offer.

"Oh, come now, young man, what can be the harm in it?"

And despite Alejandro's evident reluctance Hernandez challenged him. "We will try something easy first. I will let you be the one to find a resting place where there is water."

Wary though he was of participating in his escort's little game, and weary though he was of their discussion, Alejandro loved a challenge. But water was not a luxury, it was a necessity. "And if I do not find water, what then?" he said to his companion. "Will we be in danger?"

"Then I will show you my own wisdom by being the one to find it."

"All right, then," Alejandro said.

As they rode on, Alejandro kept his eyes moving in search of the kind of greenery that would naturally be found near water. Several times he thought he'd found it, but on closer inspection every one of his "finds" had no water above the ground. Finally, from a distance, he spied a lush green enclave of vegetation, bigger and heartier than the previous sites. It came into closer view as they rode through the shimmering heat of the mostly brown Aragon countryside.

It did not take them long to reach the greenery. Their reward was a delightful spring bubbling up in its center. "You see?" Hernandez said. "You have natural skills. I shall help you to improve them even further."

With Hernandez instructing his charge in the proper means of doing such things, they removed the saddles from their horses and hobbled them near the spring where the animals could drink at will. Bowlegged and stiff from their extended travel, each man stretched, then they arranged their few possessions a few paces away. After a few minutes of rest Hernandez removed a slingshot from his pack and carefully untangled the straps.

"I'll be back in no time with our supper, God willing," Hernandez said. He tossed Alejandro a flint. "Light us a fire for cooking." He took a few steps, then turned back and said, "You do know how, I assume. . . ."

"Indeed," Alejandro said, feigning insult. "You will no doubt be surprised to find that I can also eat without assistance."

"I had no doubt," the Spaniard said, laughing, "for I have seen you eat." He stepped into the brush and returned a short while later with a large buck rabbit. He pulled out a hunting knife from his belt sheath, and butchered the animal against a large flat rock nearby. Alejandro watched in fascination as the small rodent was eviscerated. Hernandez was about to toss the innards away from their campsite when Alejandro stopped him. He reached into the slimy mass and pulled out the heart.

"This was a mean-spirited rabbit, for the heart is small," he said.

"Then he well deserves to be eaten," the Spaniard said. "I will leave it to you to be the judge of such matters. Of one thing I am sure, however, and that is that a man with a slingshot will never go hungry, even if he eats rats." He flung the remaining innards as far away as possible so they would not attract unwanted predators. "He can hunt game that the bow and arrow cannot touch. Better a small unsavory meal than no large tasty one, eh?"

Alejandro reluctantly nodded his agreement, but thought to himself, *I will starve before I eat a rat.* But to his surprise the roasting rabbit smelled like the chicken his mother cooked nearly every day. It tasted as good as it smelled, and he ate it with great relish, hoping that God would forgive him for any dietary indiscretions he might commit in the course of surviving this journey. He offered a silent promise to God that upon safe arrival in Avignon, he would become the most devout and obedient Jew who ever lived.

Hernandez brought out another loaf of bread and they devoured it without leaving so much as a crumb behind. Some dried figs made a fine end to the meal, and Alejandro thought he had never eaten so well before. They filled their flasks with fresh water from the spring and drank until they would burst.

"I swear to you that I shall never pass by water again without taking my fill," he said, recalling how dry his lips had become during this three days in the monastery silo. He wiped his lips on his shirtsleeve.

"Then neither shall you pass by a shrub or a tree without leaving your mark upon it."

Alejandro surprised himself by laughing. As he lay down on his blanket, exhausted by the day's long ride but full to bursting with good food and clean water, he wondered, *How have I come to be out here under these stars, when I should be home in Cervere, sleeping in my own soft bed?* The events of the previous few days raced through his mind. *How could everything have turned out so badly?* He considered the dramatic changes in his once sheltered life: branded, separated from his family, perhaps forever, and forced to flee the town where he had been born and raised, he was no longer the same person he had been just a few days before.

But what burdened him most was the sudden emergence of a side of himself he had never known to exist. *Today I killed a man*, he thought ruefully, *without hesitation.* It struck him as odd that he should feel so little regret for what he had done to the bishop, and wondered if it was madness that prevented him from recoiling in horror at his own deed. But in his heart he knew it was not, for it was the simplest of justice. Did not the elders teach that an eye must be taken for an eye? Alejandro doubted that the cleric would ever have been punished for his unholy treatment of the Canches family, as the Canches family had been unduly punished for having served him faithfully for many years, and forgave himself momentarily for acting as the man's judge and executioner. But it troubled him, and he found sleep elusive. Staring up at the stars, he lightly fingered his crusted wound, reliving the shock of its delivery, the shame of his helplessness still fresh. Then, remembering his gold, he got up from his blanket and retrieved it from among the small pile of possessions lying nearby. He placed the saddlebag under his head and used it as a hard pillow.

Hernandez, whom he had taken to be asleep, said, "You are wise to do that. I see that wariness is a skill I shall not have to teach you. Sleep well, Jew."

"And you, Spaniard," he said. *So he knows, then*, Alejandro thought, relaxing more with the knowledge that his escort was a man of sufficient honor to resist such a temptation. *And he has not left me on the side of the road to die, fortuneless, while he rides off a wealthy man.*

He was guaranteed a smooth settlement into Avignon with this treasure. He could immediately set up practice in a well-equipped surgery with paid assistants, and could afford servants to establish and run a household. If his father and mother were by some miracle to survive the journey to Avignon, they would be welcomed into the comfortable home of a prominent physician. His dreams washed over the pain of his last few days, and floating through fantasies of a sweet and comfortable future, he fell asleep.

Hernandez shook him slightly just before dawn. "I would like to end my employment with the House of Canches sometime this year. Your sloth and laziness will keep me in your hire for far too long! I will end up working for pennies a day if we continue to travel at this rate," groused the burly Spaniard.

Alejandro stretched his limbs, careful not to split the healing skin of his circular wound, and rose up stiffly. With Hernandez's help he removed his shirt and checked the wound for festering. Finding none, he washed it carefully in the cold spring water, trying not to disturb the newly formed scabs. While it was still wet and somewhat pliable, he dabbed oil of clove on the wound, being careful to conserve his small supply. He winced briefly at the initial sting, which was blessedly followed by numbness.

After a small breakfast they rode without incident until the sun was high in the sky, then began to look for a convenient place to rest and shade themselves from the midday sun. They came upon an area of scrub trees, too small to indicate a ground source of water, but high enough to shade them and their horses from the worst of the day's heat. Hernandez magically produced some dried meat from his pack, which was disagreeable in flavor but satisfying to their hunger, and they followed it with a drink from their flasks.

As they rested, the Spaniard aimlessly whittled a small dry twig. Alejandro watched closely as the twig began to take shape, marveling at how quickly it was transformed into a sinuous snake with smooth skin and a finely pointed tail.

"Señor, where did you learn such a fine craft as this carving you do?"

"I have not learned, my young friend, but practiced. After carving so many pieces, I think I can do it without looking, by feeling only. I love the distraction, for it enables me to think more clearly."

"I beg you to share your thoughts with me now."

Hernandez spat before replying. "I am pondering our route."

"Are roads so plentiful that we are given a choice of routes?"

"Not so plentiful as you might think. We can choose to pass through the mountains or travel by the seacoast. Though the mountain route is shorter in distance, it takes only a bit less time than the coastal route. And there are many fearful treacheries awaiting the mountain traveler."

"Name them, and I will ponder them as well."

"The people can be none too friendly. They care for neither Franks nor Spaniards, but would be known as Basques. Travelers are fair game for their highwaymen, who know the routes well, and sometimes lie in wait in hidden alcoves of the mountains. And the weather can rise up like an angry steed, pounding down upon you with sharp hooves. Hail and lightning abound, and thunder rolls through the peaks roaring like the very gods."

"Surely there is some advantage to this route, or why else should it be considered?"

Hernandez elaborated. "It can be very pleasant in this season to travel in the cool hills, for along the coast there is little respite from the sun and its damages. But we are only two, with one carrying much gold, and we make an easy prey for marauders."

Alejandro eyed his scrupulous escort. *Father must have paid him very, very well, he thought, or perhaps, he is simply a very, very honorable man. I have lived beside Christians all my life, yet how little I know of them. . . .* Alejandro had always relied on the tales of his elders for information. Often what was offered was less than flattering, and seldom did he hear a story that did not arise from some controversy or scandal. Now this man with whom he traveled was showing him that gentiles were capable of a very different sort of behavior. Hernandez did not behave like a devout Christian, more like a Christian of convenience, and Alejandro could easily see that he was not filthy or uneducated, but that his knowledge of the world was actually quite substantial.

Hernandez continued. "Of course, the safer route will take us north of Barcelona, around the eastern tip of the Pyrenees, and into the Languedoc. From there we simply follow the shoreline, through the cities of Narbonne, Béziers, and Montpellier. Not much past Montpellier is fair Avignon, where your fate awaits you."

"I have traveled to Montpellier. It is there that I was educated."

"Ah, you are not the innocent I supposed, then." Hernandez grinned as memories of youthful forays into unknown cities were revisited in his mind. "Nor, I must confess to you, am I. I have seen many cities, my friend, and they are much the same. In every one there are delicious foods, exotic and willing women, wondrous edifices, and many fine goods to be had. It is all a matter of knowing how to expose these riches."

"And of course, you do," commented Alejandro.

Hernandez laughed heartily. "I have a sharp nose for sniffing out those things worth smelling. If we travel by the coastal route, you may acquire this skill from me as well. Your journey, though I fear you may find it long and wearying, will be filled with more interest and, might I add, far more comfort than if we travel by the mountain route. You may find as well that it seems delayed. You will not want to pass too quickly through these places of delight. You will want to stay and sample their treasures."

Alejandro considered the choices. "I am torn, señor," he said. "If I travel as my people usually do, which is no doubt the intent of my family, I would shun these dens of Christian iniquity and follow the less-traveled route. We Jews are always in danger of being the victims of those who are downtrodden by the rich of their own kind. They seek their revenge on those who are not able to defend themselves. It is my duty to travel to

Avignon, and to establish myself in the hope of welcoming my family."
But he knew that he would reach Avignon far ahead of his elderly parents,
even if he were to take the slowest route possible. They would have to
rest in every town along their route. It might take them a full year to
reach Avignon under the best of circumstances.

"Remember, young man, that you no longer look like a Jew, and
forgive me for saying, *God be praised!*"

Alejandro wondered if perhaps Hernandez was already tired of the
cities' debauchery, and longed for fresh mountain air and cool nights. He
might be eager to engage some Basque marauders in combat, needing to
keep his skills sharp. But Alejandro was not.

"Well, Jew, what say you?"

"By the sea, señor! I am confident that I can see these alien ways
without falling prey to them. And some new methods of surgery may be
fashionable in these cities."

"Aye, they'll cut out your purse in the wink of an eye!"

Alejandro laughed, but patted his saddlebag for reassurance,
prompting Hernandez to say, "Your first purchase with that fortune will
be a set of more suitable traveling clothes. We will instruct the tailor to
sew several small pockets with buttons atop them, therein to divide your
coins, so you'll never lose all your money at once."

Alejandro thought this to be a wise course of action. He was rested
now, and the sun had lowered a bit, making travel more comfortable; he
began to fidget some. Seeing this, Hernandez resheathed his small whit-
tling knife and tucked the snake into one of his bags. Taking a last swig of
water, he swung up on his horse, and his charge followed suit. They
retraced their path to the road, and set off at a fast pace toward the
northeast.

They made steady progress, always riding northeast toward the
coast. The seacoast road was now within one day's ride, and their contact
with civilization increased with every passing hour. As they neared the
coast the air became cooler and cleaner, without the dust of the hot
Aragon countryside. The vegetation became more lush and bountiful,
and the journey more pleasant because of the shade it provided. They
stopped as needed, taking on fresh water whenever possible, Alejandro
drinking like a rabid dog wherever there was a spring or stream.

His wound had blessedly not festered, and now, as it healed, was
more inconvenient than painful. The skin on his chest had stiffened
somewhat, even though he had applied emollients whenever possible to

try to keep it supple. There was, however, simply no way for him to prevent the huge ugly scar that would be his lifelong companion. He knew he would be ashamed of his unsightly disfigurement when he was again among people other than Hernandez, who politely tried not to notice the mass of ugly scabs. But he blessed his good fortune that the scar would be carried on his chest, and not his face, as had been the intent of his branders. His chest he could hide with clothing; his face he could not.

As the distractions of the road became more plentiful, Hernandez sat up a little straighter in his saddle and paid more attention to the sights and sounds around them. "It has been a long time since I've been in a city where the cantinas are worthy of my patronage!" he said to Alejandro. He pointed out some places of interest as they rode. "This bodes well, Jew! Perhaps we will find some food worth blessing here!"

As their shadows lengthened eastward in the late afternoon sun, they neared the small city of Gerona. Hernandez was amused to see the fascination with which his inexperienced companion regarded the bustle of people busily tending to the last of their day's business. Though most were harmless enough, he knew well that there were some who would as soon smile and lift their purses as smile and say hello. "You'll make an easy meal for those who would prey on your pocket, I think," he said, and laughed loudly. "You had best beware."

This comment brought a stony glare from his charge, who after the successes of his journey was feeling quite sure of himself. "I may be untutored, Hernandez, but I am no simpleton. Do you think me incapable of riding through this city with my possessions intact?"

"It's not the ride that concerns me, my young friend. It's the time when our horses are tethered and our spirits are not that will be the most dangerous. Take care not to fall victim to some luscious young thing with an invisible partner in thievery!"

Alejandro was incensed at Hernandez's implications, and thought it far more likely that the older man would find himself in such a predicament. He told him so in no uncertain terms. "You'd best pay attention to your own warning," he said to the older man. "Remember what you yourself said! I am the one who is young and handsome, and you bear the mark of many wars! Consider again who might be the easy prey!"

"By the Gods, Jew," Hernandez bellowed, "you are right! You are no simpleton. And if I am frugal after the surprisingly pleasant task of seeing you safely banished from Aragon, I can live well for the next few years. Provided, of course, I do not squander too much on women!" He laughed again, and when his laughter subsided, he said, "I am growing too old to be wasting my means on such nonsense anyway. Better left to you young handsome ones, eh, Jew? And now," he said, "I think it wise for us to find a place where we can rest our weary bones for the night."

He inquired of a few passersby for an inn with good stables, and they were directed to an establishment on the north side of the square. A small cantina, they were told, was just a few doors away.

As they headed in the direction of the inn, the pounding of approaching hooves could be heard. Soon the horses and their armored riders entered the square in a cloud of dust. Alejandro stiffened upon seeing the soldiers; Hernandez watched him, saying nothing, but observing his every move carefully.

The soldiers dismounted in unison, each one entering a different establishment in the center of the small town. They strode from door to door with brusque authority, searching for something or someone, knowing no success. Hernandez and Alejandro stood at the hitching post tying up their horses; neither one made any attempt to move from their spot as the soldiers milled all around the square.

He is delaying, Hernandez thought as he watched Alejandro tie, then untie, then retie his horse again. *He fears an encounter with these riders.* He put his hand on the young Jew's shoulder, and then looked again at the soldiers, who had reformed into a unit near their horses. "Perhaps we can rest here a few moments before we settle in?" he said.

Alejandro was not surprised by his guide's clever perception of his fear, and he was grateful for the man's deference to his wish to remain unnoticed until the soldiers departed. They remained by the horses as Alejandro continued his pointless fussing about the details of their equipment, first tightening a random strap, then loosening it again, and then removing his water to take a drink, sloshing the water around in his mouth, then spitting it out before drinking again. Always the physician's eyes remained glued to the soldiers, and he did not relax his silent vigil until they had remounted their steeds and roared out of the town square.

Hernandez looked directly into Alejandro's eyes and said, his brow raised curiously, "Perhaps you will need that new suit of clothing immediately, eh? We will see to it after we find suitable lodging."

Alejandro nodded as he slung his saddlebag over his shoulder. He had started walking in the direction of the inn when Hernandez took him by the arm, holding him back. The big Spaniard said sternly to his charge, "Young man, I am no lover of Jews, but you are a good man and I am paid to deliver you safely to Avignon. You had best tell me if there is reason for us to beware of soldiers."

The young Jew met his gaze steadily. He did not wish to be dishonest with Hernandez, for the Spaniard had proven himself to be a worthy companion. But until he could be sure that the Christian would not betray him, Alejandro intended to keep his secret about the murder of the bishop. He nodded again, leaving Hernandez to wonder what the nod meant.

He was surprised when the Spaniard roared in laughter and slapped him on the back, nearly knocking the wind out of him. "You've more lead in your pants than I thought! Let's settle ourselves in!" They resumed their progress toward the inn.

The landlord showed them a room with two large straw beds, each covered with a rough but clean-looking woven blanket. The low table, set beneath the window looking out onto the square, held a basin and pitcher.

"Clean enough for a couple of vagabonds, eh, señor? We will be your grateful guests tonight. A bath before supper will do us both good. And please tell us how we may find a good tailor in this town."

They went as directed, and Alejandro was measured for a shirt and trousers. Alejandro flinched as the tailor placed the end of the measuring string between his upper legs, noting with irritation the grin of amusement on Hernandez's face.

"My young friend, you show your ignorance! How else can the tailor outfit you like a gentleman? Would you have your breeches so tight that you sing like a girl? Stand still, and let the man proceed."

Embarrassed by his own timidity, Alejandro did as he was told.

"We must have this clothing first thing in the morning," Hernandez said to the tailor.

"Señor," the tailor protested, "that is not possible, there will not be enough light to complete the work in time! I must find the necessary goods. . . ."

Hernandez reached into his pocket and took out a gold coin, which he waved seductively under the tailor's nose. "Perhaps this will buy the necessary cloth and candles," he said. He saw the tailor's greedy eyes drink in the sight of the coin, so he pressed it into the man's hand and said, "There will be another in the morning when the clothes are ready."

Having settled the matter of Alejandro's new clothing, they returned to the inn and climbed the stairs to the room they shared. A partially full tub of water had been set between the two straw beds. There was a soft knock on the door; Hernandez grunted his permission to enter, and the landlord's wife came in, carrying another heavy bucket of steaming water. This she added to the tub, after which she left, returning quickly with a large cake of green translucent soap and a loofah sponge.

Hernandez motioned to Alejandro to use the tub first, saying he would go to the cantina for a draft of wine before he bathed himself. Once again he instructed Alejandro to mind his possessions.

Having properly attended to his duties as the young man's escort, he disappeared out the door, closing it behind him. Alejandro slid the bar across, guaranteeing his privacy, and undressed carefully, ever mindful of his sore chest. The warm water was at first painful to the red skin of the circular wound, but as he grew accustomed to the temperature, he found it to be extremely soothing. After shaking the dust out of his clothing, he dressed again, and removed the bar from the door. Then he looked out the window and watched Hernandez stride with great bravado through the square, obviously having enjoyed his refreshment.

The great Spaniard was singing loudly as he mounted the stairs to their room. His jollity was contagious, and Alejandro smiled, liking the man more and more each day. He was glad to see him as he blustered through the door, just slightly drunk, and friendlier than ever.

"Ah, my boy, this bath will be a gift from heaven, I think." He disrobed with great ritual, scratching lazily. He slapped away an annoying insect, then said, "Thanks be to God for this new baptism," and guffawed at his own joke. Alejandro did not understand, but chuckled politely, entertained by the huge man's childish antics.

Hernandez bathed with lusty ostentation, vigorously scrubbing the accumulated dust of the road from his body with the rough loofah. Having immersed his entire head in the water, he blew out his nose and rubbed his eyes, and scratched his ears with the smallest of his fingers, taking advantage of this rare opportunity to have all the parts of his body clean at once. The cake of soap was clearly diminished by the time he finished.

"The landlady will charge us more for that bar of soap," Alejandro observed.

"Aye, and a worthy expenditure it will be!" Hernandez said. "I am gloriously clean because of it!"

The Spaniard shook himself off like a dog, head to behind. Alejandro jumped away to avoid the spray, marveling at the muddy color of the small amount of water remaining in the tub.

Having tended to their exterior needs, the two men went down the stairs, Alejandro clutching his precious saddlebag, and headed to the cantina for supper. The noise and intoxicating bustle were quite intriguing to him. He had been carefully kept away from the cantina in Cervere by his overly cautious parents, who feared the influence of gentile ways on their children more than almost anything else. Now he stood in the doorway of the forbidden place, afraid to enter, but enticed by its exotic mystery. Hernandez was well inside, being greeted by several new "old friends" acquired over the flagon of wine he'd had before his bath. Alejandro saw him playfully grab a rather plump and buxom woman, pulling her into a rough embrace, kissing her dramatically. She resisted, but not too much, with coy exclamations of modesty and chastity, like a shy maiden in her first encounter. When he entered, Alejandro could see, at closer inspection, that she was no maiden.

As the young Jew observed the scene from his place at the great table, what he saw was a group of harmless-looking people, engaging in harmless behavior. They laughed and drank, perhaps a bit too much, and toasted one another in loose celebration. Fantastic stories were thrown about, Hernandez revealing his past deeds of bravery and heroism to attentive listeners. The Spaniard entertained his new-made friends with all his heart and soul, captivating them with tales that went far beyond the common daily experience of their ordinary lives. The listeners appreciated the storyteller's gift to them, for these things could not be known otherwise. The tales would be passed on to the relatives and children of those who had heard them here, and small legends would be born. Alejandro counted himself among the appreciators.

Soon Hernandez was too full of wine to continue, and after a brief lull the sounds of slurping and chewing were replaced by the voice of a young man who had been listening to Hernandez with great attention.

"I have a tale of my own," he said, " 'Twas told to me by a sailor in the port of Marseilles."

"Then let us hear it," Hernandez slurred. But unlike the crusty soldier who'd regaled the crowd before he spoke, the young man was not a natural storyteller, and he had to be coaxed into continuing.

"Perhaps a glass of wine will loosen your tongue," Hernandez said, gesturing to the landlord to bring one around.

And after a few minutes it was plain that Hernandez had been correct in his estimation of the wine's effects. The young man said, "The sailor was hovering about the docks in Marseilles, looking to join a merchant crew, for his own company's ship was to be refitted and would be dry for a while. Having nothing else to relieve him of idleness, he took to laying about in the *taverna*, hoping for word of a ship in need of mates."

The crowd, having heard the effusive Hernandez, looked bored by this ordinary tale. But fortified by another gulp of wine, the teller bravely continued. "I heard him one afternoon, talking about a galley that had drifted into port in Messina, anchoring well out. It was owned by a Genoese trading company, and was long overdue, so its safe arrival was heralded as a great blessing. But when the galley was boarded by the representatives of the *compagnia*, they found that all but six of the crew were dead, and the remaining six were dying."

A hushed exclamation went through the crowd, their interest suddenly piqued. In a low voice, one man said, "A plague ship!"

"Aye," agreed the teller, "and a plague like none seen before, according to my sailor friend. The man told a tale of black necks, with swellings as if a melon were stuck in the throat!"

The listeners moaned, gesturing in disbelief, chiding the man for this fantastic story. Alejandro stood halfway up in his seat, raising his hand to quiet the crowd.

"Shhh! Please, I will hear this tale to its completion."

The others regarded him quizzically, but his interference gave the storyteller the courage to continue.

"The sick ones had bruises covering their arms and legs, and their hands and feet were black like an Ethiope, and burning with pain. Not a one among them could bear to be touched, and all screamed for merciful death to deliver them from the misery of their awful afflictions. The foul smell of death and disease exuded from all their pores, and sweat drenched their garments until they nearly dripped. Of the fifty on board when they first cast oars to the water, all were afflicted, and only one survived. And now he is mad, unable to remember his own mother's name."

No one spoke. Hernandez drunkenly crossed himself, and others followed suit, some invoking the name of the Virgin to come to their protection. Against such a malady there was no other defense.

Somehow, Hernandez managed to regain the attention of the silent crowd, and brought them back to revelry. The Spaniard did not notice his traveling companion, lost in his thoughts, in a mood quite apart from that of the others. Later Alejandro grilled the news bearer for more details of the rumored disease, but the man had little more to relate, and Alejandro finally let the inquiry go.

That night, by the light of a single candle, Alejandro wrote in his book the details of the story they had heard in the cantina. As he scribbled furiously, Hernandez snored, grunting and tossing in his straw bed. He was glad for the dearth of other travelers, for the two might have been forced to share a mat, and Alejandro paled at the thought of the drunken Spaniard's flailing limbs crashing down on him like sacks of flour in the night. Clean, full of food, his head brimming with the evening's news, he fell asleep clutching his bag to his belly, soon to dream of Carlos Alderón.

In his dream the giant blacksmith was even larger and more imposing than in life. He came to Alejandro in the light of day, dead but still walking, each limb separately wound with the coarse fabric of his shrouds, his unshrouded chest a mass of cuts and slashes. The hands and feet that protruded from the wrappings were as black as the cast iron of the shovel that was used to disentomb him. Carlos shrieked out grisly accusations at the doctor who had failed to cure him, blaming his death on Alejandro's desire to later exhume and dissect his body. He came closer, reaching out his arms, but just before he was overtaken, Alejandro jolted awake. He lurched violently to a sitting position, trembling, with cold sweat dripping from every pore. He rubbed his face hard with one hand while supporting his shivering body with the other, and turned aside to see Hernandez sleeping peacefully, untouched by the sense of dread that had awakened him.

The tailor bowed and nodded his way backward out the door, clutching the gold coin Hernandez had pressed into his hand, grinning in disbelief at the fantastic sum he had been paid for such simple work. After settling their bill with the innkeeper, the Spaniard and the Jew headed to the bakery, where Hernandez bought several loaves of the day's first batch of bread, stuffing the long thin loaves into every available crevice in his clothing and packs.

As he was about to mount his horse, Alejandro said, "This shirt is heavy from so many coins!"

Hernandez laughed heartily. Unsympathetic to the young man's enviable plight, he said, "May God burden me with the affliction of having too many coins! And may I never be cured!"

They traveled intently until midday, when they reached the small town of Figueras, still well inland on the coastal road. They left the horses at a stable, where a small boy wiped and watered them well.

The cantina was dark and cool, a welcome interlude in the day's blazing heat. They ate heartily, Hernandez washing his meal down with rather copious quantities of ale. Alejandro was again quite subdued as his companion regaled the locals with his heroic tales and war stories.

"Enough of my lies," he concluded. "I am tired of boasting. Who bears news worth hearing?"

Reports of various harvests were made. One man described in great detail the passing of a sumptuous wedding train, which bore a young noblewoman from far away to her waiting bridegroom in Castile. He entertained his rapt audience with tales of the lavish excess of the wealthy, barely imaginable to the peasants who surrounded him.

Ever mindful of his fugitive status, and not wishing to draw attention to himself, Alejandro remained quiet, his disinterest rapidly turning to boredom. He and Hernandez had managed so far to outride the news of the bishop's murder, and he fervently hoped they would continue to do so. He had not yet found the trust to tell Hernandez what he'd done while the Spaniard awaited him outside the monastery, but he assumed that the older man knew it was not his purpose to thank the prelate for his charitable treatment.

It was not until a ragged pilgrim began speaking of the plague ship that Alejandro sat up attentively. The man had been sitting quietly in the corner, making short work of his bread and cheese despite an apparent lack of teeth. Gray stubble covered his chin, and his rank smell hinted that he had recently been in close company with mules.

"The disease is no longer confined to the crew of the ship," he said, stunning his listeners. A hushed murmur went through the inn's occupants. "The representatives of the *compagnia* waited a few days, then sent out a crew to bring the ship's cargo ashore, much against the wishes of the Messina harbormaster, who has vowed to take the matter before the magistrate for adjudication."

Alejandro was surprised at the man's articulate speech, expecting it to be more in keeping with his rough appearance. The man continued, embellishing his account with precise detail of the disease's progress.

"Within a few days several members of the unloading crew had fallen ill, their first complaints being tender necks and scratchy throats. Soon, they were all feverish, their tongues swollen and white. One by one they took to their beds, and not a one rose again."

The occupants of the cantina were all paying strict attention, horrified by the man's story. "After several days one man's extremities turned blue, then black. The swelling in his neck became an apple-sized lump, filled with thick yellow pus, the whole area surrounded by blue-and-black mottling. The same vile eruptions soon came forth in his groin and armpits, and he was in constant pain. A doctor was called in by his family, and the huge boils lanced."

The rest of the crowd moaned in revulsion, but Alejandro paid strict attention, considering carefully the possible diagnoses. He heard the traveler describe delirium and sweating, periods of unconsciousness, then bouts of shivering as if the victim were on ice. The teller told of the poor man's inability to retain any bodily fluid or solid, and how his appearance rapidly became skeletal as the body consumed itself in its final attempt to survive. The man's last indignity, the teller said, was deep despair, followed by a thrashing convulsive death.

Forgetting for the moment his reluctance to speak, Alejandro questioned the pilgrim. "Did you see this with your own eyes?" he asked.

"No, sir, I did not, for the story was told to me by another traveler from Messina. But I have no doubt that he spoke the truth."

Nor did Alejandro, but it was not the firsthand account he had hoped for.

All were silent now, reflecting on the frightening tale they had just heard. The news bearer returned to his supper, dipping his remaining bread in a cup of ale and gumming it resolutely. Even the normally effusive Hernandez seemed somber and reserved. He reminded Alejandro that they still had a long journey ahead of them, and that it would be wise to take advantage of the remaining light to reach the next village before nightfall. They set off at a fast pace, heading for the coastal town of Carbere.

The deep cerulean blue of the Mediterranean gleamed with the reflection of the last light of day, the sound of waves caressing the shore soothed the weary pair, who by now had heard quite enough of the sound of pounding hooves. Not since he had journeyed back from his years at medical school in Montpellier had Alejandro seen the ocean, and it was a welcome sight.

In Carbere they'd refilled their water flasks and had bought some steamed fish wrapped in large leaves, and now they sat quietly on the beach just before sunset, enjoying their fish, which would be followed by one of Hernandez's innumerable loaves of bread.

Unlike Hernandez, Alejandro was not sobered by the rumors of plague, but agitated and excited. He speculated about its cause, worrying out loud about the difficulty of treating such an affliction.

"I have never," he said, "even in my time at medical school, come upon such a ghastly set of symptoms. Surely the stories have been exaggerated in the repetition—I simply cannot believe that anything so hideous could just appear out of nowhere."

Hernandez had seen plenty of typhus and cholera in his warrior years. "Despite my glorious tales," he told Alejandro sadly, "the truth is that war is seldom a glorious occurrence. These stories of mine often help me forget the misery by keeping the honor of victory in the front of my mind. Were I to remember the blood and pestilence as often, I should lose my sanity from the burden of the sorrow. Many die, as many from the sword of disease as by the sword of the enemy."

Alejandro knew that these thoughts must weigh heavily on Hernandez, for his usual lighthearted manner was replaced by grim silence. As the sun was leaving the sky, the old warrior rose and gathered up some dried beach grass, then lit a small fire to give them another hour of light.

They slept on the soft sand, their blankets beneath them, lulled to sleep by the thrumming of the nearby ocean. Alejandro awoke to the glint of the sun's first rays peeping over the horizon. The sea birds fought vainly to be heard above the crashing of the early morning waves, screeching and shrieking as if to waken God Himself.

He looked around for Hernandez, shading his eyes against the bright sun. He found the huge man splashing in the waves, refreshing himself in the cool salty water. Hernandez motioned wildly to his charge to come into the water, and eventually Alejandro rolled up his trousers and waded a few feet out, liking the feel of the sand and water between his bare toes. He went back ashore, stripped off his clothing, and plunged in.

And for a few moments they were both untroubled and carefree, Hernandez shaking off his disturbing memories of wars past, and Alejandro recapturing the safer time when he had not been a fugitive. Neither man could name the shapeless dread that had crept uninvited into their journey. It settled slowly in the pits of their stomachs, this nagging undercurrent of fear, and became an unwelcome companion. Each one knew that this brief idyll was a calm before some turbulence, yet the tempest remained hidden, not ready to reveal itself.

The beach was firm and well suited to riding, so they rode at water's edge as much as possible, enjoying the cool spray of the surf, returning to the road only when the beach became too rocky for the safety of the horses. They made fair progress, Hernandez hoping to reach the Languedoc sea town of Narbonne by nightfall, for he knew of no fresh water source after Perpignan.

It was in Narbonne that they heard of the disease's arrival in Genoa. Alejandro was not entirely surprised to learn of its spread to the region's most important trading port. Genoa had been the plague ship's original destination, and its pestilential cargo had been sent there on another galleon. Within a few days of its arrival some members of the crew, who had dispersed into the community after their short voyage, began to experience the same illness as the crew of the ghost ship. Others among the ship's sailors and trading agents had already boarded galleys bound for other ports, among them Marseilles, taking along the unknown cause of the pestilence.

The malady first spread to the ship's rowers, and gradually the entire lot of them was abandoned in their chains, either dead or dying. A gruesome tale was told of one galley slave who could be heard screaming for days, begging to be released, for he had managed miraculously to escape the contagion. Instead he died of dehydration at his oar, surrounded by his shipmates' stinking bodies, as no one would board the ship to move the water barrel within his reach.

They passed that night in the coastal town, having found a suitable inn with room to spare. New accounts of the plague's spread comprised the entire evening's conversation in the village cantina, no other topic being of nearly as much interest. The tone of the talk was hushed and anxious; there was great fear among the citizens that the mysterious ailment might spread to their region.

Alejandro and Hernandez set out again at first light, having reprovisioned the night before, for their journey now seemed somehow more compelling and urgent. Although their pace had already been brisk, they resolved to travel even more intently, for Montpellier was now only one day's hard ride away.

And as the sun was setting, their lathered horses carried the two men over the last small rise before the gate to the ancient monastic town where Alejandro had spent that portion of his youth given to formal education.

"It comes back to me so clearly now," he said to Hernandez, "though the place is much changed! There are houses now where once there was empty land, and some of the streets have stones!" They rode farther into the town and Alejandro pointed out the house where he had boarded with a prominent Jewish family. "Perhaps I should present myself to them," he said to Hernandez. Montpellier was part of his past, and reminded him of a happy time in his life. He found himself with a sudden and unaccountable ache for something familiar.

"It would be wiser if you did not," Hernandez said soberly, "unless, of course, there is no reason for you to fear discovery."

Alejandro would not meet his eyes, and let the matter fall without decision. They rode away from the house in silence. Farther along the same road they came to the beginnings of the university, and Alejandro became visibly excited. "Here a Jew can study without fear of mistreatment," he said. "And yet this is a school founded by priests. The family who cared for me kept me under tight vigil, so I did little more than study while I was here. I regret now that I did not take the time to learn more about this city."

There was much activity in the city as they rode through the crowded streets. They were eager to find accommodations for the night, and stopped many people to ask for recommendations. Most were polite, but some seemed distracted and hurried off after brief excuses. Alejandro's little-used French was weak at best and Hernandez, having even less, relied on Alejandro to speak and hear for him.

When at last they were settled, Alejandro questioned the innkeeper about the flurry of activity in the city.

"Monsieur, there is a terrible affliction that has visited our region. We thought it confined to Marseilles, but this morning a farmer came into town to report that his entire flock of sheep lies dead in the field, having succumbed en masse. People are anxious to leave town, fearing contagion, for no one knows who brings this pest or how it travels. And though I am glad to have your coins, you would be well served to travel on, hastening yourself away from this place."

After this conversation Hernandez took Alejandro aside. "I agree that we would do well to leave this city as quickly as possible, but we will stay the night. I am not heartened to be in the company of a physician, for you may be pressed into service by a priest or magistrate in authority. Hide your profession from anyone who inquires, or say you are a scholar."

"Hernandez," Alejandro said to him, "you ask too much of me! I am bound by my oath to serve the sick and injured without concern for myself."

"Young friend, I implore you to protect your own health now. If you have such a desire to serve, you may find yourself far more useful if the plague spreads farther. When you are dead you can be of help to no one, least of all yourself."

Hernandez's last statement sent a chill of foreboding through Alejandro's spine. *When you are dead,* he repeated in his own mind.

"When I am dead, Hernandez, I will no longer be your responsibility."

"Then I humbly request that you allow me to fulfill the terms of my employment with your family by delivering you safely to Avignon, as my full payment will not be received until you present yourself intact to the banker who will honor the letter of credit I carry from your father."

Alejandro assured Hernandez that he would stay out of harm's way until they were safely in Avignon. "Please forgive me, Hernandez; I had no idea of the arrangements. You have been a noble companion and a creditable escort. You have protected me and I am humbly grateful. You shall have your small fortune, for you deserve it well. Alone on this journey I would have certainly perished."

Hernandez bowed majestically, sweeping his arm before him, saying, "I am at your service, señor. It has been my privilege to assist you on your journey to a new life."

The quarrelsome mood now dissipated, the travelers both prepared to settle into bed, and agreed to leave in the early morning for their final destination of Avignon.

Six

Ted found the microbiology lab empty except for the security guard.

"There was a young lady just here looking for you, sir," the guard said, "asking about some work she had in here. She was interested in that item there," he told Ted, pointing to the fabric circle on the microscope. The man stood nervously waiting for some sort of response from the director, who was notoriously spare with his comments to lower-level Institute employees, most of whom felt rather uncomfortable in his presence.

He looked down his long nose at the guard. "Did she say where she was going?"

"To find you, she said, sir. I assume she went directly to your office."

"Then I imagine she'll come back when my secretary informs her I'm here." Ted gave the man a halfhearted smile, a stiff little curl at the corners of his mouth. He had meant to put the man at ease, but his disjointed facial gesture had the effect of making the man even more nervous.

"Well," said the guard, stepping backward toward the door, "I have my other rounds to make. If I should happen to see the young lady again, I'll tell her you're here." The guard turned and completed his escape.

As he waited for Bruce, Ted looked around the lab. *True self-esteem comes from real accomplishment,* he told himself, and in this building, Ted had accomplished a great deal. Since the Outbreaks he and Bruce had built the Microbiology Department into a scientific establishment of immense importance, not only for the experimental research that flowed out of it, but for its staff's quick response capability in the face of a field crisis. The staff in this department had developed all the guidelines for the Biological Police Unit—he hated the word *Biocop,* but it had stuck like cold dried oatmeal the first time it was used by a journalist—and had trained the first officers assigned to that division of the Metro London Police Force. In his office Ted had a folder of résumés at least two inches thick with applicants waiting for the rare opening that came along in the Microbiology Department, and on Monday he intended to open that folder with the notion of separating out the best dozen as he began the process of replacing Frank. One lucky microbiologist would be getting the opportunity of a lifetime: he or she would happily work in England's finest laboratory, surrounded by glass and chrome and white plastic laminate, with every piece of equipment, every new program, every robotic gizmo, that money could buy. Since the Outbreaks, when the flustered and overwhelmed minister of health saw what public health benefits could be derived from such a facility, funding had not been a problem.

Ted had shrewdly built it up with Bruce's support; it was sort of their baby together. Bruce, who insisted on keeping his hands on the actual work, was more in touch with its day-to-day operation. "I'm jealous, you know," he'd once told Bruce. "You get to play with all the toys." Bruce had countered, with similar envy, "Yeah, but you get to pick them out."

As he looked around at all those toys, Ted's eyes came to rest on what had been Frank's workstation. It was, in a true reflection of its former occupant, messy and unkempt, a marvel of contemporary chaos. He walked over to it and poked around among the piles of papers and stacks of research reports, looking for the list of preparations that needed to be made for the upcoming work, but it wasn't readily visible. In an age when paper's importance was dramatically diminished, Frank had managed to hold on to far more than his share, most of it, by Ted's estimation, trivial. Ted hated this kind of disorder, and had frequently spoken to Frank about it. He had been about to make another attempt at correcting this glaring flaw in the otherwise superb technician when the man had the impertinence to expire inconveniently. He realized he'd have to get someone in here quickly to tie up the loose ends. *Should've done it yesterday when I found out,* he thought. But it hadn't occurred to him that even Frank would leave such a mess behind.

He began searching the area on the perimeter of the workstation. Lying on a nearby table was a reference book, obviously out of its proper place. He wondered what would happen if it were needed and could not be found. No doubt the party guilty of leaving it there would have been the first to complain. He picked it up and looked at the entry on the open page. *Yersinia pestis.* It didn't ring a bell in any recent work. *Oh, well,* he thought, *maybe the pages were blown over by the fan.* He closed the book and continued looking around.

He wondered if the preparation list had been in Frank's pocket when he died. Stranger things had been found in the pockets of lab coats by the laundry staff. Of course his clothing and possessions would have been cataloged by the police. What would they do with such an article if they found it? He made a mental note to find out the name of the officer in charge of the postmortem investigation. He was grateful, at least, that the untimely death hadn't occurred *in* the lab—it would've been weeks before the Biocops would let him back in, those very cops whose medical-training routines were developed in that lab. They would not hesitate to cause whatever delays they deemed necessary, and he couldn't afford to wait that long to get started.

Getting started would be a lot easier if I had that blasted list! he thought, his level of irritation rising. He decided that the logical place to look, outside of Frank's pockets, would be the main office cubicle in the lab.

Only seconds after Ted passed by the small table on which it rested, the edge of the tube of *P. coli* began to fizzle, exuding tiny frothy bubbles around the rim of the stopper. Thawed and warm, the bacteria had reached new heights of reproductive excess; the gases released by the flurry of microbial activity had increased dramatically. The vibration caused by Ted's passing footsteps jostled the table just enough to get the gases moving around inside the tube. They swirled and frothed, destabilized, and approached a state of volatility. The stopper, though well enough secured for ordinary cold storage, reached the limit of its holding power; it clung precariously to the smooth glass of the tube until the lab's automatic venting fan came on, subjecting it to one more wave of vibration. Then it quivered and let go, spraying foamy droplets of *Palmerella coli* all over the near surroundings in the lab.

Had Ted actually seen the event as it took place, he would have been surprised by how far the spray carried. But his back was turned, and he didn't see the frothy liquid fly out in an area about eight by twelve feet, roughly elliptical in shape, to contaminate nearly everything in its path, including the microscope on which Janie's recent find was mounted. A droplet of *P. coli* landed directly on the fabric circle, saturating the area in which the mystery microbe rested, dormant again after her reproductive struggles.

If Frank had been alive to watch, he would have been fascinated once more to see the newly moistened *Yersinia pestis* stretch and yawn, then begin to heave her sides again, trying with Herculean effort to divide. But this time she had a visitor who provided just the help she needed. *Palmerella coli*, true to its lusty nature, sent out a host of gene-transporting plasmids in search of a little hot sex, which it found in short order, for Gertrude, having lived in chaste dormancy for over six hundred years, was ready, ripe, and willing, opening her cell wall eagerly for the invasion of the genetic projectile. It slipped easily into her moist cell body, and they were one.

After that, reproduction by division was a simple matter. Gertrude P. Coli was born.

When he heard the shattering of glass and the popping of the stopper, Ted turned around, and almost instantly his nose was assaulted by a new odor. *Grapes,* he thought. *Grapes gone bad.* Following his nose, he came upon the scene of the small explosion. His eyes scanned the trail of broken glass and frothy liquid, and by following the increase in the intensity of debris he was able to locate the epicenter of the disaster. Shocked by what had happened to the point where he forgot the proper precautions, he picked up a large chunk of the exploded tube and turned it around and around in his ungloved hand, examining it closely. A small shred of its label still clung to the side of the tube. The letters *P* and *c* were smudged but readable.

He knew that *P. coli* had been on his list of preparatory materials. "Bloody hell," he said to the ghost of Frank, "I should have figured that you'd get around to taking the sample out of the freezer." Ted knew that the sample could have been out of the freezer for as long as twenty-four hours, plenty of time for the buildup of pressure needed to cause such an explosion.

He stared at the toxic mess in front of him, panicking, certain that his blood pressure was about to go through the roof. He'd have to clean it up himself. He couldn't even let anyone know that this had happened, much less that it had happened during a project under his direction. He was technically required to report such an event to the Biological Police, and depending on the circumstances, prosecution might result. With Frank out of the picture Ted knew that he would be the focus of any investigation that followed. Good supervisory procedure demanded that he immediately investigate any ongoing work in which Frank had been involved at the time of his death, in order to maintain laboratory safety. Ted had failed to do this, which was a tremendous oversight on his part; he had to admit that he hadn't even given it a thought.

What a mess! he thought, *and Bruce will be here momentarily.*

He had worked with *P. coli* often enough to know that it was the bacterial version of a harmless gigolo, and that on its own it was not toxic or particularly dangerous. But Ted was more worried about the microbe's rather outgoing social behavior, the behavior for which it had been developed and was now cherished for research purposes: it was shamelessly willing to share its genetic material, and often did so with microbes that were the biological equivalent of complete strangers. He immediately ran back to the glass-enclosed office and reviewed the posted schedule of ongoing work, and was relieved to see that there were no open bacterial procedures listed. He went to the lab's utility closet where he found an appropriate assortment of antibacterial cleaners, all of which were used regularly on the lab floors and flat surfaces. He gathered up an armful of spray bottles, then grabbed a roll of disposable towels and returned to the scene of the disaster.

He carefully wiped all the nearby surfaces with a towel saturated in the strongest cleaner he could find. The chemical smell almost overpowered him; it was far worse than the fruit-gone-bad smell of the bacterial contamination. He disposed of each dirtied towel in an approved biohazard plastic bag. He wiped down the computerized microscope setup, but had to remove the small circle of fabric that had been on the plate in order to reach to the surfaces that were obscured by its overlap but not protected from contamination. He looked at it briefly as he turned it over in his hands. In his panic it didn't occur to him to consider that it might have importance in and of itself. He placed it back in the correct position before finishing the wipe-down.

And as if Ted didn't have enough on his mind, he still needed a *P. coli*–type microbe for the work he and Bruce were about to begin. Now there was none and somehow this would have to be explained. He rummaged through Frank's drawers looking for a pen and, when he finally found one, ran to the freezer area. He flipped quickly through the list for the location where *P. coli* was ordinarily stored and directed the camera to the slot. It brought up a close view, close enough to read the marker. It had Frank's name on it.

He'd have to explain where Frank put that sample if he didn't change the marker. Carefully but clumsily manipulating the mechanical arm, wishing he had even half of the dead man's lost skills with the robotic retriever, Ted grasped the marker and brought it out through the decontamination pass-through. On a blank marker he quickly wrote, *Sample contaminated due to cracked tube. Neutralized and disposed of on . . .* He stopped and counted back to the day before Frank's death. He finished the note by writing in that date, then scribbled Frank's initials on the signature line. He placed the forged marker in the pass-through, then picked it up with the mechanical arm. With a lot of maneuvering he managed to slip it into the proper slot. He grabbed the old marker and brought it out through the disinfecting pass-through, then placed it in the bag with the towels for disposal. If anyone asked why the disposal of a live microbe was not recorded in the daily log, he would explain truthfully that it was sometimes Frank's habit to do all his weekly paperwork on Friday from personal notes kept over the course of the entire week.

He set the venting fan to high power and opened the outer door a crack to get rid of the antiseptic smell. After a few minutes the odor diminished to the undertone level that was always present in the lab, for a day never passed without an antibacterial solution being used somewhere within its walls. As he was sealing the top of the plastic bag he heard a tentative knock on the outer door of the lab. The unfamiliar voice of a woman called out softly, "Hello?"

After quickly tucking the sealed bag under a nearby table, he glanced back at the area he had just cleaned and decided it would not arouse suspicion in a casual observer. He was a bit disheveled, so he ran his hands over his hair quickly and smoothed out his rumpled lab coat before he turned to face the unexpected intruder. He wiped the sweat off his forehead with the sleeve of his lab coat, but some had trickled down to the corner of his eye, so he flicked it away with the tip of one gloved finger.

Ted turned around and put on his warmest smile when he saw that the interloper was not Big Bad Bruce but a lovely red-haired woman who looked to be about thirty—probably the same woman the security guard had mentioned to him. He took a deep breath before speaking in an effort to calm himself—his heart was still pounding—and gave her a warm greeting.

"Good morning. May I help you?"

"Maybe you can. I'm looking for the director, Dr. Cummings."

"Well, fortunately, you've found him," he said, gratified to see how happy this seemed to make her.

She extended her hand. "I'm glad to meet you," she said. "My name is Caroline Porter. I'm supposed to meet a colleague of mine here this morning. We have some items in this lab for analysis. But when I got here earlier the security guard told me I'd have to talk to you about it. I've been running around this building like a chicken with my head cut off looking for you!"

He made a show of pulling off his glove and throwing it in the proper container, then extended his bare hand to her. "Sorry about that," he said. He glanced around to make sure again that his cleanup was not obvious. "I've been sort of preoccupied," he continued, struggling to hide his nervousness.

He looked the young woman quickly up and down, taking care not to make it a leering look, and made a quick mental assessment of her threat factor. She was a little shy of average height, and of medium build, with a conventionally pretty face and a very pleasant smile. Her attire was conservative, simple and on the casual side. He decided, after a few seconds of consideration, that this young woman represented very little threat of discovery to him. She did, however, represent a serious distraction from the completion of his cleanup, and he needed to get rid of her. He would try to solve her problem and send her packing as soon as possible. "What sort of items do you have here?" he said, trying to sound eager to help.

Caroline motioned with her hands, drawing long narrow lines in the air to demonstrate the shape of the items she sought. "Big tubes of dirt. We're completing an archaeological dig requiring soil analysis, and the chemistry work is going to be done here." She frowned and added, "Under Frank's direction, as luck would have it."

"Not especially *good* luck, I'm afraid. You stumbled onto a rather inconvenient situation, to say the least." For sympathetic effect he added, "What a tragedy. We'll all miss him; he was a good worker. I'm here now trying to get a handle on some things he started for me. I don't know what I'll do without him."

Caroline, feeling uncomfortable discussing someone she barely knew, politely turned the conversation back to the matter at hand, saying, "I wonder if you can help me sort out where our samples are stored. They would have to be refrigerated. They were also quite large, about a meter long and ten centimeters in diameter."

"And how many were there?"

"Fifty-four."

"My goodness, that's quite a lot! I shouldn't imagine that we have room for that much material."

"It was all brought here, and we didn't get any notification that it was moved elsewhere. Although Frank might have intended to send us a notice if he moved them, and just didn't get around to it."

"Unfortunately, that is a distinct possibility. There were a few things he left undone. But all samples for external work are stored in the refrigerated unit over there. They weren't biorestricted for any reason, were they?"

"Not that I'm aware of," she said.

"Then they'd definitely be in there. All the other storage areas are for restricted materials." He pointed to a bank of units against the far wall of the lab. "That would be the most logical place to look."

"I'll start looking there, then," Caroline said with a smile. "Thanks for your help. I have one little thing to take care of before I start there, though," she added. As she moved in the direction of the area he'd just cleaned up, Ted felt his heartbeat start to accelerate. When she pointed at the fabric circle on the microscope his knees began to weaken and his throat to constrict. She set her purse down nearby and explained, "This came up from the ground with one of our soil plugs. We were looking at it on Thursday just before Frank, uh . . . expired. He did a little bit of computer work on it and made us some marker files. It was probably the last work he did here."

She was touching it, trying to remove it from the mounting tray! *Why isn't she wearing gloves?* He moved toward her, frantically trying to think of ways to keep her from handling the fabric, but it was too late; her fingers were already all over it. He could barely hear his own voice when he said, "Did you find anything of interest?"

"At first, no, but then we stumbled on this big fat microbe. We didn't get as far as figuring out what it was, but Frank said he would check into it for us. He put a dye marker on the actual microbe so we could find it more easily later on. We should have some fun with it when we get back to the States."

Somehow Ted Cummings controlled his rising nausea, but his knees were another matter. Nevertheless Fortune smiled on him: as they buckled and he teetered, Caroline turned away and looked toward the door in response to a new voice calling her name. She didn't see his distress. He looked up as he regained his balance and saw a tall woman enter; he heard Caroline greet her as he clutched the back of a chair to steady himself.

"I'm sorry that took so long," the new arrival said, "but I had a devil of a time convincing the accounting department that they should use the credit exchange rate on the day they post my bill, not the day it happens to be most in their favor. So I got to spend a few minutes with a rather annoying billing clerk explaining the concepts of math and foreign exchange."

"Lucky you."

"I guess! And we thought things were bad back home!"

Ted stood back, wobbling slightly. With a massive effort of will he regained his composure and came forward to introduce himself. He smiled too sweetly when he extended his hand, but the response he got from the woman who'd just entered was all brisk professionalism. "How do you do," Janie said simply as she gave his hand a brief shake. He cleared his throat nervously and said, "Miss Porter has told me about your samples. I've told her where you might start looking for them. If I can be of any further assistance, please don't hesitate to ask." They thanked him and headed for the storage unit.

He sat down, his blood literally racing through his veins, as he waited for Bruce. What would he say when Bruce finally arrived? *Sorry, old boy, I seem to be having a small fit of apoplexy. . . . I've developed a bit of a problem here, although at the present time I'm not prepared to discuss it.* In the background he could hear the exchange that took place between the two visitors as they searched the refrigerated storage area. He should have been standing right behind them, making sure that procedures were being followed, but here he was, glued to a chair, the very personification of the human physical response to stress. He sweated, his heart pounded, he felt horribly nauseous. And his senses betrayed him; he could hear that they were talking, but not the actual words they said. He was in far too much of a panic to focus on anything so specific.

Soon they were back again. "Some of our materials are missing," Janie said. "We counted the protruding ends. Our tubes are much larger than anything else you have in storage there, and we were able to locate the stack quite easily. But we counted three times, and neither one of us could come up with more than forty-eight."

"I'm terribly sorry," Ted said, but he was secretly glad that a distraction had presented itself.

Janie moaned. "One I could understand, but six?"

"As I told Miss Porter, it's quite possible that they were moved," he said. "There's not a lot of space in there. You know, I seem to recall hearing Frank say that he was going to reorganize the storage units a few days ago—it was one of the things he was doing to get the lab ready for some rather complex research we're about to start. One of my associates might know about the things that were moved. He's going to be heavily involved in an experiment here and he needed additional space."

"Can we speak with him?" Janie asked.

Ted glanced at his watch and said, with stiff courtesy, "He's on his way, supposedly; he should be here momentarily."

"May we wait for him?"

This is getting too complicated, he thought to himself. He finally said, somewhat stonily, "If you'd like."

Just as he finished uttering his halfhearted assent, the lab door flew open and Bruce Ransom made a rushed, dramatic entrance, breathing heavily. His lean, narrow body looked even longer dressed in black pants and dark gray shirt, buttoned at the neck with a matching tie. As his one concession to professional attire, he had covered his street clothing with a long white lab coat, his ID tag clipped to its pocket. His unruly dark hair, falling in soft waves over the collar of his lab coat, looked almost as if he hadn't bothered to comb it that morning. Ted always told him that he looked more like a jazz musician than the assistant director of a high-security government-operated medical research facility.

"Ah! Here he is!"

"I'm sorry, Ted," he said, "I just wanted to get this entire outline on paper before we got started today." He waved the file folder at the director. "It's finally done. . . ."

He was aware of the presence of two strangers standing nearby, and thought gratefully, *Ted won't get on my case about being late in front of anyone else. . . .*

He glanced over at the two women. They appeared to be waiting for someone, and by their expectant looks it occurred to him that they might be waiting for him. Something was familiar about the taller woman, and he wondered if he knew her from somewhere. He searched his memory for a match, but all he got in the first run-through was a few quick hits of recognition, nothing solid enough for identification. *Attractive,* he thought. *Nice legs.* But then he saw that the same woman was staring at him as well, her eyes working him over. They settled on his security pass; when she read the name, a smile crept onto her face.

"Oh, my God. Bruce Ransom. We were in medical school together. I'll bet you don't remember me."

He looked at her again and gave her a slight smile as he studied her face. He looked at the visitor's pass clipped to the collar of her shirt. It had no name, only the date and time of entry. "Well, it would be easier if I had the advantage of knowing your name too."

"Sorry," she said. "Of course. Janie Crowe. You would have known me as Janie Gallagher."

"Crowe?" he said, with a smile of amusement. "We've gotten about a hundred faxes from you in the last two months."

Janie was not amused. "You guys made me jump through hoops to get authorization for this lab. You must know my shoes size by now."

"Well, I wouldn't be surprised, but I didn't handle it, so I don't know the first thing about it. Authorizations come out of my department, but I don't look at any of them myself. One of the clerks in my office took care of your request." He chuckled. "I don't know if I should tell you this, but she's taken to calling you *Faxkreig.* I had no idea it was you. I mean, the different name and all."

Janie laughed. *Faxkreig?* "My whole *being* is different. Medical school was twenty years ago."

"Don't remind me," he said with a smirk. "I'd rather not think about it."

"Oh, cut it out. I happen to know how old you are, and you look terrific."

"You do too." He looked her up and down. "What a surprise this is! So what brings you to the Institute?"

She sighed. "It's a very long story. Long and sad and not terribly interesting. Suffice it to say that I've had to change professions. I'm doing an archaeological dig to get certified in forensics and I've got some soil samples here for chemical analysis. Frank was going to oversee the work. We came in to see if we could get a different technician assigned, that is, we being Caroline and I. . . ." She gestured in the direction of her assistant, who smiled and said hello as Bruce nodded back at her. "Caroline's working with me on this project. Anyway, when we checked our samples, we discovered some are missing. There are supposed to be fifty-four and we can find only forty-eight. We're on a pretty tight deadline and we have to get things moving. We're trying to find out where they might have been moved, and your colleague here"—she gestured toward Ted—"told us that someone was coming to the lab who might know where they were."

Bruce looked at Ted. "My guess is that someone would be me."

Ted nodded. "Since you worked with Frank regularly, I thought you might have some firsthand knowledge that I don't. I recall Frank telling me that he was doing some reorganization of the storage units before we start our new work."

"He was," Bruce said, "but I don't know specifically what he might have done or how far along he got in the project before he died. Just that he was doing it."

Janie sighed, her frustration clear. "I just find it so odd that he never said anything to us about it when we were in here yesterday."

"When were you supposed to start the analyses?"

"Monday."

"Then it's quite possible that he moved them temporarily and was planning on having them back here by then. He wouldn't have any reason to mention moving them if that was the case. Frank could be very scatterbrained, but he had his own way of doing things. They always seemed to get done, somehow." He looked at Ted, as if seeking confirmation of his assessment of the late lab technician's work habits. Ted nodded his agreement.

Janie found her frustration slipping over the line into anger. *Too many things are going wrong,* she thought to herself. *This whole project seems to be jinxed.* Her tone was more snippy than the occasion might have warranted when she said, "That's all very well and good. I'm sure he had the best of intentions in moving them, and I'll even venture a guess that he would have had them back here bright and early Monday morning." She glanced back and forth between Bruce and Ted. "You both seem to have had a lot of confidence in him, so I'll have to accept your explanation." She smiled rather sardonically. "Graciously, even. Unfortunately, your very good explanation of *why* the tubes aren't here doesn't do much to solve the problem of *finding* them, and then *getting* them back here."

Bruce and Ted exchanged glances and performed a silent mental coin toss. Janie watched them, and thought, *So which one of you gets to deal with this crank?*

A midair decision took place. Bruce looked back at Janie and said, "I'd be happy to check into it for you. There are really only a few places where things that big might have been taken."

"I'd really appreciate that, Bruce. Our schedule is already tight as it is. I'd hate to lose time over something like this."

"It's no problem. I'm happy to do it for you. But I might not be able to get to it for a few hours or so." He looked at Ted briefly, then turned back to Janie and said, "Ted and I have some things to go over right now. When we're done—"

To Bruce's surprise Ted interrupted him. "We can postpone it for an hour or two. I'm not sure just how much of the prep work Frank managed to get done, and I could use a little while in the lab to figure it out. It doesn't make much sense for us to proceed if we don't know where we stand in terms of the background work."

Bruce looked at Ted again, this time with eyebrows raised in curiosity. "Are you sure?"

Ted smiled. *Oh, yes, very sure,* he thought to himself, relief flooding through him. "It'll mean a slight delay in our own work, but things have pretty much come to a standstill anyway, what with the funeral and all coming up. Most of the staff will want to attend. I don't see where a few hours are going to make much of a difference. And there's another problem. I went to the freezer for the sample of *P. coli* while I was waiting for you this morning, and unfortunately it's been destroyed. The tube had developed some sort of crack and Frank disposed of it. He left a disposal marker in the slot. I haven't found any record of him ordering a replacement before he died."

Looking very pleased, Janie said, "Well, that settles it." She turned to Bruce. "How can I reach you?"

He took his wallet from the back pocket of his pants and fished around in it for a moment, finally producing a card, which he handed to Janie. "Here's my number. Why don't you give me yours too."

From her purse she extracted a small notepad and wrote the hotel number on it. "There's voice mail. If I'm not in, just leave me a message. I'll get right back to you, I promise."

"Okay." He looked at Ted again. "I'll get right on this." He glanced at his watch. "Shall we meet back here later, maybe two-thirty or so?"

Ted nodded.

Janie said, "We're just going to write down the tag numbers on the samples we've got, then we'll have to go back to the hotel to compare them to the list. I didn't think to bring it with me."

"Good enough. I'll talk to you later, then."

"I'll look forward to it," Janie said.

Before leaving, he said, "It was good to see you again after all this time."

Janie smiled. "Yeah, it was."

As he headed back to his office, Bruce contemplated the morning's strange and confusing events. When he finished the mental replay of his chance meeting with Janie, he realized that a far more interesting story was taking shape, and he'd nearly missed it in all the excitement. *Why isn't Ted foaming at the mouth?* he wondered. This kind of screwup ordinarily sent Ted on a rampage. He wanted to say to the obvious imposter he'd left back in the lab, *Who are you and what have you done with Ted?*

Ted was sitting down near the microscope workstation, the scene of his earlier fiasco, waiting for the two women to leave so he could complete his cleanup. He was still trying to compose himself when Caroline returned from the bank of storage units. "One more thing," she said, "—I almost forgot. I have to get Gertrude."

"Gertrude?" Ted asked.

Caroline turned toward the microscope and extracted a small plastic bag from her purse. "The microbe. The one Frank found on the fabric. We named it after Janie's grandmother."

Ted leapt up off his chair and reached in her direction, his outstretched hands ready to stop her from touching the fabric. "Here, let me help you with that. . . ." He hoped his voice would not give away his growing panic. He tried to move deliberately, not desperately, toward her. But he was not quick enough; she already had it firmly in hand. There was nothing he could do to stop her.

"Thanks, but I can manage," she told him. "I'll just seal it up in this bag and store it in the unit with the tubes." She smiled at him. "Hopefully no one will move it on us."

I will never get used to independent women, he swore to himself. He swallowed hard and said nothing, but watched her carefully and noted exactly where she put the fabric in the storage unit. He would return later to retrieve it.

He was careful to maintain a veneer of perfect politeness, and considering the volume of adrenaline pumping through his veins, he did quite well. He sat down again and closed his eyes, hoping to open them again in a few minutes to find this nightmare over. He didn't think it likely.

"It looks so puny in there," Janie said. Placed flat on the plastic-coated wire rack in front of the stacked tubes of dirt, it seemed almost pitifully lost. "Maybe we ought to take that with us now," she said. "We don't need to be losing anything else today."

Caroline looked back at the unit. "You're right," she said, and tucked the sealed plastic bag into her purse.

Just before leaving the Institute that night, Ted slipped back into the lab to retrieve the fabric. He would burn it, and be done with it, and its potential to cause disaster would be forever neutralized. If they asked where it had gone, he'd play dumb, and he wouldn't give them the opportunity to search as they'd done before. But when he opened the storage unit, the prize was not immediately visible in the section where he'd seen Caroline place it. He pawed anxiously through an assortment of nearby containers and boxes, but couldn't find it. After a few minutes he gave up and arranged the items back in their original positions, not wanting to leave a visible path of disturbance.

He wondered if Caroline had moved it, or if he had remembered incorrectly. He had been in a panic when he watched Caroline place the small plastic bag in the unit; perhaps his memory of what had transpired was untrustworthy. *Well, no matter,* he thought. They would be back, and he would make sure he was informed of their arrival. Perhaps he would drop in casually while they worked, to socialize, then turn the conversation toward their work and ask to see that item. Then he wouldn't let it out of his sight.

Seven

This was to be the last day of their long travels, so the Spaniard and the Jew rose from their comfortable beds at the inn in Montpellier and rode out energetically well before dawn. Both were eager to leave the ancient monastic town and complete the journey to Avignon.

They stopped in a small farming village to water their horses after covering a good amount of distance. The sun was not yet high enough in the sky to burn off the dampness of the night before, and they were enveloped in rolling clouds of fine gray mist. As they stood at the trough, removing what they could of the road's grit, Alejandro splashed water on his face and said, "I will be glad to live through a day when I am not required to rise up from a soft bed and settle my haunches on a hard saddle."

"Do not complain, my friend," Hernandez said, chuckling. "A less fortunate man might have been forced to *walk* to Avignon."

"Ah, but were I *truly* fortunate, I would not have made the journey at all."

"You tempt fate, my friend, with such a declaration. There are those who think there is some sort of divine plan to the course of a man's life. I am inclined to agree. You do not know what awaits you at the end of this road; perhaps it will be a pleasant situation. Perhaps you will find a means to understand that you are *not* unfortunate. For the meantime, be thankful that you can ride."

Their attention was drawn to the sound of groaning wheels. Out of the mist, a short distance away, emerged a mule-drawn cart, creaking under the weight of its burden.

"*Madre de Dios,*" Hernandez whispered, and made the sign of the cross.

They exchanged shocked glances. Hernandez pointed toward the cart and said, "Now, a *truly* unfortunate man might have traveled thus."

As the cart emerged slowly from the mist, Alejandro began to see the shape of hands and feet protruding from its sides. A man in a hooded black robe, crop in hand, walked before the mule, turning every few steps to whip the reticent animal, who seemed intent on waking the passengers in the cart with his pathetic braying.

The physician felt his curiosity rising. *At last!* he said to himself silently. *Now I will see for myself if the tales we have heard are true.*

As the cart came closer, his eyes were glued to it. "See how ragged and filthy they all are," he said to Hernandez. "They must all have been poor in life. And look!" he said, pointing. "Not a one wears shoes!"

"One cannot infer poverty from a lack of shoes," Hernandez said, his tone cynical. "Most likely the thieves are the poor ones, looking for a bit of comfort for their feet." He crossed himself again, the second such unusual gesture for a man who was customarily so lax about observing his religion. "God grant that I may never know such depravity."

Alejandro noticed the protective ritual and said, "You are far too resourceful for that fate to befall you."

Hernandez gazed somberly in the direction of the cart. " 'Tis true, I think, and may the Virgin be praised," he said, his voice low. "But I would gladly give up my fortunes for the certainty that I will not end up like *those* poor souls."

No such certainty may be had, Alejandro thought to himself. *We will all be equal before this scourge.* He started to move closer to the cart, and Hernandez immediately began to protest.

Ignoring his escort's outcries, Alejandro edged closer still, until he was as near as his own fear would allow him to go. An obscene stink emanated from the cart and he was forced to retreat a few steps. He turned his head away, nearly retching, and gulped in several deep breaths of fresh air. When he approached the cart again, he breathed through the fabric of his shirtsleeve.

Inside the death cart he saw the twisted bodies of women and children and old men. They were tall and short and fair and swarthy, every variety of humanity he could conceive of. *Hernandez is right,* he thought to himself. *They were not all poor.* Some showed signs of leftover plumpness, and might have been prosperous in life; others were as skinny as broomsticks and weathered, a sure sign that they had labored long and hard for their daily bread before meeting an ignominious end. He peered curiously at the bodies, looking closely at the swollen necks and bloated fingers of the unfortunate victims, and decided that none of the tales he had heard were exaggerations.

"Where will they be taken?" he said to the driver.

The man looked up at this questioner, and stared with eyes so full of fatigue that they were nearly as dead looking as those of his gruesome passengers. A chill of foreboding passed unbidden through Alejandro's spine.

"They will be taken to a field north of town, where the priest will say a funeral mass over all the dead together. God grant that they did not die unshriven!"

And though he did not really understand what it meant to be unshriven, Alejandro nodded, implying sympathy for the plight of these unshriven dead, hoping privately that the Christian God did not determine the worth of the soul by judging the appearance of the corpse. He would ask Hernandez to explain that condition to him later. He rejoined his escort at the trough, shivering slightly, disturbed by the cart's grim cargo, and continued his ablutions.

The majestic arches of the grand bridge of Saint-Bénézet curved gracefully over the Rhône, the beautiful stonework softly reflected in the shimmer of the water. Alejandro caught his breath when it came into view. They had been passing through a stand of trees skirting a bend in the road, when the bridge suddenly appeared as if out of nowhere, massive and magnificent. Over the river lay the city of Avignon, and high on a hill, keeping watch, stood the magnificent papal palace. And after all he had been through—his capture, the branding, the separation from his family, and the murder—Alejandro was still as excited as a child to be there, for Avignon was the place where his new life would begin.

The towers of the papal palace reached up majestically, great white arms, supplicant, straining toward heaven itself. The dazzling white walls gleamed in the afternoon sun, blinding the observer to the sights around it. Alejandro thought it was more beautiful than anything he had ever seen. Scaffolding ran up one of the walls, but Alejandro saw that it was unoccupied. "Do you find it strange, Hernandez," he said, "that there are no workmen on the ladders on such a fine day as this?"

Hernandez looked at the palace. "You are right," he said. "There are no stonemasons in sight. Perhaps Avignon has not escaped this plague either."

As they rode into the city, they saw all around them evidence that Avignon had not, in fact, escaped. People rushed swiftly past them, as if some urgent business compelled them onward. The citizens of Avignon showed none of the open friendliness Alejandro had hoped he would find, but instead skulked by, avoiding contact with the riders, distrust and outright hostility in their expressions. Bodies lay on the ground in front of nearly every third house they passed, awaiting the cart. The carts themselves passed by in rapid succession, like some macabre caravan on its way to the burial grounds. Always they were full, their wooden wheels bowing under the weight.

"Wherever will all these dead be buried?" Alejandro wondered aloud as another cart passed.

"More important, who will bury them?" Hernandez responded. "This scourge takes so many! By all the gods, Physician, I fear it will take me too! How are we to avoid it?"

"I do not know," he said, sounding discouraged, then sighed. "I do not know."

"Are you certain that this sign says 'Rooms to Let'?" Hernandez asked. "Perhaps you have forgotten the correct words. . . ."

"I have not forgotten," Alejandro replied. The sound of the slamming door was still ringing in his ears. The widow householder had refused them entry, saying that she no longer trusted anyone to be plague free. She had told them to seek out another house not far away in their quest for lodging, so the tired pair turned in unison and stepped down the narrow stairs back onto the cobblestone street.

The second widow, an elderly woman whose husband had succumbed to the affliction just three days earlier, was only too glad to have them, for she was all alone and quite frightened, with no relatives to whom she might turn for aid. But she needed income beyond the mere letting of rooms, for the death of her husband had left her without means. She offered to rent her house to Alejandro, and to act as his housekeeper in return for a small payment and his promise to help her with things an old woman could not accomplish by herself.

It seemed a good arrangement to both, but before consummating the agreement, Alejandro took Hernandez aside, and asked his opinion of the widow's proposal.

The Spaniard approved. "A man is always fortunate to have a woman to look after him," he said, "even if she does not do so without payment." He glanced back at the widow, who awaited their word. "At least this one will not waste your time in trying to drag you to the altar."

After a brief round of self-congratulation for their fortunate discovery, Hernandez said, "I will take our horses for stabling, then seek out the countinghouse to finalize my contract with your father. I shall return before the dinner hour, and then we shall see if this widow's services are a worthy investment. We shall raise our glasses to your new home and your continued good fortune."

Alejandro brought his few things inside the small house. It was small but well appointed with sturdy, serviceable furniture. The packed dirt floors of the first story were well swept and level; there was a long, narrow table with benches on either side, a chair, and a small sleeping pallet. Upstairs, he found two separate sleeping chambers, one of which he thought, judging by the size of the bed, might have been occupied once by a child. The other sleeping chamber was large and commodious and, being in the front of the house, had a window. The straw bed was raised off the floor. On closer inspection he found the straw fresh and relatively insect free, and the linens, while obviously old, were in good condition and very clean. He set his own belongings down in the smaller room, with the intent of allowing the massive Hernandez the bigger bed while he remained in Avignon. He would occupy it himself, as master of this house, when Hernandez left.

Once settled, Alejandro set out to investigate Avignon, hoping to locate a suitable site for his surgery. Not far from his new abode he came upon an apothecary shop, and inquired of the chemist if there were any doctors practicing in this area.

"At one time there were two physicians and one barber serving the people of this section," the man told him. "But all have died of the same savage malady that killed their patients, and I fear you will find no help from them."

Alejandro explained that he himself was a physician, and was not in need of a physician's services. "I have recently come to Avignon, and I await the arrival of my family. I am interested in rooms to let for the purpose of setting up my surgery."

"Then I suggest you inquire of Dr. Selig's widow. His rooms were two blocks east of here, down a narrow street next to the shoemaker's shop. She might be willing to sell his equipment as well." He took on a sad look. "There are young ones to feed."

The apothecary leaned closer, as if to convey a great secret. "The good doctor and I had an arrangement regarding his patients. He would send them to me if his treatments failed to effect a cure, and I would prescribe additional medications and potions in a further attempt to aid the patient."

Alejandro's interest was piqued. "Have you had any luck in treating this pestilence?"

"Bah!" He laughed. "None of our treatments has made a bit of difference. No one can determine the source of the contagion! I have little success in treating even the symptoms." Again, the chemist leaned in, confiding, "There is talk of Jews poisoning the wells. I myself am inclined to believe it."

Alejandro was stunned, but tried to conceal it. This was not the first time he had heard this ridiculous accusation. Now that his appearance was not that of a traditional Jew, it seemed that people felt free to speak ill of his people in his presence. Clutching the collar of his shirt more tightly to his chest, he played along with the man, whispering, "Dreadful! What can be done about it?"

"Oh, indeed, plenty is being done already! In Arles three Jewesses were burned at the stake after a priest discovered empty vials in their homes. They had been seen at the well just hours before. Now the townspeople are in a great quandary about their water—some say the well is fine; others refuse to use it, saying that to die of thirst would be preferable to risking death by this plague."

Alejandro said, with more boldness than he felt, "I think there may be some wisdom in that preference, but I do not think this pest originates in water. We all drink water, and yet many of us live; and would not all the citizens of Arles by now have succumbed completely, to the very last one, if the poison were in the well? It seems only logical that we need not fear the water."

"But this is a scourge, a punishment from God," the apothecary protested. "We cannot apply logic to its discovery."

"We must apply logic to *all* discoveries," Alejandro said, to which the apothecary did not reply. Alejandro thought it just as well that the discussion end there. He'd heard enough nonsense from the man. Excusing himself as politely as possible, he went in search of the Widow Selig, vowing never to send a patient to a man who was himself so filled with poison.

The widow opened the door to her late husband's surgery and, after Alejandro had explained himself, invited him in. He walked about for some time, inspecting the premises and equipment carefully. Patiently waiting by the door, she kept her distance, answering Alejandro's questions with polite but brief replies.

He asked her the price of the premises and equipment, expressing an interest in buying everything at one time. The tools suited him well. They were not the best quality available, but they were far better than what he had used in Cervere. She named a price, and he hesitated a moment, thinking it too low to reflect the true value of the lot. He remarked about this to her. "Surely, madame, a higher sum would be more appropriate."

"I named this price because I need to sell quickly. I must provide for my children."

Counting out the number of coins needed to make the higher price, he pressed them into her hand. After thanking him profusely, she handed him the heavy iron door key and turned to leave. Alejandro called out to her.

"Madame," he said, "did your husband treat many patients afflicted with the plague?"

Still she would not look directly at him, but spoke instead as if addressing the floor. "It was all he did for the last week of his life. It consumed him. When they took his body away, it was covered with pustules; but I know he died of a broken spirit." And then she left, carrying in one hand all that was left to her of her husband's years of devotion to his craft.

He stood in the empty surgery and looked around at his new possessions, feeling an odd mix of excitement and trepidation. It was larger and darker than his surgery in Cervere. He knew he would need to arrange a source of light for delicate procedures. *Light for my new life*, he thought as he locked the door behind him. There on the door was the sign with Selig's name still on it. *Tomorrow*, he thought, *I will find a signmaker, and post my own notice of trade.*

Hernandez came back to Alejandro's house in time for the evening meal as promised, and reported on the success of his mission to the banking house. "We are to report there together in three days, at which time I will be handsomely recompensed for defending your ignorant hide against the ruffians of the road." And giving Alejandro a pointed stare he added, "I am thankful that no ruffians in the guise of Spanish soldiers bothered us." Then Hernandez chuckled and said, "But I am overpaid, I think. The worst danger we seemed to face was the heat of the sun."

"Nevertheless, señor," Alejandro answered, "your task was not an easy one, and you did it well. No one begrudges you your rightful compensation. It was agreed upon in advance."

They ate their boiled meat and crusty bread by the illumination of two candles on the table between them. The widow provided a delicious wine, one that her husband had made, and they raised their glasses to each other as promised.

Alejandro queried the Spaniard about his plans for the future. "What will you do, now that your employment is over? Perhaps you should spend some time here in Avignon. This house is far too big for me, and I think the widow might be glad to have an extra coin each week."

Hernandez thanked him for the offer. "I have actually grown fond of you, young sir, and I know I will miss your company. We have come a long way from our first encounter in the monastery at Cervere."

After a sip of excellent wine he continued, "It is too much temptation for a man like me to have a fine horse and a small pile of gold. I can travel now wherever I wish, and take my fill of starry nights. Besides, I am growing tired of my old tales. I believe it is time for me to collect some more."

Then the Spaniard lowered his voice, not wishing to bring the landlady to mind of her recent bereavement. "I have it in my plan to outride this pest. I think Avignon will be more dangerous to me than a fireside camp."

Alejandro was sobered by this declaration from his brave friend. Trying to regain their previous warm mood, he made a bold prediction.

"You will return to Avignon, and I shall eagerly await your next visit. I will expect to be entertained by tales of your latest adventures. In the meantime, your fine company and conversation will be sorely missed."

Hernandez toasted his young host again with a courtly flourish. Alejandro thought about future dinners with only his landlady for company, and knew he would miss him indeed.

"And now, my friend, I shall leave you for the evening in search of the company of a lusty wench. I feel a need to repeat my old tales one more time."

The night before they were to visit the banking house, Hernandez excused himself from the table before completing his meal, and complained of a sick stomach.

"This French food is too rich for me. I have consumed more eggs and cheese this week than in my entire time in Aragon. I believe I will let my digestive organs have a rest tonight."

By midnight he was sweating and shivering alternately, one minute pulling his blanket tightly about him, the next kicking it off violently. Alejandro hoped against all reason that his friend's symptoms were only a passing influenza, or a simple bout of *la grippe*, so he treated Hernandez accordingly, administering tea and sponging the man's head with cool water.

He borrowed a lantern from the landlady, promising to refill its receptacle with oil the following day. Running quickly to his nearby surgery, he gathered together the tools he would need to deal with Hernandez's illness, should his worst fears be realized. He would need his knife and scalpel, and a bleeding bowl, some laudanum for easing the pain, and much wine, which he would buy from his landlady's supply.

By the time he returned to the house, Hernandez had visibly worsened. His breathing was shallow, and his normally swarthy complexion was pale and greasy-looking. Alejandro instructed the landlady to bring a sturdy goblet, which he filled with strong wine, forcing Hernandez to drink it. It seemed to calm him.

Then without warning the big man sat up in bed, his eyes bulging, and vomited forcefully, casting the undigested contents of his stomach fully across the room. The landlady groaned in revulsion and hurried out. Alejandro heard her hurried footsteps on the stairs but did not try to follow her.

Hernandez settled down somewhat, having purged himself of his gastronomic demon. Alejandro opened the window shutters, hoping to clear the air of the unpleasant smell, then pulled a chair up by the sick man's bed. "I will keep a vigil by you, Hernandez, and see to your needs," he said. Resting his head on his arms, he dozed fitfully, with small dreams of Carlos Alderón disturbing his repose.

He was awakened by the cawing of a blackbird on the sill of the open window. When he looked at Hernandez, he saw that the sick man was still sleeping peacefully. The coarse dark blanket was pulled close around the soldier's neck, in eerie contrast to the chalky skin of his face. "You must be warm, my good friend," he said, laying his palm across Hernandez's sweaty forehead.

"Yes, you are indeed," he answered himself, and pulled the blanket back from around the man's chin.

He had seen the ghastly swellings on the necks of the corpses, but the sight of a living man with such disfigurement turned his stomach. Hernandez's neck was grossly distended and misshapen. Patches of blue and black surrounded one large spherical growth. He reached toward Hernandez, feeling the increased warmth of the flesh as his fingers neared the neck. Resting the tips of his fingers lightly on the hot skin, he gently palpated the circular mass, and was surprised by its firmness. He knew without a doubt that it would be filled with the thick cloudy mess so frequently described by observers of this plague. He decided to relieve Hernandez of the pain of the enormous boil by lancing it.

When he called for the landlady to bring water, he got no reply; when he went downstairs he saw that the linens on her hearthside sleeping pallet were undisturbed, and he assumed that she had fled. He pulled the light sheet of linen off the pallet and quickly tore it into small rags. In the kitchen he found two water buckets, one full and the other partially so. He carried one bucket and the rags upstairs, arranging everything on the small table at Hernandez's bedside.

After quickly washing his hands and drying them on a linen scrap, he took out a small flask of laudanum. He gently shook Hernandez to awaken him, and bade him open his mouth.

"Stick out your tongue, Hernandez. I will give you a draft that will relieve your pain."

Groggily, the Spaniard did as he was bidden. Their roles were now the opposite of what they had initially been, Hernandez the helpless and ignorant child, Alejandro the wise and experienced warrior, ready to do battle with his friend's unseen attacker.

Alejandro turned away, needing a fresh breath, for Hernandez's tongue was covered with a chalky film, and the odor it exuded was beyond description. Fortified by fresher air, he said, "Steady, now, for this will taste vile," and dribbled a small amount of the drug on his friend's tongue. Trying to amuse his patient, he added, "This time it would please me greatly if you did not give it back as you did your last meal." Hernandez tried to smile, but winced instead; the simple act of curling his mouth caused his neck to throb wildly. He bravely refrained from crying out, but he could not keep the tears from coursing down his pale cheeks.

"Patience, Hernandez; soon I will apply my meager skills to your tormented neck. You will not suffer much longer."

Unable to speak, Hernandez slowly moved his hand to Alejandro's, tapping the hand lightly, then tapping his own armpit. Trying to decipher the meaning of the sick man's actions, Alejandro unlaced Hernandez's shirt, and pulled it down over the shoulder for a better look. The same mottled swellings were presenting themselves there. As he touched the apple-sized lumps, Hernandez recoiled, this time failing to stifle his expression of agony. He cried out in misery.

Slowly the laudanum worked its magic, and the patient lay quiet, insensible and drowsy from the drug. Alejandro worked quickly, not knowing how much time he would have before Hernandez came back to full awareness. He cleaned his instruments, wiping them carefully on one of the linen scraps. Another rag was dipped in water and the area around the boil wiped clean of the sweat that had poured down Hernandez's neck. Carefully, Alejandro placed several more small rags around the yellowed center of the boil, hoping to absorb the effusion of fluid that was likely to gush forth after the lancing, for he was not inclined to touch the vile exudant. He placed the scalpel at the center of the boil, wrapped yet another rag around it, and pressed down. Hernandez began to writhe slowly, feeling this agony even through his laudanum-induced haze; Alejandro kept strong pressure on the man's neck, and felt the size of the mass slowly diminish.

At last the flow was stanched, and none too soon, for Hernandez was beginning to regain consciousness. Alejandro thought he would be better off in a stupor, and offered him more laudanum. But Hernandez weakly gestured no with his hands. He seemed to want to say something.

The voice was dry and tired. "Do not waste your potions on me, Alejandro. I feel the same pain in the pit of my arm and near my manhood as I feel in my neck. Soon I will be a mass of boils, and you will not be able to help me. I despair of ever rising from this bed again. Please allow me to die with some honor."

It had taken all of Hernandez's strength to speak those few words; he closed his eyes and lay still, exhausted by the effort of making his wishes known.

Alejandro had heard that the victims of the plague suffered the terrible despair of hopelessness in their last hours, and he sensed its presence in Hernandez now, but it had not occurred to him that the same despair would have such a deep hold on their survivors. He whispered to Hernandez, clutching the man's blackened hand, "As you wish, my friend. I will not add to your suffering."

By midafternoon both of the Spaniard's hands were completely black; Alejandro had not dared to look at his feet, but suspected they were in a similar condition. He sat uselessly at the Spaniard's bedside, his mind alternately sinking into deep gloom, then racing into a frenzy of impotent anger. He thought back on the death of Carlos Alderón, and the frustration that had come from his inability to stop the progress of the blacksmith's disease. "Would you not allow me time to prepare myself?" he said to Hernandez, who could no longer hear him.

Looking at the ruined body, Alejandro recalled how burly and strong it had once been. The body had consumed itself with fever in the short course of its illness and the man appeared much smaller and bonier, as though the very life had flowed out of him. His neck was once again swollen, having filled up rapidly with black blood, which was now oozing from the wound and coagulating in grainy lumps along the side of his neck.

Desperate to maintain some contact with the man he had come to admire, now his only friend in the world, Alejandro spoke softly to Hernandez as the man slipped closer and closer to death, although he knew the Spaniard could not hear him.

"I curse my luck, Hernandez," he said; "I would be still in Cervere, among friends and family, were it not for that girl. And had the bishop behaved honorably, as you have shown me Christians can behave, I would not have known the fear of discovery on this journey." He hung his head in shame. "Nor would I have had reason to keep my secret from you. I killed him, you see. I plunged my knife into his breast. I watched the redness of his life flow out of him before me. It burdens my soul; I will need to atone somehow for that act."

Hernandez groaned and Alejandro wiped his forehead. "But had this not all come to pass, I would not have had the privilege of knowing you, my friend. It has been a greater pleasure than I could ever have imagined. I will miss you, indeed."

Hernandez died at sunset, after opening his eyes briefly for one last look around. He whispered, *"Madre de Dios,"* then closed his eyes, and his chest fell for the last time.

Knowing there was nothing more he could do for Hernandez, Alejandro covered him with the sheet, then walked slowly to his own bedroom and fell into bed exhausted, not even bothering to remove his clothes.

Pope Clement sat in his private apartment, fanning himself against the stifling heat. *Of what use is this exercise?* he asked himself silently. *There has been no new air in here since that rascal de Chauliac locked me in here, at my own orders, all irony be damned!* He wiped the sweat from his red brow with the moistened cloth that had been at his side since he began his imprisonment.

He was distracted from his misery momentarily by the soft ringing of a bell. *Oh, sweet Jesus, let it be something tasty, or honeyed, or perhaps lusty and willing! I tire of this boredom!*

But to his disappointment it was merely a scroll, albeit an impressively large one. He opened it eagerly, needing its distraction from the boredom of his routine as his physician's captive. Neglecting to review the seal before doing so, he began reading.

Your Holiness,

It is with great sadness that I write to you concerning matters of great import to the Holy Church of Christ and the Kingdom of England. We are stricken at last with the dreaded scourge that has already ravaged the whole of Europa. We had hoped by virtue of our isolation from France to escape its ravages, but it has stubbornly crossed the waters, bringing its vile poison to our fair shores. It began in Southampton not a month ago, and is now firmly entrenched in our fair city of London and its surrounds.

It is my sad duty to advise you of the death of John Stratford, our devoted archbishop, at Canterbury on the sixth day of August. His Eminence departed this earth after five days of illness, attended by his physician and several members of his family, who are greatly distressed in their bereavement and cannot be comforted.

But we must speak of our own grief now, for I am further bound to report a loss more deeply distressing to myself and my good Queen Philippa. Our dear daughter Joanna, on her bridal journey to Castile, has succumbed to the same dreadful plague. While traveling through Bordeaux she became ill, along with several members of her entourage.

The death of our beauteous Joanna, beyond leaving its unspeakable mark on our grieving family, has threatened our alliance with King Alfonso. I fear that my Isabella's refusal to wed his despicable son Pedro did nothing to promote mutual understanding between our two kingdoms, and you know that I was not in favor of the subsequent match between him and Joanna. Your Holiness may recall that there was much discord over the wisdom of this match. We expended great effort to persuade Alfonso that Joanna was a suitable substitute for her sister, and the girl herself was willing, and may God grant her the blessing in heaven she deserves for such noble willingness. Now her untimely demise has no doubt widened the rift between Castile and England. There is no remedy for the loss of Joanna, except the conjuring of another acceptable daughter of marriageable age, and my queen is now loath to let any of her progeny leave her sight, for fear of it being the last encounter. I have convinced her to allow the younger ones to travel with our royal physician, Master Gaddesdon, to Eltham Castle, there to await the scourge's passing. But she will not hear of allowing young Edward and Isabella to join them there, and in truth, neither wishes to do so.

My ministers and advisors cannot come to accord now, and all is confusion; no one wishes to stay in London, dreading the contagion that has gripped our populace in its black claws. My court is meagerly attended, and I have been forced to disband Parliament for the foreseeable future. I lack counselors of any notable ability at Windsor, and the business of my court is dangerously neglected. Scots gather in a jovial mood at my border, thinking to take advantage of our temporary weakness, falsely believing that they will not fall prey to the pest.

I most humbly and sincerely request your holy advice in the settlement of these matters. We are in special need of a successor to the late archbishop. Surely there is a suitable candidate among Avignon's capable bishops, or a prelate among our own people who can serve well in this capacity. I leave this decision in the hands of God and Your Holiness, but I remind you most humbly of our wish to fill the seat with due haste.

It is said by your envoys that your physician is wise in methods of preventing the spread of contagion. Truly, he has done well in his role as the protector of your holy person. I would have you send to us a physician well versed in those preventive crafts, for we have little experience, and must take care to protect our Isabella from the fate suffered by her sister. She is the favorite of her mother, who has already borne the pain of seeing one of her daughters precede her into eternity. I would spare my good queen another such loss, God willing.

I have begun to consider other conjugal arrangements for Isabella. There is the possibility of a marriage with the family of Brabant; the duke has proposed that his eldest son be wedded to our daughter. I hesitate to solidify the coupling for fear of weakening our bloodline; Isabella would be closely cousined to her bridegroom, and Your Holiness has made known his opinion that such matches produce weak and often witless offspring. Whilst we are convinced of the vigor of our lineage, we are suspect of Brabant. My queen and I seek your word on this tender of alliance. And Isabella herself still smarts from the shame of her recent rejection, which is brought to mind in the presence of the Brabants.

We have not yet entered a state of anarchy on our fair island, but it cannot be far away. My campaign in France is at a standstill. There is much uncertainty here, and my good knights advise against pursuing the siege just now. Every day the plague takes more victims, making no distinction between the wretched and the highborn. The farmers cannot bring in their harvests for lack of able hands to swing the scythes. Barley stands bolting in the fields, and honey goes ungathered, hence there is no mead. Our livestock are unattended; some have already fallen prey to the same pest, and their carcasses spoil the pastures and foul the air. Our whole world is writhing in the devil's hands, squirming to escape the path of the plague, but every day more and more perish horribly.

My queen and I, together with all of our royal house, await your wise response to our queries. We pray that it will be sent by swift riders, for this dreaded affliction takes its victims whimsically, having no regard for the best plans of even the mightiest lord. Prostrate at the feet of Your Holiness and imploring the favor of its apostolic benediction, I have the honor to be, Very Holy Father, with the deepest veneration of Your Holiness, the most humble and obedient servant and son,

Edward Rex

Pope Clement VI finished reading the king's letter, then fanned himself pensively with the scroll. The events chronicled in Edward's missal required thoughtful attention, and under the elaborate isolation imposed by his personal physician, Guy de Chauliac, Pope Clement had plenty of time to think.

Monsieur le docteur had decreed that the pope should have little or no contact with others for as long as the plague persisted. He had entombed Clement in his private apartment, ordering fires to be lit in all the hearths throughout the spacious suites. The windows were barred shut, and the doors were opened only with the physician's specific permission. Clement was advised to wear long-sleeved, tight-fitting garments and to keep his head covered at all times. His blandly prepared food was served in minute portions, for de Chauliac believed that the sin of gluttony enhanced a person's susceptibility to disease.

Miserably rubbing his chin, Clement thought to himself that for a man of his worldly tastes, this monastic life was worse than death. De Chauliac was firm in his conviction that infection was a result of direct contact with the contagion, but could not specify how the contagion traveled, so he had simply ordered that Clement remain isolated from everything.

Having been thus deprived of all pleasures, the pope was naturally quite irritable, a condition not improved by Edward's letter. He pulled the velvet bell cord hanging near his couch, and waited for Guy de Chauliac to enter. The physician quietly let himself in and knelt before the pope, kissing his ring in a display of submission.

"Stand up, de Chauliac, for I find your gesture ingenuine. We both know that it is I who submit myself to you, rather than the other way around. I long for the day when this pest will pass and I can properly chastise you for the punishment you have inflicted upon me."

But Clement was no fool; he knew that Avignon had lost the greater portion of its people to the plague, and he himself was still very much alive. He knew that his continued health could not be due to simple luck.

De Chauliac rose up as he was bidden to do; he towered over the sitting pope, who gazed upward in disgust. "Your Holiness," the physician said in a sugary voice, "how may I serve you?"

"Truly, monsieur, you have served me too well already. I would have you release me from this unholy captivity."

De Chauliac was always prepared for this complaint from his spoiled patient. "I humbly remind Your Grace that our efforts to protect your health have thus far been quite successful."

"I am aware of your success, de Chauliac, but I tire of your Spartan methods. Surely this will not be necessary much longer."

"Holiness, I have just this morning received the report of the medical faculty of the University of Paris, written at the command of our noble King Philip. A most learned group of physicians and astrologers have put their considerable intellect to the task of solving this very tricky question. They are of the opinion that this pestilence was ordained by a most unusual celestial occurrence. Almighty God set the planet Saturn, a stubborn yet quite impatient body, in near perfect alignment with the bawdy and jocular Jupiter, normally a rather unremarkable conjunction; their paths intersected in the heavenly area known to be under the influence of Aquarius. This heavenly meeting has in the past produced some unusual events, such as small floods, poor crops, and the like. Unfortunately, the arrival of Mars with its bellicose temperament added a deadly character to what would have otherwise gone unnoticed. Mars is enamored of war, and caused Jupiter and Saturn to do battle with one another. It is this unfortunate mix of qualities that has allowed the pestilence to dominate our lives."

Clement deplored the continued influence of astrology on the followers of Christianity, but could not seem to discourage the practice of the fatalistic science. "Are you in agreement with these findings, monsieur?"

Ever the careful diplomat, de Chauliac replied, "My Prince, I am not of adequate intellect to *disagree*. These are very wise men, the most learned in our realm, and they set their minds diligently to His Majesty's task. The heavenly conditions they describe could easily influence events on earth in a most malevolent manner."

The pope, annoyed by de Chauliac's wordy nonsense, fanned himself again. "I would still know the expected duration of my confinement here, and you have not given me your answer."

De Chauliac smiled graciously at his patron and, with his customary verbal skill, removed himself neatly from this potential trap. "We are but men, attempting to explain the plan of God, who makes His plans known to no one. I beg you to be patient, and remain in seclusion. This will pass in due time."

And though patience was not one of the pontiff's more notable qualities, Clement was wise enough to know that his advisor's words were at least half true, and he resigned himself to his hated isolation. "Monsieur, the angels will laugh when I survive this scourge only to be felled by the random strike of God's lightning. As I wing my way to heaven, I will resent this cloistering terribly."

De Chauliac allowed himself a small laugh, relieved to have the situation in hand once again.

Then Clement held forward Edward's letter and gave it to de Chauliac, who read it quickly. "These events are *most* distressing, Your Holiness."

"Indeed!" Clement replied. "It was settled, this matter of the marriage! And now all our clever diplomatic efforts are for naught. An alliance between Spain and England would have been of great benefit to our Holy Church. When Pedro is king in Spain, he will give more thought to matters affecting the Church than Edward will in England; he might have influenced Edward to be more of that mind through his daughter Joanna."

De Chauliac mused, "Has not the Princess Isabella already refused Pedro?"

"Yes! And she influences her father most disagreeably! She is altogether too headstrong. She made her dislike for Pedro known to Edward as soon as the Castilian match was proposed. The fool occasionally makes the mistake of consulting with his children prior to consummating an arrangement, as if their opinions could be of value in determining the outcome of such weighty decisions! He indulges her. I have heard from my ambassadors that the child puts him in mind of his mother."

"To whom he owes his very throne, by a circuitous route," de Chauliac observed. De Chauliac knew that Clement's "ambassadors" were nothing more than spies sent to keep a constant measure on the influence of the Catholic Church on the English court; Edward knew it too. "Then I do not understand why it is to our advantage to protect her. If she is as willful and wild as is rumored, we will be hard pressed to control her."

"But we must not underestimate her importance as a means of cementing our hold on England. That she is lavished and pampered is of no concern to us. She is most importantly the mother of future kings, and may herself be a queen of some influence someday. God willing, she will outgrow her petulant behavior as her beauty fades, and will begin to show some of her royal breeding. She is, after all, the daughter of the king of England and a noblewoman of considerable lineage."

"Then I shall pray diligently that God will guide you in these matters." De Chauliac knew that Clement would apply his considerable statecraft to Edward's requests, and would choose well for the bishopric at Canterbury. The physician's more immediate concern was complying with Edward's other demand for a doctor who could protect his children as de Chauliac had protected Clement.

He knew he had no medical craft comparable to the diplomatic finesse displayed by his shrewd patron, though he would never admit to his ignorance. Despite his extensive education and his official status as papal physician, Guy de Chauliac was certain that he knew no more about the cause of the terrible plague than did a common fishwife. All he could do was what he had already done: isolate the healthy patient in the hopes of keeping him away from *whatever* it was that brought on the illness, and continue those treatments that he *hoped* would work. He had no direct evidence that any of his ministrations made the slightest bit of difference, but Clement seemed impressed by his efforts, so he kept them up.

He knew it would be no easy task to choose a protector for Edward's children. There were diplomatic considerations, more than medical. The shrewd and cynical King Edward III, who had proved himself to be a very able ruler despite the weaknesses he might have inherited from his pathetic father, distrusted the French, and would not tolerate a French physician. Most of Avignon's physicians had already died, and many of those remaining were Jews, and therefore even more unsuited than a Frenchman for attendance on the royal family of England. He privately thought that Clement was too lenient on the Jews of Avignon, especially now when so many of the church's communicants were ready to blame them for the plague. To foster that belief would divert the common folks' attention away from the shortcomings of the clergy and the medical establishment in their handling of the pestilence.

He would simply have to see them all and then choose as carefully as possible. But not too carefully, for the physician's influence must not become too strong. "Holiness," he said, interrupting his patient's fanning, "it would be a wise course of action to issue a papal edict requiring all physicians in Avignon to appear before you. I will then be able to make a proper choice. We must be sure to send a man whose company will not be offensive to the family, especially the princess. We will train many men, and therefore have a goodly number of candidates from which to make our final selection. But since they will all be assembled, would it not seem wise to send out emissaries to all the European courts? Why limit our influence to England?"

The pope's eyes widened. "De Chauliac, you are brilliant! Surely, no one would dare to protest. Find all the available physicians and bring them here at noon on Monday next. You shall personally oversee their training."

"And while I am thus preoccupied, who shall see to Your Holiness' needs?"

The pope smiled. "You are too cunning, de Chauliac. I see that I shall not be able to escape you. Do not fear, I shall obey your edicts. But now I shall reply to Edward, for he will want to know the good news."

Clement went to his writing desk and pulled out a parchment scroll. Since his isolation had begun, de Chauliac would not allow him to use the services of his scribe, and he had been forced to write all of his own correspondence.

It will occupy my mind for a time, he thought, glad to have a task. He dipped his pen in *encre noir* and began to write.

Beloved Brother in Christ,

We are distressed to learn of the recent demise of John, Archbishop of Canterbury, and we are grateful to Your Majesty for so quickly conveying the news, that we may more swiftly act to ameliorate his loss. And we offer our prayers for your departed daughter Joanna. No doubt your anguish over her loss is limitless; it is a pain that cannot be described by words alone. And still, brave Edward, you are diligent in your stewardship of the Holy Church! Even in your bereavement your thoughts turn to the protection of Christ's influence in England. Such nobility of action will surely be rewarded by Almighty God, when you meet Him at last in your eternal rest, which we hope will be many years hence. We are grateful for your strength in these troubled times.

We receive with interest your notion of wedding Isabella to the young duke of Brabant. We admit to some concern over the nearness of the couple's kinship, and commend your patience in delaying the consummation of the match. Our prayers over this matter shall be immediately directed to heaven and, God willing, we will soon have His guidance on this important matter.

Advise Isabella to be patient, dear brother; she has yet to reach her full flower, and will soon be well and happily married. Our ambassadors tell us that she is a high-spirited beauty, with a great wit and considerable charm. She must not despair of her spinster condition.

Our physician de Chauliac receives with thanks your praise for his considerable medical accomplishments. As you have requested, we shall send a physician trained by de Chauliac himself, in the hope of protecting your cherished offspring from the terrible scourges of the pest. You must see that his orders are strictly obeyed; do not allow the princess' high spirit to lead her astray. She must follow his advice diligently and pray daily for continued health.

Noble King, we suffer here immeasurably; it is impossible to convey to you the true condition of fair Avignon. Every day hundreds die and are swiftly buried, or if no grave is readily dug, the corpses are left in the river to await their eternal repose. It is as if God would eliminate our entire race. We wonder what sin has been done to bring about His mighty wrath. Mind your health well, and follow our emissary's advice. We implore you to protect yourself and your noble family, and pray daily that Christ and His blessed Mother will watch over you continually.

Swift riders will bear this message to you, that you may be quickly relieved of your anxiety over these grave matters. We will dispatch the full expedition as soon as it may be properly organized. In these terrible times we must take every precaution that their journey is safely completed.

In nomine Patris, Filii, et Spiritus Sanctis, we send our greatest hopes for your continued welfare, and for the prosperity of your kingdom.

Clement VI
Bishop of Avignon

Clement handed the letter to de Chauliac, who read it carefully. When he had finished, he grinned and said, "Edward will think we are sending a spy into his very household. By now he has had second thoughts about the wisdom of his request. So it matters little whom we send. The man will get little cooperation from the king who requested his presence."

"But still," said Clement, "it is amusing to know that we can create such confusion in the royal household. So we *shall* send him a physician. We will send the most enthusiastic and dedicated physician we can find.

And then we shall rest well in the knowledge that we are still a thorn in the side of our dear English brother."

Alejandro awoke to the gripping pain of grief in the small silent house, which seemed cavernous to him with the widow gone and Hernandez dead. He had never felt so alone; the only people he knew in Avignon were the bigoted apothecary and the morose Widow Selig. He was lost in his sorrow. There was no one to comfort him for the loss of the gruff man who had become like a brother to him.

He felt like a weasel as he went through all the cupboards in search of something, *anything*, that felt familiar, but nothing was there except the ever-present droppings of the mice and rats that infested nearly every home, even the most pristine. And from these familiar things, he took no comfort, only revulsion. He sat in silence at the bare dining-room table, eating a crust of bread and some cheese he had found in the pantry. When he could eat no more, he retrieved his tools from Hernandez's bedchamber and washed them in the kitchen bucket. *I will need to bring his body downstairs for the cart*, he thought miserably, envisioning his friend's limbs protruding from the siderails like pale sticks. *But I cannot face it now.* Wrapping the tools in one of Hernandez's old shirts, he headed for his new surgery, thinking he would find some distraction there.

The people on the streets slunk past him as he made his way down the narrow street. As he approached the surgery, he could see a notice of some sort hanging on a nail in the door. He took it down and examined the seal more carefully, deciphering the Latin inscription that had been pressed into the rough circle of wax.

The seal said: HIS HOLINESS CLEMENT VI, BISHOP OF AVIGNON.

Eight

J anie inserted the plastic key card into the slot in the painted metal door to her hotel suite. As soon as she passed through the door, she dropped her briefcase on the floor and flopped down on a chair. She leaned back, stretching her long frame almost straight out. She dropped one arm down limp beside her and draped the other one over her forehead. Her position was one of total submission to the frustrating events of the day.

"Go ahead, world, beat me up," she said to Caroline, who followed her into the room and closed the door after herself. "I could use a few more bruises."

Caroline immediately removed the wrapped circle of plastic from her purse and put it in Janie's refrigerator. "Wallowing in self-pity just a little bit, are we?" she said as she sat down across the small table from Janie.

"Absolutely," Janie said, her arm still covering her eyes. "Under the circumstances it's the right thing to do." A moment later she sat up, rubbed her eyes, and sighed. She looked at the stack of papers on the table before her and said, "Well, we might as well figure out where the missing samples are from."

Leafing through them, she found both the grid map and the owner's list. She checked the list of the forty-eight accounted-for samples against the total list and made a separate list of those she determined were missing. Then she compared that list to the grid map and marked a small circular frowning face at each of the locations for the missing samples.

"Of course," Janie said. "They're from all over London. Why did I think I'd find a nice neat row of missing samples?"

Caroline looked over her shoulder. "Ignorance? Stupidity? Wishful thinking?"

"All that and more," Janie said. "There's no logical order to them. I guess whoever moved the tubes around just took any old six and put them someplace else."

"Someplace inconvenient, I'll bet, the way things seem to be going," Caroline said.

Janie put the papers back on the table and rubbed her eyes again. With her elbows on the tabletop she rested her face in her hands for a few moments. "I can't let this get me down," she said when she straight-ened back up again. "I'm going to start making the calls so we can dig new ones immediately. We won't need to repeat the paperwork. A verbal okay should suffice on the second samples."

Caroline was surprised. "Are you sure you want to do that?" she said. "Why don't you wait until you hear from your friend before you start repeating what we've already done?"

Caroline picked up the list of owners and scanned through, noting which ones Janie had checked. She made a little frown as she read it. "Two of these owners were difficult to convince," she said. "We might not get a second shot from either of them. But thank God that last one isn't missing. I can just see us going back to that old man again saying, 'Pardon me, Mr. Sarin, but do you remember that sample of dirt we stole from you? Well, I'm sorry to tell you this, but we've got to steal another one.' Not to mention that one trip out on that field in the middle of the night was quite enough for me in this lifetime. What a spooky place."

Janie concurred. "It was, indeed," she said. "But you know what? Even though I didn't get what I wanted from him, I kind of liked that old guy. He was very sweet while he was turning us down." She pushed away from the table and tilted the chair back, one arm folded across her chest, and chewed the end of a pencil. "I wonder what his story is. He lives alone in that old cottage, just the dog to keep him company. Seems too strange to have a wife or kids, don't you think?"

"I didn't see any pictures that looked like they might be family. I did see one of a woman and a boy, though, and it looked kind of old fashioned, maybe from the forties. It was black and white and the woman had that kind of rolled-up hair and the stumpy heels. Could have been him and his mother."

"Maybe. He seemed slightly retarded, I think. Maybe he never got married."

"Slightly something. I don't know if I would say retarded. Slow, maybe. But something's not quite right."

Before Janie could come to a conclusion about just what it was that set Robert Sarin apart from the rest of his species, the phone rang. She leapt up and answered it after the first ring.

"Hello?" she said anxiously.

A male voice said, "You'd better be careful, or I might get the impression that you're eager to hear from me."

She could almost *hear* him smiling over the phone. "Bruce?" she said.

"Yes, Bruce."

"Did you find them?"

He chuckled. "I'm fine, and how are you?"

"Sorry," she said. "Forgive me my anxiety. I'm fine too. And I am glad to hear from you."

"You're about to be gladder. I have in front of me a shipping manifest listing six metal tubes, each one meter in length."

"That's wonderful!" Janie said gleefully. "Where are they?"

"Well, that's the sticky part. I'm not exactly sure. They could be in one of two places. We have two long-term storage facilities, one in Manchester, and one in Leeds. The manifest just says they left here and things were being shipped to both places, but not specifically where those items went. I have calls in to both places already, and I expect to hear back by tomorrow afternoon at the latest."

"Not today?" she said, her disappointment obvious.

"Maybe today, but I'm not sure. But it will definitely be no later than tomorrow. Can you be patient just a bit longer?"

She sighed and slumped slightly in the chair. "I don't suppose I have a lot of choice. We need those six tubes. We set up a grid of dig sites that's six rows by nine rows, so we could drop a row of six on either end and still have a valid sample. But we didn't collect them by rows. It was a lot more random than that, mostly depending on whether or not the paperwork for a particular site was done, so they got stored in no particular order. The missing ones are from all over the grid, so we either have to get the originals or take new ones. Caroline was just telling me that two of the owners were difficult about the first samples, so I think it would make sense to wait one more day to avoid having to approach them again."

"Sounds complicated. I guess if I were you I would wait too."

"Unfortunately, that leaves us twiddling our thumbs."

Bruce laughed. "Didn't you know that thumb twiddling is illegal in London? The lord mayor finds it highly offensive. There's an entire ministry of bureaucrats who do nothing but make sure that no thumb twiddling occurs within the city limits."

"Why am I not surprised? There seems to be a ministry of everything here."

"Well, perhaps I could help you avoid the pitfalls of ennui. Have you seen the British Museum yet?"

"I haven't seen anything but the handle of a soil plugger. We've been too busy to do any sightseeing. We took all our samples in four days."

"Wow," Bruce said.

"Wow is right. I was pretty sore the second and third days. I'm not used to doing all that bending."

"Well, I haven't seen the museum myself in a while, so why don't we go together tonight? I can pretty much assure you that there'll be no bending required. Then we can have a drink or maybe even dinner afterward and catch up a bit."

She hesitated before answering, wondering if their association should be kept strictly professional. But the invitation seemed sincere, and Bruce was a very attractive man. *Loosen up, Janie,* she told herself. "Hold on a minute," she said. She placed one hand over the mouthpiece of the phone and whispered to Caroline, "Would you mind being left alone this evening?"

Caroline raised her eyebrows slightly and shook her head no.

Janie took her hand off the mouthpiece and said, "I think I'd like that."

"Good," he said. "It'll be fun. Why don't I get you about five?"

She looked at the clock; it was three-thirty. *Time enough to make myself presentable,* she thought. "Sounds good," she said. "I'll see you later."

"What's the story?" Caroline said after Janie had hung up the phone. "That sounded like a very friendly conversation, especially toward the end. I assume that means it was good news."

"It was. He found out that the tubes were sent to one of two places, and he'll know tomorrow where they are."

"Great!" Caroline said. "Oh, boy, what a relief! But what does that have to do with my being left alone this evening?"

"That's where it gets better," Janie said, grinning. "He's taking me out tonight."

"Good deal," Caroline said. "Come to London to get data, end up getting a date too."

"I haven't been on a date in almost twenty years. I'm not sure I'll remember what to do."

"You'll do fine. It'll all come back to you after the first five minutes."

"I hope you're right."

Janie and Bruce stood over a glass cabinet in a dimly lit room on the second floor of the British Museum. A cloth cover was draped over the top of the cabinet, on which was written, *Please lift cover to view document. Kindly replace cover when finished viewing.*

As she lifted the cloth, Janie said, "These Brits! Always polite, even when they're telling you what to do."

"Etiquette is the national pastime here."

"I was beginning to get that idea."

As she held up the cloth, Bruce read the placard next to the exhibit. "Letter from Pope Clement VI to King Edward III written during the Black Death, 1348, concerning a papal representative being sent to the English court to help protect the royal family from bubonic plague."

The parchment was browned with age, and the ink quite faded. Janie could make out a few of the words, but not enough to read it. "Wow," she said. "That thing is *old.*"

"*Really* old," Bruce said, replacing the cloth. "That was one of the things that took me the longest to adjust to when I first came over here. Everything is so ancient."

"Well, you come from California, don't you?" Janie asked.

"You remember that?" he said.

"I remember bits and pieces, here and there. I have to say, though, my memory's just not what it used to be."

"Mine either," Bruce said. "But, yes, I'm from California. Los Angeles. It's the polar opposite of England in almost every way. Oh, there's some old stuff from when the Spanish settled, but nothing like what there is here. And everything is small here too. Much smaller than in the States. People were smaller when London was built. You're from Massachusetts, aren't you?"

"Still am," she said. "I live in a small town on the western end of the state. I'm about a hundred miles from Boston. We have some pretty old stuff there, a few seventeenth-century houses. It's quaint, typically New England; a nice old Main Street area with buildings from the early nineteen hundreds."

They wandered on, exchanging observations about the various exhibits and general comments about their lives; eventually they came to a room of massive Egyptian pieces. There was a bench at one side of the room, unoccupied, so they sat down, two very small beings in a room full of very large objects.

"I wonder if this is how a dog feels sitting next to a couch."

Bruce glanced around. "A small dog, maybe."

Janie looked at him. *Not one wrinkle,* she thought to herself. He looked back, and their eyes locked for one uncomfortable moment. Janie broke the discomfort by speaking. "So how long have you been here? In England, I mean?"

"Eighteen years," he said.

"That's a long time."

"I don't know, it doesn't really seem that long to me. Ted recruited me right out of residency. He knew Dr. Chapman, who was chief on my rotation, and Chapman told him about me. Made me an offer I couldn't refuse."

"Which obviously you didn't."

"Nope. Here I am, after all these years. And I've never really regretted it. I've been involved in some really exciting research at the Institute."

"For some reason it sounds very forbidding when you call it that."

"It can be a very forbidding place to some people. Depending on what you do, working there can consume your entire life. But I love my work. I get up every day and I'm glad to go in there. The only fly in the ointment is that I've never actually practiced medicine, and I think I might have enjoyed that. I've been isolated from the real world inside my glass-and-chrome lab, just researching my brains out."

"I did practice for about fifteen years," Janie said.

"Did?"

"Yeah, did. I'm not practicing right now."

"Why not? Is it part of that long, sad story you mentioned before?"

"It is. You want to hear it? It takes a while."

He glanced at his watch. "They won't be kicking us out of here right away."

"Okay, then," she said. She drew in a long breath. "When the first Outbreak happened and so many people died, it was right after the whole medical reorganization took place. They hadn't worked the kinks out of the physician distribution formula—come to think of it, they haven't yet. They may never, now. Anyway, there were huge surpluses in several different types of specialties. I was a surgeon; surgeons were one of those surplus categories. The GPs came into contact frequently with people who were infected, and a lot of them died as a result of that. There was no one left to treat sore throats, so Congress passed an emergency measure reassigning some groups of specialists to general practice and a few other areas where there were shortages. But there were still too many doctors for the remaining population, and a lot of the funding for health care got eaten up by the cost of dealing with the epidemic, so to keep the federal budget balanced, a lot of us got bumped, literally."

"Bumped?" he said. "I don't understand."

"We were literally ordered to stop practicing."

"Sounds like a potential lawyerfest to me."

"Oh, it was. The suits will go on forever. I'm part of several class-action suits. But my lawyer says such a move is essentially legal under emergency conditions. War, famine, pestilence, situations like that. Congress can make anything legal or illegal by passing legislation. It's ultimately up to the courts to decide if the legislation is constitutional, and we all know how quickly they move. So the real question is not whether or not those regulations are going to stand, in my mind anyway—it's how long it will take to get rid of them. It may take a while. In the meantime they gave us the option of entering a lottery where we were randomly assigned new medical-type fields, with retraining provided if needed."

"You obviously took that option," he said.

She nodded.

"What did you end up with?"

"Forensic archaeology."

"Well, that's about as obscure a specialty as I've ever heard of."

Janie's tone became very sarcastic. "Not as obscure as you'd think. The skills run anywhere between archaeologist and coroner. The reason why there were a lot of openings is that a lot of them died too. They handled the bodies at first."

"And dropped like flies, no doubt."

She nodded.

"You mentioned certification this afternoon."

"Yeah. I have to take certain courses that I wouldn't have had a need for before, and then I have to do a thesis, which is what this trip is all about."

Bruce let out a long breath and shook his head. "I guess we have it a lot better here than we thought. Maybe I'll stay here for good."

"Have you changed citizenship?" Janie asked.

"Nope," he said, "and I don't think I ever will. I like being an American too much. Over here, at least, it gives me a certain cachet."

"How long has it been since you've been Stateside?"

"Oh, God, you had to ask . . . it's been at least five or six years."

"Pre-Outbreak, then."

"Yeah."

Janie sighed. "You might not be so anxious to retain your citizenship if you'd been there since then. Things are really a mess."

"I've heard some of it, read the papers, watched CNN. I guess you have to be there."

"I think you do," she said. "There's this sort of martial-law feel to life in the States these days that doesn't come through in the media reports. No one says much about it, but everyone knows it's there. There aren't Gestapo running around all over the place or anything like that, at least not anymore, but it's like someone sprayed *Eau de Gestapo* in the air during the Outbreaks and the stink won't go away completely. Sort of like a dead skunk. You can smell it for a long time."

"I've heard a little bit about that. I guess I've ignored it. I don't really have good reasons to stay on top of it, since I'm not planning on going back anytime soon. I've tried to maintain contact with people there, but I haven't really done a good job of it. My whole professional life has been here. I have a few old friends there, but that's about it, and none of them are terribly tuned in to politics. My parents are gone, and I'm an only child."

"My parents are gone too. It feels like we skipped a generation or two backward during the Outbreaks. It used to be that people our age had parents. In fact, I had a grandmother until two years ago. She didn't die during the Outbreaks, though. She died of old age. Woke up dead one morning. My parents weren't so lucky."

She hung her head a little and was silent for a few moments. Bruce didn't say anything more than a quiet "I'm sorry."

"Thanks," she said. "I am too. I miss them."

He wondered if it was the appropriate time to ask the other question that had been nagging him. *Well, we are talking about family,* he rationalized. "You said your last name is Crowe now. Are you married?"

"I used to be," she said softly.

"Do you have any kids?"

There was a significant pause before she spoke, and then her words were so soft, he could barely hear them. "I used to."

"Oh, dear God . . ." he said, stiffening slightly as the true meaning of what she'd said bored into him. *She lost everyone at the same time,* he thought, stunned by the crushing weight of that idea. "Janie, I—I'm so sorry. I had no idea. I wouldn't have brought it up if I had. It wasn't as bad here, and we're just not accustomed to assuming that everyone's lost someone."

She hitched in a small breathy sob, and a tear slipped out of the corner of one eye. It trickled to the end of her nose, dangled there for a few seconds, then fell into her lap. She turned her head and looked back at him, with perhaps the saddest expression he'd ever seen on the face of a human being. She tried to smile. "It's all right," she said. "You had no way of knowing."

She straightened up and sniffed, then wiped her nose inelegantly with the cuff of one sleeve. "I never seem to have a tissue," she said. "Do you think the Ministry of Etiquette will try to have me arrested?"

Bruce laughed. "I won't tell," he said. "But you're more likely to get arrested by the Ministry of Health for Public Effusion of Body Fluids. I won't tell them either."

He was joking, she knew, but something in the tone of his voice as he spoke about the Ministry of Health led her to the conclusion that dripping snot and tears in public was a serious no-no. She sniffed lightly and, she hoped, daintily. None of the people around them were looking at her with any particular interest, so her discomfort passed after a few moments. "Thanks," she finally said with a thin smile. "I want you to know that I appreciate your discretion. So how about you?" she asked, her voice firmer. "Are you married?"

"No," he said. "I never did take the plunge."

"Shame on you," she said, teasing him. She surprised herself with the realization that her moment of grief had passed cleanly, with no bitter aftertaste. *Maybe it's getting a little easier*, she thought to herself. "You have shirked your moral responsibility to reduce the population of single women."

He laughed. "You say that with such feminine authority. If the right single woman had come along, I would've been more than happy to fulfill my social obligation. But like I said, I'm really married to my work. When we've got an interesting project going on, my life gets pretty hectic. I don't know that anyone would want to put up with that."

"It sounds like you really like what you do."

"I love it. I'm the happiest camper in the world."

"I'm jealous. I've been away from surgery for almost two years."

He gave her a very sympathetic look. "Ouch. That's gotta be tough on you. Have you been able to manage?"

"You mean financially?"

He nodded.

"Everyone in my family was well insured. And they all went in the first round, when the insurance companies were still paying. Then my grandmother left me her entire estate, and it was pretty substantial. Money is the very least of my worries. And it's a good thing, because I've spent plenty of it on travel to do this project. You can't believe how complicated it is to get a visa these days. They charge you coming in and going out."

"I guess all the restrictions they put in place over here were a good idea after all."

"I think they were. You didn't get hit anywhere near as badly as we did. And the British government didn't waste any time. We didn't close our borders for almost a year after the Outbreaks started, and that was a big mistake, in my opinion. Stupid, considering that it came in over the border from Mexico in the first place. I mean, God forbid that we should take away the right of people who aren't even citizens to bring in fatal and highly infectious diseases. We wouldn't want to miss the opportunity to pay for their treatment."

"Do I detect a bit of the redneck emerging, Ms. Crowe? Whatever happened to the Hippocratic Oath?"

She gave him a hard look and said, "When people are dying by the hundreds all around you, and you can't do a blessed thing about it, the Hippocratic Oath seems like just another bunch of ancient mumbo-jumbo. You do what you have to do, regardless of the Oath."

He felt chastised. "I've never been in a situation like that. I guess I have a hard time understanding it."

"I never thought I would be. I thought I'd spend my entire career safely and unemotionally snipping pieces out and stitching pieces in. But some of the stuff I saw, Bruce, you simply wouldn't have believed. Piles of dead babies with oozing sores, all from one hospital nursery. People with visible signs of infection being held at gunpoint, being shot if they tried to run. Children, even. It was just out of control. I could go on forever with horror stories."

There wasn't much Bruce could say in response, and Janie was tired of Outbreak talk; she'd had far too much of it already. So they sat in silence, each of them staring at some point of interest. The sound of a woman's voice came over a loudspeaker with a notice that the museum would close in ten minutes.

"Well," Bruce said as he stood up, "shall we go grab a bite to eat?"

"You know, I don't think I'm very hungry now," Janie said. "Maybe I should just go back to my hotel."

"But the night is young," Bruce protested.

"Unfortunately, I'm not feeling all that young tonight. I don't think I realized how tired all these complications have made me. I don't think I'm completely adjusted to the time difference yet, anyway. I think I should try to get a good night's sleep. Can I take a rain check?"

Bruce was disappointed, and made no attempt to hide it from her, but he was quite gracious in accepting her refusal of his offer. "Absolutely," he said. "Anytime at all."

And with promises to call her the next day as soon as he heard from either of the storage facilities, he took her back to the hotel by cab. Janie went upstairs immediately, took a stinging hot shower, and went to bed. She dreamed, fitfully, of her husband and daughter.

*   *   *

When the phone awakened her the next morning, Janie didn't feel as if she'd slept for ten hours. She answered it groggily.

"Good morning," Bruce said.

Her eyes still shut, Janie said, "Are you always this cheerful in the morning?"

"Did I wake you?" he asked.

She opened her eyes and looked at the bedside clock. It was already ten-fifteen. "I hate to admit it, but you did. I must've needed the sleep. I usually get up with the gods."

"Do you want to call me back after you're more awake?"

"No. From the chirpy sound of your voice I think I'd rather hear what you have to say."

"Ah," he said with amusement, "you noticed my enthusiasm. Good. I hoped you would. I did find them, and they're in the closer of the two possibilities."

Janie had fifty questions, but she was still too sleepy to organize them in her mind. She sat up and shook her head to clear away the effects of the sandman, then asked, "How quickly can I get them back here?"

"That depends on how jammed they are up there. Your work is not going to be a priority for them. The quickest way to retrieve them would be to drive up there and bring them here by car."

"Not by plane? It's a long drive, isn't it?"

"It is, but I think you might run into a few bureaucratic walls if you try to ship them by air. I don't know what it's like back in the States, but here anything transported in the baggage hold of an airplane has to meet certain criteria. It might actually take longer to fly than to drive because of the red tape. From what I saw in the lab, your samples look a little too much like bombs."

"Okay, I'll rent a car—"

He stopped her. "There's another slight problem. You need certain types of clearances to get into that facility. I have most of what I need. Ted has the whole shebang. But if you went by yourself you'd have to sit there for a couple of weeks while some subminister decided if you were an upright citizen in your own country and scientifically qualified to handle potentially biohazardous materials. As you can imagine, you can run into all kinds of snags."

"Does your director, what's his name—"

"Ted."

"Does Ted have any influence?"

"He does. He can get things moved in and out quickly. Unfortunately, Frank was the guy with all the high cards. He knew all the people who run these places on a first-name basis. Needless to say, you wouldn't be in this mess if he hadn't died."

"Don't remind me. But, okay, so I'll have to depend on Ted to help me get in there."

"Hold your horses. You still might not be allowed inside, and you'd have to wait for them to get around to paying attention to you. Back to square one."

Every suggestion she made had some problem. "It's not nuclear waste!" she fumed. "It's plain old dirt! The kind most of our food used to grow in!" She took on the whiny tone of someone who was feeling sorry for herself. "Oh, the hell with it," she finally said. "It would be a lot easier just to forget the whole thing and go home. This has just been one big waste of time and money."

"Look, let me tell you what I've been thinking," Bruce said. "I'll ask Ted to call ahead so we can speed up the process. Then I'll drive up with you and we'll bring them back in my car. I can get in pretty easily. All you'd have to do is look in through the window and identify the tubes to make sure they're the right ones."

Janie was floored by his offer. "That's a lot of time and effort for someone who is only a casual acquaintance from twenty years ago. This is awfully nice of you. I don't know what to say."

"Say, 'Thanks, Bruce, I'd love it if you went with me.' "

She laughed. "Okay. Thanks, Bruce, I'd love it if you went with me."

"That's better."

She was silent for a moment then asked, "Why are you doing this?"

"Best reason in all the world," he answered. "Because I want to. It's nice to be able to be helpful once in a while. Makes me feel good."

Janie smiled into the phone. "It's making me feel *very* good. I needed a shot in the arm right about now."

"Glad I could give you one. But get ready to feel even better. I think I can arrange it for you to do your own work in the lab. I've got some free time until we get this project going, and I know most of the equipment. Ted already said he could get you the necessary clearances, provided neither of you has bombed a federal building in the last few years."

"God, Bruce, I'm speechless. I don't know what to say again."

"Say, 'Yes, Bruce, I'll let you work on this with me.' "

"This is the proverbial offer I can't refuse. I accept."

"Good. Now, if you can manage to drag yourself out of bed and get over here this afternoon, I can get started in showing you the ropes. If your assistant does well enough, she can work by herself, with a security person present. It won't be too much difficulty to get one assigned. That way, when you and I go to Leeds, she can be working."

"This is too much."

"No, it's not. It's just proper British hospitality."

"Then maybe I'll move here too. I'm not used to getting this kind of treatment back home. I get the feeling that they think nice treatment will actually make people happy, or something sinister like that."

"Now, now," he said, trying to restore her good humor. "The Etiquette Police do not appreciate sarcasm."

"I'll try to remember that," she said, a bitter edge in her voice. "I guess we'll see you in a little while."

"I'm looking forward to it."

They met Bruce in his private office. Janie looked around as they waited in the anteroom. The furniture was very masculine, dark and sleek, much like Bruce himself. The secretary sitting behind a black-and-chrome desk was an older woman, quite grandmotherly, with frills and pearls and very bouffant hair, a smidge on the blue side. *He probably didn't pick her out, and she certainly didn't pick out this furniture,* Janie thought, and then assumed further that Bruce himself had seen to the decoration. She liked the notion that he probably hadn't asked his subordinate to do it for him.

He came out of the inner office looking fresh faced and well scrubbed, and Janie observed to herself, as everyone exchanged greetings, that he seemed very comfortable, both with himself and the place over which he held professional dominion. Everything around him seemed to fit neatly into its place. It was obvious that he'd managed to influence his work environment to the point where it suited him perfectly. She didn't even consider that perhaps it was the other way around, and he had adapted to fit the environment; even after many years of no contact, she remembered that his personality was too strong, in a positive way, to allow himself to be shaped by his circumstances. She felt a momentary twinge of envy for the apparent ease with which he seemed to move through his life and for the shaping touch he seemed to have on the things around him.

"Very nice," she said to him.

"Thanks," he said, then confirmed her suspicion by adding, "I did it over a couple of years ago. It was a little stuffy before."

Out of the corner of her eye Janie noticed that the grandmotherly secretary stiffened slightly, as if she was highly offended by his comment but would swallow a toad before allowing it to show. Maybe *she'd* picked Bruce, Janie speculated, at a time when this office looked more as if she belonged in it, and was now suffering through his choice of furnishings with stoic British dignity. She made a mental note to add that question to the list of those she would ask him during the long drive to Leeds.

As they walked through the corridors of the Institute, Janie felt very small; the walls and ceilings were all the same matte white, and the floor was a glossy, light-colored linoleum. Overhead pipes, which she guessed had once been part of the old building's original heating system, were painted in a rainbow of soft pastel colors and were remarkably dust free, leading her to think that the ventilation system must be superb.

"What a great building this is," she said to Bruce. "It looks like it's been really well cared for. It doesn't have that slap-a-Band-Aid-on-it look that some older buildings have."

"I know," Bruce said. "They do a good job. It's been in continuous use since the late nineteenth century. It was originally built as a hospital. This place was filled to bursting during the flu epidemic in 1918. Then during World War I a lot of these corridors were filled with recovering soldiers. They literally overflowed the wards. There were surgeries all along here set up to deal with the huge numbers of soldiers who came home wounded. A lot of victims of mustard gas were also treated here."

She thought about the horror of those times and she could feel it ooze right out of the walls as she walked along. In her mind's eye Janie envisioned rows of bunks lining the corridor, each narrow bed occupied by some suffering young boy barely out of his teens, or some old woman in the hot grip of influenza. She saw the dull hospital green favored at the time with the misguided hope that the cool color would evoke a serene feeling of antisepsis, a state that would not occur until almost fifty years later with the development of antibiotics. *What a heady time the antibiotic era was*, she thought to herself. *We could cure almost anything. Gone now.* She could almost hear the pipes overhead clanking and see the coating of greasy soot, and as she proceeded forward, she imagined moaning doughboys reaching out to tug at her, pleading for something to alleviate their pain; the old women, reeking of death, simply moaning, knowing they were beyond help. The images came through so clearly that they unnerved her and she paled and shivered slightly.

Bruce was still talking about the history of the building as Janie moved out of the green-paint fantasy and back into the white-paint reality around her. After another turn they came to the lab's metal door with its small window of thick wire-reinforced glass. He pressed his right hand flat against the surface of a grayish-green panel at the right side of the door, and after a few seconds Janie heard the electronic lock click. The door clicked open and he motioned them inside. As they passed through the door Janie heard the soft hum of an electric current; she looked back and noticed that the grayish screen had taken on a bluish hue, which faded after a few seconds.

"It's cleaning itself," he explained. "After we installed those locks we noticed that lab personnel were sharing colds at a higher rate than in other departments, so we planted a harmless noninfective virus on one of the techs. We never did find it in the lab—everyone was apparently following the proper procedures. But it was all over the palm-print readers, so we had them retooled to be self-sterilizing. An electric current flashes through the surface of the screen, not strong enough to hurt anyone, but strong enough to kill any bugs lurking on the surface. It's set up so it will zap itself until it detects no more microbes on the screen."

"Very clever," Janie said. "Very efficient."

"We try," Bruce said. "Now let me show you the equipment." He led Janie and Caroline on a general tour of the facility, pointing out the restricted areas that were completely off limits to anyone but those employees with specific access to them, checking as he did to make sure that each of those areas was properly secured. He walked them through the operation of each piece of equipment they would be using in the course of doing their soil analyses, and showed them where the manuals were stashed, in case a problem arose. He explained the disposal systems, and how to alert security in case of an emergency. He showed them the communications system and explained how to reach both him and Ted.

"Most of this stuff I've used before," Caroline said, "but it's all upgraded. I don't think it will take me too long to get used to the improvements, though. Problem is, when we get back to the lab at the university, I may feel deprived working on our older stuff again."

"Can't help you there," Bruce said.

"Maybe you'll have to move here too," Janie said to Caroline. "It's a good thing you're familiar with most of this stuff, because I feel pretty lost. You'll have to guide me through it again when we get back from Leeds with the missing samples."

"No problem," Caroline said confidently. "By then I should be a real ace."

"Great," Bruce said. "When you get here tomorrow morning, there'll be a pass for you at the reception desk. Go there first and pick it up. Then have the receptionist page security for you."

On the way out Caroline ducked into the ladies' room. Janie and

Bruce waited for her in the hallway. He turned to her, as if he'd been waiting for an opportunity to speak privately.

"I enjoyed taking you to the museum," he said.

"It was fun."

"I was wondering if you'd like to cash in that dinner rain check. Tonight, specifically. I know a great Indian restaurant in South Kensington."

Inside herself Janie felt the walls going up, just as they'd risen around the man captured by the Compudoc in the medical inspection line at Heathrow. It was a completely involuntary event, one that occurred regularly and predictably since the first of her Outbreak losses; she'd grown pitifully used to it. With each additional loss the walls had become stouter and more protective, and she was just now beginning to see that individual bricks could be loosened if she worked at it. But Janie felt a certain comfort in knowing that she was safe from the potential trauma of further loss while those walls were in place, and made few attempts to peek over them into the freer emotional world beyond. Like an inmate accustomed to the safety and simplicity of imprisonment, she wasn't entirely sure that escape was in her best interest.

She didn't respond immediately, and the silence hung between them like a deadweight. The look on Bruce's face darkened in what appeared to be anticipation of rejection.

She started to explain. "It's been hard for me to venture out since the"—she groped for words—"since the bad stuff that happened to me. I'd like to go, but I'm not too steady yet in social situations. I guess I'm afraid I'll lose my composure."

He said, "I understand." He gave her a warm look with *Trust me* written all over it, and left it at that. No pressure, just an invitation with the implication that he would accept her as is.

She searched his eyes, looking for some undefined sign that it would not be wise to spend time with him. She found nothing to which she could reasonably object. "Oh, what the hell," she said, drawing in a deep breath. "I accept. What time?"

"I'll get you at seven." He smiled. "I'll make a reservation this afternoon."

"Great," she said, just as Caroline rejoined them. "I'll see you later, then." They said good-bye and parted ways.

The hours passed more quickly than Janie had expected they would, and when the phone rang in her suite that evening, she felt a little shiver of nervousness pass through her. She willed it to go away, and looked at herself in the mirror before going downstairs. She found herself wanting to look attractive and had taken pains with her appearance, something she hadn't done much since the close of the Outbreak era.

She was not disappointed with what she saw there. At forty-five she was still slim, largely because of her obsession about exercise; it seemed to be the only thing that allowed her to vent the anger and pain that hid within her. There were small touches of gray in her dark brown hair, and as she fingered a few strands, the notion of coloring it crossed her mind, not for the first time. Her skin was fair, and relatively unwrinkled, considering the stress of her last few years, although she had smile lines at the sides of her mouth and could see the beginnings of a line between her eyebrows. She frowned, and the line deepened. She smiled, and it went away, but the smile lines came out. *Can't win*, she thought. Her legs, shapely and firm from years of daily jogging, were what she considered to be her best feature. Consequently, she had worn a skirt above the knees to show them off, and shoes with a small heel to accentuate her height. She liked being a tall woman—it afforded her a view that was customarily reserved for men, and what she'd observed from that view had been quite illuminating on more than one occasion.

She was satisfied that she'd done the best she could with the raw materials she had. The only thing that disappointed her was the deeply ingrained sadness in her eyes. It couldn't be covered with any makeup she'd yet encountered.

"You look great," Bruce said as she crossed the lobby. "You look better than I remember you looking twenty years ago."

"Thanks." She smiled. "And right back atcha. I still can't believe how young you look."

"I attribute my youthful appearance to the dewy English climate," he said sarcastically. "Speaking of which, it's remarkably *undewy* this evening. The restaurant's not too far. Would you like to take a cab, or should we maybe walk?"

"I'm definitely up for a walk," she said. "I feel like I've been a slug since I got here. I usually run three miles a day at home and I miss it."

"Then a walk it is," he said, offering her his arm.

Oh, so charming, she thought as she took it. They headed out of the lobby only to encounter the revolving door, which forced them to let go of each other. Laughing, they slipped into separate cells of the door and were whirled out onto the street, where they joined arms again.

The streets of London were sparsely populated at the dinner hour, and as they progressed toward South Kensington, Janie found herself feeling very much at ease. She hadn't taken the time to explore since arriving, and as she looked into the various storefronts and office windows, she was taken by how quaint and simple everything seemed. The window displays were subdued and notably free of the garish advertising and obnoxious marketing devices seen everywhere in the United States. She recalled a series of television ads in which a crass and obviously nouveau-riche Texan shocked a well-bred British lady to the point of fainting by asking her to pass the jelly, and decided that it summed up the difference between America and England quite neatly. America had civilization, and the standards of civilization were redefined as needed. England was *civilized*, and civilized standards were not touched, ever. She realized that she wouldn't want to have to make a choice between the two.

"You've lived here for such a long time," she said. "Is there anything you miss?"

"Cold beer," he said, and laughed. "The one or two ninety-five-degree days I used to like in July. But you get used to it. I've completely forgotten what it feels like to drive on the right side of the road. I shift with my left hand. I don't waste water anymore."

"I noticed that the water's not too tasty here," Janie commented. "I've been buying bottled water."

"Everyone does, native or not," he said. "You guys are spoiled by the quality of the water in the States. By the way, I live not too far from here." He pointed to a narrow house on one of the side streets as they crossed at an intersection. "In a small town house sort of like that one. I have the top two floors. The building is narrow but the rooms are good sized for London and the ceilings are quite high. Sometimes when I walk through it, it seems way too big for me. But I like space, and I guess I'll fill it all up eventually. I bought it a few years ago, just before the first Outbreak."

"If you'd waited a year, you probably could've had it for a lot less. Housing prices took a tumble when demand went down in the States."

"They went down slightly here, but not as much as you might think. They were inflated before, anyway. Everyone sort of accepts that they've paid too much. Now prices are more like what they ought to be. But I'm not unhappy. I love the apartment."

"Is there anything you *don't* like about your life?" she asked, sounding almost miffed. "It seems so perfect."

He gave her question a few moments of thought. "Sometimes I

don't like being alone, and occasionally I regret that I don't have any children, especially around the holidays." He looked directly into her eyes. "I'm sure that must be a tough time for you."

She sighed. "That and birthdays. Anniversaries aren't exactly a piece of cake either. I have a tough time getting through those days."

"What do you usually do?"

"I try to be as far away from familiar sights as possible," she said, "but it's difficult to avoid bumping into reminders. They seem to be everywhere. When I get through with my certification, I'm hoping to be able to travel a little more, inside the United States, I mean, since it's a lot simpler than leaving the country. Once I'm settled into a new position, I should be able to schedule it. Traveling makes it easier because nothing is familiar."

"Is it easier here?"

She thought for a minute and said, "I think it may be. I feel okay right now."

"I'm glad," he said. "I was hoping you'd say that." He smiled and squeezed her arm where he held it, then led her through the door into the restaurant.

The smell of cardamom and fennel welcomed them, and the drone of a sitar played softly in the background, plumping out the Indian ambience nicely. Ornate and colorful embroideries on black velvet hung on the walls, scenes of ravens and elephants and Buddhas in the familiar flat style of the Orient.

They shared a half bottle of red wine, which warmed and relaxed them; they talked about their lives and how different their paths had been. The food tasted as good as it smelled, and Janie was surprised by her own appetite. "I haven't eaten this much since I got here," she said as she folded her napkin and placed it on the table. "I'm full to bursting."

"We'll take another walk when we leave here," Bruce said.

"Good idea."

They took a very different route from the one they'd used to get to the restaurant, and were soon in a residential neighborhood with a notable lack of commercial establishments. Bruce led the way, turning down one street then another, and Janie got the idea that she was being led to someplace specific as they progressed. Her suspicions were confirmed when Bruce stopped in front of a white brick town house with a lovely small garden in front.

"Here it is," he said, pointing to the house. "This is where I live."

Janie regarded it suspiciously. "It's charming," she said, and wondered if he was waiting for some sort of signal that she wanted to be invited inside. She decided to avoid the issue entirely, and began looking around at other buildings. "The neighborhood is very pretty."

"And quiet," he said. "A couple of dogs, but otherwise it's very peaceful."

In the brief silence that followed, Janie ran through a list of self-incriminations that would have brought her therapist to tears. *I am a forty-five-year-old adolescent*, she thought to herself, *standing in the doorway of a hot night with a great man. I could go in that door and probably have a good time, maybe blow off a little of this steam. Or I could go back to the hotel.*

They both started speaking at the same time. Janie said, "Do you know what time it is . . ." just as Bruce said, "Would you like to come up . . ." and then they crossed words again, Janie saying, "I'd love to see it, but we're leaving early . . ." and Bruce saying, "Of course, what was I thinking, you must be exhausted. . . ."

And then they both laughed at the silliness of their situation. Bruce looked at his watch. "It's almost eleven," he said. "We can walk up to the next corner. It's a main street and I should be able to get you a cab."

"I think that's a good idea," Janie said, her cheeks hot and red. "I really should get a good night's sleep before tomorrow."

As she emerged from the cab in front of her hotel, sleep was the last thing on her mind. She hopped onto the elevator and took it upstairs, where she quickly changed into running gear. Back out on the street again, she ran until the sweat poured off her, until her heart was beating so rapidly that she thought it would surely explode.

At one in the morning she turned on the shower and wasted water in the grand American tradition. She let the steaming water bore into her sweaty skin like hot sharp needles. Purged of her demons, at least temporarily, and cleansed of the sin of sloth, she dried off and slipped naked between the sheets. She closed her eyes and slept, for once, dreamlessly.

Thinking, *just in case*, Janie threw a clean pair of panties and a toothbrush into her briefcase, then went downstairs to the hotel lobby to wait for Bruce. He arrived at the crack of daylight, as he'd promised on the phone the day before. *Let's hope this mission is successful*, she thought to herself as Bruce pulled his car out of the hotel drive and eased into the London traffic.

They drove for most of the morning on major highways. She spent a lot of time looking at the map while Bruce drove, comparing the pastel two-dimensional images on the paper to the lush green reality of the countryside around London. Most of their conversation was focused on the country they drove through and the deeply personal issues didn't come up, which was something of a relief to Janie. For a good part of the time she leaned back in the bucket seat and closed her eyes, drifting into as peaceful a state as she could manage in view of her personal uncertainties. Bruce did not disturb her when she slipped into that private place. A little before noon he pulled off the highway and headed north on a side road.

Janie came out of her reverie when the surface of the road changed and the speed of their travel slowed. Looking at the map, she said, "This can't be our exit!"

"Nope," he said, "You're right. It's *my* exit."

"I beg your pardon?" she said.

"My favorite pub in all of England is here. And it's time for lunch. We have about another two hours to go before we get to Leeds. I don't think my stomach will forgive me if I don't eat something."

As they entered the small Tudor-style building, she said, "We seem to spend a lot of time eating."

"But we're eating well, aren't we?"

She couldn't disagree. When the waiter handed him a menu, Bruce promptly gave it back to him. "I already know what I want," he said, and ordered Yorkshire pudding. Janie quickly ordered a bowl of soup and a roll.

As she watched Bruce eat, Janie let her thoughts float back and forth between the man she saw before her and the boy she remembered from a lifetime ago. The man was handily invalidating any reasons she might have had to dislike the boy; he was an increasingly pleasant surprise. She wondered if she was faring as well in his imagination, or if he was even bothering to make a comparison between the girl he'd known only minimally two decades ago and the woman whose deepest secrets had been laid out for him to see. He ate quickly and with obvious delight, licking his fingers now and then as he dipped huge chunks of the doughy pudding into the drippings on the plate. Remembering an old occasion when she'd seen him dipping doughnuts in coffee, Janie silently compared Bruce Then to Bruce Now as she carefully chewed each bite of her own spare meal. It was a revealing moment, a quiet study in the differences between them, a validation of her personal belief that eating habits were the true measure of any man or woman. She wondered what this moment was for him.

As if in response to her silent question, he said, "Now, *this* is *lunch.*"

She laughed out loud.

He gave her a raised-eyebrow look and said, "It's nice to hear you laugh. I thought you might have forgotten how. What's so funny?"

She ignored his baiting and said, "Oh, nothing in particular, just life. If I'd known you were going to grow up to be such a good guy, I might have paid more attention to you when you were younger."

"Thanks. I think."

"You're welcome, I'm sure."

Though his associates frequently found him to be very charming, beneath Ted Cummings' polished exterior was an annoyingly Spartan human being who always arrived punctually for work with every hair in its proper place, never sick, never externally rumpled. When he woke up on Friday morning with a pain shooting through his right temple, he was completely unprepared. There wasn't even an aspirin in his apartment, legally prescribed or otherwise. He hadn't needed one in years.

He nearly overslept, and when he did finally manage to drag himself out of bed, it was a slow process. He hauled each leg off the bed stiffly and plunked it down on the floor with a thud. His bare feet felt as heavy as if he were wearing steel-toed boots, and he wondered for a few fuzzy moments if the force of gravity had somehow intensified overnight, thereby making his entire body feel unbearably heavy. His pillow-bent hair stuck out from his head in a hundred different directions and had to be rather forcefully tamed before it looked even remotely presentable.

For the first time in his ritualized tenure at the Institute, he arrived in his office later than his secretary. After checking his electronic mail he unplugged the speakers on his computer, for after only a few minutes of use, its voice and signal tones were already starting to sound obnoxious. Following that vein of thought, he shut off his beeper as well.

He stopped in at one of the Institute's medical offices and commandeered two aspirin tablets from the physician's assistant, who promptly teased him.

"Better go see your friendly Compudoc," she said, smirking, a suggestion that Ted rejected immediately. Despite the Institute's role in developing and overseeing their operation, Ted hated Compudocs and avoided them unless he was scheduled for the required monthly checkup. He'd seen enough people locked by the right wrist to those bloody machines, protesting violently the obligatory confinement that always followed the machine's discovery of some rogue microbe during a routine scan.

His discomfort by then was so great that he swallowed the aspirin dry, and felt the acidic burn as the tablets went down his throat. Despite his increasing malaise he made it successfully through the first half of his day's work, although he couldn't honestly say that he remembered much about it. Later, he dictated the notes of what he *could* remember of his activities, including his first glance through the list of applicants for Frank's position. He had just finished packing his briefcase with the intention of going home to bed when he remembered the circle of fabric. The idea that he was supposed to make a phone call flashed in and out of his brain, but he couldn't seem to nail it down. He searched his memory, but couldn't manage to bring out the necessary information. *Who am I supposed to call? What am I supposed to say? I must be sicker than I thought if my memory's being affected,* he thought to himself, and for the first time considered the possibility that what ailed him might be more than a simple cold. *Maybe it's an out-of-season case of flu.* He intended to treat it aggressively with bed rest, fluids, and more aspirin if he could get it *(if Bruce were here he'd just write a prescription!)* and he felt certain he'd be back at work again in a day, feeling much better, with no one the wiser.

He set aside thoughts of the phone call and concentrated on the circle of fabric. The lab was still the most logical place to look for it, so he went there, hoping it would be a fruitful effort, for as the day progressed and his condition worsened, he understood that any effort he expended would have to be spare until he felt more himself. He placed his hand flat on the gray screen outside the lab's main door and heard the soft click of the lock opening. He entered the lab and immediately heard another kind of clicking, the sound of fingers lightly working the keyboard of a computer, and found Caroline working intently at one of the computerized systems.

Having also forgotten that she would be working in the lab that day, Ted was caught off-guard by her unexpected presence. Though he'd met her only twice, he recognized her immediately from the fall of red hair tumbling down her back in soft waves. He had an impulse to reach out and grab a handful of her hair while her back was still turned, then rub it against his cheek. He wondered if she would be shocked by such an action.

As his hand reached out toward the mass of curls, he caught himself and quickly drew it back, his heart full of shame for the uncharacteristic thing he'd nearly done. He'd sooner reach out and stroke the mane of a lion than touch a woman's hair uninvited, and he was shocked at his own behavior. *Dear God, what's gotten into me?* he wondered frantically. He felt uncomfortable even being in the lab without her knowing of his presence. He announced himself discreetly by clearing his throat, forgetting that his throat was sore, and grimaced at the pain the small sound caused him.

Caroline heard him and turned around. He almost gasped but caught himself before offending her. It was certainly Caroline, but how different she looked! There was none of the rosy glow he had seen in her cheeks when they'd met before. Her skin was pasty white, except around her eyes, which were rimmed with streaks of red. She appeared to be having difficulty turning her head.

Caroline saw the look of shock in his eyes and flushed with embarrassment, in high contrast to her sickly pallor. In her mirror that morning she had seen the look of oncoming illness; like Ted, she supposed it was the onset of a cold.

"Good afternoon, Caroline," Ted said. "How are you today?"

She coughed twice, small hard barks, which she muffled with her hand. "Truthfully, I've been better," she answered. "I seem to have developed something nasty."

"We seem to share that affliction," he said. "A cold, perhaps. The undefeated scourge of modern medicine. I'm glad I'm not alone, but I regret that you're my company in misery."

"Thanks." She smiled weakly. "I think this might be more than just a cold. I've had a killer headache since I got out of bed this morning. I've got just a few more files to copy, then I'm going right back to the hotel and getting under the bedcovers. I hope I can fight this off without arousing any interest from the local Biocops. I figure if I lay low, I won't attract any attention. I'll be out of your way shortly." She turned away and blew her nose.

"Oh, you're not in my way at all. I just need to locate a few items in the storage freezer. Then I'm through for the day too. By the way, have you heard from our friends in Leeds? I was wondering if they had any success in locating those soil samples."

The word *Leeds* triggered the thought *phone call* again. There was a connection to be made there, but it escaped him. He felt a hot wave of frustration building up inside him and he began to feel angry. He missed the first part of Caroline's response to his question, and heard only the tail end of it.

". . . this evening, if they managed to pry them loose."

She was saying that she thought they might return that night. Ted knew it was highly unlikely that they'd be back so quickly because wheels of bureaucracy, especially the British scientific bureaucracy, turned very slowly indeed. But he made no mention of his doubts and instead tried to engage Caroline in a conversation about the contaminated piece of fabric. "So have you had some time to work with that thing you found in one of the tubes—that piece of cloth? Quite an interesting find. I should think you'd be anxious to examine it."

Caroline started to say, "No, I didn't have time today; I had too much to do, and anyway we—" but her sentence was interrupted by a sudden fit of almost violent coughing. She got up from her chair and bent over, still coughing, and placed her hands on her knees to ease her breathing.

Ted was alarmed and came over to her. He placed his hand on her back for comfort, and gently rubbed in circles, which seemed to calm her. In a few moments she was upright again and coughing only lightly.

When she could speak again, she laughed a little and said, "Excuse me! That was rather indelicate. I think I'd better just go back to the hotel now."

No! he thought desperately, *not until you tell me where you put that damned piece of fabric!* He tried to think of a way to maintain contact with her, but his brain felt like tapioca pudding, all thick and cloudy with big lumps of some nondescript gelid substance floating around in it. *Think, Ted!* he scolded himself. And finally, after a period of agonizing blankness, his temporary wave of thickheadedness passed and the notion of offering help presented itself. He was filled with relief to have an idea that actually made sense to him.

He put on his most solicitous face. "Is there anything I can do for you?" he asked, his brows furrowed in concern. "You might need something. Especially until your friend returns. Perhaps I can help."

Caroline sat down in the chair again, coughed a few more times, and began putting away her cataloging work. "If I get any worse, I just might need your help. The health care system here is so confusing, and I'm worried about getting myself into something more complicated than necessary if I try to get help through the ordinary channels. If I get detained we'll run into all sorts of difficulties, and Janie has this morbid fear of being bodyprinted. She's determined to get back to the States before it's required of her here."

He didn't agree about the bodyprinting. He and Bruce had had a major part in perfecting the technique, and though he would be the first to admit that the experience of being bodyprinted would not be described by any normal human being as "pleasant," few would say that it was not intriguing. But he agreed with her assessment of the potential for travel difficulties. "Understandable. It could be *quite* difficult."

Caroline elaborated. "If Janie were here she would take care of me, but she's not and I'm not sure when she will be. Could you give me the name of a real doctor in case I need to see one? One who won't turn me in? I mean, whatever I have, it seems to have come on awfully fast."

There were any number of physicians connected to the Institute who would have been glad to help out quietly, even though it was technically against the law to do so, and Ted had easy access to their private phone numbers. But he was hesitant to pass her on to someone else. Even in his state of increasing incoherence Ted knew he couldn't afford to have her running loose before he got his hands on that fabric. There was simply too much potential for disaster. He took a pen from the chest pocket of his lab coat and pulled a notepad from the side pocket, then scribbled a series of numbers.

"This is my home number," he said, offering it to Caroline. Not wanting her to know he was without plans, he added, "I'm going to be in and out, but if you need help, call and leave me a message. I should be able to scout up a doctor who can see you right away."

As she took the piece of paper from his hand a smile of relief spread over her face. "Thanks," she said, looking genuinely grateful.

"You know," Ted told her, "I really don't understand why you Americans object so strenuously to bodyprinting. It's hardly any worse than mammograms used to be, and it's *certainly* no worse than a testigram." He shuddered, thinking of the last time he'd been checked for testicular abnormalities after the initial Outbreak. "It's a wonderful diagnostic tool; we can tell so much about the body with so little effort."

"Actually, Ted, I think that's the whole problem."

"Well, I suppose it entirely depends on your point of view. But that's a discussion for another time." He smiled too sweetly and said, "Perhaps it would be a good idea for me to check in on you once or twice over the weekend if you're going to be alone. Where are you staying?"

Without giving it a second thought, Caroline told him.

"Well, I'll be in touch, then," he said. He left her somewhat reluctantly and went to the catalog for the freezer. When he'd entered the lab earlier, he'd been reminded about the necessity of finding a replacement carrier for *P. coli*, and was determined to get that task out of the way before he collapsed into his bed. The experiment seemed a million light-years away. All he did was look at the names on his list and then check to see that samples of his choices were available, which they all were. After that, all notions of work left his mind.

He went to the men's room before leaving. As he was washing his hands, he glanced up at his own image in the mirror.

His neck was beginning to swell.

For the remainder of the drive to Leeds, Janie and Bruce talked quietly. Janie took a turn at driving for a while on a section of highway where the traffic was very light. As they neared Leeds, the traffic began to pick up, and she yielded the wheel to Bruce again. Not long after, he took an exit and followed a side road to the converted toy factory. Bruce parked the car in a side lot, and as they shook off the stiffness of the second part of the drive, Janie looked at her watch. "It's two forty-five. If we can get our business done in an hour or less, we should be able to have a decent trip back."

As Bruce locked up the car he said, "There's a good chance we can. Let's just hope Ted was able to throw his weight around for us."

After asking Bruce a few questions the security guard searched through his computer files for some communication from Ted about the missing tubes. Bruce and Janie waited impatiently just outside the security scanners, so close to what Janie needed, but still on the outside. But there had been no message from Ted.

"I've made an attempt to contact his office directly on the computer," the guard reported, "but his system's not responding. Perhaps you have another way of contacting him."

Bruce immediately dialed Ted's personal beeper number on his portable phone, but there was no answer.

"Damn!" he said, his frustration evident. "He's not answering. That's very unusual. I've never seen him without his beeper."

Despite repeated attempts over the next half-hour, Ted could not be reached. They complained bitterly and the guard referred them to the chief of security, not wishing to be subjected to further undeserved abuse. They were told that if they started the paperwork at that moment, the proper clearances could be secured by the following morning without Ted's authorization.

"But what about my own clearances?" Bruce asked indignantly. "Don't they count for anything?"

"Oh, indeed they do, Dr. Ransom," the chief responded with a sugary smile. "Without your clearances you wouldn't get the materials out of here in less than a week."

Bruce guided Janie out of earshot of the guard. "I don't know what to say about this. I'm really embarrassed. And I'm *really* sorry. Ted's usually very reliable about taking care of details. I can't imagine why he didn't make that call. He's such a stickler for details and procedure."

Janie attempted to hide her frustration and failed miserably. Her forehead tightened and she suddenly felt very haggard. Rubbing her temples to keep a developing headache at bay, she stood motionless and silent for a moment. Then she looked at Bruce and said, "What *bullshit* this all is. No wonder the world is falling apart."

He said nothing, having no immediate solution to offer. After a few moments he spoke again. "As the Brits would say, '*Quite.*'"

Disgusted by the ridiculous nature of her dilemma, she dropped all pretenses of civility and said, "*Very* fucking quite, *indeed.*"

Bruce was not surprised by the vehemence of her anger. Instead, he tried to move her toward a solution. "What do you want to do now? It's your call."

Janie sighed deeply. "I guess I just really want to know the bottom line. If we can be out of here tomorrow morning, that's still better for me than having to dig new samples. I think we should just keep trying to get in touch with Ted. Maybe we can still pull this off today."

Not wishing her to labor under illusions of possible success, he said, "I think that's unlikely."

"When do they close up shop here?"

"Probably five-thirty." He looked at his watch. "That gives us about two hours to get hold of Ted and complete the paperwork. If we manage to do that, it still means we'd be driving most of the night. I'm not sure I'm up to doing that. We may have to stay here tonight, unless you want to go back right now and just start digging bright and early tomorrow."

Janie paced around in a random, meandering path, her arms folded protectively across her chest, her heavy briefcase hanging by a strap from one shoulder. "I didn't recontact the owners," she said. "I was so sure we'd get this taken care of today. I don't even know yet if anyone will let me dig again."

Her unhappiness and frustration, a good part of which he felt he'd caused, weighed heavily on Bruce. "Look," he said, "we need a plan. I don't mind staying here tonight, and even if we left right now, we wouldn't get back in time for you to accomplish anything today. There's a very nice hotel in the center of Leeds and I'm sure they'll have a room."

She shot him a glance of surprise.

"Rooms," he quickly corrected himself.

She let out a long breath. "I don't think there's much choice. We'll have to stay. And I'd be very grateful if you would fill out those forms, just in case. But if we can't get the tubes bright and early tomorrow

morning, I need to go right back to London. If I start digging the minute
we get back, I'll still have to dig like a mole for the next two days."

"I'm really sorry for all this trouble."

"It's not your fault, Bruce, and you've been a real prince about
helping me. I guess I'd better call Caroline. She can start with the phone
calls to the owners. Can I use your phone, please?"

He handed it to her and she dialed the London number of their
hotel. There was no answer in Caroline's room, so Janie left her a message on the voice mail, full of detailed instructions. Then Bruce tried
Ted's beeper again, but it rang and rang, without an answer.

Bruce and Janie drove into Leeds in stony silence after Bruce finished filling out the dozen or so forms required of him at the medical
storage facility. They asked directions and were told how to find the
converted mill, now a lovely small hotel, that Bruce remembered from a
previous trip. They found it easily, right in the heart of what had once
been the industrial center of a bustling Edwardian city, a city now struggling to maintain its tax base. The area in which the hotel was situated
was enjoying a renaissance as a chic lodging and entertainment district.
Years of grime had been sandblasted from the Victorian factory-turned-
hotel before its renovation and the neat rows of exterior brick were
uniformly reddish brown. In the early-evening sun the muted color was
particularly inviting, and Janie felt some of her brittleness wash away as
she let the warm red glow radiate through her tired body.

She'd felt so smug and prepared as she and Bruce got out of the car,
thinking about the clean panties and toothbrush tucked into her bag.
Then she saw Bruce go around to the trunk of the car and retrieve an
overnight bag, and her self-satisfaction evaporated into a feeling of complete incompetence before the trunk lid slammed shut again.

"I like to be prepared," he said as he handed the bag to the porter.
"I should've said something to you about this possibility."

She suppressed an expletive in its embryonic stages and said
sweetly, "It's okay. I'm not completely unprepared. I sort of thought we
might hit a snag. I tucked a few necessities into my briefcase."

"Good thinking," he said. "Let's get settled in, then we can hunt
down some dinner."

They agreed on a time to meet in the lounge and then checked into
two attractive rooms at opposite ends of the seventh floor. After a quick
freshening Janie walked to the nearby business district, where she found a

few stores still open. She bought a dress and a pair of nice earrings and walked briskly back toward the hotel.

My kingdom for a good long run, she thought to herself as she quickened her pace. By the time she reached the hotel, she felt almost normal again. She cleaned herself up and changed into the dress, then put on the earrings as she surveyed herself in the mirror.

"Not bad for an old broad," she said aloud to her reflected image, and headed downstairs.

As she approached the table Bruce stood up and pulled a chair out for her. He said, "I took the liberty of ordering a bottle of wine I thought you might like. I told the steward to hold it until you got here."

He barely had the words out when the steward appeared with two glasses, a bottle, and a corkscrew. He went through the ritual of displaying the label for Bruce's approval, then deftly removed the cork with a few swift turns of the wooden handle. He poured a small amount in a glass, then stood back discreetly as Bruce took in its fragrance and tasted it. Bruce nodded his satisfaction with the dark red liquid, and the steward stepped forward again to fill their glasses.

Janie watched all this with tentative curiosity and compared it to her memories of him. She decided that Bruce the Mature was a lot more elegant and charming than Bruce the Raw, that his years of living in the orderly society of England had given him an understanding of the value of social ritual that most American men simply couldn't grasp. His manners were courtly and all of his rough edges seemed to have been smoothed. He had become an altogether attractive man.

The lounge looked out over a nearby canal and the light of the setting sun danced prettily on the slow-moving water. Everything touched by its nearly horizontal rays turned a brilliant fiery red, and Janie was captivated by the warmth of it. The magic of the wine transfused itself from the glass into her veins. More than once the steward appeared without being summoned and unobtrusively refilled their glasses before stepping back into whatever shadow had previously hidden him from view. And though she tried to resist letting go of its protective walls, Janie felt the stress of the long, hard day gradually slipping out of her as she relaxed into her low chair. She closed her eyes and drifted into a state of near-serenity. When she opened them again, she found that Bruce was staring at her. She quickly turned her eyes away.

He was curious about her. She knew it without question, and to the level at which she could accept it, his unabashed interest in her felt wonderful. She knew he had no way of knowing what she'd been through, how it had hardened her, and how difficult it was for her to let herself be contacted deeply. For the first time since the day she'd buried her husband, Janie allowed the huge ache of wanting to be touched to come to the surface. She sat there under Bruce's benign gaze and let the electricity of longing sizzle on the surface of her skin, and for once made no attempt to push it back down again. Her eyes misted, and she bit her lip in a noble effort to keep the tears at bay. She did not want Bruce to see her in a state of emotional upheaval.

He placed one hand gently on her arm, and the warmth of his hand almost startled her. As if he had read her fears, he said, "Janie, I promise I won't think poorly of you. But I really want to know what happened to you."

Her lower lip quivered and she cast her gaze downward.

"It's all right," he said soothingly. "You're safe with me."

To achieve that state of loose-lipped Bacchanalian bravery where inhibitions melt, she drained her glass. After a small and delicate hiccup she said quietly, "Forty-five years old and I'm still a cheap date."

He smiled. "Not cheap. Inexpensive, maybe. But not cheap."

She returned the smile, but tentatively. "Inexpensive, then." She said, very carefully, "The story starts out pretty, but it gets ugly toward the end."

"I understand. But I'd still like to hear it if you're willing to tell it."

She spoke slowly and deliberately, as if the tale she told was fragile, knowing that the true risk of breakage lay in the teller. Her words were wine slurred. "After my residency I married a man named Harry Crowe. Harry was a pediatrician. We had a very nice life going for us, Harry and I did . . . a careful life. We did everything right. *Everything*. I used to pinch myself every morning and think to myself, *What a wonderful orderly life I have*. Sort of like the life you say you have. You know, content. Satisfied."

She paused and reached out to pour herself more wine, but Bruce took the bottle from her and said, "Let me do that for you." He poured a very small amount in her glass and said, "Go on."

She could feel herself slipping into the old familiar melancholy, but she pressed onward, knowing Bruce would not be satisfied until the story was complete. "We bought stocks in the Reagan years and sold just before the crash. We bought our house before the prices peaked and held on to it until after they stabilized. We invested in technology funds in the early nineties. We both loved our work. Our daughter went to wonderful private schools and did really well; she had music lessons and played sports. . . ."

Bruce watched her intently as the drama unfolded. As her steadiness began to disintegrate visibly he reached out and took hold of her hand. He felt it grow tense as soon as the contact was made. "Go on, Janie. . . ."

She hitched in a rapid breath and let her pain pour out. "And one morning I watched them go off together; it would normally have been my day to drive Betsy to school, but Harry was going to a seminar at the university that day, and it was right on his way. I was on call and I didn't have to go anywhere. I was still in my pajamas at eight o'clock in the morning.

"We were just beginning to hear reports of epidemics in the medical community. The CDC had already issued a bulletin, but the news services hadn't really picked up on it. So school officials hadn't been notified. Well, the day before, one of the cafeteria workers had gone home complaining of a stomachache and a fever. The last thing she did before she went home was to prepare the morning snack for the next day.

"By two o'clock all the kids who'd eaten the snacks were feeling sick, and by that time the cafeteria worker had died. When she went to the emergency room, one of the doctors had just read the CDC bulletin, and found out where she worked. He called the health department and convinced them to quarantine the school.

"I'd been called in for an emergency procedure in the middle of the morning, so I'd already contacted Harry and asked him to pick Betsy up at the end of the day. When he got there, the quarantine was already in place, but he got in somehow, probably by saying he was a pediatrician. If I'd been one of those cops, I probably would've let him in. Out of the four hundred people who were quarantined in that school, three hundred fifty-six came down with it. Three hundred forty-two of them died. Harry and Betsy were not among the lucky ones. They took all the bodies away and held them for postmortems. I never saw either of them again. The bodies were burned within a week."

"Oh, Janie, my God, that's so awful . . . I'm so sorry. . . ."

"It gets worse," she said. Tears were now freely dripping down her cheeks. "I set up a memorial service. There weren't any bodies to bury, but I needed some closure, I needed to feel like I'd done what I was supposed to do when someone dies. My parents came. They were in Pennsylvania when it happened, so they drove up to be with me and to be at the service. On the way they pulled into a rest stop on the Jersey Turnpike and got something to eat. . . ."

She hitched in a drunken sob and Bruce said, ". . . and they picked up the disease there?"

She nodded rapidly and squeezed her eyes shut. Rivers of tears flowed down her face, dripping onto her arm, Bruce's hand, and the tabletop. "Oh, God . . ." she said, "Look at me. I'm leaking again."

Bruce couldn't help smiling slightly. "I might have to report you for unauthorized release of body fluids in a public place. . . ."

Wiping her eyes with one hand, Janie sniffed and said, "It's a good thing it's not illegal in the States. I'd still be in jail."

Bruce got up from his chair and went around to the back of Janie's. Without asking her permission he wrapped his arms around her shoulders from behind, resting his chin on her shoulder as he did so. He held on to her with tender firmness, as she continued to cry quietly. She didn't resist his effort to comfort her.

All around them, people stared. They hadn't made much noise, but Bruce's abrupt rising from his seat turned heads in their direction. Janie didn't see how much attention was being paid to them; Bruce didn't want her to see it, and looked around, meeting the gaze of all of their watchers with a look that said *Please . . . don't stare . . .* and one by one the looks of disdain melted into softer expressions of sympathy.

After a few minutes she reached up and patted his arm with her hand, a signal that she wanted him to let go of her. He understood it perfectly and withdrew his arms, then sat back down in his chair.

With swollen red eyes she looked at him and, surprising herself, said, "I can't tell you how good that felt. Thank you *so* much."

"My pleasure. Anytime. I don't know that I would have managed to keep it together at all if I'd gone through what you went through. You're very brave to have plunged back into your life so quickly."

"Yeah, well, you get pretty tough after something like that. I was a very hard lady for a while after it happened. I felt like someone just pulled my guts right out, and I've been trying to shove them back in ever since."

For a few moments they sat in silence while Janie dried her eyes, the quiet of the lounge broken only by conversations from the surrounding tables. Bruce waved off the approaching steward, who carried a replacement bottle of wine. After a decent interval he said, "I was originally thinking we might go out of the hotel for dinner, but maybe we should just stay here."

"Food again," she said. "I think we're destined to eat every time we see each other. I don't know if I'm sober enough to read the menu."

"I can order for both of us," he said.

She reached out and put her hand on his. "What a nice guy you turned out to be. Order anything but snails," she said, slurring her words. "I *hate* all that grit." And she remained drunkenly silent as the wise and thoughtful grown-up who had invaded the body of the more reckless Bruce-of-yore ordered an assortment of nonsnail items.

Soon the food arrived and as she ate, Janie slowly began to slide back into sobriety. She wondered with some resentment how Bruce managed to stay sober while she'd gotten completely inebriated. But as the evening passed her mood gradually brightened a little and the conversation drifted to other details of their lives. The veneer of sadness slowly melted, and Janie found herself feeling unexpectedly comfortable with her companion by the time the meal was over.

As they walked through the lobby toward the elevators, Janie could still feel the lingering effects of their brief but intense contact. Invited into her altered state, the warmth of an attractive male presence had slipped into her belly and was proceeding slowly but steadily in a straight line toward her groin. She looked at Bruce and thought, *It's so obvious, you can feel it oozing out of me, I know you can.* It was late, and there was no one else around, and as they waited for the old birdcage elevator to reach the lobby, Bruce put his arms around her, this time face-to-face, and drew her close. She resisted, but only slightly, so he looked into her eyes and brought his lips to hers, lightly brushing them together. He pulled back and smiled, then pressed his mouth on hers again, this time closing his eyes.

But the glow of the wine had faded, and as the elevator doors opened, Janie pulled back away from him. As the heady looseness of intoxication dissipated, she remembered herself and the work that remained to be done, some of it professional, some of it personal. No matter how badly she wanted to release herself from its suffocating grasp, the fear of letting herself become attached to someone who might be taken away from her still held her hostage. She recaptured her normal voice and said firmly, "I think I'll walk up. I need the exercise." Then she squeezed his hand and said, "Thanks for the lovely evening. I feel a lot better." And leaving a bewildered Bruce staring at her retreating form, she wobbled resolutely toward the stairs.

Nine

*I*f their prophet Jesus was a poor carpenter, why are his temples so splendid? Alejandro was astounded by the sumptuous carpets and tapestries that appeared everywhere he looked in the papal palace; the exquisite paintings were more intricate than any he had ever seen. The lush figures of barely clad goddesses were strangely exciting to him; he had never seen such erotic representations of the female figure before, certainly not in his medical texts, where the flat renditions had none of the appeal of the lifelike women on these walls. *This castle is holy to them,* he thought, perplexed, for he had expected it to feel more hallowed, more spiritual; instead, it seemed almost conspicuously profane. Should he feel reverence for these Christians, whose ways he admittedly did not understand, or contempt that they had strayed so far from simplicity in their faith?

In time you will know, he told himself.

In his hand was the scroll that conveyed the order for him to report here, and he looked around for someone who might know what he should do now, finally settling on an ornately armored guard standing against one wall.

"Excuse me," he said to the guard. He showed him the scroll. "I am summoned by this notice. Where shall I go?"

The guard looked at the scroll and pointed to his right. "Over there, through those doors," said the bearded man, a scowling ruffian who, Alejandro decided, was *not* a priest beneath his substantial armor. Another guard stood outside the new doors, which were handsomely carved out of lustrous wood and larger than any doors he had previously seen. *So many guards,* he thought, and wondered, *Why does this poor carpenter need an army?* He showed the scroll again, and the new guard opened the heavy doors, admitting Alejandro to a large room, some sort of court, he supposed, where many other equally bewildered-looking men waited.

He stood in the middle of the room, overwhelmed by his surroundings, with a group of other men who seemed equally awestruck, all staring at the splendor that surrounded them. They turned in unison toward a sound at the far end of the room. Large wood doors swung open, and two more armored guards entered. Each carried a ceremonial staff, and between them walked a tall man of regal bearing. A murmur of excited whispers went through the waiting men.

The gentleman who entered was richly attired in a long red robe trimmed with white ermine at the collar and cuffs; the buckle of his belt was gold, encrusted with bright jewels and lustrous pearls. He strode regally into the center of the room, and stood there silently waiting for the attention of all present to be turned toward him. From his air of impatience, Alejandro had the idea that the pinch-faced man, scrutinizing the unruly crowd with overt disapproval, was accustomed to having attention paid to him, and quickly. His intelligent and perceptive-looking eyes, narrow-set over a long, pointy nose, moved from man to man; they rested for a moment on Alejandro, and the two physicians stared at each other for a brief time. With the barest hint of a smile the red-robed man looked away, then nodded at one of the staff-bearers, who banged loudly on the floor, and the surprised occupants of the room hushed their whispers quickly. The tall man then cleared his throat, and began to speak.

"Are there any Jews among you? If so, step forward."

Fear gripped him. *Have the Spanish soldiers reached Avignon? Am I finally to be discovered?* He looked anxiously around, waiting to see what others would do. *Why does this man call forth only the Jews here?* There had been no word that the pope's edict protecting Jews had been rescinded. He tried not to show his fear as he stood in the room full of strangers, but had to struggle to hide his trembling. If closely questioned about his heritage, he knew that he would surely lose what little composure he had managed to maintain and give himself away.

He watched in terror as, one by one, the Jews stepped forward, some of them wearing yellow circles sewn to the sleeves of their clothing. For those men there was no decision. They gathered together in a group, nervously awaiting their unknown fate. Alejandro saw the fear in their eyes, but also the proud defiance, and he was ashamed of his own cowardice.

The tall man in red looked at the group with contempt. "You are dismissed," he said.

The Jews looked at each other in disbelief, expressions of relief washing over their previously terrified faces. All quickly turned toward the door, and hurried out, stunned by their good fortune.

It was too late for him to join them. He watched with rueful envy as the Jews disappeared from the room. The tall man motioned those remaining to be seated, and all shyly looked around for a suitable place. To Alejandro's surprise they were directed to sit in a grouping of luxurious cushioned chairs he had admired earlier.

When they were all settled, the man in red sat down in a splendid

gilt chair perched on a dais before the assembled men. "Learned physicians and colleagues," he began, "I am Guy de Chauliac, and it is my
great honor to be the personal physician to His Holiness Pope Clement
VI. I act today on behalf of His Holiness, who requires your services in a
matter of utmost importance to the Holy Church and the Kingdom of
France.

"As you all undoubtedly know, we are smitten by a horrible plague
of devastating proportions. It is reported that the whole of Europa is now
afflicted by this scourge, and thousands fall daily. Reports from other
nations are as grim as those we would send out to them. Our beloved
brother Edward III of England has written to us of the pest's arrival on
his shores, and we mourn the passing of the archbishop of Canterbury as
a result.

"King Edward is himself now mourning the death of his daughter
Joanna, who was on her way to be wedded into the royal house of Castile
when she was cruelly struck down by the pestilence."

The young noblewoman on her bridal journey to Castile! He recalled
the cantina where the story had first been told on his journey to Avignon.

"His Holiness has great regard and affection for the English royals,
and recognizes their importance in maintaining the political stability of
Europa. His Holiness wishes, despite the current rancor between our two
countries, to encourage the noble leaders of France and England to set
aside their differences, and to pursue the alliances that are so essential to
renewed peace and prosperity. It is imperative that England be allied to
the other noble houses of Europa. If the royal houses are decimated,
there will be grave consequences for the order of our world, and the
Church's interests will not be served."

Alejandro looked around at the men seated with him; all were
paying rapt attention to de Chauliac, who continued with his dramatic
speech.

"I have personally seen to the health and well-being of His Holiness
during this dreadful plague. My methods have been unorthodox, and
while it's true that my patron dislikes his confinement, one can hardly
argue with the results.

"Our beloved pope has decreed that we shall be active participants
in the protection of the royal families of Europa. He has called you here
today, in recognition of your medical accomplishments and your great
learning, to enlist you in a holy war against the pestilence. Today you will
all begin instruction, under my personal supervision, in the methods
used to guard our Holy Father's health. Thereafter you will all be sent as
ambassadors to the royal houses of Europa and England. Your charge will

be to see to the health of these families, in order that they may be entirely preserved. We will not allow the plague to disrupt alliances that have flourished for many years, nor will we allow it to negate those unions we have planned for the future."

It was a masterful performance, and Alejandro was as captivated by it as every other man in the room.

"You will return immediately to your surgeries when I dismiss you to gather your equipment, for your travels will commence as soon as your training is complete. If any man here has a family in need of support, His Holiness will see to their needs in your absence. I will have your names now, which our scribe will take to the Holy Father."

Alejandro Canches knew that his real name might betray him immediately as the murderer of Bishop John of Aragon, and he knew that he had no choice but to abandon it. Sadly, he thought that he would miss it; it had served him well for all of his life, and he was proud to be known as Avram Canches' son.

When it was his turn, he looked directly at de Chauliac, focusing his gaze intently on the tall man's piercing blue eyes, and said calmly, "Hernandez. I am Alejandro Hernandez."

"A Spaniard?" de Chauliac asked.

"*Oui, monsieur,* that I am."

Alejandro and his bewildered colleagues were lavishly housed in the papal palace during their three days of intensive tutoring under de Chauliac's watchful eye. Each one lived during that time in his own room with a private toilette. They were well fed and pampered in every way, for the pope wanted to incur their complete loyalty. De Chauliac kept the men entirely under his influence and tutelage, teaching them in detail his procedures for keeping the pope free of contagion, watching them carefully for those innate qualities needed to carry out the task for which they were being trained, qualities that could not be taught.

Every day the medical ambassadors attended lectures in one of the sumptuous court chambers. De Chauliac would stand at a podium and speak for hours in his professorial voice, and Alejandro marveled that he never seemed to tire. *He loves this work as much as I do,* the pupil thought of the teacher.

"You must consult with astrologers," he said on the first day of instruction, "in order to know the most auspicious days for bathing, or going outside, or any of the other normal occurrences of daily life. Ordinary activities that your patients previously did with casual abandon must now be viewed with suspicion, for we simply do not know which activities have the potential for bringing the individual into contact with the plague. You will find that your royal patients, who are so accustomed to having their whims realized, will resist your instructions about when and where they may do certain things. Be firm and do not accept their challenges to your authority."

Alejandro tried to imagine himself telling a king what to do and when to do it, but he could not conjure up such an unlikely image. "And if they still resist?" he asked.

"Bid them to remember that you have the power of Almighty God, bestowed upon you through His Holiness, and that you will use it, if necessary, to protect their health."

Alejandro went to bed that night feeling very small and confused. *The most difficult part of this task*, he thought, *will be subduing the arrogant patients.*

On the second day de Chauliac explained his theories about contagion. "It is my firm belief based on observation that there are invisible humors and vapors in the air, and that these fumes are the means by which this plague is spread. The living victim pours these humors into the air when he breathes and disperses the evil contagion unseen, allowing the next victim no chance to escape. Therefore, the patients must be isolated. Confine them to their castles; do not allow commerce or travelers to enter without your inspection. And since one cannot see these vapors and humors as they are forming, it is the wisest course of action to allow absolutely *no* interaction with the outside world at all. My esteemed predecessor Henri de Mandeville was quite firm in his beliefs about contagion; he taught those who taught me to cleanse the hands before and after touching a patient, for it was his belief that these humors can be passed on the hands as well. In His Holiness' library there are copies of de Mandeville's texts on this matter; those who wish to do so may read them."

But this is my theory as well! Alejandro thought, excited to know that his beliefs about the importance of cleanliness were shared by other physicians. Again, he spoke out of turn.

"I have seen, additionally, that ablution in wine will cause a wound to heal more quickly. There is some part of the wine that seems to attack the sepsis."

"Perhaps the sepsis becomes drunk, and can no longer navigate its way to the wound," another man interjected, bringing a chorus of laughter from the other men in the group.

Alejandro reddened, but de Chauliac raised his hand. The group fell silent very quickly. "One must never laugh at the observations of a colleague," he said. "The wisest among us still cannot cure this pest. We are all quite equal in our ignorance." He looked directly at Alejandro. "We will speak privately of this later."

All heads turned toward the young Jew, who simply nodded to his instructor, and then lowered his eyes. "Therefore," de Chauliac continued, "though they will not acquiesce easily to this demand, you must instruct the court astrologers to tell them that every day is auspicious for bathing. . . ."

That night Alejandro was summoned from his room by a papal guard and escorted to de Chauliac's private apartment. He climbed several flights of stairs in a tall tower behind the guard, who was visibly slowed by the bulkiness of his garments and armor.

He entered the anteroom cautiously. De Chauliac waved him inside.

"Come, come," he said, "and sit down." He pointed to a softly cushioned chaise longue and said, "Enjoy some comfort."

Alejandro sat down timidly, settling carefully into the thick padding of the long chair. Gone was the pedagogue, the taskmaster, and in his place was a gracious and accommodating host. The transition was striking. "You are a different man in private, Dr. de Chauliac," he said warily.

De Chauliac offered a glass of wine in a heavy silver goblet, which was accepted by his guest. "And how do you find me different?" he asked, one eyebrow raised in curiosity.

After a hearty gulp of wine Alejandro said, "You are a stern lecturer, and your presence is quite"—he struggled for the proper word—"commanding."

De Chauliac laughed cynically. "One must appear to be in command when teaching fools," he said, "or they will not learn, and one's efforts will be wasted. I detest imparting valuable knowledge to those who do not understand its worth."

Alejandro's face took on a visible look of hurt. "Sir, I—" he began, wanting to protest.

"I do not refer to you," de Chauliac said quickly, "for you would not be here tonight were that my opinion of you. Rather, I speak of the rest of them. A bunch of dolts, I think. The plague seems to have carried off our very best and left us with idiots for physicians." He got up from his chair and seated himself in one nearer to Alejandro. He leaned closer and seemed very excited. "But there is fire in your eyes, a love of learning, and my heart knows joy to see it."

"You do me too much honor, sir."

De Chauliac peered closely at him. "I think not," he said. "I have watched you as you hear my lectures, and you cannot hide the mark of your intelligence. I have longed to talk with one who believes as I do about sepsis. I am glad you spoke today. You must tell me now how you came to your belief that wine helps wounds to heal."

Alejandro relaxed; he understood that he was not discovered, but that de Chauliac had the same thirst for knowledge that he did. "I have tried many experiments using different liquids to wash the wound after surgeries," he began, "and there are many that have no effect. A few, in fact, seem to delay the healing. But wine, even the vilest, most undrinkable wine, will always speed the healing. Or so I have observed. I first noticed this in my time at Montpellier—"

"You read at Montpellier?"

"Indeed," Alejandro said.

"I often lecture at Montpellier. When were you there? Perhaps you attended one of my lectures then."

"I was there . . ." he began, and then stopped himself; he could remember the year only as Jews counted time. He began to panic. How would he explain to de Chauliac that he didn't remember the year?

"I was there, uh, six years ago."

"In 1342."

"Yes." His forehead began to feel warm and moist.

"Ah, then perhaps we missed each other; I spent that year in Paris attending to the king. He suffers monstrously from gout. It is no surprise to me that he is thus afflicted. Despite his unaccountable slimness the man's diet is sinfully rich. He ignored my pleas for moderation." Raising his goblet with a flourish, he took a sip of wine. "His Majesty would have no other physician but me, so I was forced to give up my teaching for the duration of his illness. A pity we did not meet then. I think I would have remembered and enjoyed a notable student such as yourself."

No doubt I would remember you, as well, Alejandro thought. *But enjoy . . .*

"Ah, well, 'tis no matter," de Chauliac said. "You are here now. And how is it that a Spaniard comes to be in Avignon?"

After a brief silence Alejandro said quietly, "It is the will of my family that I should be here." He offered no embellishment.

But de Chauliac asked nothing further about his personal life; he was far more eager to speak of other matters. "You say you arrived at this conclusion about wine simply by trying things over and over until you knew of their effects? How marvelously original! So often we wait for accidents to teach us, and even then we are slow to learn. . . ."

Alejandro's panic gradually subsided and he lost himself in the discussion. They spoke back and forth over wine and delicious fruits for the rest of the evening, sharing ideas and comparing theories about surgery, disease, and treatments. Worthy colleagues, they spoke long into the night, sharing their hopes for the discovery of cures. Alejandro left de Chauliac's apartment with far more respect for his teacher than when he'd entered, and the sure knowledge that this was a man not to be trifled with.

On the third day de Chauliac gave his students an unexpected surprise. They assembled in a large airy courtyard on the first floor of the papal palace, a pleasant area with many wonderful plantings. De Chauliac stood behind a long table draped with a heavy cloth, grinning magnificently. When the students were all gathered around the table, he removed the drape to reveal the body of a newly dead victim of plague, a man who might have been thirty years old when he died.

Gasps of surprise went through the crowd of students, for it was clear that de Chauliac meant to dissect the body before them. "As you all must know, His Holiness prohibits the desecration of corpses," he said.

Alejandro stood silent, and thought to himself, *If only you knew how well I know this. . . .*

"However," de Chauliac continued, "because your need to learn is so urgent, and because of the great benefit to be derived from studying the body firsthand, he has given me permission to dissect this body. Not his blessing, mind you, although the victim was a Jew, and has no hope of salvation in any case. . . ."

Alejandro somehow managed to maintain his composure and allowed his eyes to wander to the groin, where he saw the undisputable evidence of what de Chauliac had said.

"And now," de Chauliac said, "I will require assistance." He looked at Alejandro. "Dr. Hernandez, perhaps you will help me?"

He looked sadly at the body of the Jew, the neck grossly swollen, the fingers and toes black with accumulated blood, and thought it odd that he, the only other Jew present, should be the one to cut it. *Perhaps this is a just punishment for my sins . . .* he thought to himself sadly. *Or perhaps it is just God's will that I should be given this task, for who would be more tender with the body of a Jew than another Jew?*

He moved closer to de Chauliac and silently took up the hammer and chisel. "Good," de Chauliac said. "You may make the entry."

He placed his hand on the chest to find the correct placement for the chisel. The body was not yet entirely cold; the man could not have died more than a few hours earlier. *Good,* he thought, *the stench will not be so brutal.* And as he had done in Cervere to the breast of Carlos Alderón, Alejandro placed the chisel carefully, then brought the hammer down on it. He heard the crack of the ribs, and set the tools aside. He took up the knife and made the proper cuts.

"How skilled you are, Dr. Hernandez," de Chauliac said as he watched Alejandro work. "One might even think you had done this before."

The seemingly casual comment stunned Alejandro. *What can he mean?* he wondered frantically. He was afraid to meet de Chauliac's eyes, terrified of what he would find there: recognition, perhaps, from Montpellier; the knowledge of his real name and the circumstances of his flight; the taunting look of one who watches a man perform what might be his last work in freedom. As he spread the rib cage, Alejandro remained silent. Inside the chest there was a very large heart, and all present knew what that meant: that the dead Jew on the table before them had been in life a very good and kind man. With agonizing slowness Alejandro looked up and stared at his instructor.

With no hint of emotion de Chauliac simply nodded and said, "Proceed."

Recipes for amulets and medications were copied by the pope's scribes, and given to each physician along with an ample supply of the materials required for their concoction.

Alejandro in turn copied what was given to him directly into his book, taking great care to be certain that everything he wrote was exactly as the scribes had written it first. As he was finishing, de Chauliac came upon him unannounced, and he was caught with the book in his hands.

"Once again I am impressed by your diligence, Dr. Hernandez. I have found it to be rare in the Spanish race."

Ah, if he but knew the truth . . . perhaps he does. . . .

He closed the book quickly before de Chauliac could read what he had written, and said, "It has been my habit since I was a student to record what I am taught. Otherwise I am prone to forget that wisdom for which I must be the steward."

De Chauliac did not believe for a second that Alejandro would forget even the most minute detail of what he had been taught. *This one cannot disguise his zeal. He is shrewd, and will not allow himself to fail.*

"One day perhaps we can share another repast and you will bless me with a look at this tome."

"When I return to Avignon, perhaps," he said flatly. *If* I return to Avignon, he thought.

On the morning of their departure he looked at himself in a mirror, and thought that if his mother and father were miraculously still alive, they would hardly know him in this clothing provided by de Chauliac. *What will they do when they get here and find no trace of me?* he wondered. He hadn't even had the chance to change the sign on his surgery, which would now sit idle with its tools and equipment and promise of service, until he returned. Would they think he had come to harm, or perhaps that he had never reached Avignon at all? *Will they think I have betrayed their trust?* he thought bitterly.

God curse this plague and these arrogant fools who think they can make it dance to their tunes. He scrutinized his own image more closely, hating the changes in himself, longing for the familiar flowing robes he had worn in Cervere. He had changed so much in such a short time! He was clean shaven and his hair was trimmed to just below his neck in the French style of the time; he wore tight breeches, wine-red in color, and soft leather boots, cuffed at the calf. Above his breeches was a long-sleeved tunic of fine linen in the soft green-blue of the Mediterranean Sea; it buttoned high up on his neck, for which he was grateful, since it would hide his scar, and its length was halfway between his hips and knees. Over all of that he wore a luxurious coat with voluminous sleeves and a wide lapel. It was made of rich wool in the same deep red of his breeches, and it fell well below his knees. And on his head sat a dark green wool hat, octagonal in shape, slouched stylishly to one side, a brightly colored feather poking upward a bit too jauntily for his liking. Unless the glass deceived, he was the very image of a modern French gentleman. But the most visible change was in his face. He was no longer the wide-eyed innocent he had been in Cervere. His amber eyes had a new hard look to them, a sad wisdom that he could not hide, even from himself.

The trunk de Chauliac had provided for him contained three more such complete outfits. *Enough,* he thought, *to last me the rest of my life, should I not grow portly.*

Stowed in that trunk with the finery was the clothing he had acquired while on his journey. The rough garments still had plenty of service in them, and he thought it likely that he would need them again soon. But he would ride with his own saddlebag, de Chauliac be damned if he did not like it, for therein he kept his fortune and his book, and he would not let them part from his side.

That much about myself I will not change, he thought, and left his private room to join the others.

The men assembled once again in the large room were noisily commenting to each other about the changes in their appearance when he arrived. *How different is this scene from the one I beheld only a few days ago,* he thought silently. *Now these men look as if they actually belong in this room, for they are groomed and robed and appointed as well as the wealthiest of noblemen.*

De Chauliac made another grand entrance, positioning himself in front of his newly garbed protégés, and began to speak.

"Messieurs, you are all a credit to your profession. I am delighted with your diligence and eagerness to learn. Each of you has become more skilled in your craft, and we trust that you will carry your accomplishments abroad with you when you represent His Holiness in the noble courts of Europa. Be conscientious in the application of your craft, and serve your God well. You are charged with the protection of our interests, and our prayers for your success will be ceaseless."

He then took each man aside separately, and gave him individual instructions particular to his final destination. He expressed his encouragement, and gave assurances of the pope's personal blessing. One by one the physicians left the salon to begin their travels in strange foreign lands.

Alejandro was left to the very last; the others were all gone and he remained alone in the room with de Chauliac.

"Doctor Hernandez," he said, "how marvelous you look! Just as a physician should look, prosperous and noble. I had no doubt that your appearance would improve in the proper clothing. Please sit down. I have many things to say to you and you will be more comfortable."

Alejandro did as he was bidden, wondering how any man could ever be expected to feel comfortable in such tight breeches, and found himself once again facing his undecipherable instructor and colleague. *How can such a learned man, such a fine thinker, such a purveyor of logic, be so bigoted and arrogant?* he wondered as he regarded him. *Can these dissonant qualities exist in a single man without warring to the death, or at the very least to distraction?*

"I have watched with admiration as you acquired your new skills these last days," he began, "and as I have told you, I am impressed with your intelligence and knowledge. I have therefore, in consultation with His Holiness, selected you personally to serve in the court of King Edward III, whose original request for protection led to this entire undertaking."

Alejandro swallowed and nodded.

Expecting a more effusive reaction, de Chauliac said, "Well, are you not pleased? This is a great honor for a physician."

He said quietly, "I am immensely honored, sir. Your confidence in me is undeserved."

"Again, I think not, Dr. Hernandez. I see in you a part of my own youthful self, I see that same burning desire to achieve greatness. Oh, no, monsieur," he said with near vehemence, "I do not think I overestimate you. But your task will be a difficult one because of the nature of the royals you will serve."

He paused for a reaction from Alejandro, but got none. He let out a long sigh, then continued, his tone darkening as he spoke. "I can appreciate your reticence, but please understand that your work in England is not a matter of choice. There is much at stake for His Holiness, and we will be in frequent contact with the English court to be sure that you are performing diligently. It will not go well for you if you do not."

Alejandro looked up from his hands and stared at de Chauliac. The undercurrent of coercion he had felt throughout the training period was now confirmed. The possibility of leaving the papal palace had entered his mind and he had toyed many times with the idea of escape, but all such notions now left him. *I do not know what he knows about me,* he thought, searching de Chauliac's penetrating blue eyes for some indication. What he saw there was de Chauliac's desire for him to wonder and the certainty that he would submit, and he thought with sadness that it would be the wisest thing for him to do.

With a deep sigh of resignation he said, "How are these royals different from the others?"

De Chauliac smiled almost wickedly, his thin lips curling upward in something akin to a sneer, and launched enthusiastically into an explanation. "They are Plantagenets," he said, accentuating the name as if it should have some meaning to Alejandro. "They think themselves to have the noblest lineage in all of Europa. They are all giants, and fair, with hair of spun gold and eyes of sapphire; one can see the mark of the Norse upon each and every one of them. They are haughty and ruthless and an altogether vicious lot. And they do not like to take orders that might come from His Holiness, despite their outward appearances of conformity to the will of the Church. And though Edward has asked specifically for a physician to be sent to him, he will not take your instruction without giving back an argument."

"They sound terribly unpleasant, these English royals," Alejandro said.

De Chauliac laughed. "Oh, not at all. Edward and Philippa hold the most lavish and sumptuous court in all of Europa. They pride themselves on providing the most wonderful accommodations for their guests. They have spent a fortune enlarging their castle at Windsor, and no doubt you will find it quite spectacular."

"More spectacular than this?" He gestured at the surrounding court area with its rich furnishings. "How can that be?"

"Edward would outdo the French at every turn. After all, it is only natural for him to want to do so, since he claims the French throne for himself through his mother. You will see that the French are a far more decorous and enlightened people than the English. He must be up to the task of ruling them should that honor fall to him."

He paused for a few moments to let Alejandro absorb what he'd been told. "You are to pay particular attention to the Princess Isabella, for His Holiness has designs on the arrangement of her nuptials. I warn you, she is a headstrong and willful girl, and a great beauty. She will try to charm you into leniency, but you must not let her persuasive nature deter you in the performance of your important work. You will find the others, the Black Prince, the queen, their retainers, to be of a similar nature, but less forceful. But Edward and Isabella will keep you quite busy, I think." He stood, indicating that their interview was at an end. "I do not envy you the difficulty of your work there," he said, "but I envy you the excitement. I wish it were I going in your place."

Alejandro loathed the idea that his knowledge would be put to such an offensive purpose, for he could not condone this ambitious pope's desire to meddle in the affairs of European states, and wanted nothing to do with any such silliness. Yet he could not deny that de Chauliac was right. It was an opportunity beyond compare. He silently vowed to use this opportunity to learn as much as possible.

"Sir, I will do my best," the Jew said.

De Chauliac bowed low, and approached the pope from the far side of the pontiff's sumptuous salon. He listened again to the pope's complaints and offered sweet words of sympathy, but would not relent on the confinement.

"There is a Spaniard among them," he told Clement. "He is clever and skilled, and will do better than any of the others, I think. I have sent him to England."

Clement smiled his approval and fanned himself with a fan of peacock feathers. "Well done, my friend. No doubt Edward will be pleased that we managed to send a physician who is not French."

"We shall be traveling for approximately twenty days," the captain told Alejandro. "His Holiness has given us ten guards, for in these times of anarchy the roads are none too safe. We shall travel as swiftly as possible. I do not wish to stay in one place too long, for fear of the pest."

A wise course of action, Alejandro thought as he mounted his horse, a fine dark steed wearing the handsome ornamentation of the Papal Guard. His saddlebag strapped firmly behind him, he followed the captain as he led the group out of the palace courtyard. The entourage rode out at midmorning under the pope's protective banner.

Their progress was swift and uneventful until the fourth day. Traveling roughly parallel to the Rhône, they had passed through Lyon heading to Dijon, three days north, when they encountered an eerie procession of ragged, filthy peasants clogging the road and impeding their advance.

"Why, they look like skeletons," Alejandro said, guiding his horse past the moaning caravan, breathing through the sleeve of his coat to filter out the smell. "There must be two hundred or more of them." He rode up next to the captain and questioned him. "What in God's name are these pathetic creatures doing?" he asked.

"They are everywhere throughout the countryside, traveling from city to city, flagellating themselves for all to see. The claim to be the saviors of humankind, and think that the atrocities they perform upon themselves and each other will be viewed by God as a penance, atoning for the sins of the world and thereby causing God to end this plague. Their followers grow in number every day."

"But I saw no leader before them. How are they organized in this gruesome pilgrimage?"

"Each group is said to have a master, to whom the members swear complete obedience, and all vow to remain with the group for thirty days or more. They pledge a stipend for their own support in this crusade, but God alone knows what nourishment these skinny fiends get. One need only look at them to see that they are made of bones alone."

Each one was naked to the waist, and caked with blood-soaked ashes. Their constant wailing was an affront to the ears, and it filled the air with a discordant song of desolation and woe. Anxious to proceed, the riders spurred their horses forward.

When they were safely past, the captain said, "Were *I* God, I would look down upon these wretches and send them a plague of their own."

"From the looks of it, He already has," Alejandro said, "—a plague of madness."

They rode on briskly, hoping to increase the distance between themselves and the terrible horde. In a few hours they came to the outskirts of a town, and stopped to gather their group more closely together before passing through.

Although Alejandro knew nothing more of war than what Hernandez had told him, he knew that the horrors of war could not be more gruesome than the scene that greeted them in the town's open square. Six fires raged, thick smoke billowing up around six poles, each one bearing the charred remains of what had been a human being. Encircling this atrocity were several dozen wailing demons, more gruesome than any he had seen in the caravan, stripped to the waist, the rest of their bodies covered only with rough sacks. They beat themselves with thorny branches and whips tipped in metal, and when they could beat themselves no more they turned and beat each other. Blood poured down their legs and pooled on the ground; everywhere the dirt was tracked with red footprints and shreds of bloody cloth. They circled their burned prisoners in a frenzied dance, encouraged by a large crowd of townspeople who had gathered to watch. The bells of the church pealed in wild accompaniment to their hideous hymns.

Alejandro and the captain watched in horrified fascination, their horses prancing skittishly, as one of the flagellants left the circle to whip one of the staked bodies. Alejandro nearly retched when he saw that the man strapped to the pole was still alive, writhing in reaction to the fierce whipping. He rode forward to look closer, and when he saw the sooty remains of a yellow circle on the man's sleeve, he bolted forward on his horse in anger.

The captain had been watching as his charge lost control of himself, and lashed his horse viciously to catch up. He grabbed the reins of Alejandro's horse and brought the animal to an abrupt halt.

"Monsieur! I beg you to keep your wits about you! They are only Jews!"

Alejandro tried furiously to escape, but to no avail; his captor was much bigger and stronger, and he could not break free. The captain saw the rage in his eyes, and knew that he could not restrain him indefinitely.

Through the confusion he shouted instructions to a nearby guard, who jumped off his horse and swiftly nocked an arrow in his bow. With stunning accuracy the bowman let his arrow fly, piercing the heart of the prisoner suffering at the stake and killing him instantly.

The hideous circle of penitents ceased their dancing and moaning, and turned as one to locate the betrayer who had deprived them of their pleasure. They spied the pope's entourage and, ignoring the protective banner, surged forward to confront them.

The captain once again grabbed the reins of Alejandro's horse, then spurred his own furiously to escape the lunatic crowd. The entire train sped off, quickly outrunning the demented, bleeding horde, and didn't stop until they were deep in the woods, certain of their safety.

Their horses were lathered from the hasty escape, and as dusk was nearing, the captain decided it would be wise to settle in for the night. As the accompanying guards went about the business of setting up their tents, the captain took Alejandro aside.

"That was careless behavior," he said sternly, "and the results could have been disastrous."

"But the man was suffering! They were burning him alive, and I could not—"

"I understand your compassion for those who suffer, Physician," he interrupted, "but there was nothing that any one of us could have done to save him."

"But you yourself ordered your man to kill him. You felt his suffering too."

"It was a waste of a good arrow," he said. "He was only a Jew. Jews are meant to suffer. You would be wise to refrain from such worthless heroics in the future, if you wish to complete this journey in good health."

Alejandro's rage rose within him, and he struggled to contain it. *Do not give yourself away*, he warned himself. *One Jew has died today. Do not allow yourself to be the next.*

They headed slightly west as they passed Dijon on a road that would take them north of Paris; eventually it would take them to Calais, where they would obtain passage over the Channel.

When they were one day east of Calais, one of the guards began to complain of an aching head and a sick stomach. Alejandro immediately examined him; as he feared, the man's neck and armpits were beginning to swell. He begged the captain to stop the train to allow the man some comfort, for he was growing sicker with every mile. The next morning another guard showed similar signs of affliction. By afternoon two more were ill.

Of their ten guards five were eventually affected, so Alejandro sent the remaining guards and the captain to camp at a distance. Wearing his amulet, and covering his nose and mouth as de Chauliac had instructed him, he treated the victims with the herbs and medications he had been given to bring to England.

The first man died only a day after taking ill, and the others were now in dreadful misery. The captain pressed Alejandro to move on, but the physician would not hear of resuming their journey yet. He had great hope that his newly learned treatments would have some effect on the progress of the disease. But when the second man died, the remaining guards began to grumble, and the captain, mindful of his duty to the pope, pressed even further for permission to depart.

"I will not leave until these men are either dead or recovered. There can be no compromise in this."

More grumbling ensued. The frightened guards were talking of leaving without Alejandro and their sick companions. "I am at my wits' end," the distraught captain confided in the physician. "I must see you safely to England, and I cannot do that without a decent escort. We are already down two men, and the others do not wish to stay in this place. They are certain that the contagion lurks in the air here."

"I cannot argue with that logic," the physician replied. "I can say nothing to reassure them. One more now hovers near death and the other two are sure to follow."

"How long will it be?" the captain asked.

"I cannot say. Perhaps one day; perhaps two."

The captain went off by himself for a few moments, and returned with a look of terrible sadness on his face.

"I beg your forgiveness, monsieur, for what I am about to do, but we cannot delay any longer."

Alejandro did not understand. He jumped up and followed the captain as he walked to the place where the sick guards were lying. In the brief time since he'd left them to speak with the captain, the sickest of the guards had expired; his unmoving eyes stared blankly upward, flies gathering in the moist corners, and his chest no longer rose and fell. The other two, still conscious, moaned and cried in their misery.

The captain stood between the two men and said, "Make peace with your God." Then he drew his sword.

Their pathetic looks would have tormented the soul of an angel,

Alejandro thought. *And how should I look, knowing that my time was upon me?* he wondered. *No different. They will no longer suffer, at least.* He made no attempt to interfere.

"May God have mercy on their souls, and mine," the captain said. Then he dispatched the souls of the two remaining sick guards with swift and merciful strokes.

"And now, monsieur, we shall continue, for we have wasted much time here. God will receive their innocent souls, but His Holiness will see that He does not forgive me for failing to deliver you to England. Please gather your belongings and come along." And they left the bodies in the forest, having no means of burying them. Alejandro wished with all his heart that he had brought along the sturdy shovel so finely crafted by Carlos Alderón a lifetime ago in Aragon.

And on the twenty-second day since departing from Avignon, the beleaguered group reached the port of Calais, now under English control; it had been so since King Edward's forces had claimed it in a fierce and bloody battle the year before. There was much confusion in the island town, and the pope's French guards complained that they felt as if they were in enemy territory. Were it not for the pope's banner, their progress would surely have been impeded by the English occupying force, who were not kindly disposed toward any military-looking group such as theirs crossing the water at Calais.

The captain left the remaining five guards and Alejandro in the town and went to the docks in search of passage. He returned an hour later. "It's a bit of luck, really," he said. "The weather is fine for passage. I have found a fisherman who is eager to take our gold."

The horses and men boarded the sturdy boat, and the fisherman set sail, taking advantage of the brisk wind. Alejandro had never been aboard a boat in the ocean before, and was at first excited by the prospect of sailing across to England. But when they left the protection of the shore and reached open water, he became violently ill, unable to lift his head up from between his legs. He stared at a bucket of his own vomit until it became too dark to see it anymore.

The captain showed sympathy for the physician's weakness. "It is never easy to cross," he said. "Some are never the same again after a rough passing. But we will make good progress, I think; the seas are calm and the wind is with us. Sometimes it is much worse than this."

Alejandro raised his head just long enough to say, "How could it be worse than this? I am about to toss up my very innards."

"Perhaps with no innards you will feel no pain," the captain said, "but I think not. I would advise you to try to keep them. It may make you feel better to know that you are not alone in your affliction. It is said that the mighty Edward himself is lacking in sea legs!" He laughed. To the captain, who had seen the majestic Edward, the vision of that great man violently vomiting seemed terribly funny. But Alejandro, suffering terribly, could find no humor in the notion. He dropped his head again and retched dryly.

They reached the opposite shore late the next day without incident, and the entire party quickly disembarked, walking the horses through the shallow surf to the rocky beach. Alejandro wobbled around on shaky legs for a few moments before mounting his horse.

The white cliffs rose majestically above the sand, and Alejandro watched the boat set off in the waning afternoon sun, heading back to France, leaving him and his companions on this strange foreign shore.

Pointing to a city in the distance, whose towers and spires and smoke columns were just beginning to take form in his vision, Alejandro said, "Is that London?"

"It is," the captain said.

"But it looks so small! And see the dirty air above it!" Alejandro said. "I thought it would be bigger, and more grand! It does not look like a city in which this great King Edward might live."

"The man himself is of a mind with you, I think," the captain said, "for now he only keeps his armies there, but lives to the west in Windsor. I am told he has a fine palace there. Tonight I will deliver you to the Tower of London as I am instructed to do. Tomorrow, perhaps, you will be taken to Windsor."

The language of the English people was hard and guttural, Alejandro thought, not at all like his lyrical native Spanish, or the soft fluidity of his acquired French. The rough sounds assaulted his ears as the papal envoy rode through the crowds that clogged the great bridge into the city of London. He had once heard the German language being spoken, which in an untrained ear might be mistaken for English; he didn't like the sound of either one.

Looking down to the shores of the Thames River, he could see the bodies that had accumulated there, some floating, some bobbing near the shore, and he could smell their decomposition, even at this height on the bridge. The water looked more like sludge. There were flotillas of feces and garbage, with little clear water surface visible anywhere.

The pope's banner still flew high in front of their train, and every-where people stepped aside to let them pass freely. Woeful supplicants dropped to their knees and clutched their hands together in prayer at the sight of the gold crucifix emblazoned on a red background. Alejandro was unsettled by the amount of attention their procession was receiving, and tried to become less conspicuous by guiding his horse between the guards.

At the gate of the Tower the castellan who greeted them arranged for their belongings to be taken to temporary lodgings. "His Majesty expects you, but he has gone to Windsor, where he can more graciously receive you. He bids me to invite you to rest here this evening, and journey west tomorrow, if such a course may please you."

Anxious for word of conditions outside England, the castellan in-vited them to dine with him that evening, where he hoped they would give him detailed accounts of their travel through France. The captain readily agreed, and their supper was served in the main hall of the castel-lan's residence. A long planked table was filled with steaming meats and crusty breads, and hot turnips were heaped upon a platter, which was passed from man to man. By the time they had finished their meal, Alejandro's head was pounding from the strain of trying to understand what was being said. He had picked up a few words and phrases in English from the captain on their journey, for they had little else to do but talk in the evenings at their dark campsites. The captain's English was severely limited and his pronunciation crude. Alejandro could not learn enough from him to function, and frequently requested transla-tions into French.

At first light Alejandro was awakened by his captain. "We are ready to leave," he said. "I have brought some things that His Holiness wishes you to deliver."

After rubbing his eyes Alejandro sat up and accepted the package. He said, "Why not stay a day or two and rest? Surely you and your men need not travel out so soon."

"I think not," he said. "I care not for this English soil, as English soldiers care not for the good earth of France, given a choice."

Alejandro did not want him to go. "But surely one or two days will not be too onerous. . . ."

"You forget, good sir, that my king is at war with the one into whose hands I now deliver you. There is a truce now, owing to the pest, but it will soon end. I serve the pope, it is true, but I am forever a son of France, and I am anxious to go back to my home. Surely you can understand this, so far from your own country. . . ."

Only too well . . . Alejandro thought. "Then I bid you adieu, and wish you a safe journey home," he said. The captain saluted and strolled out of the barracks.

Alone again, he opened the package to inspect the contents. Inside were several scrolls for the king and his ministers and a few small gifts, for the ladies, he thought, and a purse of gold for himself.

He dressed quickly and climbed up the stairs to where several English guards were watching the surrounding countryside. He stared disconsolately as the six riders grew smaller and smaller, and finally disappeared, and wondered who among them would not reach Avignon.

During the ride to Windsor, Alejandro stayed close to the leader of his escort, who had served with King Edward in France, and had become accomplished in the language. Alejandro pestered him continually, inquiring about the names of common everyday items, requesting advice on the proper way to greet, address, and take leave of the English royals. His tutor was at first amused, but eventually grew tired of the young man's incessant questions. He was glad to reach the gates of the castle and deliver Alejandro to his destination.

He found Windsor to be an enormous stronghold, with thick stone walls and magnificent towers rising high above the level of the surrounding forest. A man of stately carriage, attired in rich garments and with a noble air, greeted the physician in the lower courtyard.

"I am Sir John Chandos, advisor to King Edward and the prince of Wales, and I bid you welcome to our fair keep." The physician returned the man's neat bow, feeling rather clumsy. He was not accustomed to this courtly behavior.

"*Pardon, monsieur, je ne comprends pas.*"

"Ah, yes," he said in French. "Our coarse language is unknown to you. *Moi aussi, je préfère la langue française.*" He continued in French, deferring to Alejandro's need for a common tongue between them. "I am to accompany you to your apartment on the east terrace of the castle. We have prepared a suite of rooms for your stay, which I trust you shall find acceptable. The king has gone to great expense to see that His Holiness' ambassador be given every consideration while staying in our kingdom."

Alejandro followed Sir John through the courtyards, into the residential section of the castle. The rooms and passageways were all brightly lit with torches and candles, and as he passed beneath them he said, "I see that oil is not so dear in England as it is in Spain."

Sir John laughed. "Oh, it is dear enough, but our king will not tolerate darkness in Windsor."

They walked through a huge hall with an arched ceiling whose walls were hung with woven panels depicting glorious battle scenes. Three sets of swords were crossed over the hearth, encircled by several racks of giant antlers.

"What behemoth sported those horns?" Alejandro asked, pointing overhead. "And does such an animal live nearby? If so, tell me how I may avoid it."

Sir John laughed. "You need not fear, for those horns are very old, and come from Irish elk; they were brought back from the bogs of Ireland by King Edward's father. None have been seen for hundreds of years, though they were said to be twice the size of a good horse."

"They look more to have come from a good tree than a horse," he said. "Everything here is so grand! I feel myself dwarfed. Are these Plantagenets such giants, then?"

"You would think so were you to see them in battle," Sir John said, flushing with pride. "They have the look of Goliath in armor."

And I am no David, Alejandro thought.

A long table, large enough to seat several families, dominated the center of the room; it was surrounded by dozens of chairs, all richly carved. The diamond-patterned floor was made of smooth marble in alternating colors of brown and black, with woven rugs and animal skins scattered about. As they left the room, they entered a long, brightly lit corridor. Turning right at its end, they continued walking past several closed doors, finally stopping at a small alcove.

Sir John opened the door and showed Alejandro through. The physician entered, looking around at his new home, awed by the fine furnishings and rich appointments.

"I believe you will find these rooms most comfortable, monsieur. You need only pull this bell cord for service, and your manservant will arrive shortly to ask your bidding." Sir John paused, briefly allowing Alejandro to look around, then continued, "The family will gather for dinner in the grand hall at the sound of seven bells. It will be the king's pleasure for you to join his repast. I will leave you now; I look forward to your company later. Good evening, Dr. Hernandez."

At the sound of the bells Alejandro stopped his unpacking and listened carefully, counting to be sure of the time. He counted seven. Once again, he checked his apparel to see that it was in perfect order, for he had never worn such finery before, and had to think carefully about the proper wearing of each garment. With a final smoothing of the detested breeches he left his rooms and headed toward the great hall.

If he had found this room exquisite before, it was made even more so by the handsome company gathered there. A large assembly of splendidly attired people were listening to a minstrel who walked among them, his lute suspended from his shoulder by a colorfully embroidered strap.

A comely woman, fair and plump, sat in one of a pair of large wooden chairs with red velvet upholstery. Despite the radiance of her garments and jewels the woman had the pained look of deep sorrow on her face. He thought, *This is the queen, whose daughter has so recently been taken from her. It is no wonder she looks so burdened. . . .*

Alejandro looked around at the other occupants of the room. He stood back, hiding himself in the entry, observing the luminous gathering while avoiding discovery. There was much to notice here. He tried to guess which of these people were the sons and daughters of the royal couple. Nearly all were fair of skin and hair, with light eyes of blue or gray. One of the young ladies was heavily adorned with glittering jewels, and draped in lustrous satin; he took her to be a princess. One had hair of the most lustrous copper color—

Alejandro's clandestine observation was abruptly interrupted by the sound of a clarion, announcing the entry of an important person.

A man wearing a narrow gold crown in his graying hair strode briskly into the room, followed closely by a well-dressed younger man of similar appearance. Both were a good head taller than he himself, and both were blessed with fine manly figures. He would have taken them to be warriors of some note were they wearing armor. No one would fail to notice that they were father and son, nor would anyone fail to see that they were royal, or thought themselves to be. The assembly bowed nearly in unison as the king continued walking. The prince fell back and took his place among the others. Eventually, the king stopped in front of the seated woman Alejandro had taken to be the queen. He held out his hand to her, his eyes sparkling as he gazed upon her and, giggling like a girl, she placed her hand in his. He pulled her gently up to standing.

"My queen," said the king, and gently kissed her hand. He led her through the bowing crowd and saw to it that she was comfortably seated, then walked ceremoniously to the other end of the table and lowered himself into a high-backed wood chair with velvet cushions. Once settled, he exhorted his guests to do the same.

There was a general scuffling of chairs as the guests arranged themselves around the great table. Alejandro saw one unoccupied seat, and
realized to his embarrassment that it was probably for himself. He hastily
started to enter the room, when he saw Sir John rise quickly from his
seat, heading in his direction.

"Your Majesty," Sir John said as he quickly approached the entering
physician, "permit me to present Dr. Hernandez, the medical emissary
sent to us by His Holiness Pope Clement. He has arrived just this afternoon."

All eyes went immediately to Alejandro, including the piercing blue
eyes of the king. The sovereign's scrutiny of his unfamiliar guest was swift
and penetrating. He examined the young man minutely, for Edward did
not much like Clement, and trusted him even less. Despite their solicitous correspondence neither man was convinced of the other's benefi-
cent intentions.

Alejandro stood still for the intrusive inspection, not knowing what
to do. Sir John held his shoulders fast, and Alejandro remained stationary, willing to let the knight be his guide.

Finally King Edward relaxed his gaze and said, "We are delighted,
Dr. Hernandez, that you have traveled so far to be with our family. It is
kind and generous of His Holiness to see to our protection by providing
us with your services. Please join us for our evening meal. We are anxious
to hear the news from Avignon, and shall depend on you to deliver it."

The king nodded in the direction of the empty chair, and Alejandro
felt himself guided toward it by the accommodating Sir John. He sat
down and pulled his chair in toward the table. To his right was the fair
and willowy princess he had noticed earlier. He looked at her and smiled
politely.

"My father does not tolerate tardiness in his guests," she said.

She looked directly at Alejandro and smiled coyly, and he felt all
eyes turn toward him, waiting, no doubt, for his response.

This would be the impertinent Isabella, he thought. *She is all de
Chauliac said she would be.* "Nor should he," Alejandro said, "for a king
deserves the highest regard from all his subjects." Alejandro turned
toward the king and plaintively continued, "Please forgive my rudeness,
Your Majesty, for I am untutored in the customs of your kingdom. I am
an ignorant Spaniard, a long way from the comforts of my home."

He could not have done better, for the king prided himself on the
graciousness of his court and was fanatically dedicated to the perfection
of the art of hospitality. "We shall see that you are tutored in our ways,

sir, so that you may feel comfortable here. I cannot tolerate any discomfort in my guests."

Then the king laughed heartily. "According to the Holy Father, young man, you are far from ignorant. He has high praise and great esteem for your skills as a physician. But now you must forgive my ignorance, for I am remiss in my duties as your host. Please allow me to present you to my beloved Queen Philippa," and he motioned in the queen's direction.

Alejandro stood quickly, nearly knocking over his chair, and bowed deeply to the queen, who graciously nodded back. Hushed giggles rose up from the younger girls in the room, who found his sincere but clumsy bow very amusing.

"Please resume your seat, monsieur. It is I who am honored by your learned presence."

Alejandro did as the queen had requested, blushing with embarrassment at his unsuccessful attempt to be polite.

"Dr. Hernandez," the king continued, "it is my sincere hope that you can prescribe a treatment for my daughter's sharp and hasty tongue." He gestured in the direction of the girl who had earlier chastised him, and Alejandro saw the fuming look on her face. "We all suffer from Isabella's uncontrollable urge to correct our imperfections. But look first to me for the cause of her affliction. I have spoiled my Isabella, and can blame no one but myself. I will now have you meet my son Edward, the prince of Wales."

The young man who had entered with the king said, "We are blessed by your presence, Doctor," as he motioned for Alejandro to remain seated. "His Holiness has written much about your training and skills. He assures us you will bring our family safely through this scourge."

He has made too much of my skills, I fear, he thought to himself. *They did little good for the soldiers who fell ill on my journey here.* He resolved to give a more realistic description of what he might do for the royal family of England as soon as he could speak to the king in privacy, for he did not wish to alarm the ladies.

The conversation turned to news of Europa, and all ears were attuned to Alejandro's recounting of the journey from Avignon. He was grateful for the opportunity to speak, because his head was throbbing from the effort of listening to the two foreign tongues being spoken at the table. He told the group of his encounter with the revolting flagellants and of their barbaric attack on the traveling party; he described with great anguish the untimely death of the papal guards. The listeners were quietly attentive, each one absorbed in his own thoughts about Europa's bleak situation.

The prince of Wales perceived the somber change in the company's mood, and artfully steered the discourse in a lighter direction. "And how is it that you came to be in France, away from your native Spain, to capture the attention of the pope's physician?"

He stretched the truth. "I took my medical training in Montpellier. All trained physicians in the area surrounding Avignon were summoned to appear before the pope's personal physician, and he chose among us after observing our skills. Dr. de Chauliac imparted his special techniques for protecting the pope to those who were selected to go abroad."

The talk turned to other subjects, most of it beyond his understanding. A musician played lightly on a harp as a fool cavorted to the cheerful notes, delighting all, but especially pleasing one small girl who sat on the other side of the princess. Her squeals of laughter were charming, and her effervescent glee infectious. *Would that it were as infectious as the plague*, Alejandro thought.

Even though this family had lost one member to the plague, those gathered here seemed largely untouched by the cruelties happening in the rest of the world. Only the queen had the telltale look of sorrow and loss that was so common among the population of Europa. There was genuine gaiety here; the men were hale and robust, and the ladies gracious and charming. In this castle there was a miraculous immunity to the effects of the plague, and Alejandro thought that this was a most blessed and fortunate assembly. He resolved to do his best to see that their contentment was preserved.

Ten

Despite the bulge in his stomach from the big chunk of mutton he'd already consumed, Robert Sarin managed to down one more bite. Then he sat back and let out a loud, satisfied belch. He was surprised and pleased by the sudden and unaccountable increase in his appetite. He rubbed his hands over his bulging stomach while the dog sat next to him, wagging his tail and whining a little, *begging* for some of the bits left on his master's plate. The old man smiled and obliged his companion by offering him a good chunk of fat in his open palm. The dog neatly grabbed it with his teeth, never touching Sarin's skin, and swallowed it in one gulp. Sarin held his greasy hand still, and the dog licked it clean.

Knowing in his heart of hearts that he wouldn't be experiencing that or any other sensation too many more times, he allowed himself to enjoy the soft tickle of the dog's wet tongue on his calloused palm. He was learning to enjoy every pleasant sensation that came his way, and he dwelled on each of his own thoughts as if it were some great philosophical offering.

He thought it odd that fear could make him feel so alive. Now that he had dedicated himself to preparing for what lay ahead, he felt more energized than he had in years, as though a decade of aging had been stripped away in just a few days. Each breath came easier and each step was more springy. He had been out into his mother's garden and had put it right, more right than it had been in the very long time since she herself had been able to see to it. He had always loved the smell of its rich black earth; it smelled so fertile and damp and musky, as he imagined a woman might smell.

Each day he looked at his mother's book and committed the rituals more perfectly to memory. He had never known such memory before! The power of knowing things and then learning more things was nearly intoxicating to him. He knew there would come a time soon when he would be expected to use the things he had learned, and he was excited beyond anything he'd ever experienced. *If only*, he thought with sad regret, *she could have been alive to see it.*

When the meal was more settled in his belly, he rose from his chair to stretch his arms and legs. The cottage smelled wonderful, and Sarin was constantly flooded with memories of his mother now that the condition of the place had returned to what it was when she had still been in full command of herself. He called to the dog, and the big scruffy animal returned to his side, his pink tongue hanging out of a big doggy grin. Sarin patted the animal's head and said, "Sometimes it feels like she's not really gone." The dog wagged his tail in agreement and whined softly.

"It's like she's still right here helping me," Sarin said. He'd spent a good deal of time putting things right, feeling all the while as if she were looking protectively over his shoulder as he went about the work of maintenance, and it was only after he'd finished it all that he realized how far he had let things slide.

He knew that she had prayed for the task to come in her time of stewardship, and that no matter how carefully she instructed him—her only child—she would never believe that he would be ready if it happened in his time. "I should've known," she'd said bitterly as she neared her death. "I had a son. I should have known." And she was right, he thought, for he was the only male ever in a direct line of capable women through several centuries. Each daughter had borne a daughter by virtue of an old and closely guarded ritual, and had given the child her own name.

But she had told him that he had come from love, not ritual. He wondered how horrified his mother must have been to look down between her own bloody legs, there to see the small wailing wrinkled thing he had been after the protracted and difficult birth. He wondered if she had panicked and cried, and, most horrifying, if she had considered doing away with him. He could almost sense her defiance in that moment of decision, her unwillingness to do what was required of her by tradition and custom. She was an angry young girl, struggling with an imperfect baby, shaking her fist at six hundred years of compliance on the part of her ancestors. And as time passed and her defiance dissipated, he had sensed her regret. "I knew what was required of me," she'd told him once, "and I didn't do it. There is no one to blame but myself." And thereafter she had complied with everything that was required of her, in all matters but the care of her impaired son.

That son, now a man of great age, stooped down and stepped through the low door into the cool outside air. His old eyes followed the darting silhouette of a ragged man who slipped between the trees. He reached down and patted the dog's head. "There's one of them now," he whispered to the panting, grinning canine. "I wonder why they don't come to visit more often."

Why, Janie wondered with great annoyance, *does the telephone al-ways ring when I have a mouthful of toothpaste?* She was tempted to let the hotel's voice mail pick up the call, but remembering that it might be Caroline, she spat and ran instead, catching the call just before the fifth ring when the system would have automatically kicked in. After a minty smack of her lips she said, "Hello?"

Bruce said, "Good morning."

She thought about pretending not to recognize his voice, just to throw him off track. But she was determined to be a kinder, gentler Janie, especially in view of his princely behavior the night before.

Actually, she thought to herself, *a hornier, more hormonal Janie, with a newly reawakened libido, would be more accurate this morning.*

"Good morning to you too," she said.

"How did you sleep?" he asked.

She wondered if she should tell him that she had managed to dislodge the sheets from the bed without meaning to, and that what she had experienced for eight long and markedly lonely hours could hardly be called sleep, but more of a semiconscious toss-a-thon. She decided not to reveal the pounding headache that threatened to split her brain right down the middle every time she moved her neck even slightly. *Maybe he has aspirin,* she thought, and reconsidered her position.

"Oh, pretty well," she finally said. It wasn't a blatant lie, but she followed it up with one. "I feel very rested this morning. It must have been the wine."

"Lucky you," he said. "I tossed all night for some reason. Maybe it was the unfamiliar bed, I don't know. I usually do pretty well in unfamil-iar beds."

"Is that so?" Janie said, giggling. "Can you produce witnesses to support that claim?" Her giggles blossomed into full-fledged laughter.

There was complete silence on the other end of the line for a few seconds. "I set myself up for that one, didn't I?" Bruce finally said. "Maybe I should avoid engaging in conversation first thing in the morn-ing."

"Oh, I don't know about that," Janie said. "It was a cute thing to say. It feels good to start the day with a little laughter. And I'm sorry you didn't sleep well. Truth is, I could've done better myself. I think I just had too much wine."

"Maybe I didn't have *enough*. But a quart or two of coffee will probably cure what ails me. I'm going down to the coffee shop for some breakfast, if you care to join me."

"I'll be down in a few minutes, as soon as I finish getting dressed."

"I'll call the storage facility before I come down. Maybe they'll have heard something from Ted finally."

"Good idea. I think I'll try Caroline again too."

"Let's hope we both have good news to report when next we meet," he said, and they hung up.

Ted pulled the skin-patch thermometer away from his hot, clammy skin and looked at the gauge. "One-oh-three point seven," he said aloud, though there was no one to hear it. "Dear God." He sat down on the edge of his bed. As he lowered himself, he noticed that his knees ached. *Another symptom?* he thought silently. *What will be next?*

He was certain that he was suffering from much more than a cold. He'd slept fitfully, getting up several times in the night to drink water, and yet on awaking, his first thought was to drink more. He was hot and clammy, and his eyes had the rheumy look of disease, but what worried him more than anything was the swelling in his neck. It hadn't gone down at all; in fact, it had become more noticeable.

Now as he examined his neck, he saw dark areas where the swelling was more pronounced. He'd seen the symptoms of most modern diseases firsthand in the course of his work, but never had he come across anything like what he was now seeing in his own mirror.

He ran his hand over his neck. The lumps felt hard, and the slight pressure he applied produced the kind of dull ache he would have associated with a large, unresolved boil. "Ow!" He winced as his fingers dwelled on a particularly painful lump. He thought perhaps he should seek some medical help, but wondered how he could do so without attracting notice. He didn't like to let his coprofessionals know there was a chink in his armor of perfection, and if his undiagnosed ailment did in fact turn out to be more than a cold, the last thing he wanted was to be swallowed up in the slow-turning wheels of the medical system. With one misstep he'd be sucked into its great grinding gears, and he would not emerge until the authorities were satisfied that he was absolutely no threat to society. The irony of the fact that he himself was frequently one of those stern authorities was not lost on him.

He decided instead that the safest course of action would be to try self-diagnosis. He knew that all the programming he needed to chart and analyze his symptoms could be found in the medical library's computer system; he had selected that system himself. He knew he could rule out the worst possibilities before going any farther.

Every inch of his body ached as he struggled into his clothing. He winced as he pulled on a turtleneck sweater, but was satisfied to see upon looking in the mirror that it covered his neck bruises nicely. *Unfortunately,* he thought to himself as he tried to loosen the knit fabric hugging his neck, *it's bloody uncomfortable.* Before leaving the apartment he grabbed a light coat. Once outside he discovered that he needed it immediately, for despite the day's relative warmth, the air felt cold and raw to him. Not trusting himself to drive in his unwell state, he took a taxi, and sat shivering in the backseat during the entire trip.

The Institute's library was closed for the weekend and Ted assumed it would be unstaffed, though he knew there were a few people working in other sections of the building. Without the warmth and noise of human activity the Institute always seemed huge to him, like some giant cave into which he was absorbed every working day. But it was a cave of his own making, and it usually felt quite safe to him. Today, it seemed entirely too cavernous. As his concern over his condition grew, his surroundings took on false proportions; he began to feel very small and fragile, more and more out of control.

He let himself into the deserted library with a handprint. Looking around, he called out, "Hello?" When no one answered, he wasted no time in powering up the computer and logging on to the database. The program moved him along from frame to frame, asking for specific information in a pleasant, soothing voice. In the field marked PATIENT NAME he typed "Instructional session" so the computer would not record in its permanent database any of the information he was about to enter. This ploy also enabled him to bypass the time-consuming statistical data fields and proceed directly to the field marked SYMPTOMS. *Get this done before you're too sick to do it,* he cautioned himself. In the symptom section he touched on the boxes provided for fever, headache, swollen neck, stiffness, nausea.

The machine made him wait for a few moments as the information was sent out over the wires. The wait, no more than fifteen or twenty seconds, seemed interminable to him. Distortion had spilled over from his physical self and invaded his sense of time, and as he waited he began to feel slightly disoriented. He felt almost rescued when a list of potential diagnoses came up on the screen and the computer then asked him to touch the boxes for which he wanted additional information.

But the list before him was far from comforting. His panic grew as he read through it.

Hodgkin's disease: a lymphatic cancer. . . .

He passed it by.

Influenza: a viral upper respiratory condition. . . .

He marked it.

Mononucleosis: a viral disease causing marked fatigue. . . .

Maybe. But probably not.

Mumps: a viral childhood disease characterized by. . . .

Been immunized.

Plague: a bacterial condition caused by the bacterium Yersinia pestis. . . .

He stopped reading and stared at the screen. *Yersinia pestis.* He had
seen that name recently but couldn't make his brain connect it to anything. He sat back and concentrated, and was soon enormously frustrated
by his inability to recall this small but apparently important detail. He
didn't yet know that a newly born relative of the bacterium with the
familiar but intangible name was in fact the cause of his infuriating
lapses in memory.

When it finally came to him where he'd seen it, he quietly disconnected from the network and shut down the computer. He sat in the
chair staring blankly at the gray, unlit screen, trembling, his heart beating
wildly, and though he didn't move for several minutes, sweat literally
poured off his forehead and upper lip. He stood up, and a wave of nausea
overtook him, so he heaved into a nearby wastebasket. His retching was
dry and unproductive, for he'd had no appetite since taking ill and there
was nothing in his rebellious stomach that could be expelled.

When his belly finally stopped lurching, he closed the library and
walked slowly to the lab. He was terrified of what he would find when he
got there, but he had to know. It was simply too much of a coincidence
to be ignored.

He walked slowly through the white-and-pastel hallways, one hand
on the wall for balance, the other holding his aching belly. During the
weekend the automatic timers turned on only every third bulb, and

though cheerful when fully illuminated, the corridors seemed gloomy as he passed through them. His own brain felt as dim as the spare light; every footstep he took echoed off the freshly polished floors and reverberated in his ears, jarring him, dulling him even further.

When he reached the lab, he went straight for the book Frank had left lying open next to the computer system containing the Microorganism ID program. He picked up the book and had started to flip the pages toward the enterobacteria section when he noticed a piece of paper with a large graphic left lying under the book. He picked it up and examined it more closely. In the lower left corner was the file and date information. Printed there he saw the date on which Frank had died, and the name "Gertrude."

The file name brought on another frustrating neural tweak. He closed his eyes and searched his brain, willing it to drag up the information he needed. *My head feels so thick,* he thought, and wondered if what he was feeling approximated what a naturally stupid person experienced every day. In a moment of triumph he finally recalled questioning Caroline about the name Gertrude. She'd told him it was name they'd given to the microbe Frank had discovered on their fabric sample.

The same sample that had been exposed to the explosion of *P. coli* earlier that morning.

He had handled the sample, and so had Caroline. Ted didn't recall seeing either Janie or Bruce touch it. He thought it unlikely that Bruce had had any contact with it, but the other woman certainly could have.

I've got to find that fabric . . . if I can just wade out of this mental swamp. . . .

He powered up both computers. Each one, at his insistence, had a "prevops" function allowing the user to recall any previous operations performed on the system, enabling that or any subsequent user to get right back into any program exactly where it had been exited. The dates, times, and operators were listed to streamline the search. Ted had responded to complaints that it was an insidious way for supervisory personnel to keep tabs on what the techs were doing and when they were doing it by ordering the programmers to add the same function to every computer at the Institute. Two technicians immediately resigned. He had promptly replaced them with more compliant personnel.

He went first to the microscope system where Frank had left the fabric sample. He called up the prevops list and went back to the day Frank had died. On the list were three files: Gertrude, Frank, and Frank2. Then he moved to the system where MIC was installed.

Right there on the list, just after "Frank2," was the entry "MIC ID *Yersinia pestis.*"

His mind raced with the horrifying possibilities as he entered the MIC program and called up the file for the *Yersinia pestis* graphic. He held the print of Gertrude in his hand, ready to make a visual comparison between the graphic due up on the screen and the print itself. In a few seconds the image scrolled onto the screen from top to bottom. They were nearly identical; he didn't need a computer to tell him that they were the same microbe.

His fingers trembled on the computer keyboard as he exited the program and logged back in to the database he had explored in the library. He was blubbering softly to himself, hovering on the edge of tears. *They'll find me somehow. They'll come for me in their green suits and put me in one of those big yellow biohazard bags and just haul me away. . . .*

This time he bypassed the symptom search entirely and went directly to the file for plague.

> A *bacterial disease caused by the enterobacterium* Yersinia pestis, *plague is still found in significant pockets throughout the world, specifically in Southeast Asia (Vietnam, China) and the American Southwest. Bacteria are carried by fleas living on rodents and small mammals; large mammals such as deer and cattle are occasionally found to be carriers. If the bacterium is transferred to the flea when it bites the carrier, it multiplies in the flea's digestive tract until the insect's stomach becomes engorged with bacteria. Upon biting another animal, the flea regurgitates the microbe into the bloodstream of the bite victim, who is then infected. Disease may also be spread by direct contact with infectious material such as body fluids or contaminated clothing.*

Sweat dripped off his face, drenching the front of his turtleneck.

> *There are three forms of the disease, all caused by the same microbe. In the bubonic form, early symptoms include fever, headaches, minimal swelling of the lymph glands, especially in the neck and groin areas. If untreated the disease progresses rapidly to more pronounced symptoms, including massive swelling of the lymph nodes, with bleeding into the surrounding tissues. Pustules (buboes) form within the nodes themselves and often appear as raised boils on the surface of the node area. There may be marked pain, especially in the joints and extremities.*

Patients may experience memory deterioration and may exhibit antisocial or uncharacteristic behavior. Profound depression may occur.

Ted touched his neck involuntarily, palpating again, as if his head refused to believe what he already knew in his heart to be true. He read on.

If left untreated bubonic plague frequently develops into pneumonic plague, in which bacteria overwhelm the respiratory system by coating the inside surface of the lungs. In this form the disease is most contagious, for the aspirated sputum and fluid droplets exhaled during normal respiration often carry viable bacteria.

He placed his hand over his mouth as he breathed.

Septicemic plague occurs when the bacteria spread to the blood-stream and vital organs. As the bacteria complete their normal life cycle and die off, large quantities of toxic effluent are released directly into the bloodstream; the kidneys and liver may become necrotic in their attempt to purge the system of toxins. The victim eventually succumbs to toxic shock. The course of this form of plague is usually very rapid, and it is almost invariably fatal.

He was sweating even more profusely now; he wiped his brow with his hand and then wiped his hand on his pant leg. He held up his hand and stared at it, wondering with horror how many millions of bacteria he had just introduced to the fabric of his pants. . . .

The treatment of choice is a prolonged course of oral and parenteral antibiotics. Most effective are streptomycin, chloramphenicol, and tetracycline. Boils may be lanced to relieve pressure and flushed with sterile saline solution in the bubonic form, but care should be taken that secondary infections do not occur as a result of the surgical procedure. In most cases treatment must be started within seventy-two hours of the development of symptoms to be effective. Serum containing antibodies from previous victims can be used to augment or replace traditional antibiotic treatments.
All patients should be isolated and any patients exposed to the disease should be quarantined until the maximum incubation period has passed (usually three weeks). Health-care providers should use universal

precautions when handling tissue or body products from infected or exposed persons.

By international agreement all cases of plague must be reported to the World Health Organization. The U.S. Centers for Disease Control can provide further information via its info-fax system.

Now completely frantic, Ted tried to count backward. With great difficulty he determined that it had been nearly forty-eight hours since he'd started feeling ill. He sat back and closed his eyes, his head pounding as bacteria-laden blood rushed through it. *This is wild,* he thought, panicking, *this is completely insane. This is the twenty-first century, not the Middle Ages! How did this happen?*

But Ted already knew the answer to that question. He had screwed up; he was entirely responsible for this mess, and there was a very tangible paper trail to prove it, some of which was not within his immediate control. As a result of his own incompetence he was suffering from a potentially fatal and highly infectious disease, and if he sought treatment through normal channels, the whole scientific community would discover what had happened. He would never be able to reconstruct his orderly, precise life.

He knew he needed treatment; he would probably die without it. But it was impossible for him to go to his assigned physician. He knew he would have to go directly to the Institute's medical offices and get what he needed without anyone else knowing he had done so.

He left the lab and stumbled his way down the poorly lit corridors to the medical offices. *Please don't let anyone see me,* he prayed to any god who would listen. His frantic prayer was answered, for he arrived undetected to find the offices completely shut down. He could simply wade right in and help himself to whatever pharmaceuticals he needed. He knew the medications were stored by type, so he went directly to the area in which all the antibiotics were shelved, including those now obsolete and the few that were still slightly effective.

He pawed his way through row after row of pathetically useless vials, and wondered why they were still in storage. *Hope springs eternal,* he thought. *We were so stupid. Why weren't we more careful in using these drugs?* One by one all the antibiotics on which humanity had once depended had become ineffective against the bacteria they'd been developed to control. The days were long gone when a child was brought by a slightly worried mother to a clinic for a strep throat only to be sent home with an armload of antibiotics. Now, he knew, those children died in isolation wards, their bodies completely ravaged by feasting microbes that had made better genetic adaptations for survival than their human hosts.

But this is an old disease, and an old drug might do what I need it to do. The thought reassured him, but only briefly, and then he began to panic again, wondering what he would do if there was no supply of at least one of the drugs he needed. The three antibiotics named in the computer program were more archaic than most. All three had ceased to be effective on most strains of bacteria more than five years ago, and no new supplies were being manufactured. He hoped desperately that some pack-rat pharmacist with a sense of history had stored some for posterity, just to drag it out every now and then to impress some young trainee with the difficulties of archaic treatment regimens. *We walked ten miles each way to the pharmacist in the snow and wind every day . . .* or, the more likely scenario, he hoped that someone had been lazy about cleaning out old frozen samples. *Oh, dear God, please let there be some still here . . . it's my only hope!* He would have to do a lot of explaining to obtain the antibodies of a previous victim if the drugs were not available.

Hair of the dog that bit you, he thought, and despite his sheer terror he almost laughed.

Ten achingly long minutes passed before he found three frozen vials of injectable tetracycline in the back of a freezer. His hands were numb and he had to stop to warm them before he risked taking the precious vials out of the unit. If he dropped any one of them, he would probably die, as would Caroline if she were also infected, and perhaps a lot of other people.

He had to rest; his heart was beating rapidly again and his head was feeling even thicker than before. He reflected miserably on the fact that he had gone to a computer for diagnosis and treatment without ever speaking with a human being. Compudoc franchises were springing up as McDonald's restaurants had just a few decades earlier, their neon green caduceus signs now as recognizable as the Golden Arches once were. He could see the whole horrible scenario in his mind's eye: thousands of plague victims attached at the wrist to those computerized monsters, their necks swelling, their eyes bulging, sweat pouring off of them and onto the surrounding street or floor, each victim guarded by a merciless Biocop who would shoot before asking questions.

Stop wasting time! he told himself furiously, forcing himself to stand up. *You don't have any to waste!* He grabbed a handful of syringes from a supply cabinet and stuffed all but one in his pocket. He would use that one to inject himself with a good dose of tetracycline as soon as it thawed. *This time I'll be careful to loosen the stopper before too much pressure builds up.* . . . Out of the corner of his eye he spied a bottle of aspirin in a glass cabinet. He grabbed it and stuffed it into his pocket along with the other items. Armed with a complete arsenal against his silent attacker, Ted turned off the light and headed back to the lab again. There were tracks still to be covered.

He could destroy all the evidence of his ineptitude except the list of supplies he had given to Frank, but without the associated computer files, it wouldn't mean much. He knew he could easily destroy the files and the programs that supported them. Without hesitation he powered up both systems.

He bypassed the operating system completely and went straight to the root directory. *God bless the ghost of DOS,* he thought gratefully. At the prompt, he typed in:

Delete *.*

He pressed enter. A message came up on the screen.

All files will be deleted! Are you sure? (y,n)

He typed *y.*

Please enter your password.

After he complied, there was a moment or two of soft whirring as everything on the hard disk self-destructed. Then the screen went blank, signifying the death of an artificial intelligence. A million dollars' worth of software development expired in a brief blip of electrons. He repeated the procedure on the second system, without mercy, without remorse.

Then Ted got up and walked unsteadily to the storage unit where he thought he'd seen Caroline store the sample of the fabric, and looked at the shelf where the smaller items were kept. But the fabric still wasn't there. After fifteen minutes of tearing the unit apart he gave up. He tried to think where Caroline might have moved it. There was no other logical place at the Institute to store it. The remainder of the freezer units were secured because of the toxic nature of their contents. He thought it ironic that of the items that had passed through this lab, that sample, perhaps the least well secured, was among the deadliest. Nearly half of the population of Europe and Asia had fallen prey to bubonic plague in the fourteenth century. *And it could happen again,* he thought, *now that different strains of bacteria regularly shared genetic material encoded for drug resistance.* Enraged, he kicked a nearby chair. His foot throbbed miserably, and incoherently blubbering, he sat down.

The parking lot was full when Janie and Bruce arrived at the storage facility in Leeds, so Bruce parked the car just outside the gate on the access road. They retrieved their briefcases from the backseat and walked to the main security area, where Bruce resumed negotiations with the security guard, picking up where he'd left off the day before. He had found out in his earlier call to the facility that Ted had not made contact with them. Still, there was a hopeful sense of anticipation in the air as he and Janie entered the building. One way or the other they would soon know the nature of the beast they faced.

The guard flipped through the pile of papers Bruce had filled out. "I've run all the clearances, and I'm happy to say that you're in good shape. Sorry we couldn't clear you yesterday afternoon. You understand we can't be too careful. You can come right through and we'll bring the items up from the holding area." He glanced at Janie briefly. "Your companion will have to wait out here, but it shouldn't take too long. Step this way, please."

The guard turned and walked toward the entry door to the waiting area. Bruce gave Janie a smile and made the thumbs-up sign; she smiled back at him and mimicked his reassuring gesture. She was immensely relieved to know that the soil samples would soon be in her possession again. And she was filled with gratitude for they way Bruce had helped her; he'd revealed an admirable depth of character in seeing her through her difficulties. She found herself liking and respecting him more every minute.

She stood in the waiting area and fidgeted impatiently as Bruce followed the guard away. She flipped her hair nervously and tucked a few unruly strands behind her ear. Suddenly she was aware of something falling lightly on her chest. She looked down and watched with annoyance as one of her earrings fell to the floor and started rolling away. It tumbled crazily toward the security gate with surprising and alarming speed. Instinctively, Janie stepped forward to stop it, and reached down to pick it up.

It went just a centimeter too far. As soon as her hand crossed the vertical plane of the security gate's scanner, it read her genetic material and compared the readings to a database of bodyprints. It would record that she had passed through the gate at the precise date and time when the scan had occurred. But unlike the match that occurred when Bruce passed through, the computer found no match for Janie, and became understandably annoyed. Within a few seconds a loud electronic alarm blared, *You can't do that!* and the guard whipped around to see what was setting it off. In less than a second he had his weapon drawn and aimed at Bruce, who stood between him and Janie.

"Don't move, either of you," he said sternly.

As were all guards at medical facilities, he was trained to assume the worst possibility in each situation and then downsize his reaction as dictated by a cautious analysis of the circumstances. *Use your last resort first,* they'd told him in boot camp. He pointed his weapon directly at the "intruders," leaving both Janie and Bruce with no doubt that any sudden move would bring a quick end to both of their lives.

When his captives were immobile enough to satisfy him, the guard said, "Step aside, please, Dr. Ransom." Though his words were polite, Bruce knew that this man meant business. But he remained calm and stood his ground, stupefying Janie with this dangerous act of protection. He said to the guard, "What are you going to do to her?"

"I'm afraid I have to take you *both* into custody, sir."

"*Both of us?*" he said in disbelief. "What about my clearances?"

The guard looked down the barrel of the weapon and said, "Sir, as you know, access to this facility is strictly limited. Some professional civilians such as yourself may enter once the proper clearances have been secured, but we never allow unprinted individuals to enter. *Never*," he repeated for emphasis. "That alarm indicates that the lady is unprinted."

Bruce was furious. "This is outrageous! I've never heard this regulation before." And just as he was about to protest further, four more Biocops ran into the entry area, their chemical rifles drawn. Janie and Bruce were quickly surrounded.

Soon thereafter they found themselves marching down a long corridor to the far end of one wing of the building, urged on by the hard tips of the rifle barrels on their backs. They entered what looked like an old jail area with barred cells. Janie was placed in one cell, and Bruce in another a few feet away. After closing both cell doors the Biocop walked to a small wall panel just out of reach of Bruce's cell and inserted a plastic card. He then pressed two buttons, and loud clicking sounds followed from both cell doors. The Biocop came back to each cell and rattled the door to be sure it was locked. As he left the room he said, "I'll be back later for your belongings." The main door slammed shut and the thud echoed menacingly through the small, sparsely furnished room.

Janie slumped down against the wall and hugged her knees, stunned at this sudden turn of events. Bruce just stood in his cell with his hands on the bars over his head, saying nothing. The silence between them was like a deadweight.

"Bruce?" Janie said quietly.

He didn't answer, but looked up and met her gaze with an agonized expression on his face.

"I don't think we're in Kansas anymore."

Eleven

Alejandro had his first audience with King Edward III in the dressing room of the king's private apartment.

Still attired in his dressing robe, a garment of lustrous cloth-of-gold that Alejandro thought a lesser king might covet for his robes of state, the monarch was engaged in his lengthy morning toilette. He waved Alejandro into the room without a word, then resumed his tasks, leaving the physician to wait in the corner.

Laid out before him was an assortment of fine garments, handsome shirts with full pleated sleeves, velvet breeches, doublets with intricate borders of pearls and gemstones. The king strode past the array and pointed decisively at his choices, and the servants took the rejected pieces away. Then they brought forth a stream of long stockings and fancy garters and silk underthings, and the handsome monarch scrutinized them with obvious pleasure.

He seems far too jovial for a king burdened with such woes, he thought privately. De Chauliac had said that England was at war, and if the whispers he had heard on his journey from Avignon were true, had nearly been bankrupted by the cost of it.

And then, too, there was the pestilence nipping at the very heels of Windsor.

"Sit down, Doctor," the king said. "We shall speak as my men dress me."

Alejandro looked the servants over carefully and decided that none had the look of a minister or advisor who might take offense at being excluded from the discussion of an important matter. *The tongues of servants can be easily made to wag for a small price*, he thought to himself. He said to the king, "Your Majesty, I think it advisable for us to speak first in private."

The king regarded him with surprise for a moment or two, and noted the serious look on the physician's face. "Very well," he said. He dismissed the servants, and they left the room immediately, the second one closing the door behind him. He gave Alejandro a pointed stare and said, "I am not accustomed to having my morning routine interrupted. I will make an exception owing to your lack of familiarity with our customs. You would be wise to learn mine. Now speak."

Perhaps not so jovial after all, Alejandro thought miserably, recon-

205

sidering the accuracy of his previous observations of the king. This was a far less hospitable monarch than the one who had so warmly received him the night before. He cleared his throat nervously. "Your Majesty," he began, "I am concerned about the glowing reports you have had from the pope. I fear that His Holiness may have made too much of my skills. In truth, Sire, neither I nor anyone else, de Chauliac included, can cure this pest. I am trained only to prevent infection by isolation. I did not want you to think otherwise."

Edward poured himself a tall goblet of watered-down wine and then offered one to his guest, who declined. After a sip he said, "Surely, Doctor, you are not as powerless before this plague as you would have me believe."

"Your Majesty, I am as adept at curing this pest as a snake is skilled at flapping its wings and flying."

The sovereign's sharp-featured face took on a look of exasperation, neatly conveying his annoyance. "Then in God's name, why did Clement send you here? 'Tis a long journey for no purpose."

"I have never been given the privilege of raising such questions to him directly, Your Majesty. It was my understanding that this journey of mine was made at *your* request. De Chauliac was always the intermediary. All of my instructions were given by the learned physician, whose enthusiasm for this work was truly zealous."

The King did not comment. He rubbed his forehead as if attempting to soothe away a headache. "This de Chauliac I do not know. Clement I know. Tell me about de Chauliac."

He could feel the king's blue eyes almost burning into him. He could not believe that this king, said by all to be shrewd and manipulative, would not have sufficient information about a man as important as de Chauliac. *Perhaps he tests me,* Alejandro thought, *to see if I will speak truthfully.* "He is a powerful man in his presence, and clever. He has a skillful way with words. He is a most learned man, a brilliant thinker, and an originator of ideas. He seems to have the complete confidence of the pope. But I think he changes skins as does a chameleon when the need arises. One minute honey passes through his lips, the next it is vinegar. As is meet to his end."

The king smiled slyly. "I had heard as much from other sources."

I have passed his test, Alejandro thought with almost visible relief, his suspicions confirmed.

Then Edward's grave look returned. "But what are we to do now, if you are unable to secure our safety?"

The physician tried to reassure the concerned monarch. "I am not completely without skills for the protection of your family. De Chauliac has armed me with the entirety of his knowledge of preventative methods. It was in this way that he thought I could serve you best."

The king made no immediate reply. Instead, he glanced at Alejandro, narrowing his eyes, and the physician felt himself being appraised again. He could almost feel the king wondering to himself, *What is the measure of this man?* He found it ironic that he was perhaps the most trustworthy physician that the pope could have sent to England, for he had no allegiance to the Church or any other kingdom. But there was no proof that he could offer without giving himself away as a Jew.

Finally the king broke his silence. "Speak to me then of what you must do. I will not allow any more of my children to fall to this curse."

"Sire, you desire that outcome no more than I. And I have come prepared with a method to achieve it. It is a complicated regimen combining careful isolation and various preventative treatments, and I am quite certain that it will *not* please those who are forced to follow it. My greatest fear is that your children will chafe at the rigors of the regimen. My hope for its success lies entirely in the willingness of the patients to cooperate."

Edward's look of frustration intensified. "You have met my son and daughter, Dr. Hernandez. What say you to your chances of controlling their behavior?"

The physician would not allow himself to be trapped into an admission of impotence with his work not yet even begun. *There will be time later for that . . .* he thought soberly. "Truthfully, Sire, I dare not say. The royal children, I am told, have become accustomed to considerable free will and independence. De Chauliac readily admits that the pope despises his confinement, labeling it an intolerable imprisonment."

Edward smirked, betraying his unflattering opinion of the pope's sybaritic habits. "He misses his chatelaine, no doubt. The good pontiff has never been one to deny himself the luxuries of a secular life. It is a wonder that he has not yet retracted his patronage from his physician as a way of evading the responsibility to behave sensibly."

"All wise men fear this pest, my lord, and one who is pope must be wise, no? The rich and powerful fall just as readily as the poor and helpless. The affliction makes no distinction between them."

Edward agreed. "I am a wise king, I assure you. I fear it more than the bloodiest battle." In a firm voice he said, "I have survived more than my share of those."

"This battle we now face will not be bloody, but it will require bravery and resolve."

"England has both in great measure, be sure of it."

"Well, then," Alejandro said, standing up, "this is what must be done. We must begin by closing off the castle entirely. No one is to go in or out without a period of quarantine; no goods may pass through the gate without first resting outside for a period of time. You must tell the warders to bring in whatever supplies will be needed for three months, at the very least." In a deep state of concentration he began to pace around the audience room. "Staples of food must be stored, and more animals brought in to be slaughtered for meat. You must prepare, it seems to me, as if you were to be under siege. Bring in everything you might need. Then keep everyone and everything else out."

When he finished speaking, Alejandro looked at the king, waiting for a response. The monarch looked terribly distressed. "You are right, Physician; this will not be well received. Is there no other way?"

"None that has been made known to me, and you know the success of my teacher."

Edward went to the window and looked out at the surrounding countryside. He sighed deeply. "Do what you must," he said. "I will make it known that you have my authority."

The king dismissed him after discussing only a few more details, leaving Alejandro to his own devices. The physician took a few hours to stroll around the grounds of Windsor, making note of all the entries and exits, looking into conditions in the kitchens and laundries, inspecting the privies. It was an enormous keep and made the papal palace seem small in comparison, and though it was no less lavish in its appointments, Alejandro thought that de Chauliac's observation was correct: the French sense of beauty was more refined. The stones of Windsor were larger and more crudely cut, the tapestries more roughly woven, the boards of the floors less perfectly smooth. At Windsor, too, there was scaffolding, for the king was in the process of increasing its size dramatically, to be more in keeping with the greatness he intended for the English realm. It was a magnificent work in progress, evolving daily in accord with the dreams of its master, who would one day soon be able to claim that England's rulers were majestically housed.

He began his implementation of de Chauliac's regimen later that day by convening an assembly of the royal astrologers. While the king dismissed their ministrations as foolish quackery, Queen Philippa relied heavily on their daily forewarnings, and Edward was begrudgingly tolerant of her dependence on them.

"I retain three practitioners," the queen explained at their first interview. "My husband considers this to be an extravagance. He says one should suffice, but I will not hear of parting with them." She smiled sweetly, showing signs of the great beauty she had been in her youth, and said, "Of course, he would not give up one of his dressing-men for all the gold on Cleopatra's barge. Nor shall I give up any of my own pleasures."

"Then, if it pleases you, Your Majesty," he said, "please ask your astrologers to prepare a schedule of times when it would be auspicious for each member of the household to bathe and eat, and ask them also to advise us on what foods would preserve the health as well."

"An enormous task!" the queen said. "They will surely protest."

"But necessary," Alejandro said. "I beg your indulgence to convince them of the importance of this intelligence. The health of Windsor's occupants may depend on it."

Begrudgingly, the queen agreed to his request, but their efforts were not as fruitful as he'd hoped they would be. The immediate result of their occult divinings was a kitchenful of very cross cooks, and a family of cross diners, for seldom could the astrologers and their patients agree that one dish would be beneficial to the entire family on a particular day. Nor were the chambermaids pleased to be carrying buckets of hot water to the tubs of their mistresses at the odd hours when the astrologers deemed it appropriate for them to bathe.

But those problems seemed mere annoyances on the day when one of the practitioners said to the queen, "There are certain days when marital relations between yourself and the king will be most beneficial to your health. Unfortunately, there are others when the opposite result may be expected. I have prepared a calendar for your use."

When the apologetic queen relayed this information to her husband, he exploded in outrage. "The sniveling heretics! How dare they even *think* to instruct me in matters of my bedchamber! Enough of this nonsense. I will hear no more of it!"

"Edward, they think only to protect us. The physician said—"

He interrupted her. "Perhaps they could use their skills to find me another lady whose company would be deemed appropriate by the heavenly guides when yours is not favorable."

The queen left in a huff, and the astrologers' practice was limited thereafter to those matters not concerning the king's intimate enjoyment of his wife's company.

Having determined the limit of his ability to influence the behavior of the king, Alejandro, already somewhat discouraged, turned his attention to the amount of access given to those who did not live on the castle grounds, hoping for more cooperation from the captain of the king's guard. But he discovered when he went looking for the man that he had decided to leave Windsor to return to his family, with the reluctant permission of the king. In his place Alejandro found Sir John Chandos, who had agreed to take the captain's place temporarily.

"I rejoice to see you in such employ," Alejandro said. "The sight of a reasonable man is welcome indeed. I have had much resistance from others, and having barely begun my tasks, I feel thwarted already."

"I shall try to accommodate you, Physician," Chandos said, "where it can be done."

"I expected nothing less from you, sir," Alejandro said. "Now, this is what we shall need to do. We must close the castle completely, and allow no one to enter without a strict quarantine."

"Of what duration?" Sir John said.

"A fortnight, I think, will suffice."

"And if one leaves, what then?"

"No different," he said.

"Then where shall the king's men practice at arms?"

Alejandro looked around the grounds. "Here, I think."

"In the courtyards? There is not room enough!"

"It will have to suffice, unfortunately, Sir John. Once the gates are closed, no one may go out and return without quarantine, no matter how brief the duration."

"What of repairs to the armaments, and supplies for the barracks?"

"Can they not be arranged in advance? Is there an armorer willing to come in for the duration?"

"Willing or not, I will find one and convince him," Chandos said.

Another man pressed into service by necessity, he thought, considering his own indenture under the pope. "Do what must be done, Sir John, and we will hope for a short internment," he said. "God willing, we shall not be bound up in here for long."

Then the workers of the castle were assembled and told of the plan to encapsulate Windsor into a self-contained unit until the plague passed. Objections were immediate and strenuous. Saddlers, bow makers, tailors, and all manner of craftsmen were to be kept outside the barred doors at Alejandro's insistence. All foods and grain supplies, including feed for the animals, were to be discarded and fresh supplies brought in to replace them. All cupboards and closets and containers were to be emptied and washed and in pristine condition before they were refilled.

Every edict he announced before the crowd brought grumbles of discontent, but with patience and carefully chosen words, he managed to convince Windsor's occupants that the harsh restrictions imposed upon them would keep them from falling to the plague. Then he delivered the coup de grâce.

"Henceforth, all occupants of the castle shall bathe daily and don fresh garments. All worn garments are to be washed immediately. The laundresses shall keep a cauldron of water heated at all times for such purpose."

A virtual howl went up from the castle's residents. Alejandro clapped his hands angrily to get their attention. When he finally had it again, he said, "Would you all survive this pest to return to a state of normal sanitation, which seems to please you more?"

There were low grumblings, but none of the vehement objection he had heard a few moments before. "Then you must do as I say. I have the support of His Majesty in these matters."

As the crowd dispersed, Sir John, who had watched from the side, said, "You will be an unpopular man inside these walls."

Alejandro shrugged. "I have been unpopular before, far more so. But they will all forget their inconvenience when the gate opens again, and they are alive to see another year."

As he continued to enforce his mandates, Alejandro found to his amazement that the more forcefully he conveyed his orders, the more readily they were obeyed, even by the royal children, whose legendary lack of respect for authority seemed more truth than legend to him. But as de Chauliac had predicted, it was not long before their somewhat cheerful acquiescence began to change into resentful compliance. The war with France had been temporarily suspended, and the young men of the castle, championed by the Black Prince, grew restless from inactivity. They pleaded to be allowed to take their horses and armaments into the countryside for weaponry practice, and the king was in favor of this, claiming that the continued strength of his fighting force was equal in importance to their avoidance of the pestilence. Alejandro disagreed vehemently and would not hear of it, insisting that they be limited to refining their skills within the castle's courtyards.

The king seemed to grow more suspicious of his intentions every time they met. Alejandro began to wonder if Edward thought that he had some secret mission, that he was not a physician at all, but instead an agent of war for the French pope, perhaps trying to set in place restrictions that would reduce England's readiness for battle with France when the time came again, as all knew it would. It was not long before the physician's concerns were realized, and the king issued a stern warning.

"Physician, these things you make us do begin to seem treasonous to me. If your orders begin to sound to me like the insidious influence of the king of France to dilute the strength of my forces, I shall have you returned to His Holiness in chains."

Once more Alejandro felt the sting of the king's distrust, and the frustration of his own inability to substantiate his ambivalence. He could only say, "Sire, I am a Spaniard, and I bear no allegiance to France. Neither am I unduly directed by papist influence. I implore you to trust that my interest lies only in doing my task well and thoroughly. I am entirely dedicated to my craft, and my loyalty lies there alone."

This declaration seemed to satisfy the king for a time, and matters became relatively peaceful again. But it was not long before some of the king's retainers requested Alejandro's permission to leave Windsor's grounds and return to their own dominions.

When they approached him he said, "That is not for me to permit or refuse. That is the king's decision. What is mine to permit is your reentry. If you wish to come back after leaving, you must be quarantined in isolation until I deem it safe for you to mix with the other occupants again. If you become infected while outside, you may not show signs of infection until well after you are resettled, for it seems to me always that there is a time between when one victim shows signs, and then the next falls ill. It is the opinion of the pope's physician, who taught me his skills personally, that mere eye contact can pass the contagion from one person to the next." He did not add that he disagreed with this theory, for he was loath to compromise his own success in isolating the castle's inhabitants from the outside world by invalidating any superstition that worked to his benefit.

Still, many decided to go home to their families. Having already allowed the gate captain to depart, the king could hardly refuse, and gave reluctant permission for many of his best retainers and favorite knights to depart for their own keeps. One by one his comrades-in-arms left Windsor's comfort and safety on the uncertain journey to their various estates, most not knowing what would be found or what they would bring with them if they were fortunate enough to reach their homes.

The royal household having been thus diminished, the days passed more quietly than ever before. Alejandro thought it fortunate that the older royal offspring had suites of their own, or they might have made great nuisances of themselves in the constant search for entertainment. Prince Edward had three servants who attended to his needs, and the companionship of Sir John Chandos, who made a valiant effort to keep the prince and his comrades busy with sword practice and lessons in strategy. The younger Edward managed to amuse himself quite well, stoically accepting his fate and enduring it like that brave warrior he claimed he would one day become. The queen's ladies, accustomed to the entertainment of poets and minstrels and storytellers, kept themselves busy with embroidery, and took up the tasks of singing and reading to each other. Sweet soft voices and tentative strums of the lyre were always heard from their apartments. Alejandro even heard that some of them had taken up the dice, a thing that ladies rarely did, which he thought might account for the sudden increase in laughter he heard coming from that section of Windsor's living quarters.

The Princess Isabella, however, proved to be a great challenge to Alejandro, whose authority and rules she tested continually.

One morning he heard a timid knock on his door, and opened it to find a small maiden, just a child, whom he had once seen in Isabella's apartment, requesting his immediate attendance upon the princess. She curtsied neatly, her small hands holding the sides of her skirt as she did so. She brushed away an unruly golden ringlet and tried to tuck it under her cap. It disobeyed and fell free again, and she put one hand in front of her mouth and giggled. He could not help but smile in response.

"Yes?" he said.

She waited for a moment, then said, "Sir, will you not return my curtsy with a bow?"

"Ah, yes," he said, reddening, "Forgive me." He bent deeply at the waist, and then straightened. He saw her look of disapproval and said, "I have not yet mastered this skill of bowing. My apologies to you."

With a smile she said, "I accept your apology with thanks." Then she tried to take on the seriousness required for the mission on which she had been sent. She stood taller and said in a firm but tiny voice, "My lady is greatly distressed and in a foul humor because of Nurse's scolding." The little girl fidgeted impatiently while waiting for Alejandro's response.

"And what would the lady have me do to correct this intolerable situation?" he asked.

"She would have you settle certain matters in the presence of Nurse, who has invoked your edicts in order to restrict the princess' activities."

He smiled at her, amused by her self-assurance. "And what would be your own opinion in this dispute?"

The child smiled impishly, leading him to believe that she would like to make some naughty revelation disguised as her own opinion. "Sir, my opinion is of no consequence, for I am just a small child, and a female," she said, "but I will confess my belief that Nurse is continually seeking reasons to keep my sister in her cradle. She means to keep Isabella a child forever."

Ah, her sister! he thought, intrigued by the child. He pressed her further. "And of what age is your lady, that she has acquired sufficient wisdom to run her own affairs?"

"Sixteen" was her confident reply. "My sister is already twice betrothed, and now keeps her own household."

"Then I am not surprised by your obvious pride in her independence, for she has accomplished much at her tender age."

The child, now more at ease with her mission, beamed up at him, pleased with her own success in conveying the message. "Now we must hurry," she said, extending her hand to him, "or Isabella will be cross with me for delaying your arrival. She is rarely pleasant if she is kept waiting."

He took her hand briefly, then let it go. "Then let us be off at once, to see to Her Highness' needs."

As they neared Isabella's private apartments, Alejandro could hear the shrill cries of a young woman in the full fury of a tantrum, accompanied by the clatter of items being thrown around the room. The strained replies of an older woman could be intermittently heard above the racket. Outside the door the child motioned for him to stop, then held her finger to her lips to hush him, adding in a low voice, "Please wait here, sir. I shall announce your presence to the princess."

By the time the child returned, Alejandro had counted every stone in the wall and memorized the pattern of the tiles on the floor. Seated on a rather uncomfortable bench outside the princess' anteroom, he listened to the scurrying of servants beyond the door, and speculated about the mess that the rebellious Isabella had so audibly made. The child curtsied once again, so Alejandro politely stood up, proffering a slight bow.

"Will you have a seat, Princess?"

"Ah, thank you, sir. I am not inclined to sit just now. My lady awaits us. And please permit me to correct you: I am no princess. My name is Catherine, and I am called Kate by the members of our household."

"May I then have the honor of addressing you thus?"

The child giggled, relishing her grown-up role as Isabella's intermediary. "Sir, it is I who would be honored. Now let us enter the princess' apartment before she grows restless enough to make a shambles of the place again."

Kate opened the outer door and led Alejandro into the anteroom. It was large, full of light, and quite exquisitely appointed. The colors and patterns used in the rugs and tapestry gave the immediate impression of an extremely feminine occupant. He had passed by before, but he had not entered. He stared like a dumbfounded child.

"Do you admire my taste in furnishings, Dr. Hernandez?"

Alejandro was caught off guard by the princess' light voice at the other side of the anteroom. He turned to face her, prepared to bow in salutation. Since his first evening at Windsor, after nearly toppling the dinner table, he had practiced bowing over and over again, hoping to perfect the unfamiliar technique and avoid another embarrassment. His bow to Kate had been better, but before Isabella he was no more successful than the first time, for he stopped in midbow to catch his breath and stare in wonder at the young woman standing quietly next to Isabella. She had sat far away from him at his welcoming dinner, and he had not been able to see her features clearly in the evening light. But he remembered her hair.

He had seen hair of that burnished copper color before, but never on a woman whose skin was so nearly transparent. She was standing just slightly behind the tall, willowy princess, a small and delicate-looking lady wearing a rose-colored dress embroidered with white flowers. She appeared to be slightly older than her mistress, and though her carriage was clearly noble, she showed none of the imperious affect of the princess. Around her neck was a single strand of small gold beads from which dangled a gold cross with one gleaming ruby in its center. She kept her distance behind the princess, standing quite still, with her large eyes downcast, as if mesmerized by the intricate and colorful pattern of the woven rug below. Isabella, correctly aloof and waiting patiently for Alejandro to regain command of his senses, made no polite offer of introduction but looked directly at the doctor, who was completely lost in gawking at her companion.

"Dr. Hernandez? Are you feeling ill, sir?" she said, sounding annoyed. "Shall we pretend that you are the princess and I am the doctor?"

He managed to extricate himself from the entrancing spell of the quiet young woman well enough to respond to her mistress. "My apologies, Your Highness. The great beauty in this room simply held me captive for a moment." The bold but solicitous comment slipped off his tongue like honey, and he was startled by his own audacity.

The copper-haired woman at Isabella's side caught her breath, and brought her hand to her mouth, hiding what Alejandro thought might be a smile. He reluctantly dragged his eyes away from her enchanting face and looked at Isabella again. "I believe you summoned me. How can I be of service to you?"

"Well, since you have *finally* inquired, you may serve me best by allowing me to contact my personal clothiers and jewelers. Under your plan of confinement I have had to make do with garments that I would rather discard than wear, and they are degraded from this *nonsense* of constant washing. I am in desperate need of my tailor for immediate improvements in my wardrobe. Surely his presence here cannot be objectionable to you."

Her condescending tone of voice and contemptuous manner, her hauteur, were precisely what he'd been told to expect, but although de Chauliac had warned him, Alejandro was still not prepared for her acid tongue. *Take care not to offend her,* he thought. He wished with all his being that de Chauliac had given him some training in diplomacy as well as medicine. It would have been a great pleasure to say, *Take two drops of this vegetal potion in your wine, Your Highness, and your arrogance will be promptly cured,* but he suspected that such a prescription would not be well received.

"Is it not possible for the garments to be left outside in the prescribed manner, and then brought in for your inspection? Surely they will not go out of fashion in that short time."

He instantly regretted this barb when all the ladies in the room caught their breath in unison in anticipation of another tantrum. The woman at Isabella's side turned her head away, her hand still at her mouth. This time Alejandro was sure he saw her stifle a laugh. He looked furtively around the room, desperately seeking an ally in this battle of wits, finding no one willing to stand with him.

Remarkably, the princess did not explode in rage, but made a visible effort to contain herself before all the witnesses. She looked directly at Alejandro, and raising her chin in an affectation of superiority, she calmly delivered what he thought might be a killing blow.

"I shall speak to my father about this incident."

She turned away and looked at her titian-haired companion. "Come, Adele, we shall retire to the salon," she ordered, and led the way out of the anteroom. The red-haired lady finally raised her eyes and cast them in Alejandro's direction, meeting his gaze with one of equal intensity. But instead of the expected trepidation there was a twinkle of gaiety. She quickly followed her mistress, hurrying to catch up as Isabella strode determinedly away from the physician. She looked back once again before disappearing into the privacy of Isabella's salon.

Her eyes were green. Alejandro was speechless.

Kate escorted him back to his rooms, chatting brightly as they progressed. "My sister enjoys the fussy attention of her tailor nearly as much as she likes to wear the fine garments he makes for her. It will not satisfy her to have new finery simply sent in. Nurse suspects the tailor of bringing only those items that are plain but merit further beautification so that Isabella can spend even more of her income on fancy embroideries and buttons. The tailor himself would choose meaner baubles of bone and baked clay, Nurse says, thereby lessening his cost on the garment. Isabella invariably selects the choicest gold and silver, and the tailor's profits are increased without any effort on his part. Isabella is so enamored of his efforts that she fails to notice when he overcharges her." She giggled and snickered at her own scandalous revelation, as if it were a well-kept secret.

"And what says your mother about such extravagance?"

Kate hesitated before responding. At last she said, "My mother is not a member of this household, and her opinions are of even less consequence in matters pertaining to Isabella than are mine. She lives in London, and rarely hears the gossip concerning the royal family. When I visit with her, I always relate the intrigues of the court as best I can, but I don't always hear the most interesting things. Those things which my father deems inappropriate for a maiden's ears are kept from me."

So this child and Isabella share a father, he thought, *and it pains her to speak of her mother.* He decided to let his inquiry rest for a while.

Unaware of his musings, Kate said, "Do you enjoy chess?"

"I have never played, but I imagine that I would enjoy doing so if I only knew how."

"Shall I teach you, then?" she asked brightly.

"I would be delighted to learn such a valuable skill from such a charming teacher," he replied.

"Lovely!" she said. "I shall await you in the ladies' salon after dinner, then. I shall be glad to have a new partner, for none of my sister's women can match my skill, and I grow weary of letting them win."

"Does your sister's lady Adele play chess with you?" he asked.

"She does, but she cares little for the game, and is only a fair player. I think she prefers to read or embroider, and Isabella frequently monopolizes her time. I expect that your skills will quickly exceed hers, though you are a novice."

Alejandro laughed. "Do not expect great skill from me, Kate, for I know nothing of the game save what I have observed while here in Windsor. You will be sorely disappointed if you anticipate a good match immediately."

"Ah, monsieur," she finished, "I shall confine my expectations to the minimum for the immediate future, but tonight we shall see if you show any promise. My mother says I must always be prepared for the unexpected."

With the appropriate polite bows and curtsies, they parted.

Sir John Chandos appeared at his door not an hour after Kate left. Alejandro had grown friendly with the affable man, whose outwardly gruff appearance camouflaged a pleasant and cooperative demeanor.

"I do not envy you, monsieur," Chandos said, "for Isabella has been railing at King Edward for the better part of an hour, trying to convince him that your treatment methods are ill advised and not to be tolerated. She would have you sent back to Avignon immediately."

To what? he wondered. By now everyone in Avignon could be dead, for all they knew here in England. He regretted that he understood so little of the intrigue between the pope and this willful king, and how it might affect him.

He *did* know that France's king, whom Edward claimed was a usurper to his own rightful position on that throne, was far more strongly influenced by Pope Clement than his secular cousin Edward. He had been told this around the campfires on his journey to England. The captain of his escort knew many such wonderful intrigues, and there was little else to do after dark but tell lengthy and descriptive tales, which no doubt grew more illustrious with each new telling.

How Hernandez would have loved these campfires! he thought. But they had verged on treachery for Alejandro. On more than one occasion he had been forced to think quickly to create a personal history that would not betray his true identity, and when it came his turn to speak, he frequently astonished himself with the inventiveness of his fables. The captain had spoken at length about the war of more than a decade's duration, now in truce because the pest had carried off so many warriors, far more than had the fighting.

Emerging from his brief distraction, Alejandro replied to Sir John, choosing his words carefully, "I have noticed that the princess is a spirited woman. She seems to tolerate her confinement no better than the pope tolerated the one my patron forced upon him."

Sir John laughed. "I have known her since a tender age. The effects of her father's overindulgence are plainly evident. He freely admits to spoiling his children, especially Isabella. There is frequent grumbling among the lot of them that Edward favors her far above his other children, even my lord the prince of Wales, who is heir to his father's throne."

Emboldened by Sir John's casual talk of the royal family members, Alejandro decided to inquire about Kate. "I have met a delightful little girl who refers to the princess as her sister, and speaks as if the king is her father. May I inquire as to her position here?"

The older man smiled. "She is a remarkable child, is she not?"

"Yes," Alejandro replied, "and she possesses a marvelous quick wit."

"She is the king's daughter by one of the queen's former ladies. The lady's husband once served the king in France, but was killed in battle while Edward himself was here in Windsor tending to other matters. The king developed a rather strong 'courtly' admiration for the lady, who at first, it is rumored, resisted his advances. But eventually she submitted before receiving word of her lord's death. It is said she wanted to protect her husband's position in the king's retinue.

"Just less than a year after her husband's departure for France, she gave birth to Catherine. Her husband never returned. Edward's fascination for the lady was well known within the household. There was little doubt in anyone's mind that Kate was his child, and she was born with the unmistakable look of a Plantagenet. Naturally," he said, "the queen was enraged that her husband would flaunt his infidelity right under her own nose. Her revenge on Edward was to send the lady in question back to her family in London. Her punishment for the lady was to keep the child, placing her with Nurse in Isabella's apartments, to be raised as a lady-in-waiting to the princess."

Alejandro was shocked. "Had the queen no pity that the woman had lost her husband as well? The punishment seems unusually cruel."

Sir John shrugged and sighed. "The queen is powerless in areas that are customarily under the king's control, but it is entirely proper for her to manage her own domestic affairs without his approval. This was not the king's first indiscretion. Some years before, he became enamored of the wife of one of his most ardent supporters, the duke of Salisbury, while Salisbury, too, was out of his dominion on the king's business. I do not blame him," Chandos said. "I remember that lady well. She held her castle against Scottish invaders for more than a month without benefit of her lord's presence. When the king came to her aid, she greeted him in her finest garments, with the glow of victory on her face. Naturally, His Majesty was smitten. What man would not succumb to such a woman?"

Alejandro wanted to say, *What king would take the wife of his supporter, when she had held his border for him?* He said instead, "She seems a noble example of womanhood."

"Indeed," Sir John said. "A magnificent example. Nevertheless, there was a great scandal, to which it seemed all the world was privy, and ultimately Salisbury was forced to dispose of all his holdings and leave the country. The countess, it is said, has never recovered from the shame, and mourns her former life constantly. Edward was loath to be involved in another such scandal, so he did not interfere when Philippa took care of the business of Kate."

The physician wondered out loud, "And yet the two seem to be a devoted couple with great admiration for each other."

Chandos said, "They are greatly devoted. They chose each other. Such a match is rare among royals."

"But how can such an incident not mar their mutual affection?"

Sir John thought for a moment, then said, "There is much to be lost and little to be gained in concentrating on the distasteful events that have occurred in the past. I suspect each of them has both the will and the means to forgive the other, and does so frequently. But it is a wonder that you paid any attention to Kate. She is notoriously chatty."

No wonder at all, Alejandro thought to himself. *I am sometimes so lonely that I would strike up a conversation with the house cat about his recent acquisition of dead rats if I thought the cat would talk back.*

They reached the entry to the great hall, and were announced by the sentry to the king. Edward motioned them forward, and Alejandro saw to his dismay that Isabella was seated on a cushioned stool near her father. His mood soured at the knowledge that he would have to make his argument against her request to the king in her presence.

After Sir John's departure King Edward turned to Alejandro and began his inquiry into the morning's disruption. "Dr. Hernandez," he began, speaking in a slow and deliberate voice, "my daughter informs me there is some disagreement between you and her on the matter of her tailor's access to the castle. I would have your insight regarding this situation."

Alejandro cleared his throat nervously. "Your Majesty, a tailor is as likely as a baker or blacksmith to carry the plague's causative agent, whatever it may be, into the castle. As I have plainly stated, I believe that only one diseased person can infect the entire castle, and we must be ever vigilant against such unwitting introduction of the pestilence to the safe haven that we have achieved here at the cost of our liberty."

Isabella was ready with her response, and when she spoke, it became obvious to Alejandro that she had already consulted with her father, and had ascertained the limits of what she could hope to gain, for the proposal she put forth was softer than he'd expected it to be.

"Dr. Hernandez, I suggest a compromise. Can we not hold him and his goods in quarantine within the castle until we are certain that he harbors no contagion? You have spoken of this possibility before." She rose from her cushioned seat and began pacing around, wringing her hands while she spoke. "If after a period of, say, six or seven days, the man has shown no signs of disease, might we not assume that he is harmless?"

"Regrettably, Princess, I cannot say for sure. There is simply no way to know with certainty that the man cannot infect you and every other unsuspecting soul within these walls. And the time you propose is far too brief."

She looked at her father with a pleading countenance, silently asking for his help. This was a much different woman from headstrong shrew he had observed this morning. She was completely charming and innocent again, as she had been at their first meeting, and Alejandro could well understand why her father doted on her so shamelessly.

Her imploring look was not lost on the king. He himself turned to the physician and said, "I believe that Isabella's suggestion has some merit. And I would not see her suffer. Perhaps we can reach a beneficial compromise."

She suffers, from a lack of tailoring? he thought incredulously. He thought of the ragged homeless children he had seen in the streets of Avignon, children who had no families alive to care for them, and was disgusted that this woman, princess or not, should consider her situation anything short of marvelously fortunate. His resolve hardened.

"Sire, I must remind you there is no possible benefit in compromising my restrictions. There is only the bleak potential for great tragedy, which will benefit no one, least of all your daughter, who can otherwise look forward to a long and prosperous life, and no doubt a brilliant marriage." He saw Isabella wince when he spoke of marriage. *Let her suffer a moment's embarrassment,* he thought. *It will do her good to know some discomfort, however brief.* "I cannot help her to survive by allowing possible carriers of the infection to enter these walls. I beg you to remember that in the time I have been serving you, although the world outside the gate continues to suffer massive losses, we have not lost one member of the household to the plague. Clearly my restrictions are having the desired effect. I cannot cure the disease if it enters while we are lax in our vigil, but I believe that I can keep it out."

But the king, having grown extremely weary of his daughter's whiny supplications and the constant carping of her servants, finally gave in to her and ordered that the tailor be allowed to enter the castle.

"Do whatever is necessary to see that the safety of the castle is maintained," he said to Alejandro. Then he turned to Isabella and said, "I will hear no complaints about this anymore. The tailor will be quarantined for whatever period he deems suitable."

So Alejandro explored the castle grounds again, seeking an appropriate place in which to quarantine such a visitor. After much indecision he finally decided on a small, little-used chapel located on the eastern side of the lower ward. Its many windows enabled the physician to observe the occupant closely without actually having contact with him. After a questioning of the remaining castle guards a man was found among them who was handy with tools, and by his crude but effective efforts the windows and doors were refitted with wooden bars.

As the preparations were nearing completion, the princess repeatedly summoned Alejandro to her apartment, for the purpose of probing him about the length of the tailor's initial confinement, each time trying to get the physician to agree to a shorter period of incarceration.

Though he was always glad to have the opportunity to catch another glimpse of the elusive Adele, Alejandro grew weary of her mistress' tirades. One day he finally told her, "Princess, I have determined that the suitable period of confinement shall be six months. Only then can I be sure that no contagion has been brought into the castle."

Isabella paled in fury at the doctor's obviously impertinent remark. "How dare you toy with me, monsieur! Do you forget who I am?"

To which he replied, "Certainly not, my lady. You are my patient, and you will abide by my rules for preserving your health. However, I do not wish to prolong your anxiety, so perhaps we can reach an agreeable compromise, as we have so effectively done in our past negotiations."

"Explain your proposal, then" was her guarded reply.

"I propose that the quarantine be limited to one fortnight, in exchange for which you will agree to abide by my restrictions for your behavior without negotiation or objection for the six-month period that was to be the tailor's original quarantine. And may God grant that our confinement shall not last that long."

Isabella renewed her complaints, loudly denouncing the "intolerable" conditions of the bargain proposed by Alejandro. The physician reminded her that the king had quite clearly given him the authority to confine the tailor for as long as he wished, and she finally acquiesced to his proposal.

"Then bring forth one of your ladies, and I will summon Sir John, and we shall seal this bargain before witnesses."

She stomped off rudely, heading to her private chamber in what Alejandro thought was a most unprincesslike manner, muttering and complaining all the way, to await the arrival of Sir John.

Isabella's nurse had observed the goings-on with wicked satisfaction, pleased that someone had finally gotten the better of the impertinent princess, wishing to herself that she might get some similar revenge for all of the rude insults Isabella had heaped upon her in her years of service. Alejandro interrupted her enjoyment by asking for Kate to be sent to fetch Sir John. Then Nurse retired, and Alejandro was left alone in the sumptuous parlor.

Almost immediately he heard a door open. Looking toward the sound, he saw that it was Adele, and he felt his heart skip a beat.

Her steps were so light that she seemed almost to float toward him, her skirts rustling behind her, small and delicate like a china figurine in her pale dress. Cascading from her close cap was a filmy veil, which settled softly around her shoulders when she came to a stop before him. Wisps of her titian hair escaped the cap's enclosure, and he longed for more of the wondrous stuff to break free and tantalize him. She stood before him, smiling sweetly, and he drank in her image.

In his imagination he reached out with one arm and encircled her waist, drawing her close to him, while pulling away the cap and veil with the other, releasing the glorious tresses to fall freely down her arched back; as his fantasy proceeded, he gathered up the silky mass of locks in his hands and pressed his face shamelessly into it, breathing deeply of the intoxicating scent. In reality he stood quickly, and gave her a courtly bow. She responded to his respectful gesture with an equally graceful curtsy of her own, then astounded him by holding out her hand. Without thinking he reached out and took it in his own, and brought it to his lips for a lingering kiss, all the while staring intently into her green eyes. She did not flinch, or recall her hand, but kept it raised. Finally Alejandro could no longer stand the fierce beating of his own heart, and fearing it would burst and thus deprive him of further joy, he slowly lowered her hand and let it go with anguished regret.

What strange and enthralling possession forces my blood through my veins as if it were lightning? I have seen this lady only rarely, and never conversed privately with her, yet I am a prisoner of her charms. Alejandro fought to maintain his composure, and remained awkwardly silent, in the sure knowledge that should he try to speak at this moment, the sound issuing forth would be as dry as the croaking of a frog. His spittle had entirely deserted him.

"Good day, Dr. Hernandez," she said.

And why, he swore inwardly, *has God granted her the voice of an angel, to further enchant me?*

The heavenly voice continued. "I am Adele de Throxwood, and I serve the Princess Isabella as her companion and confidante. She has requested that I stand as witness to a bargain between you, and it is my pleasure to oblige her."

Finally finding his voice, Alejandro thanked her, then added, "Sir John will join us as well."

Then the full weight of his discomfort descended upon him, stunning him into silence. He had never in his life kissed a woman before this day, even on the hand, and had assumed as was the custom among his people that the first woman he touched would be his bride. What would this elegant lady say, were she to discover his true identity? Would she recoil in revulsion, horrified by his wicked deception?

How complacent he had grown in this short time away from people of his own kind; how easily he could simply forget his past and live this privileged life, serving a foreign king, reinventing himself as his circumstances demanded it. The dividing lines between Christian and Jew were sharp and seldom violated. He knew it would be completely unthinkable for him to engage in a romance with a Christian lady of noble birth. He shuddered to think of what his punishment would be at the hands of her liege lord, which in the case of Adele was King Edward himself, since she lived in his daughter's household.

She must assume that I am of the Spanish nobility, and think it suitable to engage in this flirtation with me. She does not realize that I am not of her station in life. Dear God, why have You brought me safely this far, only to torment me with something I cannot possibly have?

Adele took a seat on a thickly padded bench, and gestured Alejandro to join her, which he did at once. When they were settled together on the seat, Adele leaned toward him and confided, "My lady complains incessantly about your restrictions on her freedom, as though she is the only one who bears the burden of confinement."

She had artfully led him to a matter on which he could speak without nervousness. "I know of no other way to guarantee your safety. My patron has managed to keep the pope alive while more than half of

Avignon's residents have perished around him; his success can only be due to his strict guardianship of the pope's daily routines. It was rumored in the palace at Avignon that Clement's complaints could make those of your lady seem weak and inconsequential."

"This I cannot imagine, for our Isabella has become nothing short of a shrew with her relentless whining. She can be such a pleasant companion in gentler times; I adore her spirited company, but she bears this poorly, and has grown quite sullen." She sighed, casting her eyes somberly down. "I miss her former gaiety and will be glad when limits are no longer imposed on our activities."

"As will I, Lady Throxwood."

Kate appeared at the outer door of the anteroom, with Sir John in tow. After the customary greetings and courtesies Kate disappeared through another door, and Adele excused herself to announce Sir John's arrival to the princess. Sir John watched as Alejandro's eyes eagerly followed every step of her departure, then saddened when she disappeared behind Isabella's door.

Alejandro was caught unprepared when Sir John said, "A lovely lady, is she not?" He had not realized that his infatuation was so obvious to others. The amorous regard Alejandro suddenly felt for Adele was meant to be private, for it was a new thing to him, and he had no experience in the ways of love. He simply didn't know how to respond to Sir John's inquiry without giving himself away. It had never occurred to him that other men might find her as enticing as he did, and this surprising thought gave rise to a few moments of jealous uncertainty. His cheeks reddened involuntarily, causing Sir John to laugh.

"Do not be embarrassed, my friend; and do not fear, I have no interest in the lady myself."

Alejandro was visibly relieved, but still unsure how to respond. He finally asked, fearing an unwanted answer, "Has she a paramour, or is she betrothed?"

Sir John put his fears to rest. "The princess cherishes Lady Throxwood's company, and has promised to support her so long as she remains in her service. Since Adele's family is gone, her father lost in France and her mother a victim of the plague, it is up to the king to see to her marriage. Edward is in no great hurry to displease his daughter, as you have seen, and hence no one has spoken for Adele."

He continued, happily enumerating the lady's charms. "I have known her since her childhood, for we are distantly related, and I applaud your appreciation of her fine qualities. She is notably patient with her tempestuous mistress where others have collapsed in frustration. Perhaps this is the reason for Isabella's sincere admiration for Adele. She alone seems capable of prying out the princess' gentler nature."

He smiled knowingly at Alejandro. "But enough of my elaboration. You are already aware of the best in her, and from your smitten look, I suspect that any unkind gossip I might conjure up about the lady would pass by your enraptured ears unheard."

When Alejandro did respond, it was to only express his uncertainty. "I fear she will find me wanting in the amorous arts. I have little experience with women, having devoted myself slavishly to my profession. Until now I have not found a lady whose virtues are sufficient to tempt me to set aside my consuming interest in my work. It is a disconcerting state of mind for an innocent such as myself."

"In this castle it is a formidable task to maintain a state of complete innocence."

"As you have said before," Alejandro replied, recalling the tale told of Kate's arrival in the household.

Once again the physician felt his forehead grow tight, and his head ached dully from the constant strain of deciphering the guttural language and understanding the confusing customs of the English people. Painfully aware of the differences between them, Alejandro retreated into his own thoughts, drifting back in time to his safe and comfortable home in Cervere. *I will never be one of them,* he thought. *We are worlds apart.*

But suddenly Isabella and Adele were before him. He wondered how long they had been waiting for him to break free of his trance. When she finally had his attention, Isabella looked directly at Alejandro, almost challenging him, and said, "Sir John and Lady Throxwood shall be witnesses to our agreement and to your promise that my tailor's quarantine shall be only one fortnight. Please repeat the bargain we made earlier."

The physician stated the terms again, and Isabella questioned the witnesses as to their understanding of the bargain. Finally satisfied that she had an unbreachable contract, she turned to Sir John, and instructed him carefully. "Choose a swift rider, one who will have the best chance of success, and tell him to make ready for a journey on my behalf. I shall send Lady Throxwood with further instructions shortly."

Chandos bowed to her and departed for the gate.

Then she turned to Adele. "Proceed at once to the gate in the company of Dr. Hernandez. You will order the rider chosen by Sir John to ride out immediately and summon the tailor James Reed. Bid him to carefully describe the conditions of the service I require to Master Reed. Should he be hesitant to attend me because of the quarantine, instruct the rider to remind the tailor of the considerable value of my continued patronage." She turned to Alejandro and said, "You will, no doubt, see that Master Reed is comfortably lodged during his quarantine. I will not have his treatment any less noble than it is when he attends me under less restrictive circumstances. I count on his goodwill. As I count on yours now, Physician."

Alejandro bowed, and Adele curtsied, and they left together. They walked slowly and deliberately through the vast castle, taking an unnecessarily long and winding route to the gatehouse, each one wishing to prolong the time spent with the other. *Merciful God*, he thought, *she does not resist my company, but enjoys it as I do hers.*

Despite his aversion to the onerous task at hand, he thought that this was perhaps his best hour since the glorious morning when he and the true Señor Hernandez had splashed in the warm waters of the Mediterranean. Time stood still now, as it had then, and in the presence of this woman, his demons seemed at rest.

Twelve

C aroline awakened in the middle of the night with a fresh dream hanging in her memory. Bits and pieces of it teased her, making her want to remember much more. She struggled to shake off the haze that clouded her consciousness and obscured the dream's details.

A horse. A long ride.

She lay in the bed and slipped back and forth between two antithetical states, one in which she would swear that she could actually feel the rise and fall of her own body on the running horse, so stunning was its reality, and another more clouded mind-set in which she would not have claimed with any certainty that her own arm ended in a hand. In and out of the dream she floated, feverishly tossing in the bed until the covers were hopelessly tangled around her, restricting her movements and pinning her in place. The details of the somnolent tale became more vivid, and she left the edge of the dream to plunge fully into it at last.

The great beast moved in a rhythmic cadence beneath her and she lowered her body to decrease the drag of the wind. Strands of windblown mane-hair stung her face as she leaned closer to the horse's long neck.

But I've never been on a horse! her mind protested. *How can I know what these things feel like?* She struggled to come awake, but was too firmly a captive of her own imaginings. The pace of the ride became more brisk, and it seemed to her that there was some urgency to it, some great need for the rider to be far from that beach. As the horse's speed increased, she became aware of the discomfort this caused her, and she wished her breeches . . .

Breeches?

. . . weren't so tight, and that the linen of the shirt she wore weren't so rough; the exertion of the ride brought forth an uncomfortable dampness and the fabric felt scratchy against her skin. She tightened the grip of her thighs against the side of the horse and was aware of a sharp irritation in her groin. Still riding, she rose up a few inches from the saddle, the muscles of her thighs hardening as she did so, and adjusted her testicles so they would lie more comfortably against the saddle. . . .

Oh, my God . . .

She wrenched herself free of the dream and clawed her way frantically out of the restricting grip of the sheets. Once free of her damp mummy-wrap she sat bolt upright in the rumpled bed. She quickly placed her hand between her legs, where she found, with enormous relief, no physical evidence of masculinity. She ran her hand along one thigh, measuring it against her memory of the size it ought to be, and was grateful to find its familiar softness. It was not the hard alien limb she had imagined to be gripping the heaving sides of the horse only a few brain ticks before.

"Sweet Jesus," she said aloud, her voice shaky. She could have sworn it was all real, all part of her own body, and that it was the most natural thing in all the world for her to be riding along that unknown beach with tight breeches and testicular discomfort. She remembered a companion in her dream, a fellow rider about whom she couldn't recall any details except that he, too, was a man; his presence lingered, vague but insistent, and she knew somehow that he was important, that her dream-state survival depended upon him. Something about his name . . . it hovered in her memory, but wouldn't come through. But she remembered clearly the physical image of the man whose consciousness she had occupied, however briefly, in that dream.

She closed her eyes and let the image flood back into her; it was one of great physical beauty and youthful power. In her mind's mirror she saw handsome dark Mediterranean features on the serious-looking face of a youngish man, mid-twenties or thereabouts. His face was sunburned and he was tall and wiry, with no fat, lean as an athlete; he had fine lithe hands with elegant fingers, more feminine than she would have expected, but with a few healing cuts as if he had done some demanding work recently. He had long dark hair caught up in some sort of string, a few curly wisps rebelliously escaping at the temples. There was a feeling of surprising strength and of heightened senses about him, and a constant undertone of wariness. *Is he running from something?* she wondered. His eyes were always nervously in motion, darting here and there and assessing what he saw around him, never resting in one direction. Fear. Worry. Concern. Anguish and grief. Hope so tightly cherished that it was almost painful.

A wave of nausea passed through her and her head began to pound. She opened her eyes and placed one hand on her stomach. Trying to stand, she swayed dizzily. "Whoa!" she said aloud as she steadied herself against the bedpost. Once she was fully vertical, she felt an urgent need to urinate, but after groping her way to the toilet, she managed to produce only a thin brief stream. She left the bathroom quite unsatisfied, still feeling the urge. There seemed to be something pressing on her bladder, although her nightdress was loose and ordinarily quite comfortable.

She went back to bed, where she drifted in and out of sleep. When the day's first thin rays of light appeared through the window, she'd been in bed for many hours but still she felt unrested and brittle.

With great difficulty she made herself a pot of coffee, but despite her normal addiction to the aromatic dark liquid she found it unsatisfying, and was left with the sense that she'd drunk nothing more than hot dirty water. Her head still ached, and her neck was even stiffer than it had been the previous day. She tried to eat a cup of yogurt but it tasted unpalatably metallic and she couldn't make herself finish it.

Well, maybe I'll lose a pound or two before I shake off this . . . whatever this is, she thought. But even the hope of slightly looser jeans did nothing to ameliorate her growing misery. She went to the closet and extracted the illegal bottle of ibuprofen from the toe of one shoe. She poured out three tablets into the palm of her hand and swallowed them with water, then sat down in an overstuffed chair to wait for the painkiller to take effect. Half an hour later her headache had improved slightly, but had not disappeared altogether; even so, the medication had a slightly numbing effect and she became more relaxed. She went back to bed and was soon asleep again.

The ringing of her phone brought her back to consciousness; *Janie,* she thought happily, with visions of chicken soup and thermometers. *She'll bring me ginger ale and Vicks VapoRub and tuck me in, and I'll feel better in a day or two.* She answered the phone in relieved anticipation of speaking with her employer, and was surprised by the weakness of her own voice. She was even more surprised when she realized that it was not Janie's voice that she heard on the other end of the line.

"Caroline, this is Ted Cummings."

Caroline was a momentarily confused. She was still not thinking clearly and it took a few moments for her to remember that Ted had promised to look in on her in Janie's absence. She leapt immediately to the conclusion that Janie must still be absent, and that there would be no chicken soup or ginger ale. She felt almost palpable disappointment.

"Oh, hello," she said after a brief pause. "I'm sorry if I sounded confused. I forgot you said you would call. I'm still really foggy this morning."

"No apology needed," he said, "but you might want to look at your clock. It's afternoon."

Caroline started to turn her head toward the bedside clock, but her neck was far too stiff, so she turned most of her upper body and discov-

ered that it was well after three P.M. "My God, I woke up earlier and then
went back to bed. I seem to have misplaced about six hours."

"Are you feeling any better now?" he asked.

"Not really," she said. "I just tried to turn my head and it really
hurt. This is one killer cold."

You don't begin to know, Ted thought. "Which is the purpose of my
call," he said. "I've just spoken with one of my colleagues in the Institute's medical office this morning. I mentioned that you might need
some attention and I told him you thought you might have some sort of
flu. He was quite concerned. He said there's a bacterial strain we've just
started tracking, and its initial symptoms mimic the flu. Unfortunately, it
gets quite a lot worse than the flu if it's left untreated. It can be quite
deadly and he assured me that it's nothing to fool around with. They
haven't pinpointed the source of the outbreak yet, so it could be picked
up anywhere."

Caroline began to feel quite panicked and it came through clearly
in her voice. "What are the other symptoms?"

"Neck stiffness, to begin with," he said. "High fever, even at rest.
Swelling of the glands around the throat and groin. Dark splotches that
look almost like bruises."

"I've *got* those symptoms! Every one of them! Oh, my God . . ."

"Now don't panic," he said, using his most reassuring voice. "It's
bacterial, and it's apparently one of those rare bugs that still respond to
antibiotic treatment."

"Thank God," she said. The relief in her voice was enormous.
"What do I need to do now? Do I need a test or something like that?"

"Unfortunately the Institute's medical offices are going to be closed
for a few days, since we have no resident patients in the building right
now. I won't be able to arrange for a test until they reopen."

"But don't I need a test to get the treatment? You triage *everything*
here."

"Yes, we do, but that wouldn't make any difference in your situation. This is an emerging disease and it won't be in the triage system
yet."

"Why not?"

"Not enough cases, probably. It has to hit a certain threshold before
we enter it into the whole system."

"Then how come there's a test already?"

He didn't like the way she was asking all these difficult questions.
Of all the luck, he thought. *I happen to infect someone with a brain in her
head. Be careful, now. . . .*

"It's not precisely a test. It's just a means of detecting the specific bacterium we're looking for. We use something like polymerase chain reaction to grow enough material for identification purposes. It's very quick and quite accurate."

Then he hesitated, for proper effect; he wanted her to think he was hiding some important detail from her, something so terrible she wouldn't be able to cope with it.

Caroline took his dangling bait and jumped right into the silence. "But I've got to get this treatment! I'll have to go to a facility. If this is such a terrible thing, I don't think I should wait—"

"Now, calm down," he advised her. "Panicking isn't going to solve anything." But panic was just what he wanted from her. He wanted to get control of her, through her own fear if necessary, while Janie was still out of town. He had to keep her in that hotel room and out of circulation. He would get control of her by insinuating himself into the solution of the problem he had created. "That wouldn't be a good idea for *us* right now," he said, joining himself to her with a pronoun. "It might put us in a delicate situation. If a triage unit supervisor thinks there's something contagious, your alien status would be a great liability."

"Oh, God! What would happen?"

Another loaded hesitation. Then carefully, "Biopol would be required to quarantine you until a definite diagnosis was made. These days their processing systems are so overloaded that it's taking several days just to see each patient. It could mean a long wait in a holding facility. And nine times out of ten they deport their detainees even if it's just a cold. I don't think we want to get into that sort of spot right now, especially if you're really sick and you're in a lot of discomfort."

She said, "I am. I can barely move my neck."

And your groin is swelling and your armpits are sore and the skin on your neck is darkening, he thought. "That *is* one of the symptoms he told me to look for. And there's another thing to consider. If you haven't been printed yet, they'll do it while you're being quarantined. It's not a terribly comfortable procedure to begin with. I think it might be quite an ordeal if you're already ill."

Caroline's silence was just the response he wanted. He knew she was imagining the dire consequences of seeking medical treatment outside the channels he offered. Exaggerated and inaccurate images of the horrors of bodyprinting were running through her mind, alongside fearful thoughts of being held against her will while the medical authorities decided what to do with her. He hoped she was imagining cattle pens with unsanitary conditions and lots of filthy, contagious people. In truth the facilities were quite modern and clean, and the detainees were well treated, but he wanted her think otherwise to solidify her idea that he was her protector. He wanted her so scared that she would do whatever he told her to do, so he could treat her for plague without anyone but himself knowing that she had contracted it.

He continued, drawing her into his web. "I could pay you a visit this afternoon and get you started on the medications. Then you'd need a repeat dose tomorrow."

"Oh, Ted . . . I can't tell you how much I appreciate what you're doing for me. It seems like a lot of trouble for someone you hardly know."

"Not at all, really. I'm quite happy to help you. I know how trouble-some these things can be . . . things are so difficult these days; you're in a foreign country and you don't know the system. It's really no bother."

"Are you sure you won't get into hot water over this? I mean, it seems to me that this all might be illegal. . . ."

He was quiet for a brief moment. "The legality is questionable, certainly, but I don't think I'm going to run into any problems. There is a sort of 'underground' that happens in medical situations every now and then. Sometimes we're forced into it because of the complexities in-volved. I often find myself very frustrated by the burdens that have been placed on us by our government. We figure out our little ways to circum-vent them when necessary. And I assure you my colleague will be very discreet. He doesn't even know your name." He wished he could give her a smile, but her hotel did not have videophones.

"Well, I guess it's okay, then. . . ."

"It will be fine," he assured her. "Just fine. You must trust me when I tell you that you'll be all better in a couple of days and no one will be the wiser. Then you can go about your work, and Bruce and I can get started on our project."

"I didn't even think of that," she said, her tone apologetic. "He's helping Janie when he should be working with you. I guess we just arrived and mucked things up pretty badly, didn't we?"

He said nothing to dispel her guilt. "It's all right. I understand that these things happen now and then. Can't be helped. But you'll be better soon and things will get right back to normal."

"I hope you're right."

"Oh, I *know* I am. Now we should get this treatment started. I'm going out in a little while and I can just stop by, if that's okay. Let's see . . . it's about three-fifteen; I think I can be there in about an hour."

"I really appreciate what you're doing."
My pleasure, he thought.

The old dog lay on the grass next to Sarin, his head resting across his front paws and his eyes half-shut. Every now and then he twitched, and his master would look down at him, wondering how fast the bunnies in his doggy dreams might be running.

He looked out over the sloped plain and watched the light of day fade, a recently added habit that had become part of their late-afternoon walk routine. They paused every day to sit in this particular spot and watch the sun slip below the horizon. It was the simplest way for Sarin to envision the passage of time, which had taken on new meaning to him since the arrival of the American women. He knew that his was limited, and he wanted to *see* it pass.

The sun set; his heart soared. It never failed to thrill him, the wonder of it all. He could imagine each of those who came before him doing the very same thing, all the way back to the very first.

He doubted that the field looked much different now. Except for the city lights in the distance and the scruffy-looking people who always seemed to be loitering on the perimeter, it was essentially unchanged. In this little protectorate things never seemed to change much, regardless of how well one might visualize the passage of time as the sun descended. Time moved on, oblivious to the small intrigues of those on whom it cast its dark shadow.

But time would claim him, he knew, and soon. In the last few days, after the burst of energy that had inspired him to put things right again, he had once more begun to falter, as if the air had suddenly gone thin on him. Each day was closer to his last, and it seemed to him now that the sun literally raced down from mid-sky to plunge madly below the horizon. He was afraid, and he was alone, except for his dog. He looked down at his sleeping companion and envied the gentle creature for the simple peace in which he always seemed to dwell.

Ted walked down the seventh-floor hallway in the old hotel, unsteady as a drunk, and balanced himself with one hand on the wall as he progressed. His condition had worsened dramatically since his earlier conversation with Caroline, and he needed to support himself. By now he thought he should surely be feeling better; he'd taken his first dose of antibiotic many hours previously and it should have started to affect the bacteria that had invaded his body. He could feel no improvement at all, not even the slightest increase in energy, and he was growing more concerned with every hour that passed.

He finally came to the door bearing the number Caroline had given him. Behind him on the wall was a mirror. He turned to look at himself before knocking, checking to be sure that his careful preparations had done the job of disguising his own worsening condition.

Thank God, he thought as he appraised himself. *My fever gives me a nice ruddy tone. . . .* He pulled out the cowl of his turtleneck sweater to loosen it. It had become even more tight and constricting than it had felt the day before. He'd managed to get here by cab without arousing suspicion, but no one had really gotten close enough to look into his eyes. He would be in much closer contact with Caroline, but he hoped she would be too concerned with her own situation to pay any attention to his.

He raised his hand to knock but stopped. He looked up and down the hall until he spotted a DO NOT DISTURB sign hanging from a nearby door handle, and retrieved it. Holding the sign behind his back, he knocked, then stared at this own feet while waiting for Caroline to answer.

She's taking her sweet time, he thought nervously, hoping no one would pass by and see him waiting there. If things didn't go right with Caroline, he wanted no witnesses.

"Who is it?" came faintly from the other side of the door.

He leaned as close to the door as he could and said in a hushed voice he hoped only she could hear, "It's Ted."

He was relieved when Caroline opened the door, and relatively sure that no one else could have heard him from within a nearby room. As he entered he slipped the DO NOT DISTURB sign on the door handle without her knowledge.

Ted's jaw dropped in shock when he saw her. Her flaming red hair was matted and snarly and her skin was pale to the point of ghostliness. She looked unmistakably sick, and he was certain that no one who saw her would be fooled. He was filled with shame for having been the cause of her illness, but he slapped the guilt aside, for he couldn't let it be the overriding concern at that moment. There was damage control to be done, and his first order of business would be to try to get her appearance improved. He needed her complete confidence and didn't want to alienate her in any way, so he knew he had to be delicate in his suggestions. *She'll be offended if I suggest that she clean herself up,* he thought anxiously, *but I can't let her be seen looking like that.*

He needn't have worried. Caroline mistook his confused and guilty stare to be one of disgust over her appearance, so she pulled the folds of her robe around her more tightly than before. "I look awful, I know," she said. "Let me clean up a little."

Thinking that it was truly amazing what one could accomplish with a properly disapproving look, he said, "Nonsense," and entered the hotel room. "You just look a little tired, that's all. That's only to be expected. A few days' rest will take care of that."

But she was already stumbling off to the bathroom clutching a pair of jeans and a flannel shirt, and a few minutes later she emerged looking somewhat fresher. Her hair was neatly combed and pulled back into a ponytail, which worried him, because now that it was off her neck, he could see that the discolorations there were no longer faint. It would be only a matter of time before she took notice of them herself.

"There, that's a little better, I hope," she said. She sat down slowly on her rumpled bed and Ted could see the stiffness with which she eased herself into a sitting position. "I feel a little more human, but not much." She rubbed her neck with one hand and winced visibly. Looking up at Ted, she noticed he was staring at her, and began to feel uncomfortable under the weight of it. She smiled weakly, hoping to break the spell he seemed to be in. "Tell me about this medicine," she said.

What's to tell? he thought. *It's very simple. I'll shoot you up, and you'll either get better or you won't. But either way, you won't be leaving this room for a while. . . .*

"I've brought two antibiotics, and I'll give you an injection of both. I'll have to give you follow-up injections again tomorrow." One of the supposed "antibiotics" was in fact a heavy-duty timed-release sedative intended to keep her immobilized for a while. "They're both pretty powerful. I wouldn't be surprised if you felt quite drowsy as a side effect."

Her face took on a cast of suspicion. "I've never heard of an antibiotic that had drowsiness as a side effect."

It took Ted a few seconds to come up with a plausible explanation. "Er—" he stammered, "it's, uh, not exactly drowsiness as you'd normally think of it, it's just that one of these medicines is very powerful, and it can sometimes 'shock' the body to the point where the patient feels quite tired. You really should stay in bed while you're recovering, if that's at all possible."

It was clumsy, he knew, but it seemed to satisfy her. "Believe me, I'd like nothing better," she said. "But pretty soon I'm going to have to be up and about. We've got a deadline and Janie's going to need my help. And I don't want to make her any more unhappy than she already is."

Ted had no doubt that Janie would be unhappy, but not for the reasons Caroline thought. He hadn't answered any of the messages Bruce had left from Leeds, nor had he made the requested call to the storage facility on Janie's behalf. When they finally got back to London, there would be some accountability expected, but Ted had already decided that he would explain to Bruce (confidentially, of course, and with the hope of understanding) that he'd been ill and didn't want to reveal it. He'd say that he'd stayed home with his beeper shut off so he could recover without being disturbed. Bruce *would* understand. He didn't care whether or not Janie understood.

"Well," he said, moving his chair closer to the bed where she sat, "let's get you better so you can get back to work on your project and I can get back to work on mine. Roll up your sleeve, please."

She did as he requested. He tore open an alcohol wipe and swabbed an area on her upper arm. He filled one of the syringes with antibiotic from one of the vials, then tapped the side of the syringe until the air bubbles floated to the top. He worked the plunger slightly until all the air was expelled and then took hold of Caroline's wrist. "Hold still, now," he said. "This will just take a second." He pressed the tip of the needle quickly into the flesh of her upper arm and pressed the plunger home.

Caroline hated injections; it always felt to her like a tiny little rape when the probe entered her skin. She watched Ted's emotionless expression as he held her arm and pulled out the needle.

"One more, and then you're through," he said.

Thank God, she thought. She felt the twinge and felt the liquid disperse into the muscle of her upper arm, and finally, blessedly, the needle was out. Ted placed both used syringes and the used alcohol wipes in a plastic bag and then put the bag in his pocket.

"Now I'll just stay a few minutes until I'm sure you don't have a reaction, and then I'll be off. I'll call you in the morning to see how you're doing. You won't need to see me out. I can make sure the door locks behind me."

Caroline felt herself slipping into sleep, and was shocked that an antibiotic could have such an effect on her. She lost more and more control as the seconds ticked away, and finally she closed her eyes and slipped over the edge.

She fell instantly into a renewed dream state; again, she was the dark young man in her dream, and she found herself in a manor house or some other large stone building. She was watching someone who looked just like her as she dried her hair before a fire. As the dream man, she looked at the dream woman with aching love and she groaned in her sleep as she struggled with the conflict of her discomfort and his desire.

Ted watched her from a chair near the bed and wondered why her hand suddenly went to her throat as if concealing something. *Perhaps she's dreaming about her bruises,* he thought. He was incredibly tired; he could barely move from the chair. It had taken almost all his energy to get through his ersatz treatment of Caroline without collapsing from his own illness. His own heart beat rapidly, but he couldn't tell if it was from sickness or anxiety.

With effort he went to Caroline's refrigerator to look for the fabric sample. He poked around, moving things roughly out of place, his anger and frustration deepening as it became plain to him that the object of his search was just not there. He knew he would use up whatever reserves of energy he had if he allowed his anger to keep a grasp on him, so he sat back down in a chair by the bed and tried to calm himself. He stared at Caroline as she slept.

She tossed and turned in her fever. She threw off the covers, revealing a long pale leg where her nightdress had become disarranged. The sight of her naked leg brought forth feelings he wouldn't normally have associated with a situation such as the one he now found himself in. It stirred him, made him want to touch her, and he was momentarily ashamed of himself for such inappropriate sensations. Was this the beginnings of the dementia the medical book had promised? He shuddered briefly, an involuntary spasm, and shook his head to try to clear it. Then he leaned forward and reached for the bedcover; when he finally had it in his grasp he pulled it toward him to cover her again.

Fatigue and discouragement overwhelmed him. With every moment he could feel himself slipping deeper and deeper into depression and fear—yet another symptom, according to the book. The antibiotic he'd given himself didn't seem to be having much of an effect, and he wondered if it would be a good idea to double the next dose. He considered the idea for a moment. There was little danger that he would react badly to the drug, and some hope that it would do its work more quickly. He peered through slit-eyes at the clock on Caroline's bedstand and saw that it was nearly time for another dose. *Perhaps I ought to go home first and get settled,* he considered, *maybe take in some nourishment.* But as soon as the idea of eating crossed his mind, he began to feel nauseous, and he decided that this was as good a place as any to inject himself with the curative drugs. *Why wait?* he thought. *It will just get to work faster if I do it now.*

With a heavy sigh Ted rolled up the sleeve of his shirt and swabbed the surface of his skin with an alcohol wipe. He pulled a vial out of one pocket, and a clean syringe out of the other, and drew ten milliliters of liquid, double the required dose of five, into the clear plastic vessel of the syringe. Squeezing his eyes shut, for he, too, hated injections, Ted pressed the plunger in as quickly as possible, then pulled the needle out again.

It was only after he'd pulled the needle out that he took a closer look at the small vial. Instead of the name of the antibiotic, written across the front of it was the name of the sedative. Instead of the recommended one-milliliter dose, Ted had unwittingly injected himself with a ten-milliliter dose.

In that instant he knew that he had no choice but to call for help, for the sedative was powerful and fast-acting; he had chosen it specifically for those properties. He wasted a few precious seconds in clawing at the skin of his arm as if he might scratch out the lethal liquid, which was now silently but steadily spreading into his body. Everything he had tried so carefully to cover up would soon come to light as a result of his blunder; the truth would have to be revealed to those who answered his call for help. He would be ruined—there could be no doubt about it. *So be it*, he thought to himself as the sedative began to take hold. *I'd rather be alive and ruined than a well-respected dead man.*

These woeful thoughts passed through him in a mere instant, and he surprised himself with how easily he decided to give up everything he'd worked for in exchange for just a few more breaths. *I am the Anti-Faust*, he thought with some amusement, *bargaining with God so I can keep my soul. I'll do better with another chance*, he promised. In a desperate attempt to maintain his life he rose up from the chair and headed toward the small table on which the telephone, his lifeline, sat waiting for his dying fingers to dial it.

He almost made it, but the sedative finally overtook him in the few steps needed to cross the small room. His knees began to buckle and he felt his consciousness slipping away. His last recognizable thought was an angry *Too damned short*. He slumped down at the side of the bed, still trying to balance himself, though he was completely unaware of his own instinctual efforts to remain vertical. After a few seconds more of precarious teetering he fell forward and came to rest sprawled across the sleeping Caroline, who was too drugged herself to notice the weight of his body. He breathed his last with his head on her chest.

Thirteen

Alejandro regarded the king's troops as they filed past him in the courtyard at Windsor, every one eager for some task that would take him outside the walls, out to freedom. At his side was Sir John Chandos, who wore the subdued look of one who has resigned himself to some distasteful obligation, but still prays privately for a reprieve.

"How eagerly they line up to brave this pest," Chandos said sadly. "They think it some honor to make this ill-omened journey."

They are so young, Alejandro thought; *every one of them younger than I myself.* He turned to Sir John and said, "Who among them is likely to return unscathed?"

The knight's eyes wandered down the line, scrutinizing each volunteer, and came to rest on a hearty-looking, handsome young man. He regarded the soldier soberly for a few moments, then barked out an order.

"Matthews, your king does you great honor. You will represent him on a mission of some importance to the Princess Isabella. Come with me."

Alejandro used the last of the herbs he had brought from France to make two protective masks for the riders. He admonished Matthews to drink nothing, eat nothing, touch nothing, and to keep moving at the swiftest pace possible.

He and Adele watched from a parapet window as Matthews mounted his horse, then turned to his observers and saluted. He rode quickly out of the gate, vanishing in his own trail of dust.

"May God be with him," she said.

"And keep him steady on the path," Alejandro added.

Alejandro sent a message to Kate canceling their chess match that evening, for it was his duty to see that Matthews and the tailor Reed were settled into their temporary quarters, and Sir John had told him to expect their return by sunset.

As he fussed about the converted chapel seeing to last-minute details, the physician wondered if either man would ever emerge alive.

Outside Windsor's walls half of all humanity had perished, and it was therefore only logical that one of the two travelers should contract the pestilence. God alone knew which one it would be. Alejandro said a silent prayer that both would be spared.

But if the plague ends, I will have no purpose at Windsor, and my welcome will grow thin. My service here will be forgotten by those who will owe me their very lives and futures. And I will not see Adele.

He thought of Kate, who at a tender age was already hardened by the uncertainty of her position. How had this small child found the strength to thrive in the face of her own powerlessness and anonymity, while all the others around her could command what they wished by simple virtue of their birth? *Her bastardy, my deception—they are not unalike,* he thought. *Neither of us is who we are; we are nameless.* It was that possibility of namelessness, that he would live his life without memorable accomplishment, then die alone and unmourned, that Alejandro feared most.

"Riders approaching!"

The lookout's cry was heard in the last few minutes of daylight, and resulted in a flurry of excited activity in the castle's courtyard. Squinting into the fading light from one of Windsor's towers, it was a few minutes before Alejandro could discern the red doublet worn by Matthews when he had left earlier. The man riding beside him was bouncing up and down on a horse that was far too heavily laden with parcels. Wearing their hawkish masks, the pair were a bizarre sight indeed.

But they were no less welcome for their foolish appearance. So starved were the castle's occupants for news of the outside world that they waited as if for some foreign dignitary or high church official.

The physician hurried down the stairs to the courtyard. He found Sir John and instructed him on the procedure for their reentry. "Matthews and Reed must unload all of their possessions and lead their horses to the outside holding pen. There they will remove their outer garments and boots. Upon entering through the portcullis they must walk directly to the chapel, touching no one. Inside they will find fresh clothing, and can once again assume a state of proper modesty."

Despite Alejandro's seriousness Sir John chuckled. "I think Matthews has little dislike of being unclothed, even before the ladies, for he is well aware of his own charms, and can be quite the braggart about his abilities with women. He's more likely to strut like a peacock than slink through the courtyard in shame."

"Nevertheless, the man must not stop or approach anyone. His path must be swift and direct."

He turned his attention to the gathering crowd, which had grown in size quite dramatically in the last few minutes. Both Isabella and the Black Prince were already among the curious and excited onlookers. Adding to the confusion was the crier's announcement that King Edward himself approached. Even though he was heavily occupied with the business at hand, Alejandro could not keep himself from looking around for Adele. His searching eyes were rewarded with a glimpse of the gleaming copper hair, and when their eyes met, she flashed him a smile, a momentary respite from the confusion surrounding him.

It strengthened him. *I must gain control of this crowd!* he thought, panicking. *Otherwise, the reentry will not go as I have planned!* He leapt up onto a stone bench and waved his arms frantically, shouting out for the buzzing crowd to listen carefully. When the noise finally abated, he surprised the listeners by making his statement in halting but understandable English.

"All those who do not wish to risk infection by the plague should stand clear of the path."

There was an immediate hum of alarm, and Alejandro jumped down to the dirt again, then strode firmly to the portcullis. Borrowing a flagpole from one of the guards, he drew a line in the dirt, directing the crowd back out of his path as needed, from the gate to the chapel. Then he drew a parallel line back from the chapel to the gate, creating a wide path on which the riders would make their way to the chapel.

"Clear the way for these men. Their progress must not be impeded for any reason; do not reach out to them or pass any object to them or accept an offering they may make to you. Anyone who steps over this line will most certainly be afflicted with any contagion carried by either of these men."

The onlookers quickly rearranged themselves behind Alejandro's imaginary wall and soon settled down in quiet anticipation. Alejandro approached the king, who with Queen Philippa stood well back of the line in the center of the courtyard.

"Your Majesty, I regret this inconvenience. We will have the men settled in just a few minutes and the guards will disperse the crowd if it is your pleasure."

"In truth, Dr. Hernandez, I would have a word with both men when they are at last in place. And I would not deny the crowd their pleasure. They are as eager as I am for outside news. It is quite impossible for me to rule my kingdom without knowing what is happening in it."

Alejandro knew he should have anticipated this obvious possibility, but he had not, and had no response prepared. Now he would have to rush things to please the king. "Your Majesty," the physician said, making up his explanation as he went along, "it will be some time before they are ready to see you. They must be properly secured; their belongings must be dealt with. I implore you to be patient." But Edward, already nearly as tired of his own confinement as his impetuous daughter was of hers, glared at Alejandro with a distinctly hostile look, and spoke in a restrained voice. "Very well," he said, "I shall return to my private apartments now. But within the hour I shall expect your summons for my interview with our 'guests.' They had best be prepared for my arrival. Good evening, Physician."

Though he smarted from the king's rebuke, Alejandro brushed it off and returned to the gate. There was too much to be done to allow the chastisement to affect him. *One hour!* he thought. *Not nearly enough time.* He ran back to the gate and opened the small window in the portcullis. Matthews and Reed stood outside, looking like huge birds with their beaklike herbal masks. Alejandro instructed them to remove the masks, and they did so, tossing them aside. One landed just outside the short fence that enclosed the horse's holding area. Matthews' curious horse lowered his head to the ground and gave the item an inquisitive sniff, then picked it up in his teeth. Deciding that it was not to his liking, he dropped it and moved away to nudge the other horse in a brief but playful interchange.

Alejandro thought little of the incident, being too preoccupied with the goings-on inside the door to make much of it. He used the end of the same flagpole that had marked their path as a means of passing out two hoods made of coarse cloth, with which he bade them cover their heads.

The returning soldier and his charge looked both comical and bizarre in their strange costumes. They would have been mistaken for participants in some ancient heathen ritual, or perhaps a circus farce, were it not for the observers' knowledge of their mission. Matthews walked through the open gate with swift determination, but the tailor was fearful and hesitant, and looked around in near panic as he made his way to the chapel. His prior visits to Windsor had elicited a more elegant and stately reception, and he was keenly embarrassed to pass his patroness in this disheveled state.

Emboldened by her parent's departure, Isabella jumped up and down, clapping like an eager child, at the sight of her tailor. "Welcome, Monsieur Reed, and well done, Matthews! I shall reward you both handsomely for your bravery!"

After Isabella's declaration the crowd felt freed to engage in their own display of approval, and a resounding cheer went up into the otherwise calm twilight, revels of welcome that would have seemed suitable for a returning war hero and a rescued hostage. Matthews gloried in his momentary celebrity, waving his hand in acknowledgment of the appreciation and bowing like a courtier. He strode cockily into the chapel with the meek and confused tailor following him, and disappeared from the crowd's view.

The chattering throng quickly dispersed, but Alejandro remained behind to speak with the travelers. He stood some distance from one of the barred windows, and called out to Matthews.

"My congratulations on your successful mission and safe return, Matthews," he said. "There is fresh clothing and a supply of bread and ale in the cupboard. I have tried to anticipate your every need in advance, so that you will be comfortable during your forced confinement."

Despite that fact that he faced two weeks immured with the dour-looking tailor, Matthews remained in good spirits. He joked, "You seem to have forgotten the willing maid, Doctor."

"Of course, how stupid of me," Alejandro apologized, appreciating the man's good humor. "For now you will have to be content with Monsieur Reed."

Matthews snickered and shrugged in the direction of the tailor, who was sitting on his bed, staring at the floor in a state of bewilderment over the situation in which he suddenly found himself.

"Perhaps later," the soldier said. "Right now he is still getting accustomed to his new home. And I myself am nearly spent from this day's rough journey, so I shall retire soon to my sumptuous bed"—and he gestured toward the straw mat—"regrettably alone."

"I must ask you to remain awake for a short while longer, for the king himself would speak with you."

Matthews shrugged again, and commented, "I suppose I can keep my wits about me for a little bit yet, but Master Reed may not be in any state to pay his respects tonight."

The king appeared almost immediately after Alejandro's summons. Though he was eager to hear what passed in the outside world, the stories Matthews told were not encouraging. "Deserted cottages are everywhere," Matthews told him. "Fields of grain stand unharvested and will surely rot, Sire, if they remain unattended. But the population is so diminished, I fear there are no able men to do the work."

Matthews then related what he had seen during his brief wait for the tailor to pack his materials and belongings. "There is a plain nearby where it is said that hundreds are interred; indeed, the field looked as if it were freshly plowed, such was the extent of its coverage with new graves. The abbey has only two priests remaining, and there is little business transacted there, God's or otherwise. The dead meet their Maker unconfessed for lack of priests to hear them, and those who survive stay inside their houses, fearing the contagion."

Standing nearby, Alejandro observed the exchange between the king and his soldier. As the report progressed, and the severity of England's plight outside the safety of Windsor became clear, he saw a look of great distress and sadness spread over Edward's face. The king said nothing, for there was little he could say after such news.

Matthews politely kept his silence for a few minutes, waiting for his sovereign to speak. When no comment came from the pensive monarch, Matthews requested permission to speak again. The king grunted his distracted approval.

"Surely, Sire," said the soldier from his cage, "this is the end of the world as we have known it."

Princess Isabella managed to stay away until the following morning. Alejandro, awakened on his cot in the nearby gatehouse, sighed heavily when a soldier advised him of the princess' presence outside.

"Good morning, Dr. Hernandez," she chirped gaily. "I would like to ask you some questions about the terms of Master Reed's confinement."

As tired as he was, Alejandro knew that he could not put her off. She would continue to pester him until she had the information she wanted. "Yes, Princess, how can I advise you?" he asked, more politely than he felt.

"I would like to know how closely I may approach the chapel windows, or if I might pass through sketches of my ideas for new dresses for Master Reed's perusal. Surely it will shorten his visit here if he can do some preliminary work while remaining in his temporary 'suite.' I am not of a mind to bring him too much inconvenience."

As *if a fortnight of confinement were not inconvenient*, he thought. "Your sketches may be given to Master Reed," the physician stated rather coolly, "but not by your own hand. We will pass them through the service opening. I will be happy to arrange for their delivery if you will give them to me."

Elated, the princess advised him in a happy tone that she would send a folio of parchments of her own creation, which she said should be treated with the utmost care and given directly to her tailor as soon as possible. *Does she even remember our bitter disagreement?* he wondered as he watched her walk away. *She behaves as if this entire undertaking has been a pleasant and cooperative effort toward a mutually agreeable end. She finds it completely normal for this much fuss to be made in reaction to her demands.*

Not long after Isabella left, Adele arrived with the rolled drawings. Alejandro was delighted to see her, for she afforded him a momentary escape from his vigil. As he took the scrolls from her, he said, "Lady Throxwood, your presence warms my heart."

"It is my heart that is warmed, monsieur. I readily offered my services when the princess sought a messenger for her drawings. She was at first hesitant to send me on what she deemed to be a menial errand, but I convinced her that such important works should be carried by someone who understands their value."

"Adele," he said, boldly using her first name, "I can think of no one better suited. I regret that we have so few opportunities to meet, for your company is most pleasing and welcome."

They conversed briefly about recent events, cherishing the rare stolen moment. Then Adele excused herself reluctantly, saying that Isabella awaited her, and would soon send another lady to find her if she did not return.

"I regret that our paths cross so infrequently," Alejandro said sadly.

"Then we shall have to find reasons to change those paths so that they are more to our liking," she answered. "I bid you good afternoon, Doctor, and I look forward to our next meeting with much anticipation."

His heart pounded as he watched her walk away; he had to force himself to return to the business at hand. After checking on the condition of Matthews and Reed, Alejandro found Sir John and told him, "All seems to be well and calm here. Please pass these scrolls through the service opening to Master Reed. I am in great need of cleansing and refreshment, so I shall leave you now for my own quarters."

After thanking the knight for his diligent efforts, the physician walked back toward the south wing of the castle, where he could bathe in the privacy of his own apartment. He dismissed the manservant who had prepared his hot bath, then removed all his clothing and lowered himself into the tub of steaming water. He scrubbed every inch of his body vigorously as if to wash away his distaste for the ludicrous exercise in which he had just participated.

Months after his branding the circular scar was still an angry red; soon it would begin to fade. Although the scar would never completely disappear, he might someday—*if I live*, he thought—wear the collar of his shirt open again.

Just after dawn on the fourth day of the riders' confinement, in the middle of yet another dream of pursuit by agitated ghouls, Alejandro was roughly shaken awake by his manservant, who poked and shook his arm like an anxious child requiring its mother's attention.

"Monsieur! *Monsieur!* You are summoned to the gate! Arise, for Sir John requires your attendance!"

Still groggy, Alejandro rubbed his eyes and peered through his mental haze at the toothless elderly man whose hearty breath betrayed his proximity. He arose quickly and dressed, then followed the guard through the labyrinthine corridors to the main courtyard. The quickness of the soldier's pace indicated the importance of the mission. Evidently something of great significance had occurred during the night.

He returned the knight's brisk salute with a quick bow, and asked with trepidation if the cause for his summons was Matthews or Reed.

"Neither," replied the distressed man, "it is the horse."

Matthews' horse was prancing about the pen for no apparent reason, wildly snorting and frothing. He would turn in a wide circle, then abruptly rear up and down and head in the other direction. Now and again he would run up to the railings of the low fence and rub his lathered neck against the rough wood, scratching himself until his neck was raw and bleeding, but finding no apparent relief from his agony. His ankles were visibly swollen; each movement caused the poor animal terrible pain.

"How long has this behavior been going on?"

"I noticed last night before retiring that the animal was skittish and nervous, but it is not entirely unusual for a stallion to behave so, especially if he catches wind of a mare in season. I thought little of it then and went to bed without concern. But this morning he was still prancing. I have not seen this odd behavior before, either in the water-dreading malady or the twisted-stomach disorder that so frequently torments even the strongest horses. I do not understand this animal's strange dance. But I am certain he is not well. I fear that this one behaves as if he had the plague, and I thought to consult you immediately."

"And well done," Alejandro assured him. "If this animal is pestiferous, I fear the worst for Matthews and the tailor."

Sir John glanced at the chapel, then turned back to Alejandro and said, "Then surely I have sent him to his death, and it will be on my head."

Alejandro looked at him, pitying his untenable position, and said what the man could not untreasonously say for himself. "It is not on your head or mine, good sir, but that of the princess and her overindulgent father. And time will give us the answer we seek. If we are lucky, there will be no blame to be borne. Let us watch this animal carefully. Perhaps he will recover soon, and our fears will be put to rest. For the time being let us keep this between us."

Their fears were not put to rest. For the next few hours the horse continued to prance about in a similar manner, but his already frantic pace had quickened, and the frequency of his neck-rubbings increased until there was barely any skin left intact. Soon he began to slow down, but the change of tempo could not be attributed to any improvement in the animal's condition. He had simply exhausted all of his energy. Finally, the horse was calm, and stood still in the middle of the small pen, his rasping breath quite audible even from the small gate window. His sides heaved erratically with each shallow breath. The animal began to sway slightly, and tried valiantly to maintain its balance, but was finally forced by its own fatigue to give up the brave fight. The sickening sound of a snapping bone accompanied the horse's crumpling fall to the ground, and Alejandro covered his hands with his face, unable to watch the final death throes of the once magnificent stallion.

"Keep this to yourself yet, Sir John." He left the old soldier standing there, his head bowed in shame, and headed toward the chapel. There he found Matthews standing with his face between two of the wooden bars, staring out into the courtyard, watching the activities of his comrades as they practiced at swordplay. The man looked well enough, and had made no specific complaints, but Alejandro didn't want to rely on Matthews' ability to recognize a symptom worthy of report. He greeted the man, and inquired about his condition.

"I feel quite good, thank you, sir," was the soldier's quick response. "Mostly I feel envy that my fellow guards are out there practicing without me. My belly grows fat from this inactivity and I am as sluggish as an old worm."

His interest piqued by the report of sluggishness, the physician queried him further. "Are you feeling tired, or lethargic?"

"As I said, sir, I feel sluggish, but I am certain it is from the indolent life I lead in this small cell."

"Has your head ached, or is your neck stiff?"

The soldier replied, "Thankfully, no. I assure you, Doctor, I am unafflicted."

Alejandro ended the interview with Matthews, and looked around the dim cell for signs of Reed. His eyes finally settled on a round figure bent over the table, intently studying what looked to be the princess' drawings. He thought to call out to the man, but hesitated, not wishing to alarm him unnecessarily. But he stayed in the area for the remainder of the day, and kept a close eye on the men's activities, just in case their conditions should suddenly change.

When he was summoned again the next morning, he knew it was not to attend to the horse.

On his arrival at the chapel he found Sir John standing well back from the wooden bars, the entire company of soldiers assembled behind him, all buzzing with alarm. More members of the household arrived every minute, some still in their nightclothes, for the word had quickly spread that something was amiss in the courtyard.

Matthews was huddling in one corner of the chapel, his back pressed against the wall, a look of sheer terror on his face, for the tailor James Reed was slumped over the table, his plump cheek flat against the princess' parchments, eyes still open and staring out as if their vision persisted through the veil of death. A dribble of vomit clung to the corner of his mouth, which was twisted at the odd angle that could occur only when the body had no ability to countermand it. Were it not for the horror of his situation, the physician thought the patient looked almost bemused, as if he had been surprised in the night and was now contemplating some odd occurrence.

Matthews, quite conversely, found his own situation to be completely without humor. He ran to the barred window when he saw Alejandro, and began to rattle it violently, seeking escape from the ghastly corpse with which he shared occupancy.

"Physician, I beg you, let me out, or I shall surely die!"

Alejandro turned and walked away, steeling himself to the soldier's screams and frantic pleas for mercy, though his heart ached with pity for the terrified man. He asked Sir John a few questions, then left to seek an audience with the king.

King Edward received Alejandro in his comfortable sitting room and directed him to a well-padded chair. He immediately noticed the look of grave concern on Alejandro's face.

"I doubt that you would have had me disturbed for good news, Dr. Hernandez. What grim tidings do you bear?"

"Sire, the tailor Reed has been found dead this morning in the chapel, and although Matthews is yet unafflicted, I fear that he will soon follow Reed."

Edward contemplated this news for a moment without expression, then asked Alejandro, "What is the proper course of action in this situation?"

"Your Majesty," he answered, "my inclinations are abhorrent to all civilized men, but we must consider the following course to protect those within these walls." He paused, and drew in a deep breath, then outlined his plan. The king listened intently.

"You may order it done under my authority. And God grant that your actions are truly justified, or you shall surely burn in hell."

Alejandro did not doubt that he would.

As Matthews' screams continued, the courtyard was cleared of on-lookers, and the soldiers began piling wood in the very center of the open area. *Where is this man's former lusty bravery?* Alejandro wondered, for his incessant sobs and pleas offered a very different view of the otherwise stalwart soldier.

Sir John ordered the remaining soldiers to encircle the pile, which was now covered with twigs and dried leaves as well.

"Make ready an arrow and draw your bows!" he shouted, and his legion quickly obeyed.

He walked to the door of the chapel. He unfastened the bar, then returned to where Matthews could easily see and hear him, while the horrified confinee watched every step.

"Matthews! Remember yourself, and the king you serve," he said. When Matthews' whining supplications finally ceased, Sir John ordered, "Drag the tailor's body out through the door and lay it over the pile of wood."

Matthews looked back and forth between the faces of the physician and Sir John, looking for some sign of pity in their stony expressions. Alejandro could not let himself look into the man's eyes, else he knew his resolve would crack. He stared vacantly at the ground as Matthews pushed Reed's body out of the chair and picked it up at the ankles.

With considerable effort, for Reed had been a portly man, Matthews dragged the limp and uncooperative body across the stone floor until he reached the door. He let go of the ankles, and opened the door slowly. He was greeted with dozens of ready arrows pointed in his direction by men with whom he had honorably served in many fierce battles. Not one among them responded to his pleading looks.

He dragged Reed's plump body across the dirt courtyard. After an arduous effort he arranged the body on the pile of wood, and stood up to face his encircling companions.

His sword upraised, Sir John called, "Ready!" and the bowstrings were drawn in unison. Matthews did not stir.

Then the knight said, "Aim!" and the archers sighted their arrows. Matthews covered his eyes with his hands.

He lowered his sword, and dozens of arrows hissed through the air, nearly every one piercing Matthews' body before the blink of an eye.

After Matthews fell, Sir John took the bow from the nearest man, and unsheathed one of his own arrows. He wrapped the front of the shaft with a piece of paraffin-soaked cloth, which he then held to a torch. Taking careful aim, he let fly the burning missile, which landed neatly in the pile of dry wood. The leaves and twigs caught immediately, and the flame roared up to devour the bodies of the dead men.

Looking around the circle of archers, he said, "God alone knows which bow loosed the fatal arrow. We shall leave it to Him to judge us all."

"Fiends! Monsters! What horrible thing have you done?"

Isabella stood helplessly watching the raging bonfire outside the castle gate, fueled by bolts of silk and linen, and countless lengths of beautifully tatted lace. Pacing back and forth, she stared in pained frustration as the fire consumed her long-awaited finery. It was more than she could bear, and she wailed out her pathetic grief as she clutched Adele for balance.

Alejandro watched from a distance as Adele made an attempt to calm her enraged mistress. *How futile!* he thought angrily. Adele was powerless to stop Isabella's splendid performance, so skillfully given for the benefit of the assembled throng. Where, he wondered, was her grief for the tailor Reed? The physician shook his head in disgust, and turned away from the sickening scene.

That night, with renewed fury and increased vigor, his dream of Carlos Alderón returned to disturb his sleep. But this time he was joined by the ghoulish figure of Matthews, filled with arrows like a target stump, running urgently after him, the shafts of the arrows clicking together in a bizarre and disturbing musical performance.

Alejandro would not release Isabella from their bargain, regardless of the fruitlessness of Matthews' mission. With unexpected wisdom the king refused to hear his daughter's whining petitions, and it was rumored that she had begun to disgust even her adoring father. Only patient, loyal Adele seemed capable of tolerating the princess, who had alienated nearly everyone else in the castle. Finally, during one of their increasingly frequent but still clandestine meetings, Alejandro found the courage to query Adele about this situation.

"I am torn between two warring thoughts," he said. "I both admire your tolerance of the princess' testy nature and abhor that she requires you to be so eternally indulgent. I doubt that I would have such success in bearing her insults."

Adele blushed at his florid compliment. "I beg you to consider her circumstances before you pass judgment on her. Despite the remarkable advantages of her position she has no true admirers or suitors, and she is sixteen years old! I, at least, am blest by the admiration of a fine gentleman who is a skilled and attentive physician. Poor Isabella has no luck in love, and neither does her father in his attempts to make matches for her. She is twice betrothed, and yet remains a spinster."

His heart was warmed by her confession that she enjoyed his attentions.

"But surely," Alejandro said, "she need not be concerned at her age. You yourself are older than she, and yet unwed; I hear no complaints from you on that account."

Adele's look was troubled, and Alejandro instantly regretted his clumsy remark.

"I do not bemoan my state," she said. "No one has spoken for me, it is true, and it will likely remain so until Isabella herself is busily occupied with her own wedding arrangements. It is her father who must give my hand to the man of his choice, but it will not be done without the princess' consent. She will not agree until she no longer requires my companionship."

Alejandro did not reply, for there was nothing to be said. Isabella would not part with her dearest friend and only supporter until it was in her interest to do so. He was embarrassed by his own lack of discretion, and apologized for any distress he might have caused Adele.

"My dear," she said, her eyes cast down, "you must not be concerned for me. I have not been dissatisfied with my position here. I have never given much thought to marriage. There is no advantage to be gained by my betrothal, for I have no family left to whom a fortuitous match might be beneficial. Isabella is my family. I enjoy privileges in her household that few in this world will ever know. I have been content." She looked directly into his eyes. "Until now."

And finally he reached out and held her, as he had wanted to do since first seeing her, desperately clinging to her fiery hair with his trembling hands.

Alejandro sat at the small table in Edward's private apartment, watching the long shafts of afternoon light play upon the opposite wall. This audience had been at the king's bidding, and the anxious physician pondered the reason for the abrupt summons. Suddenly the door flew open and Edward strode briskly into the room. Rising immediately, Alejandro bowed, and the king waved him back into the chair. *This will be a brief interview. He is preoccupied and rushed.*

"Physician, I am in a difficult position, and I require your assistance."

With suspicion in his voice Alejandro said, "Sire, how may I serve you?"

Edward caught a huge breath, as if preparing for a long response, and launched into his story. "You are aware that there is a young girl in Isabella's household who is my child by a woman other than my queen."

"I have been told so, yes. I thought it not my concern to inquire further, Your Majesty."

"You possess and display much wisdom for a Spaniard, Dr. Hernandez."

Alejandro gave no hint of his anger at the thinly veiled insult about his heritage, for the king's remarks would have been even more biting had he known the truth. "It is no doubt due to my French training, Sire."

The king locked eyes with the physician, knowing that his own glaring insult had been bested, but so subtly that he had no basis to claim offense. "Ah, yes, your schooling in Montpellier," he commented. "But let me continue." He paced about, wringing his hands.

"The child's mother, who resides in London, has taken ill. A message was brought this morning that the lady is in the clutches of the plague."

"I am sorry to hear that, Your Majesty. It is a truly horrible way to die."

Anxious remorse came through in the king's voice. "I fail to recognize, Physician, that there is a pleasing way to leave this world, and despite her distance, I still bear this lady considerable affection. It was not my choice that she be sent away to London. To this day I feel great anguish over the circumstances of her departure. I would not have had it so, were it my decision."

Alejandro was somewhat embarrassed by the king's expression of regret and wondered how he planned to atone for his misdoings. He said, "Your Majesty, I fail to see how I can be of assistance. I cannot cure the lady, though I would give my soul for that ability."

Impatiently the king said, "I have no such expectation. I would have you take the child to London to her mother's deathbed. I can no longer live with my anguish over their separation. You are best qualified to oversee her journey. There is at least some hope of her safe return to Windsor if your best skills are given to her protection. I already have far too many reasons to fear for my eternal soul. I would be relieved of the burden of this guilt."

Alejandro was stunned. Surely this was a death sentence for both the child and himself. How could Edward justify this request?

But it was not a request. "Make ready for an immediate journey, Doctor," the king said, "for there is little time, and you will leave at first light."

Adele's already china-pale face lost all its remaining color when Alejandro told her of the king's "request."

"Dear God . . . why can he not send one of the guards?"

"He believes that by accompanying Kate I can increase her chance of surviving the trip to London and back again. He is heavily burdened by guilt in the matter of her separation from her mother."

"And well he should be. He made no effort to intervene on her behalf when Queen Philippa took the child, but simply washed his hands of the entire matter. Now he compounds his sin by sending Kate to her sure death, and you with her!" She stifled a sob. "A curse on this plague and the wretchedness it has caused!"

"Adele," he whispered, with far more certainty than he felt, "do not fear for my return. I have been through many trials, with little hope of finding joy or contentment. Now at last I have a reason to carry on, for I am inspired by my hopes of winning your love in time."

He was nearly trembling with the fear that she would not share his hope, but would scorn his profession of love. *God curse my inexperience! I have spoken too soon.*

But Adele did not scorn him, or make haste to retreat. "I have longed to hear you say these words, for I, too, would win your heart. I am loath to let you go from within these walls, for I fear that some harm will come to you outside their safety."

"I shall return, be certain of it."

She was not convinced. "Yes, of course you shall, just as Matthews did, and Reed with him! I shall not watch your body burn for the sake of helping the king rid himself of his past sins!"

Adele sat down on a stone bench, her mood pensive and quiet. At length she looked up at Alejandro, and made a determined declaration.

"I shall go with you and Kate."

"That is quite impossible! Even if the king would allow it, which he surely will not, Isabella will object mightily to losing your company. I cannot see how you have any hope of accompanying us. Nor should you. This is not a mission for a lady of great delicacy."

"Do not be deceived into mistaking me for delicate, Alejandro. I am a woman of great resolve and no small means. Since I was a small child," she said deliberately, "I have served my lady admirably, and never given a thought to my own happiness. For all my life I have been her friend and trusted confidante, never asking a favor. She will not deny me. Nor will I ask permission of King Edward. Isabella would rather die than lose the only companion whose love for her is genuine, and not merely an instrument for gaining royal favor. She will let me go, and will make excuses to the king for my absence."

Alejandro was in awe of her sudden boldness; he had not guessed that this quality dwelled within her. *Where has she been hiding this adventuresome spirit?* he wondered.

Then his reason returned. "I cannot allow you to risk your health for the sake of accompanying me. There is a terrible danger that none of us will survive."

"I have no fear of losing a life that is devoid of nearly all I hold dear. If you are lost, and Kate, too, then I shall be alone in the world, save Isabella. I will be bitter and dry and without hope. I fear such loneliness far more than I fear death."

Sharing her fear of loneliness, he could understand her determination. "So be it, then," he said. "We are together in this."

As Adele had predicted, Isabella did not deny her. She was unwilling to risk the demise of Adele's friendship by refusing her permission to leave, but still tried mightily to persuade her to remain in the safety of Windsor's walls.

"Dear Adele, would you leave me for a Spaniard? Are you sure that he is worthy of your affection and confidence?"

But Adele was firm with her. "He is worthy of even your affection, Isabella, but I doubt that you could see it, for you are blinded by your anger."

Chastised, Isabella asked, "Have I wronged you in some hidden way?"

"No, dear friend, but I will wrong myself if I do not follow my heart in this matter."

The tiny young woman hugged the willowy princess and tried to calm her. "If it be God's will, I shall return, in the company of a good man and the child, for surely all three of us are under His loving protection." She fingered her ruby cross, and hoped with all her heart that she was right.

Alejandro went immediately to the guardhouse and advised Sir John of their journey. A strong horse, but a gentle one, he said, would be the animal of choice for the young girl, who had little experience in such travel. He did not say that the horse would in truth be carrying *two* small ladies.

He gave many instructions for their return, for he and Kate would be subject to the same strict quarantine as Matthews and Reed had suffered. He had not yet considered how Adele would safely be brought back into the castle, but there would be time on their journey to devise a plan. This time the preparations would need to accommodate the more delicate needs of a very young lady.

With his usual efficiency Sir John made the necessary preparations, taking great care to select an appropriate mount. The horses were waiting by the gate when Alejandro arrived before dawn with the sleepy little girl in tow. He helped her up onto the saddle, and was alarmed at how small and lost the child looked on the huge horse's back. He checked the provisions one more time, and prepared to mount his own horse. Then Sir John put a hand on his arm, and spoke earnestly.

"See that you shield her from harm, Physician, for should your journey end as Matthews' did, it will not be me or any of my soldiers who put an arrow in her breast. Not even for the king."

And with that advice Alejandro took the reins of Kate's horse, and they rode out just as the sun cleared the horizon.

Adele hid a hundred paces into the forest, dressed in the rough clothes of a common traveler. She had made her escape from Windsor earlier by using a narrow tunnel that she and Isabella had discovered as girls. Alejandro almost missed her, for her brown tunic and gray breeches were nearly indistinguishable from the dry twigs in which she hid. Kate shrieked with delight when she saw Adele, for she had not been told of the extra company she would have on this morbid journey. In their rough travel garb they appeared to be a common family on the run from the plague. No one would mistake them for two ladies of nobility and a renegade Jew.

Fourteen

As soon as the guard left, Janie rushed to the edge of her cell and gripped the bars with white knuckles. "What is going *on* here?" she whispered urgently to Bruce. She saw more fright in his expression than she wanted to see.

"Just try to stay calm," he said quietly. "This is just some sort of misunderstanding. I'm sure it will all be worked out very quickly."

"But why are we locked up like this? All I did was drop an earring, for God's sake! It wasn't as if I had some kind of terrorist bomb or anything—"

Bruce interrupted her in midsentence. The look of fear on his face intensified. "I don't think we should be talking right now," he said. He cast his gaze around the area as if he were looking for some sort of listening device.

Idiot, Janie chided herself silently. *Of course they can hear every word we're saying.* She nodded, indicating her understanding, and said nothing more.

Almost immediately the same Biocop who'd first trained the weapon on them opened the door to the cell room and entered with an air of brisk authority. He slipped his magnetic identification card into the wall slot as he'd done when locking them into their cells and pressed one button, a different one this time. There was another click, this one smaller than the one they'd heard when the doors closed, after which the cover plate on a small pass-through bolted into the bars of Janie's cell slid up with a soft *whirr.* The guard passed through a flat plastic container, which appeared to have some sort of garment folded up inside it. Janie stared at it for a few wary moments, then reached out tentatively and took the sacklike container out of the open bin. She turned it over a few times in her hands, examining it, and then looked up at the guard. Bruce watched silently from his own cell.

"What is this?" she asked.

"A suit of sterile clothing," the guard replied. "You are to remove all your own clothing and put it on," he ordered.

She looked at Bruce in alarm, and he immediately said to the guard, "Can you please explain what's going on here?" His tone was firm and conveyed clear displeasure, but Janie was surprised by the lack of anger she heard in it. *He's holding it down intentionally,* she found herself thinking, and decided that she would be wise to follow his lead. *What does he know about this that has him so worried?* she wondered with alarm.

"The lady made an attempt to enter this facility, which as you know, Dr. Ransom, is a secured storage area." He turned to Janie. She could barely see his facial features through the thick plastic of his mask. "You are not authorized to enter, madam."

All notions of personal constraint left her. "I didn't try to enter your facility," she said angrily. "I dropped an earring and I picked it up."

The guard was infuriatingly polite to her. "Nevertheless, madam, your arm crossed the plane of the scanner and it read your presence. It considers any reading, however incomplete, to be an entry."

It considers . . . she thought. *It* seemed to have taken on a life of *Its* own, and *It* clearly had a great deal more authority than the guard who operated *It*. "Oh, for God's sake," Janie said, exasperated, "do I look like some kind of terrorist?"

"I daresay there's no consistent look to a terrorist, madam, and it would not be for me to say what it is in any case. That falls under the authority of a different ministry altogether." He pointed with his gloved hand to the plastic container she held in her hands. "Now, if you will kindly remove your clothing and put on the suit, please. You can place your own clothing in the empty container. You'll be collecting it later."

But Janie just stood there looking distinctly noncompliant.

The guard was still polite, although his tone of voice was growing more serious. He said firmly, "I'm sorry, madam, but this is not a request. Please do as I've asked."

"No," she said quietly, and drew back in the cell until her back was pressed against the rear wall.

The guard was becoming less pleased with every moment of delay. Bruce paid close attention from his cell, but said nothing until he was certain that Janie was not going to cooperate with their captors. "Janie," he finally said, "it would be a good idea for you to do what he's asking you to do. We may have some problems if you don't."

The guard looked at Bruce and nodded. "That's right," he agreed. "It's best not to be difficult. We're just going to go for a little walk to—"

She didn't allow him to finish his sentence. "*Fuck you,*" she said quietly.

"I beg your pardon?" the guard said in surprise.

"I said, *Fuck you!* I am *not* going *anywhere* until you tell me what's going on here. I haven't done anything to warrant this kind of treatment and I demand—"

Abruptly, Bruce cut her off. "Janie! Please! *Calm down!*" And when he had her attention he said, "They're just going to print you. Anyone who's detained is printed if it hasn't already been done. They're not going to hurt you."

She knew the process was not painful or dangerous. But no one, even its most ardent proponents, would deny that bodyprinting was the ultimate invasion of human privacy. She pressed herself even tighter against the wall, as if by doing so she could melt right through it into blessed freedom again. She said, hoping she would appear to be more defiant than she actually felt, "I won't let you do that to me."

The guard calmly pulled his weapon out of its holder and pointed it directly at her. "Very well, then," he said, "but I urge you to reconsider that position. I must advise you that refusal to cooperate will place you in violation of Section 236 of the International Biosecurity Treaty. The British government has the right to try violators for a variety of crimes under that treaty, some of which carry a mandatory death penalty. We are not squeamish about that here in Britain as we once were."

Desperate, she said, "I demand that you contact the U.S. ambassador."

The guard said, "Violations of the treaty cannot be mediated through diplomatic channels, madam, I'm sorry to say."

Janie looked at Bruce again. He looked nearly frantic. "Janie . . ." he said, "please cooperate with him."

The guard said, "Of course, all this depends on my report of the incident . . . if you should change your mind and cooperate, things might go somewhat better for you."

Her eyes went back and forth between the guard and Bruce, both of whom waited for her to say something, both of whom, for different reasons, hoped she would stop her resistance. She swallowed hard and dropped her gaze to the ground, saying nothing.

Frustrated, the guard said, "Very well." His tone darkened. "From our conversation so far it's my understanding that you wish to skip all the formalities of our justice system and proceed directly to execution." He pulled the trigger on the weapon forward with a click. "But don't be afraid. This is a chemical bullet and you won't feel anything. Your brain will cease functioning before your head hits the ground."

Her eyes went back and forth between the Biocop's mask and Bruce's pleading face. "Please, Janie . . . don't be foolish . . . it's only printing. . . ."

Finally Janie understood that she would not win this battle, and reluctantly gave it up. She looked up at the guard and said, "Can you at least turn around so I can have some privacy while I'm changing clothes?"

"I'm sorry, madam, but I have to observe. I must keep you in my sight at all times."

"I will, Janie," Bruce said as he turned away. "I'll turn around. Just don't do anything foolish. It'll be all right. Everything will be all right."

Caroline remained suspended in the fuzzy space between sleep and wakefulness for what seemed to her a very long time. Her chest ached and she felt as if a huge weight had descended upon her in her sleep. She felt terribly cold, though she knew from the weight that she was still covered.

Oh, God, I'm so sick, and this blanket feels like a layer of bricks. . . .

She couldn't open her eyes. Even if she'd had the energy, they seemed to be stuck together with dried crust, as though she'd been crying in her sleep. Bits and pieces of her continuing dream came back to her as the drugged haze slowly dissipated. She tried to move her arms again. They seemed to be pinned to her; she could not move them. She gave her position more hazy thought and decided that something was keeping her from moving her arms. *If I could only open my eyes to look . . .* but the effort of moving facial muscles, however small, seemed too much to even consider. She lay there, semiconscious, and waited for more clarity.

She was cold, but covered. Her mouth was dry, but her skin was clammy and damp. She was almost awake but she could not move. She struggled again, and finally managed to raise her eyelids.

The first thing she saw was a mound of something lying across her chest. The heavy object was wrapped in some sort of dark cotton fabric. . . . Then she saw a shock of graying hair, and part of an arm. . . .

Someone is on top of me.

Using all her strength, she heaved herself upward and struggled to push him away, but she couldn't do it even though her interloper was not struggling to remain in his position. With a great heave she finally managed to push the body off of herself, and it started to slip away toward the floor.

Mother of God, I've been covered by a dead man. . . .

The body finally rolled completely off her and thumped loudly onto the floor. Gasping for breath, she clutched at her throat and tried to scream, but could not. She looked over the side of the bed and saw the pale stiff body of Ted Cummings staring up at her, his expression a twisted grimace of horror.

She stood up too quickly and her head felt as if it would split. The horror of revulsion rose up in her gorge and she stumbled to the bathroom, where she heaved dryly for over a minute before getting hold of herself. She saw her jeans and flannel shirt lying there where she had left them earlier and dressed quickly, leaving her sweat-soaked nightdress on the floor of the bathroom.

She had to find help. Her first thought was Janie, but she had no idea if she'd returned yet from her mission in Leeds. She ran out of the bathroom, swaying and unbalanced, and looked again at Ted's corpse.

She had no idea how or why he had died, no notion of whether or not she was involved in that death in some way. A quick look at the body gave her no clues as to the cause of his death. There were no obvious marks or blood, and although he looked pale and bloated, those conditions didn't account for his death. She'd been unconscious for what she thought might have been a very long time; who knew what she might have done in her sleep? She was in a foreign country where she had virtually no protective rights, a country whose severe policies on situations of the sort she found herself in were almost always immediately applied. Suddenly the seriousness of this situation came crashing down on her and she panicked; she could think of nothing but leaving the suite and dissociating herself from the horrible thing that lay on her floor. She quickly ran out the door and heard it click shut behind her as she hurried toward Janie's nearby door. She knocked as loudly as she could, but there was no response, so she tried again. This time she came as close to pounding on the door as her weakened state would allow. Still nothing.

She turned back toward her own flat, but realized that she had no key. Hoping she had left the door unlocked, she tried the handle, but it wouldn't give; she rattled it harder but it still held. *Christ, Janie, where are you?* She turned around and leaned against the door and began to weep in frustration.

It was then that she caught a glimpse of herself in the mirror mounted on the wall opposite her door.

Her hair was in matted disarray. Her face was a mass of yellow bruises, and the neck below it was covered with dark blue-black splotches. Her fingertips were dark and visibly swollen. Her eyes were rimmed with deep blue-black and the whites were tinged with red.

As she gaped at her own terrifying image, the elevator bell rang, announcing its impending arrival at the seventh floor. She knew she could not allow anyone to see her in this condition. She ran crazily toward the exit sign at the end of the hallway and struggled with the door, tugging frantically. It seemed to weigh a ton. Just as she crashed through to the fire stairway, the elevator door opened. She closed the door behind her, and tumbled down the stairs.

Janie walked slowly down the same long corridor they'd used to reach the cell room. She was naked within the big plastic suit that enveloped her body like a huge condom, and the cold plastic rubbed against her skin, sending shivers through her entire being with every step she took. She wore paper slippers, which she knew would later be discarded. They were the same type she had always worn into the operating room, a million years ago when she had a happy life as a surgeon. She imagined herself opening the swinging door with her hip, nurses on the other side with gloves waiting for her scrubbed hands, Mozart playing on the sound system, the promise of an imminent cure. . . .

Instead, two heavy metal doors slid open automatically, withdrawing into the walls with a *whoosh* and then coming together again after her entourage had passed through. Two Biocops walked behind her, weapons drawn, ready to take her out of *this* life, unhappy though it might be, if she misbehaved. That she was about to undergo a forced bodyprint in just a few moments was completely abhorrent to her. In the United States it was a rare practice because of the privacy laws, although those laws were weakened by Congress with every new Outbreak. Still, very few people had suffered the indignity of the procedure, and she wished with all her heart that she could somehow turn back time and avoid it.

One of the Biocops said, "Turn left here," and she obeyed, although she felt anything but obedient. She wanted nothing more than to turn and run away to some lush pastoral place where birds chirped and pollen made her sneeze. The filtered sterile air in this facility was devoid of all the sweet-smelling earthy things that made her want to take breath after fragrant breath; it was dry and irritatingly pure, it had no *life* in it.

After the turn she faced another long corridor and kept walking past numerous side doors toward a set of double doors at the end. *This must be the place*, she thought. When she reached them one of her escorts entered a code into a wall-mounted number pad and the doors slowly swung open. He said, "Go in, please, and do nothing until the doors have completely closed again. We'll give you further instructions by intercom."

The *whoosh* and *click* of the closing doors signaled the demise of any possible escape. Janie stood in the small room and stared at the small pedestal in the center of it. *That's where it will happen,* she thought, and she began to tremble.

There were mirrors on every wall of the stark enclosure. Janie had no doubt that they were two-way mirrors, enabling the Biocops to watch the procedure though she wouldn't be able to see them. She wondered, *Which mirror will it be? Or will it be all four? Do they all drop what they're doing and come out to watch?*

A voice came from a small speaker in the ceiling. "Please state your name."

For a moment Janie wondered why they didn't know her name. Then she remembered that she'd never been asked since arriving at the facility. Bruce had done all the negotiating. Perhaps they thought she was simply Bruce's traveling companion. And she'd left her own papers in Bruce's car. She thought slyly, *These Einsteins didn't even ask for my papers!*

Anything you say, Adolf, but I'm going to have a little fun with you and your storm troopers. . . .

She cleared her throat and said in a loud clear voice, "Merman. Ethel Merman."

There was a moment of silence before the voice returned. "Dr. Ransom referred to you as 'Janie.'"

Ha! They really don't know! "Jane is my middle name. I hated the name Ethel when I was a kid, so everyone called me Janie."

"All right, Miss Merman. We have a few other questions for you before we proceed."

I'll just bet you do, she thought.

"Date of birth."

Make it a good one, Janie. "November 22, 1963."

"Place?"

"Dallas, Texas. *USA.*"

Behind the glass the guards exchanged glances. The leader flipped off the intercom button and said, "Like she's going to put one over on us. She thinks we have to be told she's American."

He flipped the intercom back on again. "Very good, Miss Merman. I understand Dallas is a lovely city. Now if you could please tell me your permanent U.S. residence."

"Yawkey Way, Boston, Massachusetts."

"Could you spell that, please?"

"Yawkey. Y-A-W-K-E-Y . . . Way. W-A-Y—"

"Thank you very much," he interrupted her. "Postal code?"

Oops! she thought. She invented a nine-digit number. *They'll never know.*

"Social status?"

Painful memories flooded through her. These were the questions she always hated. "Widowed."

"Thank you, Miss Merman. Now we'll need a brief medical history."

A flash of concern went off in Janie's head. *They'll know everything about my medical history when this is over. Why ask now?*

Maybe they're just checking. They want me to know they'll check what I say against what they find.

"Number of live births."

"One."

"Number of living offspring."

Oh, God, please stop these questions. "None."

"Reproductive status."

"Sterilized."

After that response there was silence in the pedestal room as the guards conferred briefly in privacy to assess Janie's responses.

One said, "She seems to have settled down. What do you think we should do with her?"

They knew they had a difficult situation on their hands, and their decision on how to proceed could have major ramifications. Their captive was not a British citizen, but claimed to be American, a claim that was bolstered by her accented English and her impudence. She had no identification on her person, but neither had she been carrying any weapons or other suspicious items.

"Maybe we should call upstairs for some advice on this one."

The other guards groaned in response to that suggestion. One said, "Oh, Christ. Not *upstairs*. He'll make a bloody mess of it. And then we'll have to answer for it when it turns out to be nothing."

They discussed the difficulties they'd had when their supervisor, a political appointee with good ancestry and poor decision-making skills, had leapt to unwarranted conclusions and arrested an innocent American citizen for a minor infraction of biosecurity regulations. His bungling had nearly caused an international incident, and one of their erstwhile colleagues had taken a fall for it, losing his job and his pension. None of the guards handling Janie was eager to let their current situation reach that state. They knew they were obliged to process her, but wanted to keep the procedure as local as possible unless further investigation was warranted.

One of them said, "I think she's telling the truth. Look at the numbers here." He pointed to a diagnostic readout of the time when Janie had answered the questions about her parental status. It measured her bodily reactions to the questions they asked and compared the biological indicators to what would be expected for the type of response she gave, like an old-fashioned lie-detector. "Looks like she lost a kid in the Outbreaks. She should be upset by that question. This leap in the line says she *was* upset. I think we should just get on with it. I don't think we have a terrorist here."

"Probably not," the other said. "Maybe she *did* just drop an earring." He pressed a few keys on the board of his computer and looked at the screen. "Merman," he said. "There's no history of any kind of criminal activity; no association with any known group, at least not in Europe. I wish we could get that information from the U.S. I don't understand why they don't let us look at it."

"They want us to ask nicely first. At least they let us look at biologicals. And she didn't match up with anything on file when she hit the scanner. If she'd been arrested or even investigated over there, it makes sense that we'd get some sort of a hit, even a small one. There's nothing. Let's just print her and be done with it." Everyone nodded accord.

He flipped on the intercom button again.

"All right, Miss Merman, that will be all the questions. The matron will come in to hook you up now."

Caroline lay confused and frightened in a heap in the stairwell between the sixth and seventh floors of the hotel, trying desperately to remember the circumstances that had led to her present predicament. Her fall down the stairs had knocked her senseless for a few moments, and she was slowly coming out of it. She knew she was in a stairwell, but she didn't know why. The best idea she could come up with was to get out of there as quickly as possible. Since it was much less strenuous to go down the stairs than up, she headed in that direction, using a disjointed combination of crawling and sliding to drag herself over the cold concrete steps.

When she finally came to the bottom of the stairs, she saw a door with a red-lit exit sign over it, and decided to make her escape through that door. She had no idea what lay on the other side of it, but it couldn't be any worse than a dark concrete stairwell. She stood up and balanced herself against the steel door, then pushed hard against the handle. As soon as she succeeded in opening it a loud alarm sounded directly over her head, sending her into a state of confused panic. The sound threatened to split her head; she clasped her hands over her ears and plunged out the door to find herself in a small grassy courtyard nestled between her hotel and the next building. All she could think to do was to get out of sight quickly, so she ran clumsily in the direction opposite from the well-lit street, into a dark alley behind the hotel.

She rested there for a little while, and listened as the fire brigade arrived to investigate the alarm. Looking back down the passageway to the street, she saw the bobbing flashlights of emergency personnel as they dispersed into the area. She knew she had to move to avoid detection, so she got up onto her hands and knees and crawled painfully in the direction of a darker area a few buildings down the alley.

When she thought she was out of sight and beyond the range of suspicion, Caroline lay back, panting to catch her breath and shivering from the chill. Suddenly all of the aches and pains that had been overshadowed by her fear and urgent flight came blaring back again. Her feet stung, and she realized that she had not remembered to put her shoes on. Her head throbbed, and her neck was so stiff that she could not turn her head without wanting to cry. Still, she knew she had to assess her situation, and turned her body so she could take a look around. Tears poured down her cheeks as she did so.

As her eyes slowly adjusted to the darkness, she became aware of the distressing fact that she was not alone in the dark place; there were several motionless forms nearby. Whether they were male or female, drunk or dead, she couldn't tell, but it was clear to her that none were citizens of the average, normal sort. She stayed very still and watched for a while to be sure they were all asleep.

The half hour it took for the emergency crews to determine that the hotel had not been on fire seemed like an eternity to her. Finally, they left, and the roaring sound of their powerful vehicles faded into the distance. She tried to stand, but fell back from dizziness. Landing firmly on her buttocks, she felt a jolt of pain surge through her diseased body, especially concentrated in her neck and groin and armpits. Finally she gave up on walking and crawled quietly to the nearest sleeping resident of the alley. Carefully, without waking him, she removed his shoes and put them on her own cold feet. Forcing herself to stand and walk, she lurched clumsily toward the end of the alley, in search of someplace safe.

The scruffy man whose shoes she'd stolen quietly got up and slunk over to his nearest compatriot. He tapped the equally scruffy woman on the shoulder and said, "Come on. She's moving out now."

The woman sat up immediately and rubbed her eyes. They both

got to their feet, but kept themselves in the low shadows as they quietly followed Caroline.

Just outside the alley Caroline leaned against a light pole. She held on to keep herself from falling and looked around to get her bearings. She didn't dare remain in the open for long, but she could hardly move. She saw the scrubbed faces of well-dressed diners through the window of a nearby restaurant, their skin softly lit by candle glow. They were doing something she'd done a hundred times, quietly enjoying themselves in a public restaurant, laughing, drinking, having a wonderful time. She was hanging on a light pole, wearing stolen shoes, and barely clinging to life. How was it that she had come to be so different from those people in such a short time? *I'm watching a film of how my life used to be*, she thought; *I'm not part of it anymore.*

A man came out of the front door of the restaurant. He was well dressed and clean, and his steps as he moved toward her were firm and determined. *He's coming to help me*, Caroline thought gratefully. *He's not wearing a uniform!* As he neared her she decided that he was the sort of man who could be trusted to help, and she tried to smile.

The two followers hung back, invisible in the shadows, and watched with concern as the man approaching Caroline drew nearer. "What do we do now?" one asked the other.

"Just watch," the companion answered. "And stay close. There's not much else we *can* do."

They stayed hidden and heard Caroline say, "Oh, thank God, I really need your help."

But the man grabbed her by the shoulders. "You're beyond help!" he said angrily. "Bloody Marginals! How many times do I have to move you away from my window?!"

Before she could rally herself well enough to protest, he was guiding her weak, stumbling, coughing form down another alley, where he deposited her roughly onto the cracked pavement.

Shaking his fist at her, he said, "And don't come back, or I won't bother to call the police. I'll just take care of you myself." As he walked back toward the restaurant, he brushed his hands together and wiped them on his pants as if to cleanse them. The watchers both gasped as the man coughed into one hand and then ran it through his hair in an anxious gesture.

Caroline lay stunned in the alley and slowly drifted into unconsciousness. The watchers waited until the restaurateur was completely out of sight and then slunk anxiously down the alley, hunkering in the shadows, until they were within sight of her. The scruffy woman stayed behind and sat hunched by a wall as the ragged man slowly crept nearer and nearer to Caroline's sleeping form. He sat down a few feet away from her and pretended to try to sleep, all the while keeping a slit eye on her.

When Caroline finally came back to consciousness, the thin light of dawn was just beginning to come into the alley. She dragged herself to a sitting position and looked around, her eyes settling on the dozing man nearby. Had he been there when she'd passed out last night? *I can't remember . . .* she thought. *Why can't I remember?*

She took in a long deep breath, preparing to stand, and as the air streamed into her lungs, her chest muscles tightened in revolt. The sudden tight pain made her cough, and she hacked out a short burst of wheezing barks. When her coughing settled, she struggled to her feet, but fell back to the ground almost immediately.

I'm going to have to crawl out of here. She got onto her hands and knees and moved slowly and steadily past the vile-smelling man beside her, heading toward the end of the alley, her too-big stolen shoes dragging behind her.

As soon as she was safely away, the smelly man crawled back to where his female companion waited. "She's heading for the end of the alley," he whispered to her. She nodded and said, "I'll just get the cart and be off, then. Wish me luck."

"Luck," he said, and watched as she took off in the opposite direction.

As Caroline half crawled, half stumbled to the street she saw a bench. To her dazed mind it seemed a worthy goal, an improvement over her current situation, which was near desperate. It was unoccupied, and she thought she could rest there for a while with her ravaged body off the ground while she tried to think of what she might do next.

She dragged herself up onto it, and curled up on one side of it. A flock of pigeons swooped in and settled at her feet; she made a half-hearted attempt to shoo them away. *Rats with wings,* she thought. *Welfare mentality.*

"I don't like 'em much myself," said an unfamiliar voice. Caroline looked up and saw a ratty-looking woman standing there. She was curiously dressed and had a tattered brown bag hanging from one shoulder. She smiled and leaned against a rusty, dented shopping cart, empty but for a few weathered newspapers. "Mind if I join you for a rest? I'm feeling a bit tired."

Caroline shrugged weakly and gestured to the woman that it was all right to sit. The woman's ample form filled the remainder of the open space on the bench, and it sloped noticeably after she sat down.

"You're looking tired yourself," she said to Caroline. "A bit under the weather, perhaps?"

And although she had little energy left for polite conversation, Caroline responded groggily, "A bit."

The ragged woman smiled. "Been a long night, has it?" She leaned closer to Caroline and said, "I've had a few long nights in my time, some quite memorable, some I'd rather forget!" She laughed heartily at her own comment and slapped her own knee. "Mind you, I was younger then, and still pretty enough to turn a head or two."

With some effort Caroline looked up at her and wondered how long it had been since this woman could still have been called "pretty." The woman saw Caroline's look and continued, "Oh, I know what you're probably thinking. You're wondering how this stinky hag could ever have turned a head. Well, you must always be prepared for what you don't believe to suddenly become true."

Oh, God, Caroline thought, *if only I could remember what I believe. . . .* A tear slid down her cheek.

Seeing the tear, the woman placed a hand on Caroline's arm and said, "Oh, dear, now I've gone and upset you. Please forgive me."

Caroline tried to look at the woman, but her vision went in and out of focus for a few moments. When it finally clarified, she saw that the strange woman was smiling down at her. The woman's appearance would not have made her feel particularly comfortable under normal circumstances. Her clothes were grimy, her hair haphazard, her age indeterminate, and her smile was full of gaps where there should have been teeth. *Not my usual circle. . . .* Still, she felt oddly comforted.

A port in the storm, she thought. She shook her head to let the woman know that she'd done nothing untoward.

"Well, something seems to be upsetting you. Are you lost, then?"

With great pain Caroline nodded. Then she grimaced.

"Been lost myself a few times," the woman said, "but somehow I always find myself." She patted Caroline's arm. "I suspect you will, too, in good time."

Good . . . time . . . find . . . The words ran together in Caroline's mind as she slowly slipped out of consciousness. The burden of wakefulness was suddenly too much for her ravaged body to bear. It wanted to be rid of the burdens of thought and movement, for those simple activities somehow seemed to take more energy than she had.

The woman said nothing and did nothing, but waited patiently until she was sure Caroline was asleep. Then she reached out a chafed hand and stroked Caroline's oily hair. "You rest now," she said, "and I'll take care of you."

With hands clasped firmly on the brown bag resting in her expansive lap, she sat in silent vigil over her sleeping charge, watching as people passed. Prosperous Londoners paid them no attention whatsoever, for most would rather not acknowledge their disturbing presence; to do so might necessitate a sympathetic response. Now and then she checked Caroline's breathing and, when it had taken on the cadence of sleep, got up from the bench and placed her belongings in the bottom of the cart. Gently, and with surprising strength, she lifted Caroline up from the bench and placed her in the cart on top of the other items. She whistled softly and looked down the alley, where her companion waited. He waved back at her in acknowledgment.

She dug around in the pocket of her filthy dress looking for some crumbs. After tossing a few handfuls to the milling pigeons, she grabbed the handle of the cart and, mumbling incoherently to herself, headed down the street with her dreaming passenger.

A smiling woman in an abbreviated version of the green Biocop suit entered the pedestal room through a sliding mirrored panel in one wall.

Bionurse? Janie thought. *Para-Biocop?*

The woman pushed a metal cart of medical-looking supplies forward. Despite her fear Janie looked curiously at the contents of the stainless steel tray resting on top of the cart. There was an odd and somewhat threatening assortment of long metal probes and clamps, a few adhesive patches, and other such items, none of which inspired Janie to feel particularly comfortable about what would happen in the next few moments, but every one of which caught her interest.

"Please remove your transfer suit," the woman said.

"But I'll be naked."

"Yes, madam, I understand that." The nurse looked sympathetic but sounded firm. "I apologize for any discomfort this might cause you, but you will not be able to wear clothing during the procedure. It's just like any other medical examination. Clothing can lead to inaccurate results."

How many naked patients have I stood over on operating tables? she wondered. *Have I always treated them with absolute dignity?* She remembered one male patient on whom she'd performed lower abdominal surgery. When they'd prepared him, she and the other members of her team had noticed his small penis and she recalled with shame how they'd all snickered, knowing that the patient was under general anesthesia and couldn't hear them. *Probably* couldn't hear them, she thought, feeling even more ashamed.

She tried to think of what was about to be done to her as just another medical procedure, but her efforts to fool herself weren't successful. *Karma,* she thought unhappily, *payback.* She looked nervously around the small room, staring into the mirrored panels. She felt the invisible eyes of the guards staring back through those mirrors and burning into her as she slipped the plastic suit down around her ankles and stepped out of it. The woman picked it up immediately and stuffed it into a yellow plastic bag.

Then the woman handed her a shower cap and a clear plastic necklace with the name "Ethel J. Merman" inscribed in it. "Please put your hair into this cap and place the identification necklace around your neck, then stand on the pedestal and remain stationary. You'll be getting a cleansing rinse now to sterilize your skin."

Janie heard the scraping noise of a door sliding open overhead. She looked up and saw a large panel disappear into the ceiling. As soon as it was gone, a big circular tube not unlike a miniature missile silo descended and settled itself around her. Thousands of minute nozzles lined the inside of the tube.

"Please reach up and take hold of the overhead hand grip. Close your eyes and keep them closed until the spray stops."

The tiny jets of bluish liquid, the same temperature as her skin, bombarded her body. She'd neglected to take a deep breath before the jets began to spray and she was near to sputtering when the liquid stopped needling her. Strong blowers came on and hard bursts of dry air forced the blue liquid off her body onto the base of the pedestal. A vacuum drain opened and the blue pools were sucked down into the base. Then the blowers softened, like a hair dryer on a cool setting.

When Janie's body was quite dry, the woman handed her a thin blue towel of light fabric and instructed her to dry all the folds of her body that the air might not have reached. "You probably won't like the next few minutes, but I'm going to have to ask you to cooperate," she said. Janie thought she saw another look of sympathy in the woman's face. "It's best if you don't resist. Then it will go very quickly. And they'll get a good picture. You don't want to have to go through this again."

And then all those probes she'd seen on the tray were inserted into every available cavity in her body. Each properly shaped probe was fitted first with a thin plastic cover—*machine condoms,* Janie thought—and then lubricated before being slipped into every available orifice. Adhesive patches were affixed to her navel, to several places on her chest, over her closed eyes, on her nipples, and to the tips of her fingernails. Each one was a minitransmitter, designed to radio out an image of the area to which it was attached.

"Almost ready now, try to stay steady," the woman told her. "It'll all be over soon."

Janie tried to remain calm but she couldn't entirely contain her shaking. She could no longer see what was happening to her, but she heard the woman say, "Just one more thing now."

The woman stepped up on a stool and removed the cap from Janie's hair. She pulled the hair up to the top of her head, and it was sucked up into a vacuum cap. As if to comfort Janie, the woman said, "We used to have to shave the heads. This is better, don't you think?"

All Janie could say with the bulb-shaped probe in her mouth was *"Gluph glunk."*

"Here we go, Miss Merman. Almost done now . . ."

Eight panels descended slowly from the ceiling opening and settled together into a new silo around Janie's body. Janie couldn't see them, or clearly hear the sounds they made, but she felt the slight vibration of the pedestal as the heavy objects were lowered.

She wanted to scream, but it was impossible. She wondered how the real Ethel Merman, a wonderfully gutsy broad, might have reacted to such a horrifying situation as this.

She'd sing, of course, Janie thought. Songs of comfort started playing in her mind. *When you walk through a storm, hold your head up high. . . . I simply remember my favorite things. . . .*

Soon there was a soft whirring sound as thousands of tiny metal prongs slid out from the panels. Each one stopped automatically when it reached her skin, forming an exact mold of her body.

"Now stay very still, please! Just a few more seconds."

But trapped as she was in the machine of her nightmares, touched menacingly by ten thousand electronic probes that would record all her secrets, Janie could not have sung if her very life depended on it. She was immobilized by the metal protrusions, and as she stood there, unable even to tremble, she heard several clicks and whizzes as the transmitters sent out their data.

And so she remembered a favorite thing, her sixteenth birthday, when her aunt, a successful jeweler, had given her a single strand of perfectly graduated pearls. In the privacy of her childhood bedroom Janie had stripped down to her underwear and stood in front of her full-length mirror wearing the luminous necklace. Laughing into an imaginary microphone, she'd said, "I'd like to thank the oysters of the world for their help in making this day possible. . . ."

She called on that memory to preserve her sanity as she stood there naked, encased in metal prongs, wearing not pearls but a necklace of clear plastic. She gripped the overhead strap, white knuckled and afraid. She imagined she was that young girl, firm and innocent and hopeful, in the early bloom of eroticism. To be where she was, a middle-aged woman, cold and slightly sagging, in this bare room being stared at by unseen strangers with questionable intent, was unimaginable. As the tiny metal prongs sent a buzz of current through her skin and into her body in perfect synchronization, recording every cell, every molecule, every *atom* of her physical being, Janie cried inside for the loss of that innocence and the death of her hope.

Fifteen

They rode along the rutted, dusty road from Windsor to the estate where Adele had lived with her parents as a child, before being sent to Windsor to serve the Princess Isabella.

"I have traveled this route so many times that I know every tree and rock," she said. "I think I could complete the journey with my eyes closed, were the horse obedient."

"Do you find this one to be so?" Alejandro asked.

"He's a very gentle mount. See for yourself," she said.

Since she knew the route so well, he had been riding behind her on the narrow road. Now he rode up beside her, and saw that the child Kate was asleep against Adele's bosom. *Would that it were me*, he thought with some envy.

"Sir John chose that horse well," he said.

"Indeed," Adele said. "He treads so evenly that I could be lulled off myself."

The woods were cool and quiet; their occasional words and the clop-clop of the horses' hooves were all that disturbed the stillness. When a hawk cried overhead, it seemed an intrusion into their privacy.

The air that Alejandro breathed was warm and sweet, and although he knew that the journey he now undertook could not possibly end happily, he felt at peace. "It is difficult to believe that such a world as this could be filled with so much turmoil."

Adele sighed deeply, her chest rising and falling as she did. Kate squirmed a bit in response, and Adele clutched her more tightly. "More turmoil awaits me ahead, no doubt."

"How so?" Alejandro asked.

"Since my mother's death, I am the sole proprietress of my father's lands and holdings," she explained. "They are not insubstantial."

"I do not understand," he said. "How can it be troublesome to have such good fortune?"

"As my father was fond of telling me, fortune makes itself. One must work to create prosperity. He was a shrewd and careful steward of his lands, and having no son, he passed his wisdom on to his daughter. Now I am the mistress of these holdings, and I am obliged to see that my tenants and overseers care for it properly. And that they themselves may prosper. My father always told me that the best way to inspire loyalty among one's tenants is to treat them fairly. He was a good lord to his subjects."

"Are you as good a lady to them?"

"I try to be," she said. "I am fortunate to have in my employ an excellent overseer, one who served my father before me. Of course, there will still be many affairs requiring my attention when we arrive there. Nearly a year has gone by since my last visit. It was when my mother died, and was laid to rest in the sarcophagus, may God have mercy on her soul. I brought some of her possessions back with me to Windsor, among them the ruby you seem to admire so much."

"You have noticed, then."

"I watch your eyes; it matters greatly to me where they settle."

"Then you should be a happy woman, since they are only for you."

"To the degree that one can be happy in such a world as this, I am."

"As am I," Alejandro said.

They rode on in silence, each one content to be in the quiet presence of the other, until Adele pointed to a tree ahead of them and said, "A road comes off to the right just ahead of that tree. We are not far away now."

As they rode into the courtyard of the manor house, a fat housekeeper came out to see who approached. She shouted out a happy greeting when she saw her mistress. Adele waved back to the woman, who ran to a nearby bell and rang it loudly for a few moments.

"The others will come quickly," she said. "The bell will summon them."

"That bell would summon the devil, I think." Alejandro jumped down off his horse and took Kate from Adele. As he brought her down from the saddle, she awakened, and seemed lost for a moment. He held the small child in his arms and cooed reassurances into her ear, until she was fully awake and aware of her surroundings. By then Adele was off her own horse and at his side.

The housekeeper waddled toward them, clucking out an effusion of grandmotherly joy. Soon Adele's overseer appeared from one of the outbuildings, and added his own voice to the greeting. There was a flurry of welcome in the courtyard, which continued well into the house.

Then there was the bustle of settling in. Adele was an impressive mistress and directed the servants to do her bidding with firm but gentle authority. "Make ready my own chamber, and settle young Kate there," she instructed the housekeeper. "I shall be quartered in my mother's suite, and Dr. Hernandez will be given the master suite."

"As you wish, my lady," the old housekeeper said. "It is good to hear friendly voices in these rooms again."

"And I warm to the sounds of my childhood home," she said. Out of Kate's hearing she added quietly, "But sadly, we shall be here a short while, for we bring young Kate to her mother's deathbed, after which we shall promptly return to Windsor."

Then she raised her voice again and said, "See that a good board is laid for supper and send out for all of my stewards. Let them dine at my table tonight," and winking at Kate, added, "with some sweets for the child if such can be found, for when we have shaken and washed off this dust, we shall all no doubt be very hungry."

As Alejandro watched Adele busy herself with the tasks of management, he imagined a small redheaded child, no larger than Kate, giving her laughter to these cold walls. It was a delightful image that lightened his heart. He had never given much thought to Adele's own station in life outside her service to Isabella, and she had said little of it. This estate was nearly a kingdom in itself! He thought, *It is plain that she has no need to marry. As long as her holdings are well managed, she will never want.* And in that moment it was also distressingly plain to him that with such an attractive dowry, the king might be tempted to force her into a loveless match for the sake of a beneficial alliance. Alejandro shuddered at the thought of Adele as the wife of some man who might care nothing for winning her heart, and everything for winning her wealth.

When they had finished the supper, Adele commented on the variety and quality of the foods that the housekeeper had managed to assemble before them on such short notice. "You have set out a remarkable board," she said, "complete with honey cakes for all, I see! We shall all become too sweet, I think."

The housekeeper winked and said, "Ah, Lady Adele, you may be right for the old ones among us, but can a little girl be too sweet?"

Adele looked at Kate, whose face and hands were smeared with honey. The child's drooping eyes betrayed her fatigue. "I think not, but a little girl can be too tired," she said. "Perhaps it is time for this one to go to sleep."

The child made no protest as the housekeeper led her away to Adele's childhood chamber. As soon as the child was gone, Adele turned to her chief overseer, and asked for his report.

"As you can see by the contents of the board, my lady, we are still fortunate. We still have help to bring in the yield."

"I take it to be your meaning that others are not so fortunate."

"With so many dead, many other estates do not have enough hands to bring in the harvests!" he said. "We have lost four farmers, but their parcels were not the best, and the others have rotated parts of the labor to see that their crops do not go to seed. For a small consideration, of course."

"Naturally," Adele said. "No man shall work uncompensated on my holdings. And the wool? How goes the shearing?"

"We are blessed again this year," he said. "The yield is very high."

"And the prices? How is the market with so many dead?"

"Prices have fallen, of course, but no doubt they will rebound as things get settled. I see no reason for us to sell our stores too quickly, though; we can hold them for a year or even two if necessary. There is enough other income to see to all of your expenses, and we can afford to wait for wool to rise again."

"Then that is what we shall do," she said. She looked around at the gathered stewards of the various parts of her estate. All had the same anxious looks on their faces. "Now, I sense that there is much more you would all like to tell me. Please speak freely."

With great urgency in their voices the stewards described the daily uncertainty of their existence. Everything familiar had changed, or soon would, and their lives had none of the simple solidity of the recent past. The local dead from outside her holdings were named, and it seemed to Adele that every other person she knew was among those taken by the scourge.

"Everyone is numbly inured to the grief of losing a loved one," the overseer said, "for it has become a common occurrence. The shock of death has begun to lose its power, and the passing of a single human being is hardly worth noting anymore."

The sad news weighed heavily on Adele, and left its mark on her face. She excused all but her housekeeper and main overseer, to whom she gave the tasks of preparing for the next morning's travel. After asking Alejandro if he required any additional preparations, which he declined, she dismissed them both, with her sincere thanks for jobs well done. Finally, they were alone.

Alejandro could feel the very coursing of the blood through his veins; sitting across from him at this table was the first woman he had ever touched with true affection, and he knew that in time his love for her would grow to something he could no longer contain.

Here there is no princess requiring attendance, and no manservant who might tell tales to his prince in return for a few coins in a cloth purse, he thought, his heart pounding. *In this place Adele is the mistress of her own fate and, God be praised, mine as well.*

"Adele," he said softly, needing to hear the sound of her name, "I cannot say what is in my heart right now."

"Alejandro . . ." she breathed. "You need not say it. It passes through the very air without a sound. My heart is full of the same nameless thoughts."

So lost were they in each other that the freshening of the evening's light breeze to a chill night wind went unnoticed, until the flame of a nearby torch flickered. Alejandro rose quickly and closed the shutters against the noise and the sudden chill. Turning back toward the table where they had been seated, he suddenly found Adele only an arm's length away, never having heard her footfalls behind him. *She moves like a cat, so quietly, and with such grace.* She reached out to him and took his hand, then lightly traced a pattern of swirls on his palm with her small finger, and they stood, engrossed in the simple pleasure of that touch, for a long while. Humming softly, she closed her eyes and swayed to her own tune, until Alejandro finally broke the spell by lifting his other hand to touch her cheek.

"Adele," he said, "I fear that if we do this thing, I shall not be able to bear the solitude of all the nights after this one. When we are again at Windsor, it will be no simple task to find a private place."

"And I fear that if we do not, I will eternally regret my own foolishness, for God alone knows if we shall have another chance."

Alejandro could not define the end of his fear and the beginning of his joy, for the two ebbed and flowed and were inseparably blended in his heart. The battle between his faith and his freedom raged potently within him; in one moment he was an independent young man in the arms of his lover, in the next a devout Jew with an obligation, even a longing, to uphold the customs of his family and ancestors. And he could not forget that the mark of his faith was cruelly burned into the skin of his chest.

It will be dark, he assured himself, *and she will not see it. . . . I will keep her hands so busy that she will not be able to feel it. . . . And what if she does?* he asked himself. *Will she betray me?*

She will not, he told himself. *She loves me; of that I am certain. And does not the Talmud say that each man, when he meets his Creator, must account for the pleasures of this life that he has not experienced?* His God demanded that he live his life with as much joy as possible, and had made it painfully plain that the life in question could be snatched away at any moment.

"And God alone knows if we shall live long enough to feel that regret," he finally said. "Suddenly I have lost my willingness to leave it in His hands." He took her in his arms and said, "I have not been with a woman before."

"Nor I with a man."

"Then we shall learn from each other," he said, and drew her into a kiss.

It was but an hour's ride to where Kate's mother lay dying, and as they neared their destination, Kate grew whiny and fussy. Alejandro wondered what disturbing thoughts were shattering the child's peace. *She must be terrified,* he thought, *as I myself would be by the prospect of watching my mother's life fade away.*

Perhaps, he thought, *what she really fears is losing the hope of ever knowing the lady well enough to call her "Mother."* Kate hardly knew this woman who, with the help of England's king, had given her life, and soon the opportunity would be forever lost. The child might not really understand what it was that caused her own unrest.

But I understand your fright, little one, he thought, *for I, too, am without a true home.* He marveled that she had any of her wits about her. She could not be enjoying this journey and the inevitable misery at its conclusion.

But *he* would never forget this journey for the indescribable ecstasy it had brought him. All of the pain of the past few months had been erased in one sweet night and replaced with joy, and despite the chaos of the world around him, all was well within his heart. He and Adele exchanged glances again and again, reliving the deep joy of their discovery of each other. Their eyes would meet, and a thrilling rush of emotion, almost painful in its intensity, would course wildly through him like a raging but welcome flood.

She had not noticed his scar. And were she not as virginal as he himself was, she might have known the difference between him and a man who had not given a piece of his flesh to God, but she had said nothing. All she had uttered were words of love and moans of ecstasy, sounds that still echoed in his ears.

Now as they rode along, Adele spoke almost formally, not wishing to betray the new intimacy between herself and Alejandro while Kate was able to observe them together.

"We have arrived at our destination, monsieur," she said stiffly, and nodded in the direction of a modest but solid-looking house just before the next crossroad.

Alejandro dismounted, then lifted Kate off the horse that she and Adele shared. He cleared his throat nervously, trying to find his gentlest voice to tell Kate the sad things that needed saying before she went inside.

"I know Nurse has told you that your mother is gravely ill," he said to the small child. "Soon God will claim her as His own and she will live among the angels."

Kate's eyes squeezed tightly shut and she fought to contain her tears. Searching around his many pockets, Alejandro found a small cloth and offered it to the frightened little girl, who was trying bravely to maintain her composure. She accepted his kind offer with a weak but grateful smile, and wiped her eyes.

"Kate," he said, "your mother may not look the same as she did the last time you saw her. No doubt this heinous blight has diminished her beauty."

The little girl nodded, eager to convey her understanding, but failed to convince her skeptical escorts that she would be unaffected by what she was going to see.

"The king has strictly ordered me to use all of my medical skills to protect you from contagion, in honor of the great affection he still bears your mother. He could not accompany us himself, but he is anxious for you to have the opportunity to see your mother again."

The small child sniffled, then slowly raised up her eyes and looked directly at him.

Alejandro smiled. "Good, brave child! I have brought some herbs in a mask that you must promise to wear faithfully while you are inside this abode, for otherwise you are in danger of contracting the contagion yourself. And sadly, Kate, I am afraid you must not embrace your mother, or even touch her, for such actions might allow the pest to travel from her body directly into yours. The king's wrath will be huge if you disobey me in this matter, and I have no wish to be subjected to any more of his anger."

Kate nodded again, with terrible seriousness, then wiped her nose on her sleeve.

"Would it help you to know that I understand your suffering, my small friend?" the physician asked. "I was separated from my own mother and father on a journey to France, shortly before I was pressed into this service by the pope's physician."

Finally she spoke, flashing a temper that betrayed her kinship to

Isabella. "But they must have been old! My mother is young, and beautiful, and it isn't fair for her to die!" She sobbed, and fell into Alejandro's
arms, and he comforted her as best he could.

Before knocking on the massive door the three travelers donned
their cloth masks, which were filled with a protective mixture made from
what remained of Alejandro's dried medicinal herbs and leaves. When
the serving girl opened the door to them, she stepped back abruptly. The
three travelers bore a distinct resemblance to giant birds of prey in their
beaked masks and winglike cloaks. Suspecting chicanery, and knowing
that in this house of women they were ill prepared to defend themselves,
she started to slam the door shut again.

But Adele spoke quickly. "Wait!" she said. "We are envoys from the
king, and here is the lady's child, as she requested. God grant that we
have not arrived too late."

In a dramatic gesture of realization the servant girl raised her hands
up in the air then clasped them together quickly, whispering, "Thank
you, blessed Virgin, for bringing the child safely here, and God curse King
Edward for his neglect!" then reopened the door rather quickly, and
rushed them into the house. "There's chill enough in here already, and
the lady cannot seem to find a moment of warmth! Come in, and close
the door to cold drafts and evil vapors. Quick! Before the bad air gets in!"

As she took their cloaks, the servant took on a grave expression and
said, "It is not too late, but I fear that she will not be long in this life.
There have been few words from her since she awoke this morning,
mostly just moans and grunts and the like. She complains of the chills, so
I cover her, then before a blink she's thrown off the spread again. She
mutters like a lunatic, then clamps her jaw tightly shut. It can't be long
now."

Adele rephrased this communication so Alejandro could understand, for she knew he would have difficulty with the servant's rather
common dialect of English, then she advised the servingwoman that the
gentleman was a *medicus* who had been sent to protect the young girl.

The servant gave him a sneering look of disapproval, followed by
some harsh and cynical words. "We've had all the doctors here with their
fancy educations and their potions and such since the lady took ill, but
the lot of them couldn't cure a pimple, by my soul! The midwife is the
only one that's brought relief to this poor woman. Better than all them
physics, if you're asking me."

At this, Alejandro paid strict attention, for never had he heard, except from the inflated de Chauliac, a report of any success in treating this dreadful scourge. After a few animated words with Adele he turned to the woman and asked, in shabby but understandable English, "Where is this midwife, that I may ask about her methods? I am anxious to hear of any new treatments."

The servant replied, "She'll be calling here on the morrow, if you care to come back. But she's a strange one, our Sarah. I'll wager she won't like your looking over her shoulder."

Alejandro wanted to question her further, but Kate was growing more impatient with every minute of delay. She tugged on Alejandro's sleeve, and asked through her mask to be brought to her mother. The servant said, "Follow me, then, but step quietly, mind you! I'll not have you upsetting her." Then she turned and led them down a dark hall.

As they groped their way through the dark passage toward the bedchamber, the servant explained, "We keep the windows covered, to keep out the evil influences. My lady is already ill enough without inviting in more pestilence."

So successful had she been in this endeavor that the battened house was dank, stuffy, and airless. As they neared the lady's sickroom, the familiar odor of plague humor invaded Alejandro's nostrils and sickened him; it had been a long time since his last proximitous encounter with the disease, and the memory of its horrible effects had dimmed. Now he was instantly reminded of all of its miseries.

He stopped and held out a hand behind him, bringing Kate and Adele to a stop themselves. He removed his mask and sniffed the air lightly, then wrinkled his brow in concentration as he tried to identify the odor. "This is more than the smell of disease," he said. "There is something more here. Something I have smelled before." He sniffed again. "I know!" he said. "It is the smell of eggs gone bad!"

The servant explained, "Mother Sarah has left some small pots of a secret substance burning in the bedchamber. She uses this and many other means to keep the pest at bay. She has managed to keep the lady from the grasp of death now for more than a fortnight, God be praised."

"A fortnight!" he exclaimed excitedly. "I must meet this woman, this Sarah, to question her immediately!"

Adele added, "Has she a surname, that we may more easily find her?"

The servant furrowed her brow, and gave the question some obvious thought. She finally answered, "Never a one's been told to me. I have known her since I was a wee one, and she has always been called Mother Sarah. Even by my own mother, God rest her soul."

"But where can she be found?"

Again the servant gave much strenuous consideration to their question, after which she directed them over the river to a nearby plain. "It's a goodly ride," she said. "You must cross the open meadow, and you'll find a pair of oaks with twisted gnarled trunks. Pass between them, where you'll find another path, this one narrower, leading to a clearing in the woods. At the edge of the clearing stands a small stone cottage, next to a yellow steaming spring, which the local people say has magical qualities. It is rumored that the Mother draws some of her power from those hot waters."

Upon hearing the reference to magic Adele covered the child's ears with her hands and exclaimed, "Blasphemy and heresy! God protect us from all magic and witches!"

Alejandro turned to her quickly and said, "Witch or not, if the woman has even the smallest power over this plague, we shall visit her immediately, for I shall not leave any possibility of curative treatment uninvestigated."

A surprisingly headstrong and defiant Adele, no longer silken, demanded, "And what of the child? I insist that she remain out of the evil influence of witchcraft!"

"Adele, we do not even know if this woman practices the black art, for the servingwoman says she is a midwife! It may be that the tales of her success have so impressed the ignorant local people that they speak of her in terms of their own suspicions. She sounds to be more nearly a *medicus* than a witch, if her cures are so good."

The child was caught up in the argument over her care, and followed the animated conversation as it continued going back and forth between her two companions. Finally she asked, "Can I not remain here, in my mother's house?"

Their dispute interrupted, Adele and Alejandro exchanged looks, each awaiting the other's opinion. The serving girl said, "The child is welcome to stay here as long as she doesn't disturb my lady's rest."

"That she will not do," Alejandro said, "for she has been strictly instructed not to touch her mother or even approach her too closely. Our good horses will bring us there in easy time, and we shall return before sunset to gather up the child. By then she shall have had a private visit of fitting duration, and we will begin our return journey to Windsor thereafter. What say you, Adele?"

Adele looked suspiciously at the servant, wondering if she could be trusted to properly supervise Kate's time in her mother's house. She was certain that this girl had until very recently been no more than a scullery maid, elevated to household maid only because of her employer's dire need for close service.

But if they were to find the mysterious Mother Sarah, they had no choice but to leave the child behind. Adele opened her small purse and extracted a gold coin and handed it to the servant. "See that she stays a good distance from the sick woman, and there will be another of the same for you when we return to find her safe."

The servant's eyes widened, for she had never had so much money at one time, and she knew that she stood to see it doubled! "I will, lady; be sure of it. No child could be safer," she assured them.

Nevertheless, Adele was full of doubt. She embraced Kate and said, "We shall return for you before sunset." After taking their riding cloaks from the ragged servant, they watched as she and the child walked down the dark hallway to the bedchamber. Alejandro whispered a silent prayer that no harm would come to the little girl, then they quickly let themselves out of the house, and headed west on the road.

The plain came in sight at the top of a hill not long after they had crossed the river. Alejandro turned his horse onto the open meadow and Adele follow closely. As expected, they soon came upon the noble old oaks in their motionless embrace. Alejandro had the sense that he was intruding on the privacy of the venerable trees as he slipped between them onto the path.

Immediately after their passage into the dense woods, they knew that everything had changed. The very air was different from that which they had breathed in the meadow; it was warm and sweet, though they were in what should be the cool of a thicket. There was no sound other than the thud of the horses' hooves on the dirt path, no insects buzzing, no frogs chirping, and no human voices calling out.

Alejandro looked around in wonder and said to Adele, "I begin to understand why you thought it best to leave the child behind. I feel almost enchanted by this place . . . truly there is some unnatural presence here."

They broke through the forest so suddenly that they had to shield their eyes from the glare of the sunlight. Alejandro could not remember any details of the path beyond the oaken gate, but he knew that he had traveled its entire length. He had no idea how long it had taken; was it moments ago that they had passed between the oaks? *He couldn't remember . . .* he was too charmed by the mystery of the place.

But Adele was not nearly so taken with the place as her companion. Though she wanted desperately to cry out to Alejandro that they must turn back and leave, her speech had completely deserted her. While on the forest path, she had felt as if some beckoning hand literally pulled her horse through the trees to the bright clearing. She had wanted to protest, but she suddenly found herself unaccountably mute and powerless to make even the feeblest utterance.

Spellbound, the victims of some glamour, they stared at each other in wonder. With slow and heavy movements they dismounted and began to walk toward the stone cottage. Soon the two found themselves standing on a stone walk that started at the door of the house and led directly to the warm yellow spring; they saw the waves of heat rising from the tepid waters, and were mesmerized by the golden glint of sunlight dancing on the smooth surface. A moist intoxicating smell permeated the warm air, and Alejandro felt compelled to inhale it in great gulps, again and again. The more he breathed of the fertile perfume, the more he wanted. It was sweet and heavy, and smelled of living things, of dying things rotting, of moisture and dampness and life.

When he finally regained his voice, he said to Adele, "If this is evil, then may it smite me forever. I am spellbound by this place."

Then a dreamy voice broke through the silent haze. "I welcome you to my home, honored physician and gentle lady."

Seemingly out of nowhere there appeared before them an old woman whom neither one would imagine to be the possessor of such an enchanting voice. She spoke again, her words like those a mother uses to soothe her child. "I have been expecting you to come," she said, "but I knew not when."

Alejandro's logical mind, fighting to retain superiority, told him that in the real world, such foreknowledge was not possible. But the peaceful stillness, the rich fecund smells, the strangely calming presence of the old woman, all together gave him a sense of inner serenity and abandon that had not been his since the safety of his childhood in Spain, and he gave himself over to it. In this tranquil place butterflies floated so slowly through the air that it seemed to him they should fall to the ground, despite their lightness. He saw no sun, yet there was brightness all around, but no shadows. Nothing was brown and withered; everything was fresh and perfect, except the woman herself, who bore the mark of time as if it were more a grace than a burden. Here he could remember how it felt before the curse of contagion had been visited on the world. Outside this place, beyond the twisted oaks, there was no such magical serenity, only chaos.

"You have come to learn of a cure," she said.

He nodded his head eagerly, his eyes wide in hopeful anticipation.

"Very well, you shall have it." She handed him a sack of finely embroidered linen. He turned it over in his hands, examining it carefully, his face full of childlike wonder.

"I did not expect to have it placed in my hands," he said. "What is this gift you give me? Is the cure contained herein?"

Her laugh was deep and ancient, almost musical in its enchanting effect on him. She said to him, "You must be eternally prepared for that which you do not expect, Physician. If you would know the cure, open it and satisfy your curiosity."

He did so, eagerly. He showed the sack to Adele, who regarded it with a look of mistrust, but joined him in examination of its contents nevertheless. He removed each item carefully and with great reverence, and Adele followed his example. Inside there were several small pouches, each one filled with a supply of rare herbs, among them ones like those de Chauliac had given him at the outset of his journey in Avignon, which were now depleted. There was a larger pouch, filled with a foul-smelling grayish powder. He took some of it between his fingers and let it drift like sand back into the pouch. There was a small flask, filled with yellowish liquid, stopped with a cork. There were red ribbons, and a walnut shell and a few other odd items, none of which he knew to have any medical use. He clutched the precious package tightly, feeling it in his hands to be sure that it actually existed and that he could really touch it, beyond his mind's perception.

He looked back at the woman, wanting to thank her for the gift. "Woman, I know not even how to address you, to offer my thanks. We came here seeking one called Mother Sarah. . . ."

"And it is she who you have found."

His suspicions about her identity confirmed, Alejandro could hardly contain his excitement. "It *is* you, then!" He turned to Adele and said, "It is she!" He turned back to the old woman. "In my wonder of this place I almost forgot the true purpose for our coming. We have seen the lady you attend, and have heard of her fortnight's progress! Speak to me of your cures, for they are great knowledge! I thirst in my very *soul* to learn your methods."

"Physician," she replied, "you must be patient. All will be revealed in time. You will know the answer you seek when it is necessary for you to know it."

For the first time in this dreamlike place Alejandro did not feel completely calm. "I fear it will pass me by, and I will not recognize that which I am intended to see."

"You must trust that you will" was all she said. "You hold the cure in your hands, and soon you will hold it in your heart. Go now, and quickly see to the well-being of the little girl, for her soul is in grave danger. I cannot see the outcome of its journey, but she will have a difficult trial in the days to come. Above all things, remember to have faith, and believe that all will end well."

Alejandro would have liked to ask her a thousand questions, but he could see that Adele was very agitated and concerned.

"She speaks of a child," she said. "She can only mean Kate. We must return to her!"

It did not occur to him to ask the old woman how she knew about Kate; it simply seemed natural to him that she should. They found their horses just where they had left them, happily grazing in the sweet dark green grass. Alejandro carefully stowed the beautiful purse of healing herbs in his saddlebag, then they mounted and started back through the dense forest again, heading for the oaken doorway back to the rest of the world.

They stopped their horses just before the gnarled gateway. Alejandro could feel the chilly wind on his face, blowing in from the world they were about to enter, and the warm sunlight on his back, painfully reminding him of the world they were about to leave.

He said, "I fear that when we cross this gate, we shall not remember what transpired on the other side of it." He looked out pleadingly at Adele and said, "I fear that when we pass through it will all be forgotten, and there will be no cure strapped behind my saddle."

With wisdom beyond her age Adele cast away her own doubts and consoled him. "It cannot be so. We held it in our hands. It cannot disappear. Remember what the woman said, that there would come a time when you would use it. . . ."

Still, he remained stationary. He looked back into the forest at the streams of brilliant sunlight pouring down through the tall straight trees, coming to final rest upon the soft pine needles on the forest floor. Then he turned again, and looked toward the meadow, where the thin gray light of the cool afternoon made no such enchanting image. He felt the wind whip through the oaken gate, scattering dried leaves around the horse's ankles, and he was loath to ever move again. He stayed there, paralyzed by his fear of losing what he had gained.

"Alejandro," Adele said urgently, "we must go! Remember what she said of Kate! We must return to her now!"

She turned toward the meadow and kicked the sides of her horse, and the big gentle mare plunged forward at her bidding. She cried out, not in pain, but in the shock of feeling the cold raw air that filled her lungs in her first breath beyond the gate. She stopped her horse, which was similarly gasping, and coughed in loud objection to the assault on her breathing.

Seeing her distress, Alejandro forgot all his fears and spurred his own horse forward. He, too, felt the attack of the cold wind upon his unprepared body, and struggled for breath briefly. But his discomfort soon passed, and he found himself astride his mount at the edge of the meadow, Adele at his side. Neither one moved. Alejandro looked into the sky for the sun's position, and saw that it had barely moved from the place it occupied in the heavens when they had first passed through the oaks. He saw the soft shadows, hardly changed, and he knew that very little time had passed. It was as if they had hardly moved from the spot.

But to his overwhelming joy, he remembered. He remembered the warmth of the sweet air, and he could envision the old woman in his mind. He turned to Adele and said anxiously, "Beloved! Please say that you remember what has transpired!"

"Aye, my love, it stays with me as if I were still there."

Overjoyed, he jumped down from his horse, and opened the tethers on the saddlebag. Reaching his hand inside, he found the item he sought. He grabbed the fabric sack that he had placed there while still in the glade, and extracted it eagerly.

But this sack was not of fine embroidered linen, only rough combed flax, coarsely woven, brown and worn, near to breaking. *What is this trickery?* he thought. *Has this woman deceived me?* He looked at Adele in dismay, then loosened the drawstring. Inside were the same precious herbs, only now in rougher pouches. The exotic contents of the tattered treasure bag were blessedly intact, and had survived the transition.

He replaced the sack in his saddlebag, then jumped energetically into the saddle, and they set off at a fast gallop across the wide meadow. The horses neighed and snorted in loud protest at their fast pace in the cold air, and Alejandro wondered if they, too, would have liked to remain.

Sixteen

The matron gave Janie a hot disposable towel to wash the residues of lubricant off her body, and when she had removed as much of the taint of bodyprinting as possible with the small cloth, she handed it back. She watched dazedly as the matron placed it in the yellow plastic bag with her first sterile garment, then sealed the bag shut. She tagged it with a label—Janie could see that it said "MERMAN, ETHEL J.—and set it aside. Then she gave Janie a fresh sterile garment and disposable slippers.

Janie covered herself immediately, for she had no doubt that the eyes behind the mirrors were still looking at her; she could almost feel those eyes boring into her flesh. She wrapped her arms around her upper body and hugged herself for warmth, for the temperature in the printing room was quite cool, and she was covered with goose bumps. The light plasticky fabric of the sterile garment did little to warm her, and as she walked back to the cell between two silent Biocops, she shivered visibly. The cold shame of violation lingered with enough intensity to make her feel as if the body she occupied were not her own anymore, that it was somehow foreign and different, that it belonged to someone else now. She returned to the cell in that disjointed state of mind, much more docile than when she'd left it in the company of the Biocops. They would have found her quite manageable had they returned with any more requests.

The floor of the cell was tile, and when Janie picked her clothes up again they were infused with its chill. "Turn around, would you?" she said coolly to Bruce, who complied in silence. "I'm going to change back into my *dirty* clothes."

There was much he wanted to ask her, but he'd seen the humiliation and anger in her expression when the Biocops had brought her back, and thought it best not to disturb her until she'd had a chance to recover a bit. He'd hoped that she would speak without being prompted or questioned, but she remained quiet, her teeth chattering as she paced around the cell.

Eventually his patience ran out and the desire to know how she was faring overtook him. Still facing away from her, he said, "Janie?"

She continued to pace. "What?"

"Can I turn around again?"

"Be my guest."

He turned around and looked at her. She would not meet his eyes. "Are you all right?" he said quietly.

She hesitated for a moment then answered in a soft voice. "I suppose you could say I'm all right." She sighed deeply. "I've definitely had better days." When she finally looked up at him through the cell bars, her expression revealed defeat and fatigue. She let out a long breath and said, "That was without a doubt the most degrading experience of my life."

He looked at her with true remorse, as if he were somehow personally responsible for her trouble. "I'm sorry this happened to you. I know you disapprove of printing. It's rough, but I don't even think about it anymore." He hung his head and continued, "Sometimes I forget how difficult it is for some people. . . ."

Janie sat down on the cold cement floor again and hugged her knees tightly to her chest. "I don't see how it could be easy for *anyone*. All those probes and sensors . . . and the places they put them . . . I felt like I was on a roasting spit, like the flames would start licking my ankles any second."

Bruce was quiet for a few moments, almost contemplative. When he finally spoke, his voice was contained. "How long did the printing take? I mean, the actual imaging."

She sniffed. "I couldn't tell you. I didn't see a clock the whole time I was in there. It might have been half an hour. It felt like an eternity. But I really don't know."

"It's been a long time since my last print. . . ."

Janie sat up a little taller. "Your *last* print? I'm don't understand. I thought only one was required."

He held back a few seconds before responding, hoping to find just the right words. Eventually he settled on the plain, unembellished truth. "I volunteered."

She rose to her feet. "Run that by me again," she said. "I'm not sure I follow you." Her eyes narrowed on him. "You *volunteered* to be printed twice?"

He felt small under the intensity of her stare. "It's been more than twice. Actually, I've been printed ten times."

She gripped the bars of the cell, incredulous. "Ten times? For God's sake, *why*, Bruce? It's an awful thing to go through! Are you some kind of masochist?"

"I had to be sure we had it right!" He was upset now, and his voice betrayed the conflict he felt. His involvement with the development of bodyprinting had been intoxicating for him, but as he told his story to Janie, it felt uncomfortably like a trip to the confessional. "I was on the team that developed the earliest printing techniques. It wasn't my idea, though I have to admit I've been intrigued with it from the start. Our first efforts were very rudimentary, and not terribly useful. But it didn't take long before we started getting really meaningful results and it just sort of mushroomed from there. From concept to working model it was only six years."

Then his voice became calmer. "I've been printed ten times because in those days it was a struggle getting anyone to volunteer, even prisoners. We all used our own bodies for experimentation, to test the controls and the radiation levels on the light probes. For the longest time all we printed was ourselves and whatever cadavers we could get access to . . . then we built a few beta machines and we sent them out all over the world for test runs. Eventually almost everyone who died in the first Outbreak was printed, even in the U.S., though that's not widely known. We just used the same machines over and over again until we were satisfied with all the adjustments, and then we destroyed the first group and built new ones from scratch."

"I don't know how you could allow yourself to be involved in something like this."

Bruce began to lose patience with her. "I don't think you're seeing this clearly, Janie. You seem awfully narrow minded about it. You're a surgeon and you certainly must have benefited from—"

"Correction," she said indignantly. "I *used* to be a surgeon before all this regulation came into being. Before all this technology, *bodyprinting included*, made pure simple medicine almost obsolete."

"How could a superb diagnostic tool make medicine obsolete?" he said, his frustration building. "If you know precisely where you need to cut, isn't your surgical technique improved? Doesn't the patient heal faster with a smaller incision? Isn't there less pain and less potential for infection? Isn't *everything* better?"

"Of *course*, everything's better. I loved being able to make a smaller cut and then slap a Band-Aid on it. It's not that part of it that I object to. It's the invasiveness of it."

"You make it sound like cutting open a person's body isn't invasive. You probably did it several times a day."

"Yeah, I did. But when I did it, it was only seen by the people in the room with me at the time. And though we weren't always totally respectful about the people we worked on, we didn't send out a report afterward on some computer network. It happened in one room, with a limited number of viewers, and with the patient knowing that his personal business wasn't going to become part of some big computer file."

"You're overreacting. The information's out there, but we're developing regulations for limiting access to it."

"You know as well as I do that any halfway decent hacker can break into almost any network on earth. There's no privacy in computers anymore. What happens when some overly enthusiastic entrepreneur figures out that people can be blackmailed with information gathered in bodyprinting? Don't you remember what happened to people who were HIV positive in the early stages of the AIDS epidemic? They were treated like pariahs, for the most part. They had no protection initially."

"That's not going to happen, and you know it."

"Do I? Do I really know it? Do *you*? I think you might be giving the powers-that-be a lot more credit than they deserve. There are some really smart people out there with the brainpower to poke into a lot of other people's lives. You wait—it won't be long before someone figures out how to tell who's got compatible organs for transplant. All that information is available in a bodyprint. Think how much money could be made by arranging an 'accidental' death so the organ could be harvested. There are also a lot of desperate people willing to pay anything to keep their lives going."

"We're only five or ten years away from being able to grow organs for transplant," Bruce said. "It won't matter after that."

"But don't you see? It matters *now* and it will continue to matter until then. There are just too many opportunities for people to be hurt by this. And now my own bodyprint is getting fed into that computer along with millions of others. I don't know if I'm ever going to feel safe again." She crossed her arms in front of her chest. "You should have given a lot more thought to what you were doing before you did it."

Her remark stung him, and he lashed back defensively. "We *did* give it thought. We thought about all the good that might come of it. And who made you the guardian of world morality all of a sudden? There are a lot of people, some of them in a position to make solid, informed decisions about this stuff, who think bodyprinting is the best thing since the microscope. When we were in the thick of it we all knew we were developing the technology that would replace MRIs and CAT scans. It was very exciting to think that we might get to look at the whole body, to actually see it in full three-dimensional form. We were like a bunch of overgrown kids with a big new toy. No one was thinking about the Orwellian potential. That wasn't our job at the time; we had politicians for that. We were just doing good science so we could improve the future of medicine for everyone in the world. None of us ever dreamed it would seem so insidious to some people,"

"Well, you *should* have given it some thought! You might have projected ahead—"

He interrupted her. "My God, Janie, how did you get so jaded? I can't believe what a cynic you've become." He reached out his hand through the bars of his cell as if he might touch her by doing so. "Try to take it easy about this. It's not so sinister as you seem to think it is. I know you've been hurt, but it might do you some good to lighten up a little bit. You make it sound like the Apocalypse is right around the corner."

She lowered her head. "That's how it feels to me most of the time."

"Then I'm doubly sorry about what you've been through. I wish there were something I could do to change how you feel. But there's not."

She looked up at him again. "I know; I *know*." She resumed her pacing. She moved around the small cell like a caged tigress, back and forth, hating the limits of the walls and bars. "Everything seems so weighty to me. My future just seems so bleak and all these changes just make it seem bleaker."

"Then think about this," he said, "if you want something to be hopeful about." His voice took on a tone of excitement. "You remember my mentioning a project that Ted and I were going to start, the one that's been delayed?"

She nodded.

"Well, it's based directly on information developed out of bodyprinting. I'm working on a way to customize artificial neurological impulses based on an individual's neural print. Eventually people with neurological damage can have electrical implants done that will stimulate their nerves in a specific way to bring about natural movement. Like a pacemaker, but for specific nerves. They won't have to wait for fetal transplants anymore." His anger gradually shifted to excitement and his hands moved energetically as he spoke. "We'll be able to do it because the print allows us to separate out the nervous system so the impulses can be timed and sized precisely. Right now I can simulate facial movements on the computer. I've got a bacterium that dances a jig in 3-D based on its print—"

"Oh, my God, Bruce, I never imagined—"

"Neither did I until we had a few years' worth of printing data. Then the idea just popped into my head one day. I thought, what if we could use this information to send impulses so precisely that we could do a sort of electronic choreography? We could program people for specific movements so they could perform certain necessary tasks. It can all be controlled from a tiny chip implanted near the site of the injury, a sort of command center hooked up to the spinal column."

His eyes grew wide and Janie could see the enthusiasm building in him. "There will come a time soon," he said, "when people who can't move because of neurological damage will be able to move again without assistance, using just their own bodies. Just think of it! Think of the joy someone will feel to rise up out of a wheelchair and walk for the first time in years. Think how exciting it will be to someone who's been fed like a baby to be able to use a fork and spoon. I'd work the rest of my life to be able to make those things possible."

She heard the passion in his voice, and understood his fervent belief that what he was doing was the absolute right thing to do. "I think I might be jealous," she finally said. "When you speak of what you're doing in those terms, it sounds like such wonderful work. I'm not sure how I'm going to feel about my work—that is, if I ever get certified to do it."

"You will," he said. "I'm sure of it. This whole mess is just a snag. And now that you've been printed, the pressure's off. You don't have to meet a go-home deadline. You can take your time."

"But Caroline does," she said. "And I'm not sure it's just a matter of having been printed for me. My visa has a time limit. And I have Attila-the-advisor waiting back in Massachusetts to breathe down my neck as soon as I get home. He didn't even want me to do this project. Said it was too complicated to dig out of the country. I thought it would be a nice change for me. It's been a change, all right, but nice, I'm not so sure."

"I'm sorry it hasn't been nice for you," Bruce said quietly, "but it's been really nice for me getting to know you again." He smiled expectantly.

Janie forced herself to set aside the last remnants of her anger at the events that had transpired over the last day. "I'm glad we've had the time to talk," she said.

And when the guard finally came back a whole day later, they'd said more to each other than they had ever dreamed they would.

The rusty cart bumped over the London streets, rattling noisily on the cobblestones, but the ragged woman who guided it by the handles kept pushing it as she had for the better part of the day, mumbling happily to herself as they progressed.

Despite the jarring bumps Caroline did not awaken. She hovered just below the surface of consciousness, looking up through the film of a dream as if she were underwater. At times her dream was so beautiful that she prayed in her delirium for it to become reality; at other times it was so violent and wretched that her sleeping mind tried desperately to awaken her, but with no success.

No one paid them any attention or tried to stop them. They were just two among thousands of ragged, lost "Marginals" living outside the norm of London's bright society. No one called them "homeless" any-more, but despite their updated name they were still the ones who could not find a proper fit anywhere in the rigid social structure of post-Outbreak England.

The woman now pushing the cart had grown accustomed to being shunned by so-called "normal" people. She chose to live as she did because the life was more pleasing to her than the demanding alterna-tive. She reported to no one except her extended family of other Marginals. There were several "families" throughout London, clans al-most, some of whom lived under bridges or in abandoned buildings. Her own had settled in a wooded area on the outskirts of a field on the south side of the Thames.

"Rest in peace," she mumbled to herself, thinking about the former owner of the property near which she lived, an ancient woman who had recently passed over, leaving behind an addled son who was himself quite an old man by the time his mother died. She took one hand off the cart's handle and crossed herself, then whispered a brief prayer for his poor befuddled soul, adding at the end a blessing for her passenger.

A siren sounded in the distance. She stopped the cart to still its creaking and listened carefully. The sound was growing louder. She looked ahead for a place to hide and saw an alleyway situated between two tall buildings. She stepped up her pace and hurried toward it.

She slipped the cart in between the two buildings and then stood in front of it, her large form blocking it from easy view, and watched ner-vously as the Biocop van sped past her en route to some virulent crisis. When she was sure it had completely passed, and there was no more danger of discovery, she emerged back into the daylight again, and pulled the cart out behind her.

And so it was that the shopping-cart woman with her bedraggled redheaded cargo passed quite invisibly through London, weaving through each street and alleyway according to a predetermined plan.

Now and then she stopped, only briefly, for she knew that haste was important. Sometimes another Marginal would push the heavy cart, and she would walk alongside. During these respites she would dig around in her tattered brown bag and find a bruised apple or a dry crust of bread, or another prize from some household's leavings. Ever mindful of Caroline's worsening condition, one or the other of the accompanying Marginals would try to force small sips of water into her mouth, a difficult and trying task. No observer would imagine that such ruffians could provide the tender care they gave to their unconscious charge, but they had sworn long ago to do so, in gratitude for the care they'd received themselves in the household of the one to whom they'd made that oath.

The woman who now pushed the cart had been watching on the night when Janie and Caroline dug up the bedeviled fabric artifact, had stood in the shadows not a meter away from them as they hid in the woods to avoid discovery, and had understood how serious would be the consequences of their disturbing the soil. She knew that Sarin would need their help now more than ever. It was time to pay back his mother's karmic kindness, and though she knew the price might be a heavy one, the Marginal woman was prepared to pay.

The Biocop used his magic card to open Janie's cell door. "All right, Miss Merman, we've got your results. Would you follow me, please?"

And before Bruce could say, *"Miss Merman?"* Janie shot him a warning glance. He read it clearly. After a day and a half of uninterrupted communication they were reading each other almost sublimely well. He managed to suppress the snicker he desperately wanted to let loose and wisely kept his mouth shut.

The Biocop, however, had more to say. "I don't know what the law is in your country, miss, but here we must show you the results of your print and provide immediate counseling for any questions you might have."

As he led her away she said, a bit too imperiously, "We give our citizens a choice. We're still unregulated."

He gave her a patronizing look and said, "Naturally. Your country has *always* been unregulated, at least since *our* country let it go. It was a regrettable lapse in judgment on the part of King George." He smiled as he opened a metal door for her, and motioned her to enter.

She thought to herself, *Polite to a fault. They've obviously decided I'm no threat. Only one guard, and a comedian at that! He's hardly even watching me.* Then she saw the chemical pistol strapped to the guard's belt and understood why she was allowed to walk with only one escort. Armed as he was, this one guard was quite capable of keeping her in line without help.

The small room they entered had obviously once been an office in the toy firm that had occupied the building in the pre-Outbreak days. There was a desk with a chair, and another chair on the opposite side of it. On the desk was a computer console. The Biocop directed her to the far chair and, when she was seated, sat down at the desk. Janie saw two projection machines, one mounted overhead, and one mounted on the floor. He flipped a switch that lowered the light level dramatically.

"Ready?" he said to her.

Am I ready? she wondered. *Will I ever be ready to see all my own flaws?* She sat silently for a moment and thought about what she was going to see. She had always taken her health for granted; illness was rare for her and she'd never been seriously hurt. When people all around her were dropping like flies, she had managed to survive the Outbreaks. Suddenly, she was filled with fear. *What if my luck's run out? What if there are tumors there? What if there's some genetic time bomb that's all set to explode? Do I want to know these things?*

Yet despite her fear and uncertainty there was a part of her, the part that loved medicine, which wanted to know all there was to know. *The only thing I really can't change is the day I'm scheduled to check out,* she thought to herself; *almost anything else can be fixed.* She knew that even a sophisticated tool like a bodyprint couldn't determine the length of her life, so she gathered up her courage and nodded yes.

"You'll want to pay attention to the area between the two projection devices," the guard said.

As she watched, a holographic image of her own body slowly took form before her. Suddenly she was standing in front of herself in all her middle-aged naked glory. The image clearly showed her tension and the grimace on her face at the precise moment the print had occurred. Seeing her look of dismay, the Biocop said, "Don't worry. No one ever looks good in these things."

"Some people look good in anything," she countered. "I just don't happen to be one of them. But never mind about that. What did you find?"

"Let's see now. . . ." He flipped through a series of pages, saying "Normal, normal, normal," then he stopped and pushed a few buttons on the console before him. Everything but Janie's circulatory system melted away, leaving behind a Janie-shaped mass of veins, arteries, and capillaries. A tiny light glowed in one vein in her lower right leg. "There." He pointed. "You've got the potential for a varicose vein."

Janie watched, astonished, as he pointed out several minor glitches in her physical being, small abnormalities that had little significance. A protruding middle toe on one foot, the result of an ancient toe-stubbing, memorable still for the throbbing pain it had produced years before. Her appendix, still present, but tucked up under her intestine.

"Ever have indigestion?" the guard asked.

"Oh, yes. . . ." she answered.

"That's probably why," he said. Then he smiled and said, "But I'm not telling you anything you don't already know, am I?" As he passed through the image of her reproductive system, he said, "Sterilized, I see . . ." then stopped on that page.

He peered at the image and then glanced back down at the written page before him. By adjusting a few knobs on the console he made the image more transparent, then grabbed a pointer.

"Here's something you're not aware of, though. . . . I'm not sure if you can see it from here, but just there"—and he extended the pointer right through the image to a specific spot on her left breast—"something microscopic shows up. It might be a developing lesion of some sort. Or more precisely, a tumor-in-waiting. You should have it excised as soon as possible." Janie winced as he withdrew the pointer, as though it were actually leaving her flesh.

She looked at the small dot on her breast, and considered that before bodyprinting, it would not have been noticed until it was large enough to show up on a mammogram. Had she lived earlier, before advances in breast-cancer treatment, that small unchecked lesion might have been the cause of an untimely and painful death. She also considered that once her image was entered into the system, everyone on earth with access to her print would know that she had some sort of breast lesion. She suddenly felt very confused, but she could not deny that she was grateful to have found out in plenty of time to have the poison dot removed. *After all, I know plenty of surgeons. . . .*

The Biocop looked at her in smug satisfaction, knowing that he'd justified what she'd gone through by showing her the immediate benefits of such a procedure. "Are there any questions, then?"

She was too flabbergasted to think of anything germane, and too realistic to consider an attempt at escape, so she simply followed him out of the room and went compliantly back to her cell.

*   *   *

The scruffy woman was simply too tired to push the cart any more that day. She was having difficulty seeing after the descent of the sun, and decided to seek a safe place where she could rest. Her companions had all deserted her to seek rest for themselves. They would find her in the morning, she knew, but she needed help now. There was an overpass not far ahead, with a well-established clan living under it. By this time of night, she thought, everyone would be settled in to await the blessing of daylight. She had a friend or two there who might help.

She stopped the cart and leaned over the railing, then softly called out a password. In a few moments two dirty men appeared from under the overpass and they all exchanged quiet greetings. She asked for their help, and they willingly gave it. Together the Marginals lifted Caroline gently out of the cart and carried her down the embankment. Under the bridge other Marginals readied a place for her to sleep by piling up an assortment of blankets and extra clothing, until the resulting bed was soft enough to please a princess. They set her gently down on the make-shift bed and covered her with newspaper. The woman sat down beside her and talked quietly with the two men; a small fire in a metal pot cast an eerie glow on their weathered faces. Finally the woman leaned close to Caroline and listened to her breathing, then placed her dirty hand over Caroline's forehead. Though terribly ill, her charge seemed stable enough, so the woman propped her ratty brown bag against a pile of bricks, then curled up on it and went to sleep.

Once again the door to the holding area opened and a Biocop entered, this time alone and with no visible weapon. He said to Bruce, "We've found the materials you were looking for. They've been processed and you may take them with you." He pushed open the door to Janie's cell and then did the same to Bruce's. "By the way, Dr. Ransom, I sincerely apologize for putting you through all this. I had no choice, really. The regulations are quite specific about what we must do. And you might be interested to know that we were never able to contact Dr. Cummings in London. It's a good thing you had the necessary clearances. Otherwise you'd be spending a lovely week in Leeds." He laughed and said to Janie, "Miss Merman, I do hope you'll come back to visit Leeds again. I'm certain your next trip will be more pleasant."

Not bloody likely, she thought silently, but she gave him a saccharine smile and said, "Thanks. It's been grand. And highly educational. But I think I'll pass."

"Suit yourself," the guard said, and motioned for them to follow him. He escorted them to the main reception area where the missing tubes were stacked neatly in a pile, each one wrapped in protective yellow plastic and sealed with red tape. Bruce and Janie shared the heavy load, and as they walked out the door, one of the Biocops deposited another yellow plastic bag on Bruce's pile.

"Your watch and other personal items," he said.

They were surprised to discover that it was full dark outside. With no windows in the building they'd lost all track of time. But the cool night air was invigorating, and the freedom was heady, and for a few moments they both felt renewed and energized. After storing the tubes in the trunk of his car Bruce took his watch out of the bag. "Holy smokes, it's almost midnight!" he said.

"Damn!" Janie said. "I wanted to call Caroline! She's probably already asleep."

Bruce handed her his phone, which he'd left in his case in the car. She dialed Caroline's number in London, expecting to apologize for waking her.

"She's probably wondering what the hell happened to us," Janie speculated as the phone rang. But the hotel voice mail came on and Janie said with great irritation, "Where can she be at this hour?" She looked at Bruce as she listened to the message and said, "I'll bet she turned her phone off."

"Sounds like something Ted would do," he said, thinking of the difficulties they'd had because Ted had not responded to his pager. "Here's a thought!" he said. "Maybe they're together!"

"Not a very *pretty* thought," Janie commented. "From what little I know of Ted, they'd be like oil and water."

As soon as they were settled into the car with their belongings stowed and the maps ready, the adrenaline of finally being released was replaced by the brittle weight of fatigue and disorientation. Bruce reached wearily forward and punched in the car's ignition code. As the engine hummed to life he looked over at Janie and said, "Do you think we should attempt to drive back to London tonight?"

"I think we should get as far out of Leeds as we can right now. I don't like it much here."

They drove off, and Janie looked back through the rear window as the distance between them and the storage facility widened. She waved and said, "Good-bye, Ethel. . . ."

* * *

Not far out of Leeds it started to rain, a sweet good rain, steady and calming. Janie closed her eyes and leaned her face against the cool damp glass of the car window and slipped in and out of consciousness. Bruce leaned forward and switched on the wipers. It wasn't long before their rhythmic *thrum thrum thrum* had an unwanted soporific effect on him. His head nodded up and down as he stared over the steering wheel into the dark wet road ahead of him, and for a few seconds he closed his eyes. He snapped back to alertness just in time to avoid hitting a signpost and steered the car back to the delineated roadway. Knowing he could no longer drive well enough to get them back to London safely, he pulled off at the next exit and found the nearest lodging.

As the car came to a rest in the gravel drive of the old stone inn, Janie woke up in the passenger seat. "Where are we?" she said sleepily.

"An inn," Bruce said. "I'm falling asleep at the wheel." He shut down all the car's systems and pulled out the locking card. "Why don't you stay here, and I'll go in and see if they have any rooms."

"Okay," she said. But as he was getting out of the car, Janie reached over and put a hand on his arm. "Wait," she said. "Wait a minute."

He turned back and looked at her. "What is it?"

She searched his eyes, looking for an answer to a question she hadn't asked yet. He looked terribly tired and drawn. She hesitated, wondering if it was the right time.

Do it, Janie, she said to herself. *It's been too long and you might not get another chance.*

She squeezed his arm gently. "Why don't you just get one room," she said, then quickly added, "I mean, maybe that's something you want to think about. . . . I don't know if it is. . . ."

He laughed softly and gave her a warm smile. "Right now it's just about the *only* thing I'm thinking about."

Relieved, Janie said, "I guess I don't want to be alone right now."

He placed his own hand over hers, then leaned over and kissed her gently on the forehead. "You're not," he said.

They stood with their arms wrapped around each other in the shower and let streams of hot water wash the foul contamination of imprisonment off their tired bodies. They kissed long and hard and clung fiercely to each other, melting and blending together in an almost desperate act of coupling. When they emerged from the shower, cleansed and renewed, into the cozy room of the friendly old inn, they dried each other with soft towels and embraced again. Together they pulled down the quilt. The sheets below it were cool white cotton, and the bed looked wonderfully inviting. Janie slipped her freshly showered body between the sheets and pulled the soft quilt up to her neck. As soothing warmth spread through her aching, drained body, she watched Bruce look through his travel bag in search of his alarm clock.

She hated the notion that it would ring in a few hours and take them away from the quiet perfection they'd found, back to the uncertainty and the frustration of the real world, out of the comfort of privacy, to the jarring reality of schedules and demands and limits. *It's always an issue of time*, she thought. *There never seems to be enough of it to do what needs to be done.* His slim silhouette moved before the moonlit window and she thought, *Time's been very kind to him; he's still a good-looking man.* She wondered briefly what he would say about her, then shoved that insecurity out of her mind for what she hoped was all eternity. It didn't matter. He'd already said plenty with the way he'd touched her.

He climbed in beside her and she felt herself being gathered up in his arms. They shifted their positions until the hollows and bones of their bodies were lined up as closely as possible, then lay there, experiencing the strange new fit of each other. "This is the first time I've shared a bed in a very long time," Janie whispered. "It doesn't feel as small as I thought it might."

He kissed her lightly. "It feels just right," he said. And soon again, though they were both desperately tired, they rolled in each other's arms, and rocked away whatever distance remained between them. As dawn was breaking over the lush green hills, they were asleep in each other's arms, and until the alarm rang, all was well in that tiny part of the world.

Janie listened to the unanswered ringing on the other end of the line and felt her patience growing thinner with every repetition. "She's still not answering," she said to Bruce, who was brushing his teeth in the bathroom. "It's the middle of the morning! I can't imagine where she'd be."

"She's probably just out sightseeing," he said, "or maybe she got lucky. You aren't the only one that can happen to, you know."

She raised her eyebrows and smirked. "Me, lucky? Or you?"

Bruce put away his toothbrush and crossed the room. He took the receiver from her hand and replaced it, then scooped her up in his arms and kissed her fiercely.

"Hey, listen. We were *great* together. We should have done this twenty years ago."

She kissed him back with equal passion, and soon their hands were roaming all over each other and groping for pleasure points. She breathed deep, the scent of his skin filling her lungs, his scent, the unique essence of Bruce. *Oh God, let me just lose myself in this, just for a day or even an hour . . . let all this other stuff just disappear. . . .*

But unbidden, tubes of dirt danced through her consciousness, all fifty-four of them in a neat, unbroken row, followed by lists and letters and computer files; the distraction proved too much, and the exploratory mood snapped. She pulled away slowly, a sad look on her face, and said, "I'd love to do this now, but we really should go back."

He smiled, a little what-might-have-been grin, and nodded his agreement. "I know. You're right. But it was a nice thought, wasn't it?"

"*Really* nice," Janie said. And then another thought, a big, resented Nazi of a thought marched into her brain and called her to attention. *What will you find when you get back?* it demanded to know.

The glow of the previous night was slowly replaced by the pressure of her now even tighter schedule. "I just hope Caroline isn't out there digging up more dirt," she said to Bruce as they gathered up their bags. "We've got enough trouble with what we already have."

Seventeen

I t began to rain as they neared Kate's mother's house, so Adele and Alejandro stopped momentarily under a tree to lift the hoods of their riding cloaks. Still dazed and somewhat shaken from his leap through the oaks, Alejandro shivered and drew his cloak more tightly about himself, then leaned over and rearranged the folds of Adele's. As he fussed with her garment, she reached up with one hand and stroked his cheek.

"Tell me why you're so sad," she said.

He sighed sadly as he buttoned her collar. "How well you read my mood. You are a lady of many talents."

"It would take little talent to see the melancholy on your face, for *you* have no talent in hiding it."

"I *am* sad," he admitted, "and to the very core of my soul. I feel as though we have left Eden, and are cursed with the knowledge of what might have been. We were innocent there, and everything was beautiful; now we know far more than is bearable. And we return to a place where more sorrow awaits us."

"But we *shall* bear what we know," she said softly, "for *this* is the world in which we must live, not the one we have just left. And look about you. Do you not see beauty here? Consider the beauty of this rain." She extended her hand to catch a few drops. "I need only hold my hand out and soon I shall have enough to drink. Sweet rain to cool my thirst."

"It is a *cold* rain."

"It is a gift from God, Who would have us know the trees and flowers that even a cold rain brings us."

"It is autumn, and you have said it grows cold here. I begin to feel it for myself. Will the trees and flowers not turn brown soon?"

"Only to be born again in green with the spring."

"But why must everything wither and die?"

She shrugged. "Your questions are beyond my simple ken. Surely you would do better to consult a philosopher or a priest on such divine matters. But I will tell you what I have always believed. Things wither and die before us so we may better savor that we *live*."

But Alejandro would not be comforted. To him England was a cruel, forbidding, unwelcoming place. He no longer knew where his home was, or to whom his allegiance belonged. To King Edward he was the pope's spy, cloaked in the guise of physician, yet to the pope he was a Spaniard to be toyed with, one who could be counted on to annoy the English royalty as much as he protected them. "Now I have the promise of a cure," he said, "but it comes from a place that seems unreal, not of this world, and from a woman who could not be more unlike the other healers I have known. I bring it from the pale, but I must use it in the darkness. And who knows if it will even work! A fortnight's delay in dying does not necessarily make a cure."

Adele said quietly, "It will work if it is God's will for it to work."

With anger in his voice Alejandro said, "I curse God's will. All around us lie His victims."

She reached out and took one of his hands. Squeezing it gently, she said, "Curse it you may, but you will never change it. Things die because it is God's will that they should." She nodded in the direction of their destination and said, "Let us hope that it is God's will that we get to Kate before He reaches down to claim her." Without another word she rode off, with Alejandro close behind.

They were admitted to the house by the same servant, whose expression was even more grave than before. "Come in quickly," she said. "Mother Sarah is here! The very one you rode out to see. Had I known she was on her way already, I would not have sent you out to seek her. To have ridden all that way for naught, when she arrived right after ye left! Can you forgive this poor ignorant wench?"

Alejandro looked at her with genuine bewilderment. "Foolish woman," he said, "what are these inane mutterings?"

"As I've told you, Mother Sarah is here!" she said. "She arrived not a piddle's time after you left. I've been cursing myself since, and I hope you'll not whip me."

With their riding cloaks dripping on the wide planks of the entry floor, Adele and Alejandro exchanged confused looks.

"How long has she been here?" he asked the servant.

The servant peered at him suspiciously; "Did ye not hear me, sir? Since shortly after you rode out to seek her, I said."

He looked at her in shock and disbelief. The servant mistook his expression for anger and continued her pathetic confession of ineptitude. "Oh, forgive me, sir! I didn't mean to speak so harshly. And now the Mother is saying I'm a simpleton for missing some doses of medicine! The lady refused to drink that yellow swill, and who can blame her? It smells of death itself and would never cross my lips, even for the saving of my soul! Such foulness has never been kept in a vial, for the vial itself would break from the revulsion of containing it."

Completely confused, Alejandro looked around for Kate, remembering the old woman's dire prophecy. "Where is the child?" he growled.

"Why, she's within, as is the Mother, who attends my lady."

Alejandro pushed roughly past her, followed closely by Adele. They rushed into the bedchamber, not knowing what to expect. There they saw a ragged figure bent over the bed, upon which lay the thin remnants of a once beautiful woman. The child stood against the far wall with a cloth in her hand, her herbal mask discarded, her eyes red and swollen. Upon seeing Alejandro and Adele she bolted away from the wall and threw herself, sobbing, into their mutual embrace.

"Oh, Blessed Virgin be praised that you are here! I am so afraid!"

The physician comforted her as well as he could. *God curse the king for ordering this travesty to take place! His conscience be damned, as it well deserves to be!* He said to the little girl, "Find your strength, for you must tell me what has taken place in our absence. . . . Who is this hag attending your mother now?"

She sniffled as she composed herself. "Why, this is no hag, but the midwife!" she protested. "This is the Mother Sarah!"

This cannot be! Alejandro's thoughts raced wildly. *She cannot have left her cottage after we did, only to arrive here before us. . . .*

He stood up, leaving Adele in the corner with Kate in her arms. "Woman, turn around and let me see your face," he ordered.

Briefly glancing over her shoulder, the crone said impatiently, "Physician, do not order me about as you would some common underling. I am not your apprentice. If things were as they should be in the natural order, you would be apprenticed to me." She shuffled forward toward the head of the bed. "Sadly, the natural order has been disrupted of late. Now, I have important work here! If you cannot be helpful, take care not to get in the way!"

"This can't be," he cried again in disbelief. "We left Mother Sarah at her cottage and came directly here. No one overtook us on the way!"

The bent grimalkin slowly turned away from her work and faced the physician. He studied her closely. It was the same lined and ancient face, the face of a thousand years' wisdom.

"You must always expect the unexpected," she said, shaking her finger in his face.

Stunned by her repetition of the remark he had heard so recently, he peered closely at her wrinkled features, searching for some reason to discount the likeness. She stared back at him, overpowering him with the strength and steadfastness of her gaze. With a knowing smile she said, "Now, if you wish to learn, watch closely here. You will see these things nowhere else."

Shocked though he was by her presence, for he could not believe that she had traveled so quickly, he did as he was told. He came around to the side of the bed and looked more closely at the helpless patient and saw the telltale blue and black blotches on her swollen neck. *She is near to death,* he thought; *yet she has lived so long with the affliction. . . .*

"There is not much time now," she said quietly. "The stupid wench I trusted to care for her has allowed the lady to pass over dosages of a critical tincture, and now I must use all my skills to undo the damage. Be prepared to assist me!"

The voice, the stance, the clothing, they were as like to those of the woman at the stone cottage as was the face. He had no choice but to believe that she was the same woman. Flustered, he said, "What would you have me do? I will do anything."

From a nearby tray she took a long reed filled with powdered yellow stone, and gave it to him. "Hold this to the candle," she said, "but be sure to keep it at arm's length. Set it in the hole of that stone." She pointed to a flat gray rock resting on a small table.

He did as she directed, and immediately the room was lit by a blue-white sparkling flame. The light it gave was harsh, and as the blue fingers of flame sputtered out from the tip of the reed, shadows danced eerily. The odor of rotten eggs again filled the air.

He came back to the bedside, and watched as the old woman began a droning chant in a language he had never heard before. He thought it sounded like English, or some combination of that rough language and one containing more Latin, but he could not really understand.

Adele cradled Kate in her arms and watched intently, stupefied by what she was seeing. So stunned was she that she almost failed to hear Alejandro's urgent plea. "Adele! Please, if you can understand what she is saying, try to remember for me. . . . I will recall her motions later. Please recall her words for me!"

"I will!" she said, hugging the child closer.

Mother Sarah addressed each of Kate's mother's symptoms in turn. "Three crumbs of a crust baked on Good Friday last, to solid up the bowels." She broke three small clumps off a nearly petrified crust of bread and laid them on the lady's lips.

From a small vial she dripped seven drops of a milky fluid on the lady's forehead. "The balm of Gilead, as rare as the gift from Sheba to Solomon." Alejandro recognized three words from the Torah, and though he did not comprehend the remainder of her invocation, he knew this ritual, for it had been used for centuries by Jewish physicians to treat digestive and melancholy disorders. *How had she come by this knowledge?*

"A coin of gold, placed in the hand, to buy back the health from the devil." The old woman pried open the lady's clenched fingers and closed them again around the coin.

"The blood of the lamb, to ward off the pest, marked upon the lintel as in ancient Egypt." Mother Sarah dipped her thumb in a small bowl of bright red fluid, then smeared the headboard of the bed with a long streak of the substance.

Now the old woman held the shell of a walnut in her hand, and passed her other hand over it in slow circular motions as she whispered indecipherable chants. She placed the shell on the lady's abdomen and lifted the upper half, revealing a large black spider with a white diamond on its back. The confused creature scampered immediately toward the lady's chest and quickly disappeared under the bedclothes. Watching from the corner, Adele crossed herself again and grimaced, and Kate cried out, each one imagining how it would feel to have the furry-legged black thing crawling on her own chest.

Then the old woman bent stiffly and retrieved a small package that had been resting by her feet. The small brown sack was tied with a cord dirtied by many openings. Onto a nearby board she poured out a small pile of a grainy grayish powder. Pinching a quantity between her fingers, she said, "A knuckle's worth." She sifted it from her fingers into a small bowl. Then she picked up a vial and said, "Half of a cupped hand." She poured some of the yellowish water into her cupped hand and allowed it to drip into the bowl containing the powder. Mixing the two together carefully, she made a disagreeable gray-green slurry, which gave off a musty odor and would not be welcomed by even the most desperate patient.

First she dipped her finger in the potion, and smeared a small quantity on the lady's forehead, then she ladled the rest into the objecting patient's mouth. Even in her state of great weakness the lady attempted to spit the foul mixture back out again, but the old woman covered her mouth with surprising strength, forcing the lady to ingest the medicine. The weak patient swallowed, then resumed her irregular panting.

Mother Sarah gently wiped the sweat off the patient's cheeks and the dribble from her chin. "Soon we shall be through, and you can rest again," she cooed reassuringly. She slipped a silver ring on the finger of

the gasping patient, intoning, "A ring made from pennies begged by
lepers!"

Then with a sigh of resignation Mother Sarah pulled the last of her
implements out of her satchel. A small woven strip of red cloth, much
like a ribbon, was folded once to form a small loop with a crossed tail,
and pinned to the nightdress over the patient's heart. "To ward off the
spirit of the plague maiden," she said, "who fears the color of blood and
will not disturb a heart protected by its wearing."

Finally the old woman collapsed into a nearby chair, depleted and
exhausted from her efforts to cure her failing patient. She did not move
or make a sound for many minutes; even her breathing was so shallow as
to be barely noticeable.

Alejandro shook the old woman's arm gently. So motionless was her
trance that he feared she might have diverted death onto herself from
the lady. But her eyes fluttered open, and she righted herself in the chair.

"I can do no more," she said. "Now we must pray."

And so they prayed, each in the way of his or her custom, for the
lady's recovery. But as the sun lowered in the sky, it became plain to all
that the spirit of the Plague Maiden had not been dispelled. The lady
began her journey to the other side of life. Her eyelids began to flutter
and her gaze shifted around the room.

The physician knew there was no focus to her gaze, much as the
loved ones would like to imagine, and that the patient had little control
over herself. He was not surprised when she pulled her legs up near her
body as would an infant and lay on her side in a huddled pose, as if
protecting her plague-distended belly. He heard her gasp in one last
breath, and then saw that she was still, her unseeing eyes staring out from
between her slightly parted lids.

In keeping with the local custom Mother Sarah closed the woman's
eyes and placed a penny on each one.

Kate, sobbing uncontrollably, her small body completely enfolded
in Adele's arms, cried out, "*Mama!*" with pitiful grief and anguish. Alejandro was about to wrap the bedclothes about the dead woman's body,
but Kate begged him to stop.

"Please, Physician, let me kiss her one more time."

Kneeling down and holding her by the arms, he said gently, "I
cannot, child, for the contagion may pass from her lips to yours."

But her pitiful and plaintive expression was more than he could bear. He watched as she wiped away her tears one more time with the cloth he had given her.

"Kate, kiss your handkerchief," he said.

Between her hitches and sobs she said, "But why?"

"I will show you."

She wiped her eyes one more time and then kissed the cloth.

"Now give it to me."

He reached out with her small hand and placed it in his larger one. He smiled reassuringly and stroked her hair. Then he rose up from his crouch and went to the bedside. He touched the handkerchief to the dead woman's lips, then tucked it into her hand.

"Now she will take your kiss with her into all of eternity."

Alejandro stood by, fidgeting impatiently, and watched as Mother Sarah splashed cool water against the wrinkled skin of her face and neck again and again, trying to remove the foulness that had settled into her pores during the failed ritual of healing.

Still bent over the basin, she turned her head toward him and said, "Would you not allow an old woman a moment's respite?"

"I would question you about—"

"Aye, I know, there is much you wish to ask me." Water dripped from her face and hands and she wiped them dry on her apron, sighing deeply. "Very well," she said. "You have my attention now."

"What I wish to know first is how—"

"Is how it is that you could ride on horses from my home while I stood and watched you leave, and then, horseless myself, arrived here before you?"

"Yes!"

"In truth, young man, it did not happen that way."

"But I saw it with my own eyes, as did my companion. . . . Adele!" he called.

She came from the next room with Kate in her arms.

"Please tell this woman what we saw."

"Alejandro, the child . . ." she said, concern on her face. "I would not have her hear this. It is blasphemy!"

He took Kate from Adele and handed her to the servant, who took the child away. With Kate safely out of earshot Adele related the events of their earlier ride to the old woman.

"You did not see me pass as you first rode out?"

Alejandro and Adele looked at each other. Adele shrugged, and Alejandro said, "I do not recall seeing a woman such as yourself."

"But there were travelers on the road, were there not?" the old woman said.

"There were," he said almost angrily, "but none such as yourself!"

"In my years of treating those with disorders of both the body and soul, I have known many people who see what they wish to see, in total disregard of what is actually before them. It must have been powerfully important to you to see me in that glade today, or surely you would have seen that the house and clearing were quite empty."

"Woman, I assure you," he responded, his anger now unbridled, "that my soul, body, and mind are all equally sound and I have no doubt that you were there at that cottage, as my companion has verified."

He waited for her to respond, but she simply remained silent, her hands folded across her ample bosom.

"Well? What have you to say now?"

"I have to say, impertinent stripling, that though I do not doubt you believe your tale to be true, it is in actuality your recollection of a most pleasing dream. How can one be sure that your weary minds did not conjure up the entire occurrence, simply for the joy of having something wondrous to contemplate in these trying days?"

"I have brought out the things you gave me, the medicines—"

"—which you cannot say for sure that you acquired from me . . ."

Exasperated by her repeated denials, Alejandro threw up his hands. He paced restlessly around the small room, muttering to himself. Finally he said to her, his voice bitter with disappointment, "Then at least let me understand why your efforts failed to save the life of the lady. By the telling of the servant, she had lived with the affliction for over a fortnight! This is remarkable. I have never seen such success. What went wrong in the final hours? I must know!"

The old woman sat down, and breathed a deep sigh before answering. "Physician, do you ever use your skills on a patient who cannot possibly survive?"

He said nothing, but his thoughts went instantly to Carlos Alderón's slow wasting.

"Aye, I thought you might have," she said, recognizing his shamed look. "Your eyes betray you, though you cannot speak of it."

He hung his head and said, "You are right. I have made such wasted treatments."

Her voice grew gentler and more soothing. "Never consider those treatments wasted, for their effect on the living is of far greater consequence. If I simply walked away from this lady today, my disregard for those who cherished her would have been as deadly to them as the plague itself. I will not take away the hope of a child. But I would be lying if I claimed to have a cure. I have long delayed the dying, but a cure eludes me."

Alejandro said, rather rudely, "Then all of those ridiculous charms and incantations were nothing but cheap tricks, when in truth you have no better skills than I!"

She flashed him an angry look but held her temper, then gave him a knowing grin and stroked her chin. "I recall quite clearly, my young friend, that you were as much in awe of the rituals as was the overly pious lady who accompanies you. Do you deny that for at least a while, you had faith in the cure?"

He could not deny it. He recalled the intense fascination he had felt while observing the crone's performance. She was right. For at least a short while he had believed that the lady would live.

"And that," she said with confidence, almost smug in her tone, "is the sole source of my healing powers. People are prepared to believe what they want to be true. You are no different from any other in that regard."

But I want to be different, he thought miserably. *I need to believe that because of my training and dedication I can ease the suffering of the afflicted. There is nothing more to my life than that.*

She saw his shamed look, and understood what was behind it. "Do not be too hard on yourself, Physician, for you have not had enough lessons from the best teacher, which is nothing more than the daily practice of your art. Experience will teach you more than any patron or mentor. And while there is much experimentation yet to be done, I believe a cure is at hand. Each time I treat a patient, I have come closer and closer to success. I change the proportions of the powder and liquid, for therein lies the key."

She busied herself with putting away her tools and medicines as she spoke, but left two containers out of her satchel. "Now rise up from your self-pity, young man, and pay attention, for I shall not repeat myself.

"A long time ago I noticed that the animals who drink from the warm spring by which I make my home seem to resist the ravages of all contagions, whereas others of their species fall prey and die rapidly."

She picked up a large jar of the cloudy yellow water and placed it on a table near him. "I observed that it had a rather noxious odor, which is fainter but similar to that given off by the strange yellow rocks that are brought up with the ore from the copper mines."

"The ones that remind me of eggs gone bad."

"Yes, exactly! You are a quick study when you are not mired in sadness! I fancied that the yellow water contained small bits of the yellow rock finely powdered; through what force, I know not, but what matter? The animals who drink from that spring must have large amounts of the pungent yellow rock absorbed in all of their bodily humors by now."

"What is this yellow powder called?"

"It is called sulphur. When it is burned, the flame sparkles and turns blue. Witches have long used it to dazzle the ignorant into believing in their special powers."

"As you did today, with the reed."

"Guilty I am of that sinful chicanery," she said with a grin, "but all for good cause." Then she placed the small brown sack next to the jar of water. "You must add this gray powder, for it strengthens as a sword strengthens a knight!"

She took one of his hands in hers and poured a tiny mound of the grainy gray stuff into the palm. Alejandro rubbed it between his fingers and felt its granular texture. He looked questioningly at the old woman.

She whispered with great reverence, "It is the dust of the dead, and it imparts their powers to the ill one."

The dust of the dead? Surely this is forbidden. . . .

She continued with her instructions. "Mix a knuckle of the powder into a half a cupped hand of the water, and give the patient a good swallow at sunrise, highest noon, and again at sunset. Should the patient be awake, and yourself as well, one more swallow at midnight will not do harm. But conserve your supply, and use it wisely, for these things are found only by my abode; God alone knows when you may need them again."

"God alone," Alejandro repeated, and prayed that such need would never come to pass.

They placed the lady's body along the side of the road where the teamster could not fail to see it. The five people who had been present at her death watched as the cart came to a stop and the driver dismounted. The teamster and another man picked up the body, still warm and pliable, and callously heaved it to the top of the pile of those who had succumbed that day.

The cart began to sag in the middle from the weight of its gruesome load. One man looked down the road at several additional bodies similarly awaiting their last earthly journey, and said to the other, "That's all now, the rest'll still be dead when we come back later."

"Aye," his helper agreed, "let's be off. The stink is addling my brain, and I'll soon be a simpleton."

"Soon, you say?" joked the other. "I see no sign of brilliance coming from you now. Although there is always hope of a miracle. I'll put you in my prayers."

They climbed back into the front seat and lightly slapped the reins along the horses' backs. Neighing in protest, the horses began their grim march to the burial ground, carrying Kate's mother as their last passenger.

They followed the same path as Adele and Alejandro had earlier, and soon came to the open field, near where Adele and Alejandro had visited Mother Sarah; the oaks still stood guard, but now their shadows were long and straight. As the horses dragged the creaking cart across the plain, its wheels bogged in the fresh-dug ground, and the lifeless passengers were jostled quite roughly about, but the teamsters paid no mind, knowing that none was likely to complain. In the course of this irreverent bouncing, the bedclothes covering the lady's body were loosened, and as she had not yet stiffened, her arm fell free of the wrapping. In her hand was the handkerchief that had carried her child's last kiss to her lips.

A few meters farther the cart groaned to a stop next to a shallow pit, hastily dug that afternoon in the peaty soil. The teamsters, already aching from the labor of digging the hole, lowered themselves slowly down from the high forward seat, and set to the hideous task of laying the bodies side by side in the open grave. When the pit was full, a priest would be summoned, if one could be found, and the sins of the dead would be remitted en masse. Then the peat would be thrown back into what was left of the pit, and the ground smoothed as much as possible.

"Let's hope the dogs don't dig up this bunch too," said one of the men, and they returned to the cart, ready to make their way back to London's outskirts, dreading their next load of passengers.

Mother Sarah gathered her strange assortment of cures and talismans and stowed them away in her ragged satchel. She threw a red shawl around her shoulders and took up her walking stick and headed toward the door. But before leaving, she turned back to Alejandro, and admonished him one last time, "Physician, mind you to be prepared. You must always expect the unexpected."

*   *   *

The stableman rushed out to tend to their horses when they returned to Adele's estate that night, and the drenched trio ran quickly up
the stone steps into the manor house. The roaring fires laid earlier by the
overseer had warmed the house and taken the wet chill off the air inside;
still, Alejandro trembled as he removed his dripping cloak. He could
barely control his shivering, and hurried to the fire to warm himself. Kate
followed closely, and held her small hands out to the blaze to soak up the
welcome heat, while small puddles of water formed around the hem of
her thin frock.

Suddenly, she sneezed, three times in rapid succession.

"Child?" Alejandro said with alarm. "What ails you?"

She sniffled and said, "I am cold, and weary from the ride, and my
stomach begs for food."

Relieved by her ready explanation, Alejandro relaxed. "Well, I am
glad that you have only three complaints. By great good fortune all three
are curable." He took her hand and together they sought out Adele. They
found her in the kitchen giving instructions to the housekeeper.

"It seems our small companion is cold, hungry, and tired, and I
have brazenly promised her a cure for all three afflictions. Can a dry
nightdress be found, and some supper?"

Adele nodded. "See to the child," she said to the housekeeper. "We
will speak again later."

The housekeeper led Kate away, saying, "First we'll get you dry and
warm, then we'll come back for some supper."

Kate rejoined them in a fresh nightdress, one Adele had worn as a
little girl. After a supper of soup and crusty warm bread, Adele led Kate
off to her old room and tucked her safely into the clean bed, singing
tenderly to the little girl until she was asleep. When she returned to the
table, it was cleared and deserted.

She found Alejandro in the salon, where a flickering fire cast shadows on the walls as it danced in the huge hearth.

"Shall we have some wine," she said, "to further warm our bellies?"

"I shall never feel warm again, nor dry, I fear," he said.

"The curse of our fair isle, I think," she said, pouring the wine. "I
have never traveled to your land, but I hear it is warm there, even in
winter."

As she poured the clear dark liquid, a stray beam of firelight sparkled on the ruby cross resting on her bosom. It was nearly the same color
as the wine, and the flash of red caught Alejandro's eye; he took pleasure
in the comparison.

As they sat before the fire, Alejandro carefully recorded the rituals

Mother Sarah had performed on Kate's mother, with Adele's help in recalling the things she had said and done. When the words were all on paper, he made a sketch of the woman herself. He wrote, *Mother Sarah,* on the page, and showed it to Adele.

"It's a fair likeness," she said. "It catches her spirit, I think."

"Hers is a spirit that will never be completely caught, I fear, but I shall not soon forget it." He closed the book and set it aside.

Slowly, as the fire warmed his skin and the wine his belly, Alejandro felt the distress of the day gradually leaving his weary body, and he sank back in the cushions to watch Adele brush her remarkable tresses before the fire. He allowed himself a few moments of joyful speculation on what his life could be like if she were his. He watched as she arranged her hair about her shoulders, and realized that she was doing her best to make herself attractive to him. She was having great success in her endeavor, for the physician's heart beat as if it would burst; they would be lovers again tonight, he was sure of it. *Dear God,* he prayed, *let this journey never end.*

Adele rose from her seat before the fire and came toward him. She settled herself on the soft rug in front of him and placed her head on his knees. The thick red hair fell in great waves over his lap, and he ran his eager hands through it again and again; it felt cool and soft and incomparably sensual, and he could not believe his joy.

She lifted her head off his knees, and he opened his mouth to protest its withdrawal, but before he could speak, she pressed one of her fingers over his lips to silence him. "Do not speak," she said, "for I would busy your lips with other things." Then she raised herself up and insinuated herself between his legs. She drew him close and pressed her soft body against his trembling one, then gently wrapped her arms around his back and held him tightly against her. They kissed, deeply, with a passion that knows no time. It might have been just one minute, or even ten, that their lips were together. He could not have said if his very life hung on the answer.

And then Adele placed her hands lightly on his shoulders, drawing them down along the front of his chest. He stiffened as her fingers neared the neck of his shirt, beneath which lay the telltale scar, and he was filled with the icy fear of discovery.

Speak! he admonished himself, *before the opportunity is no longer yours!*

Adele, forgive me for the lie I am about to tell you. It is not my intent to deceive you, only to survive to know your love, he thought silently. He reached his own hands up and gently caught her wrists, then brought all four of their hands together in a loving clasp. She looked at him quizzically, wondering why he had stopped her gentle exploration.

"Adele," he said carefully, "I am disfigured by a scar, and I would not have its ugliness frighten you."

She drew back a bit and said with alarm, "What scar is this you speak of?"

He unfastened one button at the neck of his shirt, and pulled the neckline slightly open. There Adele could see only a small portion of circular wound, now pink and well healed. She gasped. "Oh, my dear, how did this happen?"

He was weary of lying, but he knew there was no other choice; the truth would bring all his joy and hope to an end. "There was a skirmish on my journey from Spain to Avignon. I am ashamed of the outcome, and I would not speak further of it. I beg you to understand my modesty. I have kept this from you because I myself find the scar revolting, and I believed that you would find it so as well. And I did not wish to frighten you." He cast his eyes downward, and said, "I am humiliated before you. Please forgive my deception."

To his immeasurable relief she said, "It was not your choice to be so scarred. We will not speak of it again, for it has no import to me."

In her bed they spoke softly of the sweet things that new lovers cherish, each one blushing quite invisibly in the dark room, and finding small sweet surprises of pleasure in the other. Their simple union cemented no kingdoms together, only two people who dearly wished to be so joined.

So accustomed was he to his dreams of Carlos Alderón that to sleep without them was an anomaly to him, and when Alejandro felt a small warm hand touch his cheek just before dawn, he thought it was just part of another dream. But the touch was insistent, and eventually he opened his eyes. He saw Kate standing at the bedside.

"My throat is sore," she moaned, and touched her neck lightly. He looked at her more closely and saw to his horror the beginnings of a bruise beneath her chin.

Panicking, he began to throw off the bedclothes, then remembered that he was naked except for a light shirt. He said to the child, "Kate, you must do exactly as I tell you now. Return to your bed and I will attend to you as soon as I am decently covered. Do not touch anything as you make your way back to Adele's room, or speak with any of the servants. Breathe shallowly and try not to cough if the urge should come upon you."

She nodded, a look of terror in her eyes, and left the dim room, padding lightly away on her small feet. He glanced over at Adele's sleeping form and decided not to disturb her rest until he had investigated Kate's complaint further. After drawing up his breeches he searched out the saddlebag containing the gifts Mother Sarah had given him, and went to the pantry for a cup and a spoon.

When he entered Adele's former bedroom, he was shocked to see how tiny Kate looked in the huge bed. The canopy curtains were wide open, so he closed them at the far side and the foot of the bed, leaving open only the one that faced toward the door of the bedroom.

"Now, let me examine that neck of yours, my fine lady," he said. "I shall untie the top of your nightdress, but do not fear for your modesty. I am presently only interested in your neck."

He gently touched the darkened area under her chin. "Does it hurt when I touch you there?"

She winced, and he pulled his hand away. "It hurts there, and in my arm as well."

He lifted her arm up with one hand and with the other felt the area under her arm. He felt his heart sink as his fingers found the beginnings of a lump.

A *curse upon all that walks, flies, swims, or slithers,* he thought angrily. A *curse upon all that is holy!* He heard the soft rustling of a gown behind him, and looked around to see Adele silhouetted in the doorway.

"Rest here, child, and I shall return shortly." He closed the remaining canopy curtain, and left the room, taking Adele by the elbow and leading her in the same direction.

Her eyes full of fear, she said to him, "I see by your look that the news is not good."

He confirmed her suspicion with a nod, and she buried her face in his shoulder and wept. As he comforted her, she looked up at him through her tears and said, "I cannot bear to see her die."

"Nor can I, my love, but for once I am not helpless. At least we have some means to try to save her."

"The medicine!" she cried. "Where is it? I shall fetch it!"

"It is already in the room, on the bed table."

"Then let us waste not one minute in treating her."

Eighteen

Janie and Bruce walked slowly through the lobby of her London hotel, savoring their last few private minutes together. "Mission accomplished," he said.

Janie faced him and grinned. "Not prettily accomplished, but accomplished nonetheless. The trip had some high points, though. Toward the end there I was beginning to forget why we went in the first place."

Bruce laughed. "Me too. It was those soil samples, wasn't it? I'll make sure they get put in the cold storage unit," he said.

"And put a guard on them," Janie said.

"Oh, don't worry," he said. "I plan to oversee their security myself." He stopped walking and took her by the hand. They stood in the middle of the lobby, with people passing all around them, and looked at each other. "I have to say I think it ended rather well," he said.

"I'd have to agree. I'm surprising myself by feeling sorry that it's over."

"I'll ride up with you," he offered. "See you to your door."

"Actually," she said, "I was thinking about taking the stairs. I could use the exercise." She smiled and touched his cheek. "It would take longer. I'm not quite ready to let you go yet."

Still, at the notion of climbing seven flights of stairs, Bruce groaned.

"Wore you out, did I?" Janie teased. "And here I was thinking you looked like you were in such good shape. Must've been a trick of the moonlight."

He grinned. "Come to think of it, I do feel pretty achy this morning. Okay, I confess. You *did* wear me out. I guess I should be trying to build up my reserves."

"In which case, we should definitely ride."

They emerged from the elevator on the seventh floor still smiling and glowing, and walked slowly to the door of Janie's suite. Bruce wrapped his arms around her and started to kiss her good-bye, when they were interrupted by the sound of a latch turning. It broke the rhythm of the kiss. They pulled apart abruptly and looked in the direction of the sound. A few doors down a hand emerged to snatch up the newspaper lying on the carpet, the first concrete evidence that the real world would indeed try to extinguish the afterglow of their one-night idyll. Then the hand disappeared back inside, and the door closed again.

Janie frowned. "Let's do this inside the room."

"Good idea," Bruce said.

She withdrew the key card from her wallet and opened the door, but before entering she looked next door to Caroline's suite and noticed the DO NOT DISTURB sign still hanging there. She tapped Bruce's arm and pointed in the direction of the sign.

"Bless my soul," she said, sounding a bit miffed. "The wanderer seems to have returned, and it looks like she's sleeping something off."

"That's Caroline's suite?" he said.

"It is. I guess you were right. She must have met someone. There's probably a message from her waiting for me." They went in and Janie took off her jacket.

"Wait one minute while I clear up this mystery, and then I'll kiss you good-bye properly," she said.

"No problem," Bruce said. "You're the one with the tight schedule."

"Don't remind me," Janie said. She went to the phone and called for her voice mail, but there were no messages. She dialed the extension number for Caroline's room, but got no answer.

She hung up the phone. "She's either not in there or she's with someone and not answering. But that doesn't make any sense. She knows I'm trying to get hold of her, even if she is otherwise occupied."

"She might have different priorities," Bruce said, grinning. He walked over to her and took her in his arms.

Suddenly his lips were on hers, and she felt the warmth of his kiss rising up from her toes, spreading through her thighs and belly, the quick tease of his tongue, and his hand on the back of her waist, urging her gently closer to him. She felt her exasperations melting away, her resistance crumbling, and she pressed her body into his.

"Hmm," he said—*light kiss on the tip of her nose*—"maybe we should"—*soft little peck on the forehead*—"put the"—*nibble on her cheek*—"DO NOT DISTURB sign—"

The DO NOT DISTURB sign, she thought silently.

"—on this door too . . ."

Janie's brain-wheels were suddenly spinning. "What did you say?" she said.

He pulled back from her a little. "I said maybe we should put the DO NOT DISTURB sign on *this* door—"

The DO NOT DISTURB sign . . .

She pulled away from him abruptly, leaving him empty-armed and wondering. "Bruce, if you weren't in your room, why would you have a DO NOT DISTURB sign hanging on the door?"

He shrugged his shoulders. "I wouldn't. Maybe she just forgot to remove it before she went out."

"Not Caroline. She's a compulsive detail freak. That's why I asked her to come along to help me on this project. She doesn't miss a thing." Janie stared at the floor in a moment of indecision. Then she looked up and resolutely declared, "That's it, I don't care if I catch her in the act. I'm going in," she said.

"How are you going to do that?" Bruce asked.

"We have keys to each other's suite," she told him. Her face tightened with worry and she said, "I just hope everything's all right."

She quickly went out of the room and left her own door open. She tore off the DO NOT DISTURB sign and slid the plastic key card into the lock. When the lock clicked, she opened the door a crack and said, "Hello?" rather tentatively, hoping that she would find Caroline there but occupied. There was no reply.

She opened the door farther to go in, but the smell that greeted her drove her back into the hallway gasping for breath. She bumped backward into Bruce, who was right behind her, and closed the door again.

They both knew what that smell meant. She looked at Bruce pleadingly. "Do you want me to call the police?" he asked.

She'd seen lots of dead bodies, hundreds perhaps, in various states of wholeness, but Janie had never actually discovered one before, even during the Outbreaks. She stood in the hallway outside Caroline's room, trembling with fear. "No," she said, with more decisiveness than she felt. Her voice quivered. "I think I'd rather see what's there first. But I'm really scared of what we'll find."

Bruce pulled her close to him and held her for a few seconds. "I'm with you, Janie. We're here together."

Comforted by his presence, she took a deep breath of clean air and reopened the door, and together they entered the room. When she flipped on the light switch, a swarm of flies rose up from the floor area on the other side of the bed.

"Oh, God, Bruce, what if she's dead. . . ." They rushed to that side of the room and saw the stiff body of Ted Cummings lying there on the floor, just as it had landed when Caroline pushed him off her own body.

Janie stood there slack-jawed, staring in disbelief at the sight before them. Bruce turned aside and vomited into a wastebasket, then wiped his mouth with his hand.

Gagging from the vile smell, he said, "My God, what *happened* here?"

Janie rushed to the window and opened it as wide as it would go. "I don't begin to know," she said frantically. "Why on earth would Ted be in Caroline's room? *And where the hell is Caroline?*"

Bruce knelt down to take a closer look at the body. "We'd better not touch anything. We might be disturbing evidence."

Janie looked at him in shock. "Evidence of *what?* Are you implying that you think Caroline did this?"

He looked at her intently and said, "Janie, it's her room, and he's dead, and she's not here. What else am I supposed to think?"

Fighting off her anger, she knelt down beside him. "We don't know a thing about how he died." She leaned closer and looked at Ted's face. "I don't see any signs of trauma, and there's nothing to indicate that they might have struggled." She leaned closer, holding her breath, and looked carefully at the body.

"Damn," she said. "I need to get closer." She stood up and wiped her hands on the fabric of her pants, though she hadn't touched the body at all. "I've got some gloves and masks in my room. Let's go get them." She gave him a pointed stare as he rose up. "Caroline did *not* do this, you know," she said heatedly.

As he followed her out of the room, Bruce was not convinced.

The envelope from London had been staring at him from the corner of his desk for way too long, John Sandhaus thought. *They grow eyes after a while if you don't pay attention to them,* he thought, and picked it up. *Right.* The printout that Janie Crowe had sent him. The cacaphonous noise of children playing drifted into his office from another part of the house. He yelled to his wife, "Cathy, can you please keep those kids quiet so I can do some work?"

Cathy promptly invited him to engage in self-copulation, so he shut the door to his study in an effort to block out the din of family, and then felt guilty because he knew there would come a time when he would miss the comfortable noise of his children playing. He knew that someday, way too soon, its absence would seem far more disturbing than its presence.

As he waited for his computer to log on to the university database, he looked out the window at the beautiful New England countryside.

Soon enough, he thought, the colors would be magnificent, but then, of course, there would be the inevitable and never-ending leaves to rake, and all thoughts of magnificence would fade.

The computer said to him in a soothing, calm voice, "Welcome to Biocom. Please enter your password."

He typed in a few digits, then said back to the computer in a sarcastic voice, "Here's your bleeping password, you big pile of plastic! And stop talking to me! You are *not* human."

As if in direct contradiction to his edict the computer replied, "You may enter. Thank you for using Biocom."

And what else am I supposed to use? he thought. *You guys run everything. There's nothing else to use.*

In a few seconds he was on-line to the CDC's Atlanta database and the computer was searching for a match to the graphic image Janie Crowe had sent him. The program came back and asked for further information, but he had none to give it. She'd only sent a print; there had been none of the usual accompanying chemistry or genetic information. He made a mental note to speak to her about incomplete data when she returned, then wondered if such a chastisement might not be worth an international phone call right at the moment. But the note she'd attached to the print had said, "Have fun!" so he doubted that this piece would wind up being part of her final data. He decided against calling.

Reverting to the original file, he ran it through three different filters, hoping to sharpen the image so it would be more readable. His efforts were successful, because the next time he ran it through the program a new screen came up and told him it had identified his mystery bug as *Yersinia pestis.*

Yersinia. Enterobacteria, he thought. *Pestis* didn't ring a bell. "Have we met?" he said to the image on the screen. "No, I didn't think so. Not recently, anyway. Okay, then, let's see what else they have on you." He called up a list of options from the database, then scanned through the list and selected "Pathology." The file came up on the screen and he began to read it. It wasn't long before his eyes widened and his heart began to beat faster.

Holy shit, he said under his breath. He closed the file when he finished reading it and reverted quickly to the graphic image of the microbe. "*Yersinia* fucking *pestis,*" he said aloud. "*Holy shit.* You are *not* supposed to be loose in London."

She sent a print, he thought, his mind suddenly racing. But what did she make the print from, and where was that object now? *Does she know what this is?*

Of course not, idiot! That's why she sent it to you in the first place!

Wishing with all his heart that he hadn't left the envelope sitting on the corner of this desk for more than one minute, he searched around in his file on Janie's project for the phone number of the hotel she'd booked. As soon as he found it, he reached for the telephone.

He heard his teenage daughter on the line talking to several of her friends in a conference call. Without even saying hello, he ordered, "Get *off.* I need the phone *now.*"

"But, Daddy . . ."

John borrowed a phrase from his father. "But nothing!" he thundered, and everyone hung up without another word. As soon as he had a dial tone, he punched in the number, and waited impatiently for her to pick up on the other end. "Oh, Christ, Janie, answer the phone, *please. . . .*"

As she crossed the threshold into her own room, Janie's phone began to ring. She almost leapt on it.

She yanked the handset off the receiver. "Caroline?" she said, a little too quickly.

But it wasn't Caroline. "Janie? Is this Janie Crowe?"

Janie was disappointed. "Yes," she said. "Who is this, please?"

"It's John Sandhaus. From Amherst."

"Oh, John, oh my God . . . Hello. Listen, I'm afraid you're calling at a bad time—"

"It's pretty important. I'm calling about that graphic image you sent me."

It took her a moment to remember that she'd sent him a print and another moment to remember what had been on it. *That microbe,* she thought. And in view of what she faced in the next room, it seemed glaringly trivial. "I'm sorry, John. I appreciate your getting back to me about that. But I can't talk right now. Can I call you back later? I've got a problem here and it can't wait."

"I'll say you've got a problem." His voice was full of exasperation. "I don't know what your problem is there, but your problem here is pretty enormous. I think you'd better listen." Without waiting for her to agree he launched right into his explanation. "I got a firm ID on that bacterium from the CDC database."

Big fucking deal, she thought angrily. *How dare he think his opinion is more important than my problem here. . . . I've got a dead man in the next room. Top that, John Sandhaus. . . .*

325

Incredibly, he did top it. "That microbe you dug up was not your ordinary household bacterium. It's *Yersinia pestis*. It causes bubonic plague."

She gasped and put her hand to her mouth. Then she pulled it away just as quickly and stared at it.

"And Janie, there's something else very strange about it. The CDC files show that the last known case of plague in all of England occurred in 1927. There were some slight but significant differences between the sample of *Y. pestis* in the database and the print you sent me. Where did you get it?"

The sense of dread she'd felt on that field that night returned in full force. She said quietly, "I dug it up from about a foot and a half down."

"There you have it, then," he said triumphantly, and issued his opinion. "You've got a very old bug on your hands. It's obviously the archaic strain. I should probably be congratulating you for such a major find, but I think I should console you for major trouble instead. That bug is probably far more virulent than what's around today, just based on the differences in the symptoms we see in modern plague and the symptoms described in history books. Right now it looks like it's still in a sporified state, but if the right conditions occur, say it gets wet or it's warmed up just right, it could desporulate and revert to its active state."

"*Dear God*" was all she could say.

"You can say that again. It would be a *very big problem*. You have to call the proper authorities in London and notify them right away if there's any possibility that it might have gotten loose. We can cure modern plague, but I don't know about the old version."

She was silent.

"Janie?" he said again, but got no answer.

He said very calmly to the silent phone, "You have to do the right thing here. Don't think about whether or not you're going to get into trouble. This is bigger and more important than you. And, Janie? Do yourself and the rest of the world a favor. *Wash your hands before you get on the plane home.* This bug is just different enough that it might not make the sensors react."

He hung up.

"What was that all about?" Bruce asked anxiously.

She swallowed hard as she replaced the receiver. "Do you remember that fabric sample I dug up? Frank found it in one of our tubes just before he died."

He nodded. "I remember. What about it?"

"I sent off one of the prints Frank made for me to my reeducation advisor back in the States, thinking he might enjoy looking at it. He's a forensic pathologist, but he specializes in bacteria, and he's one of the best in his field. Well, that was just him on the phone." She looked into his eyes, her own eyes full of fear. "It seems that I've managed to dig up the archaic form of the bacterium that causes bubonic plague."

Bruce sat down, stunned. "Where is that sample now?"

She nodded her head in the direction of her small refrigerator. "Right over there."

"It's here in this room?"

"Right here. Don't worry, it's sealed up tight. But I'm not worried about the sample contaminating anything while it's in the refrigerator. What worries me is that Caroline's been handling it. And did you get a good look at Ted while we were in Caroline's room? He didn't look so good. And why on earth would he be wearing a turtleneck in such warm weather?"

"I don't know," Bruce said. "In all the years we've worked together, I don't ever recall seeing him wear anything like that."

Without another word they both got up and headed toward the door. Just before they went out, Janie grabbed Bruce by the arm. "Let's not forget these," she said, and went to her briefcase for two masks and two pairs of gloves.

Properly protected, they crouched down next to Ted's odiferous corpse and examined it visually.

"He's very pale," Janie said.

"He's very *dead*," Bruce pointed out.

"But still, he's paler than he should be." She pointed to the back of his hand. "Look at the difference. His face is much paler than his hand, and his position wouldn't account for it. His pallor could be the result of some illness."

She searched her memory for the symptoms of plague. "The one thing I remember about plague is the dark swellings in the lymphatic areas. I don't think they taught us much else."

"There wasn't much need. It was basically a dead disease by then."

"Let's hope it's not dead like tuberculosis," she said cynically.

"But that bacterium evolved into drug resistance. Plague is still treatable."

"*Modern* plague is treatable. It's my advisor's opinion that what we dug up is *archaic* plague."

"Shit."

"*Very* shit."

"But we don't know if that's what killed Ted."

Janie reached over and with one finger pulled the cowl of the turtle-neck shirt away from Ted's neck. Beneath it were dark bruises and lumpy swellings. "Look at this," she said. "Dark swellings in the lymphatic areas."

Bruce looked and swallowed hard. "We still can't be sure. We need to verify the presence of the bacteria. And there's something else too. I agree that it looks like he had plague, but it doesn't look like the disease was advanced enough to cause his death." He pointed to Ted's exposed neck. "I mean, I agree that the signs of infection are there. But look at these buboes. They're just beginning to resolve. I'm certainly no expert, but I just don't see this stage of disease as being fatal."

Janie couldn't argue; he looked as if he might have been sick before he died, but not fatally sick. But the possibility that Ted had died of some other cause was something she didn't care to consider; instead of simplifying things, it made her situation even more complex.

"This is getting very confusing," she said. "He's dead. She's not here. There's plague in the refrigerator next door. We know for sure that Caroline handled it; Ted certainly might have. It was in the lab; so was he. I don't know what to do next."

And how well did she know Caroline, after all? *Could she have done this?* Janie wondered. There was an undeniably dead man in her room, and Caroline was nowhere to be found. Until they found her, they wouldn't know for sure what had happened. Janie knew that she and Caroline would be spending *far* more time in England than they'd origi-nally planned if there was a question of wrongful death. The pit of her stomach started to lurch.

She looked around the room for anything that might sway her from the conclusion that there had been some criminal aspect to Ted's de-mise. "Nothing jumps out at me and screams, '*Evidence!*'" she said. "I'm not even sure what I should be looking for. And I'm *studying* this stuff." She went into the bathroom, where she found Caroline's nightdress lying on the floor and the toilet seat up, flecks of spittle splashed all around the rim. Though she couldn't feel the fabric through her gloves, she could tell from its weight that it was soaked with sweat.

She went back into the main room and showed the nightdress to Bruce. "I found this on the floor in the bathroom. It's drenched. I wonder if she was sick too."

She folded it neatly and laid it on the dresser. Out of the corner of her eye the refrigerator caught her attention. She looked at it more closely.

"Someone left the door of the refrigerator open," she said. She looked inside the small unit. "And it's a mess in here. Someone was looking for something."

But Bruce had his own discovery near the bed. He had begun looking through Ted's pockets and had found one of the vials.

He stood up and showed it to her. "Janie, look at this. It's tetracycline."

She looked down at the corpse. "Obviously it didn't work," she said. "And where's the syringe? Why would he have the tetracycline with him and not have some way to administer it?"

"I don't know," Bruce said. "Maybe it's lying around here somewhere."

They looked around on the floor and checked the wastebaskets, but saw nothing suspicious.

"He might be lying on top of it," Janie said. She bent down and placed her two hands under the side of Ted's body. "Give me a hand. Let's roll him."

"Should we be moving him? What if we're disturbing evidence?"

"What if we're *missing* evidence by *not* moving him?" Her voice was full of exasperation. "We can put him back in position when we've looked underneath."

Reluctantly, Bruce helped her. They tipped the stiffening body up on its side and beneath it they found the syringe and another vial. Janie moved the two items out from beneath the body very gingerly with one hand, taking care not to touch them any more than necessary. Ted's deadweight was heavy, and they were both almost sweating by the time they replaced his body in its original position.

Bruce handed Janie the partly full vial of tetracycline, then picked up the other almost empty vial. "Look at this."

She read the label on the vial and let out a long, low whistle. "This would give an entire troop of Boy Scouts some very sweet dreams for a day or two."

Stuck to the vial he had given Janie was a single long red hair, obviously one belonging to Caroline.

Janie sat down on the bed, considering everything they knew. Her head ached and she rubbed her forehead. Ignoring the pain, she went through the evidence, listing it aloud. "We have the dead body of a man who looked sick but wasn't sick enough to have died of his disease and who had no other overt signs of fatal injury. We have a missing and possibly sick woman. We have a half-full vial of an antibiotic and a nearly empty vial of a sedative. We have a syringe."

"We have, in other words, nothing that makes any sense at all."

"One thing makes sense to me," she said. "Whatever happened in here was initiated by Ted."

He came to Ted's defense almost instantly. "Janie, how can you say that? There's no way to tell who did what here."

"Come on, Bruce, think about it! How is she supposed to *get* these drugs? She has no access to any of this stuff. They took my *aspirin* at the airport, for crying out loud!"

It's true, he thought; *Ted could just walk into the Institute's medical office and take whatever he wanted, as long as he wasn't too greedy about it. . . .*

"I've been staying next door to her, we've been working together," Janie continued, growing shrill, "and I can't tell you how out of character this would be for her. She's almost pathetically normal." She took the vial of sedative from Bruce's hand. "This is a class-five drug! She has no possible way to get hold of it." She held it up in front of Bruce's face. "And it's almost gone! You can't tell me that she planned all this, obtained the materials, pulled it off, and then ran!"

She picked up the soaked nightgown again. "And if you want evidence, check this out." This time she tossed it at him; he missed it and it hit the floor. "Maybe Ted knew she was sick. Maybe he had something to do with it. Maybe he's been sedating her and *that's* why she didn't answer the phone. She was probably out like a light."

She could see the look of disbelief on Bruce's face. "Then where is she now?"

"*I don't know.* She could be anywhere. But if I woke up from a drug-induced sleep to find a dead man in my room, I'd get the hell out as fast as I could."

"All right, all right," Bruce said, "you've got a point. Maybe there's more here than what we're seeing. But it's all just so unfathomable." He threw up his hands in disgust. "I haven't got the faintest notion of what we should do now."

"I think the first thing we should do is get out of this room. I can't think anymore with this stink. It's giving me a headache." She thought about the ibuprofen in the toe of Caroline's shoe and went to the closet. She opened the door and saw four neatly arranged pairs of shoes on the floor. As she was checking through each one, she remembered something Caroline had told her. With the bottle of ibuprofen in hand, she stood up again.

"If Caroline bolted, she bolted shoeless. I remember she told me she brought four pairs of shoes. There are four pairs in the closet. And she hasn't had time to buy new ones, so she had to have been drugged or delirious. Maybe both," she said.

Taking their evidence with them, they returned to Janie's room. "My head is swimming," she said. "There are just too many possibilities. But my primary concern is for Caroline. She's probably out wandering around in a state of semidelirium, either from sickness or from shock at what's happened to her. We've got to find her, either way."

Bruce took on a trouble look. "You're right," he said, "but London is a pretty big place, Janie. We're going to need help. And if she's got plague, she's probably incredibly contagious. Plague is a level-four bio-hazard. We have to call Biopol."

"Wait a minute, Bruce. If it's a level-four, you know they'll shoot to kill if she tried to resist. She probably doesn't have any idea what's happening to her. She *will* resist, I assure you. And we don't know if she's got plague or not. It's certainly a possibility, but it's not a sure thing by any stretch of the imagination. If we alert the Biocops, they'll probably operate on the assumption that she does, and worry about it later. We can't tell *anyone*."

Bruce looked shocked. "What do you mean, we *can't* tell anyone? We *have* to tell Biopol. If we suspect there's bubonic plague loose in London, if there's even the slightest possibility that it's true, then we don't have a choice!"

He headed for the telephone. Janie moved toward him.

"Bruce, please, we might be wrong . . . they'll kill her . . . we can't let that happen if she's not a threat. . . ."

His hand was on the receiver. "That's the problem, Janie—we *don't know* if she's a threat. I don't think that assuming the worst is an unreasonable position in this type of situation! Look what happened in the U.S. when reasonable assumptions were ignored in the case of the Outbreak—"

"That was *different!*"

"*How* was it different? It was a contagious disease with a short incubation period. . . ."

For a few more tense exchanges Bruce's hand remained on the telephone. "Bruce, please," Janie finally said, "I'm *begging* you. *Please* don't."

"Janie, I'm a public official in a position of responsibility and I have information that leads me to believe that the public is in jeopardy! What do you *suggest* I do?"

"Look," she said frantically, "we *can* find out for sure. We have stuff we can test. We have access to one of the best labs in England, and we can go there right now and do it in a flash . . . then we'll *know!* We won't just be guessing anymore."

"It'll mean too long a delay. This should be taken care of immediately."

"It won't take more than an hour or two at most! Bruce, please listen to me. . . ." She picked up the nightdress and extended it toward him. "If we find *Yersinia pestis* on this nightdress, then we'll call Biopol instantly. I won't give you an argument. I just don't want to see Caroline imprisoned for no reason. They might *shoot* her, for God's sake . . . please just think about it before you do anything that might get her hurt."

Finally his stony resistance to her plan melted. "All right," he said. "But I have to tell you that I'm really opposed to this . . . if there's bacteria on her nightdress, we call immediately."

"Agreed," Janie said with relief. *It'll buy me some time,* she thought frantically. *But what if it's loaded with bacteria? What then?*

She didn't know. The thought of it being free of bacteria was no more appealing.

"Before we leave," Bruce said, "we have to make sure no one is going to go into that room. And we have to take that piece of fabric out of the refrigerator in *this* room. We can't run the risk of someone from housekeeping getting their hands on it."

He went to the refrigerator and pushed the door open with the tip of his elbow. In the center of a wire shelf was the circle of fabric, wrapped in plastic. He removed it carefully, taking great care not to touch the shelf itself with his potentially pestilential hands. Janie took a sealable biosample bag out of her briefcase and Bruce dropped the wrapped fabric into the bag. She put the nightdress in another plastic bag.

She removed her gloves, turning them inside out as she did, and Bruce followed suit. Janie set hers down on a piece of paper. "Put your gloves on here," she said. "I'm going to burn them."

"Good idea," he said, and did so; she wrapped the paper around the contaminated gloves and placed the entire crumpled assembly inside a water glass. Then she opened her window and set the glass on the ledge. With one match she lit the paper, which caught immediately and burned brightly.

Without warning, the glass cracked from the molecular strain of the sudden heat. It broke into two neat pieces, one of which began to tumble into the room from the window ledge. Bruce leapt forward to catch it, exhibiting surprising athletic skill as he broke the fall of the glass with his right hand. Then he said, "Ow!" and let the hot glass fall onto the carpet. In the center of his palm, Janie saw a half-moon-shaped burned area.

She rushed to his side and took hold of his hand. "Are you all right?" she asked.

He grimaced. "Not really!" he said through his gritted teeth. "It hurts like a sonofabitch!"

She looked to be sure that the fire had extinguished itself and that nothing else had caught fire when the glass fell. "Come into the bathroom and run some cold water on that," she said to Bruce.

The welt was red and angry, and Janie knew it would be even more painful when the initial shock wore off. She cleaned it and bandaged it as well as she could, then took another latex glove from her briefcase and put it on over the bandage.

"Sit down for a few moments," she said, and he complied without resistance. "I'm just going to call downstairs." She picked up the phone and pressed the number for the front desk. As he fought off the pain of his burned hand, Bruce heard her say, "This is Caroline Porter in Room 708. I'd like to ask that the housekeeping staff stay out of my room for a while. I've got some research papers spread around and I don't want anyone to disturb them. I'll put the DO NOT DISTURB sign on the door handle." The desk clerk said something Bruce couldn't hear, then Janie said, "Thanks very much," and hung up the phone.

"Okay," she said, and quickly put both the fabric circle and Caroline's nightdress into her briefcase. "Now let's get going."

"There's one small problem," Bruce said.

"What?" Janie said. "We've covered everything. The room, the fabric circle . . ."

"It's none of those things," Bruce said, still grimacing. "We won't be able to get into the lab."

"Why not?" Janie almost shrieked. Her plan was about to crumble; she could feel it coming.

"I need to use my right hand to open the lab door. With this burn, it won't read properly. Ted and Frank are"—he stopped and corrected himself—"were the only others with unlimited access. We'll have to get a security guard to open it for us."

"Do we want a guard seeing us go in there?"

"I don't think we have much choice."

She could feel it all unraveling. Then an idea came to her; she surprised herself by even thinking it.

"We'll take Ted with us," she said.

"Come on, Janie, this is no time for jokes. How are we going to do that?"

"I used to be a surgeon, remember? We're only going to take the part we need."

And before Bruce could recover enough to speak, she was poking around in her briefcase for the knife she kept in her field kit.

She left him there with his jaw hanging open, and went to do what she did best, thinking how good it would feel to have something resembling a scalpel in her hands again.

There was nothing they could do to completely mask the vile smell of Ted's hand, and in keeping with the rest of the day's luck, the London traffic was bumper-to-bumper when Janie and Bruce raced out of the hotel lobby.

As they hurried to the nearest Underground station, the heavens opened. They just managed to catch an outgoing train. It was crowded with homebound commuters, most of them dripping wet, and there were no seats. The pungent smell of wet wool rose up from dripping overcoats all around them, but inevitably people began to move away from Bruce and Janie, whose hidden cargo was quite a bit more fragrant.

At the beginning of the ride they stood holding overhead straps to keep from falling, wobbling back and forth as the train pulled away from the station and gathered speed. As the ride smoothed out, the rush of adrenaline subsided and shock began to set in. A numbing surge of dread rushed through Janie and she bit her lip to keep her tears in check; misty-eyed, she looked up at Bruce and found him staring at her, the same look of horror on his face, the look of *dear God what have we done.*

She looked back down at the briefcase. *There's a severed hand in there,* she thought, *a hand I once shook in greeting . . . a hand I watched smoothing the hair of its former owner, not some medical school plastic part, but a real human hand that's signed a Mother's Day card or two. . . .*

Finally a seat came available and Janie sat down wearily, shaking from the horror of her own thoughts. She left the briefcase on the floor at Bruce's feet. She looked up at him and caught his eye again, then nodded at the briefcase almost imperceptibly, indicating that he should keep watch over it. He nodded his acknowledgment.

The train sped closer and closer to the Institute; there were just a few more stops until they reached it. Bruce's hand was throbbing from the burn, and for one brief moment he gave in to the pain and closed his eyes. It didn't take long for a young local predator to notice that the bag was unwatched. The teenager stood up and walked closer to Bruce as the train neared a station, his eyes nervously darting all around to see who might be observing. His nose was too far gone from snorting various white powders to notice the offensive smell wafting up from the brief-case, and as the train ground to a stop, he grabbed the case's leather handle and leapt toward the opening door.

As she watched the boy, the bag, and its toxic contents fly out the opening, Janie felt the hot bile of fear rise up in her gorge. Her heart pounded as adrenaline poured into her bloodstream. She jumped up and gave chase, calling out to Bruce as she left the train. He jerked to atten-tion from the commotion and joined in after them, just making it out the door before it closed. The thief bounded over the turnstile as if he were running hurdles at a track meet, and Bruce stared in awe as his middle-aged companion did exactly the same, never missing a step in her crazy pursuit.

She couldn't take the time to look back, but Janie could feel that Bruce was losing ground and falling behind. Suddenly, she felt terribly vulnerable and small; *I can't stop now to wait for him*, she thought, her horror growing, *I'll either catch this guy on my own or not at all.*

Three miles a day for the last ten years . . . this is the payback. . . . She ordered herself to run faster, and forced her legs to pump harder. Her fitness notwithstanding, she was no match for the light-footed young man she pursued. Janie knew she would soon begin to lose steam, but she didn't dare call out for help. Try explaining to a Biocop why the briefcase they had recovered for her contained a severed, pestif-erous hand. Or why, despite the obvious danger, she had pursued it so vigorously. As her feet pounding rhythmically on the wet cobblestones, in shoes not suited to the task, she saw the boy gain ground. He was the master of this game and clearly in his element, and Janie knew that unless something unexpected happened soon, he would surely win the race.

He turned a corner, and she followed, hoping that this was not his own neighborhood, with hiding places known only to himself and a few other locals. She was losing him, she knew it. *Yersinia pestis* would indeed be set loose in London as Bruce had feared it would. No doubt the thief would toss the case the instant he opened the sealed plastic bag and saw its gruesome contents, without concern for where it might land. Soon flies and fleas and rats would come, and then it would simply be a matter of time before the rats transported their infected fleas throughout the city, and history would repeat itself.

Those who do not learn from history, she thought to herself as she surged forward, *are destined to repeat it. It will be the Middle Ages all over again.*

Fighting off the searing pain in her thighs, Janie tried to concentrate on running faster, but all that came to mind was the vague remembrance of an urge to pack up that small circle of fabric sample and leave it alone when they were preparing to examine it in the lab with Frank. That fateful day, less than a week before, seemed like a lifetime ago.

She was completely out of breath. Her throat screamed for water, and the beating of her heart almost drowned out the shriek of her quarry as he hit the cobblestones somewhere up ahead of her with a sickening thud. The clamor of voices came through the noise of her heartbeats and she looked ahead to see several people standing over the crumpled thief, one holding the pointed end of a cane, the hooked end of which was looped around the thief's ankle. Janie came upon them in a few more steps, and stood for a moment bent over with her hands on her knees, gulping in air as if each breath would be her last.

Between gulps she managed to pant out a wheezy "Thank you." She retrieved her case and stumbled back down the alley again, leaving behind a very bewildered group of gawking heroes who felt justifiably unappreciated.

She had just turned the corner back onto the main thoroughfare when Bruce nearly slammed into her. He embraced her joyfully when he saw the case in her hand, knowing what might have happened had she failed to reclaim it. They stood together in the rain, Janie shaking and panting, Bruce enfolding her, and let the cold water wash over them.

A few minutes later they managed to flag down a taxi. Once inside, they both slumped down in the rear seat, motionless and exhausted from the pursuit. When she was more composed, Janie loosened her fierce grip on the case and set it down on the floor of the cab. She reached over and took gentle hold of Bruce's injured hand. He offered no resistance. They rode on in silence until the Institute's ornate facade appeared through the cab's windshield. Bruce paid, tipping the driver far too generously, then they stood together in silence looking up at the forbidding entrance for a few minutes before either one spoke.

Finally Bruce said, "You or me?"

Janie answered, "It has to be you. If anyone sees me trying to open the lab with a handprint, they'll know something's up."

Bruce's stomach tightened into a knot as he envisioned himself holding Ted Cummings' severed hand up to the palm-print reader outside the lab's door. They stepped to one side of the entry walk between two trees and turned their backs to the street, willing themselves some privacy. Janie pulled out another pair of disposable gloves and helped Bruce put them on. He opened the briefcase and removed the white plastic bag, and as he held it still, Janie slit it open with her knife. Ted's hand was bled out and completely white, utterly unlike the ruddy tone of Bruce's own skin.

"Better put your other hand in your pocket so no one will notice that it's gloved," Janie said. "It looks a little suspicious. I'll get the door for you when we go in." She looked directly into his eyes. "Ready?"

He nodded, but Janie could see the fear and reluctance in his sober expression. Bruce grasped the dead thing with his own gloved, injured hand. He hunkered down and slid the sleeve of his jacket lower, hoping that anyone observing from a distance would think that the hand protruding from his sleeve belonged to him.

Janie closed the briefcase and picked it up. They walked up the stairs, trying to look as nonchalant as possible. She held the door and together they entered the building.

They walked quickly through the corridors, dreading a chance encounter, and fortunately met no one; Janie began to think that the day's luck was really changing. After three turns and three long hallways, they were within sight of the lab.

A security guard rounded a corner perhaps thirty feet ahead of them as they approached the lab. He stopped and peered closer to see who was there. Janie saw him squint and start heading in their direction, but after a few steps he stopped and waved. "Oh, good evening, Dr. Ransom. I didn't recognize you all wet like that. Rotten bit of weather we're having, isn't it?"

"Rotten," Bruce agreed nervously.

"Nice to have you back. How was your trip?"

Janie whispered to Bruce, "You'd better answer him."

Feeling sicker with each passing second, Bruce tightened his grip on Ted Cummings' hand. He smiled thinly and said, "It was very interesting. I wish I could get out of here for a few *more* days." The guard, satisfied that all was well, laughed and agreed. Then he turned and walked away, continuing his rounds down the corridor in the other direction.

They watched until the guard was completely out of sight. Shaking and nauseated, Bruce raised up the dead hand and pressed it against the palm-print reader. He waited a few seconds for the green light to appear, but the indicator remained unlit. He tried again, but the hand had stiffened and would not flatten against the glass surface enough to make a successful print. With a grimace of distaste he reached up with his other gloved hand and pressed the rotten hand flat. The green light came on. They hurried through the door and locked it behind them.

They put the hand back into its plastic bag and Janie set it on the floor inside the door with the intention of disposing of it in a biosafe container before they left. As Bruce was removing his latex gloves inside the lab, the palm-print reader on the wall outside began its electronic cleansing routine. It sent a thin current of electricity across the surface of the glass, and then ran through a diagnostic scan to determine if any live bacteria were still present on the reader. It would repeat this procedure, after a warning beep, until there were no living cells detected on the surface, each repetition taking about one minute.

Twenty minutes after Bruce and Janie entered the lab, the reader was still self-cleaning, and still beeping. The security guard was too far away to hear the disturbing repetition, and Janie and Bruce heard nothing inside their well-insulated high-tech womb.

Bruce swore as he tapped on the blank computer screen. "There's nothing in here. Nobody's home. Someone must have wiped out the memories completely."

"This is just getting too weird," Janie said. "Are there any other systems we can use?"

"Not with the same programming. These are the only two in here set up for the type of identification operation we need to do."

"Can we go to one of the other labs and do the same thing?"

Bruce sighed. "We can," he said, "but it will take too long to get to what we need from them. There's another setup at the far end of the lab—not as sophisticated, but it'll do the trick for the sort of comparison we're making." He got up from the chair and started in that direction. "Come on with me," he said.

She followed him to a bank of microscopes. He selected a stereoscopic unit capable of showing two images at once. He mounted the original fabric on one side and a cut square from the nightdress on the other, then turned on the illuminators and started raising the magnification. As details emerged on the fabric sample, he adjusted the focus to sharpen the images.

There were literally thousands of microbes on the surface of the fabric circle. Some were obviously alive, heaving and quaking and dividing as he watched, but many others were dead, having burned themselves out after repeated reproductions. The hand now resting in a plastic bag on the lab floor was probably teeming with millions of the same microbe and oozing biological toxins as the tiny creatures went through their strictly ordained life cycles, dividing exponentially, then dying in poisonous masses when there was nothing more of the host to devour.

Janie brought the nightdress section to the same magnification and sharpened the focus. At first nothing showed up, and she began to hope that the call to Biopol would not have to be made. But that might mean that Caroline had done something terrible to Ted. . . .

She had to know. She kept stubbornly scrolling the section around under the scope, the uncertainty torturing her with every new inch of the fabric that she examined. She wasn't sure what to hope for. What she really wanted was time, enough time to think the situation through more carefully, time to start looking for Caroline on her own. For a few minutes nothing was visible but an unblemished field of cotton fibers, and the notion of having that time seemed distinctly possible. Finally a few cells scrolled into the field, then a few more, and soon the field was replete with scattered cells. She compared the microbes in both eyepieces. After glancing back and forth a few times, she said to Bruce, "Take a look at this. I'm pretty sure these are the same."

"Let me see," Bruce said. He looked back and forth between the two fields of vision. "I think you're right," he said finally.

Janie sighed. *Now comes the time when I'm damned if I do and damned if I don't,* she thought sadly. "Caroline was probably sick, but Ted probably drugged her. Looks like nobody wins," she said.

Their eyes met and locked. Each one waited for the other to come up with a better solution to their dilemma. A few silent seconds passed.

"I'll make the call," Bruce said wearily, and headed for the nearest phone.

Nineteen

Alejandro wiped the drool from the corner of Kate's mouth and then passed the cloth over her sweaty forehead. He picked up a bowl of porridge from the bedside table and dipped a spoon into it. It looked terribly unappealing to him, but he knew it was mild and well tolerated, a food that his tiny patient was unlikely to throw back at him, as she had done with almost everything else he had tried to feed her.

"Kate," he said softly, "open your mouth, child. You must take some nourishment if we are to succeed. You need the strength to fight. . . ."

But the thin lips remained resolutely closed, so he set the bowl and spoon back down on the table, then got up and left the room.

Adele waited in the hall outside the room, her face distraught and her hands clutched together. "Well?" she said.

Alejandro removed his herbal mask as he left the room. "She has eaten almost nothing for three days," he said. "Three days. It is a marvel she is alive."

Her voice hopeful, Adele said, "Then perhaps the medicine is working?"

"Perhaps," he said, "but I think it is too soon to tell. How many times have you turned the hourglass since we last administered it to her?"

"It is coming up on the fourth turn."

"Then you had better call the others."

She nodded, dreading what she knew would soon come, and turned away.

Alejandro pulled his mask back in place and reentered the sickroom. "Four knuckles and half a cupped hand," he said aloud as he mixed the powder and the yellow fluid for Kate's next dose. He stirred the thick slurry, then held up the spoon over the bowl and watched a thick glob of the slurry plop back into the bowl again.

Adele came into the room with a mask on her face, followed by both the housekeeper and the overseer, similarly masked.

"Ready?" Alejandro said.

All three nodded.

"Very well, then, hold her down."

The housekeeper and the overseer each held down one arm and shoulder while Adele forced Kate's lips apart by squeezing the sides of her face. Alejandro spooned the gloppy mix into her mouth, then quickly set down the bowl and pinched closed both her lips and her nostrils.

The small child sputtered and struggled with surprising strength, trying to spit the disgusting mess out of her mouth; the adults, all talking at once, tried to calm her, but she would not stop her thrashing.

"Swallow, for the love of God!" the physician said as she stubbornly held the medicine in her mouth. Finally, when he saw that she was beginning to turn blue, Alejandro gave the order for everyone to stop. As soon as she was freed from the grips of her tormentors, Kate spit out the gray-green mess, fouling her bedclothes and nightdress.

No one spoke; they had been through this frustrating ritual many times, sometimes with success, sometimes with exasperating failure. The housekeeper started to leave the room, but Alejandro stopped her.

"Wait," he said.

"I am going to the cupboard for fresh linens and nightdress," she said, her voice muffled by the mask.

"No, wait," he said. "We will try again. This time I will mix it thinner, and perhaps she will swallow." He picked up the bowl and started measuring the ingredients. "This time we will try four knuckles and a full cupped hand."

"Will those proportions work?" Adele asked.

"I have no idea," Alejandro said, "but I am certain that the proportions we are using now are useless if we can't get the vile stuff into her."

He mixed the powder and liquid together, but this time it dripped easily off the spoon. "She will have no choice but to swallow this," he said.

They repeated the detestable ritual again, but this time Kate could not fight it off. As soon as Alejandro pinched her airways closed, she gulped hard and took the whole mouthful into her stomach at once. She gagged and coughed, but kept the medication down, as the adults around her cheered and clapped.

Adele and Alejandro removed her soiled nightdress, and as the housekeeper changed the linens on the bed, they bathed her in a tubful of warm water. All thoughts of modesty were cast aside as Alejandro examined her, looking for signs of changes in her condition.

He looked at her neck and armpits carefully. "The bruises seem no larger than they were two days ago. Nor have they formed into pustules," he said. "This is a hopeful sign."

But by the seventh day of her treatment, with the better part of the medicine gone, Alejandro was forced to admit to himself that there was the possibility that they would not succeed. "She has not come around as I had hoped she would," he told Adele. "I had hoped for better results by now."

"But it is a quarter turn of the moon," Adele said, protesting his pessimism. "I have seen many succumb in less than half that time."

He remembered the papal guards who had come with him on his journey from Avignon. One had lived only three days from the time he took ill. He knew it was true that Kate not sickened with the same devastating speed, and her illness was not nearly so grave. But that nearly miraculous success would not satisfy him. *I will have her live, and live in health*, he thought, *or I will die myself in trying to make it come to pass.*

He stood at her bedside that night, long after everyone else had retired, and held in his hand the diminishing vial of grayish powder that Mother Sarah had told him was the dust of the dead.

The hair of the dog that bit you, he thought to himself.

No sooner had the thought left his mind than he sat up and stared at the vial again. *The hair of the dog that bit you. The dust of the dead.* One and the same! *Perhaps each contains some invisible substance with powers against the contagion*, he thought excitedly. He left the bedside and found his book of wisdom to record his ideas.

Having done so, he took the time to read back through what he had written after observing Mother Sarah. *Such strange measurements!* A "knuckle" of the powder, and half of a "cupped hand" of the water, indeed! Should it be Adele's knuckle, and his own cupped hand, the mixture should be far different than the one he had first used. Should it be the knuckle of Adele's smallest finger, and the cupped hand of her overseer, it would be different still. The mixture used by Mother Sarah had been only partially successful.

But if the powder were less, and the water more, did it not logically mean that the medication was weaker? he wondered. *And is there not some way to counteract that weakness? If one now gives four strong doses in a day, might not eight weak doses be as effective? And why not give ten, or twelve, or even more doses?* He sat up straighter, his excitement growing, and scribbled furiously in the book. *Truly*, he thought to himself, *this is a night of bold thoughts!* Surely it would not harm Kate to ingest that very thing of which she herself was made; and although all civilized societies forbade the practice of eating the flesh of man, did not the Christian Jesus give of his own to his followers?

He picked up the bowl in which Kate's medicine was mixed. A small amount remained. He added more of the yellow water, and then a small amount of powder, until he had a thin, watery mix. He would begin giving her that mixture when it was time for her next dose.

Rarely did the child awaken. Her small body curled into an infantile position, as her mother had lain near the end. As needed, her vigilant companions washed her bodily wastes away and cleaned her bedding. Sometimes she would twitch, and Alejandro wondered if Carlos Alderón had found his way into Kate's dreams too. It seemed that the blacksmith had tired of visiting the physician, perhaps because he could not get his full attention anymore, now that Adele was by his side.

But gradually, Alejandro started to notice improvement. The swellings in her neck began to diminish in size and in the depth of their color, and she slept more peacefully. Finally, on the thirteenth day after taking ill, Kate opened her eyes and looked around, and saw Alejandro asleep by her bedside, with his mouth hanging open and his head lolled over the back of the chair. Through her cracked lips she managed to squeak, "Physician . . . Physician . . ."

Alejandro bolted awake and shook his head to clear his senses. He quickly put on his mask. For a moment he was not sure where the small voice had come from; had it been another dream?

"Physician . . ." she said again.

This time there was no mistaking the source of the sound. "How now?" he said. "What great good news is this! The sleeping beauty awakes!"

Kate managed a thin smile, though it hurt her cracked lips. She said weakly, "Am I home in Windsor? Where is Nurse?"

"No, little one, you are still in Adele's bedroom. You have slept for many, many days, and we have been watching over you. Windsor is several hours' ride, but I'm sure Nurse is still there, anxiously awaiting your return."

She closed her eyes again, and lapsed back into a thin, restless sleep. Moments later she awoke again, this time with a bit more clarity. "I am so thirsty. Please, may I have a drink of water?"

Alejandro poured a cupful from the pitcher on the bed stand. He helped her ease up to a sitting position, and held the cup to her crusted lips. She drank too eagerly at first, and some of the water dripped out of the sides of her slack mouth, which was weak from the ravages of the disease, so she wiped off the stray drops on the sleeve of her nightdress.

Thank God she cannot see herself at this moment, he thought. *Not a soul would take her for the same being.* Her eyes were red, and her skin white as the cold morning ashes of last night's fire. Now that she had begun to move her lips again, they cracked more deeply, oozing blood. She had not taken sustenance in such a long time that Alejandro wondered why she had not perished of starvation.

"I shall return shortly, brave lady, with some salve for your lips and some food for your belly."

In the kitchen he found a jar of thick yellow goose fat. Ignoring Kate's weak objections to the unpleasant taste of the makeshift salve, he smeared some of the fat on her rough lips, disliking the feel of the skin under his fingers. *I hope these lips heal without scarring,* he thought to himself, remembering his own mortification at a scar that was far more easily hidden than one on the face.

Soon there was a knock on the door. Alejandro called, "Enter!" and the housekeeper came in.

"Have we missed her dosing?" the woman asked timidly. "The hour is past, and I had not been called. . . . I feared the worst. . . ."

"As you can see," he said, extending his hand toward Kate, "quite the opposite has happened! The best has come to pass!"

Warily, she crossed the room, so the physician told her that there was no danger in coming closer. "The contagion has left her, as you can see from her pretty smile!"

"Praise God!" the housekeeper said. "Shall I bring food?"

"Will you eat, child?" he asked.

She nodded.

"Bring hot broth, and some bread," he said. "Then find your lady and tell her the good news!"

She returned quickly with a tray, and Alejandro balanced it on his knees. He tore off small chunks of the dried bread. He dipped each one in the hot broth and, after allowing it to cool a bit, carefully fed it to the little girl.

She had some difficulty at first, for her lips would not part easily, and the cracked corners of her mouth began to bleed again. But he was patient and gentle with her, and eventually she was able to consume the entire meal. The shadows on the floor of the room had moved significantly in the time it took to feed her.

When she was through, he tucked her back into the covers and went in search of Adele. He found her rummaging through the same trunk where the pink nightdress had originally been found, looking for other garments that might be of use. She hummed sweetly as she sorted the finery, and gave Alejandro a beaming smile when she saw him.

He had not seen her smile for many days. Even their lovemaking had been quiet and somber. *How I delight in her beautiful smile,* he thought.

She set aside her sorting and stood up. They embraced joyfully, almost desperately, and held each other for a long and tender moment. "Oh, my dear love," she said, her voice almost trembling with emotion, "I feel that there is reason to hope that all will be well again, that the world may at last return to sanity and goodness. I am dreadfully weary of the constant news of cruel death." She pulled free of his arms and went back to her sorting. "Am I wrong to hope this way?" she said. "Are we finally to be done with the menace of this plague?"

He touched her hair, and stroked it lightly a few times before giving her his answer.

"Sadly, I remind you that we have no more of the powder."

"But surely, more can be had!"

"Rest assured that I will convince Mother Sarah that it *must* be had! And I will learn from her how to make it for myself. I believe it has the power to cure that has evaded us for far too long! But I will see you and Kate safely back to Windsor before I ride out again on that quest. Soon we will be able to judge her progress, and plan for the trip back to the castle."

"How glad I will be to see Isabella again," Adele said, touching his cheek tenderly. "You are so sweet and kind; I actually miss her acid tongue, and you have no hope of ever being able to replace her in that regard."

He reached up to take hold of her hand. "May God be praised for smiting me with such a noble deficiency." He was glad for the chance to interject a small amount of humor into their discourse, for what he had next to say would not be to Adele's liking.

"Beloved, it will not be so simple to return as you think. We cannot simply go back to Windsor and announce that Kate is cured. Remember what was done to Matthews. He lacked any signs of infection, and no one hesitated to comply with my request that he be killed to protect the rest of Windsor's occupants."

It was the first time he had admitted to anyone but Sir John and the king that putting Matthews to death had been his idea. Adele said nothing to him, but pulled away slightly.

He gave her a look of infinite sadness, and completed his confession. "In all likelihood he would have acquired the contagion, and soon, so in my heart I believe that my decision was necessary. But I will never be convinced that it was *right*. I am reminded every day of how I failed him. I am bound by my oath to prolong life, not to shorten it by my own hand."

Her heart softened. "My dear," she said soothingly, "I have often seen you darken since that day, and I suspected that this was the cause."

Ashamed, he hung his head. "Matthews is not the only patient I have failed. There was a patient in Aragon for whom I would have traded my own life, so angry was I at the impotence of my best treatments." He stopped short of explaining further, for it could only lead to trouble, and he did not wish to invite the specter of Carlos Alderón back into his dreams.

"I don't believe that God expects anyone but His only son to perform miracles."

"It has never been God's expectation for me," he replied, "—only my own."

Adele touched his cheek again. "Then you must release yourself from this impossible obligation, for its weight will destroy you in short time."

Sighing wearily, he acknowledged that she was right. "But now," he said, "we must continue to discuss the matter at hand, I am afraid. There are plans to be made."

Patiently, he explained to her what he thought would happen on their return, that he and Kate would be greeted as had Matthews and Reed, and then quarantined. "But as soon as anyone finds out that Kate had been afflicted with the pestilence, I have no doubt that she will either be banished or killed, and even the king himself will not object."

"King Edward would never allow that to happen to his own child!"

Alejandro looked into her eyes and said, "I have heard it said that he did not stop the taking of his own father's life."

Adele's silence confirmed the rumor.

"We must keep this our secret, Adele, and Kate will never be able to tell anyone either. It would be in keeping with my own previous edict about Matthews to see her put out or destroyed, and the castle's residents will look to me to initiate the act. How can I justify sparing her when Matthews has already paid with his life? I cannot help but suspect that King Edward would be glad to be rid of the daily reminder of his past indiscretions. Surely it would improve the queen's view of him if the child was not such a visible irritant. No one with the means to do so will come forward to save her."

She set aside her previously happy work, and walked slowly to the tall window. Looking out on the cold day, she said softly, "Tell me how you would have me help. I will do what I can to make this easier for all of us."

"We must hope that Isabella has managed to hide your absence from her father. You will have to find your way back to her without my help, I fear."

"Fortunately, that will not be difficult. She will provide a separate room for me during a quarantine that I shall impose upon myself. When I reach the secret passageway, I will send a message to her through the cook, all the while keeping my distance, and she will see me safely but separately housed."

"You have no doubt of this?"

"Alejandro, I assure you, the princess loves me like a sister, and it shall be done."

Though Alejandro doubted that Isabella was capable of loving anyone with such selflessness, he did not contradict her. "You can safely rejoin the daily life at Windsor in a fortnight. Kate and I will, of course, be quarantined as were Matthews and Reed. I will explain our prolonged absence by saying that I took it upon myself to remain outside the walls for longer than originally thought because of the closeness of our contact with Kate's mother, which is in part true. No one will be displeased at my extra caution. I imagine that few will say they have missed my daily harangues about taking precautions against infection."

She made no comment, knowing that her confirmation of his statement would not improve his spirits. She simply asked, "How long will it be before Kate is well enough to resume the journey?"

"I cannot truthfully say; I have never known anyone to recover from this scourge before, and I have no experience on which to base even a reasonable guess. In a few days I will be better able to tell. At present she is quite weak, and it is out of the question for her convalescence to end now. She is young, and will heal quickly for that, but right now she is unspeakably tiny and frail, and I have seen this work against a rapid recovery."

"Then I suppose we shall just have to watch and wait, and pray for her health to return speedily."

"Aye, I suppose we shall" was his resigned reply.

Kate surprised them all with the rapidity of her healing. In six or seven days, she had regained a good measure of her formerly exuberant demeanor. Her lips were no longer miserably cracked and her bones did not protrude so pathetically. She was beginning to show some color in her cheeks, and her delightful smile had come back in full measure. She chattered incessantly to anyone who would listen.

Alejandro knew that it was time to leave. Though he was eager to be done with the king's unsavory business, he knew that their return to Windsor would mean the end of the blissful private time that he and Adele had shared. He was sure that Kate could be convinced to keep their secret, but others at Windsor might not look so kindly or enthusiastically on their liaison.

"We shall leave for Windsor two days hence," he finally said to Adele.

"Blessed Madonna! How I have longed to hear those words!" She called enthusiastically to the housekeeper to begin organizing their belongings.

He watched her with great sadness, knowing that she could not be blamed for feeling as she did, regardless of the effect it had on him. He turned away and went to tell the groom to make their horses ready for their journey, his heart burning with grief for a love that surely had no future.

On their route back to Windsor there was a small monastery with a chapel. As they neared it Adele said, "Let us stop here. I wish to make my confession. It has been far too long since I have been absolved of my sins, and I would have God smile upon me again." Without waiting for Alejandro's reaction she dismounted from her horse.

"Shall I wait here, then, with Kate?" he asked, still astride his mount.

The look she gave him in response to his question was curious and questioning. "Why can you both not come inside as well?"

There can be no acceptable explanation, he said to himself. *I have no choice but to go.* He made a simple shrug with his shoulders, then dismounted, and took Kate down from the horse she and Adele shared.

The bell they rang was answered quickly by a small and frail-looking monk in a brown robe.

"Father, I wish to make confession," Adele said.

He looked first at Adele and then at the tall man with the little girl by his side. Alejandro felt the priest's gaze settle on him, scrutinizing, appraising.

"And you?" the priest asked.

He hesitated a moment before speaking. "I shall pray while we wait for the lady," he said.

"As you wish," the priest said, and led them inside.

It seemed to Alejandro that he waited for a very long time while Adele bared her soul to the priest. *What can her sins have been, that it requires so much to recount them?* he wondered. He looked all around the chapel with its vaulted ceiling, his neck craning to see the details of the ornate ceiling.

Even their small temples are luxurious, he thought to himself. *And the windows, so tall, so colorful!* Though seven other priests were praying at the front of the sanctuary, the chapel was nearly perfectly silent. *They pray noiselessly,* he thought, remembering the droning chants that his father would recite at the Sabbath table.

Then the seven priests stood up in unison, and began to walk slowly down the center aisle of the chapel. The first began to sing, his voice clear and sweet, and the six others sang the same phrase in unison after him. The sounds of their voices rose up to the ceiling and were amplified within the peaks. It was haunting and almost painfully beautiful, and Alejandro found himself feeling unaccountably blessed by the soothing tones of their joined voices. As they filed out of the sanctuary in a long row, the priests continued their singing; the sound faded as they disappeared into the monastery, until it was no more than a whispered afterthought.

He felt a hand on his arm; he had not realized that his eyes were closed. He opened them quickly and saw Adele standing before him, with a look of radiant peace on her face. "I am absolved," she said.

He stood and faced her. "What sins have you committed that you should be so long in obtaining forgiveness?" he asked gently.

She smiled sweetly, a woman once again reconciled to herself. "I have been with a man who is not my husband."

He almost winced before her. "Then that sin is on me as well," he said.

"I have been untrue to my king."

"He well deserved your untruth."

"Nevertheless, he is my king. My family swore loyalty to him. And I have betrayed my lady Isabella by staying away so long."

"Was it not your wish to do so?" he said.

"Therein lies the sin," she said. "It *was* my wish. And because of the gravity of these transgressions, I required additional instruction beyond my penance. This gentle priest was kind enough to teach me."

She turned and watched as the priest rose up from the place where he was kneeling at the altar. Then she turned back to Alejandro and said, "And now I am prepared to return to Windsor."

* * *

To the relief of those they had left behind in Windsor, Alejandro and Kate both emerged healthy from their confinement a fortnight later, and by that time the child had regained all of her high spirits and the rosy glow of her cheeks. Adele resumed her place in Isabella's household, the king never even having noticed her absence. Kate resumed her incessant pestering and tall tales and made endless demands for chess matches. Even patient old Nurse, who had seemed at one time to have limitless tolerance for the child, wished aloud for a few moments of blessed silence.

The rich autumn, whose windblown brush had not yet begun to touch the landscape with gold and copper before their departure, was now nearly spent. Cold gusts blew gray twigs and dry brown leaves all around the stark countryside. Nearly three months had passed, and Windsor Castle's gloomy occupants settled into their winter routine, already quite bored with the entertainments that would ordinarily have seen them through the long darkness of the cold season.

One gray day Alejandro was summoned to the king's private apartment. When he arrived, the monarch was waiting for him. A pile of scrolls lay on the table.

"You must read these," the king said. "Time and again they report the plague's dissipation outside Windsor. Perhaps it is time to investigate these reports. What say you to the notion of a mission of discovery? Shall we send out a party to ride through the countryside and bring back firsthand reports?"

Alejandro looked quickly through the messages. "Sire, these are but a few reports, and from scattered locations."

"My retainers have sent messages enough, and all say the same thing: new cases of the disease are virtually unknown since the first falling of snow."

Alejandro knew that he needed to explain his fears to the king in terms that the brave but anxious monarch, a man who had been denied access to the kingdom he ruled for far too long, could more easily understand. "Imagine," he began, "that you are fighting a great battle, and your spies have ridden out ten leagues in each direction, and found no waiting army within that perimeter. Think then, of what you would do if only one of those spies ventured but one league farther than the others, and there found a well-equipped army, poised and ready for a bold attack on your forces."

The king grew impatient with Alejandro's long-winded allegory. He grunted his displeasure and said, "You are quick to cast down my conclusion as unmerited, learned Physician, but you offer no other alternatives. Knowing my responsibility to my subjects, what would you do if it were you in my place, with a castleful of irate prisoners, and a kingdom in need of attention?"

"I would send the outside retainers back along their previous routes for a ride of two hours' time, to be sure there are no other armies nearby. Remember, Your Majesty, that the pope has borne a far longer isolation than you. He remains well, last we heard."

The king sighed in frustration. "I have no doubt that I am one hundred times as unhappy as Clement; I am in the middle of a war, and I must see to the winning of it!"

"Sire, I know that you desire to resume your full and natural life, and that your kingdom would benefit from your attentions. I, too, would love to venture outside these walls without limitation, but it simply must not be done! Be patient, I implore you; give it more time."

Edward's frown of disappointment was dark and threatening. "How much time will satisfy you?" the king said.

He will not tolerate this much longer, Alejandro thought. *When, indeed, is the best time to start a new life? What would de Chauliac say?* "Perhaps the astrologers ought to be consulted," he said.

The king made a gesture of dismissal with his hand and said, "Charlatans and hucksters, every one of them. They will tell me what best suits their own ends. But you have no such bent, Physician. It *will* be your decision. Name the time."

A new beginning, he thought. *Springtime.* He looked at the king and said, "How long will it be until the first flowers appear here?"

"Five or six weeks, at most," replied the king.

"Then, if all goes well, we shall venture outside to pick the first flowers without restriction."

Alejandro and Adele met as often as they could; considering the demands for companionship made by the bored Isabella on Adele, their occasions were far too few for either of their liking.

But their fortune turned when Alejandro's elderly manservant became enamored of one of the cooks. He requested frequent leave to visit with her, and Alejandro was only too happy to oblige him. On one such night in January, Adele came to him in his apartment, having managed to steal away from her demanding mistress.

"Does she mean to monopolize your time entirely?" he said, pulling her close to him.

"She keeps me busy with planning the expenditure of her allowance once she has found a new clothier. I am constantly looking at sketches. My opinion on fashionable attire seems to have increased in value suddenly."

Alejandro sighed. "It will soon be spring. My time here grows short. I would have you to myself for what little time we have left together. I would tell all of Windsor, no, all of the *world* of my love for you, and let them think what they will. It is a secret too heavy to bear anymore. I grow weary of keeping my joy to myself."

"Alejandro, the king . . . we must think of his reaction. I simply cannot predict what his response will be."

"But you have spoken to Isabella—"

"And she has held her thoughts to herself. She will not say what her opinion is on the matter of you and me."

"But surely she can understand your feelings for me . . . surely, she herself has loved."

Adele took his two hands in hers and brought them to her lips for a kiss. She looked up at him with great sadness on her face. "I fear that you do not understand her position. Hers is not to love. Hers is to marry as her father chooses for her. She knows only too well that love may elude her, for the sake of duty. Oh, the king is mindful of her opinion when he considers nuptial arrangements for her, but if a fair match presents itself, he will do as he wishes, regardless of her thoughts. He will tell her what all princesses are told, that she will find love in her husband if God means for her to find love."

"And yet there is love between the king and the queen. I have seen it with my own eyes."

"But Edward's marriage was arranged by his mother, who detested his father. She was a woman of strong will and considerable diplomatic ability, and she found ways to put her son in situations where he might find a proper bride on his own, and think it his choice. He found Philippa among four daughters of a Flemish nobleman, one who was allied to the royal family of France, from whom she herself sprang. She was very clever about it. Her own son, our most noble king, seems not to have inherited that skill."

"So Edward loved Queen Philippa before they were wed."

"Indeed, and well, it is said. But I bore you; surely you know this history already."

He said nothing, allowing her to believe that he came from the segment of Spanish society where such things would be discussed. To admit otherwise would be to give himself away. "But still, Isabella must realize—"

"Do you not understand women at all?" she said. "I am stymied by your innocence! Isabella is jealous of our love. I know it! She changes the subject when I speak of you. I long to confess to her the depth of my feelings for you, for she is my dearest friend, and I depend on her for sympathy. Sadly, I get little. I know it is because she is envious. She has become hardened to the notion of love, and is constantly on guard against it. She knows only too well that should she love incorrectly, it will come to no good."

Alejandro allowed his resentment to show. "She is a princess. She has wealth, and great beauty, and every imaginable advantage. Surely she knows that when Europa has been freed from the grips of this plague, a match will be found for her? Even my mentor de Chauliac spoke of it— he said that the pope had arrangements in mind for her."

"Then when that happens, I think it will bode well for us. While Isabella is preparing for her own wedding, she will be too preoccupied to give any thought to my joy, as will her father. We need only wait. *Please* have patience, my love."

Wait until I am on my way back to Avignon, to be greeted by God knows what? "But I must leave before then. My work here is nearing an end. The king will not tolerate me here for one minute more than is necessary."

"Then you must tell him that there is work to be done on curing the plague. Surely he will understand the value of that work and become your patron. And surely enough time has passed since Kate was cured that she will no longer be in danger of his reaction."

"I am not prepared to trust him on that account."

She sighed in frustration. "Then you must simply tell him that you wish to stay. That you shall support yourself with your medical work."

Suddenly her voice became animated, and her eyes sparkled. "I have an idea," she said. "There is lambing to be seen to at my holdings. I will tell Isabella that I must be present to oversee it. There is only a short time left until the flowers bloom, and then she will be so preoccupied with her wardrobe that she will have little time for me. I shall petition her for permission to travel out again. I know she will grant it. Petition the king for permission to travel out for some reason. . . ."

The possibilities she presented were beginning to excite Alejandro as well. "I could say that I am in need of fresh supplies of herbs for medications . . . it would not be a lie. . . ."

"Even if it were," Adele said gleefully, "he will not know otherwise! Then you shall join me at my holdings. It will give us time to plan our campaign for Isabella's approval."

It was more than he dared to hope for. A tiny flame of optimism began to glow in his heart, warming him. What had seemed once an impossibility might now be within his grasp. *And as Adele sees to the running of her estate, I will make sure that I have what I need to cure this pest, should it revisit us,* he thought. *There will be the time and the freedom to see to it.* His heart began to swell with joy, in the knowledge that his two most precious wishes might come true.

On a clear day in mid-February the portcullis groaned upward, and Windsor's occupants poured out of the gate, a frenzied horde of prisoners suddenly and unaccountably freed from their long and torturous confinement. Alejandro watched as the celebrants snatched up the white and purple crocuses, then danced about, hugging each other; riders galloped off on long-awaited hunts, or anxious journeys home. Within a few days hungry tradesman, upon hearing that access to the castle was once again available, came calling in droves. Isabella spent all of her time reviewing their wares, her eyes hungrily roving from one fine item to the next. Thus preoccupied, she readily granted Adele's request to travel away from Windsor.

In conspiracy with his lover Alejandro petitioned the king for permission to go on an extended journey in search of spring herbs to renew his apothecary supplies, which had been dangerously depleted over the winter.

"So, Physician," the king laughed, "you are no more immune to the deep longing for some air that has not been previously breathed than are the victims of your harsh restrictions! By all the saints, this winter has been miserably long. Go ahead, bring back wagonloads of such herbs as you like! And when you come back, we shall talk of making arrangements for your return to Spain, for happily, your own good work has rendered further service unnecessary. I'm quite sure that you miss your home and those you love in Aragon."

But in the ever-increasing idle hours available to him since the plague's apparent cessation, Alejandro had begun to believe that what Adele had proposed might work, that he might find a good life here in England, perhaps as a medical practitioner in a nearby township. There was nothing in Aragon to which he could return, and Avignon held little more promise for him.

Has this beleaguered monarch had enough of me? Will he balk at the request I am about to make? He had no way of knowing save to ask. "Sire," he began timorously, "I am perhaps of a mind to settle in your country. I do not know what I will find in Avignon if I return."

"Indeed, Physician? I had not thought of it. But it might be a noble thing, your settlement here. We suffer from a dearth of skilled practitioners. Still, what of your family? How will they fare?"

"Ah," the physician said, "it was so long ago when we first spoke of such things! I am yet a bachelor, Your Majesty, and I have come to the sad belief that I am orphaned. My last knowledge of my father and mother was at the beginning of their own journey to Avignon, where we had planned to reunite. But they never arrived; I presume they were afflicted with countless others. I despair of ever finding them or of even having real proof of their demise."

In contrast to the monarch's relaxed slouch Alejandro sat stiffly upright in his chair, his tension easily visible to even a casual observer. His future was in the hands of this man, on whom he had forced severe and unwanted restrictions for many months. At this moment, in view of the king's immediate power over his future, he very much regretted some of the harsh rules he had imposed on the royal household. *Pray God that he remembers his survival, not his discontent.*

But Edward did not hold Alejandro's strictness against him, such was his glee at the lifting of restrictions. He said to his nervous petitioner, "These things considered, Physician, I see no valid reason why you should not stay, if it is your sincere wish."

With the weight of uncertainty lifted from his shoulders Alejandro proclaimed quickly, "It is, Sire; it truly is."

"Then so be it," said the king.

He was elated. "Sire, I cannot properly express my thanks. With your leave I shall go out in search of some of the necessities of my new practice." He rose up from his chair, and bowed to the monarch, who remained seated. As he was about to pass through the doorway, King Edward called his name. Alejandro stopped, and turned, taking a few steps back into the salon.

"My lord?"

"I would say more, Physician, but your haste robs me of the opportunity."

His tone was not that of a monarch issuing orders to a subject, but simply one man speaking to another. "Lest this go unsaid, Physician, I owe you a great debt of gratitude. You have performed with as much bravery as any soldier serving under my flag, though your courage was not always of the kind that is lauded by those to whom its benefits inure. I am thankful that of all the children my queen has borne me, only our beloved Joanna has fallen to this scourge, and I own that it is because of your efforts I am able to make this happy declaration. You are a fortunate man to have been blessed with such great skills, and we thank God for His wisdom in sending you to our kingdom."

The king then proceeded to make an apology, which from his bumbling manner Alejandro took to be the more difficult admission. "I regret that there have been occasions on which we gave you good cause to feel misunderstood or maligned. You have been more valuable to me and the whole of England than you will ever know."

Then the air of royalty returned to his voice, and Edward brought out a map. "Now, come forward before I change my mind, for I have a sudden notion to improve your position here. Since you have decided to stay in my kingdom, we must see that you are properly settled. Had I known before now that you wished to stay, I would have set aside a choicer parcel for you. But there are many handsome ones still to be had. You will enjoy this one, I think."

Alejandro did not understand what the king meant. "Your Majesty, I am confused. . . ."

The king smiled. "I am making a gift to you, Physician; you shall have this estate and its holdings for your very own." He set the map down and showed Alejandro the parcel he had in mind. "Here, to the north a bit—the squire who owned it has died leaving no heirs, and the right to its title has reverted to me."

Alejandro was stunned. "My lord, I am speechless. You do me a great honor."

"You will honor me in return by accepting my gift. Of course, this will depend on the goodwill and efficiency of the gentleman's advocate. Now that one plague has passed, there seems to be a new pestilence upon this land, the primary symptom of which is a sudden increase in the already excessive number of lawyers, whose chief contribution to our society seems to be the spread of the disease of greed. Would that the vicious pestilence had left more physicians, and taken more lawyers!" He roared in laughter at his own joke. "Ah, well, I am wishing for things that I cannot hope to have. The arrangements for your possession of the property shall be made by the time you return from your expedition. You shall, as well, be invested with the title that goes with the estate during the ceremony to be held at Canterbury in three months' time. I have had a message from His Holiness that our new archbishop will arrive by then, and his investiture will be made at the same time."

Alejandro assumed that the pope had long ago forgotten de Chauliac's army of physicians, but he could not stop himself from asking. "Am I to assume, then, that there were no directives for me in His Holiness' recent message?"

"You were not mentioned."

Well, then, he thought, *my mission is at long last completed.* "Thank you, Sire. I beg your permission to take my leave now."

"One thing more, Physician, and you shall have my permission. I have considerable largesse yet to expend, and some of it shall fall on you. Since you are a bachelor, are you of a mind to be married? Perhaps I can be of some service to you in that regard. There are many fine ladies unattached in my kingdom."

Alejandro was taken aback by the king's unexpected question. *Think carefully before you answer,* he told himself. "Have you a lady in mind for me, Your Majesty?"

"Presently, no," the king said, "but there are many candidates of suitable station, some orphaned, some widowed, who would be acceptable matches for you. In view of your new holdings I doubt that your Spanish ancestry would be objectionable. And if your lands are well managed, you shall have no difficulty supporting even a wife enamored of luxury."

Noting the physician's silence, the king questioned him. "Well?" he said, disappointed by Alejandro's evident reticence. "Are you not pleased? Or is there a lady upon whom you have favorably cast your eye? Only name her, and I shall arrange it."

It is too soon to ask for her, he thought, though he was sorely tempted. *Let some time pass first. Do not stray from the plan.* "Truth be told, Sire," he said, "until your offer now, I have had little thought of marriage. I have always thought first of my profession, and I had not thought to stay here. Give me some time to think on this."

The king nodded. "As you please, Physician. But be well warned! I am greatly relishing my role as a maker of marriages! Soon I will have given away all the most desirable ones, and you shall have to choose among toothless, dried-up old hags!"

When he had finally tired of his own joke and stopped laughing, the king looked at the physician, and said, "Then our immediate business is concluded. Go forth as you wish, with my blessing and thanks. I myself shall go to London; Windsor will be empty, I think, and none too soon." He made a gesture of dismissal with his hand. "Go with God, Dr. Hernandez."

*   *   *

Adele rode out to her estate in the massive traveling party that accompanied the king on his ride to London. Though she offered the party the hospitality of her home for the night, Edward declined, for he was most anxious to get back to running his country and to resume the various wars that had occupied his time prior to the plague.

"So many have died," she explained to Alejandro when he arrived a day later, "that he must restructure his entire army. Many of his advisors are gone, and he must replace them with new ones. There will be much vying for his attention in London by those who would be elevated! I do not envy him. He will long be occupied with the work of governing."

To the preoccupied physician it was all just so much silliness. Things of this nature had never been of great import to him. And so it was that he failed to recognize one of the most obvious benefits of his newly granted status in England. When he finally thought to tell Adele of the king's gift, she surprised him by falling immediately to her knees and praying fervently.

"Beloved, what is this? Are you not pleased for me?"

"Alejandro! You are a simpleton, and I am even more a fool for cherishing you! Do you understand what this means? When you are knighted, you will be of the nobility, even though you are not an Englishman. Oh, my love, we can be wed!"

He soon became lost in the daily pleasure of Adele's company, and their schemes for consolidating their future, and even though each day held a longer period of light than the last, the three weeks Isabella had allowed for Adele's absence passed all too quickly. He forgot about returning to Mother Sarah's glen to replenish his supply of her strange medications, for other sweeter things attracted his attention. Soon he would have an estate of his own to manage, and there was much to be learned by watching Adele and her overseers conduct the daily business of her property.

"When the time is opportune," Adele said on their last day together, "I shall speak privately with Isabella about our betrothal. It will then be your obligation to petition the king directly for my hand, but I swear you shall not go before him without Isabella's blessing to support your claim. It can only be to our benefit to make her our ally in this matter."

"I regret now my earlier diligence in confining her," he said.

"She will not remember it when she is busy with other concerns."

He remembered Isabella's sometimes vicious treatment of him, privately thinking that he did not share Adele's trust in the mercurial princess. "Let us hope you are correct," he said.

As they stood in the courtyard, ready to depart, the spring air was fresh with the scent of pine and flowers, and the breeze played with the loose ends of Adele's flaming hair, which gleamed like polished copper in the bright sunlight. He kissed her hand, as he had done at their first meeting, and once again his lips lingered hungrily on her fragrant skin.

"I shall think of nothing but holding you until we meet again," he said softly.

And again, he did not give the day to the task of searching the countryside for apothecary necessities. Nor did he return to Mother Sarah's cottage in search of the pathway between the oaks, which he knew in his heart was far more important than the mission on which he now sallied forth.

As he rode over the muddy roads, Alejandro cursed their dismal condition, in the same disparaging manner once used by Eduardo Hernandez. But despite its condition Alejandro was very glad to have found this road, for it would keep him on proper course toward the place to which he traveled, a place he had been only once before.

And reach it he did, wearily, after a hard ride. Before him was the small church where he and Adele had stopped on their first journey back to Windsor. At the top of the steps he pulled a bell cord, and waited nervously, staring down at his dirty boots without focus, his heart alternately full of joy, then painfully heavy. He had known of many Jews who had abandoned their faith and their God in order to prolong and simplify their lives. He had always despised such weakness. Now, as he stood ready to do the same, his heart softened, and he understood that there are some things that drive a man to redefine himself and leave his past behind.

Still, he burned with shame, and he recalled those unfortunate Jews in France who had died on the stake, saved from their fiery agony only by the well-aimed arrows of a sympathetic Christian soldier. He remembered, too, the distrusting look that gruff captain had given him after the regrettable incident. *Had he known about the murder of the false-hearted bishop, it would have been my own soul departing for their fiery hell.*

359

It seemed to be his inescapable fate to fall short of complete contentment in this life, he thought with sad resignation. He knew that whichever faith he chose, there would always be something for him to hide or regret. *Ah, well,* Alejandro mused, *their Jesus was nothing more than a renegade Jew, and so am I.*

In the midst of that thought, the door before him opened, and there stood the same priest who had heard Adele's confession. The candle in his hand flickered gently in the soft evening breeze, casting a strange and frightening glow on the cleric's stern features.

"Yes, my son?" he said slowly, eyeing the physician suspiciously.

"I am Alejandro Hernandez, a heathen from Aragon. I seek instruction in your faith."

Two days later, as he rode back to Windsor, he mulled over the strict lessons he had been given. So few people had come to the monastery seeking conversion or instruction since the onset of the plague that the priest had stored up an enormous amount of religious zeal for just such a challenge.

Emboldened with righteous fervor, the cleric made a diligent attempt to scare Alejandro into subservience with his threats of hell and damnation. Wisely holding his tongue, for to speak truthfully would arouse suspicion, Alejandro would say only, "I confess my sins," but would not elaborate. "Such matters are between myself and God alone, and God is surely wise enough to know the sins committed within His creation without having to be advised by those who have committed them," he had told the insistent cleric.

Moreover, he thought, his anger beginning to rise as he rode along, *one needs to be a complete fool to believe some of their ridiculous teachings.* That one could buy admittance to everlasting glory was a claim too outrageous for any intelligent man to accept. And the matter of this supposed virgin, the mother of their Jesus, and her "immaculate" conception by the visit of the Holy Spirit, was beyond logic.

This was a woman who truly deserves worship, he had thought to himself as the priest railed at him, *for through her quick wit she managed to accomplish one of the most fantastic ruses of all time!* A poor peasant woman is unfaithful to her betrothed, and makes up an incredible story to justify her pregnancy, so that half of the world will follow her delusional child when he is grown. And she manages to convince the duped "father" to help her raise this child to believe the story himself. *Too remarkable!* How different she would have been in real life from the suffering, mystical martyr the priests painted her to be.

She was a crafty and clever Jewess, using her considerable wits to survive, as had many of her ancestors, as would many who came after her.

As Alejandro himself did now. Thoughts of Adele, and the peace he hoped they would know together, were all that had kept him from laughing aloud at the priest as he raved on and on about the certain doom and desolation Alejandro would face for his failure to confess. *Bless me, Father, for I have sinned. I am a lonely Jew trying to find a home after wandering across the whole of Europa, a journey that I undertook after the vile duplicity and betrayal of your pompous bishop, who richly deserved exactly what he got from me. I seek peace by falsely converting to the preposterous Christian faith in order to establish a home with a woman whose blind adherence to your madness is little deserved, for she is far too good to be tangled up with the likes of you! And though I will confess to great shame over my eagerness to deceive her, she will always know that my love for her is the truest love of all.*

So lost was he in these considerations that he did not realize how far he had traveled, and suddenly, to his surprise, Windsor Castle was visible against the greening landscape. *Here,* he thought joyfully, *a truly new life awaits me!* He kicked his heels sharply into the horse's sides, and the animal neighed loudly before dashing down the hill toward the distant fortress.

Amen, he thought. *So be it.*

Twenty

The palm-print reader was now on its thirtieth repetition of the cleaning ritual. Each time it self-scanned it detected bacteria that had survived the last zapping, so it kept on shocking itself. After so many jolts the program became punch drunk and looped hopelessly into the shocking cycle, completely bypassing the customary cooling-off period between zaps. The wiring overheated, and on the thirty-first round of self-immolation it finally shorted out. There was a small flash of blue electricity as one of the wires melted, and a tiny puff of smoke rose up to the ceiling.

It was enough to set off an overhead smoke alarm wired directly into the London office of Biopol. The signal also went over the airwaves to the local Emergency Response Unit, and within a minute there was a full company of ERU field personnel on the way to the lab, sirens blaring as their vehicles sped through the crowded streets of London.

At Biopol headquarters the response was not quite as fast, but far more deliberate. The members of the responding unit took the time to climb into their protective gear before heading off to the scene shown on their computerized map. Within five minutes ten men and women in bright green spacesuits climbed into the back of a biocontainment vehicle. As they sped off, each Biocop grabbed a weapon from the mounting rack on the van's inside wall and checked to see that it was properly loaded.

Bruce was dialing the number to report the presence of *Yersinia pestis* when Janie put a hand on his arm to stop him.

"What's that?" she said.

Bruce stopped in mid-dial and listened. "Some sort of alarm," he said. He listened more carefully. "It sounds like the smoke alarm system." He hung the phone up before completing the sequence of numbers.

Janie ran to the lab's main door and tried to open it. "We're locked in!" she said. "I can't get the door to open!"

"Then the smoke alarm must have gone off in the hallway," Bruce said, coming to her side. He pressed a few buttons in a wall panel to try to override the automatic lock, but when he tried the door himself, it wouldn't budge. "The security system automatically activates the lock to keep the fire outside the lab." He tried the override again and failed to get the door open. "We won't be able to get out this way."

Janie rushed to the lab's small window and looked out to see the ERU team arrive. As soon as their siren stopped, she heard another one in the distance.

Bruce was at her side by then, and he, too, heard the second siren. "Those will be Biocops. We've got to get out of sight right now."

"My God," she said. "Why are they coming here?"

"I don't know for sure," Bruce said, "but by sheer dumb luck I think we managed to be in here when the smoke alarm went off. I don't think we should stick around to find out if I'm right."

Across the lab they heard the handle of the locked door as someone tried to open it. Janie looked at Bruce in alarm and pointed toward the door. "Someone's trying to get in!"

They heard the muffled sound of a voice from the corridor calling Bruce's name. "Probably the same security guard we saw before," he said.

She looked around quickly, searching for another exit, but saw none. "How are we going to get out of here?"

She did not like Bruce's silence or the look on his face as he considered her question. "It's not going to be easy, is it?" she said.

Bruce furrowed his eyebrows in concentration. "There's only one other way I can think of to get out of here, and it's going to be a tight fit. We'll have to go through an air duct in the main storage freezer. There are a lot of filters in the way. It's actually only supposed to be an outflow for releasing purified air back outside again, but we may be able to get through. Come on," he said, waving her toward the freezer. "We don't have much time. And don't forget to take your briefcase! They'll be able to place you in here. . . ."

She stopped short when she saw the red trilobed biohazard warning on the door, with its doomsday message:

ALL PERSONNEL MUST WEAR COMPLETE BIOSUITS
WHEN ENTERING THIS UNIT

"Bruce!" she said as she held him back. "We can't just go in there! It's hotter than hell!"

"Janie, if we don't get out of here now we're going to be in *very* big trouble!" The look on his face said, *Don't argue.*

But she continued to protest. "But that room is crawling with bacteria and viruses! We'll die, anyway!"

"Not if we don't touch anything or breathe any unfiltered air." He opened a small cabinet next to the unit's door and took out two masks.

Handing her one, he said, "Put this on. It's rated for plasmids. Nothing big enough to hurt you is going to get through it if we're careful."

She took the mask from him and stared at it. It weighed only a few ounces; once inside the freezer, the lightweight plastic contraption would be all that separated her lungs from untold billions of infectious beasties. She looked back up at him apprehensively. "But it's so small, and there's nothing to it. I just can't believe it's going to be enough—"

The door rattled again.

"Come *on!*" Bruce said.

She slipped it on and tightened the strap at the back of her head. They had just enough time to add gloves and boots.

"Take a deep breath!" he told her. He opened the door to the airlock and they hurried inside. As they waited precious seconds for the automatic air exchange to be completed, Janie looked aside and saw the mechanical arm, now at rest, with its weirdly human fingers. She imagined a skilled technician maneuvering the delicate device to retrieve a sample rather than risking exposure to the deadly agents stored in the freezer, a thought that served as an immediate reminder that she was about to enter a place she had no business entering.

They passed through the second door, which clicked closed behind them as they entered the actual freezer unit. Almost immediately, their masks fogged with condensation. "Shit!" Bruce said. "We should've cooled them before we came in. They'll clear in a minute or two, but we'd better stay still until they do."

Janie looked around through her own rapidly fogging mask as they stood in a forest of glass tubes. It was eerily beautiful in the silent freezer, everything was clear glass or brushed chrome, and softened by the haze of condensation on her mask. Here and there, renegade icicles, unauthorized in the dry treated air, clung rebelliously to the sides of the tubes. Their breath came out of the mask filters in small clouds, which crystallized to invisibility almost instantly, and Janie realized where the occasional icicles came from: they were the residue of warm, moist human breath.

Farther on she saw an assortment of randomly placed storage tanks, all bolted to the floor. She suspected they contained some of the deadliest samples, stored separately and at even lower temperatures.

She heard a noise, and turned around quickly. Her mask was defogging but her vision was still cloudy enough that she couldn't determine the source.

"Get down!" Bruce whispered as he pushed her down with his gloved hand. They crouched behind a large storage tank and looked back out as the security guard they'd seen earlier in the corridor came into view through the glass partition. Just as Janie's mask finally cleared, she saw something explode on the back of his neck and the man collapsed instantly.

They both gasped through their masks; the sounds were distorted and muffled, but the meanings were clear.

"My, God, they shot him!" Janie said.

"Oh, Jesus," Bruce said, "and with a chemical bullet!"

"They killed him, just like that?"

He held his finger to his mask in a shushing gesture and whispered, his eyes always on the glass partition, "They assume that everyone is infectious in a lab incident. That's been their policy since that arbovirus accident two years ago. Shoot first, justify later."

"And that's what will happen if they find us here?"

"There's no way to tell," he said nervously. "They might think twice about shooting blindly into this freezer. Take a look around—even a chemical bullet could do a lot of damage."

She didn't have to look far to understand what he meant. Marked on the tank that shielded them were the words *Ebola Zaire*, followed by the name of the African nurse who had been patient zero in a five-hundred-death miniepidemic several years earlier. Janie remembered reading a medical-journal report describing the swift progress of the symptoms, which caused the victim to die horribly by bleeding from every organ and blood vessel in the body. The virus had since undergone multiple mutations and the current version was even more deadly.

"But then again, these guys are good, and the guns have heat sensors set for 98.6, so we can't assume that they absolutely won't shoot," Bruce whispered, his eyes still fixed on the area where he'd seen the guard fall. "They don't miss too often."

Janie hung her head and said, "That should have been one of us instead of the guard."

And that's just the beginning, she thought, her stomach tightening. *Ted is dead, too, and Caroline is out there somewhere, pestiferous and on the move, perhaps infecting hundreds of people, the newest member of the Patient Zero Club.* Yersinia pestis *will hook up with some other microbe and pick up a plasmid with the gene for antibiotic resistance, and it'll be the fourteenth century all over again. Only, this time the rats don't have to wait for sailing ships. They can ride on airplanes now.*

This doomsday message looped through Janie's brain like an endless tape as they waited to see what might happen next. With aching legs they crouched behind the tank for what seemed like an eternity, listening to the electronically amplified voices of the Biocops outside the glass wall. Finally, unable to crouch any longer, they sat on the cold lab floor with their backs resting against a chrome storage unit. The temperature in the freezer was well below zero and the air was brutally dry. Janie shivered in her light, wet coat, which had begun to stiffen. As she moved her arm, tiny slivers of ice cracked off the sleeve and landed on the tile floor below.

Across the main pathway through the freezer she and Bruce could see the bright green of spacesuits reflected in the shiny steel surface of the cabinet opposite them. They waited in still silence, hoping and praying that the Biocops would not come up with any reason to search the unit.

After a few agonizing minutes Bruce said, "I don't think they have any idea that there's anyone else around. They'd be in here by now if they did. The guard was the only one who saw us come in."

But Janie wasn't convinced of their safety. "Wait until they find the hand," she said, just loudly enough for Bruce to hear her. "Then they'll tear this place apart. I didn't have time to put it back in my briefcase before we ran for it. It's still sitting on the floor in a plastic bag. If they get bacteria detectors going, they'll find it in a flash."

"Oh, they will—in a lab incident they're required to. Then they'll do a laser DNA scan and they'll know it's Ted's hand," Bruce said, "and they'll figure out anyone who's been in contact with him from residue on his skin. Then the real fun will start. Everyone who works here will be questioned, including me, and they'll round up anyone else who shows up in the scan."

Two green images suddenly appeared and came close to the glass wall. Janie and Bruce drew their legs up and huddled closer together. They held their breath for a few moments so the fog of condensation wouldn't reveal their presence. They couldn't move, because if they did, they might draw the notice of the searching Biocops, and their lack of movement made the cold seem even more biting as their circulations slowed. Despite the rush of adrenaline flooding into her system, Janie felt drowsy from the extreme cold. She looked over at Bruce and saw that he, too, was beginning to fade. It dawned on her that if they didn't get out of there soon, they might both freeze to death, with Caroline still loose in London.

She looked over at the reflection on the cabinet, and saw that there was now only one green figure reflected in it; the other had gone. That one turned abruptly and walked out of her field of vision. She tapped Bruce's shoulder and pointed at the reflection.

"They're gone," she said. "I think they may have found the hand."

He sat up quickly and got to his feet in a crouching position. "That should keep them busy for a few minutes," he said. "Maybe we can get out of here." And when the reflection had been free of green images for a few seconds more, he said, "Follow me."

They moved quickly down the central path of the freezer, keeping very low to the floor, passing stack after stack of tubes and a veritable forest of chrome containers. Janie read the labels as they passed, and cringed. She saw a white canister marked *Marburg*, and thought of the terrible accident that had occurred in a German lab many years before. A sample of an obscure and deadly African virus of the Ebola family had arrived at a lab in Marburg, Germany, in a broken vial, and had turned the internal organs of several lab workers into cream-of-human soup in a matter of days. She held her breath through the mask as they moved past it.

Bruce was at the air duct already. His stiff, gloved fingers clumsily unfastened layer after layer of clamps and filters, and Janie thought to herself that the burn on his hand must be excruciatingly painful with all of this activity. Each layer of clamps was designed to thwart an intruder trying to enter from the outside. Soon they were surrounded by a pile of filters and screens. Bruce reached inside the vent and pulled out the last thick filter. He went into the opening feet first and kicked away the outside panel when he reached it, hoping there were no observers nearby. But as he slid out into the darkness, he found himself behind a stand of bushes, quite out of sight of anyone, so he turned back and helped Janie squeeze out.

"Get your gear off and stow it in the shaft," Bruce said to Janie. "Don't touch the grate. We'll have to leave it off."

Bruce could hear Janie's teeth chattering. He wrapped his arms around her. "Here, let me warm you up," he said. "A few more minutes in there and we would have been in big trouble."

"We *are* in big trouble," Janie said. "How the hell did we get into this mess?"

They spent a few minutes behind the bush shivering, their teeth clicking as they tried to warm themselves. When he could move a little more easily, Bruce stood up cautiously and looked around.

"We're in the side garden," he said. "It looks deserted." Janie stood up and they brushed off their clothing. Hurriedly, she ran her fingers through her hair. They left the safety of the garden and walked out to the street to see what was happening there.

Trying to blend in, they hung back from the main crowd of people.

A rapidly increasing throng of curious onlookers had gathered outside the front entrance of the Institute, held back by a bright green tape barrier, and they eased forward, never pushing enough to raise an objection from any of the other observers. When the view was clear, they stopped and observed from their safe distance as Biocops entered and left the building. Not long after they secured their positions in the crowd, they saw the long, narrow box containing what was probably the body of the guard being brought down the front steps by four not-so-jolly green giants.

"They're not taking any chances," Bruce whispered in her ear. "They've got him sealed up tight. They'll test him later, then he'll be cremated."

Janie's eyes filled with tears; she wept quietly as she stood there. She sniffled and watched in silence as another Biocop carried a smaller box down the entry stairs without assistance. *Probably the hand*, she thought to herself.

Bruce must have read her mind. "It'll take them about half an hour to figure out who it belongs to. We'd better get away before anyone recognizes me."

A few blocks away they found a grocery store with a phone booth. Bruce dialed Biopol's emergency number and told them anonymously about the unsealed grate outside the lab. He didn't even mention Caroline or the plague bacterium; their situation had become too complicated. Even considering Biopol's fancy technology, he knew they would be safely away by the time the Biocops found the gear and traced down the phone booth, so he placed the call without hesitation. But seeing the worried look on Janie's face, he said, "Too many people use that equipment for trace evidence to be conclusive. We won't be implicated."

Neither one spoke of what they might have done if they could have been identified by reporting the gear's location. As they slipped off into London's darkness, Bruce wondered if he could have sacrificed himself for the greater good. He didn't know. He didn't want to know.

Lieutenant Michael Rosow of the London branch of the International Biological Police stood in the decontamination chamber and let the sterilizing fluid pour over the outside surfaces of his green suit. It rolled down the channels and folds of the slick plastic armor in deep aqua rivulets. It reminded him of the antifreeze they used to use in cars, back before solar temperature regulation was introduced.

This was the part he always hated, this long, slow process of coming away from a contaminated area and reentering the sterile world. When the light finally flashed to signal that the airlock was about to open, he breathed a sigh of relief and turned to face the door, anticipating the *whoosh* of the pump as it drew the chamber air into the filtration system. He stepped out and stood still over the drip pan as two gloved, masked, and booted technicians began to remove his suit.

When all the layers were finally peeled off, he stood naked and closed his eyes as one last decontaminating rinse washed over him. The techs used hand-held sprayers to direct the shower of warm liquid into his body's folds and crevices; this part of the decontamination was more than a little erotic, and he had, so to speak, risen to the occasion more than once, much to his great embarrassment.

He dried off and dressed in "normal" clothing again, then headed straight for the examination lab. His pace was brisk, reflecting the excitement he felt. As much as he hated the protracted sterilization procedure, he loved what he was about to do, and it more than balanced out his dislike of bathing in antifreeze.

He had already scanned the hand for DNA identification. Three positives came up—the first being the apparent owner of the hand, one Dr. Theodore Cummings, director of the lab in which it had been found, apparently missing, and, if the condition of the hand was any indication, now probably dead. The second positive was an enterobacterium, of sufficient quantity to read as a "being" on the scanner; he had not yet run an identity on it. And the third was an unknown female who obviously had not been printed because the scan of her DNA compared to all known matches throughout the world was inconclusive. Rosow knew that such a result could mean any one of three things. She might be quite old, enough to grandmother the law requiring that she be ID'd, but he doubted this because of the good condition of the cells in which the identifying pattern was found. Or she might be a Marginal, one who had somehow managed to avoid printing. There was no way to discount this possibility, so he kept it mentally open. Or third, she might be an unprinted citizen of a foreign country, in Britain on a limited visa, in which case she would not have been required to submit to a print until she'd been in the country for four weeks.

He sat down in the swivel chair in front of the computer and settled himself in. He brought up the DNA interpretation program and stared intently at the screen as he typed in a series of short commands. A gentle sexy female voice spoke reassuringly to him.

"The operation you have requested will be completed in six minutes. Please wait. Would you like to listen to some music during the processing time?"

Rosow answered, "Yes."

The voice said, "Please choose from the list on the screen. Speak your choice slowly and clearly."

He reviewed the choices quickly, comparing the duration times to the expected length of the procedure, then said, "Brahms German Requiem track five."

The computer replied, "An excellent choice. One moment please."

As the big voice of his favorite soprano soared above the choir, he watched the large screen intently. Bit by bit the picture formed; he was entranced, and could not drag his eyes away. Slowly organizing before his eyes was the image of a woman. As each bit of genetic coding was interpreted from the cells found under the fingernails of Ted Cummings' severed hand, she changed and reshaped and morphed as he watched.

"Come on, darlin'," he said, "let's have a look at you."

As the music crescendoed and climaxed with the rub of the soprano note against the harmony of the choir, the final details of the image fell into place. Red hair, blue or green eyes, about five four, slim if she hadn't gone to fat. A real beauty; a stunner.

"Oh, baby, baby, baby!" he whispered as he sharpened the image. Rosow wondered how she would look after living in the real world for however long she had lived here. He'd never had the nerve to bring up his own image, to see how life had beaten him down in comparison to his unsullied potential. He'd done it to a few acquaintances (without their knowledge or consent, he regretted to say) and had been shocked by the way gravity, weather, and worry affected all humans. But this woman had started out with a lot of potential. The cell generational interpreter confirmed his estimate of her age.

He isolated her facial features and enlarged them on the screen. He brought up a data entry form on the screen and highlighted the bits of data he wanted sent out over the wire. When he was satisfied with the assortment of information, he clicked on the "send" icon and waited a few seconds as the system sent out a facial image and a list of identifying characteristics for this woman to all the Biopol offices and mobile units in England.

Michael Rosow couldn't wait for the programs, rumored to be in development at the Institute, that would allow him to make the reconstructed image move as a living, breathing human would.

The sexy voice returned. "The transmission was successfully completed. Will there be anything else?"

Rosow laughed and said, "Yes, there will, luv. Show me what *you* look like."

* * *

The ragged woman was perhaps the oddest of the hundreds of silhouettes visible against the setting sun as she pushed the cart over the bridge. Cars whizzed by, occasional colored spots in a fast-moving herd of black taxis, carrying fortunate people toward their comfortable suburban homes. Other people, only slightly less fortunate, walked to edge-of-London apartments, so there was still a good deal of foot traffic crossing. And though she knew her companions were once again watching out for her, the woman pushing the cart over the bridge was somewhat frightened. She would have felt far more comfortable being back within the group that could be found under the bridge, in a very different sort of society.

"I don't like crowds much," she said to Caroline, who hadn't moved in a while, and was well beyond the condition where she might be expected to respond. "Never did have much use for big groups of people." She slowed her pace and thought about other routes she might take, routes with less exposure to the dreaded masses of civilization. Every route she considered had some problem, and all of them meant a dangerous increase in the amount of time it would take to deliver her ailing cargo. She had to get south of the river somehow, and this bridge offered the fewest obstacles, for like a wheelchair, her purloined shopping cart could not negotiate stairs; on this bridge the sidewalks, like the road, were smooth and level.

The bridge was all steel girders and beams, sleek and new, a stronger replacement for the original stone-and-concrete bridge that had been destroyed, along with a good deal of history, by a terrorist's bomb a few years earlier. The woman had liked the old one better; it had been a beautiful, stately coupler for the two sides of the river, and it fit in with the surrounding buildings.

"Such a shame, the way things change," she muttered. She leaned closer to Caroline, as if the younger woman could really hear what was being said to her. "Time was I knew my way around this city, but no more. It's like a foreign country to me now. Too many big buildings. Too many people."

Already she was not feeling well, and she was surprised at the speed with which the unseen but expected invader took control of her body. It had been only a short while since she took hold of Caroline's destiny, and she had already made a long journey, having been forced to double back on more than one occasion when faced with an insurmountable obstacle. She was beginning to grow weary of the constant walking, and would have liked to rest, even if only for a few minutes. The rapidly worsening condition of her passenger, however, did not allow her the luxury of stopping to consider her own. She maintained a slow but steady pace, knowing it was her only hope of arriving at her destination before it was too late to do what needed to be done.

"Go ahead, you little blighter, *be* difficult." Lieutenant Rosow was not having much success identifying the bacterium he'd read on Ted Cummings' hand, and he was feeling quite frustrated. As he did with many of the objects he examined, he talked to it, sometimes nicely, sometimes with obvious anger, as if by doing so he could cajole the stubborn object into revealing its inner self and all of its secrets.

He was confused. This bacterium showed similarities to a number of species, but there was no exact match in the database. It had been a very long time since he'd run across something that he simply couldn't identify. He'd developed a knack for backtracking mutations, then extrapolating those mutations onto existing bacteria, and he'd been very successful in getting matches that way on many different occasions.

But this little baby, frantic multiplier though it was, did not seem to have evolved out of anything he had on file. He set up ten different mutation options, some of them multigenerational, but nothing registered. Baffled, he instructed the computer to search for a crossmatch with other unidentified samples on file. He did not expect to get any matches.

How wrong he was. After only ten minutes of searching through millions of samples, there were six positive matches. All currently unidentified.

All six in the last two days.

He sat bolt upright and looked intently at the screen. The records for each of the cases were being assembled from the various input sources. Five of the matches had come from different hospitals, and one from a routine Compudoc exam. Three were Londoners and the other three resided in nearby suburbs. The carriers were completely dissimilar; they did not share professions or domiciles or habits or vices. All fell ill at about the same time, and complained of identical symptoms. High fever, swollen glands, dark blotches around the neck and groin; no exact diagnosis had been made. Four had already died when the last data update had been processed, and the other two were gravely ill.

It took ten unidentified matches to set the computer into automatic action. Rosow knew he would not have discovered this potential epidemic if he had not actually come into contact with Ted Cummings' hand and subsequently gone hunting for matches. Eventually there would have been enough victims to attract the notice of the system, but by then, whatever he had stumbled upon with his characteristic blind luck might already have been out of control.

He thought, *Maybe now they'll listen to me.* He had tried unsuccessfully several times to get the epidemic threshold changed to four cases, but he was the only one who believed it necessary. The Biocop Workers' Coalition felt it would increase their workload dramatically, and had blocked the suggested change. Rosow had been furious at the Coalition leadership at the time and still was. He no longer even attended the meetings.

He continued to search for a pattern among the victims, but none was immediately evident. It was not until he read through all the interviews with the next of kin that he finally found what he needed.

The first victim to die was the owner of a very chic London restaurant, and three of the others had eaten there on the same night. Rosow immediately called the next of kin for the remaining two, and discovered that one of them had also been there.

This suggested a food-related toxin to him, and that was his first avenue of inquiry, but one of the victims had not eaten anything, only sipped wine while his companion dined. There was absolutely nothing in his stomach when they'd opened him up. Examination of another bottle of the same wine showed no indication that the wine was contaminated. His dining partner had ordered a different wine.

"Hope you enjoyed it, being your last glass and all," he said aloud. "Myself, I would have had a stout." Then he added, "Had I *known.*"

Not the wine, not the food, no professional or residential pattern. Just their presence in the restaurant that bound the victims together. The restaurant had no air conditioning, or he might have considered a form of Legionnaires' disease. But the symptoms weren't right for that.

Rosow was even more baffled than before. He didn't know how to proceed. But of one thing he was sure: He needed to find that redhead.

Ahead in the distance the tired woman saw a pair of bright green Biocops standing on the sidewalk near the place where the foot of the bridge met up with the main road. They were, whether they knew it or not, very close to the place where most of the local clan of Marginals entered the under-bridge community. And though that knowledge bothered her on general principle, their presence near the underworld entry had no direct effect. She was not planning to stop for a visit. There wasn't time.

She would, however, have to get around them somehow, for they were directly in her path. She stopped pushing her cart and thought about what she should do. She couldn't see clearly enough to determine the reason for their presence. She would have to keep moving forward until she could make a determination. She looked around nervously for any sign of her furtive companions, knowing she would need their help for this leg of the journey.

After a quick look at Caroline the old woman realized it would be unwise to leave her here and go ahead alone to check things out. She leaned over and said, "Won't do to have anyone poking around in this cart while I'm otherwise engaged, now, will it?" The situation worried her; there seemed to be no alternative to proceeding. To suddenly turn and double back now might arouse more suspicion than proceeding, if one of the Biocops had already noticed her. Naturally, they'd want to know who was in the cart, and why. If she simply went ahead, they might be too distracted by their immediate task to pay much attention to her.

As she approached the Biocops, the reason for their presence became obvious. The body of a man, obviously a Marginal, was lying across the sidewalk. They were examining the body, and had rerouted traffic around their parked van; but worse yet, the body was obstructing her path on the sidewalk, and she would have to figure out some way around him.

There was simply too much traffic to try using the road. She could stop and stay where she was and wait for the Biopol van to take the body away, but considered Caroline's condition and rejected that idea. Time was growing short.

She walked on, the rusty cart squeaking inharmoniously as she neared the obstruction on the sidewalk. She was terrified but would not allow it to show, for then they would certainly suspect her. Summoning all her courage, she wrapped her shawl dramatically around one shoulder and lifted her chin proudly. She approached one of the Biocops and said to him, "See here, young man, this carcass is in my way, and I've got appointments to keep! Boys still help old ladies get across the road, don't they?"

Her brazen entreaty stunned the two burly cops, and they were caught off-guard. One came up to the cart and pushed the papers aside, peering at Caroline as the woman stood and watched, trying desperately to keep her shaking under control. He looked up at her and straight into her eyes. She summoned all the steel she could find in her soul and said,

"Sleepin' one off, she is. Guess I didn't bring her up right." At that moment Caroline groaned, as if to verify her false mother's claim.

The scruffy woman used that groan to her advantage. "All right, now," she cooed to her charge, "you'll just toss up that bad stuff and we'll be off again." She looked at the nearest cop and said, "You'd be wise to stand back. She's a hurler. Always has been. You don't want to mess up that pretty green suit." And she was right; it was the last thing the cop wanted. "Messing up the suit" required a mountain of explanatory paperwork and an extended sterilization session, and no one liked that regimen.

Suddenly two of her rough companions, bedraggled saviors, appeared from either side of her and made a fuss about helping. Their confusing arrival was just the distraction she needed. The Biocops turned their attention away from Caroline and looked warily at the sudden congregation of Marginals. Together they lifted the cart up and over the fallen man, chattering amiably as they did so. The woman, though surprised by their abrupt performance, played along with them and made a great show of thanking them for their help. Then the helpers disappeared just as suddenly as they'd shown up.

Seeing an opportunity for a clean escape, the woman launched into a crazed narrative of gratitude, proclaiming her thanks to everyone in the immediate area, including several disgusted passersby, who hurried suspiciously past. Leaving the cart momentarily, she pranced up to the two cops and said, "Give us a kiss, now, and I'm off!" They both raised up their hands in protest and waved her away. Feigning indignity, she stomped off and returned to the cart, leaving behind two shaken but relieved green-suited men.

She shook violently as she pushed the cart away from the scene. *So close, too close. . . .*

Up ahead was the last hill, the hardest part of their journey, and already she was exhausted. She stopped and took a swig from her water bottle, then poured a little over Caroline's face to cool her. It was the best she could do for the young woman, since she could no longer force her to drink. Up the hill she started with a heavy sigh, wishing all the while for a miraculous return to her unsullied youth. The effort of walking uphill made her feel quite warm, so she removed her filthy shawl and placed it over Caroline. It gave one more protective layer against the prying eyes of passersby, some of whom glanced curiously into the cart. She didn't suppose that Caroline could feel much of anything right about now, nor would she have been aware of or concerned about the deficiencies in her personal grooming. The woman looked back one more time, wishing she'd covered more distance from the bridge, then turned and continued her groaning progress.

She was just leaving their field of vision when a third Biocop came out of the van with a color print in his gloved hand. He passed it among his peers, one of whom looked more carefully at it than the other. He looked in the direction he'd last seen the ragged woman go, but didn't see her. He gave the print back to his comrade and went back into the van, where he typed a quick message to Lieutenant Rosow, who'd transmitted the image. He pressed a few buttons on the computer keyboard and sent the message off, indicating that he'd had a possible sighting of the quarry.

Panting and groaning, the woman was finally forced to stop pushing. Within a few moments a member of her clan appeared and took the handle of the cart in her stead. Before setting off on the remainder of the journey, he gave her a hug and wished her well. As soon as he started pushing the cart away, another Marginal came and started leading the woman, who was now both shivering and sweating with fever, to a place where she would be safe. She leaned wearily against him and together they walked away.

The new Marginal pushed onward. Not far ahead there was an old iron gate, and beyond that the barren field, where Caroline and Janie had shivered in the darkness. He moved forward with great energy and resolve, elated that the task would soon be complete and that he had played such an important part in its completion. To anyone watching him he would have seemed far too thin to have the strength for this task, but he felt inexplicably joyful and inspired, and he performed admirably.

He looked down at his cargo and said, "I guess there's a bit of fire left in me yet. Now, what shall we do about you?"

He opened the iron gate and pushed the cart through it onto the field. "This is going to be bumpy," he apologized. "You might even like the cobblestones better."

But Caroline was lost in a feverish dream. She was in a wooden cart being pulled across a muddy field by a team of worn horses, and she could feel the drops of mud splash up on her hand, which was extended over the edge of the cart. In that hand was some unidentified precious object; she held on to it with what little strength she had left.

As this dream wound to a close, her Marginal courier lifted her out of the cart and laid her gently on a dry rise in the ground. He positioned Caroline slightly upright against a rock, hoping that the elevation would keep her from drowning in the fluid that was near to filling her lungs. He covered her with newspapers again, then laid the woman's small brown cloth sack beside her.

Having completed his mission, he turned the cart around. It was much easier to push without the burden of Caroline, and he moved quickly toward the perimeter of the field. He wondered how long it would be before he, too, felt the chills and sweats, as his woman friend now did; he wondered, too, if others would soon join him in his pain. He stopped momentarily and looked back at Caroline, wondering if saving her was worth the cost to him and his community.

"Guess I'll never know," he said to the empty night. His debt to Sarin's mother paid, he ditched the cart behind a stand of bushes. In a few minutes he had disappeared completely into the London darkness, heading north toward the river and the comfort of the bridge.

Twenty-One

Upon returning to Windsor, Alejandro quickly organized and packed the few belongings he had brought with him when he first arrived. Everything he would take with him to his new home could be easily transported on one additional horse hitched to the saddle of his own mount, and still there would have been room for more.

With the hour of departure approaching and his readiness assured, he began the sad task of saying farewell to the people with whom he had lived so closely for the trying months of their confinement. He went among the servants, giving to each one a gold coin, for in all of his travels he had not spent a hundredth of what his father had given him at the start of his journey.

His obligation to the staff complete, Alejandro walked slowly toward Isabella's suite in the southwest section of the castle, deliberately delaying his arrival so he might postpone the inevitable sadness of leaving Adele until they were reunited in Canterbury.

Isabella herself was the first to greet him. He bowed to her flawlessly, having finally perfected that courtly ritual. The princess grinned and clapped lightly.

"Monsieur, your improvement is to be commended! We admire the progress you have made in acquiring our customs. Not all exotic foreigners learn so well as you have! And now you shall leave Windsor. It is a pity you shall not be able to use your skills here."

Exotic? he thought. Would her snipes never cease? When he and Adele were married, would this snide princess not be like a sister to him, in view of her closeness to his intended? *I shudder at the very thought!* He suppressed his dislike of her yet another time and said, "Thank you, Highness, but you give me too much credit. Were it not for the selfless and diligent tutelage of the fine lady at your side, I should have failed miserably, and you would forever be laughing at my clumsy attempts."

Kate peeked out from behind Isabella's skirt, where she had been pretending to hide, and looked up at her sister.

"Isabella, may I give it to him now?"

"Oh, yes, all right. God curse your impatience! I have yet to bid the good doctor farewell, but go ahead."

Kate stepped forward and held out a rectangular wooden box,

which Alejandro accepted with great drama, emitting many "Oohs" and "Ahs" as accompaniment to his close examination of the gift.

"How beautiful it is! And what fine craftsmanship. But what can be inside?" Fumbling momentarily, he found the latch and eased the cover off the base of the box, marveling at the snug fit. He caught his breath in surprise. Smiling at Kate, he said, "The box alone would have been far too generous, but look at the treasures I find within!" One by one he removed each exquisitely carved chess piece and examined it minutely.

"You are pleased, monsieur?"

He scooped up the child in his arms, saying, "I shall be more pleased if you will visit me in my new home sometime to teach me all the secrets of successful play. This *trousse* must be used by only the best players, in keeping with its own fineness. If you teach chess as well as you do the courtly bow, I shall soon be winning our matches."

The child hugged him tightly, and whispered in his ear, "I shall miss you so! Please, monsieur, can I not go with you now?"

He set her down gently, and saw the tears filling her eyes, and thought, *Indeed, I shall miss her as well.* "Who knows how long it will be before my home is suitably outfitted to receive a young lady of your stature?" he said. "You must allow me adequate time to prepare. We shall see each other at Canterbury, and discuss it then."

Isabella was uncharacteristically patient while Alejandro gave his attention to Kate, but now she reclaimed it. "I thank you for seeing me and my family safely through the scourge, and although you have been a plague yourself at times, I am deeply indebted to you for the excellence of your work."

Alejandro had the surprising sense that her expression was genuine. Then her kind tone darkened, and after looking around to ascertain that their conversation was private, the princess continued, "I advise you to take care that Adele is not hurt, for you shall quickly incur my displeasure if any harm should befall her at your hands. You shall not be treated lightly in that event."

And what should I say to such a preposterous statement? How could she even think that I would do anything to bring Adele pain? Why, I have already given up my faith to be with her! What more can I possibly do? "Adele shall never want while I am by her side," he said simply.

"Take care that you speak the truth, Physician, or it will be yourself who is wanting." Then she raised her voice again, conspicuously, and added, "I bid you a safe journey, and may God protect you. I know that Lady Throxwood would bid you good-bye, and I shall send her out to you. See that you take your leave gently, for she is a woman of deep sensibility." She turned and made a grandiose exit. Alejandro looked around, but no one would meet his glance.

I must leave this room, for I cannot remain another minute in it. He searched for a sympathetic face, just as Nurse came through the door.

"Nurse," he said with the hint of a plea in his tone, "please tell Lady Throxwood that I shall await her on the west balcony. I require some air, for the room has grown stuffy."

When Adele found him, he was gazing off into the distance, admiring the lush green of the English countryside. When he heard her approach he turned and smiled, saying, "Even after the chill of winter I find the coolness of your spring quite pleasant. At this time of year in Aragon it would be quite warm, and the greenery would already be near to browning."

She came up next to him and slipped her arm through his. She breathed deeply of the spring air. "It is a pleasure to breathe the cool air, especially after our long winter ordeal. This year the freshening of spring and the greening of the countryside seem unusually lovely and welcome."

With a loving look he said to her, "Once again we are in agreement. Can we also agree to meet in Canterbury, where I shall petition the king for the great honor of taking you to wife?"

"My love, you need not even have asked."

"In Canterbury, then."

"Yes," she agreed, "in Canterbury."

Alejandro mounted his lead horse, and checked to see that the packhorse was secured to follow. He rounded the corner of the wooden stable building, heading for the gate. Before him in the courtyard was an unusually large number of soldiers, all seemingly awaiting someone's arrival. He had not heard that an important party was expected today, and was surprised by the throng of milling guards.

One soldier saw him, and shouted, "Attention!" and the remainder quickly formed two opposing parallel lines, about a man's height apart. Alejandro was quite impressed by the skill with which these troops put themselves into perfect order. He had only once seen them perform as a uniform fighting force, when the pitiable adversary was their doomed comrade Matthews.

He halted the horses, and stood his ground, watching to see what happened now that they had so ceremonially formed up. *Who can this important visitor be?* he wondered.

And then he saw that the entire company was looking directly at him. Sir John Chandos, Alejandro's erstwhile fellow jailer, stood at the end of the line, and waved him through.

As he rode between the lines of rigid soldiers, each man took out his sword and raised it up to meet the sword of the man facing him, creating a tunnel of flashing swords through which Alejandro slowly rode. Stunned, he gawked awkwardly at the men who honored him with their arched salute. And as he neared the end of the tunnel where Sir John waited, the soldiers broke their silence and began to cheer and whistle, and the knight himself bowed deeply to Alejandro.

"On behalf of the men who serve under me, I thank you for saving our lives, and for giving us the opportunity to serve our king in France once again. Godspeed, Physician; may Providence guide your way."

He had never known such exhilaration. He waved his hand back at the lines of soldiers, who cheered lustily in response, then turned his horses away through the gate and headed north. He was still within hearing when the portcullis groaned to a close on his time at Windsor Castle.

Riding north on the Stepney Road, tired and dusty and worn from the hard travel, Alejandro began to wonder if his holdings were far enough away to be a form of banishment. He was considering stopping for the night when he finally came upon the set of landmarks that Sir John had described in his directions. Now he knew it would be only a short distance, and he resolved to finish it quickly.

He nearly passed his "estate" by without notice, for the road was badly overgrown from months of neglect. So, too, was the courtyard; there was plenty of growth for the horses to graze on. *I shall live here,* he thought, as he slowly opened the door; *this is my home.* It creaked open on rusty hinges, and he entered cautiously. Out of the musty darkness a bat flew erratically past him, causing him to drop quickly to the floor, where he crouched nervously for a time, hoping to avoid further contact with the evil little creatures. *Dear God, You have seen me through many months of plague unharmed. Please do not sneer at me now by allowing the bat's foul drooling malady to take me out of this world.* It would be too ironic, too unbearably cruel, after all he had survived.

To which God should this prayer be directed? he wondered.

"Well," he said aloud, needing only to hear a voice, "perhaps one or the other of You will grace me with survival of this night. Then tomorrow I shall see what needs to be done."

He laid out a blanket on the hard surface of a large table in the great room, for he dared not sleep in any bed, should he find one, before seeing to its cleanliness. There would be time enough tomorrow to explore, he knew, and to begin settling into his new home, but now he needed rest.

That night his dream of Carlos Alderón returned, and though the giant blacksmith had not disturbed Alejandro's peace in some time, his reappearance was so clear and real that it seemed as if he had never left, not even for one night. Again, the massive man dragged his shrouds behind him, and again, Matthews grinned at his side, the weird percussion of his clicking arrow shafts accompanying the ghoulish chase. But this time a new horror was added to Alejandro's unconscious turmoil: the pale ghost of Adele, attired in the bloody remnants of bridal finery, rode behind them in a rickety cart, which bumped along the rutted road, jarring loose the dead blossoms of her bouquet.

He thrashed awake, and rolled violently off the tabletop, landing with a thud on the stone floor below. There he remained, his heart pounding, his skin clammy and cold, his shivering body motionless, until the welcome dawn.

Alejandro resumed his practice of medicine, and every day at least one person from the surrounding countryside came to him with an ailment needing his attention. One day he set the broken arm of a young boy, whose futile attempt to preserve the balance of an overloaded cart had failed disastrously. Alejandro winced when he remembered his own past experience with a toppled cart, so many months ago in Aragon, and sincerely hoped that the boy's life would not be as dramatically altered as his own had been after that fateful event.

"I have seen many such injuries, and I fear I will see many more," he said to the boy's angry father. "The bone is broken."

"I had hoped it would only be a bruise, but the boy claims it is useless."

"As well he should," the physician said. "I fear that the boy will require at least one full turn of the moon to rest, sir. Thereafter his arm will be sufficiently mended that he can work again, but he is of a tender age, where the bones can fail easily. My advice would be to put him to less strenuous tasks when he is healed."

"Aye," said the unhappy man, "if he doesn't starve before he mends. I cannot get a crop in without his help! He'll have to do his share. I cannot excuse him for his poor arm."

"Then be warned that he'll be of little use to you next year with a bent and fragile limb at his side. Best you let it rest, and soon he'll be well again. God gives young children the gift of quick mending, where those well on in age require much more time."

"Then why is it," asked the angry farmer, "that so many of the young have perished by the pestilence? Just last week another was taken in the village north of my pastures. The landlord is complaining that none will be able to pay the rents if all the tenants perish."

Alejandro, who had been giving his attention to wrapping the child's arm in a cast of clay and hemp fibers, stopped what he was doing immediately and grabbed the man by the shoulder.

"What say you now? Another taken by the plague? Are you certain it was the same pestilence?"

"I know only what I was told by the boy's mother, who begged me for some nails to close the coffin. She told of the neck swellings, and the blackened fingers, and I doubt not that it was the plague."

The physician quickly finished his work and washed his hands, then dug the hardening clay out from beneath his fingernails with the tip of his knife. "I will ride with you," he said, "for I would question the woman at greater length."

"Suit yourself, Physician, but I do not doubt her word. She has lost seven of her nine children now, and she knows the pestilence well enough when it strikes down another of her offspring."

Alejandro bade them ride his extra horse, for the man and boy had walked the long distance to his house, and he knew that his own impatience would not allow him to travel slowly.

When they reached the woman's farm an hour later, Alejandro saw the seven freshly dug graves, with only new sprouts of greenery growing, and his heart ached in sorrow for this family's deep suffering. He tethered his horse to a tree and walked up to the window of the wattle-and-daub cottage, and peered through the cracks in the window shutters. Though his vision was impaired by the bright outside light, he could make out three motionless human forms. The largest, whom he took to be the mother, was on the straw bed, and two smaller ones, both little girls, were slumped on the dirt floor nearby. Swarms of flies circled around each one, and even through the crack Alejandro could see the dark discolorations about the necks and throats.

"It is as I feared; they are all dead," he told the farmer, describing the scene within. "We must halt the spread of this outbreak by purging the site with cleansing fire. Have you any oil in your possession?"

"Only at my own farm, which we passed on our journey here."

They rode back to the farmer's longhouse, which he shared with his livestock, and soaked a rag with some of his precious supply of oil.

"Enough!" the man said. "The price of oil is dear!"

Angered that the man would protest the use of oil to such good purpose, Alejandro proposed a barter. "I will trade my services to your son for your oil. It seems a fair exchange."

The farmer grumbled but accepted the offer. Alejandro rode off with the oil-soaked rag strapped to the saddle of his extra mount, knowing that father would have the child back to work again as soon as possible, and that the boy would be forever disfigured as a result of his father's shortsightedness.

When he reached the cottage again, he wasted no time. He lit the oiled rag with his flint, and tossed it up onto the dry thatched roof. It caught quickly, and soon thick smoke was billowing into the sky. Quickly he jumped onto his waiting mount and grabbed the reins of the other horse. Then he rode a short distance away, stopping to look back briefly before returning to his own home. As he squinted through the sunlight at the growing inferno, he could see rats scampering quickly out of the house, squeezing through the remains of the cracked outer walls, scurrying off to find some new hiding place.

Rats. Always rats, everywhere.

Always rats, where people are afflicted. Rats on ships, rats in houses and barns. Rats with their accursed fleas, tormenting any poor soul standing still long enough.

And with the same sense of revelation that had rushed through him when he saw Carlos Alderón's hardened lung, he knew that rats and their fleas were a part of the curse of plague.

He heeled his horse and rode off at a fast pace, wishing to put as much distance between himself and the horrible scene as possible.

Safely back at his own house, Alejandro quickly settled his horses and cleaned himself of the road's debris, then went immediately to the large table with quill, ink, and parchment.

To His Majesty King Edward III,

In a village north of my fine home, for which I am in your great debt, a family of nine has died, all showing signs of the pestilence that we thought had finally deserted us. While I have seen no other cases, I cannot discount the possibility that this incident will not remain isolated. I have taken all precautions against the spread of the malady by burning their cottage, but as it was being consumed in flames, I saw dozens of rats escaping. I have noticed the presence of these vermin almost everywhere that plague shows itself and I cannot help but conclude they may transport the disease to its victims. Surely this is how the pest migrated to England; I cannot imagine that there is any lack of rats in the holds of the ships that regularly cross from France. You must therefore take immediate measures to rid your palaces and fleet of rats.

I have also learned from a wise old woman, a most venerable healer, that a powder can be made from the remains of one who has succumbed, which, when administered to a living victim, imparts the power of the spirit of the departed so the victim may live! I humbly request your permission to desiccate the corpse of one who lost the battle for life to plague, that we may have the means of keeping the newly afflicted alive.

Pray God that this occurrence is only the last gasp of a pest that is as reluctant to die as its unfortunate victims. It would be my honor to be of service to your family again, should it become necessary; may it please the Almighty that such necessity does not arise, and that the eradication of rodents may put an end to this scourge.

I await your reply with great eagerness.

Your most humble servant,
Alejandro Hernandez

He sent it by hired messenger that day. And for the next few days he asked around his region if anyone had heard of the reemergence of the plague in the surrounding countryside. He received no reports of the pestilence, though he had patients enough with other complaints. Still, he was not entirely reassured.

Well, perhaps it is just my nature to see doom ahead where others see the light of hope, he thought. *Still, it would be a comfort for once to feel truly safe, and I wish this sense of foreboding would leave me.*

"Blast this scourge!" the king cried. "Will its destruction never end? I cannot walk the streets of my own city without stumbling on the dead body of some poor soul, nor breathe the air for the foul stench! Send at once for the lord mayor! I will have an explanation for these vile conditions."

His joyous mood upon returning to London had soured as soon as he went about to inspect the city, and saw the truth of its condition. Rotted bodies from the plague's autumn rampage through the city were in many places still lying uncollected in the gutters and the Thames was a solid mass of sludge composed of garbage, feces, and bodies, all of which left little room for water. And despite the delight King Edward took in governing his fair realm, the problems that faced him now were far too numerous to attend to immediately. So when Alejandro's letter arrived in the hand of a breathless courier, His Majesty was not amused.

"Rats!" he bellowed. "He would have me rid the palaces of *rats*? An *impossible* task. I could rid all my palaces of stones with less effort. Have you ever heard such nonsense, Gaddesdon?"

His regular personal physician, having rejoined the king in London after a year-long banishment to Eltham Castle with the younger royal children, scoffed at the danger and tried to minimize the threat. "We cannot allow this Spaniard to set the kingdom into renewed panic! I have not seen one new case of the pestilence since the frost moon. I believe that he speaks too soon and with too much conviction. It is my firm belief that we have nothing to fear. I assure you that we can safely proceed with plans for the archbishop's investiture before the Solstice. Do not allow this foreigner to dissuade you from your planned course."

But the king was uncertain. He was a shrewd man, accustomed to weighing one risk against another. He gave more thought to the contents of Alejandro's letter. "Master Gaddesdon," he said, "perhaps we are too hasty in our judgment. Please remember that the good Dr. Hernandez, while admittedly an otherwise ignorant Spaniard, was infuriatingly cor-rect in his predictions regarding the pestilence during his time at Wind-sor. And as I ride around London, I see thousands of rats! Perhaps this theory of his may not be so mad as we seem to think! And if there is a cure, should I not grant him his request to use a corpse?"

"The archbishop will not permit it, Sire."

"There *is* no archbishop," Edward reminded him, his voice terse. He stood up to his full and imposing Plantagenet height; all of the courtiers in the room jumped to their feet immediately, including Gad-desdon. "He was felled by this plague, or had you forgotten? And if there were an archbishop, is this not my kingdom, wherein I may do as I see fit?"

"Sire, I beg you to listen . . ." Gaddesdon said.

"Give me good reason why I should listen to you rather than the Spaniard."

Stung, Gaddesdon replied, "I, too, protected your family, though not in your presence. All of your younger children lived well and thrived under my tutelage at Eltham. And in Eltham we had no lack of rats. And, Sire, even without the advice of an archbishop, how can a Christian king permit such desecration as the uprooting of the earthly remains of one who has already suffered?"

"We do not lack for dead peasants, Gaddesdon. Look about you on the streets of this once fair city! There are corpses rotting everywhere! Why not put them to good use, if Hernandez is right?"

"Have not those dead ones suffered already? Why add to the curse by endangering the holy rewards of those who are not even buried?" In a hurt voice he added, "I have seen no cure for this scourge, and I bristle at your willingness to make light of my achievements in protecting the health of your other children."

"Do not misunderstand me," the king replied in an exasperated tone. "I do not belittle your good work. But there is a fear that springs from my gut, not my intellect, that our lives shall once more be interrupted by the horror of this scourge, especially now when I am finally back at the business of ruling this weakened realm."

"Then, I pray you, Your Majesty, do not allow his tales of doom and fantasies of a cure to get in your way. Do what you must do, and let the plague reveal itself, if it shall. God will provide a cure, if it is His will to do so."

He sighed, revealing his frustration to those all around him. "All right. Enough of this arguing; we shall have no more of it." He ordered that a letter should be sent to Alejandro thanking him for his vigilance but declining his offer of assistance and refusing his request. Then he sent for his daughter Isabella, hoping that the good news he had just received would be as joyful to her as it was to him.

"Father," Isabella cried, "I beg you! Do not do this to me! I shall forever be unhappy in that backward land!"

"Isabella, I warn you," the king said angrily, "do not challenge me on this, for I shall not renege on my promise. You shall wed Charles of Bohemia as soon as I can make the arrangements for your travel."

"Dearest God, have pity on me," cried the frantic princess, "for my heartless sire sends me on two months' cruel journey into the arms of an unenlightened savage!"

The king spring up from his seat. "Silence!" he hissed, now more angry than ever at his headstrong progeny. "You speak of the future emperor of Bohemia with that vicious tongue of yours!"

"As I recall, he is yet uncrowned," the princess countered defiantly.

His anger crested, and he rushed forward, raising his hand as if to strike her in the face, but stopping his feigned blow just short of it.

Shocked by her father's violence, Isabella turned her cheek and squeezed her eyes shut. When the feared blow did not materialize, she opened them again and saw her father's large hand hovering inches from her nose. Everyone present in the court saw clearly the ancestral origin of Isabella's notorious temper.

"Do not contradict me, child, for that is all you are, *my child, to marry off at my whim*, at which time you shall become your poor husband's cross to bear! I shall wed you to the very Prince of Darkness, if that is my pleasure, though I doubt that the Evil One himself would have you for fear of your shrewishness! Now return to your quarters and begin to prepare for your bridal journey. Spend even *more* of my money on baubles! I shall tolerate your ungrateful presence no longer."

Her pride completely crushed, Isabella wept openly before the assembled court, and stayed where she was against her father's direct order to do otherwise. She walked closer and pleaded, "Father, I beg a private word with you before I depart this room."

Edward looked at the unhappy girl, his favorite child, the cherished daughter who had grown into the very image of his formidable mother, and for all his rage, he could not find the heart to refuse her request to be heard. With a swift wave of his hand he dismissed the court. Those present made haste to leave the hall, amid hushed whispers and the rustle of robes.

Isabella knelt at her father's feet and made a dramatic plea for clemency. "My lord and father, why do you punish me with this distant and wretched banishment? Have I displeased you of late? Tell me my sin against you; is there nothing I can do to attenuate my unknown offense?"

Edward's heart was breaking. He did not truly wish to send his daughter so far away, but the opportunity to wed her into such an alliance was too great to be passed over.

In a voice that he hoped would convey more determination than he actually felt, the king said, "You denigrate your position as princess of England with such behavior as you have shown today. It is already said among my advisors that I pamper you and forgive your failure to perform the royal duties for which you were raised, which duties include the willing acceptance of advantageous nuptials, regardless of your distaste for the bridegroom. My enemies will think me weak, and contrive cunning methods for swaying me from my chosen course. Would you be the cause of this malfeasance?"

The girl had no answer for her father, who was undeniably correct in his assessment of the effects of her behavior. She hung her head in shame before him, and wept once again, desperately trying to win his sympathy. And while the king had never been unsympathetic to his willful daughter's desires, in this instance he neither could nor would shift his policies to her benefit.

Isabella's mind raced with desperate ideas for manipulating this situation to be more tolerable. Shaken by the failure of her attempt to change her father's mind, she decided to try to make her banishment as comfortable as possible. And to this end she became as clay in her father's hands, willing to please him and help his cause abroad. For the better part of an hour they talked privately of his plans for her, leaving the waiting members of Edward's court wondering about the outcome of the earlier dispute. Edward was delighted with his daughter's sudden and unexpected change of heart, and privately thought that he should have been firm with her long ago, if this blissful accord was the result of such rough treatment.

When their discussion neared its natural end, Isabella rose and, after kissing her father on his forehead, thanked him for tolerating her childish outburst. But before departing she added, "There is one more thing that will greatly ease my pain at leaving my beloved family."

"Only name it, and if it is within my power, you shall have it."

"Please send Lady Throxwood to Bohemia with me as my companion."

The king hesitated. "I had thought to arrange a favorable union for her as well, and there are many good candidates whose allegiance will be welcome in our quest to reclaim France. After all, you are no longer little girls in constant need of each other's company."

"Father, please," she begged. "How can I be expected to learn to love my husband if I am otherwise miserable? She will be a great comfort to me. And there is yet time before her age becomes a consideration."

"She is nineteen. My Philippa was thrice a mother by that age. My own mother was wed at thirteen. How can her age not be a factor? Her childbearing years slip away."

"Father, I beg you, do not separate me from all that I love and cast me into the arms of an unknown man. . . ."

His heart nearly breaking, he gave in to her. "All right," he said. "But she will stay with you for only one year. Then she shall return and be properly wed. I must make all the alliances I can, and her holdings are a valuable dowry."

"Oh, thank you, Father!" She kissed him again. "But I beg you, do not tell her that it was my idea for her to accompany me. I believe that she already feels greatly indebted to me for my generosity. Let her think that this honor comes from you, for I would not have her gratitude overshadow our friendship."

He hesitated, wondering what had prompted his daughter to make such a strange request. "Very well," he finally agreed, though the small voice of curiosity still nagged him. "I shall tell her that it is entirely my doing. Send her to me when you return to your quarters. I would like to make the announcement of your betrothal at Canterbury."

Twenty-Two

J anie and Bruce sat on a bench in a small park not far from Janie's hotel, regrouping after their narrow escape from the lab's freezer. Instead of cabbing, they'd walked. It helped to work off the afterburn of adrenaline, and restored their sluggish circulations after the harrowing spell in the freezer. Still, Janie could not seem to get warm. She huddled up against Bruce, shivering almost violently, and said, "All I want to do right now is crawl into a bed and close my eyes. When I open them up again, I want to be in Massachusetts."

Bruce put his arm around her shoulder and rubbed it. His voice was desolate. "That sounds pretty good right about now. But I'm not going to be able to avoid questioning for too long."

"We've got some time, though," Janie said, her voice deceptively hopeful. "They probably won't call you right away. Maybe not even until tomorrow. I can't imagine you'd be considered a suspect right now. The only person who can put you in that lab around the time of the alarm is the security guard, and he's dead, and there would be evidence of your presence all over that lab, even if you *hadn't* been there today. You *work* there. It would be odd if there *wasn't* any sign of you. As far as anyone else knows, you've been in Leeds. The cops at the storage facility and the clerk at the inn will confirm that we were both there. If you stay out of sight you might not be suspected at all."

"But they'll still want to talk to me." He sounded weary and brittle. "These people are very thorough, and they don't care whose toes they step on. That's not my biggest concern, though. I still have no idea what we should do *right now*. We can't go to my apartment and we sure as hell can't go back to your suite."

Janie sat up straight and looked at him in surprise. "Then what are we doing here? Why did we even bother to come here?"

"I don't know," Bruce said, sounding terribly confused. "I feel almost *homeless* all of a sudden. It seemed like a good idea to come back to the hotel when we left the Institute. Now I'm not so sure."

"But this is the place where Caroline's most likely to try to reach me. The only other place she'd try to reach me would be the Institute. We almost *have* to go back in there. And in case you need reminding, which I assume you don't, there's a dead body in her room."

"You assumed correctly." Bruce's tone was short; their exchanges were beginning to sound strained. "I *don't* need to be reminded. But the notion of dealing with it seems almost crushing to me right now."

"We have to do something with it. If it's found in there, Caroline will never get out of England," Janie said, disliking the shrillness she heard in her own words.

Bruce leaned forward with his elbows on his knees and put his head in his hands. He drew in a deep breath and let it out in one long frustrated sigh. "This has gone beyond Caroline now," he said. "Not only do we have to find Caroline and confine her, we have to do it without implicating ourselves. Who knows what they'll find in the trail we've left behind? You can take it to the bank that they'll find *something,* and they won't be afraid to use it to build up a case against us. You and I know that we had nothing to do with this whole fiasco, but the green guys don't. And if we get locked up before we find her, then God knows where she'll go or what she'll do. She's like Typhoid Mary out there. She could traipse through half of London before anyone figures out what's happening and stops her."

He sat up and looked directly into her eyes. "We may have to think about the bigger picture. There are *fifteen million people* living in and around this city. And one thing I *do* remember about plague is that, left untreated, it has a mortality rate of about ninety percent."

Janie knew that everything he'd said was true. The realist in her said, *Give it up; there's no hope. Walk away now, when they still might believe you.* She remembered John Sandhaus saying, *Do the right thing, Janie.* She thought about how it would feel to be released from the nearly unbearable burden that had settled, uninvited, on her shoulders, so quickly and without the slightest warning. The sense of lightness she imagined was sweet and seductive, and she wanted it desperately.

She could see that Bruce was waiting for her to respond to what he'd said. *He's a good man,* she thought, *and I could love him, when this is all over.* She knew that what she did right now would largely define their future together. *It might already be too late,* she thought, *but I can't do anything about that.*

The night sky was beginning to lighten just slightly. Dawn was only a couple of hours away. *Maybe the light of day will make things seem clearer,* she thought hopefully. "Just give me till dawn," she said. "If we don't hear from her by then, I'll call."

She could see his reluctance and expected that he would say no. He surprised her by saying, "All right. Dawn." He nodded in the direction of the hotel. "In the meantime let's try to figure out what to do with Ted's body."

He rose up from the bench and stretched, then reached out and took her hand. He pulled her to standing, and she was glad for the help. His grip tightened briefly as, reunited for the moment, they headed toward the hotel.

Sarin grew increasingly impatient. Like a woman heavy with child whose time was close at hand, he'd had another burst of energy and had gone over everything one more time to be sure all was as he wanted it to be. He was nesting, preparing, digging in to ease his passage through the hard time ahead of him. No longer afraid, he was instead anxious to begin his tasks, and as the hours of the day passed, he began to think that the waiting was more draining than the preparation had ever been.

The dog had picked up on his master's heightened state and followed him around the cottage with concerned eyes. Their normal daily routine had been disrupted by the flurry of activity. A creature of habit, the shaggy beast had spent the day in a state of confusion. It was unlike the old man to expend so much effort in one day.

At dusk Sarin grabbed the dog's leash from its hook and waved it at him. "Shall we, then?" he said. Their evening walk was the first sign of normalcy in the oddly paced day, and the elated dog was soon as animated as a puppy, jumping up and down gleefully and wagging his tail.

The sky was unusually clear and Sarin looked above the treetops for the evening star. His mother had once told him that it wasn't actually a star, but something more like the earth itself. He looked for it every night, and its presence was always a comfort to him, a sign of stability in the sky, evidence that though darkness was about to descend, lightness would follow it in due time, and all would be well. At this time of year he knew it would be found above a certain tree, and there it was, twinkling and friendly. He soaked up the image of it and imprinted it on his memory, for he wanted to take its comfort with him when he passed over.

They passed through the oaks. As they took their customary route around the perimeter of the field, Sarin let the animal lead and allowed himself to be dragged along. The dog did his business rather quickly, but contrary to his usual habit he did not continue to trace the edge of the field. Instead, he stood quietly and picked up his ears, obviously straining for a sound in the distance. Suddenly he started pulling on the leash, almost violently, and the old man nearly stumbled trying to hold him back. The dog wanted to run, and leapt around wildly to free himself, trying to move toward the center of the field.

"Whoa," Sarin said. "Hold on there!" He grabbed the dog's collar and tightened it, hoping to get better control of him. The dog would have none of it and continued to strain in frustration. Sarin was forced to drop the leash, and no sooner had he done so than his pet bounded off at a frantic pace toward the center of the field, leaving his master to stare after him in wonder. "Slow down!" he called out to the racing animal; he'd never seen the dog run so fast before. "I'm coming!"

He ran as fast as he could, guided by the sound of the dog's barking up ahead of him. He stumbled once or twice on rocks and roots. *Be careful, old fool,* he said to himself, *there is important work yet to be done.*

He'd always thought that when he grew old he would naturally be wiser than in his youth, but he was still as uncertain as a teenager, and the thought of what lay ahead of him seemed suddenly overwhelming. He pressed on, aching and panting, every step over the rocky ground a jolt to his spine.

Suddenly the dog bounded out of the darkness and leapt around at Sarin's feet, then dashed back in the direction from which he had appeared. Sarin followed him with his eyes, and saw that the dog stopped on the crest of a small rise, not far from the familiar spot where the mud oozed up each spring. He knew there was a large rock there, embedded deeply in the ground, its rounded crown protruding just enough to be visible. As he drew nearer, he thought he made out another rounded shape near where the rock should be. When he was just a few meters away, the shape moved.

He finally reached it and came to a stop, panting and wheezing. He bent over and pushed the dog away. Peering through the darkness, he could just barely see the woman at his feet. He directed the flashlight at her face and recoiled immediately.

"Dear God!" he cried in shock. He looked again, trying to determine which of the two previous visitors had returned to him. The red hair, although matted and filthy, gave its owner's identity away immediately.

Her condition was far worse than he'd expected it would be. "There's no time to waste," he said to the dog. "She's very bad!"

The newspapers with which she had been covered had all blown away. He buttoned her ragged jacket closed, then removed his own sweater and covered her legs with it. She groaned and tried to turn suddenly, and he jumped back, frightened by her unexpected movement. He began to whimper, but quickly chided himself for his lack of courage. Gathering his wits, he raised a finger to his lips and said, "*Shh!* Be still now, you've no need to move." He thought it unlikely that she could understand him, but he felt compelled to try to comfort and reassure her. "Everything will be fine," he said. "You'll be well soon. You'll see!"

The dog whined and cocked his head; he bent down to Caroline's hot, filthy face and starting licking her again, as if to cool her. Sarin pushed him away and shook his finger in the dog's face, saying, "Bad dog! We must be careful with her. Now, stay here! I'll be right back. You stay here like a good chum!"

He stood up and started a slow trot back toward the cottage. The dog took a few steps in his direction, then thought better of it and returned to Caroline's side. After a few more confused whines he lay down next to her, warming her with his own fur. He stayed there, panting, every now and then licking her face, and waited for his master to return.

A few minutes later Sarin returned with poles and blankets. He tied two corners of one blanket to each pole and made a simple travois with which to transport Caroline to the cottage. He laid it on the ground next to her and spread it flat. As gently as he could, he lifted first her feet, then her midsection, then her upper body, onto the blanket. She started to move again, as if resisting him, so he stroked her forehead gently and said, "Be still! It will only be a few more minutes, then I'll have you safely inside." Using another blanket, he tied her to the makeshift stretcher so she wouldn't slip off during the bumpy ride over the field.

"I'm sorry, miss," he said to her before picking up the poles. "I don't think this is going to be a comfortable ride."

He pulled slowly in the direction of the cottage. The travois scraped over the rocks and their progress was grindingly slow. The distance seemed enormous to him from where he stood. He knew it was really just a short walk, but with the burden of Caroline's leaden weight he had to stop frequently to catch his breath and shake the stiffness out of his arms. He looked back at his passenger many times during the journey, checking that she was still secured to the blanket, each time thanking God that she was unconscious and unable to feel the pain of movement.

A wind came up, not the fair wind he was accustomed to, but a crisp, harsh wind with a distinct chill to it. He bent lower and squinted against the leaves and bits of dirt suddenly whirling all around him. The cruel force of it threatened to push him backward, and for a few minutes he made no forward progress at all. Then he renewed his efforts, leaning into the wind and pressing ahead. Finally, he reached the oaks, and as he passed between them to the other side, he could feel the wind change. It softened and then dissipated altogether, and suddenly he was warm again.

* * *

By the time Janie and Bruce reached the lobby of the hotel, they had developed something resembling a plan; it was incomplete, but it would get them started. It required a luggage cart, so Bruce grabbed one as they passed by the bell station and they brought it upstairs with them on the elevator.

Ted's body was more decomposed than when they'd left it, but the smell had lessened somewhat, since they'd left the window open. Being as careful to avoid contamination as was possible under the circumstances, Janie and Bruce rolled him onto a blanket and wrapped him up tight. Avoiding thought, they struggled until they were able to bend it at the middle, and shoved it unceremoniously into Janie's plastic garment bag.

When they had finally managed to hoist Ted's bent, bagged body onto the luggage cart, they went to the bathroom and scrubbed their hands almost until they bled. Bruce sat down on the bed and stared at the cart with its grisly cargo. Then he buried his face in his hands and rubbed his eyes. His voice was muffled as he said to Janie, "I can't believe what I just did. And I have no idea what I'm going to do."

"We should burn the body," Janie said.

"We'll have to take it out of London to do that."

She looked at her watch; it was nearly four A.M. Dawn was just an hour away. She needed an idea.

"We can put it in the trunk of your car and take it out of London later today. At least it will be out of sight."

He sighed deeply and stood up. "Well, we can't leave it here."

After another look around they wheeled the cart out of the room and took the elevator down.

In the lobby they separated. Bruce took the cart and the body and went to the car, which was parked where they'd left it across the street. Janie stayed behind and rang for the night clerk. When he came out of the back office, he had the tousled look of someone who'd been awakened from a sound sleep. Nevertheless, he was polite to her. "Yes, ma'am?" he said.

"Sorry to wake you up," she apologized nervously.

"That's quite all right, ma'am," he said. He looked at her through half-slit eyes, and Janie wondered briefly if it had been a mistake to ring for him.

She mustered what she hoped was a convincing smile. "I'm going to be doing some field trips over the next few days," she said. As an explanation for the early hour she added, "I wanted to get an early start today. I won't be checking out, but I'm going to be leaving some important research papers in my room. They're scattered all over the place, so I'd prefer not to have any housekeeping done while I'm gone. I know Miss Porter in the room next to me requested the same thing and housekeeping has been very accommodating."

"Of course, ma'am, I'll be sure to tell the housekeeper. Now, what room was that again?"

"Seven ten," she said. As he wrote down the room number, she looked over her shoulder and saw Bruce closing the trunk of his car. The luggage rack was empty.

"Well, thank you very much," she said, and turned to go.

"Just a minute, ma'am. Seven ten, you said?"

She turned back, fear gripping her belly. "That's right."

"You've a message here. A gent called earlier. Didn't seem to want to use the voice mail."

That would be Sandhaus, notorious crank that he is, she thought, and her fear was replaced with annoyance. *Your timing is impeccable as usual, John. . . .*

He held out the paper to her and said, "I took the call myself. If you don't mind me saying so, ma'am, the gentleman seemed a bit upset."

She took the proffered piece of paper and unfolded it.

Robert Sarin, it read. *Very important come immediately.*

Moving stiffly, for he'd almost thrown out his back when he lifted Caroline onto the small bed, Sarin removed all the wet rags from her body and threw them into the fire. He watched until they caught and saw the flames leap up in protest, as if some vile force had been put to the torch and was fighting to reclaim its power. He washed her entire body with a cloth dipped in fragrant herbal water, keeping all but the part being tended modestly covered with a light blanket as he did so. It shamed him to see certain parts of her. He had never seen a woman completely undressed, not even his mother, and he was too old now to be stirred by the sight as he once might have been. The layers of accumulated grime gradually began to disappear and her skin finally showed. *So terribly white,* he thought to himself. He wondered how she could be this sick and still be breathing.

From an ancient wooden chest he removed a delicate white nightdress, fashioned from fabric so fragile that it seemed almost translucent. He raised her head up with one hand and pulled the nightdress over it with the other. He had to struggle to get her uncooperative limbs to do his bidding as he drew the gown over them. When he was satisfied that he had made her as comfortable as possible, he pulled fresh bed linens up over her thin form. Then he arranged her hands together, one over the other resting on her belly, and placed a bouquet of dried herbs between them.

He stood back and regarded her thoughtfully. "I hope you recover your beauty," he said to her, confident that she could not hear him. Then he thought about what he had just said and prayed quietly, *Dear God, I would be happy if she would simply recover. That would be more than enough.* He suspected that the extension of her life, should it be granted, would not be an isolated occurrence, but part of some larger purpose.

He sighed aloud, then reached out and patted her reassuringly on the leg. *If only I could see it played out.* Would she still be young when it happened, and perhaps bear an important child? Or would she be an old woman, ancient like himself, before any role she might play became obvious to her?

Would this woman, should he manage to heal her, perhaps become a healer herself? He had always known what would be expected of him, but until the object of his well-rehearsed attentions was actually put before him, he had never bothered to wonder why it was so important for him to succeed. "Well," he said quietly to the dog at his side, "I probably wouldn't have understood anyway."

The room was awash with the pale glow of candlelight, for his mother had said that too much light would be painful to her eyes if she opened them again. If he was still at this work in the morning, he would draw the shades to protect her from the harsh rays of the sun.

Through the dim light he saw her stir and went to her side immediately. He placed his hand on her forehead; though her skin was still clammy, she felt cooler. He was pleased and gratified that something he'd done, perhaps the herbal wash, might have made a difference in her comfort.

"I wish they would come," he said to the dog. He looked at his pocket watch and sighed. "It's time to get started." The dog whined softly in response, and Sarin took a big deep breath. "I'll just have to get on with it without them, then." He hoped he would do well.

Twenty-Three

Alejandro was confused by the king's ambiguous reply to his urgent message.

We are once again in your debt, Physician, for the diligence with which you apply yourself to your craft. Please continue your good work in advising me of your discoveries. I, too, shall listen for news of the pestilence from the entirety of the kingdom, and together we shall soon know the truth of this supposed new outbreak. I shall consider your request and give my answer at Canterbury.

The reply said nothing! *How is it that even educated men can use so many words and say so little with them?* the physician wondered. The king had no plans to pursue the rumors aggressively, nor did he seem interested in Alejandro's news about a possible cure. *He is too caught up in kingcraft and fails to see that there will soon be no subjects in need of his monarchal service. But I do not share his casual indifference.*

He rode back to the burned cottage and walked among the blackened ruins. In the center of what was once their home, he found the charred skeletal remains of the woman and her two daughters, and thought momentarily of adding their graves to those already scattered about the yard. But he dared not touch the unburied corpses, in fear of inviting the stealthy contagion to infect him as well.

This cannot be the end of it. There must be others nearby. I am missing something.

He thought of going ahead with the desiccation without official sanction, but the memories of his experience in Aragon kept such thoughts in his head. He spent the rest of the day inquiring among the local people, and he grew ever more frustrated by the disparity between what his logical mind told him should be true, and what reality presented instead. As the shadows gradually grew longer, he turned toward the safety of his home, having neglected to prepare for overnight travel.

Thirst and hunger were gnawing at his belly when he came upon a small monastery, and as it was the custom of some Christian orders to give hospitality to the travel worn, he rang the bell, hoping for some refreshment before continuing. When no one answered, he rang again, but again his request for entry went unheeded.

When he could no longer politely contain his growing curiosity, he tried the door, and found it unlocked. He opened it, planning to enter the monastery uninvited. But before he was through the door, the familiar stench hit his nostrils with enough force to make him turn and run back out again, gagging and gulping for fresh air as if he were drowning. He did not need to investigate further, for there could be no doubt about the origin of the choking odor. And though it was only two days before he was to ride to Canterbury, he resolved to leave at first light, for he knew he must convey this knowledge to the king.

But when he awoke after a fitful night, he looked out his window to see a strong wind whipping the trees around, causing them to shed branches and limbs as if they were mere twigs, and the rain poured down in ceaseless torrents. He was forced to delay his departure another day, until there was a reasonable chance that he would arrive at his destination unscathed, for in this mission he could not risk failure.

Adele refastened the buttons on her sleeves, then rearranged her skirts over her chemise. Nearby, Nurse wiped her hands on a linen towel, sighing heavily as she did so. This was a difficult turn of events, and she feared for the soul of this lady.

"There can be no doubt. Your menses have ceased for two moons, and your womb is soft to my touch. By midwinter, God willing, you'll hold a babe in your arms."

Lost in turmoil, Adele made no comment on receiving the news. When she had first begun to suspect that life grew within her, it was a terrifying thought, for this fatherless child could not reside in Isabella's household. The child Adele carried was no Kate but the bastard of a Spaniard, and until he was knighted, Alejandro would be considered a poor match for the aristocratic Lady Throxwood. She would have to keep her condition secret until after his dubbing.

"If you love me well," Adele said to Nurse, "as I know you loved my gentle mother, please do not say one word of this to anyone, especially my lady Isabella. I would share this knowledge with the child's father before it is known in the palace."

"Lady," Nurse said with some hesitation, for she was certain of the child's paternity and feared for the mismatched pair, "if you are of a mind to be rid of this burden, it can be arranged. Many a midwife has plucked an unwanted seed from its mother's womb, even among the highborn."

Adele already knew that it was possible for women of stature and privilege to terminate an undesirable pregnancy but, in her confusion, had not even considered it. She almost resented the additional complication introduced by the well-meaning old woman. Now that her condition was a certainty, there was much to reflect on. Her head began to ache, and she rubbed her forehead lightly. And even though she felt concern for her situation, she had already spent many happy hours dreaming of the fine life that she and Alejandro might soon enjoy, and their child, too, if things went well. Most of her life had been spent in service to her friend, but it was time that she had something of her own. Surely Isabella could not resent it.

"There is simply too much to think about!" Adele said, and rolled over, hiding her face from view.

Nurse stepped away from the small bed and began to bustle around the room, tending to small tasks, busying herself with meaningless chores so as to afford the lady some privacy. "God curse all fleas!" she said, slapping the back of her hand. "May I live to know just one spring without the annoying little blighters!"

Adele did not reply but groaned as a cold wave of nausea spread over her. She rolled over onto her other side and drew up her knees to offset the discomfort. Hearing the sound of distress, Nurse rushed back to her side.

"Many women who are newly with child suffer torments of the belly," she said, "but it will pass. In two turns of the moon you will feel no discomfort. And the child will quicken within you! You will feel his small kicks. It is the most wonderful pleasure when that joyous time comes."

"Ah, gentle nurse, how you comfort me," she said, holding the old woman's hand. "I had thought these pains were God's punishment for my failure to be chaste."

"Not so," Nurse said sympathetically. "Few escape. I venture to guess that the Holy Virgin herself suffered so."

Adele closed her eyes, prepared for a new onslaught of cramping, and said, "Then I shall pray for her guidance and protection."

By late morning Adele felt more nearly herself. She ate a small repast, and spent some time at embroidery. She was bent over her stitching when Isabella returned from court and told her that King Edward wished to speak with her privately.

"But you look so pale," the princess said. "Are you ill?"

"A bit tired, perhaps," she said. Looking in Isabella's mirror, she saw that what the princess had said was true. She pinched her cheeks with her fingertips, and they reddened. She turned to Isabella, who smiled with approval.

"Why in God's name does he wish to see me?" she asked.

"I do not know," Isabella said lightly, pretending ignorance.

Oh, dear God, no, Adele suddenly thought. *It cannot be. Not now.* Timidly, she asked her mistress, "Has he an offer of marriage for me?"

Seeing the look of concern on Adele's face, the princess laughed. "Do not be concerned, my dear companion. I have heard nothing of any offer. I would speculate that he wishes to speak with you on matters concerning your holdings. But do not let my father's love of hearing his own voice keep you in court too long. When you return we shall try on our robes for the ceremonies. They have finally arrived, and not a moment too soon!"

Dragging herself to the king's court, Adele wondered if she should have left the chamber at all. Her stomach ills returned in full force, and she had to stop to balance herself against the wall. She fought off her urge to retch and gathered her composure, then proceeded toward the great hall.

"Why, you are as white as the purest linen!" the king said when he saw her. "What ails you, lady?"

"It is just a passing grippe, Sire. I am, in truth, much improved over this morning. I beg your indulgence of my pallid appearance."

The king declined to inquire further, though he was pleased to hear that she felt better. He offered her a seat, which she gratefully accepted.

"There is a mission of great importance which I beg you to consider," the king began. "I would ask you to help in making some important preparations regarding Isabella's upcoming nuptials."

Confused, Adele said, "Your Majesty, I do not understand. Is my lady newly betrothed?"

"What, has the neglectful upstart failed to advise you of our great good news? Why, you would be her first confidante! How unusually gracious of her to allow me the joy of being the first to tell you! We have nearly completed arrangements for Isabella to be wed to the Bohemian Charles, who will soon be crowned emperor. You are to travel there with her, and remain for a year as her friend and comfort. This will allow adequate time for her to make an adjustment to her new husband. She would not impose this travel upon you herself, but it is my sincere belief that your presence will give her much joy, and will enable the union of England and Bohemia to be more firmly cemented."

When the color drained even further from her face, Edward said, "Lady Adele? If you are unwell we may discuss this later. . . ."

Shaking, she said, "No, Sire, my discomfort will pass. . . . I am unaccustomed to good news these days. . . ."

"I will not keep you, then, for two such bits of good news, one for yourself, and one for Isabella, must be more than your constitution can bear. Tell me, then I will give you leave, can I count on good service, as your father gave me in France, from his daughter in Bohemia?"

Adele could not answer, for it was not within her power to do so. Overwhelmed by the implications of the king's request, she fainted and slumped over in her chair, unconscious.

Sir John Chandos was nearby. The great warrior rushed over and picked her up easily. He carried her back to the women's quarters unaided. There, Nurse took charge, and instructed him to deposit Adele's limp form carefully on the bed. When he had done so, she promptly and boldly ordered him to leave.

"Be off, now. This is no place for a man, or are you of a mind to learn more about the women's curse under my tutelage?"

The good Sir John, unaccustomed to the intimate ways of women, was only too glad to depart. As soon as he had gone, Nurse began to undo the bodice of Adele's dress and called for Isabella to help.

The frightened princess fumbled at the laces, but her clumsy fingers were of little use. "What ails her?" she demanded of Nurse.

Nurse said nothing and would not meet Isabella's eyes.

"Speak, woman!" Isabella ordered.

When Nurse remained conspicuously silent, Adele, who had regained consciousness, relieved her of the promise to keep her secret from the lady she served. "I will explain for myself," she said thinly. "My malady is little more than that of any breeding woman. I carry Alejandro's child."

Borrowing Adele's habitual gesture, Isabella crossed herself. Shocked by Adele's admission, the princess withdrew from the bedside and left Nurse to minister to Adele's needs. She paced about the room like an angry cat; she was confused, and desperate to keep her situation under control. First she felt rage, that her dearest friend would commit an act of such underhanded betrayal; and then jealousy of the closeness Adele shared with the father of her child, while she herself, a royal princess, had no success in love.

When she had calmed herself a bit, she returned to the bedside, where Adele lay with a damp cloth draped over her forehead. "Oh, Adele,

I thought you loved me well! Among those around me, I thought you would be the last to abandon me."

Adele tried to sit but managed only to rise up on her elbows. "Isabella, how can you doubt me? I have been by your side since we were but little girls!"

"But you have let your love for me be sullied by the love of that ungodly Spaniard. First my father succumbs to his restrictive influence, and then the vile trickster steals your precious affection and loyalty from me!"

"You judge him too harshly! And I gave my love willingly."

Isabella took Adele's hand in hers. "He is beneath you. He does not deserve you. You are of the most noble lineage, and he is a common *Spaniard*."

Her anger beginning to rise, Adele defended Alejandro. "You are blinded by your dislike for the restrictions he imposed upon us, the very restrictions that saved our lives. You cannot see past your anger! And if you knew him as well as I do, you would find him far from common."

"No doubt you know him very well," Isabella said, "judging by your condition." Then she turned and ran angrily away from the bedside, leaving Adele stunned by the viciousness of her remarks and alone in her misery.

How could this have happened, and at the worst of all possible times? Isabella asked herself. She knew that a woman with such a burden in her belly presented a grave danger to the rest of a traveling party, whose need to move quickly could be dramatically compromised by such a vulnerable member. And what monarch would send an unwed lady to a foreign court, with the visible evidence of sinfulness protruding from her swollen abdomen? Not King Edward—of this Isabella was certain.

What to do? O Blessed Virgin, what is my proper course of action?

Her melancholy self-absorption was interrupted by Kate's small tug at her sleeve. Isabella snapped at the child, "Oh, you! What is it now?"

"Please, sister, what ails the lady?"

"She ails with the curse of being female, which you yourself shall soon enough know, and then perhaps your childlike pestering will finally come to an end! Now, get out, and do not bother me today!"

Accustomed though she was to Isabella's abuse, Kate was nevertheless stung by her sister's hurtful invective. Feeling more than usually unwelcome, she curtsied quickly, and ran out of the room, fighting back hot tears of rejection.

Later that day, when Adele's color had returned a bit and the urge to retch had finally released her from its grip, Isabella approached her.

"I would not have us angry at each other," the princess said. "We are far too long together to let anything come between us. Can you forgive me for my cruel treatment of you?"

"Oh, Isabella," Adele said, greatly relieved by her mistress' apparent change of heart, "I would forgive you almost anything. And I would share my joy with you, for despite the difficulties of my situation, I am more joyful than I ever dreamed possible." She gripped her friend's hand and squeezed it tightly. "Oh, please, Isabella, can you not intervene for me with your father? Help me to convince him that I must remain behind; help me to show him that Alejandro will be a deserving husband for me."

So, Isabella thought, *you will choose him.* She drew her hands away from Adele's grip and said quietly, "All right. I will try. If it will make you happy."

Adele reached out and hugged her with all of her might. Isabella, smiling weakly, broke free of the embrace and said, "Now we must try our gowns for Canterbury. They have arrived just this afternoon, while you were confined to bed."

And all the while, as the ladies of her entourage tried on their finery, Isabella feigned gaiety, and falsely assured Adele that she would do her best to intervene on her behalf with the king. In her soul she boiled with the humiliation of rejection, but her pride would not allow her to show it, even before her most intimate companion. Like a wounded child she made her quiet plans for revenge, but like a cunning princess she kept them to herself. Soon enough Adele would know the heavy cost of her betrayal, and Isabella was sure it would never happen again.

After the pounding storm of the previous day the sky had blued prettily, but nothing good could be said about the condition of the muddy roads. Alejandro's plan was to ride directly to the Tower, and there seek an immediate audience with the king. Fearing the king's rejection of his plea for an audience in favor of more pleasing petitioners, Alejandro resolved to do his best to convince him of the importance of his news.

Evidence of the storm lessened as he neared London. By the look of the improving roads Alejandro assumed that the vicious storm that had delayed his departure had not touched the city. Still, the conditions he found there were shameful, completely offensive to the fastidious Jew. *If this is England's best city, what can be said of the poor ones?* he wondered. He stopped to ask the way, and was saddened by the hollow look on the faces of the residents. It would be a formidable task to set things right in London after the plague's devastation, and Alejandro was sure that recovery would not happen quickly with a diminished and weakened population.

He persevered through the drab, cluttered streets, but stopped abruptly when a flash of bright color caught his eye. He saw a haggard crone shuffling wearily in the opposite direction, a bright red shawl wrapped tightly about her shoulders; it was the very image of Mother Sarah. *How can it be she, so far from her cottage?* Still, he turned his mount around. She was nowhere to be seen, and he could see no easy place where she might have hidden herself.

And why should such a traveler feel compelled to hide? he wondered, confused by her disappearance. He cast his gaze up and down the street again in search of the elusive midwife, but he saw nothing of her. The horse pranced nervously in place, and lacking any further reason to linger, Alejandro resumed his ride toward the Tower, feeling more than slightly unnerved.

The vile odor of the river and the Tower moat had not improved since his first trip over the drawbridge, now nearly a year ago, and in fact had worsened. *The king should be glad,* he thought, *for that odor is weapon enough to keep all but the most insensitive enemies away from him.* Inside, the courtyard was nearly deserted, with only a few sentries in evidence. He recognized one of them as having been in the party that escorted him to Windsor, so he dismounted and approached the man.

"Fellow!" he hailed. "Good day!"

The sentry brightened with recognition. "Good Doctor! I rejoice that God has brought you through this long and bitter winter; what purpose brings you to our fair and scented city?"

"The king's business," he answered. "But why so quiet here? Why is no one about?"

"Ah," the man said, "the king's party rode out yesterday! Quite a handsome parade they made, especially with all the ladies. It was perhaps the biggest party I've seen in a year. They were heading for the cathedral, on account of the archbishop's investiture, no doubt. We've had little excitement here, save the plague, and the people will be wanting a good show of color from their king to inspire them!"

"Was the Princess Isabella among them, and her ladies?"

"Indeed, she was, sir, and a grand parcel of cartons as well!"

I have missed them, then . . . I have come too late to catch them here. "I must leave immediately, then," he said to the sentry. "Where is the gatekeeper? I must see his map."

And after committing it to memory, since the gatekeeper would not part with the precious map even for the outrageous price of a gold coin, Alejandro set off on the last leg of his journey to Canterbury.

Twenty-Four

S arin brought the wooden box of ancient items to the bedside. He sat down in a chair and balanced the box carefully in his lap. Mindful of its great age and fragility, he lifted the cover very slowly and set it on the floor next to his chair. There was an odd assortment of items within, a seemingly random group of small things with no obvious relationship to one another. One by one he removed them and placed them on the table by the bed. He muttered the name of each thing as he set it down, reciting his memorized checklist so that the backward order would be precise, for the item last removed would be the item first used. He had practiced it that way many times in the course of preparing for this night. When all the items were set in their proper places, he looked them over until he was satisfied that his reenactment of what he'd practiced was flawless.

"Now the book," he said to Caroline's sleeping form. He got up from the bedside chair—it creaked slightly as he pushed off from the caned seat—and shuffled stiffly into the next room. He found the ancient volume precisely where he'd left it and brought it back into the bedroom with him. He'd marked the proper page with the same feather his mother used to use, and he was careful not to dislodge it. He placed the book on the edge of the bed and opened it to the correct place.

He read slowly, for the candlelight was very dim and his eyes had not completely adjusted to it. He needn't have bothered, for he'd nearly memorized the instructions, and this reading was but one more repetition of what he'd already studied and learned well. He was stalling, he knew, out of fear, for once he started, there could be no stopping. *Stop wasting time*, he told himself. *Get on with it.*

"First, the ribbons," he muttered, reassuring himself. They were tied together in a bundle with a small piece of twine. He loosened the knot in the twine and the ribbons tumbled free, falling onto the bedcover in matted bunches. They were musty and smelled of mold, but the fabric from which they were fashioned so long ago was still sound and did not fray or ravel as he handled them. He pinned the ribbons all over her nightdress and the bedclothes, then sat back and regarded his own work appreciatively. *One step accomplished*, he thought. He said aloud to the dog, "Come have a look, chum. The young lady looks quite festive. One day she'll be a comely lass again, don't you agree?"

The dog did not appear at his master's side as Sarin expected he would do. *Sleeping, probably,* the old man thought. *He's had a time of it, just as I have. Best to let him rest.* He returned to his tasks.

Tied around a hollowed-out walnut shell was a white ribbon; he'd fastened the bow himself only the day before. Now his stiff fingers struggled clumsily with the small bow and he wondered to himself how he'd ever tied it so tightly. Finally, after a few inept and frustrated tugs, it came loose. Holding the shell just above Caroline's chest, he separated the two halves and set them down on the bedcover. A hairy black spider scampered out and scurried off in great haste.

Sarin watched the creature disappear under the bedcovers, and thought about how much harder it had been to get the insect into the shell. He'd been enormously relieved when the two halves of the shell had finally come together, the spider safely captured. "Feisty little bugger, wasn't he, eh, chum?" he said to the dog.

He expected a whine of accord from his pet, but instead, there was empty silence. He looked around the room again, hoping to see the animal. *Still sleeping,* he thought. *A very long sleep, indeed.*

Second step done, he thought. He returned the empty shell to the box along with its ribbon. *Just in case it's needed again . . .* He whispered a brief prayer that it would not be. *Dear God, let it not be needed, let it come to an end here. . . .*

He broke a few crumbs off a crust of bread so dry that it almost powdered when he touched it. "Three crumbs from a loaf baked on Good Friday last . . ." he said, pressing the bits of bread to her lips. It didn't matter if she swallowed, he knew; it was enough just to make the offering. *Third step complete . . .*

And now the fourth. He took a small copper ring and placed it on one of her fingers. A ring made from pennies begged by lepers. . . .

What could be keeping the other one? Had she not received his message? He got up from the chair and went into the main room of the cottage. After pulling aside the curtain on the small window, he looked outside into the depths of the night, wondering when the headlights would finally round the corner and make the slow turn into the drive.

"I can do it myself, you know," he said aloud, almost defiantly. "After all, I've practiced properly . . . haven't I, chum?"

The cottage remained silent. He called aloud to the dog, but the animal did not appear. He went to the door and opened it, thinking perhaps the dog had been left outside. This was not inconceivable, considering the hurry he'd been in, but he simply couldn't remember. He whistled into the silent night, and waited. Finally he closed the door, confused and worried. He went to the place where the dog usually rested, a worn old blanket that the beast always rearranged with his teeth before settling in. Every night he would ritually turn three circles over the rumpled layers of wool, his tail wagging, then flop down smiling and place his head on his own front paws. But the blanket was unoccupied, empty but for the few stray hairs that clung to it, and the slight doggy aroma that lingered, especially on wet days. He surveyed the rest of the room quickly, but found no trace of his pet.

"You have to be in here," he said aloud. And though it was difficult to hide much of anything in the small cottage, Sarin started moving things aside and lifting things up off the floor in his search. It was difficult work, and he was not accustomed to it. In a very few minutes he was quite tired. Exasperated, he headed back into the bedroom. He could not allow his attendance on the young woman to be delayed for too long.

Protruding from under the end of the bed was the tip of the dog's tail.

"There you are!" he said, his fears allayed. "What's got you so frightened, old chum? Come out, now."

The dog did not move. He whistled softly, a signal that he knew would bring the dog out of even the deepest sleep. Sarin waited for the dog's head to rise and the ears to perk upward, but the animal did not stir.

The old man knelt down on the floor and put his hand under the bed on the dog's back. *It should rise and fall . . . why does his back not rise and fall?* Panicking, he took hold of the dog's tail, pulling and dragging him until he was out from under the bed. Small bits of dust clung to the motionless shaggy body, and without thinking that there might be something more important to do, Sarin began to remove them. "Oh, dear God . . ." he said. "Please, *no* . . ." He placed his hand in front of the animal's half-opened mouth, hoping that a whisper of breath would gently brush the surface of his palm. No breath came.

Somewhere in the distance he heard the ringing of a telephone. He ignored it completely and stayed with the dog. He knew who it would be on the other end of the line. If he answered, she would demand an explanation for his summons, and would never believe what he would tell her. Better, he thought, that she should just come as he'd asked.

Anger filled his heart, then terrible pain; *This was never supposed to be part of the plan! No one prepared me for this!* His mother had never told him this might happen. *Why have they taken my dog?* He gently stroked the soft fur of the dog's head, and with his other hand brushed away his own tears. He picked up the animal and cradled him carefully to his chest. Sarin leaned against the foot of the bed and sat there, weeping and rocking his dead companion for a long time, until he fell asleep.

Several vans with flashing neon-green lights came to a simultaneous halt in the square at the foot of the bridge. People watching from the windows of their apartments pulled their shades down quickly as soon as they gleaned the nature of the commotion. No one wanted to be noticed for paying too much attention to the business of the Biocops.

They'd arrived within minutes of the call from the field unit on the bridge. Lieutenant Rosow considered it a bit of good luck that he'd gotten a report of a sighting so quickly. These things were always a matter of luck, he knew, and it could just as easily have gone the other way. There might not have been a sighting for several hours, or even days. *Must be fate*, he thought. *Or my good karma.*

Van doors flew open and approximately thirty green giants emerged, each carrying communication equipment and a loaded chemical weapon. Foot traffic in the square came to a standstill. Those people already in the square when the vans arrived left quickly and cautiously, and no one who was not there already dared to enter. In a few minutes the group had been reassembled into several teams, Lieutenant Rosow spoke quickly to each of the team leaders, and shortly thereafter each team moved out in a different direction.

He led his own team down the slippery embankment and under the bridge, just below the spot where the Marginal had fallen on the sidewalk. The body was gone now, neatly zipped into a green body bag and stowed in a refrigerated van; it was no longer an impediment to anyone's progress. Under the bridge they found the rough belongings and accoutrements of a very different sort of society from the one Rosow himself moved through daily. *How can they live like this?* he wondered to himself as he and his team poked through the shabby appointments of the under-bridge world.

But there were no Marginals to be found. "They must have figured we were coming," he said to his team. "Just as well—we should roust them more often anyway, then come down here with hoses." Using the tip of his rifle he pushed aside a few more items, not really sure what he was hoping to find. "There isn't much of anything here," he said, and signaled his team to climb back up the embankment to the main square.

They regrouped and headed in the woman's last known direction,

ANN   N   B   E   N   S   O   N

although the officer who'd reported the sighting to Rosow had said he could not be sure that she hadn't taken a side street. "She seemed to disappear into the darkness," he'd said when Rosow questioned him. He'd mentioned a shopping cart. The trail was getting cold, and they would need even more luck to find her and the mysterious redhead in her cart.

He asked a lot of people before one finally admitted seeing a shopping cart being pushed up the hill. *Not a woman, but a very skinny man,* the witness reported, *probably not even seven stone. But there was definitely someone in the cart, with red hair.* Rosow got on the radio to the other searchers and notified them of the probable change in the appearance of their quarry.

A *ninety-eight-pound weakling,* he thought to himself sadly. *And a beautiful young woman. And we're just going to pickle them both, no questions asked.* When he'd scanned the body of the dead security guard from the Institute, the unfortunate man had come up completely clean, no detectable problems, not even a pimple. *Such a tragic waste!* From the looks of his stomach, Rosow had surmised, the man might have had a little gas now and then. *But then farts aren't contagious. Or illegal.*

He completed his thought grimly: They're not illegal *yet.*

He led his team up the hill, as the witness had directed him. With their heavy suits and equipment weighing on them, the Biocops were all huffing and puffing by the time they reached the top. "How the devil did someone supposedly so skinny push a shopping cart with a body in it up this bloody hill?" he asked, and got a silent chorus of shrugs in reply from the team.

When they came to the field, he saw the open gate and was inexplicably drawn to it. *What is it?* he wondered. *There's nothing here.* Tracks in the mud, two widely spaced but narrow ruts, certainly consistent with a shopping cart, led away from the gate toward the center of the field. But they seemed to stop at a small rise and then turn back around again. He looked quickly around the immediate perimeter of the field but saw no dwellings, and decided that the person pushing the cart probably thought better of this bumpy route and turned around to find a better way to cross the field. *But why would anyone want to cross this field?* he wondered. *It leads to nowhere.* Baffled, he led his team back outside the gate again, where the tracks disappeared when the path rejoined the paved road.

* * *

The phone rang and rang. Janie finally gave up hope and flipped the small cellular unit closed. Disheartened, she tossed it back to Bruce, who caught it and tucked it in his pocket.

"There's no answer," she said, "but she must have contacted him. There'd be no other reason for him to leave a message like that."

"Then what do you want to do?" he asked.

"I think we should just go there. Either he's not there or he's not answering. He might leave a message directing us someplace else. I don't know. He's a very odd old man."

"All right. You're finished with the desk clerk."

She nodded.

Bruce made sure the trunk was securely closed and then they got into the car and drove off. The streets were nearly deserted in the wee hours but for a few City of London workers who paid them no notice, and Bruce made very good time, expertly guiding the small fast car over the narrow streets. As he drove, Janie tried to calculate what Caroline's condition might now be.

"There's no reason to think she was any less sick than Ted," she said as they careened around a corner. She counted backward, and decided Ted had probably died three days earlier. Her voice grew more anxious. "Plague is a lot quicker than many other diseases."

"But remember," Bruce said, "your advisor thinks this is an ancient microbe. What we see around today might not be a good model. We don't know what we're going to find. Don't let yourself get too upset until we do know. She might be in better shape than you think."

Her voice was almost frantic. "I don't believe that," she said. "Even though I've never seen an active case of plague, I just don't believe that it's going to be less nasty than we think. Oh, God, Bruce, *what a mess*. She might even be dead already." She buried her face in her hands and began to cry. "Everything that's happened to me since I found that stupid piece of fabric has been bad. Everything but *you*."

He took one hand off the steering wheel and took hold of one of hers. She leaned back in the passenger seat and closed her eyes. He watched the occasional car speed by in the opposite direction as they crossed over the bridge and wondered how Caroline had managed to make the protracted journey, or if in fact she had managed to complete it.

When Janie opened her eyes again, they were at the far side of the field. "We're almost there," she said, shifting her position in the bucket seat. She sat up straighter and started giving directions. "You have to drive around, that way," she said, waving her hand frantically. "There's a drive on the opposite side. We can get pretty close to the cottage."

He turned down the drive and brought the car to a skidding halt as close to the thicket as he could. Acorns flew out from under the tires, striking the undercarriage with sharp pings. They jumped out of the car and headed down the dirt path.

As they hurried toward the twisted oaks, the same wind that had challenged Sarin earlier came up to protest their intrusion. Bruce pulled his jacket tighter around himself, and Janie shielded her face from flying twigs and leaves.

"Where did this wind come from? Do you remember this from when you were here before?"

"No!" Janie shrieked. "There was nothing like it! We just walked right through the trees."

Another gust blasted through the opening between the oaks, pushing them back. "It's like something doesn't want us to go through there!" Bruce yelled.

Janie stopped, paralyzed. "Oh, God, I'm so scared . . ." she shouted. She stood in the wind, clutching her jacket around herself, her eyes closed to the protect them from the flying debris.

Bruce turned around and took her arm, pulling her forward. "Come on," he shouted above the howl.

She just stood there trembling as the wind whipped her hair around her face. "I can't go any farther," she shrieked.

He pulled her forward again, but she resisted. The wind swirled furiously around them, chilling them. She started to turn and run. Bruce grabbed her arm and pulled her back. Shouting to be heard, he said. "You have no choice. And I'm in this as deeply as you are now. And I'm just as afraid. We need to get this finished."

He pulled her forward toward the cottage. "Ready?" he said.

She gave him a tentative and unconvincing nod, but it was good enough for him. With a mighty effort they leapt through. As they passed between the trees, the wind died completely. They stood together in the warm, calm air and brushed away the leaves and twigs that clung like seed burrs to their clothing and hair, then they took each other's hand and proceeded at a fast run to the cottage door. Without knocking Janie pushed it slowly open with one hand and they stepped through with great caution, ducking their heads as they entered.

They stood in the small main room of the cottage and looked around silently. Bruce was awestruck by what he saw before him. He pursed his lips and made a low whistle of amazement. "Hello, Middle Ages," he said.

Everything was old, and small, and very carefully arranged. A stone fireplace stood with a slate hearth before it; a steaming kettle hung from a hook in the center. There were no electric lights, only lanterns and candles; the only sign of modern civilization was an old black metal telephone of the stand-up type with a rotary dialer.

"I feel like I just stepped back in time," Bruce said.

The room was only dimly lit, but Janie noticed immediately the striking changes that had been made since the first time she'd been there. "This looks like a completely different place," she whispered. "When I was here before, it looked like no one had cleaned in about ten years. Now it's as if it's been turned into some sort of a shrine." She glanced around anxiously for the old man who'd summoned them. "I wonder where Sarin is."

Her eyes were drawn to the soft light of many candles, spilling from a small room off to one side. "Look over there," Janie said, pointing in the direction of the open door. Like a moth she was instinctively attracted to the light and found herself crossing the room. Bruce followed and was soon at her side in the doorway.

Janie drew in a soft gasp. Lying on the bed, her red hair glowing, in crisp linens festooned with red bows, was the still body of Caroline Porter.

Janie whimpered and brought her hand to her mouth. "Oh, my God, Bruce," she said as she clutched him for support. "We're too late."

Bruce gently removed himself from her grasp and went to the bedside without her. The woman who lay there was barely recognizable as Caroline. Her skin was as pale as chalk, but around her neck was a hideous necklace of pus-filled blackish lumps. Her lips were cracked to bloodiness, and her fingers, neatly folded around a bouquet of dried herbs, were nearly purple.

Janie stepped forward timidly and came to his side. When she saw the extent of Caroline's deterioration, she began to cry again. She reached out and would have embraced Caroline's still form, but Bruce restrained her.

And though what she saw with her eyes was Caroline, what appeared in her mind were the bodies of her child and her husband. *They died too quickly; I never touched either one of them.* Her personal tragedy came crashing back again with the devastating force of a freight train, and she began to struggle against Bruce's grip, trying to reach the bed.

"Please let me go. I just want to touch her for myself, just once," she pleaded.

Bruce grabbed her more tightly, but he was surprised by the strength of her resistance. "Janie, no," he said. "You can't. We've already been too close to this." He held her back almost fiercely. "You can't risk it."

Finally she gave in and let him hold her. They stood there in the silent glow clinging desperately to each other. Janie's nightmarish memories of the Outbreaks flooded through her, but she fought them off bravely, surviving the horror again by getting through first one second, then the next, with a strength she did not recognize as her own.

There was no sound but Janie's quiet crying, until a low soft moan came out of the darkness. Bruce looked around quickly, sure that he'd heard something, a human sound, but he saw no one. He listened intently for another moment and heard the sound again; this time he paid attention to the direction from which it came. He let go of Janie and moved to the end of the bed. As he looked downward, his eyes came to rest on an old man, who rocked back and forth, cradling a motionless dog in his arms. He touched Janie's arm and said urgently, "Look! At the end of the bed!"

Shocked back to the present, Janie wiped the hot tears away from her eyes and rushed to Sarin's side. She crouched down next to him and touched him gently on the shoulder.

"Mr. Sarin?" she said. He kept rocking, ignoring Janie's attempt to get his attention. "Mr. Sarin!" she said more forcefully. "Please, Mr. Sarin!"

He looked at her blankly, dazed and confused, but soon a weak smile of recognition appeared on his face. "Oh, hello, miss," he said slowly. He cradled the dog's head and raised it a little, as if offering the animal to her. "Look, here. My dog's passed over."

Tentatively, she reached out and touched the dog's head, not knowing what to say. She finally said, "I'm terribly sorry."

"It's a hard thing, death, when it's not expected. . . ."

His statement brought a new flood of tears from the woman beside him. "I know, I know," she sobbed. "My friend over there . . ."

Sarin looked at her quizzically, still dazed. "But she's not dead," he said.

Twenty-Five

sabella's ladies chatted gaily as they attended to the unpacking of the baggage. Their lives had been bleak and colorless since the arrival of the plague, and the bright new finery represented the long-awaited end of its dismal influence. Thrilling tournaments and brave knights awaited them on the morrow, and the ladies of the court could barely contain their excitement. Only Adele had not given herself over to the pleasantries in which her companions now readily engaged, for her thoughts were focused on extricating herself from her own indelicate predicament.

"Despite your malaise, I do not excuse you from the festivities," Isabella had said to her. She had firmly insisted that Adele attend, asserting that it would lift her sagging spirits, and that her own pleasure would be increased by Adele's presence.

But how can my heart be light and gay, how can I add to her pleasure, when Isabella herself has been the cause of so much of my unhappiness? Even after their supposed reconciliation Adele could not forget that it was for Isabella's comfort that the king had decided to send her along on the long journey to Bohemia.

With great pain Adele realized that she no longer trusted the princess, and that their once deep friendship had been replaced by uneasiness. *I do not trust that she will petition her father on my behalf,* Adele thought to herself, and as the truth of the realization dawned on her, she began to feel great anger toward the woman she had once loved as a sister.

Another suspicion gnawed at her even more deeply, one she hardly dared voice, even to herself. *Was it truly your father's idea to send me,* she wondered, *or was it yours? Would you sabotage my happiness because you have none of your own?*

But the princess went about her preparations for the festivities as if their once intimate sorority remained intact. Nothing further had been said of the proposed betrothal, nor was there any mention of plans for Isabella's promised attempt to help Adele overturn the king's decision. Each woman went about her separate business, with no unnecessary words passing between them.

Old Nurse watched these goings-on with a heavy sense of resignation. She had always feared that it was within Isabella to be heartless and cruel, for she had witnessed the cruelty with which the queen had treated Kate, and doubted not that the princess was made of the same stuff.

Adele lay low while the other ladies saw to the tasks of adorning their mistress. For some time they huddled around her, tucking and pinning and smoothing, until all but Isabella's jewelry and shoes were in place.

"I shall just be a minute in seeing to the final touches," Isabella said excitedly, and left the huddle of ladies to enter her private chamber. And true to her promise, she returned shortly, completely decked out in the official robes of the Order of the Garter. Her long gown was entirely made of shimmering velvet, in a deep sapphire, the same wondrous clear blue as the precious gems set into the crown upon her head. Small silver embroideries decorated the bodice, sleeves, and hem of the magnificent garment, and a filmy veil trimmed in silver cascaded down the graceful curve of the princess' back. She lifted the skirt of her gown, causing a flurry of giggles among the observers, and showed her dainty feet, shod in embroidered silver slippers, the toes encrusted with tiny gems.

Applause rose up from the ladies in the room, and the gown was examined minutely, for each lady would wear a less ornate but similar dress of her own, furnished at royal expense, as a gift from Isabella. All praised the fine workmanship and intricate detail, all except Adele, who sat quietly, too preoccupied by her rising nausea and her growing revulsion for Isabella.

Her disdain was not unnoticed by the princess, who walked through the group of ladies toward her favorite. The conversation hushed, and there was complete silence by the time Isabella stood before Adele, whose skin color was once again as white as the linen of her chemise. Isabella turned a graceful circle in front of her pale companion, and the hem of her gown rustled softly as it settled back around her. Adele made no comment.

Her eyebrows raised in suspicion, Isabella said, "You are strangely quiet, Adele. Are you still unwell?"

"More so," she said, "for now my heart is breaking too."

Isabella eyed her curiously. "I do not understand," she said.

"It is your doing, so you must understand," she said. Then, quietly, Adele revealed her suspicion. "It was not your father's idea to send me along with you. It would do him no good to do so. It must have been yours."

Isabella's smile faded. "We shall take this up with my father at another time, dear friend, for tonight we shall celebrate."

"And why should I celebrate?" Adele said bitterly. "What wonderful things will happen to us that we should celebrate? You are to be betrothed to a man you do *not* love, and I am to be dragged away unwilling at your pleasure from the one I *do* love. What cause for celebration is this?"

"Adele," Isabella said, "this matter shall be discussed at another time."

Her anger now fully blown, Adele said, "There shall be no other time, for I shall leave your service immediately."

Isabella stiffened and said, "I forbid it. My father shall forbid it."

"You and your father be damned."

Isabella reached out her hand and slapped Adele firmly on the face. As Adele stood there, her hand to her cheek, tears welling up in her eyes, Isabella smiled and said, "Lady Throxwood, I am still waiting for your opinion of my gown." She looked Adele straight in the eye, and asked, "Am I not a fair sight to behold?"

Adele stared back, battling back the rising bile, returned her lady's rude stare with equal malevolence, and said, "Truly, Princess, you are beyond all description."

She noted with great satisfaction the furious look on Isabella's face when the true meaning of her reply became clear. Shocked into speechlessness, Isabella picked up the hem of her gown as if she were going to depart. But before the princess could turn to leave, Adele gave in to the plague within her and, laughing bitterly, vomited all over Isabella's dainty silver feet.

As he crossed the drawbridge into Canterbury Castle, Alejandro saw the workmen erecting observation stands in the field nearby, and knew that soon many brave knights would be showing their skills before the crowds. Adele had told him so on one of their last nights together, trying to prepare him for the benefits and obligations of knighthood.

He explained himself to the warder, and was directed to the captain of the guard, who he was told would know the king's whereabouts. He took only his saddlebag with him and left his horse loosely tied to the post, with instructions to the groom to leave the animal there until he sent word to stable it.

"He's out on maneuvers with some of his troops, I'm afraid," said the captain. "There'll be no audiences until tomorrow."

"Is there no minister I can see? I bring word of the resurgence of the pestilence in the countryside."

The man's jaw dropped in stunned surprise. "God in heaven!" he cried. "Truly, then, this cannot wait. You must speak with Master Gaddesdon! He's physician to the whole royal family, just returned from Eltham with the younger children. He'll know what to do."

Alejandro finally found his unmet colleague in the anteroom of the king's quarters, and introduced himself immediately, saying he had urgent business.

"Ah, yes, Master Hernandez! The king speaks generously of your medical skills. I am honored to meet you."

"No, kind sir," said Alejandro, keeping in mind the rituals the English used in their socializing. "It is I to whom the honor of our meeting belongs."

Alejandro hastened to give a detailed accounting of the events that had led him to think the plague had resurfaced in the outlying areas, and explained his theory of how new victims might be cured. "I have written it all to His Majesty in my letters. Surely he showed them to you."

"He did," Gaddesdon said, "but pray elaborate." He gave the appearance of listening carefully, nodding gravely when it was appropriate for him to do so, seeming to pay strict attention.

Alejandro finally concluded, "I have good reason to believe that these cases are the beginning of the widespread return of this scourge, for it begins as it did in Europa, progressing several leagues each day, until its effects are felt to the very edge of the ocean. There is no reason to think otherwise."

Gaddesdon was briefly silent. "Master Hernandez," he began, using the title that equalized them, although Alejandro's education was far superior, "we are of the opinion here that the few isolated cases you report do not indicate enough of a threat to alarm the citizenry. King Edward is anxious to see that things get back to normal as soon as possible, for his revenues are projected to be quite poor this year as a result of last year's events. We are waging a war, which I am sure you know to be an expensive pursuit. I'm afraid there is nothing to be done until there is much greater proof."

"Is not the demise of an entire monastery enough? And what of the family who perished previously? Is not that sufficient evidence?"

Gaddesdon said, "How can you in fact be sure that those inside the monastery did not perish last autumn and remain unburied?"

"The smell was that of new death, not old."

"All death smells vile, and enclosed in a hot edifice, I daresay even the keenest sense could not discern the difference."

"And what of the cure? Will the king support me in this discovery?"

"His Majesty is of the opinion that it would be a great sacrilege to further harm those who have already died. I have advised him that I know of no such cure for any other malady, and that I doubt the merit of your treatment. But he has agreed to give it his consideration, as I believe he has already informed you. You must be patient, and await his pleasure."

Then the sting of unwelcome understanding hit him and Alejandro thought, *This man believes I usurp his position with the king! And because of his pettiness many will die.* Furious at Gaddesdon's unwillingness to support his theory, he said, "I shall take this up with the king personally upon his return."

"Of course you may do so," Gaddesdon said, "but you will find him quite busy this evening, and disinclined to listen to your tales. Tomorrow he will be busy with the installation of many new knights, yourself among them, I am told. You are to be congratulated, of course, and I have no doubt that the honor is richly deserved. But as to this other matter, bring us more proof, and then you will have his ear."

He did not know what to do. He would have to find Adele, and with her usual wisdom, she would advise him.

Twenty-Six

J anie gripped Sarin by the shoulders and shook him. "What do you mean Caroline's not dead?" Her eyes were wild with disbelief.

Sarin recoiled, frightened by her sudden explosion of anger. He was confused; he'd been certain she would be pleased to hear what he'd told her. He repeated himself, hoping she would not react so violently. "She's not dead." His own voice sounded distant to him, as if he had drifted off somewhere. "There's something I'm supposed to do, but I can't remember. . . . I'm so tired. . . ."

But by then Janie was at Caroline's bed, with her head pressed against Caroline's chest.

"There's a heartbeat!" Janie took Caroline's nearly black hand in her own and searched the wrist for a pulse. Thin and thready, it was still there, beating on with a determination Janie would not have thought possible in a body so ravaged by disease.

"Mr. Sarin," Janie cried, "I'm going to need some things. I'll need some towels, a pan of hot water, strong soap, and a sharp scissors—"

Before she had finished her list, he interrupted her. "They won't help."

She stopped short. "What do you *mean*, they won't help? I'm a doctor, and I know what I'm talking about—"

He looked straight at her; Janie could see that he was beginning to come out of his haze. She was astonished at how sharp his stare felt as it burned into her.

"There is nothing *you* can do to save her. That was supposed to be my job, and I was going about it when my dog died. . . ." He looked down at the animal in his arms, and fresh tears welled up in his eyes.

"I don't understand . . ." Janie said.

Sarin set the dog's body back on the floor and stroked his head one more time. He rose up unsteadily, with Bruce helping him, and began to explain.

"All my life I've been preparing for this moment. It's been foretold for over six hundred years that a day would come when the scourge would rise up from the ground again and attempt to reclaim the world." He furrowed his brow. "That was why I couldn't let you take the soil . . . I knew it would come to this. . . ."

Visions of that night came swimming into Janie's head when she and Caroline had surreptitiously dug up a tube of dirt from the field outside. Feelings of dread, the sense that they were being watched, all the memories returned. She thought, *Why didn't I pay more attention?*

"Oh, my God . . . this is all my fault. I knew it . . ." she moaned.

Sarin bumbled on, trying to make her understand. "Since that time—oh, dear, my mother told me—there's been someone in this cottage, watching over this field . . . she was one of them . . . someone was always making sure the souls of the departed were not disturbed."

"The departed?" she said. "I don't understand—what departed?"

"There was to be another time . . ." he said, "another time . . . we've been waiting for it, and now it's come . . . oh, dear. . . ."

"What do you mean 'we'? We who?" she asked, stunned by what he was telling her.

Her questions were confusing him. They were coming too fast for him, he couldn't seem to make his mind work properly anymore. He began to mumble almost incoherently, and he saw with great fear that the woman was growing more agitated.

Then he remembered. *The book.*

"Wait," he said, "I think I can show you. . . ."

He went to the bedroom; she followed. He picked up the crumbling, musty manuscript, and handed it reverently to Janie.

She turned the pages quickly, trying to make sense of the ancient scribblings, prompting him to say, "Take care with it, please. It was given to me by my mother." He took the book back and gently turned pages until he came to a specific place. "There," he said. "Look at these." He handed the book back to her.

As Janie leafed through the brown ancient pages, he told her the story. His voice grew calmer as he spoke and he seemed more sure of himself. "The last one is my mother. And the one before her is her mother, and before that is my grandmother's mother. And so on back to the time when the vigil first began."

The last three images were photographs. Every one before that was either a drawing or a painting, some simple and almost childlike, some exquisitely fine in their rendition. And beneath each one was the name "Sarah." The very last one, in black and white, showed Sarin's own mother as a young woman. She was shading her eyes from the sun and smiling; she wore a dress from the 1930s and she was holding a small child in her arms—no doubt Robert Sarin himself.

No men at all, except Sarin, Janie thought.

She began to think Sarin could read her thoughts when he said,

"Every one of these women, from the very first, has been ready to give her own life to keep the scourge at bay. They have guarded the secrets of the cure for the time when it would be needed. My own mother died a bitter woman. She was desperate for it to be in her time; she never had a daughter, only me. . . ."

Janie placed a hand on his arm, stopping him. "The secrets of a cure . . . ?"

He seemed disturbed by her interruption; he'd been reciting the explanation, Janie realized. *He may not even understand what he's telling me,* she thought.

He took the book from her hands and went to the very beginning. "See?" He pointed at a page. "Once there was a physician. A very long time ago. This was *his* book. And what he learned from the very first Sarah he used to work a cure. He wrote everything down and it's been passed on. Yes, every one taught the next how—"

Again she interrupted him. "Then you know how to cure Caroline."

He acted surprised that she hadn't known. "Indeed!" he said, his voice growing more excited. "I was about that very business when I discovered the dog. Look here . . . it's all in the book!" His tone grew dark and uncertain, and he spoke in the voice of a worried child. "When I found him I knew it had come back and taken him to keep me from attending to my duties, like it was defending itself by distracting me."

Janie felt her voice tremble as she asked the next question. "Is it too late?"

Sarin's head dropped in abject humiliation. "I can't say . . . I'm so ashamed. It's all I've ever been trained to do, and I fear I may have failed."

Janie slowly realized that Caroline's fate lay entirely in the hands of this very simple man, who had apparently never been entirely right, even before his great age had impaired him further. She felt a discomforting mix of sympathy and rage toward this poor soul. She was sad that he'd lived such a limited life, and angry that he had not managed to do the one thing that he seemed to think would give his life meaning and purpose. *Be careful with him,* she warned herself—*Caroline needs him to survive.* She said gently, "You shouldn't be so hard on yourself; you haven't finished trying! You must go back in there!"

"I can't," he said. It was still the voice of a child.

What she needed to do became clear to her. She took him firmly by the shoulders and raised herself up to her full height. Calling on painful memories, she summoned up her most commanding, maternal voice and firmly said, "You must. I'm telling you that you must."

He stared back at the younger woman who had just commanded him to do what he thought he couldn't, and said, "All right. I'll try, but it may be too late."

She grabbed Sarin by the arm and led him firmly back to the room where Bruce was still watching Caroline. "Bruce!" she said, her voice agitated, "Sarin knows a—"

He cut her off with a sharp wave of his hand. "Shhh!" he said. "Look!" He pointed at Caroline.

Her eyes were open. They followed Janie's movement as she drew closer to the bedside.

"Caroline? Can you hear me?"

"I don't think she can," Bruce said. "I've been talking to her while you and Sarin were looking at the book, and she hasn't responded. She seems to be in some kind of trance."

Janie looked at Sarin. "Do you know what this means?"

Trembling, the old man approached the bedside. "I think it means that we'd better get to work."

Twenty-Seven

When Alejandro knocked on the door of Isabella's suite, the door flew open immediately, and there stood the princess herself, in her magnificent attire, with a look of smoldering anger on her face.

Her jaw dropped when she saw him. "You!" she hissed. "I thought you were the laundress, the lazy wench! But I am not surprised by your sudden appearance. It is entirely meet that you should be here, for this is entirely your doing, and you have much to answer for!" She pointed to the hem of her dress, which was discolored, and then picked up the skirt slightly, revealing shoes that had obviously been fouled with the contents of some poor soul's stomach.

So this is how it will be for me here. Still shaking with anger after his frustrating meeting with Gaddesdon, he now faced this unforgiving harridan in her ruined shoes. "I came to seek Adele," he said finally, "for I must speak with her immediately. And I fail to see how I am the cause of the ill fate that has befallen your shoes."

"Follow me, then, and it shall be made quite plain to you," she ordered, and he did, to the sleeping chamber. "Here lies your lover. As you can see, she is unwell, and it is *your* fault."

He did not understand what she meant, but there on the canopied bed was Adele, pale and limp, undeniably unwell as Isabella had said she was. As he rushed to her side, the distraught princess continued her harangue, her hands clasping and unclasping nervously as she paced around the room.

"I have loved her well, and I thought her my dearest companion, and now she has betrayed me, deserted me at the hour when I most need her. She threatens to leave my service because of her love for you, a love that has brought her to tragedy! Where is her loyalty to me, and to my family? Can it ever hope to match the loyalty I feel for her?"

Her pathetic diatribe was no more than a dim drone to Alejandro, an annoyance in the background; he was too caught up in his examination of Adele to pay it any heed. It was not until he heard the words *lustful misuse* and *delicacy of her condition* that he paid more attention to what was being said behind him. He turned around abruptly and interrupted Isabella.

"What did you say of her condition?"

"Surely, you jest, monsieur. It is *you* who are the physician. Adele is with child. She claims it is *your* child."

Alejandro rose up from his kneeling position and faced Isabella. "She is with *child?*"

"Aye," interjected Nurse, nervously keeping an eye on the physician, whose anger was all too visible, "I have determined it myself to be true." Taking his hand, she led him slowly away from Isabella, away from any possibility of an outburst, and placed it firmly on Adele's belly. "See how she softens. She will give birth during the frost moon."

Alejandro looked at her sadly, his face the very image of grief. "Good Nurse, I doubt not that what you say is true, but I fear the lady has a more immediate problem."

He lifted Adele's chin gently and pointed to the small but clearly visible bruise. Kate, who had been hiding behind a chair during the whole scene, now rushed forward, and flung herself at Alejandro, who was barely quick enough to open his arms to receive her.

"Oh, Physician," she wailed. "Please cure her! Cure her as you did me!"

Isabella and Nurse both looked at him, shocked by Kate's blurted admission, seeking an explanation. Isabella said, *"Cure* her?" She turned quickly to Kate and said, "Is this true? Were you afflicted, and was the contagion purged from your body?"

Alejandro stood speechless, unsure of what might be safely said. Isabella was already terribly agitated, and he did not trust her to listen to the voice of reason.

But Kate would not wait for him to answer, and cried excitedly, "Yes! Yes! It is true! For a fortnight I lay afflicted, and they gave me a foul-tasting medicine, and see for yourself that I am well again."

Isabella looked back at Alejandro. "They? Who were *'they'?*"

He hung his head, and answered quietly, "It was myself and Adele, on our journey to see Kate's mother. The child became afflicted on that journey. While at her mother's house, we learned of a means of curing the plague, and sought it out. It was by this means that we were able to save her life. It was the reason for our delay in returning."

"Adele knew of this, yet she said nothing to me!" She looked at her companion, her girlhood friend, who lay helpless on the bed, and choked back a sob. With tears in her eyes she turned to Alejandro and said, "Was this according to your instructions?"

"We agreed between us that it was best to remain silent. We feared for the safety of the child."

Deep pain was etched on Isabella's face. "Oh, what cruel duplicity," she said bitterly. She looked at Alejandro, her own beautiful face now almost as pale as Adele's. "You were wise to conceal it, for had my father known of her affliction, she would not have been allowed to return. And now I am afraid I must speak with him about what is to be done." She looked at the child and said sternly, "You are not to leave this room until the matter is settled."

Nurse, who had been speechless with shock from the tale she was hearing, finally found her voice again. "Can you now cure the Lady Adele?"

"God alone knows, good woman, if I am already too late. I will go to my death trying." He turned back to Adele and placed his hand tenderly on her belly. "But I fear she will not keep the child. This illness kills all that is good and holy."

He looked quickly around the room for a flask or vessel to carry the precious water back from the spring by the cottage, and saw a large vial of perfumed water, scented with Isabella's favorite flower, the lilac. He overturned it, and the contents splashed wildly all over the stone floor.

"Perhaps this stinking stuff can eradicate some of the foul smell in this room," he said angrily. "I will need this vessel to carry the mineralized water that is part of the cure. I do not have what I will need with me; I will have to ride out in haste to obtain it. I shall return as soon as possible."

And before opening the door, he turned and said to the tearful princess, "Pray God that she lives to conceive another."

After Alejandro's crazed rush through their midst in the anteroom, Isabella's other ladies buzzed with curiosity. Isabella herself soon came out of the bedroom, and closed the door behind her, leaving Nurse and Kate alone with Adele. She shrugged her shoulders, saying, "See how men run from slightest hint of women's troubles, even this learned physician!" Then she admonished them, "Say nothing to anyone outside this room. I would not embarrass Adele or upset my father on this important occasion. I will be mightily displeased if this private matter becomes idle gossip. Now see to your tasks, and forget what you have seen just now!"

The princess returned to the bedchamber, where she found Kate and Nurse sitting together on a bench near the window, crying and holding each other for comfort. She moved along the edge of the room, staying as far away from Adele as she could, until she came to the window. She spoke first to Nurse, her tone dark with suspicion. "Were you privy to this betrayal of my trust?"

The frightened woman replied, "On my soul, Princess, I knew nothing of it!"

Kate supported the old woman's claim to innocence. "It was only myself, and the physician, and Adele who knew."

"You shall remain here with the child," the princess said to the woman who had attended her from her birth. She flashed the trembling servant a threatening look. "You will help the physician when he returns. I and my other ladies will hasten from here; they shall not know of these events. It is best if they do not find out, I think, so you had better hold your tongue. And should you, too, become afflicted, it shall be God's just punishment. Tonight we shall see what my father has to say about these unhappy events."

She took a key from a small box on the mantel, and locked them in as she left.

Twenty-Eight

Janie and Bruce did everything Sarin told them to do as he went through the ritual page by page. One after the other he'd used each of the items he'd laid out on the small table, except the last. Despite the oddity of his actions Janie and Bruce never questioned his foul-smelling potions and poultices. They cast occasional uncertain glances at each other, but did as they were told. Janie watched in complete fascination as the feeble old man rose above his own sorrow and fear in a virtuoso performance on behalf of his frail patient.

But as the candles burned down and the sun came up, he neared the end of what he could do for her. Caroline's eyes remained open, and although she blinked occasionally, she did little more. It was painfully obvious that her condition had not improved much, if at all.

Sarin slumped down into his chair again, and Janie saw both frustration and shame on his face. "It doesn't seem to be working," he said. "I don't understand. . . ."

"But you're not done," Janie said anxiously, "are you?"

He was immensely tired; his aching body wanted only to sleep, and had Caroline not been lying on the bed, he would have stretched out there himself. *Sweet rest*, he thought dreamily. *How good it would feel!* Somehow he managed to shake his head no. Then he closed his eyes and said, "There's one thing yet to do, but I must just rest for a moment. . . ." All through the first steps he had felt the energy flowing out of him, and he was in desperate need of renewal, however small, before he continued. "Just a minute's rest, then we'll finish it."

Janie shot a silent, worried glance at Bruce. She reached out her hand and touched Sarin's shoulder. "Mr. Sarin . . . I don't think we should stop now—there's only one thing left to do. Then you can rest as long as you like, and you won't be disturbed."

He didn't respond. "Mr. Sarin . . ." she said, touching him again.

He drifted; he felt a soft touch, but it did not last and he moved away from it. He was out on the field, playfully following his mother as she gathered herbs in her apron. The sun was well up in the sky and very bright, for it was high summer, and life was lush. Insects buzzed lazily around them, and he reached out his hands to catch one as it winged by. Laughing gleefully, he cupped his hands around the small white butter-

fly, then ran to his mother, telling her she must stop and look at what he had. He opened his hands and the butterfly flew off lazily, as if it had not been aware of its own captivity.

She smiled and laughed, sharing his delight. She was young and beautiful, and full of love, all of it for him. She scooped him up in her arms and twirled him round and round, his small legs flying out and cutting through the soft warm air. He closed his eyes, and the light of the bright sun shone through his thin lids, filling his vision with the warm light.

It was the whitest light he had ever seen, the pure light of joy, and he gave himself over to it completely.

Janie shook him harder. "Mr. Sarin?" she said.

Twenty-Nine

A lejandro's wild ride through the countryside scattered other
travelers who were unlucky enough to be in his way. He
whipped the horse mercilessly and made the half day's journey in only three hours, and soon found himself approaching the twisted
oaks from across the large meadow. His lathered horse snorted in displeasure, but Alejandro cared only that the animal complete the journey. He
shouted aloud to the snorting animal, "If you run your heart out, another
horse can easily be found. I will not find another Adele."

He drove the horse between the venerable trees and followed the
path to the clearing. Jumping from the horse, he ran to the front of the
cottage and came to a sudden halt. There he stared at the dried-up bed
of what had been a bubbly spring on his other visit here; he saw only
sludgy mud, with the vile sulphurous odor to be sure, but it was not the
cloudy liquid he had seen here before. He ran back to the horse and
retrieved his journal from the saddlebag, and began leafing through the
pages, desperately looking for guidance in his quest for a cure for Adele.

He heard the old woman before he saw her. Her footsteps, though
soft, sounded on the stones behind him.

He turned around to face her, and she smiled at him. "Must I once
again steer your hand, Physician?"

The red shawl still tied about her shoulders, even on this warm day,
marked her unmistakably as the woman who had eluded him earlier.

"How is it," he asked frantically, "that you were in London so
recently, and here now? It would seem too far for one who travels as
slowly as you surely must."

"Have you time for such idle chatter, or shall we tend to the urgent
business for which you came here in such haste?"

She turned and went into the cottage, returning shortly with a
bottle of the cloudy yellow liquid, which she handed to Alejandro.

He set down his journal and accepted the bottle from her. "And
what of the dust of the dead?"

"I've only a small amount of that for you. I was preparing more
when you arrived here, and can provide it on the morrow." She handed
him a tiny sack, which he quickly opened. When he saw the small
amount of powder it contained, he looked back at Mother Sarah in
disbelief.

"What? So little? *Then how shall I cure my beloved?*"

There was great sadness in the old woman's voice. "I cannot say how you will accomplish it. Waste not one drop of the cure. Do not let her disgorge even the smallest amount, for all of the medicine must enter her body."

A foreboding of doom flashed through him, and he thought, *This will fail.* He staggered with the weight of his realization and swayed slightly as he stood there. Mother Sarah reached out and placed her hand on his arm, and although she could not have supported him, her touch seemed to steady him; he reclaimed his balance.

Her words were as gentle as her touch, and they gave him strength. The stern teacher she had been before was gone; in her place was a kind grandmother. "You have the power to do what needs to be done. Your strength will not fail you when you truly need it. But I would say to you again that you must prepare yourself for what you cannot readily comprehend. Things seldom go as we think they will. I implore you, do not be alone in this. *You will need help in order to save this life.*"

He examined the two items he held in his hands; they represented his only hope of curing the woman he loved. Then he looked at Sarah and asked, "Will I know success in this endeavor?"

How can I tell him of my own uncertainty? she wondered. *Will the medicine be less powerful, without his faith to support it?* She lowered her gaze, not wishing to meet his as she told what she feared might be an untruth. "I believe a life will be saved. Now go, and work your own magic. I can help you no more."

And as he rode away, she saw that he had forgotten his journal at her feet where he had placed it, and wondered if she should follow and return it to him.

No matter, she thought. He would know success or failure without it. She picked it up and carried it with her into her cottage, where she looked at what he had written. She decided that it was best for the book to remain with her.

Few people were about when Alejandro returned to the castle late that evening. A guard was posted outside Isabella's suite, and when the physician arrived, he was given a key by the man, who then departed in haste, wanting no part of whatever problem lay behind the door.

Entering the anteroom, he found it deserted. Remembering that the king was giving a banquet in honor of the new archbishop's arrival, he assumed that the entire court would be in attendance. As he himself should have been, with Adele at his side. *So much the better,* he thought. *I shall do my work uninterrupted.*

As he used the key to enter the bedroom, Nurse and Kate rushed forward to greet him. While he laid out his necessities Nurse told him what had transpired and of the lie she had heard Isabella tell, having pressed her ear against the wood door.

"What of Adele?" he asked anxiously.

"She moans, and flings her arms about, but she does not speak. There is bleeding from her womanly parts, and I fear that the contents of her womb are dislodged."

The pain of the loss of his child pierced Alejandro's heart like the arrows that had brought Matthews down so long ago in Windsor. He struggled to speak, his voice wavering. "Take this vial and the powder contained in this sack and mix the contents together in a suitable vessel." He handed her the items and added, "Take care not to spill even the smallest amount. I fear we may not have enough; I cannot even be sure we have mixed it in the proper proportions!"

She returned a short time later with a bowl filled with the yellowish slurry, wrinkling her nose at its foul odor.

Alejandro gently wiped Adele's forehead with a cloth, then accepted the bowl from Nurse. He looked at the vile concoction, which he would soon try to force into Adele's mouth, a thought that horrified him. He leaned close to his ailing lover and whispered in her ear, "When you are well again, my love, we shall feast on the sweetest delicacies, and you shall forget this horrible stuff. But now . . . now you must take it without complaint."

He turned to Nurse and said, "You must help me now. I will place the medicine in her mouth, and you must hold her mouth closed. No matter what she does, do not let her open it until she swallows. Not a drop must be wasted."

She nodded nervously, her face full of fear.

"Are you ready to proceed?" he asked.

At her nod he placed a spoonful of the viscous liquid on Adele's tongue. Together they held her mouth and nose closed. Adele struggled with surprising strength to free herself. Old Nurse was no match for Adele's youth, even in its weakened state, and was soon flung away. As soon as Nurse's hand left her mouth, Adele spit all of the revolting medicine out onto the bedclothes, and only a few morsels remained on her protruding tongue. A small yellowish trickle of saliva dripped from the corner of her mouth and sullied the white linen of her gown.

"We will try again," he said.

This time they managed to get her to swallow a small amount, but not a minute later she vomited the entire dose back onto the coverlet. Exasperated, Alejandro ripped off the coverlet and tossed it aside. Her thin shift was soaked in sweat, and the delicate curves of her small body showed clearly through it. He thought of the last time he had seen her so exposed. *Perhaps it was when the child was made,* he thought, his heart aching.

Time and again they tried to force the thin curative porridge into her mouth, and at each attempt she rallied her unconscious defenses to resist their ministrations. Frantically he spooned dose after dose onto her tongue, but as soon as he removed his hand from her mouth, she ejected each one.

He slumped down in a chair by the bed, defeated and hopeless. He sat by her side, waiting impotently, hoping against all reason that she would somehow survive. He held one of her hands in his own and felt the burning heat of her flesh, and tried to will her back to health by the immense power of his love for her.

The moon had long since risen when Adele finally breathed her last and lay still on the bed, the pain of her affliction finally replaced by the calm of death. He sat there for a long time with Kate in his arms, once again a solitary man with a broken heart.

Thirty

Rosow led his exhausted team of Biocops back down the hill a short way, and directed them to search the same alleys once again. They'd followed up on every lead given to them by the fearful residents of the area, but not one had panned out; nothing of any use had been developed from the information they'd received. They'd even taken a couple of Marginals into custody briefly, then let them go again when it became clear that nothing would come of keeping them captive. Rosow got the distinct impression that one of those Marginals was toying with him, teasing him off in another direction. He'd had a notion to keep that man for further questioning, but he didn't like the looks of him. He was skinny, all right, as one witness had described the man he'd seen pushing the cart. But this one was weak and rheumy and couldn't possibly have pushed a loaded cart up a hill. Rosow noticed that the man was unsteady and had difficulty even walking. *Probably drunk,* Rosow thought to himself, *and pickled with cirrhosis.* Reluctantly, he let the man go.

Adding to his frustration was the fact that no Biocop was allowed to spend more than eight uninterrupted hours in a green suit. *Bloody Coalition rules,* he muttered in frustration as he watched the team members remove their heavy green uniforms. *Bloody knights of old wore their bloody armor till the king said they could bloody well take it off!*

So when the contract-mandated rest period finally came to an end, they took up the search where they'd left off, but by then every trail had gone completely cold. There were no wheel tracks, no footprints, no scraps of newspaper left uninvestigated. Every suspicious rock had been picked up and examined for signs that the Marginal with the cart might have passed by it. *Perhaps they're hiding in one of these houses,* Rosow thought, scanning the neat rows of bungalows and cottages that lined both sides of the hill, but with further consideration, the idea seemed ludicrous. Sheltering Marginals was heavily frowned upon, and although it wasn't exactly illegal, Rosow was certain that very few "normal" people would take the risk of doing so. But they tried a few homes anyway, frightening the residents; they found absolutely nothing.

He didn't even know if the pair he sought knew they were being pursued. One was a being on the edge, perhaps over it, completely unsuited for the complications of modern life, a natural-born fugitive. One was probably deathly ill and, if so, was by now helpless, maybe even dead. *Shame she has to die, beautiful young woman like that!* he thought. He considered it unlikely that the Marginal pushing the cart would have the mental faculties to know the difference between a dead passenger and a very sick one, or an interest in knowing the difference. But Rosow had no choice; whether they were aware of his existence or not, he had to find them and examine them and then decide what to do with them. Many lives would depend on how well he fared in his pursuit.

So, near dawn, the exasperated lieutenant led his weary team up the hill again, back to the field where the tracks ended. He split them into two groups and sent one group around the perimeter to the west; the other he himself led east. As they started their search the sun was just breaking over the horizon. It had been a long night, and he hoped the day would go better.

They stood like a pair of nervous parents over the childlike old man sleeping in the chair between them.

Bruce lifted one of his eyelids and saw the pupil contract in reaction to the incoming light. "He's out cold," he said. "It's like he just shut himself down. I don't get it."

"I don't, either, but I think we're going to have to finish this on our own."

"Maybe we should wait until he wakes up. He said he just wanted a rest."

"Who knows *what* he'll be like when he comes to again? He's been going in and out of lucidity all through this thing," Janie said. She glanced over at Caroline and then back at Bruce, a look of fearful urgency on her face.

"We've got the book," she said. "He's been using it all along to do this stuff. Like a recipe. He said there's only one more thing to use, and we can read what it says to do with it. That's all he's been doing. Reading it." The tone of concern in her voice rose a notch. "It's not like he has some magical power that we don't have."

"Janie, we don't want to do anything rash. . . . What if we make a mistake with this stuff?" He looked over to the bedside table, and was suddenly very quiet.

"*What?*" Janie said.

He pointed. "There are *two* things left."

One was a bottle of cloudy liquid, yellowish in color; it was stopped with an old, dessicated cork. The other was a small sack containing some kind of powder.

"There's not much of either of them—what if we make a mistake?"

"If this senile old man didn't make a mistake, do you think we will? He can barely read, for God's sake."

She picked up the book and looked at the page to which it was opened. There were two sets of writing on the yellowed sheaf, one faded and ancient, executed with spidery strokes and uneven pressure. Janie scanned through it, and began to feel terribly disheartened. "Oh, God, maybe you're right—part of it's in French, I think. . . ."

Then her eyes moved to the other writing, clearly the work of a more modern hand. There, the letters tiny but legible, was a passage in English. It wrapped around the old French, and here and there Janie recognized words that were common to both passages. "This has to be a translation," she said. With hope building in her again, she read the small words and recognized that they were instructions for the things they had already done. Her excitement growing, she pointed to a specific part in the English passage. "Look, this is where we left off."

Bruce read it over her shoulder. "The flesh and bones of those long dead," he said aloud. *"The hair of the dog . . ."*

She put the book in Bruce's hands and picked up the small sack of powder. Bits of it floated up as soon as she spread the drawstring and she sniffed the air above it, then turned her head away and sneezed violently. "It smells vile," she said, grimacing and rubbing her nose. But then the grimace changed slowly to a smile of excitement. "But you know what? This *is* 'the hair of the dog that bit you.' *Antibodies.* This could actually work!"

"Sweet Jesus . . . you're right . . ." He looked at the page before him and started reading again. His eyes darted back and forth from line to line, sparkling eagerly. "Let's get to it, then! It says here that we have to mix the liquid and the powder together. Then we're supposed to take some of this stuff *ourselves.* Says it will 'protect us from the ravages of the scourge. . . .'"

"I'll get some mixing stuff from the kitchen." She ran off while Bruce continued reading and returned a few seconds later with a spoon and a small bowl.

"Okay," she said, almost breathlessly, "how do I mix it? Does it give proportions?"

"Yeah, hold on, I'm coming to that part. . . ." He began to read aloud. "Join together four knuckles of powder to a cupped hand of liquid—"

"Four *knuckles? A cupped hand?*"

"Janie, I'm not making this up. It says right here"—he held the book in her direction—"if you want to read it yourself. . . ."

"Never mind. I believe you. I'll believe anything right about now."

With unsteady hands she poured a small amount of powder into the bowl and then held her hand next to it, one finger bent slightly, and decided that the amount she'd poured would suffice. When she tried to remove the stopper from the bottle, it began crumble, and she had to dig it out in two pieces with her fingernail. She filled the hollow of one hand with the yellowish liquid, which had the smell of swamp water, and then poured the handful into the bowl with the powder. She stirred it with the spoon, and the resulting mixture was a loose slurry not unlike corn-bread batter.

"How much are we supposed to take?"

He scanned the book again. "It doesn't say."

"We'll have to guess, then. Okay, we'll each take a spoonful." She scooped some of the slurry into the spoon and held it out for Bruce. "Open wide," she said.

He cast a wary glance at the gritty mess on the spoon, then gave Janie a look of uncertainty.

"Open," she said, and when he did, she shoved the entire bowl of the spoon into his mouth.

"*Ugh,*" he grimaced. He swallowed hard and then wiped his mouth with one hand. "This stuff tastes like liquid skunk!" He put his other hand on his stomach and said, "I don't know if I'm gonna be able to keep it down."

Holding her nose, Janie took her own dose; it tasted every bit as bad as Bruce had claimed, and left a gritty aftertaste.

"That was awful," she said. "How the hell is Caroline going to keep it down?"

"I think the bigger problem is going to be getting this stuff into her. I don't know if she's still capable of swallowing. And even if we had a syringe, there's no way we can dissolve this stuff into any kind of solution. It's just way too granular. She's going to *have* to swallow it."

Bruce stirred the mixture again and tried to place a spoonful in Caroline's mouth. He rubbed her lower lip with the tip of the spoon in the hopes that she would open it, but she didn't. After a few frustrating attempts he looked up at Janie and said, "I don't think this is going to work."

"Here, let me try." She took the bowl and spoon from his hands and sat down in the chair in his stead.

"Come on, Caroline . . ." she said. "Open up wide for me." But the stimulus, so effective in getting babies to eat, failed to elicit the desired response in an adult. Caroline remained closed lipped.

"Maybe Sarin's got a funnel," Bruce said. "I'll go look."

He came back from the main room empty handed. "I couldn't find one. We're going to have to wake him."

Janie nodded. She knew they couldn't wait any longer.

He gently placed his hand on Sarin's shoulder and was about to shake him, but as soon as his fingers made contact with the old man's body, Bruce knew that the spark had left it. The old man was still warm, but the energy, the life force, the *being*, was no longer there. Only the body remained. He took his hand away slowly.

"Janie," he said softly, "he's gone."

She got up from Caroline's bedside and came to where Bruce stood. Placing her fingers on the old man's wrist she searched unsuccessfully for a pulse. "Now we're *really* on our own," she said.

They stood over the old man in a momentary wake. "He deserves more than this," Janie said, "but right now . . ."

"I know," Bruce said. "We need to get on with it, here. I still need a funnel."

Another quick search of the kitchen failed to produce one, or anything that might be substituted for it. Then Janie offered another possibility. "We can make a funnel out of paper. I used to do that to decorate cakes when I was a little girl. We can close up the funnel and squeeze it like a pastry tube."

But the slurry was too loose and leaked from the paper funnel almost immediately.

Suddenly Bruce said, "Damn! Why didn't I think of this before!"

"What?"

"There's a drip tube for condensation on the air conditioning in the car. We can intubate her and let this stuff drip into her stomach."

He was up like a flash and out the door before Janie could say anything.

He ran down the path past the oaks and on toward his car. As he neared the vehicle, something in the distance caught his attention. He stopped running and looked off across the field.

Battling the wind between the trees, he ran back inside and called out to Janie, who was sponging Caroline's forehead. She looked up and saw him gesturing for her to follow him. She stopped what she was doing and they went outside together.

"Oh, no!" she said when she saw the Biocops in the distance. "How did they find us? *How do they even know?*"

"I don't have a clue," he answered, "but I think we'd better take Caroline and get out of here."

"Where are we going to go?"

"We'll have to go to my apartment. I just hope there's no one there waiting for us."

"What about Ted?"

"We'll leave him here with Sarin and the dog. Janie, we have to burn this place. It's going to be infectious anyway."

She looked at him gravely, wondering if it would all ever end. "All right," she said, "let's do it."

Thirty-One

As she stood weeping near the window in Isabella's bedchamber, Nurse began to hear the sounds of merriment drifting up from the courtyard. Wiping her eyes, she looked out the window to investigate. Below she saw a stream of knights and ladies pouring out into the torchlit darkness of the courtyard. She heard their bawdy laughter, and the clap of wooden heels on the stones, observed the drunken weaving and the stolen kisses. The clamor of innocent joviality rising up from below seemed almost profane to her in its disruption of the quiet sadness of the death room.

Then she saw the king and queen, bidding good-night to their guests, until the next day's tournament. The Black Prince was by the king's side, but Isabella was nowhere to be seen in the crowd. "Oh, dear God in heaven!" she gasped, her hand going to her mouth. She rushed back to the bedside, where Alejandro and Kate still sat consoling each other. Tapping the physician's shoulder with great urgency, she said, "The festivities have ended! The princess will return soon, I fear!"

No sooner had the words passed her lips than the door to the bedchamber flew open, and the still gloriously attired Isabella rushed into the room. She gasped in shock when she surveyed the scene before her. Without a word she turned and closed the door that separated the chamber from the anteroom. Then she turned back again, and slowly approached the bed, her footsteps barely audible, her hands clasped tightly together in fear.

Adele lay there, the bedclothes twisted and flung about, her diminutive size made more conspicuous by the huge bed. Her copper hair was damp and matted against the pillow, her shift clinging to her thin body, and all of her gentle spirit gone, flown, vanished. As Isabella approached the pale remains, her eyes filled with tears and she said, "Oh, my dear friend, you have been robbed of your beauty. . . . I can no longer perceive the warmth of your soul . . . how I curse myself for the cynical and undeserved repudiation you have gotten from me . . . oh, what have I done to you?" She began to cry, and soon her wrenching sobs were nearly convulsive. She clutched her arms about herself tightly and began the keening wail of grief.

She must not alert the king's guards until I have had time to think of what to do! Alejandro thought desperately. He set Kate gently down at his side, then stood up and said, "Princess, please listen to me, you must stop your wailing—it will do her no good now. . . ." She began to sway, and he reached out, thinking to steady her.

To his astonishment, no sooner had his hand touched her than she fell into his arms, pressing herself against him, her pitiful sobs racking against his chest.

"Oh, what am I to do, what am I to do? She is gone, my dearest friend, my sweet companion! I had thought to make things right with her, but I am cruelly robbed of the opportunity. Oh, why did you not save her?"

"Princess," he said, pleading with her, "you must calm yourself, you will injure your own health. . . . I did everything there was to be done. . . ."

"But it was not enough! Oh, my dear friend, gone . . . it cannot be. . . ."

She took hold of the front of his shirt and began to wipe the tears from her eyes. Alejandro began to stiffen with alarm as he felt first one button on the travel-worn shirt come loose, and then another, and soon Isabella's cheek was pressed against the bare skin of his chest. Then to his horror he saw her pull her head away from his chest, and open her eyes; directly in front of them was the telltale arc of red and mottled flesh inflicted on him by the monks in Aragon.

She caught in her breath, and whispering a nearly silent curse, she drew back from him. "I have seen such scars before, in paintings . . ." she said. Her eyes wide, she pulled herself free of his comforting embrace and backed away from him slowly. Her voice trembled as she pointed at his chest and said, "Is this the mark of a Jew on your flesh?"

He stood motionless, the shirt open, his deceit finally exposed, the icy blood of fear rendering him speechless.

"Your silence speaks to condemn you," Isabella said, her anger rising. "I begin to understand why my hackles have always risen in your presence! Oh, how could I have not seen this? You are a master of deceit, Physician, a talented thespian, and by your craft and cunning you have weaseled your way into my father's confidence. But your true self is uncovered now, and you can no longer cloak yourself in gentility! You are nothing but a despicable Jew," she hissed through her teeth, "and you have entered my household, and eaten at my father's table, and touched things that I myself have touched. . . ." She looked at her own hands and shook them as if to fling off his essence where she had touched him, then wiped them on her skirts. "You have ravaged my cherished companion; you have stolen her loyalty from me, and misused her heart! You have ruined her and, with her, a part of me! I swear on my future children that I shall haunt you for all of your days for this! Your deceit shall be *your* ruin, too, and on my oath, *you shall suffer!*" She picked up her voluminous skirts and ran swiftly out of the room, calling for help from anyone who could hear her.

He looked over at Adele's body, and tried to remember how it had felt to hold her in his arms, to feel her sweet warm breath on his neck. It seemed a lifetime ago, and as he stood there, he felt utterly disconnected from everything around him. *This is not real. . . .* he said to himself. *If I reach my hand out to touch the bedpost, there will be only air. Those voices I hear are just part of the same horrible dream, and soon they will stop, leaving me in peace. Adele will rise up, and come to my side, and together we will leave this land to go to someplace where no one knows us, where there is no plague. . . .*

He was jolted out of his fantasy by an urgent tug on his sleeve.

"Physician . . . Physician . . . you must leave now. My sister will return with guards to arrest you, and you will surely be burned. . . . Jew or not, you are a good man, and Adele loved you well. . . . I love you well, too, and I would not lose you. . . . Physician, please . . ."

He looked down and saw Kate's pleading face looking up at him. "Yes, I must leave," he said vacantly, "I will leave now. . . ."

She tugged harder on his sleeve. "There is no time to waste," she said desperately, "and you must take me with you. . . ."

He came completely out of his stupor and gripped her small shoulders. "Child, you ask the impossible. I know not how I myself will live, let alone how I could provide for a child such as yourself!"

"Please!" she wailed, begging him. "I will never be welcome in this kingdom again! I shall run away alone if you do not take me!"

"No, child," he protested, "you must not—"

"I will, I swear it!"

He swallowed hard. It would be difficult enough to escape on his own, but with a small girl, he knew it would be near impossible. "Kate, I have but one horse."

"Then I shall ride with you, I am a good rider! Oh, please do not leave me alone to face my father. . . ."

Please do not leave me alone. Her words stung him, and he reached out to her. She fell into his embrace. "All right," he said gently. "I shall not desert you."

✳   ✳   ✳

Nurse tied the hood of Kate's riding cloak securely under her chin. "I shall call for a litter to remove Lady Adele's remains," she said, "and God grant it will serve as a distraction while you escape. But you must run now, and never look back. You have little time."

He looked at Kate, and said, "Are you ready, child?"

The little girl nodded somberly.

How bravely this child casts herself into the unknown, and at such a tender age, Nurse thought. She hugged the little girl one last time, and kissed her cheek, then, with a sob, pulled away. "Go now," she said, "and may your God watch over you both."

And she herself watched from the window, to be sure of their success. After a few minutes she saw their crouching forms slip out of the shadows, the man pulling the child by the hand as they sneaked across the courtyard to the waiting horse. She saw the physician look into the bag hanging from the saddle, and caught her breath as he mounted the horse and pulled the child up in front of him. She did not release that breath until they were safely out of view, swallowed by the velvety night.

With the fugitive pair safely gone Nurse turned her attention to what remained. She cleaned up Adele's soiled bedclothes as best she could to hide the muddy results of Alejandro's failed efforts, and when the scene was presentable, she pulled a bell cord. A servant appeared moments later.

"Send immediately for a pallet," she said, sniffing and dabbing her eyes, "for the Lady Throxwood has expired of womanly troubles, and we must remove her remains before my lady Isabella returns to be shocked by the sight."

When the pallet arrived minutes later, she made a great fuss of her sorrow and toiled over the preparation of the body. Just as the bearers were finally carrying the pallet out of the room, a group of soldiers arrived, led by a stern-faced knight, his drawn sword in hand. He strode into the room with brisk authority and demanded to know the whereabouts of the man Isabella had sent them to arrest.

Nurse wept into her hands, sobbing inconsolably, trying to delay her response to the soldiers so Alejandro and the child would have more time to make their escape. The leader finally shook her roughly by the shoulder.

"Calm yourself, woman," he said impatiently, "for with every moment of delay he increases the distance between us."

Indeed, she thought to herself. As she continued her sobs, Nurse took one hand from her face and, still wailing loudly, gestured in the direction of the door. The soldier, frustrated by Nurse's feigned inability to direct him, had no time to wait for her moaning to cease, so he ordered the others to follow him, and they rushed out the door, their armor clanking.

Alejandro whipped the horse with the leather strap, hoping to get as far away as possible in a short time. The worthy steed responded by running like the wind, though he was carrying two passengers. After an hour's ride the physician knew that they must rest or the horse would be ruined; unlike his earlier trip on the animal's back, he had no hope of finding another should this one be rendered useless. They could not return to his estate, which by now was no doubt forfeit, for he was certain that the king's men would seek them there, and soon. He knew that they would have to make their escape only with what they carried, and that they would have to stay off the roads.

They found a dense wood with a small stream, and dismounted there. Alejandro wiped down the lathered horse as best he could, and led him to the water, where the exhausted animal drank greedily. Then he spread a thin blanket on the soft pine needles of the forest floor, and lay down with young Kate to try to sleep, but the numbing effect of the day was not enough to bring them respite. Neither one closed an eye; daylight found them still awake, and filled with crushing grief.

Sir John Chandos could barely contain himself as he listened to the orders. King Edward's booming voice made the hateful mission known to the assembled men before him, every one of whom owed his continued life to the man he would now be hunting. It would be his dishonorable duty to lead out a party to hunt down the fugitive physician, now known to be a Jew, who had abducted the little girl after assaulting the Princess Isabella.

He stared coldly back at the king, and thought gravely that the soul of the man before him had just acquired another sin requiring atonement. The sin of bearing false witness. *Did I not honor you for your bravery, King Edward, and your gallant son as well, I would now bear witness against you myself to prevent this travesty! You speak of the rape of Lady Adele, but I know it is not so! That physician had not a rape within him. Already such a litany of lies,* the warrior thought; *will this king ever get out of purgatory?*

"Your Majesty, I beg a word," he said when the king had finished his announcement.

"Speak, then, soldier, for you must quickly be off."

"I beg your indulgence, Sire. You know I am your loyal servant, that I have served you well in Crécy and imparted my best skills to the prince—"

"Get on with it, Chandos," the king said impatiently, "for I am anxious to catch this man!"

"My lord, I only wish to say that, Jew or not, this physician had shown himself to be a good man. None among us suspected him of being anything other than the pope's emissary until now, and certainly not something so foul as a Jew! He bears none of the customary despicable Oriental qualities, and he has bravely performed his duties in the face of incessant opposition. I believe we are alive now because of his constancy and fine service."

"And what would you have me do, knight? His deceit is nothing short of treasonous, and you know the penalties for treason. By rights I should have the man drawn and quartered." He narrowed his eyes and looked at Chandos. "But that shall not be his fate when you catch him, though I admit I would relish it, for it would deprive me of the immense pleasure of watching him burn."

The soldier bit his tongue and bowed to the king, but cursed him in his heart as he went to prepare for the chase.

Alejandro and Kate traveled hard all the next day, stopping only for food and water. They kept to wooded, unpeopled areas to avoid discovery. The few people they passed took them for father and daughter, as it was not unusual in the wake of the plague to see fractured families deserting ruined towns for a more hopeful life elsewhere. No one who witnessed their flight bothered to wonder how such a dark and swarthy man should come to have such a tiny, fair child, until they were queried by Chandos, who led his band in hot pursuit. Then it was an easy task to recall the strange traveling pair, and the news of the fugitives raced quickly through the area between Canterbury and London.

As they stopped for water on the second day, Alejandro crouched at the edge of a still pond and looked into the glassy surface to examine his growing beard; he had stayed clean shaven since Eduardo Hernandez had bidden him to remove it, for the sake of disguising himself. Now he grew it again to disguise himself anew. As he stroked his neck, his fingertips found a small hard lump under his chin, and he sat down hard from the shock of his discovery, steadying himself with one hand as he hit the ground. Kate observed all this, and rushed frantically to his side.

"No!" she cried when she saw his neck. "No! You cannot die!"

Soon I will be too weak to ride, Alejandro thought to himself as he clung to both the horse and the child. And though he knew the method for curing himself, he lacked the means. He set the horse immediately on the road to Mother Sarah's cottage, hoping against all wisdom that he would arrive soon enough to seek her treatment. They rode through towns and villages without stopping; the horse kicked up a cloud of dust behind him as they sped past gaping onlookers. Alejandro knew that should the king's search party happen upon anyone who had seen them, they would easily be tracked; but he had no choice, he could not take the time to travel in a way that would discourage their discovery.

As they crossed the meadow, Alejandro could see the dark brown surface of many freshly dug graves; he wondered how many hundreds of bodies lay beneath the surface. Nearing the oaks, he felt the wind rise up against their progress, and once again he had to whip the exhausted, unwilling horse to make him continue. As they flew through the twisted gate to Mother Sarah's glen, the horse neighed and whinnied in protest, but once they were safely on the other side, the frightened animal quieted, and they finished the journey to the cottage quickly.

He had never been inside the small abode before; he found it neat and clean, and spare in its furnishings. He thought momentarily, *This will be a pleasant place to die,* then banished the uninvited thought as quickly as it had appeared. He called out to Mother Sarah, but got no response, so he continued his exploration. In a small room off to the side there was a bed of fresh straw, and a blanket folded at one end of it.

In the very center of the small house there stood a heavy oak table made of rough boards. Two benches flanked it on either side. In the center of the table Alejandro found a vial of the familiar yellowish liquid and a bowl of the precious gray powder. Beside them was his journal. It was as if Mother Sarah had anticipated his need, and gifted him again.

He told Kate to sit down on one bench and he seated himself on the other. "Pay close attention, now," he said, "for I will instruct you in the very cure I used to keep you in this world."

Kate nodded gravely and followed his movements and words carefully. As she repeated his actions, Alejandro saw how tiny her hands were and wondered if she would have the strength to do what needed to be done. He whispered a silent prayer that God would guide her small hands with His strong ones, then praised the little girl for her quick learning. She was his only hope of survival.

By nightfall he began to ache. His joints grew stiff and his limbs heavy as stone. He lay down on the straw and covered himself with the blanket, wondering if he would ever rise again, and tried to prepare himself for the swift decline he knew would soon follow. His fingers and toes grew numb, and soon the plague took even the simple comfort of vision from him, for as the night deepened, he faded in and out of consciousness, and by morning, he no longer responded to Kate when she called his name.

Thirty-Two

Rosow had still not found any new tracks, and there was no visible evidence that anyone had been in the wooded outskirts of the field. The other teams had all gone off in other directions, and he was beginning to think that perhaps he should take his group out of the area completely and send out a new search bulletin. He was about to order his team to return to the van when one of them pointed to an isolated stone cottage in the distance, barely visible through the surrounding trees. *Why would they be welcomed there, if nowhere else?* he wondered. But they were already near it, and he decided it was worth a shot. It would be the last place they looked in this particular location if it didn't pan out. He led his green team away from the perimeter and back onto the field in the direction of the cottage.

Ted's body was a heavy burden after their exhausting night, which was still in progress. Janie and Bruce half dragged, half scraped it over the dirt and twigs and acorns, straining to make haste, and struggled against the now vicious wind to bring it through the oaks. The gale blew with nearly unimaginable force, shrieking and howling as if to wake the thousands of dead buried beneath the soil of Sarin's field. By the time they had managed to drag it into the cottage, the garment bag in which it was enshrouded was nearly in shreds. They dropped it with a thud in the center of the cottage's main room, and ran to the small bedroom.

They sat Sarin in his comfortable chair and placed the body of the dog at his feet. Bruce wrapped Caroline in a blanket and carried her out the door with Janie close behind.

"Make sure we don't forget anything!" Bruce shouted back to Janie as he ducked through the door with Caroline over his shoulder. She had already gathered up everything she thought they might need, the medicines and utensils, the small flask of yellow water, the pouch of gray dust. She caught up with Bruce, who was struggling against the wind with Caroline in his arms. Not satisfied with trying to keep them out of Sarin's cottage, it had changed directions, and now tried to keep them from getting away. Clutching each other and their burdens, they broke through as a single unit, a unified force of will, and made it to the other

450

side. When they finally reached the car, Bruce laid Caroline carefully in the backseat and arranged the blanket so it covered her fully.

"I'll stay here with her," he said, his breath raspy.

Janie nodded and handed him the things she had carried out with her. She turned and ran back as fast as she could, as she had run to reclaim her briefcase in the alley, but now her feet were powered not by fear, but by exhilaration, for she could feel that they might triumph and she was ready to do whatever she needed to do to make that happen. Anticipating the force of the wind, she threw herself between the oaks, but this time there was no resistance and she tumbled to the ground, rolling in a wild path toward the cottage. The wind had been stilled, and it seemed it would never blow again.

She almost hit her head on the low door as she reentered the cottage. She passed by Ted's body, lying there like a pathetic sack of stones, and went straight to the room where Sarin and the dog remained. Before Janie lit the match, she whispered to the remains of the old man. *"Thank you,"* she said. *"I owe you so much."* Then she struck the match's dark tip against a mantel stone and reached up to touch it against one of the bunches of herbs hanging from the dry wood of a beam.

She waited just long enough to see that the flame had caught. As she turned to leave, she saw Sarin's book resting on the bedside table. She picked it up and ran out the door. When she reached the car, Bruce had it running and ready, and as soon as she was in the front seat, they sped off in a wild flurry of acorns.

Rosow watched in bewilderment as the flames leapt up through the thatched roof of the small house, fanned by a furious wind that seemed to rise up out of nowhere. The air around them was still, and he could not understand how a wind could be so isolated, so directed; it sent a long, cold shiver down his spine.

His team was still a hundred meters short of the burning cottage, so he yelled, "Come on!" and waved them into a run. By the time they got there, it was fully engulfed, and throwing off a good deal of heat. The team stood outside the cottage, far enough away so their plastic suits wouldn't melt, and watched as the roof finally collapsed inward.

Bruce carried Caroline's wrapped form up the narrow stairs in the restored Victorian building where he made his home. "Let's get her into the bed," he said to Janie. "Then we can get a tube going."

Janie had carried the medicine and the plastic tubing into the apartment, and after Caroline was properly arranged, she went to the kitchen and washed out the inside of the tube. "We could still use a funnel if you have one," she said. "One with a small end to fit in the tube."

He opened a small drawer and brought out a small white plastic funnel. Janie tried to shove it into the end of the tube, but it was just slightly too big. "Damn. We'll need to spread the end of the tube so the funnel will fit," she said.

Using scissors, she clipped notches in the end of the tube. The funnel slid in neatly. Bruce found some white adhesive tape and wrapped it around the joint.

"All right," Janie said determinedly. "Let's get this thing inside her."

Bruce held Caroline steady as Janie slowly threaded the tube down her esophagus and into her stomach. As soon as it was in place, Bruce taped the funnel to a nearby wall, high enough to promote a gravity drip, and poured the contents of the bowl into the funnel.

They stood next to Caroline and watched as the gray liquid slid quickly down the tube and into Caroline's body. As the level in the funnel dropped, Janie mixed another "four knuckles" of powder and a "cupped hand" of yellow liquid and added it to the funnel. They took turns mixing and filling until most of the gray powder was gone. After the medicinal drip was finished, Janie filled the funnel with water several times and let the life-giving liquid replenish what Caroline had lost.

Janie sat down on the edge of the bed. "So now we wait," she said weakly. She slumped over and held her head with her hands. "I'm so exhausted. All I want to do is sleep."

"Then lie down," Bruce said. "Caroline won't mind. She won't know."

So Janie lay down on one side of Caroline, and Bruce on the other. They lent their warmth to the ailing woman, who was by now a mere shade of her former glowing self. As they drifted into healing sleep, they joined hands across Caroline's body and felt her chest rise weakly as she struggled for each breath. And when they awoke, they would know if "four knuckles and a cupped hand" was as good as the hair of the dog.

Janie thought she was dreaming when she heard the thin voice calling her name.

She lifted her head from the pillow and then rose up on her elbow.

Between her and Bruce, Caroline lay quite still, but her eyes were open and she was trying to speak.

Janie quickly got up and shook Bruce's shoulder. "Bruce!" she said. "Wake up! She's trying to speak! Oh, my God, I think it worked!"

Caroline's voice was hardly more than a squeak. "Where are we?" she said.

Janie took hold of her hand. "Shh," she said. "Don't try to talk if it hurts."

But Caroline would not be silenced. "I think I've been really sick. I had the most unbelievable dreams. . . ."

And when they started talking about it, a full hour passed before the entire tale had been pieced together. There was weeping and relief and hysteria and incredible joy that they'd come through it alive and relatively intact. They moved through the details, examining each twist of fortune and turn of fate.

"I'm exhausted," Janie said when they were finally finished.

"I'm hungry," Caroline said, delighting her caretakers.

As she and Bruce moved around the kitchen preparing a simple meal for their patient, Janie saw Bruce's digital calendar on the wall. Something on its numerical display struck a familiar chord, but she was far too preoccupied to pay it the necessary mental attention. As she tended to the joyful task of caring for Caroline, the blip of discord planted there by the date and time kept chipping away at her peace of mind. Finally, the source of her anxiety burst into her consciousness.

She put her hand on the counter to steady herself. "Dear God, it's four weeks today since Caroline arrived here! She's not printed!"

Janie was ready to start packing their things. "We've got to get on a flight today!"

"Janie, that's ludicrous. She's still sick. She'll never get through the gate onto the plane. And once they figure out what happened, they'll keep her in isolation forever!"

Janie was frantic. "As far as they know, *I'm* not printed."

He put the tray down and stared at her. "*You* were printed in Leeds."

"*Ethel Merman* was printed in Leeds, but Jane Elizabeth Gallagher Crowe was not! What are we going to *do*? We'll be arrested if we don't figure something out."

"Damn!" Bruce said. "I don't know if this will work, but there's something I can try." He left the kitchen and went to his study, where he immediately powered up his computer. He entered his security code and logged on to the Institute system, something he did nearly every day to check his schedule before going to work. It would arouse no suspicion for him to do so, but he usually limited himself to brief harmless inquiries. What he needed to do now would actually be a crime, another in the long list he'd recently committed.

"I'm going to try to reassign someone else's body print to Caroline. Then I'll try to change the name on yours so you can actually use it to get out of England. At least that will buy you some time."

"*Can you actually do that?*"

"I'm just about the only person still alive who can." He tapped some keys on the keyboard and began his search for a print for Caroline. "What time of day did you finally clear the Compudoc?"

"About noon," she told him.

"Then at noon today, if you haven't left the country, an order for your detention and printing will be issued and delivered to Biopol. We'll have to complete this switch before then."

"If you switch identities, how can you be sure that person won't be traveling somewhere today? Or doing something else that requires evidence of a print?"

"I'm going borrow a file for someone who's already dead. I've got access to millions of prints through the project I'm working on now. Some of them are not British citizens; we acquired print files from all over the world so we could have a truly random selection."

Janie thought of her daughter. *Betsy . . . your print out there on the Worldnet. . . .* She grew strangely quiet, and said softly, "I didn't know prints could be 'acquired.' "

Bruce was distracted by his efforts, and excited by what he was doing, so he made only a cursory comment. "The Institute bought access rights to several million prints in the last few years for research purposes. Even U.S. prints. So much for privacy. . . ."

Betsy . . . her mind screamed.

"Bruce, what you told me about in Leeds, the way you can make prints move—can you show me?"

It struck him as odd that she would want to see a demonstration of the technique he was working on, especially now when time was so critical. Something in her voice made him hesitate to proceed.

"Can you find a specific print?" she asked, her tone insistent.

Then he knew; he knew what she wanted. "Janie," he said, his voice gentle and sympathetic, "I don't know about this—it might be very traumatic for you . . . you've got a lot facing you already. . . ."

"Please, Bruce, I just want to see my daughter. She was so young, and I never got to say good-bye to her."

"Janie. Please think about this. *She's dead.* Even if you can see her and say good-bye, *she* won't hear it. And we didn't buy the names, just the prints. I might not even be able to locate her."

She pleaded with him. "Can you please just try?"

He sighed deeply, knowing he might regret what he was about to do. But he didn't have the heart to refuse her. "All right. Give me the date, location, and time of her death. Then I'll need a physical description."

She forced herself, through aching pain, to visualize her dead child. "Brown hair, blue eyes . . ." she said wistfully. "She had the most beautiful eyes, with long dark lashes. I was so jealous of those lashes. . . ."

She paused, her eyes closed, and dwelled on the face of her child.

"Go on . . ." Bruce said softly.

"She was about five six or seven, maybe even five eight, she grew so fast that last year. She was like a colt, you know, all legs and clumsy energy, but she was just starting to take on the shape of a woman. Her waist had just begun to come in a bit, she had the beginnings of a chest. . . . I remember how self-conscious she was to put on a bathing suit; I think her body felt very foreign to her. To me she was still my gorgeous daughter. . . ."

Bruce looked at the clock. "What did she weigh, if you know?" he asked.

"She was average weight, maybe one twenty-five. Not thin, not fat. Just right."

"I need the date and time and place of her death, and then I can set up the search," he said. "If you remember."

"If I remember," Janie said softly. "I will never forget." She gave him the information.

He entered everything and instructed the program to search. As they waited for the results, Bruce said, "Are you sure you want to proceed?"

"Absolutely," she said without hesitation.

The computer announced one match.

As he typed in a few commands, Bruce said, "I can't be sure this is actually her."

She smiled and said quietly, "I think I'll know if it is."

As the image of a young woman assembled itself on the screen, Bruce thought she looked as if she were just sleeping. He was astonished by her resemblance to her mother.

Janie was riveted to the image. "That's my Betsy . . ." she said quietly. "She was so young!" She reached out her hand and tentatively touched the screen, "Oh, Betsy!" she whispered. "My sweet baby!" She turned her gaze to Bruce. "Can you make her open her eyes and smile?"

He looked at the clock on the wall. "I can try. But this is still so new. I can't say it's going to be what you want to see. . . ." He typed in a long series of commands. "Please don't be disappointed if it's not what you'd hoped for. . . ."

And as if by magic the entire image seemed to soften, when in truth only the eyes and mouth had changed. Janie laughed joyfully through her tears and said, "Oh, Bruce! It's almost like she's alive!"

He said gently, "You should say good-bye, if that's what you want to do."

Her expression turned sober, and she touched the screen again. "Bye, honey . . ." and Bruce shut down the image. He put his arm around her and said, "We've got to get some prints into the system for you and Caroline."

She wiped a tear away from the tip of her nose and said to him, "Use Betsy for Caroline."

"Are you sure?" he asked.

"I'm sure. That way her death will serve some useful purpose."

And it will keep her alive in my heart, she thought to herself.

At eleven forty-five Bruce completed the reassignments and shut down the system.

Thirty-Three

The physician lay on the straw bed in Mother Sarah's cottage, and beside him the child Kate kept a silent and tearful vigil as the plague filled his body with insidious poisons and his head with terrifying delusions. He thrashed in his sleep, throwing his arms about wildly, as if by doing so he might cast off the burden of his affliction and send it tumbling far into the night, never to torment him again.

He dreamed; he ran like a wounded animal over the wooded path from the clearing outside the cottage, his feet flying as he leapt over the rocks and roots on the forest floor. He dared not look back, lest he slow himself and fall into the grasping clutches of his pursuers. Yet he feared not knowing the progress of the chase, so he turned his head far enough to catch a glimpse of the two figures in urgent pursuit. Each time he looked, the distance between them seemed to have closed, and he tried desperately to quicken his pace in response. He lengthened his stride and pumped his arms, gulping in deep desperate breaths that seared his lungs. He careened and wove and spun his way through the forest with Matthews and Alderón in primal pursuit, darting between the bushes of the ever-thickening underbrush, which closed more tightly around him with every step.

He heard the terrifying *click-click* of the wooden arrows, which still protruded from Matthews' chest, in weird concert with the heavy percussion of Alderón's thudding steps. *Surely this path was not so damnably long when I last traveled its length! By now the oaks should have appeared in the distance ahead. . . .* But still ahead of him was a long stretch of the path, with no sight of the familiar oaken gate. The terrain grew more treacherous. Roots and twigs seemed to reach up with gnarled wooden fingers and tug at his feet as he leapt ever higher to avoid them, until finally he caught his toe in a protruding root and went crashing down.

He landed with a hard thud on the floor of the forest, and the shock of the fall sent a bolt of pain deep into his joints and bones. He landed on his face, and his mouth became filled with grit and small leaves. *I must spit this out; my teeth grind against small bits of rock and I only want to retch; dearest God, please grant me just one drink of water. . . .*

He struggled with the mouthful but could not seem to force himself to spit, for some smothering wall was across his face and he could not get by it. He gagged, and could not draw in a breath. Finally, desperate to clear his tongue, he swallowed, for there was no other choice, save to suffocate on the mouthful of debris.

He could not move, not a muscle, not an inch; he was stuck to the earth like some ancient headstone. Matthews and Alderón sat themselves down beside him, grinning triumphantly, and began their macabre interview while relaxing by his side.

"So, Physician," Alderón began, "I should have listened to my family. Had I done so, I would have been saved the trouble of wasting my time with a charlatan Jew. A lot of good it did me, to spend the last days of my life in your care! I thought the barber a fool, but he had the decency to tell me there was naught to be done. 'Tis I who was the fool to place my trust in you! He didn't bleed me, or give me horrible emetics, or purge me of foul humors, but I suffered all those things in your care, and I got no benefit for my pain." He turned to his companion shade. "Isn't that so, Matthews?" he said.

"Aye," said the soldier, then Alderón continued.

"And then you have the brazen gall to uproot me from my resting place, and force me to chase you through the whole of Europa before I can finally speak with you face to face."

"But do you not see, señor? Can you not understand?" pleaded the terrified physician. "I tried to speak *for* you. There was nothing I could do to save you, I admit it. I am sorry if my treatments caused you pain. But I saw your disease inside your chest! I felt it in my hands! And someday I will tell the world about the hard, cruel thing I found inside you, and some wise man will know what to do! Others will live because I saw the disease in your chest—"

"Physician," the grave ghost of Alderón said, "my last living thought was a wish for more life. You did not obtain it for me, and God did not grant it. My first thought on the other side was a wish for eternal rest. God gave it to me, for I was a good and decent man. But *you* disturbed it."

Exhausted, the physician lay motionless, hearing the accusations of those whose blame he feared most. "Señor," he pleaded, "I beg you to forgive me—"

"And I, too, will have my say," said the soldier at Alderón's side. "What fool will trust a Spaniard, even an educated gentleman in the service of my king? Did you know, Physician, that I myself carried no contagion, and that only Reed was so cruelly touched? And despite your certainty to the contrary, I am here to tell you that had you let me live, I would now be bouncing my young son on my knee."

The specter of Matthews raised itself up and stared down at Alejandro, who remained paralyzed by his terror.

"Your skills are a mockery. You are no better than a witch! You would serve the king far better as jester than physician, so all could laugh at your piddling efforts! But what you have done is not a matter for laughter. I am dead, and yet you live."

Alejandro found his voice and cried out, "What would you have me say, soldier? I curse my own ignorance daily, I weep for the tortured souls of those for whom my cures have been worthless. What would you have me do?"

The gray shades of those who had died on his journey began to surround them. Five brave soldiers who served the pope and died by their captain's sword in France, the Jews who suffered at the hands of the flagellants, and finally, his dear companion Hernandez.

"And what of the lady, Physician? What will you say to her?" Matthews said.

In the distance Alejandro saw the gossamer shape of Adele floating toward him. He called out to her, and she drew closer, but did not respond to his voice. She continued to float, nearing him but never reaching him. He could not get hold of her, his arm would not stretch far enough, and he could not move to bridge the gap between them.

Oh, dear God, Adele, please come back, do not desert me! I am in the clutches of these two specters and I owe them a life; they mean to collect the debt right now, and mine is the only life I have left. . . . Oh, Beloved, please stop; I would have gladly given my own life then for yours, and Mother Sarah said to me that God decreed you should live . . . it is beyond me to know why you did not!

But the pale vision would not slow its movement, and passed away from him like an evaporating mist. Soon her image was completely gone.

The voice of a woman called out to him, and he turned his head toward its source, desperately hoping it would be Adele. Instead, he saw the bent figure of Mother Sarah. The old woman smiled, which brought forth hisses of defiance and fear from the specters surrounding him.

"Ah, fool," she said to Alejandro, "do you think you know the will of God? In God's service no untruth can be told. I did not lie when I told you a life was to be saved, but think carefully: Did I say whose life it would be? Did you think that it would be of your choosing? Had I told you what I feared to be true, you would have lost all hope, and you would never have returned here to preserve your own life. You wished it to be she whose love you cherished, but *yours* was the life you were meant to

459

save, and by living you will pay the debt you owe. There is much yet for you to do. God is not finished with you."

She reached out her wrinkled hands, and said, "Come. I will show you the way, one last time." He gave her both of his; he could not tell if he was feeling her skin or only the idea of it, but he cared not, for either was a comfort. He could hear the beating of her heart as if her blood flowed through him, and he began to rise, slowly and painfully.

And suddenly she pulled him to full standing with great strength, forcing his legs to do her bidding. The old woman flew before him, and he followed closely, still holding on to her gnarled hand. He could not feel his feet touch the earth, but he knew that he was running, using all that was within him to press forward.

The specters rose up in unison, shouting their protests at his escape. Matthews and Alderón hurled themselves into the chase, struggling to keep up as the old woman with inexplicably swift feet made off with their prize. Alejandro looked back at the pair as they all sped toward the oaken gate, and saw that all five soldiers and the burned Jews had joined in and were closing fast. Only Hernandez hung back, and sadly watched the macabre parade as it sped away from him.

The clicking of the arrows grew nearer, and Alderón's foul breath was hot on Alejandro's neck. "Do not look back!" she cried. "The past will not serve you!"

Just as the ghosts of his failures were about to consume him, he heard Mother Sarah cry, "Farewell, and may God protect you!" and he was propelled violently through the oaks, as if ejected from the very womb of the earth. The fresh wind hit his face like a splash of cool water, and he knew he was on the other side.

Kate stood over the wet spot on the floor of the cottage and stared at it in dismay as the yellow liquid was absorbed into the dirt. The physician had flailed about in his delirium, and knocked the bowl from her small hands, and she watched in horror as half of the remaining supply of medicine drained into the dirt.

He would know what to do, but she could not rouse him; he was beyond consciousness and would not be called back. She would simply have to do her best without his help. So she bent down and scooped the wet dirt into the bowl. After whispering a prayer for success, she squeezed his nostrils together as she had seen Nurse do with babies who required some distasteful medicine, forcing him to open his mouth wide enough to breathe. With the other hand she grabbed the entire glob of mud and plopped it into his open mouth.

He gagged and sputtered and tried to force the gritty mess out of his mouth, but she pressed down on his face as he had told her to do, covering his nose as well. He would have to swallow or suffocate.

He held out for nearly too long, for her strength was about to fail, but she persevered, pressing with all her might, and whispered through her frightened tears, "Physician, I owe you a life. . . ."

Finally, he swallowed, and she collapsed across his heaving chest, crying with relief.

Dressed in her dead mistress' finery, the servant girl who had cared for Kate's mother in her last days was an odd sight. The delicate garments once worn by the petite woman she had served were far too small for the substantial serving wench, but she had forced her ample body into them. With an unpracticed hand she had applied the lady's cosmetics to her own worn face, with predictably laughable and clownlike results.

Now as she paraded through the streets of London, unsteady on the lady's small horse, she was a bizarre sight indeed. But from a distance she appeared to be a respectable woman going about her business, perhaps out on an errand or a visit, so Sir John Chandos stopped his party as they approached her, and greeted her with respect.

"Good day to you, lady; we are on the king's business and require assistance."

She nodded politely, knowing that the moment she opened her mouth, she would give herself away.

"We seek a fugitive from the king's justice. A physician. He travels with a small child." When he gave a detailed description of Alejandro and Kate, the serving girl knew immediately whom they were seeking.

"Have you seen such a pair, or heard of them?"

Blessed Virgin, what to do? The wench knew there was no love lost between the child and her neglectful father, and it was certain that the physician would do her no harm. Even with her dim intelligence she knew there was more to this story than she was being told.

She shook her head no, then nodded politely to Sir John, who regarded her quizzically as she turned her horse clumsily and rode away. Puzzled by the woman's strange behavior, he remounted his horse and resumed his quest, thinking to himself, *Poor soul—another one gone mad.*

As soon as she had put a safe distance between herself and the riding party, the serving girl turned the lady's horse again. She would go immediately to the cottage. Mother Sarah would know what to do.

A full day passed before Alejandro opened his eyes and saw the head of the sleeping child resting on his chest. He moved his stiff arm slowly, for both disease and lack of motion had rendered it nearly useless. When it was once again functional, he placed his hand carefully upon her golden curls, and rested it there. Feeling the weight of his hand, she opened her own eyes and came back to consciousness. When she saw that he was awake, she sat upright immediately, and rubbed her eyes, then moved forward to touch his forehead.

"You are once again cool, Physician. For a full day you have burned with fever."

"Please, Kate, I would have some fresh air. . . . Can you open the door?"

She opened it wide, and Alejandro could see the horse at the post, grazing peacefully, and he heard the buzz of lazy insects as they flew around in the hot sun. He thought that the blue of the sky had never seemed so beautiful.

"A drink, if you could bring the bowl; my mouth is filled with grit."

So she told him the details of what had happened during his delirium, and he marveled at how his dream had reflected the truth of what had occurred, only dressed it in the robes of his past.

"Are you cured, Physician?" asked the child.

"Aye, child, it would seem that I am, and of far more than the plague."

Thirty-Four

I t was a week before Caroline could rise from the bed in Bruce's apartment. During that time, while her ravaged patient could do little more than sleep, Janie enclosed Caroline's hands and feet in plastic bags with maggots gathered from a nearby garbage can. After a few days she removed the bags and swarms of flies flew off, having nourished their metamorphosis with Caroline's infected flesh, such cleanup being their naturally assigned task. Then Janie applied her human surgical skills and repaired what was left. Using razor blades, sewing needles, dental floss, and tweezers, she worked near miracles on Caroline's nearly ruined appendages, saving everything but the tip of one toe.

Bruce was questioned about the incident at the lab, but because he could prove he'd been in Leeds at the time when it was finally determined that Ted had died, his true involvement was never discovered. The Board of Overseers at the Institute asked him to assume Ted's position until a replacement could be found, but he declined their request, citing his unwillingness to set aside his hands-on work, even temporarily. Disappointed by Bruce's refusal, the board had reluctantly brought in an outside consultant, one who would run things as crisply as Ted had.

Both Janie and Bruce were amazed by how well and quickly Caroline healed, considering the near-death state to which she had sunk. They agreed that a short convalescence would be in order. Janie delayed their return for a week and the three of them went to a seaside hotel in the resort town of Brighton. There the clean sea air worked its own miracles; soon Caroline's lungs were clear again, and she began to walk on her damaged feet. Janie began to hope that Caroline might return to being the person she had once been.

But in her heart Janie knew that some part of Caroline had died in that cottage, some small but vital piece of her essential spirit. Sometimes Janie caught her with a look of indefinable sadness on her face, as if she was missing something terribly.

Michael Rosow spent the time of Caroline's hidden convalescence rousting Marginals, checking customs records, and reviewing flight reservations. Through solid, plodding, and often frustrating investigation he had finally narrowed the identity of the mystery redhead to only three possibilities. The first one he had already checked, but it had simply been a dead end. Upon meeting the second he'd discovered that the passport photo shown in his computer system was several years and a few dozen pounds out of date.

But the third, as yet unprinted, candidate could not be located at the hotel she'd listed as her place of temporary residence in London. The desk clerk didn't recall seeing her for many days, and her companion had checked them both out, citing unexpected travel plans, none of which could be substantiated in computer records. Her original reason for visiting England had been listed as "scientific research," and a security guard from the Institute, scene of "the phantom hand," had identified her as having been a recent visitor. The fit was neat, almost *too* neat, and he knew this one would pan out. All he had to do was figure out which plane she'd be on when she left to go home, and meet her at the airport.

Janie pulled the collar on Caroline's jacket closed and buttoned it, mindful of her companion's healing fingers. "Are you warm enough?" she asked.

"Yeah. But this collar is itchy."

Their bags were already on the plane, or so they'd been told, minus, of course, the garment bag that had served as Ted's shroud.

A handsome and extremely well-built young steward with a beautiful smile had just reviewed their boarding documents and was about to let them pass through the laser security gate. They were nearing the security checkpoint when Janie heard a commotion in the distance.

She turned around and saw a man approaching at a fast pace. He was holding up an ID card and people were moving out of the way quickly.

Janie panicked. After all they'd been through, this was the last step in their safe return to the U.S. Hoping that everything Bruce had done would work, she held her breath and guided Caroline through the scanner, dreading the siren that would sound if their passport numbers registered as unprinted. But the siren remained silent for Caroline, so Janie whispered a little prayer and followed her through.

The alarm did not sound. *Thanks, Ethel . . . and Betsy,* she thought as they headed down the ramp.

Rosow arrived at the gate not thirty seconds after Caroline had passed through with Janie behind her. He held up his Biocop badge and showed the gate attendant the now tattered image of Caroline's face. The attendant recognized the image and said, "She just boarded."

"How could she get cleared through? She's not printed."

The attendant checked the computer records quickly and looked up at Rosow. "I show that she is."

"That's not possible," Rosow said. "I must speak with her. Please bring her out right now."

"I'm afraid I can't do that," the attendant said. He stepped aside politely to allow a tall woman with dark hair to pass back out again, then returned to his discussion with Rosow. "That plane is considered U.S. soil. I have no jurisdiction there." He grinned slyly, for it was a rare treat to be able to thwart an English Biocop. "And neither do you. You'll have to get an order from the U.S. Embassy if you want to board, unless you're a ticketed passenger or a member of the flight crew."

As soon as Janie had Caroline settled, she went back out to investigate. The man she'd seen sprinting for the plane was still arguing with the door attendant, trying to convince him to bring out one of the passengers. She checked her watch and saw that it would still be half an hour before the flight departed. She asked another attendant if she could get off the flight and then reboard.

"If your documentation is in order, there should be no problem." She showed him her papers and he said, "Go right ahead. But don't be too long. We'll be closing the door and getting you all suited up in fifteen minutes."

Recalling the crinkly sounds of the flight over to England, she said, "I wouldn't miss it for all the world." Then she turned and walked through the scanner past the loud clamor of Michael Rosow's insistent tirade. As she passed by him, he momentarily locked eyes with hers.

He was on that field, she thought as he held her gaze. *I don't know how I know, but I know he was on that field. I wonder if he knows how close he came to finding us. . . .* But Caroline was already on the plane, and protected once again by her U.S. citizenship. There was nothing he could do to her now.

She smiled warmly at the man and thought for a moment that there was a look of recognition in his eyes. But it faded, and he returned her smile with a brief nod of his head. Then he resumed his previous argument, and Janie continued on her way.

Up on the mezzanine the green men kept their silent, unwavering vigil, their weapons aimed downward at the crowd passing below. Janie

passed by, stepping briskly, on her way to a bookstore for one last purchase; they would be in transit for many hours, and she wanted the
distraction. It would keep her mind off the demons that rose up every
now and then in a cruel dance, stomping out every last bit of peace she
managed to find.

One more loss, she thought. *It's starting to feel like my normal life,*
this awful pain of missing people. . . . She wondered sadly what might
have been between her and Bruce if they could have figured out a way to
overcome their geographical challenge.

They'd said their good-byes at his apartment the night before. It
had seemed too crowded, with Caroline in the extra room, and Janie had
felt dissatisfied by the leave-taking. *It should have touched me more, I*
should have been sadder or something. . . . Instead, she had felt terribly
empty. She had convinced herself beforehand that she would not allow
the pain to get to her. *If I don't let it in, it can't hurt me.* . . .

But it *had* gotten in, despite her best efforts. It was in there, deep in
her heart, buried in the pit of her stomach, and lurking in her psyche,
ready to scratch and claw its way out with the slightest provocation. She
would hold it back, she'd decided, until she was safely home and in a
private place where she could cry and wail until her heart burst.

"Why don't you stay," he'd said. "There are things you can do here.
I can help you get settled . . . find work. . . ."

"I don't know, Bruce," she'd said, confusion paralyzing her. "I don't
think I'm ready to make that kind of decision right now. There's so much
confusion in my life . . ." she'd told him, "and things are changing; and
when I first came here, I thought England was heaven. But you have even
less freedom than we do. It's so far gone here that I don't think you'll ever
get it back. Back home we can still change things. I guess I just don't like
the way it feels to live under all this . . . control."

And then she'd said, "But why don't *you* come back to the States?
You're still a citizen, and you've been productive over here. You can just
get on a plane and show up at the gate. We'd be glad to have you back
again. We can always use another brilliant scientist."

He'd smiled sadly. "Maybe I'll surprise you someday."

In other words, she'd thought to herself, *no.* They'd left it like that,
a no-decision match between equally stubborn participants.

At the back of the bookstore she found an interesting-looking
novel. She read the back-cover copy and a bit of the first page, and
decided it would do. She went to the front of the store and paid, then
headed toward the plane.

Standing not far from the entry gate was the same man who'd been arguing with the attendant earlier. He looked angry and resentful. His hands were stuffed into his pockets and his shoulders were tight, as if he'd been subjected to some monumental annoyance. He gave Janie a resentful look of defeat as she passed by, as if he knew somehow that she had caused him all this frustration.

You'll never find out, she thought, a welcome sense of relief swirling through her.

The attendant was cheerfully welcoming passengers. *Back to the good old U.S.A.,* Janie thought, silently applauding his victory over the insistent Biocop.

"Good work," she said to him as she passed through for the second and final time.

He gave her a very beautiful, very broad smile and said, "And fun too."

She passed by the cockpit, and walked through the flurry of pre-flight activity toward her seat at the back of the plane. She saw women struggling with babies, and flight attendants trying to cram small pieces of luggage into the overhead cargo bins. She saw a steward with an armload of clear plastic suits working his way down the aisle, passing them out and confirming to the occasional first-time traveler that these were *indeed* the suits some passengers called body condoms. She saw confused-looking elderly people trying to figure out where all the straps and masks were supposed to go.

She saw Bruce.

"Surprise," he said.

Thirty-Five

Kate stood in the clearing and brushed the horse while Alejandro cleaned his sweaty body inside the cottage. He removed all of his ruined clothing and dropped it in a pile on the floor, then washed himself in the basin until he felt renewed—cleansed and purged of the plague that had nearly claimed him for its own. He reclothed himself in the fresher garments he had placed in his saddlebag before setting out for Canterbury, then ran his fingers through his hair and cleaned his teeth with the raveled end of a green twig.

He had decided, despite his weak condition, that they could not stay in one place long, and that they should leave Mother Sarah's cottage as soon as possible, for there was no doubt that the king would send men to pursue them. As he sat at the table considering what they should take with them, he noticed a small movement out of the corner of his eye. Looking closer, he saw the tail of a rat disappear into the pile of clothing he had dropped near the hearth. He rose up quickly, and tried to shoo the vile animal away, but it remained hidden in the pile of garments until he beat it with the heavy end of a nearby broom. Then the rat scurried away, chirping like a bird, and disappeared through a crack in the stone wall.

What to do? If he was right about the rats, those garments would now be capable of carrying the plague into the body of any unsuspecting fool who might find them and wear them. They would have to be burned before he left this place, for there were plenty of destitute people who would not think twice before wearing anything that still had even a day's service in it.

He shoved the pile of clothing into the hearth with the end of the broom. He placed a few dried faggots and a handful of leaves on top of the pile. As he was doing so, Kate came through the small doorway.

"What are you doing?" she questioned him.

"I am burning the clothes I wore while I was afflicted. I have seen a rat in the pile, and I fear that anyone who stumbles on this place and wears the clothing will be afflicted as I was. I am convinced that rats are the means by which this scourge makes its way through the countryside. To burn purifies," he told her. "I would not have it on my soul to leave these items behind."

And to secure her part in this important ritual Kate asked, "Please, Physician, may I strike the flint?"

"If it pleases you, child," he answered, and handed the dark stone to her.

She picked up a nearby rock and was about to strike the two together, when the sound of a horse turned her head. They looked at each other in alarm. She dropped the flint and the stone and they hurried to the door. Alejandro, his knife in hand, moved her gently behind himself as he peered out to see who was approaching.

Crossing the glade was a plump woman in torn clothing, wobbling precariously on a too-small horse that labored under her weight. Her headdress was tilted to one side and her face smeared with dirt. Peeking out from behind Alejandro's leg, Kate cried, "It is my mother's maid!"

Alejandro squinted through the sunlight. "Indeed, it is she! Why on earth has she come here?" he said. *And have others followed?* he thought. He tucked the knife back into his boot and ran outside to help her, for she was clearly in difficult straits.

"God in heaven, woman," he cried. "What has befallen you?"

As she slid down from the horse, landing unsteadily on sore feet in tight shoes, the maid said with irritation, "I've gone and spoiled my frock! As I entered the path, the wind pushed me right off the horse, and I landed on my behind! It's a fair thing I'm well bottomed." She brushed leaves and acorns off the hem of the gown and straightened herself up.

"But enough of me! I came seeking the Mother, but it's you yourself who'll benefit. God curse him, the king has sent a party out to find you. They passed me not an hour ago, and I sent them off to confusion, may it please the saints! You'd best move on from here, and the child too. They'll not be long in finding you."

He sent the serving girl off at once, for he would not have her found with them should her prediction of their imminent discovery come true. And it was fortunate that he did, for not long after her bouncing form had finally disappeared from view, the faint sound of barking dogs could be heard in the distance.

Alejandro frantically grabbed whatever was at hand that might be useful on their journey and shoved it all haphazardly into his saddlebag. As he was heading out the door, he looked back one more time, feeling as though he'd forgotten something. Seeing the clothing in the hearth, he put down the bag and took up the flint, intending to complete the job of burning it.

But just before the rocks came together, Kate said, "What of the smoke? They will find us by its rising plume!"

He aborted the strike, realizing that the smoke of even a small fire would give away their position, and they would quickly be discovered. He thought of leaving the items in the hearth without destroying them. As he stood there in a state of indecision, the specters of Alderón, Matthews, and Adele flashed through his mind.

No! his mind raged, *I will not be responsible for another death.* He reached into the hearth and removed the garments.

He ran outside and quickly strapped his saddlebag onto the back of the horse. Then he scooped up Kate and sat her in front of him, with the garments tucked between them. They sped down the path toward the meadow and Kate cried, "They are louder now! Oh, hurry!"

Their horse was rested and responded well to Alejandro's less-than-gentle urging. As they left the soft air of the glen through the twisted oaks and entered the colder air of the field, the running animal made no protest. As they crossed the field, Alejandro saw even more brown earth than they had just a few days before. *More dead,* he thought. *Will it never end?* His infectious clothing lay between him and Kate, a loathsome burden, but he would not leave it behind to infect others.

They entered the field and he saw the fresh-dug earth. Suddenly he knew what he must do.

He reined the horse to an abrupt halt and jumped down off the confused animal. Kate cried, "Hurry! The sound is closer still!"

He heard the sound of dogs and horns and the clatter of armor, and the urgent shouts of men in determined pursuit of a quarry. He knew that he and Kate were the object of their cruel hunt. He dug his hands into the loose earth, shoving it away with more strength and vigor than he had left. *Ah,* his crazed mind thought as he clawed frantically at the dirt, *Carlos Alderón's shovel would be useful now!* And when the small hole was finally deep enough, he deposited the clothing into it, and quickly covered it with the loose dirt. He stomped vigorously on the surface of the dirt, compacting it, then brushed his hands together a few times and mounted the horse again.

Kate shrieked and pointed ahead in the direction they were riding. Alejandro saw soldiers emerge from the woods into the clearing, so he turned his horse around and they sped back in the direction of the oaks. When they dashed between the trees, no wind rose up to rebuff them, but as he looked back, he could see the slow swirling of twigs and sticks in a building maelstrom. He stopped the horse for a moment and watched as the swirling increased in intensity. Soon the whirlpool of wind became a raging storm, and heavy debris flew about like so many dried leaves. As the dogs approached the oaks, they slowed their pace, and whined as the swirling surrounded them. The soldiers also slowed, and their horses reared up, frightened by the sudden storm.

Alejandro blessed the wind under his breath and turned his horse onto the path once again; this time they did not stop, but rode straight through the clearing and into the forest on the other side. They kept going until they were certain they had lost their pursuers for good.

They slept that night under the stars on a grassy patch atop a high cliff on the coast of England. Across the Channel lay France. When they gazed out over the water in the morning they could just barely see it, but Alejandro could feel it beckoning to him like a homeland, safe and welcoming.

His strength renewed by sleep, Alejandro packed their few belongings. As he closed his saddlebag it seemed emptier somehow than it should. He looked through the contents again, and realized with dismay that an item was indeed missing.

He had left his book of wisdom behind in the stone cottage. He could not go back to get it now.

It saddened him to think that he had lost that part of his life. As he mounted the horse and pulled Kate up to the saddle, he hoped that whoever found it would put it to the best of use. He turned the horse toward Dover, where they would cross the waters.

And there, finally, their new life would begin.

Epilogue

Caroline sat on a wooden swing on the front porch of her home in western Massachusetts and watched her three-year-old daughter play in a pile of gold and yellow leaves. On her lap was an ancient book, a gift from Janie after their return from England four years earlier. Its leather binding was cracked and dry, and she thought guiltily that she shouldn't be handling it. *It belongs in a museum*, she would tell herself every time she picked it up.

But I just can't give it up yet, she would always think. *Even after four years it's still too fresh.*

She turned the pages again, starting from the very beginning. *Six hundred years*, she thought. *Incredible that it took so long to come to completion.* She admired the fine spidery European hand of the first writer, now barely visible on the browned page. Time was, she thought, when we didn't just speak into a computer and then wait for the printed page to appear, grammar clear and concise, spelling flawless. Once people wrote on pages with feathers dipped in a suspension of carbon and diluted pitch, and their fingers turned black from it, and their wrists ached from forming the letters. This man had written as if he'd known he would someday be judged by this work.

She passed through the collected wisdom of six hundred years, the faces and words now etched into her consciousness by countless repetitions. On the very last page was a clipping from the London *Times* of an article published while she'd been recuperating in Brighton. Alongside the article was a reproduction of a computer-generated image of her own face; they had not named her, but she had known. It was her own face, and she'd known quite well why she was being sought.

The newsprint was slightly creased. She thought to herself that she must have been careless when she'd last closed the book, and vowed to herself that she would not let it happen again. *Museum*, she thought once more. *Before it's too late.*

She reread the article for the hundredth time.

Officials at Biopol are seeking the whereabouts of the woman pictured here. She is described as approximately five feet four inches tall, with bright red hair. She may have either blue or green eyes, and her skin is quite fair. She may have substantial freckling . . .

She loved the part about the freckling. *If they only knew . . .* she thought. She read on.

> *. . . on her face, especially, and in all likelihood she is of normal weight. She is believed to be a foreign national, probably American, and will be traveling on a limited visa. Anyone with information pertaining to this fugitive should contact Lt. Michael Rosow at the West End branch of Biopol. Officials further state that the woman should not be approached under any circumstances, as she is suspected of harboring the causative agent of a potentially deadly infectious disease. No one at Biopol would name the disease in question; the spokesman at the press office would only say that the unnamed condition could be "quite serious in nature."*
>
> *Meanwhile, officials of the Health Ministry declined comment on an unsubstantiated rumor that there has been a outbreak of bubonic plague, long thought to have been eradicated in London, among members of one particular clan of Marginals, and that steps have been taken to control the spread. There have been six confirmed deaths outside the Marginal population from a plaguelike disease or syndrome in recent weeks. One of the victims was a prominent London restaurateur. Biopol officials have not released the results of their investigation into these deaths, saying that the official cause of death for all six victims has yet to be determined, and that any official comment concerning the alleged outbreak would be premature and potentially inflammatory.*

Alleged outbreak, my ass, she thought, and closed the book. *I was there. It was not "alleged."* She set the book down on the wood seat of the swing and looked at her scarred fingers, shivering as she thought how close she had come to losing them. She ran them through her long red hair, loving the cool feel of it on her skin, thinking once again, *I should cut it.* But no, her husband loved it. And that was reason enough to keep it.

The sun was setting; everything was autumn gold. She called out to the little girl in the leaves, and a twig-laden head of red curls popped up out of the scattered pile.

"Sarah Jane Rosow!" Caroline called. "Come here!"

The child bounded across the lawn, scooted up the porch steps, and climbed up into her mother's lap.

Caroline kissed her daughter's forehead and hugged her, then picked up the book and opened it on her lap. "Mommy wants to tell you a story. . . ."